THE POST-TRIDENTINE
MASS PROPER

Musicological Studies and Documents

AN INTRODUCTION TO THE POST-TRIDENTINE MASS PROPER

Theodore Karp

AMERICAN INSTITUTE OF MUSICOLOGY
Paul L. Ranzini, Director

Musicological Studies and Documents, 54–1

AN INTRODUCTION TO THE POST-TRIDENTINE MASS PROPER

Part 1: Text

Theodore Karp

AMERICAN INSTITUTE OF MUSICOLOGY
Middleton, Wisconsin

AMERICAN INSTITUTE OF MUSICOLOGY

The American Institute of Musicology publishes seven series of critical editions, scholarly studies, reference works, and a journal all dedicated to the study of Medieval, Renaissance, and early Baroque eras. The publications of the Institute are used by scholars and performers alike and constitute a major core collection of early music and theoretical writings on music.

For information on establishing a standing order to any of our series, or for editorial guidelines on submitting proposals, please contact:

American Institute of Musicology, Inc.
Middleton, Wisconsin
800 736-0070 (U.S. book orders)
608 836-9000 (phone)
608 831-8200 (fax)
http://www.corpusmusicae.com
orders@corpusmusicae.com
info@corpusmusicae.com

ISBN-13: 978-1-59551-339-7
ISBN-10: 1-59551-339-6

Printed in the United States of America.
⊗ The paper used in this publication meets the minimum requirements of the American National Standard for Information Sciences Permanence of Paper for Printed Library Materials, ANSI/NISO Z39.48-1992.

Library of Congress Cataloging-in-Publication Data
Karp, Theodore.
 An introduction to the post-tridentine Mass proper / Theodore Karp.
   p.   cm. -- (Musicological studies and documents ; 54)
 Includes bibliographical references (p.   ) and index.
 ISBN-13: 978-1-59551-339-7 (v.1 : alk. paper)
 ISBN-10: 1-59551-339-6 (v.1 : alk. paper)
 ISBN-13: 978-1-59551-345-8 (v.2 : alk. paper)
 ISBN-10: 1-59551-345-0 (v.2 : alk. paper)
 1. Mass (Music) 2. Gregorian chant--History and criticism. I. Title. II. Series.

ML3088.K37 2005
782.32'35--dc22
                    2005032550

Contents

Acknowledgements

It is a pleasure to express my appreciation to various colleagues and organizations who have contributed in different ways to the creation of this book. I owe thanks to Professor Warren Kirkendale for having made me aware of riches of the Biblioteca Feininger in Trent. I am grateful for the warm reception afforded me by Professor Marco Gozzi on the occasion of my first visit to that city, and the introductions he furnished me to Dr. Franco Marzatico and Renato Scartezzini, who have charge of this library. My work with post-Tridentine chant began with a narrow focus, and it was Professor Gozzi who encouraged me to broaden my scope when inviting me to contribute a fledgling paper to the *Convegno internazionale di studi sul canto liturgico nei secoli XV-XVIII*. The staff of the Feininger library showed me many kindnesses on the occasion of my two visits.

Although I have not had the opportunity over the past dozen years to spend an extended period of time in any one European library, I have been received hospitably by many, who have shown me numerous courtesies. I recall with warmth visits to the Bibliothèque nationale de France, the Bibliothèque Mazarine, and the Bibliothèque Sainte-Geneviève. I was received courteously at the Biblioteca Apostolica Vaticana, as well as the Biblioteche nazionale, Angelica, and Vallicelliana in Rome. In Venice I was aided by librarians at the Biblioteca Marciana, and in Milan at the Biblioteca Ambrosiana, the Biblioteca Braidense (Bibl. nazionale), and the Biblioteca Trivulziana. I received similar kind treatment in Florence at the Biblioteca nazionale, the Biblioteca Mediceo-Laurenziana, and the Biblioteca Marucelliana. In Munich, I was able to profit from the assistance of the staffs at both

the Bayerische Staatsbibliothek and the Universitätsbibliothek. I recall apprecia-
tively the various kindnesses shown by Drs. Sabine Kurth and Bernhold Schmid,
the latter a member of the Bayerische Akademie der Wissenschaften. I was afforded
help by the librarians at the Bibliothèque royale in Brussels, the Plantin-Moretus
Museum in Antwerp, the Universiteitsbibliotheek of Leuven, and by Mrs. Jozefa
van Bragt at the Park Abbey in Heverlee. In Great Britain, I was given assistance
by librarians at Cambridge University and at the British Library.

I am grateful to the courtesies of the various libraries that have supplied micro-
films of items in their collections that have provided the basis for this book. I am
especially appreciative of the generosity of the Research Grants Committee of
Northwestern University in providing funds that enabled the acquisition of several
of these films.

This book has received the Weiss/Brown Publication Award from the Newberry
Library. The award supports the publication of outstanding works of scholarship
that cover European civilization before 1700 in the areas of music, theater, French
or Italian literature, or cultural studies. It is made to commemorate the career of
Howard Mayer Brown. This award has both facilitated the publication of this study
and edition and made possible the accompanying CD containing performances of
selected portions of the repertoire of post-Tridentine chant. I am much indebted to
the foresight and the broad collegial concern of both Roger Weiss and Howard
Brown.

This study and edition is much enriched by the accompanying CD containing
performances of multiple versions of selected chants, contributed through the kindness of Professor Calvin Bower and the Schola Antiqua of Chicago, which he
directs. I am most appreciative of their collaboration.

Theodore Karp

ONE

Introduction

During the three centuries following the conclusion of the Council of Trent in 1563, there was a remarkable flowering of activity in the realm of Catholic liturgical chant, much of it concentrated in the first hundred years. Indeed, within the last decade of the sixteenth century, there were no fewer than six[1] independent revisions of the entire Mass Proper. These were prompted by a changed vision of the aesthetic that should govern this repertoire.

When the Franks adopted and remodeled an earlier Roman repertory— apparently soon after the mid-eighth century—they associated with the new hybrid a legend of its Divine Creation transmitted through St. Gregory. According to this well-known story, the Holy Spirit descended in the form of a dove and, perched on Gregory's shoulder, sang the melodies to him. The Pope, in turn, dictated these to a scribe seated respectfully behind a curtain. The legend was of inestimable help in propagating the new creation—resulting in the obliteration or near obliteration of various local chant repertoires. It also helped produce a drive for the accurate preservation of this chant to the extent possible within the limitations of both the human memory and the notations that were used to aid it. One does not tamper with the work of the Divine.

The respect for this magnificent repertoire was retained well through the fifteenth century. Nevertheless, various tensions that conflicted with the uniform preservation of the melodies arose long before this time. The first of these was driven by music theory, which began to assert increasing force from the eleventh century onward. As theorists sought to fix the contents of the gamut, they dismissed those tones that lacked theoretical sanction and asserted they did not exist. As they determined the nature and structure of the church modes, they began to insist that their modal rules should govern melodic structure. Chant, of course, had originally come into being without a universally accepted gamut, and without a clearly articulated modal system. The tension between theory and practice affected the transmission of certain individual chants and was responsible for the wider-ranging revisions undertaken by the Cistercians and others who followed their lead. Nevertheless, tensions of musical origin did not have too widespread or profound an effect on the repertoire.

During the course of the fifteenth and sixteenth centuries tensions of textual origin came into being. Humanistic scholars began to focus more and more on textual values and specifically on the clear enunciation of text with proper accentuation. Composers of polyphony could accommodate the new theories by adopting changes in style. Chant afforded almost no opportunity for such accommodations. Educated people of the time were so deeply imbued with these ideas that they thought of them as timeless and universal. If chant did not follow these dictates then it was chant that was faulty. The most influential statement of this position is contained in Pope Gregory XIII's commission to Palestrina and Zoilo, dated 25 October 1577. The letter describes the chant books of the time as having "been filled to overflowing with barbarisms, obscurities, contrarieties, and superfluities as a result of the clumsiness or negligence or even wickedness of the composers, scribes, and printers."[2] These are to be purged, corrected, and reformed so that "God's name may be reverently, distinctly, and devoutly praised." It is clear that "barbarisms" referred to instances—numerous enough in chant—where unaccented syllables received a greater number of tones than those that were accented. The other charges are less certain. It is probable that "superfluities" referred to the presence of lengthy melismas. "Obscurities" and "contrarieties" may have alluded to chants whose modal structures were not in accordance with the changing tastes in modality and the nascent feeling for tonality that had come into being by the latter part of the sixteenth century. Although Palestrina devoted considerable thought to the Pope's commission during the following year, his interest apparently waned thereafter and the project remained incomplete at the time of his death in 1595. It is unfortunate that the Pope, who was served by such glorious polyphony, had so little appreciation of the beauties of liturgical monophony and so little empathy for a repertoire that accorded a substantial role to purely musical values.

As can be seen, the Pope's intent was not to order the abandonment of the age-old musical heritage of the Church. It was sufficient to charge the chant with having been distorted in its transmission. Surely one would not have thought to impute improper accentuations and effusive musical flourishes to the Saint whose name had for centuries been identified with the chant. But, following the issuance of the commission, musicians of "learning and taste" were left free to remove the numerous impurities that had supposedly accrued over the centuries, and to produce a more austere version, more keenly attuned to prosodic values. This would be consonant with contemporary taste and could be trumpeted as a restoration of the original. This attitude appears with clarity on the title page of the earliest of the French reform editions, issued in Bordeaux in 1598/99 by the press of Simon Millange, under the chief editorship of Guillaume Boni. We are told that the chants contained therein have been "carefully emended according to the oldest exemplars, restored to their pristine splendor, and corrected throughout of improper accents."[3] All of this is illusory, but it succinctly defines the goals of the enterprise and its mode of self-justification. A briefer account, which omits the claim of restoration, appears on the title page of the Angelo Gardano Gradual issued in 1591. It refers to chant as having "fallen into numerous errors through the passage of time. [These have been] emended by several of the most excellent musicians through extensive study and work."[4] The self-encomium, "Purged of errors," becomes something of a mantra for seventeenth-century title pages. A much lengthier, more passionate and detailed exposition is to be found in the *Dissertation sur le chant grégorien* by Guillaume Gabriel Nivers published in Paris, 1683.

The gambit of supposed "corrections" had, of course, been used centuries earlier in support of Cistercian revisions of chant. But now the ploy took on a new irony. By the mid-sixteenth century, secular scholars—generally those with backgrounds as jurists—had already begun to create informed editions of classical texts, and revised standards for the writing of history were emerging.[5] Had the nascent techniques been employed in the editing of chant, we might have had comparable editions of this music. However, those involved in the enterprise that we shall be discussing came from a contrasting segment of society, being closely associated with the belief system and thought habits of the church. They ignored the strides made by secular scholars. Indeed, the new techniques would not have served their purpose. Rather than employing source comparisons to locate the best available readings and thus eliminate the supposed corruptions, they instead theorized concerning the standards that should obtain in the realm of chant and projected these back to the time of Pope Gregory I. They then attempted in many different ways to bend medieval chant to their new standards or even to dispose of it entirely. (Sometimes one can find both approaches in a single source.) Their products were presented as chant as it once had been, or at least should have been.

As is well known, the mid-nineteenth century witnessed the development of historical interests in music, and a greater number of church musicians began to investigate medieval sources. By the early 1850s the now famous bilingual Montpellier, Fac. méd. MS H. 159 was drawn on for new editions of the Gradual. By the last quarter of the century, Solesmes monks, armed with a burgeoning knowledge of a broad range of medieval sources, reacted vigorously against what they perceived to be a degradation of the great musical patrimony of the Church.[6] In the aftermath of their efforts to restore this lost treasure to its earliest recoverable forms, the hybrids of the previous three centuries were essentially consigned to the trash heap.

Those seeking to acquaint themselves with the history of liturgical chant within the Roman Catholic tradition do not have access to any major secondary study concerning the period 1590–1890 as a whole. At the beginning of last century Raphael Molitor took up the study of the two-volume Gradual published by the Medicean Press, 1614–15.[7] In the relative absence of sufficient complementary information, this solitary source has until recently taken on the semblance of a standard that was at least normative, if not universal. Yet various warnings to the contrary have been appearing with increasing frequency for more than a decade.

When considering this state of affairs, we will come to realize that comparatively little is known of the history of chant for 250 years previous to this period, i.e., from ca. 1340–1590. Over the past century, scholarly efforts have focused so intently on the recovery of the earliest layer of chant that the sources best known and most highly prized are those previous to the mid-fourteenth century. This represents a serious historical imbalance. Despite the support of current aesthetic values, it involves a distortion of historical perspective that is unfortunate if not indeed intolerable.

During recent years various scholars have taken steps to remedy this lacuna. There are two noteworthy doctoral dissertations, one by Annarita Indino, *Il Graduale stampato da Angelo Gardano nel 1591* (Università degli Studi di Lecce, 1998), and another by Cécile Davy-Rigaux, *L'Oeuvre de plain-chant de G. G. Nivers* (Université de Tours, 1999). And two compilations of individual essays have been issued, *Plain-chant et liturgie en France au XVIIe siècle*, edited by Jean Duron (Versailles, 1997) and *Il Canto piano nell'era della stampa*, edited by Giulio Cattin, Danilo Curti, and Marco Gozzi (Trent, 1999). Nevertheless, no previous study has attempted a panorama of the whole. This is the goal of the present book. Notwithstanding, this project has been carried out with sharply limited objectives in mind, and the reader should be aware of these from the outset. The chronological focus is defined in the title; I am concerned primarily with the period, 1590–1890. Even within these limitations, it should be apparent that an investigation of the totality of the Mass Propers is beyond the capacity of any one individual at this time. In order to accomplish that which is presented here I have had to be highly selective. I have chosen to investigate a small group of Masses, including those for the first two Sundays of Advent, the Third Mass of Christmas, the Third Sunday after Epiphany, and Easter. The chants in this group are then supplemented by a few others in an effort to round out our view of different aspects of the chant repertoire. The Masses for Christmas and Easter were chosen because of their liturgical prominence. The remaining complete Masses were selected in order to take advantage of earlier researches that I had undertaken on the medieval transmission of one or more of their constituent chants. To the best of our knowledge, the musical content of these five Masses remained fairly constant throughout the Middle Ages. The issue of variability of content has been one concern that caused me to avoid Masses from the Sanctorale in this preliminary study. This lacuna will be addressed by means of some chants to be studied in chapter 8, "A Selected Miscellany"; these have been taken from the Mass for the Purification of the Blessed Virgin Mary. The hope is that the materials chosen for investigation will provide a representative sampling of the practice as a whole. That is the best that can be accomplished for the moment.

Obviously, the chants for the post-Tridentine Mass Proper did not come into being *ex vacuo;* the music has roots, in many instances roots reaching back eight centuries. On the one hand, it is impossible to gain a full understanding of post-Tridentine editorial decisions without some knowledge of the environment in which these were born. On the other hand, any serious attempt to deal with the history of chant as a whole will overwhelm and destroy the envisaged project. Torn between the opposite poles of a vacuum and full disclosure, I have had to make draconian compromises.

Because post-Tridentine chant—and here I refer primarily to the Mass Propers—developed out of the chant practice of the fifteenth and sixteenth centuries, it is necessary to get some information about the nature of the chant melodies during this earlier period. If carried out fully, this would entail a massive study that is entirely beyond the scope of the present work. Here, I shall provide readings from two prints. The first of these is a Gradual issued by Liechtenstein in Venice in 1580; the second is the *Graduale Herbipolense,* issued by a yet unidentified publisher in Würzburg in 1583. The two have been chosen because they are in close chronological proximity to the earliest of the "reform" Graduals now documented, the print of Angelo Gardano issued in 1591.[8] A second *desideratum* was to represent both the Western and Eastern dialects of chant. The two prints cannot possibly portray the totality of chant as it was known in the sixteenth century. (I have not, for example, had access to the French Gradual published by Barbou in Limoges in 1575.[9])

A hasty critic will promptly point out that the two sources are themselves post-Tridentine. This is true only to the extent that one focuses on the dates of publication without considering the nature of the contents. The 1580 Liechtenstein publication is a direct descendant of a 1525 publication by the same firm.[10] Although the later edition incorporates some textual revisions originating in the *Missale Romanum* of 1570,[11] a comparison of a few dozen readings in the two sources has shown the musical variants to be rare and miniscule in importance. Generally these concern the elimination in the later edition of a repeated tone present in the earlier one. Similarly, the 1583 *Graduale Herbipolense* seems to be a direct descendant of an earlier publication of 1496, issued by Georg Reyser in Würzburg, the city that witnessed the issuance of the later Gradual. This statement is made on a smaller base of comparisons. Thus, the reader is provided access to two late readings from different areas that furnish a view of selected chants that date from both before and after the Council of Trent. While this documentation is obviously incomplete, it is reasonable to hope that it provides a workable account of the nature of readings for the Mass Proper in the late fifteenth and sixteenth centuries.

The effort to provide meaningful comparisons between post-Tridentine chant readings and their medieval counterparts must deal with a still greater difficulty. A scholar working in the first decade of the twenty-first century and wishing to treat the history of drama in Jacobean England can build not only on numerous earlier works in the field, including critical editions, but also on a still larger number of studies dealing with earlier stages of the history of European drama. Equivalent statements can be made for someone now wishing to work on Dutch painting of the seventeenth and eighteenth centuries, as well as for the person working in polyphonic music of the same general period. However, the scholar seeking to illuminate a little-known area of liturgical chant has no comparable context available. If, for example, one wishes to relate a group of post-Tridentine readings for the gradual, *Viderunt omnes,* to their antecedents prior to 1300, what existing publication will provide the requisite information for the early period? The collective experiences of those working in the field demonstrate that variants exist for all chants of widespread diffusion. We know also that for stable chants these variants are relatively few and mainly of minor import.[12] We know that there are certain standard variants that distinguish the Western and Eastern dialects of chants. It is very likely that stable chants form the great majority of the repertoire. On the other hand, we know that there are also some chants whose transmission is notably unstable. These chants fall mainly into three groups: (a) those employing tones not admissible within the Guidonian gamut, thus requiring non-standard notations; (b) those of unstable modality; and (c) late chants, often of limited diffusion.[13]

This primitive information is of little assistance in selecting a basis for comparison between post-Tridentine readings and those antedating 1200. It would of course be fascinating to be able to link a given early reading with a late one from the same locale and to demonstrate thereby the influence of the former on the latter. My experience in working with the late materials treated here persuades me that such a goal is at best a forlorn hope. If we turn to the source bibliography provided in *Le Graduel romain, II,* to seek possible antecedents for prints issued by 1620 in Antwerp, Ingolstadt, Kraków, Madrid, and Tournai, we will not find mention of any of these cities. Only a single source is cited for Venice, namely Bibl. Apostolica Vaticana, MS Rossi 231, and the editors cautiously attach a question mark to the citation. The situation does not improve over the next fifteen years with the publication of Graduals in Brussels, Louvain, and Toul. As a matter of fact, we are hard put to assign a place of origin to the readings found in the Flandrus Gradual of 1595–97, brought out in Madrid. And if we search among early southern German sources for medieval counterparts to the Ingolstadt Graduals of 1618 and 1630, we will simply go astray. These sources are direct descendants of the Plantin Gradual of 1599 from Antwerp. Similarly, the Venetian Gradual of 1766 uses readings transplanted from Paris. Given the limitations of what can be placed on a single page without destroying legibility, we cannot increase the number of readings from early sources because this would entail an equivalent decrease in the number of sources that are of post-Tridentine origin. These provide the focus for this book. Generally I find it possible to present within a given example no more than one French reading. It would be eminently desirable to present also readings drawn from a more idiosyncratic French source, such as the *Graduale Bisuntinum*, edited by Jean Millet in 1682. To decrease the number of post-Tridentine sources given in each example in order to multiply the number of early medieval readings would, in my opinion, be self-defeating.

In order to present an account of normative medieval readings for a given chant I have found it suitable to use the versions of the *Graduale Triplex*. As most undoubtedly know, this 1979 edition by the Solesmes monks generally has the virtue of presenting above and below each staff the readings of two important early adiastematic sources from different geographic areas, permitting the reader to verify the editorial decisions made in presenting the pitch-readable versions of the given melody. At least one can rapidly determine the extent to which the respective bits of melody are equivalent to (or depart from) the early accounts of gestural shapes. Most readers are presumably aware that the Solesmes editions represent conflations. Many scholars find conflations to be distasteful since their component parts are drawn from different sources and the assemblage does not necessarily correspond to a verifiable historical reality. On rare occasions the Solesmes' decisions may be highly questionable, and we shall encounter one such instance in the course of chapter 8. Would it not be preferable to rely instead on the best possible reading? This editorial technique can work admirably if one is dealing with a piece surviving in six to a dozen readings. It becomes impractical when one must select a "best" reading from among a hundred or more sources, none of which has been edited previously, thus requiring the time-consuming process of transcribing afresh in order to permit comparisons. One cannot claim to have identified a "best" reading without undertaking an extensive search. This does not prevent a scholar from focusing on a given medieval reading of choice, but a choice based on the consultation of one or a handful of sources runs the danger of being arbitrary. In the end, no one reading can provide the reader with a view of the overall medieval transmission of the melody. The desire to ascertain a normative practice is one that leads naturally to the construction of a conflation. And a conflation can serve a useful purpose provided that we understand it for what it is: a condensation of the whole that cannot be shown to represent with full accuracy the historical reality of any one of its constituent elements.

In the comparative transcriptions that furnish the basis for the accompanying discussions, I normally furnish readings from the *Graduale Triplex*, the Liechtenstein Gradual of 1580 and the Würzburg Gradual of 1583 on the top three staves. The staves below are devoted to post-Tridentine readings from the period following 1590. I seek to cover each of the several traditions presently known to exist within Europe. Because of limitations of space, I give priority to the earlier representatives of these traditions. In most instances, the staff below the readings of the Liechtenstein and Würzburg prints will furnish an account of the *Graduale Romanum* issued by Gardano in Venice in 1591. The fifth staff will present the reading of the Giunta Gradual of 1596 that followed hard on the heels of its predecessor. The readings of the prints of 1607 and 1611 brought out by the Giunta press will be skipped for lack of space, although I may comment in the main text on some of the more important of the variants present in later Venetian editions. On occasion, however, I shall devote a staff to the 1610 Gradual issued by Ciera even though this is generally identical to one or another of the Giunta readings. This I do in order to document the growth of the Venetian tradition beyond the volumes issued by a single firm. Only seldom will it be possible to document the further growth of this tradition in the editions of Baba, Baglioni, and Pezzana.

The staff beneath will present the reading of the Medicean Gradual. The comparative structure of the example will demonstrate that only rarely does this famous source give evidence of influencing the performance of chant in other European centers. Later sources apparently do not take over entire melodies from the Roman print, although we encounter a few hybrids that clearly borrow portions of melodies. At present we have no information regarding any other Roman, printed Graduals or any others from central or southern Italian centers.

A French tradition may be documented beginning with the 1598/99 Gradual issued in Bordeaux by Simon Millange and able to be documented by other prints— from Toul and Paris, but also from Lyon and Grenoble—over the course of more than a century. This tradition, however, did not hold universal sway throughout France or even Paris, and one finds both modifications and alternatives in it.

Proceeding to other areas of Europe, the individual examples will treat the earliest of the reform Graduals published in the Low Countries, that issued by the Plantin Press in Antwerp in 1599. Three Graduals from 1616, 1620, and 1623 from Tournai, Antwerp, and Brussels respectively, give insight into a contrasting portion of chant practice in the Low Countries in the early seventeenth century. Germanic sources for this period appear to be quite rare. While the output of liturgical books was undoubtedly affected by the religious turmoil surrounding the events of the Thirty Years War, the dearth of volumes stands in sharp contrast to the considerable activity that had been evidence in the late fifteenth and early sixteenth centuries. The Bavarian reformed tradition that appears in two Graduals issued in Ingolstadt in 1618 and 1630 is derived from the Plantin edition, as noted previously. Even though the German publications were brought out by different publishers, they were prepared by the same printer and the readings that have been studied thus far are identical. In view of their origin it is not surprising that they lack the specifically Germanic turns of phrase that one encounters in the Gradual published by Ch[ristian] Küchler in 1671 in Mainz. We have a more easterly source published in Kraków by Piotrkowczyk in 1600, and there are two later successors to this volume. A Gradual issued by J. Flandrus (= Juan Flamenco) in Madrid, 1597, is difficult to place. We do not have the background to ascertain whether this represents a local Spanish product or an import from the Low Countries. I incline tentatively to the latter possibility. Religious Orders such as the Cistercians and Premonstratensians issued their own liturgical books. Although these bear late imprints of 1668 and 1680 respectively, it is reasonable to postulate that the Cistercian readings may have been arrived at as much as a quarter century earlier.[14] In order to make allowance for special circumstances in the transmission of individual chants, the selection of readings to be presented will not remain entirely fixed throughout.

Those who accepted the new Medicean Missal published in 1570 had, perforce, to make at least minimal changes in those few chants whose texts had been modified. But not all parties involved in the performance of chant were concerned with a more fundamental reshaping of the medium. We can, for example, trace the consistency of Carthusian practice by means of a series of prints from the late 1570s onward. Our information concerning Dominican chant derives from two prints of 1722 and 1854, respectively. They indicate very firm adherence to the late medieval Dominican tradition. In order to demonstrate this linkage, it has been necessary to treat these readings separately in the course of the chapter devoted to chant practice of the eighteenth century. There are two manuscripts of Benedictine provenance in the Universitätsbibliothek Würzburg that are ascribed to the years 1623–24; these two also show a determination to keep alive earlier traditions. In short, there was a rich mix of practice, demonstrating varied and often inde-pendent efforts at providing suitable music for Mass. Because this material is virtually unknown, its exploration will of necessity deal with very large quantities of minutiae. Only by this means is it possible to establish the range of practice and the vitality of activity during a major historical period.

The Checklist of sources that will open this study will document the extraordinary expansion in the number of publications in the last three quarters of the eighteenth century and especially throughout the nineteenth century. A number of these later sources were intended for private devotional and congregational use, a sociological development of considerable significance. A thorough exploration of this material is beyond the capacity of any one individual. Indeed, even a complete bibliographical account cannot be achieved by one person with only limited time and resources. I have not had the resources to explore the field of late manuscript Graduals. The reader will regretfully find the citations to vary in completeness and consistency. It is for this reason that I describe the assemblage as a "checklist" rather than a bibliography. However, the patent shortcomings of what is presented will hopefully act as a spur to others to advance this work, and in the meantime it will patch a glaring lacuna in our knowledge of sources.

Following a series of six exploratory chapters, an additional four will complete the volume. The first of these will deal with "*plainchant musical*" and the second with Neo-Gallican chant. The third will reflect briefly on the results of earlier chapters and on some aspects of chant in the eighteenth century. The last will consider briefly the further development of chant ca. 1800–1890 and survey various efforts to return to medieval practices occurring after ca. 1840.

The terrain to be covered in this book is vast and my objectives are, as I have indicated, limited. I seek to provide the reader with a representative panorama of the written record of chant during a period of three centuries. Even when this is in place, much more will remain to be done before we can claim to have a well-rounded account of the topic as a whole. It will be necessary to investigate the body of manuscript evidence, and it will be necessary to create a complementary panorama of the vital theoretical writings on the subject.[15] Building on the latter foundation, we must forge an understanding of the various aspects of performance practice, investigating questions of rhythm, ornamentation, improvisation, and accompaniment in a thorough manner. Then too, we ought to consider sociological questions, looking more closely into the role that chant played in the religious life of different worshipping communities and private individuals. Additionally, aesthetic issues deserve greater attention than they have received in the past.

Despite the importance of the issues which lie beyond the purview of this book, I claim that it is not possible to address these meaningfully without the grounding that will be provided here. By virtue of the numbers of copies involved in even a modest print run, the individual printed edition was used by a far greater number of persons in a far greater number of localities than any single manuscript. The evidence of theorists, however important, cannot be fully understood until we obtain some background regarding the versions of chant that were familiar to them. This we do not yet have. The same may be said of the infinitely more difficult subject matter of the various modes of chant performance that flourished during the period, 1590–1890. Such an understanding must be founded on an awareness of the music the singers had available to them. We cannot safely leapfrog past the foundation provided here in order to focus on the other fascinating issues that exist. What I present here may perhaps be viewed as the equivalent of the dry bones seen by Ezekiel, brought together with their sinews. It will remain for later studies to clothe these with flesh and to endow them with living spirit. However, without these skeletons, we cannot hope for either the flesh or the spirit.

The ultimate revival of the spirit of this large and varied repertoire will of course involve the performance of this music. The Compact Disc included with this study takes a bold and welcome step in this direction. With the exception of *Plainchant Parisien* (performed by the Ensemble Organum under the direction of Marcel Pérès, Harmonia mundi 901480) a disc containing—among other things—a Neo-Gallican Mass Proper for Christmas, extremely little has been available for interested listeners. The reader is urged to take full advantage of the CD presented here, and I express the hope that it may encourage other performers to explore the richness of this neglected repertoire.

TWO

A Checklist of Printed Graduals ca. 1590–1890

The following checklist began in 1993 as an incidental by-product of a desire—still unfulfilled—to create a history of the *Alleluia Laetatus sum*. By that time I had access to various films of Graduals and Missals created before 1400, but extremely few posterior to that date. Prior to the meeting of Cantus Planus at Eger, Hungary, I took advantage of a few days in Paris to visit different libraries and transcribe readings of this chant. I thus became acquainted with late chant resources available at the Département de Musique of the Bibliothèque nationale and visited the Bibliothèque Mazarine and the Bibliothèque Ste. Geneviève. Two years later, I had an even shorter stop-over in Vienna, and worked at the Österreichische Nationalbibliothek. Later, an independent trip afforded whirlwind visits to major libraries in Rome. Through the kindness of Warren Kirkendale, I learned of the exceptional resources of the Biblioteca Feininger in Trent. The 1997 meeting of the International Musicological Society in London afforded a few hours of study in Cambridge and London. The year following brought a two-week trip to Milan, Trent, Venice, and Florence. The opportunity to spend a few days at the Biblioteca Feininger proved to be an eye-opening experience, thanks to the kindnesses of Professor Marco Gozzi and the staff at the Castello del Buon Consiglio. This proved to be a turning point in my work, and provided the impetus for the present book. The information furnished by Gozzi's fine catalogue of the prints in the Biblioteca Feininger[1] was instrumental in allowing my collection of miscellaneous notes to coalesce sufficiently to form the skeleton of this checklist. A later visit to libraries at Munich and Augsburg provided further essential materials.

As my attention turned from the limited history of one chant to the broader endeavor undertaken here, it became increasingly urgent to obtain a workable overview of the relevant source material. Unfortunately, published catalogues of various libraries are limited in number and liturgical music is an area that may be overlooked. For the most part this investigation must be conducted by means of search engines on the Internet. WorldCat offers a convenient beginning for materials in the United States, but in this field it offers little elsewhere. At the time I was searching for sources, LibWeb (http://lists.webjunction.org/libweb/) provided convenient access to many European libraries. The number of national and regional online catalogues has continued to grow and to change. Yet not every library has completed the cataloguing of its holdings in their entirety, and a few require passwords in order to access their catalogues, rendering them inaccessible to most strangers. The holdings of religious institutions are seldom made known to the public. When searching, one must deal with the variability of the titles used by the various prints as well as the variability of cataloguing procedures. If one searches for "Graduale," one will not necessarily find "Cantus Missarum," to cite only one extreme example. Thus it is necessary to go over the same body of material multiple times as one's knowledge improves. In addition, the information provided in different entries can vary considerably. Sometimes it is quite full. The electronic catalogue of the Katholieke Universiteit Nijmegen offers the luxury of facsimiles of the title pages of their rare materials. At other times the information provided is very scant and is insufficient for secure identification. From the time that I halted my searches to the time that I read page proofs new entries had become available that I could no longer take into account. It is likely that similar improvements will be made over the next several years. I have done what I could with the materials at my disposal and within the limits of my time. I would be pleased to see others carry this work forward.

I am prompted to submit this Checklist to public view in part because of the major void in this area of our knowledge and because others have trod the same paths before me with contrasting results. There were pioneering scholars such as Amadée Gastoué and Alphonse Goovaerts, as well as more contemporary scholars who have seen editions that I have not been able to locate as of this time. Unfortunately, the circumstances of their reporting were such that we have not been given either reasonably full titles or the names of the institutions in which the volumes are to be found. I have listed these citations in my checklist, but have been unable to go beyond the information they provided. On occasion the reader may be surprised by the lack of mention of an early volume. The *Graduale Romanum* issued by Liechtenstein in 1580 has been cited in more than one place as being connected with post-Tridentine chant. The various comparisons that I have been able to make with its forebear issued by the same firm in 1525 indicate, however, that the 1580 edition gives a reasonably accurate portrayal of the earlier volume, apart from the occasional omission of a few tonal repetitions. There are also minor adjustments necessitated by textual changes made in the Roman Missal of 1570. The volume does not appear in the checklist and is instead used as a standard of comparison with later traditions.

Much more remains to be done before we can claim to have a reasonably complete and dependable bibliography of post-Tridentine sources for the Mass Proper. Library cataloguing on the Internet is a tool that is in process of coming into being. It will likely be much improved a decade hence. Close scrutiny of that which follows will reveal both inconsistencies and omissions. The field of research is deserving of a more complete and consistent bibliography. In a developing field, we should not make it necessary continually to reinvent the wheel.

A few words concerning editorial procedures followed here may be advisable. Most entries have been taken from citations on the Internet. These are human products and as such are subject to human error. I have tried to clean up a few obvious typographical errors and can only hope that I have not introduced an equal number through my own work. I have not been able to arrive at a uniform policy with regard to orthography, e.g., with the distinctions between "i" and "j" and between "u" and "v." In the citations that follow I have differentiated between "u" and "v," but the reader should understand that not all libraries do so in their cataloguing. On the other hand, I have not found it equally practical to do similarly with regard to "i" and "j" (e.g., between *iuxta* and *juxta*). This seems to be a chronological matter, with the early prints using the "i" forms and later ones making the distinction between "i" and "j." By and large I have let these matters stand as I found them. The citations for libraries use the English forms for place names. These are given mainly in the order in which I chanced upon them; this means that entries within the U.S. appear first.

Certain citations that I have seen have not been entered here, and readers might wish to be advised of these. A handful of Icelandic Graduals were published beginning not later than 1679; these are to be found for the most part in British libraries. I have entered only the 1679 print because the official religion of Iceland was Lutheran and it is extremely probable that these are records of the Lutheran rather than the Catholic rite. Those interested in this field may wish to consult the facsimile edition of a book edited by Niels Jesperssøn in 1573, *Gradual: En allmindelig Sangbog*.[2] There is an excellent possibility that the later Icelandic publications took this (or a similar work) as a point of departure. The book contains an admixture of Latin chant from the Gregorian tradition together with new chants in Danish. The Latin chants do not constitute a complete Gregorian Mass. Instead we find chants for the introit (together with the psalm verse), and the Alleluia. The latter is shorn from the Gregorian jubilus, and thus may end on a tone other than the expected final. There is a small group of sequences, all quite well known. In addition, *Mane prima sabbathi* is given, rubricated as an offertory. Perhaps because the Alleluias lack the jubilus, the opening is repeated before the singing of the sequence. There is a generous sampling of settings for the Mass Ordinary, and these are assigned to individual Masses, rather than being collected in a Kyriale placed near the beginning or the end. Occasionally a Kyrie will be given in texted form, as in the *Kyrie fons bonitatis*.

I have also omitted mention of a variety of English sources for the Gregorian Mass. Bennett Zon reminds us that the practice of Catholicism was outlawed during the reign of Elizabeth I, and was able to survive only underground and in the chapels maintained by foreign embassies.[3] An obvious result of these various prohibitions was the difficulty, if not impossibility, of publishing Catholic service books in England. When these conditions were relaxed, publishers still lacked the fonts necessary for the printing of the music. The chant had to be entered by hand in one manner or another, and these entries are often lacking. I have made mention only of *The Roman Gradual on the Gregorian Note,* issued in 1737. An extensive listing of the *Principal Eighteenth-century English Catholic Liturgical Books* is provided by Zon in his book, on pages 65–71.

During the three centuries that constitute the focus of this study, various local pamphlets containing a small number of chants used in the specific locality were also published. These often had as a title *Proprium missarum,* followed by the name of a particular locality. Others are entitled *Supplementum graduali romano pro diocese...* or *Supplément* etc., again with the specification of the diocese for which they are intended. For the most part these seem to be small pamphlets that have little bearing on broader matters of transmission. They seem to proliferate in nineteenth-century France. Unless there was evidence to show that they were moderately sizeable contributions I have omitted them. There are other publications whose titles do not securely indicate the nature of their content. What does one do with a work such as *Le Moniteur des fidèles...* 1870? This turned up as a result of a search under "Graduel romain," and has been accepted here with some qualms. Yet another volume similarly entitled has not been retained in light of the fact that it is only of pamphlet length. Equally problematic is a *Proprium officiorum ecclesiae cathedralis...Divionensis,* 1753, which surfaced in a similar search. Present-day usage would suggest that this is an antiphonary, but earlier usage was less specific, because the Mass was regarded as a liturgical office. I have tried to use my discretion as best I could, but my success in separating the sheep from the goats is open to question. One last caution: the reader will note on occasion that certain volumes held before 1940 by the British Library were destroyed during the war by bombardment. In the card catalogue these are differentiated by a special abbreviation, but this distinction is not made on the library's Internet citations. I am unable to verify whether other volumes that I located via the library's web catalogue suffered a similar fate.

In another area I have included unhesitatingly citations for prints concerned with Neo-Gallican chant. I suspect that most publications that include the name of a French city within the title subsequent to 1730 and one or two before 1730 are of this nature. One cannot, however, rely uniformly on this criterion. We shall see in due course that these sources contain numerous revisions of Gregorian melodies as well as new settings of texts used in the Roman rite. I have had access to only a handful of these sources and have no way of verifying the true nature of each.

Dated Graduals

1585   *Proprium Missarum Ordinis Fratrum Minorum*. Venetiis, 1585.
       Milan, Bibl. Ambrosiana

1586[1]   *Graduale Romanum integrum et completum: tam de tempore quam de sanctis. Iuxta ritum Missalis novi, ex decreto sacrosancti Concilii Tridentini restituti. Et Pii Quinti Pont. Max. iussu editi....* Venetiis, apud Iuntas, 1586.
       Rome, Bibl. di Archeologia e Storia dell'Arte; Fara Sabina, Bibl. statale del Monumento nazionale di Farfa
       Facsimile page in Raphael Molitor, *Reform-Choral: historisch-kritische Studie* (Freiburg in Breisgau, 1901), 65.

1586[2]   *Graduale Romanum...iuxta ritum Missalis novi, ex decreto sacrosancti Concilii Tridentini restituti....* Venetiis, apud Iohannem Variscum & Paganinum de Paganinis, 1586.
       Trent, Bibl. com.

1587   *Graduale et Antiphonarium omnium dierum festorum Ordinis Minorum, iuxta ritum Missalis et Breviarii novi per Ludovicum Balbum Venetum, ex Ordine minorum con Magistri Capel. S. Antonii de Padua, Nuperrime impressum.* Venice, Angelo Gardano, 1587.
       Berkeley (Calif.), Univ. of California; Bologna, Civico museo bibliografico musicale, R. 292; Cambridge, Fitzwilliam Museum; Cesena, Bibl. Comunale Maletestiana

1591   *Graduale Romanum. iuxta ritum Missalis Novi, ex decreto sacrosancti Concilii Tridentini restituti....* Venetiis, Apud Angelum Gardanum, 1591.
       Berkeley (Calif.), Univ. of California, M2149.V38 1591 [inc.]; Minneapolis (Minn.), Univ. of Minnesota; Chicago, Univ. of Chicago, Regenstein Library, M2149 f.A4; Cesena, Bibl. Comunale Malatestiana; Oxford, Bodleian Library

1594   [*Graduale Romanum....* 1594]?
       Heverlee (Leuven), Park Abbey
       This volume has been missing as of Jan. 2001 and its former existence is questionable; supplementary information available in the past on the Internet must be treated with great caution unless the work should resurface.

1595–97 [*Graduale Romanum*] *Proprium missarum de Tempore a Dominica Prima Adventus....* Matriti, ex Typographia regia, [apud I. Flandrus] M.D. XCVII. 4 vols. Madrid, Juan Flamenco, 1595/97.
       Austin, Univ. Texas, Gzz 783.5 C286p; Bloomington (Ind.), Indiana Univ., M2148.L4 1597; Toronto, Univ. of Toronto Music Library; Trent, Bibl. Feininger, FSG 17 (= Vol. II?)

1596   *Graduale Romanum: de tempore et sanctis ad ritum Missalis, ex decreto sacrosancti Concilii Tridentini restituti Et Pii Quinti Pont. Max. iussu editi:....* Venetiis. apud Iuntas. M.D.XCVI.
       Augsburg, Staatsbibl., 2° ThLtk 26

1599[1]   *Graduale Romanum integrum, complectens cantum Gregorianum officii totius anni, tam de tempore, quam de sanctis*. . . . Burdigalae, Apud S. Millangium, 1599.
Copenhagen, Kongelige Bibl., UA ÆS 42°

1599[2]   *Graduale Romanum: de tempore et sanctis iuxta ritum Missalis ex decreto sacrosancti Concilii Tridentini restituti*. . . . Antwerpiae, Ex Officina Plantiniana apud Joannem Moretum MDXCIX.
Alleghany (N.Y.), St. Bonaventure Univ.; Vatican, Bibl. Apost. Vat., Racc.I.Str.76; Brussels, Bibl. royale, III 98.637 D LP; Leuven, Katholieke Universiteitsbibl. (2 copies); Antwerp, Stadsbibl., H38254; Antwerp, Museum Plantin-Moretus, A1, R38.8; Oxford, Bodleian Library, B 1.10 Th. Seld; Glasgow, Univ. Library, Sp. Coll. Mu20.x–10

1600[1]   *Psalterium, hymni collectae, evangelia, epistolae, introitus, graduale et sequentiae . . . adiecta precationum.* Coloniae, Quentel, 1600.
Paris, Bibl. nat., Imp., B–16378; Göttingen, Universitätsbibl., 8 H E RIT I, 8900; Weimar, Herzog August Amalia Bibl. (It is not known at this time whether this volume survived the disastrous fire that struck this library on 6 September, 2004.)
This publication contains only texts.

1600[2]   *Graduale Romanum de tempore et sanctis ad ritum Missalis, ex decreto sacrosancti Concilii Tridentini restituti: et Pii V Pont. Max: iussu editi . . . Ad uniformem Ecclesiarum per universas Regni Poloniae Provincias usum.* Cracoviae, Andreas Petricovius (=Piotrkowczyk), 1600.
Tarnów, Biblioteka Seminarium Wyzszego; Czestochowa, Seminarium Duchownego

1602   See 1606[1]

1605   *Proprium Missarum de tempore* . . . . Venetiis, 1605.
London, Victoria and Albert Museum, National Art Library

1606[1]   *Graduale Romanum de tempore et sanctis, Ad ritum Missalis, ex decreto sacrosancti Concilii Tridentini restituti, Pii Quinti Pontificis Maximi iussu editi* . . . . Venetiis, apud Iuntas MDCVI De licentie Superiorum.
Vatican, Bibl. Apost. Vat., Racc. gen. Liturgia Str. 33; Venice, Bibl. Marciana, Misc. T. 1600; Bologna, Civico museo bibliografico musicale (according to Molitor, *Nach-Tridentinische*, II, 173).
The editions catalogued under the year 1602 at Austin, Univ. Texas, microfilm? and at Boston, New England Conservatory, may be the same. The publisher Giunta and the year MDCVI appear as part of the explicit.

1606[2]   *Proprium Missarum Ordinis Minorum.* Lugduni, Bonaventurae Nugo, 1606.
Lyon, Facultés Catholiques, Bibl. centrale, LFCC 168.C–1, Fonds ancien

1607   *Graduale Romanum de tempore & sanctis. Ad ritum Missalis ex decreto Sacrosancti Concilii Tridentini restituti* . . . . Venetiis, apud Bernardum Iuntam, 1607.
London, British Library, 3356.d.11

1608/9   *[Graduel Parisien . . .].* Paris, [Societas Typographicae librorum officii Ecclesiastici?], 1608.

Cited by Amédée Gastoué, *Le Graduel et l'antiphonaire romains* (Lyon, 1913), 186. Apparently alluded to in the Preface of 1627, with the date 1609; a surviving copy was not located.

1609   *Graduale Romanum juxta novum missale recognitum et iussu sanctiss. Domini nostri Pauli Papae V.* Editum I. Apud Joach. Trognaesium. Antverpiae, MDCIX.

Antwerp, Museum Plantin-Moretus, A 4574[2]

1610   *Graduale Romanum de tempore et sanctis, ad ritum Missalis, ex decreto sacrosancti Concilii Tridentini restituti, Pii quinti Pontificis maximi iussu editi, et Clementis VIII. auctoritate recogniti. . . . De licentia superiorum.* Venetiis, apud Cieras, M DC X.

Trent, Bibl. Feininger, FSG 18

1611?   *Graduale Romanum de tempore et sanctis. Ad ritum Missalis, ex decreto sacrosancti Concilii Tridentini restituti, Pii Quinti Pontificis Maximi iussu editi, et Clementis VIII. auctoritate recogniti.* Venetiis, apud Iuntas [Heirs?], 1611?

London, British Library, L.18.f.6; Munich, Universitätsbibl.; Bologna, Civico museo bibliografico musicale (according to Molitor, *Nach-Tridentinische*, II, 174).

The title page bears the date 1561, but the British Library Catalogue states that the "date has been altered from 1611." Since the title page mentions the Council of Trent and Pope Clement VIII (1592–1605), the date of 1561 cannot be correct.

1614/15   *Graduale de tempore. Iuxta ritum Sacrosanctae romanae ecclesiae. Cum cantu Pauli v. pont. max. iussu reformato.* 2 vols. Romae, ex Typographia Medicaea: i, 1614; ii, 1615.

Washington, D.C., Library of Congress, M2149.R7 1615; Bologna, Bibl. Comunale dell' Archiginnasio, 16cc.I.1 and 2; Vallombrosa (Florence), Bibl. dell' Abbazia; Paris, Bibl. nat., Rés. F 860; Rome, Bibl. naz. cen., 68.Banc.II.1, 68.Banc.II.2–5, and 68.Banc.II.6–7; Vatican, Bibl. Apost. Vat. (3 copies), Racc/I.Str/132, Sistine 347, and 348; Trent, Bibl. Feininger, FSG 19 and FSG 20 (2 copies); Antwerp, Museum Plantin-Moretus, R. 37.1

Facsimile publication in *Monumenta Studia Instrumenta Liturgica*, 10, 11, ed. by Giacomo Baroffio and Manlio Sodi, and by Giacomo Baroffio and Eun Ju Kim, resp. (Vatican, 2001).

1616   *Graduale Romanum iuxta Missale. Ex decreto sacrosancti Concilii Tridentini restitutum, et Clementis VIII. auctoritate recognitum. Adiectis officiis novissime editis ad exemplar Missalis romani.* Tournai, apud Viduam Nicolai Laurentii, 1616.

Wolfenbüttel, Herzog August Bibl., 2.2 Musica fol. (Schmieder, Kat. XII, #801)

1618[1]   *Graduale Romanum de tempore et sanctis, ad ritum Missalis, ex decreto sacrosancti Concilii Tridentini restituti, Pii Quinti Pontificis Maximi iussu editi,* Venetiis, apud Iuntas, 1618.

Trent, Bibl. Feininger, FSG 22 (#332); Munich, Bayerische Staatsbibl., 2 Liturg. 130

1618[2]   *Graduale Romanum de tempore et sanctis, ad ritum Missalis, ex decreto sacrosancti Concilii Tridentini restituti, Pii Quinti Pontificis Maximi iussu editi*, Venetiis, apud Cieras, 1618.

Trent, Bibl. Feininger, FSG 21 (#331)

1618[3]   *Graduale Romanum iuxta novum Missale recognitum pro ecclesiis maxime diocesios Frisingensis accomodatum.* Ingolstadium, Angermaier, 1618.

Munich, Bayerische Staatsbibl., 2 Liturg. 129 and 4 Liturg. 702 p

1620   *Graduale Romanum iuxta missale. Ex decreto sacrosancti Concilii Tridentini restitutum, et Clementis VIII. auctoritate recognitum. Adiectis officiis novissime editis ad exemplar Missalis romani.* Antverpiae, Apud Petrum & Ioannem Belleros, 1620.

Chapel Hill (N.C.), Univ. of North Carolina, Vault Folio M2148.L4 1620 (*olim* M783.23 C36g 1620 Music Lib.)

1621   *Graduale Romanum de tempore et sanctis....* Venetiis, apud Cieras, 1621.

Munich, Bayerische Staatsbibl., 2 Liturg. 131; Montevergine-Mercogliano, Bibl. statale del Monumento nazionale

1622[1]   *[Graduale Romanum integrum ...].* Bordeaux, Charrier, 1622.

Cited by Amédée Gastoué, *Le Graduel et l'antiphonaire romains* (Lyon, 1913), 186.

1622[2]   *[Graduel de Toul...].* Toul, Le Belgrand, 1622. (See 1627.)

Cited by Amédée Gastoué, *Le Graduel et l'antiphonaire romains* (Lyon, 1913), 191.

1623   *Graduale Romanum juxta Missale ex decreto sacrosancti Concilii Tridentini restitutum et Clementis VIII auctoritate recognitum....*Bruxellis, Joannis Mommartius, 1623.

Brussels, Bibl. royale, II 99.372 B LP; Utrecht, Universiteitsbibl., F Fol 168 [CBAB AB]

1626   *Graduale Romanum de tempore et sanctis. Ad ritum Missalis, ex decreto sacrosancti Concilii Tridentini restituti, Pii Quinti Pontificis Maximi iussu editi....*Venetiis, Iunta, 1626.

Berkeley (Calif.), Univ. of California; Genoa, Bibl. della Badia dei Benedettini di S. Andrea della Castagna

1627   *Graduale Romanum, iuxta Missale ex decreto Sacrosancti Concilii Tridentini, Pii V. Pont. Max. iussu antea editum....*Tulli Leucorum [=Toul], Simonis Belgrandi. [see also 1633, 1656].

London, British Library, 1885.i.2 (with 6 MS pages from 1685); Salzburg, Dombibliothek St. Peter (2 copies, one fragmentary), with handwritten corrections and additions.

The citation by Heinz Wagener in *Geschichte der katholischen Kirchenmusik,* ed. by K. G. Fellerer (Kassel, 1976), II, 177, may be to this item.

1629[1]   *Graduale Romanum de tempore et sanctis, ad ritum Missalis, ex decreto sacrosancti Concilii Tridentini restituti, Pii Quinti Pontificis maximi iussu editi, et Clementis VIII. auctoritate recogniti....* Venetiis, Cieras, M DC XXIX.

Trent, Bibl. Feininger, FSG 23 (#333); Feltre, Bibl. del Duomo

1629[2]   *Graduale Romanum de tempore sancto* .... Cracoviae, [Piotrkowczyk], 1629.
Warsaw, Bibl. Uniwersytecka; Kraków, Bibl. Jagiellonska, 311397 IV St.
Dr. (defective)

1630[1]   *Graduale Romanum de tempore et sanctis, ad ritum Missalis, ex decreto sacrosancti*
Concilii Tridentini restituti; Et Clementis VIII auctoritate recogniti. Ingolstadii,
Casparis Sutoris, typis Wilhelmi Ederi, 1630.
Munich, Bayerische Staatsbibl., 2 Liturg. 132 and 2 Liturg. 132a

1630[2]   *Graduale Romanum iuxta missale. Ex decreto sacrosancti Concilii Tridentini restitutum,*
et Clementis VIII, auctoritate recognitum. Adiectis officiis novissime editis ad exem-
plar Missalis romani. Ultimo editio multo auctior et emendatior. Tournai, apud
Viduam Nicolai Laurentii, 1630.
Cited by Alphonse Goovaerts, *Histoire et bibliographie de la typographie musi-*
cale dans les anciens Pays-Bas (Antwerp, 1880), 350.

1632[1]   *[Graduel Parisien ....].* Paris, Thiboust, 1632.
Cited by Amédée Gastoué, *Le Graduel et l'antiphonaire romains* (Lyon,
1913), 186.

1632[2]   *Graduale Romanum.* Utrecht, van Borckeloo, 1632.
Cited by Alphonse Goovaerts, *Histoire et bibliographie* (Antwerp, 1880), 353.

1633[1]   *Graduale Romanum, iuxta Missale ex decreto sacrosancti Concilii Tridentini, Pii V.*
Pont. Max. iussu antea editum. Et Clementis VIII. etiam Pontificis Max. auctoritate
nuper recognitum .... Tulli Leucorum [=Toul], Ex officina Simonis Belgrand &
Ioannis Laurentii, 1633.
Cambridge, Trinity College, c.6.16; Munich, Bayerische Staatsbibl., 2
Liturg. 132m
These two copies may vary slightly in title; see also 1656.

1633[2]   *Graduale Romanum juxta novum Missale recognitum. Ed. novissima summa diligentia*
ab erroribus expurgata. Lovanii, Bernardinum Masium, 1633.
Utrecht, Universiteitsbibl., 320 E 13 [CBDP1 ABDP1]

1633[3]   *Missae proprium festorum Ordinis Fratrum Minorum ad formam misssalis*
Romani .... Antverpiae, apud Henricum Aertssens, 1633.
Antwerp, Staatbibl., F210701; cited by Alphonse Goovaerts, *Histoire et*
bibliographie (Antwerp, 1880), 35?

1635   *[Graduale Romanum nova et accurata editione modulatum iuxta decr. Sac. Con. Trid.].*
(Paris?), 1635. [Title page lacking; date established by prefatory matter, place by
readings.]
St. Louis (Mo.), Washington Univ.
For possible additional copies, see entry under 1655[2].

1640   *Graduale Romanum iuxta Missale ex decreto sacro-sancti Concilii Tridentini, Pii V.*
Pont. Max. iussu editum, et Clementis VIII. primum, nunc denuo urbani pape octavi
auctoritate recognitum .... Paris, Impensis Societatis Typographicae librorum
officii Ecclesiastici iussu Regis constitutae, 1640.
Cambridge, Univ. Library, Peterborough U.5.2

1642   [Graduale Romanum . . . .]. [Venice, Ciera, 1642]. [Title page lacking; information
        taken from the Regestum.]
        Copenhagen, Kongelige Bibl.
        Professor Richard Agee reports that this item and 1643 are the same.

1643   Graduale Romanum de tempore et sanctis ad ritum Missalis ex decreto sacros. Concilii
        tridentini re[s]tituti Pii 5. Pontificis Max iussu editi et Celementis 8. Primum nunc
        denuo Urbani Papae 8. auctoritate recogniti. Venice, Ciera, 1643.
        Urbania, Bibl. capitolare

1644   Graduale Carmelitarum . . . . 1644.
        Modern edition by T. Chrzanowski and T. Maciejewski (Warsaw, 1976).

1647[1] Graduale Romanum de tempore et sanctis, ad ritum Missalis, ex decreto sacrosancti
        Concilii Tridentini restituti, Pii quinti Pontificis maximi iussu editi, et Clementis VIII.
        auctoritate recogniti . . . . Venetiis, Apud Iuntas, M.DC.XXXXVII.
        Trent, Bibl. Feininger, FSG 24 (#334)

1647[2] Graduale missarum propriarum festorum Fratrum Ordinis Minorum ad formam Missalis
        Romani, ex decreto sacrosancti Concilii Tridentini restituti, Pii quinti Pontificis
        maximi iussu editi, et Clementis VIII. auctoritate recogniti, redactarum. Venetiis,
        apud Iuntas, M.DC. XXXXVII.
        Trent, Bibl. Feininger, FSG 25 (#335)

1647[3] Graduale Romanum . . . . Christophe Ballard, [Paris,] 1647.
        Cited in Bennett Zon, The English Plainchant Revival (Oxford, 1999), 24
        [after Robert Hayburn, Papal Legislation on Sacred Music, 1979].

1648   Graduale Romanum iuxta novum Missale recognitum. Lovanii, B. [Bunandinum?]
        Masium, 1648.
        Novara, Bibl. dell'Archivio capitolare della Basilica di San Gaudenzio

1650?   [. . . Romanum . . . cum notis Ludovici Paschalis]. [Paris, Jean de la Caille, 1650.] [Title
        page lacking; information taken from the Privilège.]
        Valognes, Bibl. mun. Julien de Laillier, C 1150, Fonds ancien 2
        Listed as a Gradual in an Online Public Access Catalogue, this is actually
        an Antiphonal; for the Gradual, see 1666 and 1668.

1651   Graduale Romanum . . . . Cracoviae, Piotrkowczyk, 1651.
        Kraków, Bibl. Czartoryskich, 44670 IV; Kraków, Bibl. Jagiellonska, 224850
        IV Mag. St. Dr. (defective)

1653[1] Graduale Romanum de tempore et sanctis, ad ritum Missalis, ex decreto sacrosancti
        Concilii Tridentini restituti, Pii V. Pontificis maximi iussu editi, et Clementis VIII.
        primum, nunc denuo Urbani papae octavi auctoritate recogniti. Venetiis,
        M.DC.LIII, apud Franciscum Baba.
        Munich, Bayerische Staatsbibl., 2 Liturg. 133; Trent, Bibl. Feininger, FSG
        25 (#336); Bologna, Civico museo bibliografico musicale

1653[2] Appendix ad Graduale Romanum . . . . Antverpiae, 1653.
        Cited by Alphonse Goovaerts, Histoire et bibliographie (Antwerp, 1880), 358.

1655¹   *Graduale Romanum, iuxta Missale ex decreto sacro-sancti Concilii Tridentini, Pii V pontif. Maxim. jussu editum, et Clementis VIII primum, nunc denno Urbani papae octavi auctoritate recognitum. Cujus sanctitas, ne vetus graduale recudatur, gravi interminatione sanxit....* Parisiis, ex officina Roberti Ballard, 1655.
Dijon, Bibl. mun., 20758, CGA; Avignon, Bibl. mun., 8° 33101, Théologie; Solesmes, Abbaye de Saint Pierre, Bibl., LLc.7–1(1)

1655²   *Graduale Romanum iuxta Missale ex decreto Sacro-Sancti Concilii Tridentini Pii 5. Pontif. Max. iussu editum et Clementis 8. primum nunc denuo Urbani Papae octavi auctoritate recognitum....* S.l., s.n., 1655.
Rome, Bibl. Casanatense (2 copies).
According to information kindly supplied by Professor Richard Agee, the fuller of the two copies held by the Biblioteca Casanatense has a prefatory notice by the Archbishop of Paris dated 1635. The publication is obviously French and may be the same as the one listed here under 1635. Neither of us is able to conjecture how the date indicated in the cataloguing came to be.

1656   *Graduale Romanum, iuxta Missale ex decreto Sacrosancti Concilii Tridentini, Pii V. Pont. Max. iussu antea editum. Et Clementis VIII. etiam Pontificis Max. auctoritate nuper recognitum....* Tulli Leucorum [=Toul], Ex officina Simonis Belgrandis & Ioannis Laurentii, 1656.
New York, New York Public Library, *MRD

1657   *Graduale Romanum de tempore et sanctis....* Societatis Typographicae Librorum Officii Ecclesiastici iussu Regis constitutae, Paris. 1657.
Munich, Bayerische Staatsbibl., 2 Liturg. 134

1658¹   *Graduale Romano-monasticum iuxta Missale Pauli V. Pontificis maximi authoritate editum...in usum et gratiam monialium Ordinis Sancti Augustini....* Parisiis, R. Ballard, 1658.
Chantilly, Bibl. des Fontaines LB 23–4

1658²   *Graduale Romano-monasticum iuxta Missale Pauli V. Pontificis maximi authoritate editum...in usum et gratiam monialium Ordinis Regula S. P. N. Benedicti militantium....* Parisiis, R. Ballard, 1658.
Solesmes, Abbaye de Saint Pierre, Bibl., LLc.7–27(1); Vitré, Bibl. mun., T. 183.

1658³   *Graduale Romano-monasticum iuxta Missale Pauli V. Pontificis maximi authoritate editum...in usum et gratiam monialium Ordinis S. P. N. Francisci....* Parisiis, R. Ballard, 1658.
Valognes, Bibl. mun. Julien de Laillier, B 345, Fonds ancien 2

1662   *Graduale iuxta Missale Parisiense Eminentissimi et Reverendissimi in Christo Patris D. D. Ioannis Francisci Pauli de Gondy. Dei & Sanctae Sedis Apostolicae gratiâ S. R. E. Tituli Sanctae Mariae super Minervum Presbyter Cardinalis de RETZ, Parisiensi Archiepiscopi auctoritate. Ac Venerabilis Capituli eiusdem Ecclesiae consensu editum. In quo continentur Introitus, Gradualia cum Versibus, Alleluia, etiam cum versu, Tractus, Sequentiae sive Prosae, Offertoria, atque Communiones omnium Missarum Dominicarum, Feriarum & Festorum totius Anni bene disposita & ordinata in Notis.* Parisiis, Apud Sebastianum Cramoisy, Gabrielem & Nicolaum Clopeiau, 1662.
Paris, Bibl. Mazarine, 1170Q

1666   *Graduale Romanum, iuxta Missale ex decreto sacro-sancti Concilii Tridentini : cui additus est cantus missarum omnium votivarum, qui desiderabatur ante haec...opera et labor R. P. P. Ordinis F. M....Louis Paschal.* Paris, Johannes de La Caille, 1666.
Paris, Bibl. nat., Imp., B–4321

1667   *Les Messes des principales festes de l'année, avec les Benedictions des Cierges, des Cendres et des Ramaux...Pour les religieuses de la Congrégation Notre-Dame.* Toul, J. & J. F. Laurent, 1667.
Private collection

1668¹   *Graduale Romanum de tempore et sanctis ad ritum Missalis ex decreto sacros. Concilii Tridentini restituti, Pii 5. Pont. Max. iussu editi et Clementis 8. auctoritate recogniti....* Venetiis, apud Cieras, 1668.
Bologna, Bibl. del Convento di S. Francesco dei Fratelli Minori Conventuali

1668²   *Graduale Romanum, iuxta Missale ex decreto sacro-sancti Concilii Tridentini : cui additus est cantus missarum omnium votivarum, qui desiderabatur ante haec....* Paris, Ioannem de la Caille, 1668.
Lincoln (Nebr.), Univ. of Nebraska
Oxford, Bodleian Library, B 20.15Th., is likely the same print.

1668³   *Graduale Cisterciense....* Lutetia Parisiorum, 1668.
Munich, Universitätsbibl.

1669   *Graduale Romanum juxta Missale ex decreto Sacro-Sancti Concilii Tridentini. Pii V. Pont. Max. jussu anteae editum....* Lyon, Petrus Valfray, 1669.
Rodez, Médiathèque, MAG T 1 043, Théologie

1670   *Graduale Romanum, iuxta Missale ex decreto sacrosancti Concilij Tridentini, Pii V. pont. max. iussu antea editum, et Clementis VIII. et Urbani etiam pont. max auctoritate super recognitum....* Lugduni, Sumptibus Societatis bibliopolarum, 1670.
Toulouse, Bibl. mun., Fa C 2416, Fonds ancien 2

1671¹   *Graduale Romanum, iuxta Missale ex decreto sacrosancti Concilij Tridentini, Pii V. pont. max. iussu antea editum, et Clementis VIII. et Urbani etiam pont. max auctoritate super recognitum....* Lugduni, Sumptibus Societatis bibliopolarum, 1671.
Mundelein (Ill.), St. Mary at the Lake Seminary and Univ., BT 4305 1671 Folio
Chambéry, Médiathèque J.-J. Rousseau, Per D 249 Perpéchon, may be another copy.

1671²   *Graduale Missali Romano, cantui vero gregoriano-Moguntino accomodatum.* Moguntiae, Chr. Küchlerus, 1671.
Kraków, Bibl. Jagiellonska (*olim* Berlin, Staatsbibliothek Preußischer Kulturbesitz, Mus. ant. pract. 2°g 782)

1671³   *Graduale Romano-monasticum...in usum et gratiam monialium sub regula S. P. Benedicti militantium.* Parisiis, R. Ballard, 1671.
Aix-en-Provence, Bibl. Méjanes, P. 9203, Pécoul; Autun, Bibl. mun., S6039
Kraków, Bibl. Jagiellonska, 149762 I St. Dr. is likely the same print.

1671[4]   *Le Propre des festes et offices de la Congrégation des religieuses Benedictines de l'Adoration perpétuelle du Très-saint Sacrement.* Paris, Jean Henault, 1671.
Paris, Bibl. nat., Imp., B–1883

1673   *Graduale Romanum juxta Missale...cujus sanctitas ne vetus Graduale reducatur....* Lutetiae Parisiorum, Ludovici Sevestre, 1673.
Québec, Bibl. nationale

1674[1]   *Graduale: recens impressum Missis conventualibus, tam de Tempore, quam de Festo inserviens. Ad usum sacri ordinis Cartusiensis.* Lugduni, ex officina Ioannis Gregoire, Sumptibus majoris Cartusiae, 1674.
Stanford (Calif.), Stanford Univ., M2154.4 C38 G7; Cambridge, Univ. Library, MR 220.a.65.1
Trent, Bibl. Feininger, FSG 26 (#337), ascribed provisionally to ca. 1674, lacks a title page; it could be either a copy of this issue or that of 1679.

1674[2]   *Graduale Romanum juxta missale ex decreto sacrosancti Concilii Tridentini restitutum* .... Antverpiae, Apud Hieronymum & Joan. Bapt. Verdussen, 1674.
Bellingham (Wash.), Western Washington Univ., M 2148.L4 1674; Antwerp, Museum Plantin-Moretus, 4–92

1678   *Appendix ad Graduale Romanum, sive cantiones aliquot sacrae, quae ante, sub & post missam saepe cantari solent.* Ultrajecti, Arnoldi ab Eynden, 1678.
Utrecht, Universiteitsbibl., ODJ 1 dl 2 [CBDP1 ABDP]

1679[1]   *Graduale recens impressum: Missis conventualibus, tam de Tempore quam de Festo inserviens. Ad usum sacri ordinis Cartusiensis.* Lugduni, ex officina Ioannis Gregoire, Sumptibus majoris Cartusiae, MDCLXXIX
Florence, Bibl. Marucelliana, 5.C.III.3

1679[2]   *Graduale: Ein Almeneleg Messusaungs Book....* Editio V, 1679.
Oxford, Oxford Univ., English Fac. EFL York Powell, B.1.12.22

1680[1]   *Graduale Romanum de tempore et Sanctis ad ritum Missalia Pii 5. Pontificis iussu editi et Clementis 8. ac Urbani Papae 8. auctoritate recogniti.* Venetiis, apud Cieras, 1680.
Bologna, Bibl. del Convento di S. Francesco dei Fratelli Minori Conventuali [Vsmc] (2 copies)

1680[2]   *Graduale Praemonstratense, ill. ac rev. DD Michaelis Colbert, Abb. Praem. totius Ordinis Generalis, ejusdemque Capituli generalis authoritate editum et approvatum.* Parisiis, 1680: Gab. Nivers.
Paris, Bibl. nat., Imp., B–1868; Amiens, Bibl. mun., TH 1679B, Théologie; Göttingen, Universitätsbibl., 8 H E RIT I, 9144; Heverlee (Leuven), Park Abbey, AFIV/1; Pr I IV/1; Mondaye, Abbaye prémontrée
Besançon, Bibl. mun., Arch. M.II.14, Archevêché, is likely the same print.

1682[1]   *Graduale Romanum....* Lugduni, P. Valfray, 1682.
Nantes, Bibl. mun., 1093, Fonds ancien 1 (acquisitions après 1900)

1682²   *Graduale Bisuntinum editum juxta Missale illustriss. ac. RR. DD. Ant. Petri de Grammont, archiep. Bisunt., missarum omnium, tam de proprio SS quam de tempore; item et votivarum, complectens cantum: correctum et ad usum ecclesiae metropolitanae Bisuntinae reductum a R. D. Joanne Millet....* Vesuntione, typ. Lud. Rigoine, 1682.

      Besançon, Bibl. mun., 12716, Réserve Comtoise; 5427, Fonds ancien

1682³   *Graduale et Antiphonale ad usum S. Ludovici domus regiae Invalidorum.* 1682.

      Paris, Musée des Invalides, Io

1687¹   *Graduale Romanum, juxta Missale Pii Quinti, Pontificis Maximi, authoritate editum. Cujus modulatio concinne disposita; in usum & gratiam Monialium Ordinis Sancti Augustini. Opera & studio Guillelmi Gabrielis Nivers, Christianissimi Regis Capellae Musices nec-non Ecclesiae Sancti Sulpicii Parisiensis Organistae.* Paris, L'autheur, 1687.

      Chicago, Newberry Library, Estate of Howard Brown; Paris, Bibl. nat., Rés 2287; Oxford, Bodleian Library, Vet. E3 e30. (See also 1658, 1696)

1687²   *Graduale Romanum, juxta Missale Pii Quinti, Pontificis Maximi, authoritate editum. Cujus modulatio concinne disposita; in usum & gratiam Monialium Ordinis Sancti Benedicti. Opera & studio Guillelmi Gabrielis Nivers, Christianissimi Regis Capellae Musices nec-non Ecclesiae Sancti Sulpicii Parisiensis Organistae.* Paris, L'autheur, 1687.

      Nashville (Tenn.), Univ. of Tennessee; Auxerre, Bibl. mun., A 700 4°, Registres; Brussels, Cons. royale, 40.002; Dublin, Univ. College; Solesmes, Abbaye de Saint Pierre, Bibl., LLc.7–21(2)

1687³   *Graduale Romanum, juxta Missale Pii Quinti, Pontificis Maximi, authoritate editum...in usum Ordinis Sancti Francisci.* Paris, L'autheur, 1687.

      Washington, D.C., Holy Name College

1688/89   *Graduale Parisiense, Illustrissimi et Reverendissimi in Christo Patris D. D. Francisci de Harlay. Dei et Sanctae Sedis Apostolicae Gratia Parisiensis Archiepiscopi, Ducis ac Paris Franciae, Regiorum Ordinum Commendatoris, Sorbonae Provisoris, Regiae Navarrae Superiores Au[c]toritate; ac venerabilis ejusdem Ecclesiae Capituli Consensu; Editum, Sumptibus Cleri Parisiensis.* Lutetiae Parisiorum, Typos Lud[ovici] & Lud. Sevestre, Typographor. Vaenit Apud eosdem, via Mori, prope sanctum Nicolaum in Cardineto, 1689.

      Paris, Bibl. Mazarine, 1170Q².2 (*Pars Aestiva* only)

      Explicit to Temporale reads 1688 (p. 246); Explicit to remainder reads 1689 (p. 654).

1690¹   *Graduale Romanum de tempore et sanctis ad normam Missalis ex decreto Sacrosancti Concilii Tridentini restituti....* Venetiis, Sumptibus Pauli Balleoni, 1690.

      London, British Library, L.18.b.13; Piacenza, Bibl. e Archivio Capitolare

1690[2]   *Graduale Romanum de tempore et sanctis. Ad norman missalis, ex decreto sacrosancti Concilij Tridentini restituti, B Pii v, pontificis maximi, iussu editi, Clementis VIII, ac Urbani VIII auctoritate recogniti. Editio omnium optima.* Venetiis, Apud N. Pezzana, 1690.
Washington, D.C., Library of Congress, M2149.V3 1690

1690[3]   *Graduale Romanum juxta Missale ex decreto Sacro-sancti Concilii Tridentini. Pii V. Pont. Max. jussu antea editum, et Clementis VIII. etiam Pont. Max. auctoritate nuper recognitum* . . . . Lugduni, Sumptibus Societatis Bibliopolarum, 1690.
Copenhagen, Kongelige Bibl.; Besançon, Bibl. mun., Arch. P.II.124, Archevêché

1690[4]   *Graduale Romanum* . . . . Cracoviae[?], 1690.
Kraków, Bibl. Jagiellonska, 589097 III Mag. St. Dr.

1691[1]   *Graduale Romanum, juxta novum Missale recognitum* . . . . *Ed. novissima.* Ultrajecti, van Eyndam, 1691.
Utrecht, Universiteitsbibl., 319 D 17 [CBDP1]

1691[2]   *Cantum ecclesiasticum* . . . . Antwerp, 1691.
Paris, Bibl. nat., Rés. 2282

1691[3]   *Graduale Romanum* . . . . Antverpiae, 1691.
Cited by Alphonse Goovaerts, *Histoire et bibliographie* (Antwerp, 1880), 434.

1691[4]   *[Graduale Romanum].* Leyden, 1691.
Cited by Heinz Wagener in *Geschichte der katholischen Kirchenmusik*, ed. by K. G. Fellerer (Kassel, 1976), II, 177.

1691[5]   *[Graduale Romanum]* Lyon, 1691.
Cited by Heinz Wagener in *Geschichte der katholischen Kirchenmusik*, ed. by K. G. Fellerer (Kassel, 1976), II, 177; possibly the same as 1690[3].

1693   *Appendix ad Graduale Romanum* . . . . Amstelodami, Johannis Stichter, 1693.
Overbrook (Penn.), St. Charles Borromeo Seminary

1694[1]   *Graduale Romanum, iuxta Missale, ex decreto Sacro-Sancti Concilii Tridentini, Pii V. pontificis maximi iussu editum, et Clementis VIII. Primum nunc denuo Urbani pape octavi auctoritate recognitum.* Lutetiae Parisiorum, Sumptibus & typis Ludovici Sevestre, 1694.
Québec, Univ. de Laval, L.Rares M2148 L4 1694

1694[2]   *Graduale Romanum iuxta novum Missale recognitum. Editio novissima correctior.* Amstelodami, Johannis Stichter, 1694.
Overbrook (Penn.), St. Charles Borromeo Seminary; Utrecht, Universiteitsbibl., 315 C 3 [CBDP1]

1695   *Cantual Ordinis F. Eremitarum sancti p. Augustini.* Pars I–II (both parts in 1 vol.). Antverpiae, ex typographia Plantiniana B. Moreti, 1695.
Paris, Bibl. nat., Imp., B–42085

1696[1]   Graduale Romanum, juxta Missale Pii Quinti, Pontificis Maximi, authoritate editum. Cujus modulatio concinne disposita; in usum & gratiam Monialium Ordinis Sancti Augustini. Opera & studio Guillelmi Gabrielis Nivers.... A Paris, Chez l'autheur, 1696.
    Chicago, Newberry Library, VM 2149 G 73 1696; Auxerre, Bibl. mun., A568 4° Registres; Avignon, Bibl. mun., 8° 24066, Théologie
    Besançon, Bibl. mun., Arch. P.II.125, Archevêché, is likely the same print. (See also 1658, 1687)

1696[2]   Graduale monasticum, juxta Missale Pauli Quinti, Pontificis Maximi, authoritate editum. Cujus modulatio concinne disposita; in usum & gratiam Monialium Ordinis Sancti Benedicti. Opera & studio Guillelmi Gabrielis Nivers.... A Paris, Chez l'autheur, 1696.
    Paris, Bibl. nat., Imp., B-2560; Metz, Bibl. médiathèque, SE B 12, Lorraine; Nantes, Bibl. mun., 1363, Fonds ancien 1 (acq. après 1900); Orléans, Bibl. mun., A 1224, Fonds ancien 1; Solesmes, Abbaye de Saint Pierre, Bibl., LLc.7–21(3); London, British Library

1696[3]   Graduale Cisterciense, autorite Reverendissimi Domini D. Abbatis Generalis editum. In quo continentur omnia quae in Choro, pro Missarum celebratione; decantari devent; cum Hymnis, Antiphonis, Versiculis & Psalmis ad tertiam spectantibus. Lutetiae Parisiorum, ex aedibus Leonardianis. MDCXCVI.
    Kalamazoo (Mich.), Western Michigan Univ.; Rochester (N.Y.), Univ. of Rochester, Eastman School of Music; Vienna, Österreichische Nationalbibl.; Munich, Bayerische Staatsbibl.

1696[4]   Graduale Romanum iuxta novum Missale, ex decreto sacrosancti Concilii Tridentini restituti. Ante hac editum Ingolstadii: In typographeo Ederiano, nunc verò venale apud Philippum Kren, Bibliopolam Landishutanum, 1696.
    New Haven (Conn.), Yale Univ., School of Music, M2148 L4+ \ 1696

1697[1]   Graduale Romanum, juxta Missale sacro-sancti Concilii Tridentini et S. Pii Quinti Pontificis maximi authoritate editum. Cujus antiquus Ecclesiae Cantus Gregorianus è puro fonte Romano elicitus, accurate notatur.... opera et studio Guillelmi Gabrielis Nivers. Parisiis, Christophorus Ballard, 1697. (See also 1734[1].)
    Paris, Bibl. nat., Mus., 8° E 31; also Mus., X.1039 and Imp., B–4322; Paris, Bibl. Mazarine, A. 14327; Grenoble, Bibl. mun., F.27942, Supplément (CGA); Brussels, Bibl. royale, Fétis 1180; Namur, Centre de Documentation et de Recherches Religieuses, G 260; Niort, Bibl. mun., Th 499–8° 2189; Valognes, Bibl. mun., Julien de Laillier, B. 344, Fonds ancien 2; Vannes, Bibl. mun., 8°7360; Toronto, Univ. of Toronto Music Library (microfilm) M C393 1697; Québec, Univ. de Laval, L.Rares M2148 L4 1697

1697[2]   Graduale Romanum, juxta Missale sacro-sancti Concilii Tridentini et S. Pii Quinti Pontificis maximi authoritate editum.... Paris, Pierre Hérissant, 1697.
    Private collection

1697[3]   Graduale Romanum, juxta Missale sacro-sancti Concilii Tridentini et S. Pii Quinti Pontificis maximi authoritate editum.... Paris, R. & N. Pepie, 1697.
    Autun, Bibl. mun., S6029(2); Noyon, Bibl. mun., III 134

1697[4]   *Cantus diversi ex Graduali Romano, pro singulis solemnitatibus dominicis, festis et feriis*
         per annum. . . . Lugduni, apud Claudium Bachelu, 1697.
         London, British Library, D.3355.aa.3

1701[1]   *Graduale Romanum de tempore et sanctis, ad normam Missalis, ex decreto sacrosancti*
         Concilii Tridentini restituti. . . . Venetiis, MDCCI. Sumptibus Pauli Balleonii.
         Trent, Bibl. Feininger, FSG 27 (#338)

1701[2]   *Graduale Romanum juxta Missale ex decreto sacro-sancti Concilii Tridentini . . . cui addi-*
         tus est Cantus missarum omnium votivarum . . . item Cantus et Modulationes
         Kyriales, Hymni Angelici, Symbolum Apostolorum. Lugduni, 1701.
         Copenhagen, Kongelige Bibl.; Paris, Bibl. nat., Imp., 8–B–188

1701[3]   *Graduale Romanum, juxta novum Missale recognitum. Ed. novissima summa diligentia*
         ab erroribus expurgata. Amstelodami, Bloemen, 1701.
         Antwerp, Universitaire Faculteiten Sint-Ignatius, RG31305 E7; Utrecht,
         Universiteitsbibl., RIJS 095–114 [CBDP1 ABTHO]

1701[4]   *Appendix ad Graduale Romanum, sive cantiones aliquot sacrae, quae ante, sub & post*
         missam saepe cantari solent. Amstelodami, Guilielmi a Bloemen, 1701.
         Utrecht, Universiteitsbibl., ODJ 13 dl 1–2 [CBDEP BRUME]

1702   *Graduale Romanum juxta Missale ex decreto sacro-sancti Concilii Tridentini Pii 5. Pont.*
         Max. auctoritate nuper recognitum. Lugduni, Sumpt. Societatis [Bibliopolarum],
         impr. L. Langlois, A. Lauren, B. Martin, 1702.
         Turin, Bibl. Reale

1703   *Graduale missarum in festis trium ordinum Sancti Patris Francisci: ad normam Missalis*
         Romani, ex decreto Sacrosancti Concilii Tridentini restituti, B. Pii V. pontificis
         maximi jussu editi, Clementis VIII, ac Urbani VIII, auctoritate recogniti. Venetiis,
         apud Nicolaum Pezzana, 1703.
         Tallahassee (Fla.), Florida State Univ.

1705   *Graduale Romanum juxta Missale ex decreto sacrosancti Concilii Tridentini, Pii V. Pont.*
         Max. jussu antea editum. . . . Lugduni, Societas Bibliopolarum, 1705.
         Eichstätt, Katholische Universitätsbibl., 21/1 ESL III 67

1706[1]   *Graduale Romanum, juxta Missale sacro-sancti Concilii Tridentini et S. Pii Quinti*
         Pontificis maximi authoritate editum. Cujus antiquus Ecclesiae Cantus Gregorianus è
         puro fonte Romano elicitus, accurate notatur. . . . *opera et studio Guillelmi Gabrielis*
         Nivers. Parisiis, Christophorus Ballard, 1706.
         Aix-en-Provence, Bibl. Méjanes, P. 1109; Perpignan, Bibl. mun., Rés. 120

1706[2]   *Graduale Romanum, juxta Missale sacro-sancti Concilii Tridentini et S. Pii Quinti*
         Pontificis maximi authoritate editum. . . . Paris, N. Pepie, 1706
         Abbeville, Bibl. mun., 372 (in 8°); Auxerre, Bibl. mun., A 5698°,
         Registres, is likely this item.

1712   *Graduale Romanum iuxta Missale ex decreto sacrosancti Concilii Tridentini restitutum,*
         et Clementis VIII auctoritate recognitum. . . . *Ultimo editio*. . . . Antverpiae,
         Verdussen, 1712.
         Eichstätt, Katholische Universitätsbibl., 21/1 ESL III 17

1714¹   *Graduale Meldense*.... Paris, 1714.
         Besançon, Bibl. mun., Arch. G.II.182, Archevêché

1714²   *Missae sive cantus Missarum pro diebus dominicis et festivis*.... Lyon, Servant, 1714
         Milan, Bibl. naz. Braidense, Gerli

1714³   *Cantus diversi, ex graduali romano*.... Lugduni, 1714.
         Rennes, Bibl. mun., 80739, Fonds ancien

1716¹   *Graduale Romanum de tempore et sanctis*.... Venetiis, Pezzana, 1716.
         Sabbioneta, Chiesa dell'Assunta

1716²   *Graduale Romanum de tempore et sanctis*.... Venetiis, 1716.
         Munich, Bayerische Staatsbibl., 2 Liturg. 134f
         This may be identical with 1716¹.

1716³   *Graduale Romanum*.... Lugduni, Valfray, 1716.
         Avignon, Bibl. mun., 8° 19944, Théologie

1717   *Graduale sive Missale Romanum abbreviatum, ad usum Fratrum et Sororum ordinis Carmelitarum discalceatorum*. Parisiis, Coignard, 1717.
         Amiens, Bibl. mun., TH 11733A, Théologie; Metz, Bibl. médiathèque, I 75, Fonds ancien 1; Blois, Bibl. Abbé Grégoire, F 13377, Fonds générale 17è–18è siècle

1718¹   *Graduale Praemonstratense, illustrissimi ac reverendissimi domini domini Claudii Honorati Lucas, doctoris Sorbonici, Abbatis Praemonstratensis*.... Virduni, apud Claudium Vigneulle, Praemonstratensis Ordinis typographum, M.DCC.XVIII.
         Bloomington (Ind.), Indiana Univ.; St. Benedict (Ore.), Mount Angel Abbey; Trent, Bibl. Feininger, FSG 28 (#339); Amiens, Bibl. mun., TH 1806, Théologie; Troyes, Bibl. mun. à vocation régionale, Th. 1805, Théologie; Mondaye, Abbaye prémontrée

1718²   *Graduel romain à l'usage des religieuses de la congrégation de Notre-Dame*.... Toul, 1718.
         Besançon, Bibl. mun., Arch. P.II.144, Archevêché

1718³   *Graduel à l'usage des religieuses de la Congregation de Notre Dame*, 2nd ed. Toul, A. Laurent, 1718.
         Besançon, Bibl. mun., 274386, Fonds ancien

1719?   *Graduale Romanum*.... [Venice, 1719?] [Apparently lacking lower right-hand portion of the title page; hence uncertainty concerning place and date of publication.]
         Chiesa di S. Lorenzo, Mestre

1720¹   *Graduale Romanum juxta Missale ex decreto sacrosancti Concilii Tridentini restitutum et Clementis VIII. auctoritate recognitum; adjectis officiis novissime editis ad exemplar auctior et emendatior*. Antuerpiae, Apud Joannem Baptistam Verdussen, 1720.
         Washington, D.C., Library of Congress, M2149.A5 1720 Case; Bressanone (=Brixen), Bibl. del Seminario vescovile Vinzentinum; Nijmegen, Katholieke Universiteit, 665 b 1; Antwerp, Museum Plantin-Moretus, 4–74

1720[2] *[Graduale Romanum. . .]*. [Amstelodami?, Visscher, 1720].
Washington, D.C., Georgetown Univ.

1720[3] *Appendix ad Graduale Romanum, sive, Cantiones aliquot sacrae*. . . . Amstelodami,
Gerardi à Bloemen, 1720.
Washington, D.C., Georgetown Univ.

1720[4] *Graduale Romanum iuxta Missale ex decreto sacro-sancti Concilii Tridentini. Pii V.
Pont. Max. jussu anteae editum.* Lyon, Petrus Valfray, 1720.
Besançon, Bibl. mun., Arch. P.II.126, Archevêché

1720[5] *Graduale Romanum, iuxta Missale, ex decreto sacro-sancti Concilii Tridentini, Pii V.
pontificis maximi iussu editum, et Clementis VIII. Primum nunc denuo Urbani pape
octavi auctoritate recognitum.* Lutetiae Parisiorum, Apud Ludovicum Sevestre,
1720.
Québec, Univ. de Laval, L.Rares M2148 L4 1720

1721 *Graduale cantorinum sive Kyriale ad Dei omnipotentis majore[m] laude[m], gloria[m], &
honore[m].* Sorexinae: Impressum a p.f. Joan. Paulo Vertue de Sorexina Regul.
Obs. Seraph. S.P.N. Francisci, 1721.
Alleghany (N.Y.), St. Bonaventure Univ.

1722[1] *Graduale Romanum de tempore et sanctis, ad normam Missalis, ex decreto sacrosancti
Concilii Tridentini restituti, sancti Pii V. Pontificis maximi iussu editi, Clementis VIII.
ac Urbani VIII. auctoritate recogniti*. . . . Venetiis, MDCCXXII. Ex typographia
Balleoniana.
Trent, Bibl. Feininger, FSG 29 (#340); Freiburg, Universitätsbibl., TN
2.77/881; Überlingen, Leopold-Sophien Bibl., p Bd. 35 *

1722[2] *Cantus missarum totius anni ad usum Sacri ordinis FF. Praedicatorum.* Paris, FF
Praedicatores Magni conventus ac collegii generalis S. Jacobi, 1722.
London, British Library, MC.74.a; Paris, Bibl. nat., Imp., 8–B–183; Lyon,
Facultés Catholiques, Bibl. centrale, LFCC 168.A–4, Fonds ancien; Rome,
Bibl. Casanatense, Baini
Beaune, Bibl. mun., M 1649, 17–18èmes siècles, despite small differences
in the cataloguing of title and publisher, seems to be the same.

1722[3] *Graduale missarum in festis trium ordinum Sancti Patris Francisci: ad normam Missalis
Romani, ex decreto Sacrosancti Concilii Tridentini restituti*. . . . Venetiis, ex
typographia Balleoniana, 1722.
Alleghany (N.Y.), St. Bonaventure Univ.

1724[1] *Graduale Romanum, iuxta Missale, ex decreto sacro-sancti Concilii Tridentini restituti,
Pii V. pontificis maximi iussu antea editum*. . . . Lugduni, sumptibus Andreae
Laurens, bibliopolae et typographi ordinarii praetorii Lugdunensis, in vico
Racemi. . . M.DCC.XXIV [date altered to 1774].
Trent, Bibl. Feininger, FSG 30 (#341)

1724[2] *Cantus diversi ex Graduali Romano, pro singulis solemnitatibus, dominicis, festis et feriis
per annum.* Lugduni, P. Valfray, 1724.
Nantes, Bibl. mun., 22166, Fonds ancien 2 (acquisitions après 1900)

1725   *Graduale Romanum de tempore et sanctis, ad normam Missalis, ex decreto sacrosancti Concilii Tridentini restituti, sancti Pii V. Pontificis maximi iussu editi, Clementis VIII. ac Urbani VIII. auctoritate recogniti*.... Venetiis, MDCCXXV. Ex typographia Balleoniana.
Trent, Bibl. Feininger, FSG 31 (#342); Stuttgart, Württembergische Landesbibl. HBFb 179

1726   *Musica choralis Franciscana*. Köln, Caspar Drimborn, 1726.
Cited in Bennett Zon, *The English Plainchant Revival* (Oxford, 1999), 24 [after Robert Hayburn, *Papal Legislation on Sacred Music*, 1979].

1727[1]   *Graduale Ecclesiae Rothomagensis authoritate Lud. de la Vergne de Tressan*. Rouen, Jore, 1727.
Grenoble, Bibl. mun., B.231, CGA
Besançon, Bibl. mun., Arch. G.II.187, Archevêché, is likely a second copy of this work.

1727[2]   *Cantus diversi. La graduali romano*.... Lugduni, 1727.
Toulouse, Bibl. mun., 315/A, Fonds ancien 1

1729[1]   *Cantus diversi ex Graduali Romano, pro singulis solemnitatibus dominicis, festis et feriis per annum*. Lemovicis, J. Barbon, 1729.
Paris, Bibl. nat., Imp., B–6472

1729[2]   *Graduale [Romanum?]*.... Limoges, 1729.
Cited in Bennett Zon, *The English Plainchant Revival* (Oxford, 1999), 24 [after Robert Hayburn, *Papal Legislation on Sacred Music*, 1979].

1730[1]   *Graduale Romanum, juxta missale ex decreto sacro-sancti Concilii Tridentini. Pii V. Pont. Max. jussu antea editum, et Clementis VIII etiam Pont.Max. auctoritate nuper recognitum*. Gratianopoli, apud Petrum Faure, 1730.
Detroit, Univ. of Detroit; Los Angeles, Univ. of California at Los Angeles; New York, Fordham Univ.; Waco (Tex.), Baylor Univ.; Austin, Univ. of Texas; Freiburg, Universität Freiburg, Fakultätsbibl. Theologie, LIT Lr 104; Grenoble, Bibl. mun., O.14906, Dauphinois; Toulouse, Bibl. mun., Fa C 360, Fonds ancien 2

1730[2]   *Graduale Romanum de tempore et sanctis, ad normam Missalis, ex decreto sacrosancti Concilii Tridentini restituti, sancti Pii V. Pontificis maximi iussu editi, Clementis VIII. ac Urbani VIII. auctoritate recogniti*.... Venetiis, MDCXXX, apud Nicolaum Pezzana.
Trent, Bibl. Feininger, FSG 32 (#343); Freiburg, Universitätsbibl., 25/156; Feltre, Bibl. del Duomo

1730[3]   *Graduale Romanum, juxta novum missale recognitum. Ed. novissima summa diligentia ab erroribus expurgata*. 3a ed. Amstelodami, typis haeredum Viduae Cornelii Stichter, 1730.
Utrecht, Universiteitsbibl., RAR GRO 6 CONV 1 [LB LBMUZ]

1730[4]   *Epitome Gradualis Romani seu cantus missarum dominicalibus et festivarum totius anni....* Lugduni, Valfray, 1730.
    Dublin, Univ. College; Nantes, Bibl. mun., 1095, Fonds ancien 1; Valognes, Bibl. mun. Julien de Laillier, C 1380, Fonds ancien

1730[5]   *Graduale Romanum juxta Missale ex decreto S. S. Concilii Tridentini....* S.l., s.n., 1730.
    Avignon, Bibl. mun., 8° 33102, Théologie

1730[6]   *Appendix ad Graduale Romanum, sive cantiones aliquot sacrae, quae ante, sub & post missam saepe cantari solent.* Amstelodami, typis haeredum Vidue Cornelii Stichter, 1730.
    Utrecht, Universiteitsbibl., RAR GRO 6 CONV 2 [LB LBMUZ]

1730[7]   *Graduale insignis Ecclesiae Nivernensis, illustrissimi ac Reverendissimi DD. Caroli Fontaine Des Montées, episcopi Nivernensis auctoritate....* Auselianis, apud Nicolaum Lanquement, 1730.
    Paris, Bibl. nat., Imp., B–249
    Nevers, Bibl. mun., 1 N 23, Nivernais, is either the same or a related publication, although no publisher is given and place of publication is given in French.

1730[8]   *Graduale Romanum juxta novum Missale recognitum. Editio novissima summa diligentia ab erroribus expurgata.* Gerardi à Bloemen, 1730.
    Cited by Alphonse Goovaerts, *Histoire et bibliographie* (Antwerp, 1880), 469.

1732[1]   *Graduale Romanum, iuxta Missale, ex decreto sacro-sancti Concilii Tridentini, Pii V. pontificis maximi iussu editum, et Clementis VIII. Primum nunc denuo Urbani pape octavi auctoritate recognitum.* Lutetiae Parisiorum, Apud Cl. Joan. Bapt. Herissant, 1732.
    Québec, Univ. de Laval, L.Rares M2148 L4 1732

1732[2]   *Cantus diversi ex Graduali Romano, pro singulis solemnitatibus dominicis, festis et feriis per annum.* Gratianopoli, P. Faure, 1732.
    Grenoble, Bibl. mun., O.6376, Dauphinois

1734[1]   *Graduale Romanum, juxta Missale sacro-sancti Concilii Tridentini et S. Pii Quinti Pontificis maxmimi authoritate editum. Cujus antiquus Ecclesiae Cantus Gregorianus è puro fonte Romano elicitus, accurate notatur.* Parisiis, Christophorus Ballard, 1734 (= reissue of 1697).
    New Orleans (La.), Loyola Univ.; Paris, Bibl. nat., Mus. 8° E 41; Besançon, Bibl. mun., Arch. P.II.127, Archevêché; Aix-en-Provence, Bibl. Méjanes, P. 2730 and P. 7219, Pécoul; London, British Library, D.3356.bb.6

1734[2]   *Graduale Romanum, juxta Missale Pii Quinti, Pontificis Maximi, authoritate editum. Cujus modulatio concinne disposita; in usum monialium Ordinis sancti Benedicti....* Guillelmi Gabrielis Nivers.... Lutetiae-Parisiorum, Joannis Baptistae Christophore Ballard, 1734.
    Paris, Bibl. nat., Mus. Rés 2288; Versailles, Bibl. mun., F.A. in–8 O 97 b, Fonds ancien 2

1734³   *Graduale monasticum, juxta Missale Pauli Quinti...in usum monialium Ordinis sancti Benedicti....*Lutetiae-Parisiorum, Joannis Baptistae Christophore Ballard, 1734. Rouen, Bibl. mun., GS m 549, Fonds Cas; Solesmes, Abbaye de Saint Pierre, Bibl., LLc.7–21(4); Paris, Centre nationale de Pastorale liturgique, 842.OSB.1734

1734⁴   *Graduale Romanum de tempore et sanctis, ad normam Missalis, ex decreto sacrosancti Concilii Tridentini restituti, sancti Pii V. Pontificis maximi iussu editi, Clementis VIII. ac Urbani VIII. auctoritate recogniti....*Venetiis, Ex typographia Balleoniana, 1734.
　　Montevergine-Mercogliano, Bibl. statale del Monumento nazionale; Rivanazzano, Archivio della Parrochiale; Tortona, Bibl. del Seminario Vescovile

1734⁵   *Graduale monasticum ad usum ordinis Cluniacensis.* 2 vols. Parisiis, Simon, 1734.
　　Avignon, Bibl. mun., Fol. 416 Théologie and Fol. 435, Théologie

1735   *Epitome Gradualis Romani, seu missarum cantum pro diebus dominicis et festivis totius anni.* Gratianopoli, Petri Faure, 1735.
　　Grenoble, Bibl. mun., U.6191, Dauphinois

1737   *The Roman Gradual on the Gregorian Notes. Containing The Masses for all Sundays throughout the Year, in the following Manner, Part the First. The Introits, or Beginnings of the Mass, the Graduals, Alleluias, and Tracts after the Epistles, with the Sequences, Offertories, and Communions. Part the Second. The New Tones of the Kyries, Gloria in Excelsis, Creeds, Sanctus, Agnus Dei, Ite Missa est, Benedicamus: With Hymns and Antiphons, which are sung at the Elevation.* Printed in the Year MDCCXXXVII. [London?, Wade?].
　　Oxford, Bodleian Library
　　The chants are notated by hand.

1738¹   *[Antiphonaire-Graduel de Paris], pars hiemalis* [Paris, J. C. Ballard, 1738]. [Title page lacking; publisher and date taken from colophon.]
　　Paris, Bibl. nat., Mus. 8° E 34

1738²   *Graduale Sanctae Lugdunensis Ecclesiae, primae Galliarum sedis.* 2 vols. Lugduni, sumptibus cleri Lugdunensis. Et curis Claudii Journet, M.DCC.XXXVIII.
　　Paris, Bibl. Ste.-Geneviève, Fol–Z–527 inv. 418 FA; Lyon, Bibl. mun., 29622, CGA; Solesmes, Abbaye de Saint Pierre, Bibl., LLa.7–11 (1)
　　Lyon is incomplete, but furnishes the information that the printer was Christophe Reguilliat. Paris apparently consists of the Prima pars only.

1738³   *Graduale Autissiodorense complectens Missas de Dominicis ac Festis à populo feriatis, & alias quasdam tùm de Proprio, tùm de Communi Sanctorum; nonnullas etiam Votivas, & Missas pro Defunctis....*Aureliae, N. Lanquement, 1738.
　　Besançon, Bibl. mun., Arch. G.II.164, Archevêché

1738[4]   *Graduale Parisiense, illustrissimi et reverendissimi in Christo Patris D.D. Caroli-Gaspar-Guillelmi de Ventimille, ex Comitibus Massiliae Du Luc, Parisiensis Archiepiscopi, Ducis sancti Clodoaldi, Paris Franciae.* . . . Paris, Sumptibus suis ediderunt Bibliopolae usuum Parisiensium, excudebat Joannes-Baptista Coignard. . . , Pars hiemalis, 1738.
        Glasgow, School of Art

1739[1]   *Graduale Sanctae Ecclesiae Trecensis.* . . . Troyes, 1739.
        Besançon, Bibl. mun., Arch. G.II.195, Archevêché; Besançon, Bibl. mun., Arch. G.II.197, Archevêché; Besançon, Bibl. mun., Arch. G.II.196, Archevêché
        The first two of these copies are 48 cm. tall, whereas the last is only 37.5 cm. tall.

1739[2]   *Cantus diversi pro Dominicis, festis et feriis per annum, ex Graduali romano. Nova editio.* Avinione, sumptibus Societatis [Bibliopolarum?], 1739.
        Blois, Bibl. Abbé Grégoire, F 8327, Fonds général 17è–18è siècle

1740[1]   *Graduale Romanum.* . . . Cracoviae, 1740.
        Kraków, Bibl. Jagiellonska, 224992 IV Mag. St. Dr.

1740[2]   *Graduale Ebroicense.* . . . Paris, 1740.
        Besançon, Bibl. mun., Arch. A.II.3, Archevêché

1741[1]   *Epitome Gradualis Romani, seu cantus missarum.* . . . Gratianopoli, 1741.
        Auxerre, Bibl. mun., A 570 12°, Registres

1741[2]   *Epitome Gradualis Romani, seu cantus missarum dominicalium et festivarum totius anni juxta usum romanum par Dom A. de la Feillé.* Pictavi, Faulcon, 1741.
        Poitiers, Médiathèque François Mitterand, DP 261, Fonds ancien

1741[3]   *Graduale Biturcicense, illustrissimi ac reverendissimi in Christo patris D. D. Frederici Hieronymi de Roye de la Rochefoucauld, Patriarchae, archiepiscopi Bituricensis.* . . . Biturigum, Vidua J. Boyer et J. B. Christo, 1741.
        Paris, Bibl. nat., Imp., B–131 (1,2)

1742[1]   *Missae sive cantus missarum dominicalium, et festivarum totius anni, juxta usum romanum.* . . . *Editio nova, auctior et emendatior.* . . . Avenione, Delorme, 1742.
        Providence (R.I.), Providence College; Avignon, Bibl. mun., 8° 22593, Théologie and 8° 84940, Théologie

1742[2]   *Graduale Claromontense* . . . *D. D. Joannis-Baptistae Massillon, Claromontensis episcopi auctoritate ac ejusdem ecclesiae capituli consensu editum. I, Proprium de tempore; [II], Proprium sanctorum.* Claromon-Ferrandi, P. Boutaudon, 1742.
        Clermont-Ferrand, Bibl. mun. et interuniversitaire, A 300 1, Auvergne 2 [Fonds Vimont?], A 300 2, Auvergne 2.
        This item apparently consists of two volumes; these are catalogued separately, with very slight differences between entries.

1744   *Graduale Claromontense, illustrissimi ac Reverendissimi in Christo Patris D. D. Francisci-Mariae Lemaistre de La Garlaye, Claromontensis episcopi, Comistique Lugduni....* [Lugduni,] Claromon-Ferrandi, P. Boutaudon, 1744.
    Austin, Univ. of Texas; Clermont-Ferrand, Bibl. mun. et interuniversitaire, A 10403, Auvergne 1; and A 10900, Auvergne 2

1745[1]   *Graduale Romanum juxta novum missale recognitum. Editio novissima summa diligentia ab erroribus expurgata.* Amstelodami, typis Haeredum Vidua Cornelii Stichter, sub signo veteris montis Calvariae, 1745.
    St. Meinrad (Ind.), St. Meinrad Archabbey and School of Theology; Nijmegen, Katholieke Universiteit, 184 b 151

1745[2]   *Appendix ad Graduale Romanum, sive, Cantiones aliquot sacrae; quae ante, sub & post Missam saepe cantari solent.* Amstelodami, typis Haeredum Vidua Cornelii Stichter, 1745.
    St. Meinrad (Ind.), St. Meinrad Archabbey and School of Theology

1745[3]   *Graduale Bajocense....* Paris, 1745.
    Besançon, Bibl. mun., Arch. G.II.165, Archevêché

1746[1]   *[Graduel de Paris].*
    Cited in the preface to 1754[2]; no copy known at present.

1746[2]   *Supplementum gradualis metropolitanae ac primatialis ecclesiae senonensis....* Sens, 1746.
    Besançon, Bibl. mun., Arch. A.II.12 (2), Archevêché

1747[1]   *Epitome Gradualis Romani, seu Missarum cantus pro diebus dominicis et festivis....* Gratianopoli, Andrea Faure, 1747.
    Philadelphia, Univ. of Pennsylvania, M2149.5. E 6 G7; Rodez, Médiathèque, MAG T 963, Théologie

1747[2]   *Cantus diversi pro dominicis, festis et feriis per annum Graduali romano. Nova editio, correctior et auctior....* Tolosae, Gaspardi Henault, 1747.
    Barcelona, Biblioteca de Catalunya

[1747]   *[Graduel, Amiens].* 2 vols.
    Besançon, Bibl. mun., Arch. G.II.160 (1, 2), Archevêché
    Title page lacking; information taken from manuscript notes.

1749[1]   *Epitome Gradualis Romani, seu, Cantus Missarum Dominicalium et Festivarum totius anni, juxta usum Romanum, A. D. de la Feillée revisum, auctum et emendatum.* Pictavi, Joannis Faulcon. 1749.
    Baltimore (Md.), Johns Hopkins, GARRT M2148.L42 1749; Toronto, St. Michael's College Library, BQT/4305/E65/CRL; Poitiers, Médiathèque François Mitterand, DM 1159, Fonds ancien; Lille, Médiathèque Jean Levy, 89280, Fonds ancien (avant 1952); London, British Library, 3366.aa.10 (Destroyed in World War II)

1749[2]   *Epitome Gradualis Romani, seu, Cantus Missarum Dominicalium et Festivarum totius anni, juxta usum Romanum, A. D. de la Feillée revisum, auctum et emendatum.* Paris, Herissant, 1749. (Apparently another issue of 1749[1].)
Québec, Univ. de Laval, L. Rares M2148 L2 1749

1749[3]   *Graduale Romanum : juxta Missale ex decreto sacrosancti Concilii Tridentini restitutum et Clementis VIII auctoritate recognitum, adjectis officiis novissime editis ad exemplar Missalis Romani.* Joannes Baptista Damiens, ed. Verdussen. Antwerp, 1749.
Atchison (Kans.), Benedictine College; Lille, Médiathèque Jean Levy, 63595, Fonds ancien (avant 1952); Antwerp, Museum Plantin-Moretus, A 2907[2]

1749[4]   *Graduel à l'usage du diocèse de Chaalons.* . . . Châlons-sur Marne, 1749.
Besançon, Bibl. mun., Arch. G.II.178 and Arch. G.II.179, Archevêché
These two copies are slightly different in size.

1750[1]   *Graduale Romanum de tempore et sanctis, ad normam Missalis, ex decreto sacrosancti Concilii Tridentini restituti, sancti Pii V. Pontificis maximi iussu editi, Clementis VIII. ac Urbani VIII. auctoritate recogniti.* . . . Venetiis, MDCCL, apud Nicolaum Pezzana.
Trent, Bibl. Feininger, FSG 33 (#344)

1750[2]   *Graduale Romanum de tempore et sanctis.* Baglioni, 1750.
Collio, Bibl. C. Arici della Parrochia Ss. Nazaro e Celso

1750[3]   *Graduale Romanum juxta novum missale recognitum. Editio Novissima summa diligentia ab erroribus Expurgata.* Amstelodami, H. Beekman, G. Tielenburg & T. Crajenschot, 1750.
Knoxville (Tenn.), Univ. of Tennessee; London, British Library, 3365.f.4.(1.)
The publication cited by Alphonse Goovaerts, *Histoire et bibliographie* (Antwerp, 1880), 525, may be the same although only Beekman is given as a publisher and the date is lacking.

1750[4]   *Epitome gradualis romani.* . . . Gratianopoli, 1750.
Besançon, Bibl. mun., Arch. P.II.129, Archevêché

1750[5]   *Graduale Romanum: juxta Missale, ex decreto sacrosancti Concilii Tridentini.* . . . *Editio nova.* Valfray, Lyon, 1750.
South Bend (Ind.), Univ. of Notre Dame
Besançon, Bibl. mun., Arch. A.II.9, Archevêché, has the same first two words in the title, place, and date of publication.

1750[6]   *Graduale Cisterciense.* . . *auctoritate reverendissimi domini D. Francisci Trouvé Abbatis generalis editum in quo continentur omnia quae in choro pro missarum celebratione decantari debent; cum hymnis, antiphonis, versiculis & psalmis ad tertiam spectantibu.* Parisiis, apud Petrum-Joannem Mariette, 1750.
Kalamazoo (Mich.), Western Michigan Univ.; Halle, Universitätsbibl., Ih 3000; Munich, Bayerische Staatsbibl.
Munich, Bayerische Staatsbibl. has an additional copy s.l. and s.d.

1750[7]   *Missae sive Cantus Missarum dominicalium et festivarum totius anni, juxta usum Romanum. Cum missa regia Domini H. Dumont, et Missa Baptistae Domini J. B. de Lully. Editio nova auctior et emendatior.* . . . Avenione, apud Joannem Niel, 1750.
Bressanone (=Brixen), Bibl. del Seminario vescovile Vinzentinum; Milan, Bibl. Ambrosiana

1750[8]   *Le petit graduel du diocèse de Bayeux, imprimé par l'ordre de Monseigneur Paul d'Albert de Luynes. . . pour la commodité des laïques et particulièrement des personnes qui aident dans les campagnes à chanter l'office divin.* Caen, C. Lebaron and P. Chalopin, 1750.
Paris, Bibl. nat., Imp., B–41381; Orléans, Bibl. mun., 8° C9824, Fonds ancien 1; Besançon, Bibl. mun., Arch. P.II.149, Archevêché

1751[1]   *Missae novae festis solemnioribus decantandae, pluribus auctae.* . . . T. Crajenschot, Amstelodami, 1751.
London, British Library, 3365.f.4.(2.)

1751[2]   *Appendix ad Graduale Romanum, sive Cantiones aliquot sacrae, que ante, sub & post missam cantari solent.* Amsterdam, Theodorus Crajenschot, 1751.
Brussels, Bibl. royale, II 34.944 A 2

1752[1]   *Graduale Tullense; illustrissimi ac reverendissimi in Christo patris D. D. Scipionis Hieronymi Begon.* . . . Tulli Leucorum (= Toul), Sumptibus suis ediderunt Typographi, usum Tullinsium, 1752.
Paris, Bibl. nat., Imp., B–259; Nancy, Bibl. mun., 70086 CGA and 5870 Favier; Besançon, Bibl. mun., Arch. G.II.190, Archevêché; also Arch. G.II.191, Archevêché

1752[2]   *Graduale ecclesiae Rothomagensis.* . . . Rouen, 1752.
Besançon, Bibl. mun., Arch. G.II.188, Archevêché

1752[3]   *Graduale mejus Lexoviense.* . . . Lisieux, 1752.
Besançon, Bibl. mun., Arch. A.II.8, Archevêché

1752[4]   *Graduale minus Lexoviense.* . . . Lisieux, 1752.
Besançon, Bibl. mun., Arch. A.II.6 and Arch. A.II.7, Archevêché
London, Victoria and Albert Museum, National Art Library, may have the same book, although the catalogue date given is 1753

1752[5]   *Epitome gradualis romani, seu Missarum cantus pro diebus dominicis et festivis totius anni.* Tolosae, 1752.
Paris, Bibl. nat., Imp., B–42122 (1)

1753[1]   *Gradualis Romani, seu missarum cantus pro diebus dominicive et festivis totius anni.* . . . Gratianopoli, A. Faure, 1753.
Blois, Bibl. Abbé Grégoire, F 8365, Fonds général 17è–18è siècle

1753[2]   *Epitome Gradualis Romani, seu missarum cantus pro diebus Dominicis et festivis totius anni.* . . . Apud Viduam Andreae Faure, Gratianopoli, 1753.
Chicago, De Paul Univ.; Toulouse, Bibl. mun., 318/E, Fonds ancien 1; London, British Library, 3395.c.14 (Destroyed in World War II)

1753³   *Proprium officiorum ecclesiae cathedralis ac totius diocesis Divionensis....* Divione, Antonius de Fay, 1753.
Dijon, Bibl. mun., L. D. 14709, CGA; Lyon, Facultés Catholiques, Bibl. centrale, LFCC 203.B–4, Fonds ancien; La Rochelle, Médiathèque Michel Crepeau, Rés. 284 C

1753⁴   *Graduale Sanctae Ambianensis ecclesiae, illustrissimi et reverendissimi in Christo Patris DD. Ludovici Francisci Gabrielis d'Orleans de la Motte, Ambianensis episcopi auctoritate, & venerabilis ejusdem Ecclesiae Capituli consensu editum.* Ambiani, Apud Viduam Caroli Caron Hubault, 1753.
Kansas City (Mo.), Univ. of Missouri–Kansas City

1753⁵   *Graduale minus Lexoviens....* Lisieux, 1753.
London, Victoria and Albert Museum, National Art Library

1754¹   *Graduale Romanum de tempore et sanctis, Ad normam missalis ex decreto sacrosancti Concilii Tridentini restituti, S. Pii V. pontificis maximi iussu editi, Clementis VIII, ac Urbani VIII auctoritate recogniti....* Venetiis..., 1754.
Stockholm, Kungl. biblioteket, LF/56 Graduale

1754²   *Graduel de Paris, Noté, Pour les Dimanches et les Festes. Imprimés par ordre de Monseigneur l'Archevêque. Nouvelle Édition Augmentée.* [2 vols.] Paris, Chez les Libraires associés aux Usages du Diocese, 1754.
Paris, Bibl. nat., Mus. 8° E 36 (1,2)
Second edition of 1746

1754³   *Cantus diversi ex Graduali Romano, pro dominicis, festis et feriis per annum, ex graduali Romano. Nova editio, lectior, correctior et auctior. Accedunt Missae regales, novem Lectiones Jeremiea, novaque triplex Methodus Cantus ediscendi.* Tolosae, Gaspard Henault, 1754.
Toulouse, Bibl. mun., Fa D 9707, Fonds ancien 2

1755¹   *Graduale Romanum : juxta novum missale recognitum. Editio novissima magno studio ab erroribus plurimis expurgata....* Amstelodami, T. Crajenschot, 1755.
Cleveland (Oh.), Athenaeum of Ohio; Brussels, Bibl. royale, II 34.944 A 1; Nijmegen, Katholieke Universiteit, 11 d 106 nr. 1; Frankfurt am Main, Stadt- und Universitätsbibl., Mus. pr. 51/28

1755²   *Graduale Auscitanum, illustrissimi et reverendissimi in Christo Patris D.D. Ioannis Francisci de Montillet, Auscitani Archiepiscopi...auctoritate...editum.* Paris, Joannem-Baptistam Garnier & Petrum-Alexandrum Le Prieur, 1755.
Besançon, Bibl. mun., Arch. G.II.162, Archevêché

1755³   *Graduel romain, ou le chant des messes pour les jours de Dimanches et Fêtes de toute l'année....suivant l'usage romain. On a ajouté à cette Èdition divers Chants à l'usage de l'Église de Lyon....* Lyon, Aimé Delaroche, 1755.
Leipzig, Musikbibliothek

1755⁴   *Graduale de tempore....* [Sorexina], Jo. Paulo Vertua, 1755.
Alleghany (N.Y.), St. Bonaventure Univ.

1756[1]   *Graduale Romanum de tempore et sanctis*. . . . Amstelodamum, Henrici et Cornelii Beekman, 1756.
Munich, Bayerische Staatsbibl., Liturg. 532 (with 1 supplement); Nijmegen, Katholieke Universiteit, 81 c 98

1756[2]   *Graduale ad usum sacri ordinis Cartusiensis, missis conventualibus, tam de Tempore quam de Festo ac Votivis inserviens*. Castros. ex officina P. G. D. Robert, 1756.
Urbana (Ill), University of Illinois, Q.M783.23 C 286 G 1756; Vatican, Bibl. apost. Vat., Casimiri II.99; Trent, Bibl. Feininger, FSG 34 (#345); Brussels, Bibl. royale, VB 840 C; Oxford, Bodleian Library, Vet. E5 c.9 (1)

1756[3]   *Graduale Bellovacense, ementissimi et reverendissimi in Christo Patris D. D. Stephani-Renati Potier de Gesvres, Sanctae Romanae Ecclesiae Cardinales, Episcopi et Comitis Bellovacensis, Vice-Domini de Gerboredo, Paris Franciae, Auctoritate ac Venerabilis ejusdem Ecclesiae Capituli Consensu editum*. Parisiis et Bellovaci, Fratres Dessaint, 1756.
Paris, Bibl. nat., Mus. X.2084; Besançon, Bibl. mun., Arch. G.II.169, Archevêché

1756[4]   *Missae, sive cantus missarum dominicalium, et festivarum totius anni, juxta usum romanum, cum Missa Regià Dni H. Dumont, & Missà Baptistae Dni. J. B. de Lully. Editio nova, auctior et emendatior*. . . . Avenione, viduam Niel, 1756.
Alençon, Médiathèque de la Communauté urbaine, RR–3–7, Fonds ancien 2; Milan, Bibl. naz. Braidense, Gerli.2029; Eichstätt, Katholische Universitätsbibl., 21/1 ESL 204

1758   *Graduale Romanum juxta missale ex decreto sacrosancti concilii Tridentini restitutum*. . . . Antverpiae, Verdussen, 1758.
Antwerp, Universitaire Faculteiten Sint-Ignatius, RG3105 C2

1759   *Graduale Romanum*. . . . Venetiis, Bollein, 1759.
Benevento, Bibl. capitolare

1760[1]   *Epitome Gradualis Romani seu missarum cantus pro diebus Dominicis et festivis totius anni*. Lugduni, Amati Delaroche, 1760.
Mâcon, Bibl. mun., 954, Laplatte

1760[2]   *[Graduale Romanum, etc.?]* Lugduni, Am. Delaroche, 1760.
Nantes, Bibl. mun., 1094, Fonds ancien 1 (acquisitions après 1900)
This may be identical with 1760[1].

1762[1]   *Graduale Divionense, illustriss. et reverendiss. in christo patris D. D. Claud.-Marci-Anton. d'Apchon, divion. episcope. . .juxta normam ac methodum gradualis parisen. ab illustr. D. D. Caroli de Vintimille. . .promulgati*. 4 vols. Paris, ap. bibliop. Us. parisien et Divion, 1762.
Dijon, Bibl. mun., L 17378, CGA

1762[2]   *Appendix ad Graduale Romanum, sive cantiones aliquot sacrae, quae ante, sub & post missam saepe cantari solent*. 8a ed. S.l., s.n., 1762
Utrecht, Universiteitsbibl, RIJS 095–73 dl 2 [CBDP1 ABTHO]

1763[1]   *Graduale Romanum, juxta novum Missale recognitum. Ed. novissima summa diligentia ab erroribus expurgata.* Amstelodami, typis haeredum Viduam C. Stichter, 1763.
Utrecht, Universiteitsbibl., RIJS 095–73 dl 1 and ALV 27–228 [CBDP1 ABTHO] (2 copies); Nijmegen, Katholieke Universiteit, 637 c 33 nr. 1
Besançon, Bibl. mun., Arch. P.II.130, Archevêché, is an exemplar with the same first two words in title, also published in Amsterdam, 1763, but the information provided is equally suitable to the edition given next.

1763[2]   *Graduale Romanum, juxta novum Missale recognitum. . . editio novissima magno studio ab erroribus plurimis expurgata. . . .* Amstelodami, T. Crajenschot, 1763.
Kansas City (Mo.), Univ. of Missouri–Kansas City; Antwerp, Universitaire Faculteiten Sint-Ignatius, RG3105 D6; Nijmegen, Katholieke Universiteit, 247 c 94
Leuven, Katholieke Universiteitsbibl., appears to be the same; see also remarks regarding 1763[1] in Besançon, Bibl. mun.

1763[3]   *Graduale juxta Missale romanum. . . .* Lyon, 1763.
Besançon, Bibl. mun., Arch. A.II.10, Archevêché

1765[1]   *Graduel romain, ou Le chant des messes pour les jours de dimanches et fêtes de toute l'an-née. . . .* Lyon, Aimé Delaroche, 1765.
Barcelona, Biblioteca de Catalunya

1765[2]   *[Graduale Senonensis?]* 1765.
Sens, Bibl. mun., Trésor de la Cathédrale, I 56

1766[1]   *Epitome Gradualis Romani, seu Cantus missarum dominicalium et festivarum totius anni,* Joannis-Nic. Galles, Venetiis, Editio prima, cantui Romano simillima, 1766
Baltimore (Md.), St. Mary's Seminary and Univ. Library; Munich, Universitätsbibl.

1766[2]   *Graduale Romanum, juxta Missale sacro-sancti Concilii Tridentini et S. Pii Quinti Pontificis maximi authoritate editum. Cujus antiquus Ecclesiae cantus Gregorianus e puro fonte romano elicitus accurate notatur.* Parisiis, Pepie, 1766.
Amiens, Bibl. mun., Th 1398B, Théologie

1768[1]   *Graduale Bisuntinum. . . .* Besançon, 1768.
Besançon, Bibl. mun., Arch. G.II.174, Archevêché
Besançon, Bibl. mun., Arch. G.II.175, Archevêché, is another copy, four centimeters taller, but not otherwise distinguished in cataloguing.

1768[2]   *Missae sive cantus missarum dominicalium et festivarum totius anni, juxta usum romanum. . . . Editio nova, auctior et emendatior.* Avenione, J. J. Niel, 1768.
Arles, Médiathèque, AA 22659, Fonds ancien and AA 22659 M [Fonds] ancien

1769[1]   *Graduale Romanum de tempore et sanctis, ad normam Missalis, ex decreto sacrosancti Concilii Tridentini restituti, sancti Pii V. Pontificis maximi iussu editi, Clementis VIII. ac Urbani VIII. auctoritate recogniti. . . .* Venetiis, MDCCXXII. Ex typographia Balleoniana, 1769.
Zamora, Bibl. Pública, Transito Sig. CT /1. Reg

1769[2]   *Appendix ad Graduale Romanum, sive Cantiones aliquot sacrae, que ante, sub & post missam cantari solent.* Amsterdam, Hendrik en Cornelis Beekman, 1769.
Utrecht, Universiteitsbibl., ALV 29–77 and ALV 29–77 dl 2 (2 copies)

1770[1]   *Graduale Romanum, juxta novum Missale recognitum. Ed. novissima summa diligentia ab erroribus expurgata.* Amstelodami, ex typographia Henrici et Cornelii Beekman, 1770.
Utrecht, Universiteitsbibl., ALV 29–77 dl 1 [CBDP1 ABTHO]

1770[2]   *Appendix ad Graduale Romanum, sive Cantiones aliquot sacrae, que ante, sub & post missam cantari solent.* Amsterdam, T. Crajenschot, 1770.
Utrecht, Universiteitsbibl., ALV 29–102 dl 2

1770[3]   *Graduale juxta Missale Noviomense, illustrissimi et reverendissimi in Christo patris D. D. Caroli de Broglie Episcopicomitis Noviomensis.* . . . Parisiis, A. M. Lottin, 1770.
Paris, Bibl. nat., Imp., B–214

1770[4]   *Graduel à l'usage du diocèse d'Auch.* . . . Toulouse, 1770.
Besançon, Bibl. mun., Arch. P.II.145, Archevêché

1770[5]   *Graduale Romanum.* . . . Amstelodami, T. Crajenschot, 1770.
Leuven, Katholieke Universiteitsbibl.

1770[6]   *Graduale Pictaviense, illustrissimi et reverendissimi in Christo patris, DD. Martialis-Ludovici de Beaupoil de Saint Aulaire, Pictaviensis episcopi auctoritate; ac venerabilis ejusdem ecclesiae capituli consensu editum.* Pictavii, Apud J. Felicem Faulcon, 1770.
Nashville (Tenn.), Univ. of Tennessee

1771[1]   *Graduale ad usum canonicorum regularium ordinis Praemonstratensis. . . ac reverendissimo domino totius ordinis generali, ejusdemque capituli generalis authoritate edito & approbato; et nunc solicite revisum ac accurate emendatum.* Bruxellis, Franciscus t'Serstevens, 1771.
New Haven (Conn.), Yale Univ., School of Music; New York, General Theological Seminary, St. Mark's Library; Brussels, Bibl. royale, VB 846 B; Leuven, Katholieke Universiteitsbibl.

1771[2]   *Graduale Sanctae Lugdunensis Ecclesiae, primae Galliarum sedis. Pars prima.* Lyon, 1771.
Besançon, Bibl. mun., Arch. M.II.13, Archevêché

1772[1]   *Graduale Romanum juxta Missale ex decreto sacro-sancti Concilii Tridentini restitutum, et Clementis VIII. Auctoritate recognitum; adjectis officiis novissime editis ad exemplar missalis Romani. Editio novissima, multo auctior & emendatior.* Leodii, ex officina typographica Clementis Plomteux, perillustrium patriae statuum typographi. 1772.
Washington, D.C., Washington Cathedral; Leuven, Katholieke Universiteitsbibl.; Leipzig, Universitätsbibl., 39–7–1145.

1772[2]   *Graduale Cisterciense Monasterii Cellae principum.* . . . Cella principum, 1772.
Munich, Bayerische Staatsbibl.; Munich, Universitätsbibl.

1773[1]   *Epitome Gradualis Romani, seu Cantus missarum dominicalium et festivarum totius anni.* Joannis-Nic. Galles, Venetiis, Editio tertia, cantui Romano simillima, 1773.

Durham (N.C.), Duke Univ., E 4363; Rennes, Bibl. mun., 97669, Fonds ancien; Québec, Univ. de Laval, L.Rares M2148 L42 1773
In the Laval copy, the edition is given as 2a, and the publisher as the Widow of J.-N. Galles.

1773[2]   *Missae sive cantus missarum dominicalium et festivarum totius anni, juxta usum romanum, cum Missa Regià Domini H. Dumont, et Missà Baptistae D. J. B. de Lully. Editio prima.* Avenione, L. Chambeau [& F. Guibert?], 1773.
Nice, Bibl. mun., 50129, Fonds ancien; Avignon, Bibl. mun., 8° 28457, Cat. Anony. 1950 and 8° 84940, Cat. Anony. 1950

1774[1]   *Graduale Romanum juxta Missale ex decreto sacrosancti Concilii Tridentini restitutum.* . . . Antverpiae, Ex Architypographia Plantiniana, 1774.
Cleveland (Oh.), Athenaeum of Ohio; St. Louis (Mo.), St. Louis Univ., Divinity School(?); Antwerp, Museum Plantin-Moretus, A 1549; Rome, Bibl. naz. cen., 32.4.K.14

1774[2]   *Gradue[l] du diocèse de Poitiers. Imprimé par ordre de Monseigneur l'Archevêque, pour l'usage des Clercs & des Laïques.* Poitiers, Jean-Felix Faulcon, 1774.
Paris, Bibl.nat., Mus., 8° E 37

1774[3]   *Graduale romano-monasticum pro choromonasterii S. Blasii in nigra Silva.* 2 vols. s.l., s.n., 1774.
Paris, Bibl. nat., Imp., B–3089 (1,2)

1774[4]   *Graduale Ecclesiae Laudunensis, eminentissimi ac reverendissimi in Christo patris D. D. Joannis-Francisci-Josephi tituli S. Eusebii S. R. E. cardinalis de Rochechouart, episcopi ducis Laudunensis.* . . . Lauduni, Joannes Calvet, 1774.
Paris, Bibl. nat., Imp., RES ATLAS–B–1; Besançon, Bibl. mun., Arch. A.II.4, Archevêché

1774[5]   *Graduale Cadurcense, illustrissimi et reverendissimi in Christo Patris, D. D. Joseph de Cheylus, Cadurcensis episcopi, auctoritate.* . . . Francopoli-Ruthenorum, P. Vedeilhiém 1774.
Paris, Bibl. nat., Imp., B–120; Besançon, Bibl. mun., Arch. G.II.177, Archevêché

1774   See 1724[1], *Graduale Romanum.* . . . Lugduni, Laurens.

1775[1]   *Abrégé du graduel romain contenant les messes des dimanches et des fêtes de toute l'année. Nouvelle édition.* Avignon, J. J. Niel, 1775.
Zamora, Bibl. Pública, Sofías Sig. /153 Reg.

1775[2]   *Graduale juxta Missale Tolosanum.* . . . 2 vols. Toulouse, 1775.
Besançon, Bibl. mun., Arch. G.II.192 (1, 2), Archevêché
Besançon, Bibl. mun., Arch.G.II.168 appears to be another copy of volume 1, which is devoted to the Proprium tempore.

1776[1]   *Graduale juxta Missale Electense.* . . . *Pars prima: Proprium de tempore; Pars secunda: Proprium et commune sanctorum.* Toulouse, 1776.
Besançon, Bibl. mun., Arch. G.II.159 (1, 2), Archevêché

1776²   *Manuale cantorum, sive Graduale romanum juxta novum missale recognitum. Editio prima brabantica. A plurimis mendis expurgata, variis novis missis, suis locis insertis, aucta, figurisque aeri incisis ornata.* Antverpiae, typis Joannis Pauli Verdussen, 1776.
     Washington, D.C., Library of Congress, M2149.A5 1776; Nijmegen, Katholieke Universiteit, 655 c 4; Austin, Univ. of Texas, microfilm?

1777¹   *Graduale Romanum juxta Missale ex decreto sacro-sancti Concilii Tridentini restitutum, et Clementis VIII. Auctoritate recognitum; adjectis officiis novissime editis ad exemplar missalis Romani. Editio novissima, multo auctior & emendatior.* Leodii, ex officina typographica Clementis Plomteux, perillustrium patriae statuum typographi, 1777.
     Rochester (N.Y.), Colgate Rochester Divinity School; London, British Library, 1608/5518.(1.)

1777²   *Graduel à l'usage du diocèse d'Auxerre.* . . . Auxerre, F. Fournier, 1777.
     Auxerre, Bibl. mun., SX 1847, Anonymes locaux (lacuna from p. 8–23), the cataloguing gives the year as 1776; Auxerre, Bibl. mun., SY 752, Anonymes locaux; Besançon, Bibl. mun., Arch. P.II.148, Archevêché; Nevers, Bibl. mun., SM 2079, Séminaire

1778¹   *Graduale Narbonense. . . D. D. Arthuri. Richardi Dillon. Narbonensis archiepiscopi. . . auctoritate.* . . . Narbonae, J. Besse, 1778.
     Toulouse, Bibl. mun., Rés. A XVIII 101, Fonds ancien 2

1778²   *Graduale Parisiense.* . . . 4 vols. Paris, 1778.
     Besançon, Bibl. mun., Arch. G.II.186 (1, 2, 3, 4), Archevêché

1778³   *Missae sive Cantus Missarum dominicalium et festivarum totius anni, juxta usum Romanum. Cum missa regia Domini H. Dumont, et Missa Baptistae Domini J. B. de Lully.* Editio nova auctior et emendatior. . . . Avignon, L. Chambeau, 1778.
     Florence, Bibl. del Conservatorio di musica Luigi Cherubini

1778⁴   *Graduale Parisiense, illustrissimi et reverendissimi in Christo Patris D.D. Caroli-Gaspar-Guillelmi de Ventimille, ex Comitibus Massiliae Du Luc, Parisiensis Archiepiscopi, Ducis sancti Clodoaldi, Paris Franciae.* . . . Paris, Sumptibus suis ediderunt Bibliopolae usuum Parisiensium, Typis Antonii Boudet. . . , 1778.
     Austin, Univ. of Texas, microfilm
     Microfilm prepared by Baton Rouge (La.), Louisiana State Univ.; cf. 1738⁴.

1779¹   *Graduale Romanum de tempore et sanctis, ad normam Missalis, ex decreto sacrosancti Concilii Tridentini restituti, sancti Pii V. Pontificis maximi iussu editi, Clementis VIII. ac Urbani VIII. auctoritate recogniti.* . . . Venetiis, sumptibus heredis Nicolai Pezzana, MDCCLXXIX.
     Trent, Bibl. Feininger, FSG 35 (#346)

1779²   *Graduale Metense ad usum ecclesiarum parochialium et aliarum quae officio canonico non tenentur. . . Ludovici-Josephi de Montmorency-Laval, Primi Baronis Christiani, Metensi Episcopi. . . auctoritate.* . . . Mes, Joannis-Baptistae Collignon, 1779.
     Strasbourg, Bibl. nat. et universitaire, M.33.743

1779[3]   *Graduale et Vesperale Metense ad usum parochialium....* 2 vols. Metis, Collignon, 1779.
   Metz, Bibl. médiathèque, L 71 BIS, Fonds ancien 1

1779[4]   *Graduale Bisuntinum....* Besançon, 1779.
   Besançon, Bibl. mun., Arch. P.II.152, Archevêché

1779[5]   *Graduale juxta missale Montalbanense....* 2 vols. Toulouse, 1779–1836.
   Besançon, Bibl. mun., Arch. G.II.183 (1, 2), Archevêché

1780[1]   *Graduel de Lyon, noté, pour les dimanches et les fêtes.* Lyon, Aimé de la Roche, 1780.
   Chicago, Newberry Library, 3A 5158

1780[2]   *Graduale Romanum, juxta novum missale recognitum. Editio novissima summa diligentia ab erroribus expurgata. Editio quarta.* Amstelodami, F. J. van Tetroode, 1780.
   Utrecht, Universiteitsbibl., 312 J 32 [CBDP1 ABDP1]; Nijmegen, Katholieke Universiteit, 271 c 277

1781[1]   *Epitome Gradualis Romani juxta usum Romanum, a Dom de la Feillée revisum.* Pictavii, Faulcon & Barbier, 1781.
   Beaune, Bibl. mun., P 12466, 17–18èmes siècles
   Cambridge, Univ. Library, Rit.d.178.1, is likely to be another copy.

1781[2]   *Graduale Romanum juxta novum Missale recognitum....* Amstelodami, F. J. van Tetroode, 1781.
   Nijmegen, Katholieke Universiteit, 247 c 66

1781[3]   *Graduale Romanum juxta novum Missale recognitum, auctum et correctum....* Amstelodami, T. Crajenschot, 1781.
   Antwerp, Universitaire Faculteiten Sint-Ignatius, RG3097 E7; Leuven, Katholieke Universiteitsbibl.; Utrecht, Universiteitsbibl., TAA 414, ALV 29–102 dl 1; Nijmegen, Katholieke Universiteit, 247 c 58

1782[1]   *Graduale juxta Missale romanum, ex decreto sacro-sancti Concilii tridentini, Pii V. Pont. Max. jussu antea editum, et Clementis VIII. et Urbani VIII. auctoritate recognitum.... Editio nova...mendis...expurgata.* Lugduni, Typis Amati de la Roche, 1782.
   Chicago, Newberry Lib.; Providence (R.I.), Brown Univ., VM2149 G 73 1782; Québec, Univ. de Laval, L.Rares M2148 L4 1782 (2 copies)

1782[2]   *Missae, sive cantus missarum dominicalium, et festivarum totius anni. Nova ed., aucta de Missa trompette, de ea domini abbatis Bonaud, de la Thérique & de la Célestine; cum rubricis latinis.* Avenione, apud Franciscum Chambeau, 1782.
   Vatican, Bibl. Apost. Vat., Casimiri V.240

1782[3]   *Graduale monasticum ad usum congregationis SS Vitoni et Hydulphi.* 2 vols. Nancy, 1782.
   Besançon, Bibl. mun., Arch. G.II.200 (1, 2), Archevêché; also, Pars secunda, Arch. G.II.201, Archevêché

1782⁴   *Office romain noté...[avec les Messes].* 5 vols. Paris, A.M. Lottin, 1782.
Vatican, Bibl. Apost. Vat., Racc. gen. Liturgia V.241

1783¹   *Graduale Lemovicense, Illustrissimi ac Reverendissimi D. D. Ludovici-Caroli Du-Plessis-d'Argentré. Episcopi Lemovicensis, auctoritate, ac de Venerabilis Capituli consensu, editum.* Lemovicis, Apud Franciscum Dalesme, Illlustrissimi ac Reverendissimi D. D. Episcopi, ejusque Cleri, Typographum, 1783.
New York, New York Public Library, *MRD; Rodez, Médiathèque, MAG T 6 780, Théologie
No information is available to distinguish this item from the two that follow.

1783²   *Graduale Lemovicence[?]....* Limoges, 1783.
Besançon, Bibl. mun., Arch. P.II.168, Archevêché

1783³   *Graduale Lemovicense....* Limoges, 1783.
Besançon, Bibl. mun., Arch. P.II.169, Archevêché
This copy is 1.5 cm. smaller than 1783²; no other distinguishing marks have been noted.

1783⁴   *Graduel romain ou le chant des dimanches et fêtes de toute l'année....Nouv. ed.* Lyon, Perisse Frères, 1783.
Lyon, Bibl. mun., B 509067, CGA; Konstanz, Wessenberg-Bibliothek
Besançon, Bibl. mun., Arch. P.II.131, Archevêché, is likely another copy, but with a manuscript supplement of 1791 inserted.

1783⁵   *Graduale ad usum provinciae Viennensis juxta missale ejusdem provinciae. Insunt Missae Domincarum totis anni, Ferariarum Quadragesimae, (etc., etc.)...In prima parte reperiuntur ea omnia quae ad Proprium de Tempore, in secunda quae ad Proprium et Commune Sanctorum pertinent cum omnibus aliis quae ad calcem Communis apponuntur.* Gratianopoli, ex typis Vidauae Giroud & filii, [1783].
Grenoble, Bibl. mun., Section d'Étude et d'information, Hd.27, Dauphinois; also Hd.593 and Hd.681, Dauphinois
Hd.681 apparently consists of only the *Proprium et commune sanctorum.*

1784   *Graduel à l'usage du diocèse d'Angers....* Angers, Mame, 1784.
Paris, Bibl. nat., Imp., B 8368

1785¹   *Abrégé du Graduel à l'usage de la province de Vienne, contenant les messes des dimanches & principales fêtes de l'année.* Grenoble, Ve Giraud & fils, 1785.
Brussels, Bibl. royale, II 31.690ᶜ A 2 fnc.

1785²   *Graduel portatif à l'usage du Diocèse de Reims.* Charleville, 1785.
Cited by Heinz Wagener in *Geschichte der katholischen Kirchenmusik,* ed. by K. G. Fellerer (Kassel, 1976), II, 177.

1787¹   *Graduale ad usum ordinis Praemonstratensis Nanceii.* H. Haener, 1787.
Paris, Bibl. nat., Mus., 4° E 16 [Vols I & II]

1787²   *Graduale Romanum juxta missale ex decreto sacro-sancti Concilii Tridentini restitutum, et Clementis VIII auctoritate recognitum; adjectis officiis novissime editis ad exemplar missalis Romani. Editio novissima, multo auctior & emendatior.* Leodii, ex officina typographica Clementis Plomteux, 1787.

Antwerp, Universitaire Faculteiten Sint-Ignatius, RG3106 A3
Cited in Alphonse Goovaerts, *Histoire et bibliographie* (Antwerp, 1880), 514.

1788[1] *Appendix ad Graduale Romanum: of eenige gezangen die voor, onder of na de Missen gezongen worden.* Amsterdam, T. Crajenschot, 1788.
Utrecht, Universiteitsbibl., TAA 414 dl 2 [CBDP1 ABTHO]

1788[2] *Graduale Romanum....* Amsterdam, T. Crajenschot, 1788.
Antwerp, Universitaire Faculteiten Sint-Ignatius, RG3106 A3
This may be identical with 1788[1], but following a different cataloguing procedure.

1789[1] *Graduale Romanum juxta Missale ex decreto sacrosancti Concilii tridentini restitutum, et Clementis VIII auctoritate recognitum.... Editio novissima, multo auctior & emendatior.* Leodii, C. Plomteux, 1789.
Philadelphia, Villanova Univ.; Leuven, Katholieke Universiteitsbibl.; Antwerp, Universitaire Faculteiten Sint-Ignatius, RG3105 B15

1789[2] *Abrégé du graduel romain contenant les messes des dimanches et des fêtes de toute l'année. Nouvelle édition.* Avignon, François Chambeau, 1789.
Barcelona, Biblioteca de Catalunya

1789[3] *Graduale Romanum de tempore et sanctis, ad normam Missalis, ex decreto sacrosancti Concilii Tridentini restituti, sancti Pii V. Pontificis maximi iussu editi, Clementis VIII. ac Urbani VIII. auctoritate recogniti....* Venetiis, sumptibus heredis Nicolai Pezzana, MDCCLXXIX.
New York, Juilliard School of Music; Chicago, Univ. of Chicago, Regenstein Library, ffM2148.L4 1789; Trent, Bibl. Feininger, FSG 36 (#347); Venice, Archivio storico del Patriacato, Bibl. SS Apostoli, 2.B.10; Bologna, Civico museo bibliografico musicale

1789[4] *Graduale Romanum, volgens het Roomsch misboek; tot gebruik der Roomsch-Catholyke Kerken in de Nederlansche zendige. Laatste uitgave....* Amsterdam, de Erfgen. van de Wed. C. Stichter, 1789.
Nijmegen, Katholieke Universiteit, 748 b 12 nr. 1–2

1789[5] *Epitome Gradualis Romani, seu missarum cantus pro diebus Dominicis et festivis totius anni.* Gratianopoli, Andrea Faure, 1789.
Grenoble, Bibl. mun., T.1396, Dauphinois

1790 *Bylage tot het Graduale Romanum, of Gezangen die voor, onder of na den dienst der H. Misse konnen gezongen worden.* Amsterdam, de Erfgen. van de Wed. C. Stichter, 1790.
Utrecht, Universiteitsbibl., RIJS 095–55 dl 2 [CBDP1 ABTHO]

1791[1] *Epitome Gradualis Romani, seu Cantus Missarum dominicalium et festivarum totius anni: iuxta usum romanum a Dom de La Feillee revisum, auctum et emendatum.* S.l., s.n., 1791.
Rome, Biblioteca Casanatense

1791[2] *Epitome gradualis romani, seu Cantus Missarum dominicalium et festivarum totius anni juxta usum romanum; a Dom. de la Feillée revisum, auctum et emendatum.* Pictavii, F. Barbier, 1791.

Baltimore (Md.), St. Mary's Seminary and Univ. Library; Québec, Univ. de Laval, L.Rares M2148 L42 1791; Vatican, Bibl. Apost. Vat., Racc. gen. Liturgia V.1163

Poitiers, Médiathèque François Mitterand, DP 621, Fonds ancien, does not list publisher; perhaps the same as DP 261, listed as 1741[2].

1791[3] *Bijlagen tot het Graduale Romanum, of Gezangen die voor, onder of na den dienst der H. Misse konnen gezongen worden.* Amsterdam, F. J. van Tetroode, 1791.
Utrecht, Universiteitsbibl., WRT 80–272 dl 2 [CBDP1 ABTHO]

1792 *Graduale Romanum, volgens het nieuwe misboek, overzien, verbeterd, en met alle nieuwe missen vermeerderd. Vyfde uitgave.* Amsterdam, F. J. van Tetroode, 1792.
Washington, D. C., Library of Congress, M 2149.A4 1792 Case; Utrecht, Universiteitsbibl., ODB 238 dl 1–2 and WRT 80–272 NB: CON; Nijmegen, Katholieke Universiteit, 380 c 254

1797 *Graduale Romanum de tempore et sanctis ad normam Missalis, [ex decreto sacrosancti Concilii Tridentini restituti. . . .]* Torino, Ignatius Soffietti, 1797.
Milan, Bibl. de Capitolo Metropolitano

1799 *Graduale. . .commune sanctorum.* [S.l., s.n., s.d.]
South Bend (Ind.), Univ. of Notre Dame
One volume of a Spanish Carmelite Gradual.

1800[1] *Graduale Romanum, seu cantus missarum dominicalium et festivarum totius anni, juxta usum Romanum. . . .* Mes, 1800.
Strasbourg, Bibl. nat. et universitaire, M.106.181; Besançon, Bibl. mun., Arch. P.II.132, Archevêché

1800[2] *Graduel romain à l'usage du Diocèse de Québec.* Québec, John Neilson, 1800.
Ottawa, National Library of Canada; Québec, Univ. de Laval, M-fiches FC 19 C571 no. 42385

1801? *Bylage tot het Graduale Romanum, of Gezangen die voor, onder of na den dienst der H. Misse konnen gezongen worden.* Amsterdam, Wed. F. J.van Tetroode, ca. 1801.
Utrecht, Universiteitsbibl., RIJS 095–074 [CBDP1 ABTHO]

1804 *Graduale Bisuntinum. . . .* Besançon, 1804.
Besançon, Bibl. mun., Arch. P.II.153, Archevêché

1805 *Graduale Metense ad usum ecclesiarum parochialium. . . .* Mes, 1805.
Strasbourg, Bibl. nat. et universitaire, M.106.179

1806[1] *Le petit Graduel du diocèse de Bayeux, réimprimé. . .pour la commodité des laïques et particulièrement des personnes qui aident dans les campagnes à chanter l'office divin.* Caen, G. Le Roy, 1806.
Paris, Bibl. nat., Imp., B–41382; Besançon, Bibl. mun., Arch. P.II.150, Archevêché

1806[2] *Diversi Cantus Missarum. . . .* Gratianopoli, J. L. A. Giroud, 1806.
Grenoble, Bibl. mun., V.9995, Dauphinois

1808[1]   Graduale Romanum, volgens het Roomsch misboek; tot gebruik der Roomsch-Catholyke
           Kerken in de Nederlansche zendige. Laatste uitg. Amsterdam, Van Tetroode, 1808.
           Utrecht, Universiteitsbibl., RIJS 095–121 [CBDP1 ABTHO]

1808[2]   Graduale Romanum juxta missale...Editio Novissima. Leodii, L. Devillers, 1808.
           Washington, D.C., Woodstock Theological Center

1809   Graduale Romanum, volgens het Roomsch misboek; tot gebruik der Roomsch-Catholyke
           Kerken in de Nederlansche zendige. Amsterdam, Wed. F. J. van Tetroode, [1809].
           Nijmegen, Katholieke Universiteit, 777 b 8 nr. 1; Utrecht, Universiteits-
           bibl., RIJS 095–55 [CBDP1 ABTHO]

1815[1]   Graduale juxta Missale Romanum....Lugduni, T. Pitrat, 1815.
           Montreal, Univ. de Montreal; Paris, Bibl. nat., Imp., B–628

1815[2]   [Graduel romain pour tous les jours de l'année. Paris, Jacques Lecoffre, 1815].
           Information from 1874[1] and 1878[5] title pages; not otherwise known

1815[3]   Graduale Romanum, volgens het nieuwe misboek, overzien, verbeterd, en met alle
           nieuwe missen vermeerderd. 6de uitgave. Amsterdam, F. J. van Tetroode, 1815.
           Utrecht, Universiteitsbibl., ALV 28–59 dl 1 [CBDP1 ABTHO]; Nijmegen,
           Katholieke Universiteit, 634 c 93

1815[4]   Graduel à l'usage de la partie Laonnoise du diocèse de Soissons....Laon, A. P.
           Courtois, 1815.
           Paris, Bibl. nat., Imp., B–8430; Besançon, Bibl. mun., Arch. P.II.166,
           Archevêche

1816[1]   Graduel Romain, contenant les messes des dimanches et fêtes de toute l'année. Nouvelle
           éd. Lyon, Pitrat, 1816.
           Baltimore (Md.), St. Mary's Seminary and Univ. Library

1816[2]   Graduale Bisuntinum....Besançon, 1816.
           Besançon, Bibl. mun., Arch. P.II.155, Archevêché

1816[3]   Abrégé du Graduel Romain...Nouvelle édition. Avignon, A. Berenguier, 1816.
           Paris, Bibl. nat., Imp., B–5715

1816[4]   Graduale Romanum juxta missale ex decreto sacrosancti Concilii Tridentini restitutum,
           et Clementis VIII. auctoritate recognitum; adjectis officiis novissime editis ad exem-
           plar Missalis Romani. Leodii, Bourguignon, 1816.
           New Zealand, Univ. of Otago

1817   Graduel portatif à l'usage du Diocèse d'Angers. Nouvelle édition....Angers, L. Pavie,
           1817.
           Paris, Bibl. nat., Imp., B–8369

1818[1]   Petit Graduel noté en plain-chant...à l'usage...du Diocèse d'Amiens. Nouvelle
           édition....Amiens, Caron aîné, 1818.
           Paris, Bibl. nat., Imp., B–14848

1818[2]   Abrégé du Graduel Romain...Nouvelle édition. Avignon, A. Berenguier, 1818.
           Paris, Bibl. nat., Imp., B–5716

1821[1]   *Abrégé du Graduel Romain...Nouvelle édition.* Avignon, J.-J. Niel, 1821.
Paris, Bibl. nat., Imp., B–5718

1821[2]   *Graduale Romanum, iuxta Missale ex decreto sacrosancti Concilii Tridentini restitu-tum...Nova editio....* Leodii, Bourguignon, 1821.
Cleveland (Oh.), Cleveland Public Library; Leuven, Katholieke Universiteitsbibl.; Antwerp, Museum Plantin-Moretus, B 2528

1821[3]   *Abrégé du graduel romain contenant les messes des dimanches et des fêtes de toute l'an-née. Nouvelle édition.* Avignon, François Chambeau, 1821.
Paris, Bibl. nat., Imp., B–5717; Barcelona, Biblioteca de Catalunya

1821[4]   *Graduale Metense ad usum Ecclesiarum parochialium....* Metis, Collignon, 1821.
Metz, Bibl. médiathèque, O 1771, Metensia

1822[1]   *Graduel Romain, contenant les Messes des Dimanches et Fêtes de toute l'Année. Nouvelle ed. Conforme à celle in-folio de 1815, et augmentée des Matines et Laudes de Noel, et des principales Processions, de l'Absonte et de plusieurs Messes en Plain-Chant Musical de Dumont.* Lyon, Chez Perisse Freres; Paris, Chez Méquignon-Junior, 1822.
Latrobe (Penn.), St. Vincent College and Archabbey

1822[2]   *Graduale Sanctae Lugdunensis Ecclesiae, primae Galliarum sedis.* Lugduni, ex typis Theodori Pitrat.... apud Rusand...M.DCCC.XXII.
Trent, Bibl. Feininger, FSG 37 (#348)

1822[3]   *Bijlage tot het Graduale Romanum, of Gezangen die voor, onder of na den dienst der H. Misse kunnen gezongen worden.* Amsterdam, Tetroode, 1822.
Utrecht, Universiteitsbibl., ALV 28–59 dl 2 [CBDP1 ABTHO]

1822[4]   *Cantus diversi ex Graduali Romano, pro singulis solemnitatibus dominicis, festis et feriis per annum.* Toulouse, A. Henault, 1822.
Paris, Bibl. nat., Imp., B–6473

1823   *Graduel à l'usage de la province de Vienne. Nouvelle édition, augmentée et soigneuse-ment corrigée.* Grenoble, Baratier frères, 1823.
Paris, Bibl. nat., Imp., B–264

1824[1]   *Graduale Bisuntinum [Illustrissimi?] D. D. Pauli Ambrosii Frere de Villefrancon, Archiepiscopi Bisuntini, Paris, Franciae auctoritate atque approbatione editum.* Visuntione, Johannes Petit, 1824.
Rome, Bibl. naz. cen., 42.3.B.15

1824[2]   *Petit Graduel noté en plain-chant...à l'usage...du Diocèse d'Amiens.* 3rd edition.... Amiens, Caron & Duquenne, 1824.
Paris, Bibl. nat., Imp., B–14849

1825[1]   *Abrégé du Graduel Romain....* Tarascon, 1825.
Besançon, Bibl. mun., Arch. P.II.134, Archevêché

1825[2]   *Abrégé du Graduel Romain....Nouvelle edition.* Lyon, Perisse frères, 1825.
Paris, Bibl. nat., Imp., B–5719

1825[3]   *Graduale ad usum Ecclesiarum quaeritum Parisiensem sequuntur, et quae canonico offico non tenentur....Ab...D. D. Carolo de Vintimille, Parisiensi Archiepiscopo, anteà promulgati.* Divione, J.-M.-Alexandrum Douillier, 1825.
    Paris, Bibl. nat., Imp., B–626

1826[1]   *Graduale Romanum de tempore, et sanctis. Ad normam Missalis, ex decreto sanctosancti[?] pontificis maximi, jussu editi, Clementis VIII. ac Urbani VIII. auctoritate recogniti. Editio secunda Taurinensis emendatissima.* Taurini, ex typ. A Soffietti, 1826.
    Chicago, Newberry Library

1826[2]   *Epitome Gradualis Romani....* Pictavii, 1826.
    Besançon, Bibl. mun., Arch. P.II.133, Archevêché

1826[3]   *Graduel de Paris, noté pour les dimanches et fêtes de l'année.* Paris, Aux depens des libraires associés., 1826.
    Baltimore (Md.), St. Mary's Seminary and Univ. Library
    Cited in the preface to the *Graduel de Paris,* 1846.

1826[4]   *Epitome Gradualis Romani, seu Cantus missarum dominicalium et festivarum totius anni a D. de La Feillée revisum....* Pictavi, 1826.
    Paris, Bibl. nat., Imp., B–7332

1826[5]   *Graduale Molinense....* Molinis, P. A. Desrosiers, 1826.
    Paris, Bibl. nat., Imp., B–2599

1826[6]   *Graduale ad usum ecclesiae Rhedonensis....* Filceriis, apud vid. Vannier, 1826.
    Rennes, Bibl. mun., 1629 FB, Fonds régional
    This may be identical with 1826[7].

1826[7]   *Graduale ad usum ecclesiae Rhedonensis....* Fougères, Filceriis, vidua Vannier, 1826.
    Paris, Bibl. nat., Imp., B–627
    This may be identical with 1826[6].

1826[8]   *Graduale Claromontense illustrissimi ac reverendissimi in christo patris D. D. Caroli-Antonii-Henrici Duvalk de Dampierre, claromontensis episcopi, auctoritate ac ejusdem ecclesiae capituli consensu, editum.* Claromon-Ferrandi, Thibaud-Landriot, 1826.
    Bibl. mun. et interuniversitaire Clermont-Ferrand, A 10402, Auvergne 1

1826[9]   *Graduale Andevagense, illustrissimi et reverendissimi in Christo Patris D.D. Caroli Montault, episcopi Andegavensis, auctoritate, ac venerabilis capituli ejusdem ecclesiae consensu editum.* Andegavi, sumptibus et typis Caroli Mame, 1826.
    New York, Manhattanville College

1827[1]   *Nouveau Graduel à l'usage du diocèse d'Angers, imprimé par ordre de Mgr l'Évêque.* Angers, Mame aîné, 1827.
    Paris, Bibl. nat., Mus., 8° E 38

1827[2]   *Graduel Romain à l'usage du diocèse de Québec. 2 ed. rev. et considérablement augm....* Québec, Neilson & Cowan, 1827.
    Ottawa, National Library of Canada; Québec, Univ. de Laval, L.Rares M2154.2 Q 3 G 733 (2 copies) and M-fiches FC 19C571 no. 41347; Chicago, Loyola Univ.; Orono (Maine), Univ. of Maine; Montreal, McGill Univ.

1827³   *Graduel, Antiphonaire, et Processional à l'usage du Diocèse du Rennes.* 2 vols. Fougères, Ve Vannier, 1827.
Paris, Bibl. nat., Imp., B–8403 (Hiver), B–8403 (Été); Besançon, Bibl. mun., Arch. P.II.187, Archevêché; Rennes, Bibl. mun., 61964 FB, Fonds régional
The Rennes and possibly the Besançon copies contain only the *Partie d'été.*

1828¹   *Graduale juxta Missale Romanum....* Divione, J. N.-A. Douillier, 1828.
Paris, Bibl. nat., Imp., B–629

1828²   *Graduale Romanum juxta missale ex decreto sacro-sancti Concilii Tridentini restitutum, et Clementis VIII. auctoritate recognitum.* Leodii, C. Bourguignon, 1828.
Nijmegen, Katholieke Universiteit, 634 c 47 and 634 c 92

1828³   *Gradual Virdunense....* Stenaei, Templeux, 1828.
Paris, Bibl. nat., Imp., B–8367

1829   *Graduale Romanum continens Missas de Dominicis et festis, etiam novissimis, totius anni. Editio nova, usui Diocesis Argentinensis accomodata.* Argentorati, Typis Ludovici Francisci Le Roux, 1829.
New Haven (Conn.), Yale Univ., School of Music, M2153.2.S89 G7 1829; Latrobe (Penn.), St. Vincent College and Archabbey; Buffalo and Erie, County Public Library; Tübingen, Universitätsbibl., 12 A 12208; Paris, Bibl. nat., Imp., B–8353; Strasbourg, Bibl. mun., A 46928, Alsatiques

1833¹   *Graduale Romanum, iuxta Missale ex decreto sacrosancti Concilii Tridentini restitutum....* Leodii, Bourguignon, 1833.
Leuven, Katholieke Universiteitsbibl.

1833²   *Graduel romain contenant les messes....* Lyon, Paris, 1833.
Besançon, Bibl. mun., Arch. P.II.135, Archevêché; also Arch. P.II.136, Archevêché

1833³   *Graduale Nemausense....* Nimes, 1833.
Besançon, Bibl. mun., Arch. P.II.176, Archevêché

1834¹   *Graduel romain, contenant les messes des dimanche et fêtes de toute l'année. Nouv. ed.* Lyon, Perisse Frères, 1834.
Paris, Bibl. nat., Imp., B–8407

1834²   *Graduale Romanum juxta missale ex decreto Concilii Tridentini restitutum ....* Antverpiae, ex Architypografia Plantiniana, apud Albertum Moretus.
Antwerp, Museum Plantin-Moretus, A 1535; Antwerp, Staatbibl., F50593; Milan, Bibl. naz. Braidense, Gerli 224; Stockholm, Kungl. biblioteket, 173 N c Fol.

1834³   *Graduel Parisien noté....* Agen, 1834.
Besançon, Bibl. mun., Arch. P.II.184, Archevêché

1835   *Graduale Tolosanum, illustrissimi ac reverendissimi in Christo patris D. D. Pauli Theresiae Davidis d'Astros...auctoritate, ac venerabilis ejusdem ecclesiae capituli consensu....* 3 vols. *Pars prima, Proprium de tempore; Pars secunda, Proprium et*

commune sanctorum; Pars tertia, Missae pro defunctis et diversi cantus. Tolosae, A. D. Manavit, 1835/36.
> Toulouse, Bibl. mun., Lm A 34 (1), (2), (3), 1965–1992; Besançon, Bibl. mun., Arch. G.II.194 (1, 2), Arch. G.II.193 (3), Archevêché

1836[1] *Graduale Albiense.* . . . Toulouse, 1836.
> Besançon, Bibl. mun., Arch. G.II.158, Archevêché

1836[2] *Graduale Baionense.* . . . Toulouse, 1836.
> Besançon, Bibl. mun., Arch. G.II.167, Archevêché

1837[1] *Graduale Auscitanum, illustrissimi et reverendissimi de Montillet Auscitani archiepiscopi &c., auctoritate editum. . . ac typis denuò mandatum.* Auscis, apud L. A. Brun, 1837.
> Paris, Bibl. nat., Imp., B–127
> "*Graduale Auscitanum.* . . . Auch, 1837" in Besançon, Bibl. mun., Arch. P.II.163, Archevêché, appears to be the same.

1837[2] *Editio Nova Graduale Erecense.* . . . Trecis, Bouquot, 1837.
> Paris, Bibl. nat., Imp., B–244

1837[3] *Graduel à l'usage du diocèse de Nantes.* . . . Nantes, Merson, 1837.
> Paris, Bibl. nat., Imp., B–8392; Besançon, Bibl. mun., Arch. P.II.175, Archevêché

1839 *Graduale Metense, ad usum ecclesiarum parochialium in quo missae, cum cantu, dominicarum anni, festorum domini, B. Mariae Virginis, et SS. in dioecesi festivatorum, vel alias in dominicis celebrandorum.* . . . Metis, Collignon, 1839.
> St. Meinrad (Ind.), St. Meinrad Archabbey and School of Theology; Paris, Bibl. nat., Imp., B–8351
> Besançon, Bibl. mun., Arch. P.II.173, Archevêché, appears to be the same, although no information is given regarding the publisher.

1840[1] *Graduale Romanum de tempore et sanctis ad normam Missalis ex decreto Sacrosancti Concilii Tridentini restituti. P. Pii V, P. N. iussu, editi Clementis VIII. ac Urbani Viii. auctoritate recogniti. Tertia Taurinensis editio semper aucta et emendata.* Taurini, Canfari, 1840.
> Berkeley (Calif.) Univ. of California, M2149.T867 1840; Rome, Bibl. naz. cen., 42.2.F.19

1840[2] *Graduel Romain, contenant les messes des dimanches et fêtes de toute l'année. Nouvelle éd.* . . . Lyon, Perisse Frères, 1840.
> Barcelona, Biblioteca de Catalunya

1840[3] *Abrégé du Graduel à l'usage de la Province de Vienne, contenant les Messes des Dimanches et principales fêtes de l'année. Édition augmentée.* Grenoble, Baratier frères et fils, 1840.
> Grenoble, Bibl. mun., T.5562, Dauphinois; Besançon, Bibl. mun., Arch. P.II.198, Archevêché

1840[4] *Graduel de Lyon, noté.* . . . Lyon, Pelagaud & Lesne, 1840.
> Paris, Bibl. nat., Imp., B–8379

1840[5]   *Graduel noté à l'usage du Diocèse de Meaux.... Meaux*, A. Dubois, 1840.
          Paris, Bibl. nat., Imp., B–8390

1841   *Graduel Romain à l'usage du diocèse de Québec.... 3e éd., corr. et aug.* Québec, W.
          Neilson, 1841.
          Toronto, Univ. of Toronto Music Library; Québec, Univ. de Laval, L.Rares
          M2154.2 Q3 G733 1841

1842[1]   *Graduale Romanum, of Misgezangen voor de Roomsch-Katholieke Kerken in Nederland.*
          s'Hertogenbosch, Verhoeven, 1842.
          Utrecht, Universiteitsbibl., DIJNS 75–258 [CBDP1 ABTHO]

1842[2]   *Graduale Romanum, of Misgezangen voor de Roomsch-Katholieke Kerken in Nederland.*
          uitgebr. en geheel volledige uitg. onder toezigt van M. A. van Steenwijk. Amsterdam,
          A. Zweesardt, 1842.
          Nijmegen, Katholieke Universiteit, 81 b 3; Utrecht, Universiteitsbibl.,
          TAW 991, 320 B4 [CBDP1 ABTHO]

1842[3]   *Graduale Sanclaudiense....* Besançon, 1842.
          Besançon, Bibl. mun., Arch. P.II.190, Archevêché; also Arch. P.II.188 and
          Arch. P.II.191, Archevêché
          Besançon, Bibl. mun., Arch. P.II.189, Archevêché, appears to be a fourth
          copy of the same print.

1842[4]   *Graduale Sanclaudiense....* Vesuntione, Bintol, 1842.
          Paris, Bibl. nat., Imp., B–8366
          This may be identical with 1842[3].

1842[5]   *[Graduel...].* 1842. [Title page lacking; the print is assigned to Beauvais by the
          cataloguer.]
          Paris, Bibl. nat., Imp., B–8371

1843[1]   *Graduale Bisuntinum....* Besançon, 1843.
          Besançon, Bibl. mun., Arch. P.II.156, Archevêché

1843[2]   *Graduale Bisuntinum....* Besançon, 1843.
          Besançon, Bibl. mun., Arch. P.II.157, Archevêché
          This copy is 2 cm. smaller than 1843[1]; no other distinguishing marks are
          noted.

1843[3]   *Graduale Bisuntinum....* Vesontione, Outhenin-Chalandre, 1843.
          Cambridge (Mass.), Harvard Univ., C9355.206; Besançon, Bibl. mun.,
          296519, Contois

1843[4]   *Graduale Romanum juxta Missale, ex decreto sacrosancti Concilii Tridentini restitutum*
          et Clementis VIII. auctoritate recognitum, adjectis officiis novissime editis ad exem-
          plar Missalis romani. Leodii, P. Kersten, 1843.
          Dayton (Ohio), Univ. of Dayton

1844[1]   *Graduale Romanum continens Missas de Dominicis et festis, etiam novissimis, totius*
          anni. Editio emendatius recognita et usui Diocesis Argentinensis accomodata.
          Argentorati, Typis, Ludovici Francisci de Roux, 1844.

Latrobe (Penn.), St. Vincent College and Archabbey; Atchison (Kans.), Benedictine College; London, British Library, 1221.f.25; Paris, Bibl. nat., Imp., B–8354

1844[2]   *Graduel Romain, contenant les messes des dimanches et fêtes de toute l'année. Nouvelle éd.*. . . Lyon, Perisse Frères, 1844.
Baltimore (Md.), St. Mary's Seminary and Univ. Library; St. Louis (Mo.), Kenrick-Glenn Seminary; Paris, Bibl. nat., Imp., B–8413

1844[3]   *Graduel romain et recueil de messes, notés selon la méthode arithmographe de plain-chant*. . . . Par. J. E. Miquel jeune etc. pp. xvii, 421. 170 J. M. Blanc, Albertville, 1844.
London, British Library, [Music] D.427; Chambéry, Médiathèque J.-J. Rousseau, SEMM00833, Ancien séminaire; Lunel, Bibl. mun., LUY 35–1

1844[4]   *Graduale Carcassonense, illustrissimi et reverendissimi in Christo patris D. D. Josephi-Juliani de Saint-Rome Gualy episcopi carcassonensis auctoritate*. . . *Pars prima, proprium de tempore; Pars secunda, proprium et commune sanctorum.* Carcassi, apud Claudium Labau, 1844.
Paris, Bibl. nat., Imp., B–156 (1,2)

1844[5]   *Processional, Graduel, Antiphonaire et Psautier, à l-usage de l'Église Primatiale et Métropolitaine de Sens. Nouvelle édition.* [2 vols.] Sens, Thomas-Malvin, 1844.
Sens, Bibl. mun., Trésor de la Cathedrale, I 93a and 93b.

1844[6]   *Graduel à l'usage du diocèse de Nîmes*. . . . Nîmes, Ve. Gaude, 1844.
Paris, Bibl. nat., Imp., B–8394; Besançon, Bibl. mun., Arch. P.II.177, Archevêché

1844[7]   *Graduel du diocèse d'Autun noté*. . . . 2 vols. Autun, F. Dejussieu, 1844.
Paris, Bibl. nat., Imp., B–8370 *(Hiver)* and B–8370 *(Été);* Besançon, Bibl. mun., Arch. P.II.147, Archevêché

1844[8]   *Graduale Cisterciense*. . . *auctoritate et praelo R.D.D. fr. Martini Dom, abbatis, Vicarii Generalis Ordinis Cisterciensis, strictioris observantiae in Belgio, juxta illud R.D.D. fr. Nicolai Larcher.* Westmalle, Fratres Abbatiae Westmallensis, 1844.
Kalamazoo (Mich.), Western Michigan Univ.

1845[1]   *Graduale Romanum, ad normam missalis ex decreto sacrosancti concilii Tridentini resti-tuti, S. Pii V Pontif. max. jussu editi, Clementis VIII ac Urbani auctoritate recog-niti*. . . *Editio nova, accurate emendata*. . . . Divione, J.N. Alexandrum Douillier, 1845.
Paris, Bibl. nat., Imp., B–630

1845[2]   *Graduale Auscitanum*. . . . [cf. 1837[1]] Lugduni, J. B. Pelagaud & Soc., 1845, 1846.
Paris, Bibl. nat., Imp., B–8349 and B–8350
These two copies may be of different printings.

1845[3]   *Ordinarium Missae e Graduali Romano typis Plantinianis anno 1599, edito, deprom-tum. Editio altera. Accesserunt Hymni et Cantica maxime usitata.* pp. 107. P. J. Hanicq, Mechliniae, 1845.
Washington, D.C., Woodstock Theological Center; London, British Library, 3366.bb.20

1845[4]   Graduel à l'usage du diocèse de Nantes. 2nd ed. Nantes, Merson, 1845.
          Baltimore (Md.), St. Mary's Seminary and Univ. Library; Paris, Bibl. nat.,
          Imp., B–8393

1845[5]   Graduel à l'usage du diocèse de Nantes. 2 vols. Nantes, Merson, 1845.
          Baltimore (Md.), St. Mary's Seminary and Univ. Library; Paris, Bibl. nat.,
          Imp., B–635 (Hiver), B–635 (Été); Besançon, Bibl. mun., Arch. G.II.184 (1,
          2), Archevêché

1845[6]   Abrégé de Graduel romain, contenant les messes des dimanches et des fêtes de toute l'an-
          née.... Paris, Méquignon-Junior et Leroux, 1845.
          Collegeville (Minn.), St. John's Univ.

1846   Graduel de Paris, noté pour les dimanches et fêtes de l'année. Imprimé par ordre de Mgr
          [Denis-Auguste Affre] l'Archévèque. Aux depens des libraires associés. Paris, 1846.
          Paris, Bibl. nat., Mus., 8° E 49

1847[1]   Graduale Romanum de tempore et sanctis, ad normam Missalis, ex decreto sacrosancti
          Concilii Tridentini restituti, sancti Pii V. Pontificis maximi iussu editi, Clementis VIII.
          ac Urbani VIII. auctoritate recogniti. Prima editio Taurinensis. Augustae
          Taurinorum, apud Ioannem Baptistam Paravia et soc.... MDCCCXLVII.
          Trent, Bibl. Feininger, FSG 38 (#349); Piacenza, Bibl. del Collegio
          Cardinale Giulio Alberoni (2 copies); Turin, Bibl. del Seminario arcivescov-
          ile; Stockholm, Kungl. biblioteket

1847[2]   Graduel Romain imprimé par ordre de Mgr Brossays Saint-Marc.... Rennes, Vatar, 1847.
          Rennes, Bibl. mun., 1278 FB, Fonds régional

1847[3]   Graduale Sanctae Lugdunensis Ecclesiae.... Lugduni, J.-B. Pelagaud et Soc., 1847.
          Paris, Bibl. nat., Imp., B–625

1847[4]   The little Gradual, or a chorister's companion, with English translation by A. L. Phillipps.
          London, 1847.
          Cambridge, Univ. Library, Rit.c.784.1; Philadelphia, Univ. of Pennsylvania

1847[5]   Graduel à l'usage du diocèse de Nancy et de Toul, imprimé par ordre de Mgr A.-B.
          Menjaud, évêque de Nancy et de Toul. Nancy, Grimblot et Vve Raybois, 1847.
          Paris, Bibl. nat., Imp., B–8391; Nancy, Bibl. mun., 5871, Favier and 5083,
          Lorrain 1; Besançon, Bibl. mun., Arch. P.II.174, Archevêché

1847[6]   Petit Graduel du diocèse de Bayeux.... Nouvelle édition, revue et augmentée des
          oraisons, épitres et évangiles de toute l'annee. Caen, F. Poisson et fils, 1847.
          Paris, Bibl. nat., Imp., B–41697; Besançon, Bibl. mun., Arch. P.II.151,
          Archevêché

1847[7]   Graduel et processionnal du Diocèse de Clermont, reimprimés par l'ordre de Mgr...Louis
          Charles Ferron, évêque.... Clermont, Thibaut-Landriot frères, 1847.
          Clermont-Ferrand, Bibl. mun. et universitaire, A32216, Auvergne 1

1847[8]   Graduel noté à l'usage du Diocèse d'Evreux. Evreux, Cornemillot, 1847.
          Paris, Bibl. nat., B–8375

1848[1]   *Graduale Romanum juxta ritum sacrosanctae romanae ecclesiae, cum cantu, Pauli V,*
          Pont. Max. jussu reformato. Editio emendata. Mechliniae, P.J. Hanicq, 1848.
             St. Louis (Mo.), St. Louis Univ., Divinity School; Baltimore (Md.), St.
             Mary's Seminary and Univ. Library; Boston, Athenaeum Library; St.
             Meinrad (Ind.), St. Meinrad Archabbey and School of Theology; Louisville,
             (Ky.), Southern Baptist Theol. Seminary; Austin, Univ. of Texas; East
             Lansing (Mich.), Michigan State Univ.; Antwerp, Staatbibl., F266335;
             Trent, Bibl. Feininger, FSG 39 (#350); Eichstätt, Katholische
             Universitätsbibl., 21/1 ESL III 64; Besançon, Bibl. mun., Arch. P.II.137,
             Archevêché; London, British Library, 3267.b.22

1848[2]   *Graduale Romanum iuxta ritum sacrosanctae Romanae ecclesiae, cum cantu Pauli V.*
          Pont. max. iussu reformato.... Ed. F. De Voght, Edmund Duval. 1848.
             Ellwangen, Peutinger-Gymnasium
             This may be identical with 1848[1].

1848[3]   *Graduel romain....* Lyon, Paris, 1848.
             Besançon, Bibl. mun., Arch. P.II.138, Archevêché

1849   *Graduale Romanum....* Dijon, 1849.
             Besançon, Bibl. mun., Arch. G.II.157, Archevêché

1850[1]? *Graduel romain ou messes des dimanches et des fêtes de toute l'année....* Digne, Repos,
             [1850 is date of imprimatur].
             Milan, Bibl. naz. Braidense, Gerli 1767

1850[2]? *Le Service Divin pour toutes les fêtes de l'année d'après le nouveau Graduel suivant le Rit*
          Romain. Paris, Alexandre Charles Fessy, [1850?].
             London, British Library, E.162.c

1851[1]   *Graduale Romanum juxta Missale. Editio nova.* Leodii, P. Kersten, 1851.
             Yonkers (N.Y.), St. Joseph's Seminary

1851[2]   [*Graduale Romanum, complectens Missas omnium Dominicarum et Festorum*
          Duplicium et Semiduplicium Totius Anni, Necnon Officium Nocturnum Nativitatis
          Domini et Praecipuas Processionies. Cantu reviso juxta manuscripta vetustissima.]
             Parisiis, J. Lecoffre et Socios, 1851.
             Information from 1852[1]; cited in David Hiley, *Western Plainchant*, 623.

1851[3]   *Graduel romain pour tous les jours de l'année. Nouvelle éd.* Lyon, Perisse Frères, 1851.
             Baltimore (Md.), St. Mary's Seminary and Univ. Library, Tallahassee
             (Fla.), Florida State Univ.; Washington, D.C., Woodstock Theological
             Center; Paris, Bibl. nat., Imp., B–8419

1851[4]   *Graduel romain.... Nouvelle édition.* Digne, Repos, 1851.
             Paris, Bibl. nat., Imp., B–8420

1852[1]   *Graduale Romanum, complectens missas omnium Dominicarum et Festorum Duplicium*
          et Semiduplicium Totius Anni, Necnon Officium Nocturnum Nativitatis Domini et
          Praecipuas Processionies. Cantu reviso juxta manuscripta vetustissima. Parisiis, J.
          Lecoffre et Socios, Bibliopolas, 1852.

Paris, Bibl.nat., Mus., 8° E 61 (1st ed., 1851; see also 1865); Québec, Univ. de Laval, M2148 L4 1852

Prepared for Reims and Cambrai Archbishops.

1852[2]   *Graduale Romanum, iuxta missale & officia novissimi auctoritate apostolica pro universale Ecclesia approbata.* Monasterii, Cazin, 1852.

Bamberg, Staatsbibl., 0122 / Lit 537; Eichstätt, Katholische Universitätsbibl., 21/1 ESL III 73

1852[3]   *Graduel complet et noté du diocèse de Toulouse....* Toulouse, A. Manavit, 1852.

Toulouse, Bibl. mun., Lm D 365 1815–1975

1852[4]   *Proprium Missarum pro clero Archidiocesis Olomucensis atque Dioecesis Brunensis....* Olomouc, Fr. Slavic, 1852.

Bloomington (Ind.), Indiana Univ.

1853[1]   *Graduel et Vespéral romains, contenant en entier les Messes et les Vêpres de tous les jours de l'année, les Matines et Laudes de Noel et de la Semaine-Sainte et l'Office des morts, avec Propre de Luçon, imprimé par ordre de mgr. l'évêque....* Rennes, J-M. Vatar, 1853.

Vatican, Bibl. Apost. Vat., Racc. gen. Liturgia V.120

1853[2]   *Graduel romain, imprimé par ordre de Mgr Antoine de Salinis, êveque d'Amiens, pour l'usage de son diocése et suivi du propre et du supplément.* Rennes, Impr. J.-M. Vatar, 1853.

Amiens, Univ. de Picardie (Service commun de la documentation, Section Lettres), FIPL

1853[3]   *Graduale Romanum, complectens Missas omnium Dominicarum et Festorum Duplicium et Semiduplicium Totius Anni, Necnon Officium Nocturnum Nativitatis Domini et Praecipuas Processiones. Cantu reviso juxta manuscripta vetustissima.* Parisiis, J. Lecoffre et Socios, 1853.

Chicago, Loyola Univ.; New Haven (Conn.), Yale Univ., School of Music; New York, Fordham Univ.; Atchison (Kans.), Benedictine College; Washington, D.C., Dominican College; Baltimore (Md.), St. Mary's Seminary and Univ. Library

1853[4]   *Graduale Romanum ad normam missalis ex decreto sacrosancti concilii tridentini restituti... complectens missas tum de tempore, tum de sanctis, tum etiam votivas, accuratissima editio.... Cantu reviso juxta manuscript justissima.* Paris, J. Lecoffre et Socios, 1853.

Paris, Bibl. nat., Imp., B–631

1853[5]   *Graduel romain....* Dijon, 1853.

Nevers, Bibl. mun., SM 2081, Séminaire

1853[6]   *Officium defunctorum. Cantu reviso juxta Graduale et Antiphonarium Romanum....* Paris, Lecoffre, 1853.

Baltimore (Md.), St. Mary's Seminary and Univ. Library

1854[1] Cantus Missarum juxta ritum Sacri Ordines Praedicatorum ad Fidem Antiquorum
Codicum restitutus, et Reverendissimi Patris Fr. Alex. Vincentii Jandel, totius ejus-
dem Ordinis Vicarii Generalis permissu editus. Gandavi, G. Jacqmain,
Chromolithographus et Typographus, 1854.
  Paris, Bibl.nat., Mus., 4° E 17; Vatican, Bibl. Apost. Vat., Casimiri III.43;
London, British Library, 1502/10
  Stanford (Calif.), Stanford Univ., listed in RLIN, has been lost.

1854[2] Graduale Romanum juxta ritum sacrosanctae romanae ecclesiae, cum cantu, Pauli V,
Pont. Max. jussu reformato. Editio [secunda]. Mechliniae, P.J. Hanicq, 1854.
  Rome, Bibl. Angelica, H.II.53; Paris, Bibl. nat., Imp., B–8358

1854[3] Graduel Romain, contenant les messes de tous les jours de l'année, les matines et les
laudes de Noel, les processions et les obsèques. Dernière éd.... Digne, Commission
ecclésiastique, 1854.
  Baltimore (Md.), St. Mary's Seminary and Univ. Library

1854[4] Graduale Romanum, totius anni, juxta Missale, ex decreto Sacro-Sancti Concilii
Tridentini restitutum, S. Pii V., Pontif. Max. jussu editum, Clementis VIII ac Urbani
VIII auctoritate recognitum. Tolosae, ex. typ. Augustini Manavit, 1854.
  Paris, Bibl. nat., Imp., B–634

1854[5] Graduel romain à l'usage de la province ecclésiastique de Québec. Québec, A. Côté, 1854.
  Québec, Univ. de Laval, L.Rares M2154.2 Q3 G733 1854

1855[1] Graduale Romanum juxta ritum Sacrosanctae Romanae Eclesiae, cum cantu Paul V. Pont.
Maximi jussu reformato. Mechliniae, H. Dessain, 1855; Editio prima (cf. 1859).
  Rochester (N.Y.), Univ. of Rochester, Eastman School of Music; Milan,
Bibl. naz. Braidense, Gerli 47/1; Utrecht, Universiteitsbibl., ALV 27–318 dl
1, WRT 79–550 dl 1 [CBAB AB], Paris, Bibl. nat., Imp., B–632; Nijmegen,
Katholieke Universiteit, 3 a 2

1855[2] Graduale Romanum: [ad norman missalis ex decreto Sacrosancti Concilii Tridentini,]
complectens missas omnium dominicarum et festorum duplicium et semiduplicium
totius anni... Parisiis, Jacobum LeCoffre et socios, 1855.
  Paris, Bibl. nat., Imp., B–8359; London, British Library, D.3355.aaa.23
  Basel, Universitätsbibl., BibG D 165, appears to be another copy of this
work, catalogued with a variant title (Graduale Romanum ad normam missalis
ex decreto Sacrosancti Concilii Tridentini...). The discrepancies in title may
merely reflect different forms of short citations.

1855[3] Graduale Romanum continens Missas de Dominicis et festis, etiam novissimis, totius
anni. Editio nova, usui Diocesis Argentinensis accomodata. Argentinae, Typis L. F.
Le Roux, 1855.
  Paris, Bibl. nat., Imp., B–8360

1855[4] [Graduale Romanum...]. ed. by Lambillotte.
  Cited in David Hiley, Western Plainchant, 623 (cf. 1857[3]).

1855[5]   *Compendium gradualis et antiphonarii romani: continens officia dominicarum et festorum totius anni.* Moguntiae, J. G. Wirth, 1855.
Bern, Universitätsbibl. (Musikwissenschaft), MU KT d 1855/1

1855?   *Accompagnement d'orgue composé pour le Graduel Romain de la Commission de Reims et de Cambrai par M[ons.] L. Dietsch, Maître de Chapelle de L'Église de la Madeleine à Paris, et M. l'Abbé E. Tessier, ancien Maître de Chapelle.* 2 vols. Paris, Jacques LeCoffre et Cie [1855?].
London, British Library, [Music] G.132

1856[1]   *Graduale Romanum : complectens missas omnium dominicarum et festorum duplicium et semiduplicium totius anni...* Parisiis, Jacobum LeCoffre et socios, 1856.
South Bend (Ind.), Univ. of Notre Dame; St. Paul (Minn.), Univ. of St. Thomas; Alleghany (N.Y.), St. Bonaventure Univ.; Elyria (Oh.), Oberlin College; Paris, Bibl. nat., Imp., B–8361

1856[2]   *Graduel romain comprenant les messes et les petites heures....* Paris, Lyon, Lecoffre fils et cie, 1856.
Chambéry, Médiathèque J.-J. Rousseau, SEMM01315, Ancien séminaire

1857[1]   *Graduale Romanum, juxta Missale & officia novissime auctoritate apostolica pro universali ecclesia approbata.* Leodii, Spée-Zelis, 1857.
Ithaca (N.Y.), Cornell Univ.; Leuven, Katholieke Universiteitsbibl.; Utrecht, Universiteitsbibl., ALV 27–81 [CBDP1 ABTHO]

1857[2]   *Graduale Romanum....* Paris, Poussielgue fratres, 1857.
Reference from 1883 ed.; this print was not located.

1857[3]   *Graduale Romanum: quod ad cantum attinet ad gregorianam formam reductum ex veteribus mss. undique donatum....* Ed. L. Lambillotte, A. Le Clere et Soc., Parisiis, 1857.
Minneapolis (Minn.), Univ. of Minnesota; Waco (Tex.) Baylor Univ.; Baltimore (Md.), St. Mary's Seminary and Univ. Library; Québec, Univ. de Laval, Bibl.; Utrecht, Universiteitsbibl., 334 G 9 [CBDP1 ABTHO]; Paris, Bibl. nat., Mus., Recueil 11; Paris, also Imp., B–8362, B–8363, and B–40213; Eichstätt, Katholische Universitätsbibl., 21/1 ESL III 88; Sheffield, Univ. Lib., B 264.02; London, British Library, 3395.c.1 (Destroyed in World War II)

1857[4]   *Graduale Romanum... Notae veteres–Notae recentiones [sic]....* Paris, 1857.
Besançon, Bibl. mun., Arch. P.II.139, Archevêché
Without additional information one cannot tell whether the reference is to an independent print or to one of the prints listed above for the same date.

1857?   *Graduale Romanum, complectens Missas omnium Dominicarum et Festorum Duplicium et Semiduplicium Totius Anni, Necnon Officium Nocturnum Nativitatis Domini et Praecipuas Processionies. Cantu reviso juxta manuscripta vetustissima.* Parisiis, J. Lecoffre et Socios, Bibliopolas, (latest of letters of approbation dated Nov. 24, 1856).
Paris, Bibl. nat., mus.

1858[1]   *Graduale Romanum: quod ad cantum attinet, ad Gregorianam formam redactum ex veteris mss. unique collectis et duplici notatione donatum.* Parisiis, A. Le Clere et Soc. 1858.
Baltimore (Md.), Peabody Conservatory; London, British Library, L.18.b.2

1858[2]   *Graduale Romanum, juxta ritum Sacro-Sanctae Romanae Ecclesiae, quod ad cantum attinet, ad Gregorianam formam redactum, ex veteribus manuscriptis.* Parisiis, Adrianus Leclere et Socii, 1858.
Paris, Bibl. nat., Imp., B–633

1858[3]   *Graduel romain noté d'après les chants modernes les mieux estimés et les plus répandus en France.* A Valence, Abbé Rojat, 1858.
Vatican, Bibl. Apost. Vat., Casimiri IV.419

1858[4]   *Graduel Romain, conforme au missel reformé par les SS. Pontifes S. Pie V, Clement VIII, et Urbain avec les messes propres au diocèse d'Evreux. Publiées par ordre de Mgr. H. M. G. de Bonnechose, Evêque d'Evreux.* Dijon, Peutet-Pommey. Libraire-Editeur, Imprimeur de l'Évêché..., 1858.
Private collection

1858[5]   *Graduel romain, suivi du Propre d'Angers, imprimé par ordre de Monseigneur Angebault, évêque d'Angers pour l'usage de son diocèse.* Rennes, H. Vatar, 1858.
Paris, Bibl. nat., Imp., B–638

1858[6]   *Chants communs des messes d'après le Graduel Romain...*, Paris, Le Clere. 1858.
Baltimore (Md.), St. Mary's Seminary and Univ. Library

1859[1]   *Graduale Romanum juxta ritum sacrosanctae Romanae Ecclesiae, cum cantu Pauli v. Pont. Maximi jusso reformato. Editio tertia.* Mechliniae, H. Dessain, 1859. (Cf. 1855.)
Athens (Ga.), Univ. of Georgia; Collegeville (Minn.), St. John's Univ.; New York, New York Public Library, *MM; Latrobe (Penn.), St. Vincent College and Archabbey; New Haven (Conn.), Yale Univ., School of Music, M2148.L4 1859; St. Meinrad (Ind.), St. Meinrad Archabbey and School of Theology; Berkeley (Calif.), Univ. of California; Baltimore (Md.), St. Mary's Seminary and Univ. Library; Atchison (Kans.), Benedictine College; Detroit, (Mich.), Sacred Heart Major Seminary Library; Québec, Univ. de Laval, M2148 L4 1859; Leuven, Katholieke Universiteitsbibl.; Besançon, Bibl. mun., Arch. P.II.140, Archevêché; Nijmegen, Katholieke Universiteit, 740 c 44. PPL

1859[2]   *Graduale Romanum juxta ritum sacrosanctae Romanae Ecclesiae, cum cantu Pauli v. Pont. Maximi jusso reformato. Editio tertia.* Mechliniae, Hanicq, 1859.
Paris, Bibl. nat., Imp., B–18072
This may be identical with 1859[1].

1859[3]   *Graduale Romanum : complectens missas omnium dominicarum et festorum duplicium et semiduplicium totius anni....* Parisiis, Jacobum LeCoffre et socios, 1859.
Baltimore (Md.), St. Mary's Seminary and Univ. Library; Paris, Bibl. nat., Imp B–8365
Besançon, Bibl. mun., Arch. P.II.140, Archevêché, is likely the same as 1859[2].

1859[4]   *Graduel romain, contenant les meses de tous les jours de l'année, les matines et les laudes de Noël, les processions et les obsèques. Dernière éd.* Digne, La Commission, Paris E. Repos, 1859.
Québec, Univ. de Laval, M2148 L4 1859b

1860[1]   *Graduale Romanum ad normam missalis ex decreto sacrosancti concilii Tridentini....* Parisiis, J. Lecoffre et soc., 1860.
Paris, Bibl. nat., Imp., B–1144

1860[2]   *Graduel romain monastique rédigé d'après le calendrier approuvé à Rome en 1847 pour les religieuses bénédictines de l"Institut de l'adoration perpétuelle du très-Saint Sacrement.* Paris, A. Le Clere, 1860.
Paris, Bibl. nat., Imp., B–2980

1860[3]   *Graduel et vespéral romains, avec le propre du diocèse d'Amiens....* 2 vols. Amiens, Garon et Lambert, 1860.
Paris, Bibl. nat., Imp., B–17854 *(Hiver)* and B–17854 *(Été)*

1860[4]   *Graduale Cisterciense...Nova editio, juxta anteriorem, sed multis mendis emendata, in qua continentur omnia, quae in choro, pro missarum celebratione decantari debent; cum hymnis, antiphonis, versiculis et Psalmis ad tertiam et nonam spectantibus.* Westmalle, Fratres Abbatiae Westmallensis, 1860.
St. Meinrad (Ind.), St. Meinrad Archabbey and School of Theology

1860[5]   *Graduel selon le rit romain et d'après les concessions faites au diocèse de Coutances par Notre S. Pere le Pape Pie IX, redigé et publié par ordre de Monseigneur Jacques-Louis Daniel, Evêque de Coutance et d'Avranches.* Coutance, Daireaux, 1860.
Chicago, Univ. of Chicago, Regenstein Library, fM2149.C8

1861[1]   *Graduale Romanum: complectens missas omnium dominicarum et festorum duplicium et semiduplicium totius anni....* Parisiis, Jacobum LeCoffre et socios, 1861.
Los Angeles, Loyola Marymount Univ.; Dayton (Ohio), Univ. of Dayton; Philadelphia, Free Library; Baltimore (Md.), St. Mary's Seminary and Univ. Library; Paris, Bibl. nat., Imp., B–17853

1861[2]   *Graduale juxta missale romanum cum officiis propriis ecclesiae metropolitanae Rotomagensis A. SS. DD. NN Pio IX approbatis ac de mandato illuss. et. reverend. H. M. G. de Bonnechose....* Rennes, impr. Vatar; Rouen, libr. Fleury, 1861.
Paris, Bibl. nat., Imp., B–1158

1861[3]   *Graduale juxta missale romanum....* Rouen, 1861.
Besançon, Bibl. mun., Arch. G.II.189, Archevêché

1861[4]   *Graduel suivant le rit romain, à l'usage du diocèse de Bayeux....* Caen, imprimerie Poisson, Bayeux, libr. Delarue, 1861.
Paris, Bibl. nat., Imp., B–1169; Besançon, Bibl. mun., Arch. G.II.166, Archevêché

1862   *Graduale Romanum...cantu reviso juxta manuscripta.* Parisiis, J. Lecoffre et soc. 1862.
Paris, Bibl. nat., Imp., B–19304
Besançon, Bibl. mun., Arch. P.II.141, Archevêché, is likely a second copy.

1863[1]   Graduale juxta usum Ecclesiae Cathedralis Trevirensis dispositum Quod ex veteribus
            Codicibus originalibus accuratissime conscriptum et novis interim ordinatis seu indul-
            tis Festis auctum. . . . Cum approbatione superiorum in lucem edit Michael
            Hermesdorff, Presbyter Diocesis Trevirensis. Treviris, Apud J. B. Grach
            Bibliopolam, 1863.
            Eichstätt, Katholische Universitätsbibl.; Trier, Priesterseminar
            Besançon, Bibl. mun., Arch. P.II.195, Archevêché, Graduale Trevirense,
            s.l., s.n., s.d., may be the same print.

1863[2]   Graduale Romanum complectens Missas omnium dominicarum. Paris, Lecoffre & C.,
            1863.
            Turin, Bibl. dell'Istituto salesiano Valsalice

1863[3]   Graduale Romanum, juxta missale & officia novissime auctoritate apostolica pro univer-
            sali ecclesia approbata. Leodii, Spée-Zelis, 1863.
            Utrecht, Universiteitsbibl.

1863[4]   Graduel romain pour tous les jours de l'année, augmenté d'un supplement. . . . Lyon,
            Paris, 1863.
            Besançon, Bibl. mun., Arch.P.II.142 and Arch.P.II.143, Archevêché

1864[1]   Graduale Romanum: juxta ritum sacrosanctae Romanae ecclesiae. Marianopoli, Joan.
            Lovell, 1864.
            Emory (Ga.), Emory Univ., Pitts Theological Library; Rochester (N.Y.),
            Nazareth College; Québec, Univ. de Laval, L.Rares M2148 L4 1864

1864[2]   Graduel romain, contenant les messes de tous les jours de l'année, les processions, les
            bénédictions et les obsèques. Nouv. éd. Québec, G. et G.E. Desbarats, 1864.
            Québec, Univ. de Laval, L.Rares M2154.2 Q3 G733 1864

1865[1]   Cantus ex Graduali et Antiphonario romano ordinarii facultate recognito desumptus.
            Marianopoli, Lovell, 1865.
            Collegeville (Minn.), St. John's Univ.; Baltimore (Md.), St. Mary's
            Seminary and Univ. Library

1865[2]   Graduale Romanum. . . cantu reviso juxta manuscripta. Parisiis, J. Lecoffre et soc. 1865.
            Paris, Bibl. nat., Mus., 8° E 62 and Imp., B–20754 (1st ed., 1851; see also
            1852)

1865[3]   Graduale Romanum juxta Missale et officia novissime auctoritate apostolica pro univer-
            sali Ecclesia approbata, 10a ed. . . . Leodii, P. Kersten, 1865.
            Utrecht, Universiteitsbibl., WRT 79–552 [CBAB AB]

1865[4]   Proprium officiorum atque missarum pro clero vicariatus Apostolici Luxemburgensis.
            Luxemburgi, P. Bruck, 1865.
            St. Paul (Minn.), Univ. of St. Thomas

1865[5]   Graduale Romanum cantum gregorianum ad missale romanum et proprium
            coloniense. . . . Ratisbonae, Neo Eboraci, F. Pustet, 1865.
            Provo, Brigham Young Univ., SPEC M2148.L4 l 1865

1866   *Offices de l'église du matin et soir suivant le rit romain: entièrement notés en plain-chant d'après le graduel et l'antiphonaire de la Comission de Reims et de Cambrai.* Paris, J. Lecoffre, 1866.
Québec, Univ. de Laval, M2151 L4 1866

1867[1]   *Graduale Romanum juxta ritum sacrosanctae Romanae ecclesiae. Editio secunda revisa et castigata.* Marianopoli, Joan Lovell, 1867.
Cleveland (Oh.), John Carroll Univ.; New York, New York Public Library; Emory (Ga.), Emory Univ., Pitts Theological Library; Washington, D.C., Catholic Univ.; Washington, D.C., Library of Congress; North Carolina, Belmont Abbey College Library; Québec, Univ. de Laval, L.Rares M2148 L4 1867

1867[2]   *Graduale Romanum...cantu reviso juxta manuscripta.* Parisiis, J. Lecoffre filium et soc. 1867.
Paris, Bibl. nat., Imp., B–23505

1868   *Graduale Romanum continens Missas Dominicarum et festorum etiam novissimas totius anni. Editio emendatius recognita, in pluribus aucta et Kalendario perpetuo recens ad usum Argentinensis approbato accomodata.* Argentorati, F. H. Le Roux, 1868.
Latrobe (Penn.), St. Vincent College and Archabbey; Sélestat, Bibl. mun., M 75 GRA, Alsatiques 1; Strasbourg, Bibl. mun., A 56363, Alsatiques

1869[1]   *Graduel romain...Dernière édition publiée par la Commission Ecclésiastique de Digne, avec l'approbation de Sa Grandeur Monseigneur Meirieu.* Digne, Commission Écclésiastique. Cinquième tirage, Paris, Ad Lainé, 1869.
Paris, Bibl. nat., Mus., 8° E 69

1869[2]   *Graduale romanum...cantu reviso juxta manuscripta.* Parisiis, J. Lecoffre et soc. 1869.
Paris, Bibl. nat., Imp., B–22054; London, British Library, D.3365.aaa.4

1869[3]   *Graduale Romanum quod ad cantum attinet, ad Gregorianam formam redactum....* Parisiis, A. Le Clere, 1869.
Paris, Bibl. nat., Imp., B–21929

1870[1]   *Cantus Chorales juxta Missale-Breviarium-Graduale-Antiphonarium-Rituale et Pontificale Romanum....* Wratislaviae, Nischkowsky, 1870.
Greifswald, Universitätsbibl.

1870[2]   *Le Moniteur des fidèles et en particulier des Chantres de paroisse...* publié par un prêtre du Diocèse Avignon, 1870.
Paris, Bibl. nat., Imp., B–22174

1871[1]   *Graduale de tempore et de sanctis juxta ritum sacrosancte Romanae ecclesiae cum cantu Pauli V. pont. max. jussu reformato cui addita sunt officia postea approbata sub auspiciis sanctissimi domini nostri Pii pp. IX curante Sacr. rituum congregatione. Cum privilegio.* Ratisbonae, F. Pustet, 1871.
Chicago, Newberry Library, VM 2149 G 73 1871; Boston, Boston Public Library; Latrobe (Penn.), St. Vincent College and Archabbey; Dayton (Ohio), Univ. of Dayton; New York, Fordham University; St. Meinrad

(Ind.), St. Meinrad Archabbey and School of Theology; St. Louis (Mo.), Kenrick-Glenn Seminary; Santa Clara (Calif.), Santa Clara Univ.; Bologna, Civico museo bibliografico musicale; Eichstätt, Katholische Universitätsbibl., 21/1 ESL III 131; London, Univ. of London Library; Nijmegen, Katholieke Universiteit, KDCa 68 nr. 1; Rimini, Bibl. civica Gamalunga-Rimini; Turin, Bibl. dell' Istituto internazionale Don Bosco

1871[2]   *Graduel romain, contenant les messes de tous les jours de l'année, les processions, les bénédictions et les obsèques.* 3è éd. Québec, J.-B. Rolland, 1871.
Québec, Univ. de Laval, L. Rares M2154.2 Q3 G733 1871

1872[1]   *Graduale de tempore et de sanctis juxta ritum sacrosanctae Romanae Ecclesiae, cum cantu Pauli V. pont. max. jussu reformato, cui addita sunt officia postea approbata sub auspiciis sanctissimi domini nostri Pii PP.IX. Curante Sacrorum Rituum Congregatione.* [2 vols.] Ratisbonae, Neo-Eboraci & Cincinnatii, sumptibus, chartis et typis Friderici Pustet, 1872.
Austin, Univ. of Texas; Latrobe (Penn.), St. Vincent College and Archabbey; Collegeville (Minn.), St. John's Univ.; Overbrook (Penn.), St. Charles Borromeo Seminary; Vatican, Bibl. Apost. Vat.; Utrecht, Universiteitsbibl., AB 529 [CBAB AB]; Aberystwyth, National Library of Wales

1872[2]   *Graduel romain, contenant les messes de tous les jours de l'année, les matines et les laudes de Noel, les processions et les obsèques. Dernière éd., pub par la Commission ecclésiastique de Digne....* Marseille, J. Mingardon, 1872.
Berkeley (Calif.), Univ. of California

1872[3]   *Graduale Romanum... cantu reviso juxta manuscripta.* Parisiis, J. Lecoffre et soc. 1872.
Paris, Bibl. nat., Imp., B–22701

1873   *Bijlage tot het Graduale et Antiphonarium Romanum, of Verzameling van Missen, Elevatiën, Antiphonen, Hymnen, enz. ten gebruike onder de H. Mis en het Lof / meerendeels getoonzet door N.A. Janssen....* 's Bosch, Mosmans, 1873.
Utrecht, Universiteitsbibl., WRT 80–356 [CBDP1 ABTHO]

1874[1]   *Graduel romain pour tous les jours de l'année. Nouvelle éd., conforme à celle infolio de 1815.* Paris, Lecoffre fils et Cie, 1874.
Barcelona, Biblioteca de Catalunya

1874[2]   *Graduale Romanum. Juxta ritum sacrosanctae Romanae Ecclesiae, cum cantu Paul V. pont. maximi jussu reformato. Editio quarta.* Mechliniae, H. Dessain, 1874.
Charlottesville (Va.), Univ. of Virginia; Antwerp, Staatbibl., 626855; Utrecht, Universiteitsbibl., ALV 28–123, WRT 80–299 dl 1 [CBDP1 ABTHO]; Sheffield, Univ. Lib., Score res. Mn (-Aa)

1874[3]   *Graduel selon le rit romain et d'après les concessions faites au diocèse de Besançon....* Besançon, 1874.
Besançon, Bibl. mun., Arch. P.II.158, Archevêché

1874[4]   *Graduel et Vespéral romains.* Paris, 1874.
Paris, Bibl. nat., Mus., 8° E 45 *(Partie d'été)*

1874[5]   *Supplementum continens Missas proprias trium ordinum S. P. N. in usum Fratrum Minorum Recollectorum Provinciae Sancti Joseph Belgii.* Mechliniae, Dessain, 1874.
Utrecht, Universiteitsbibl., ALV 28–132 dl 2, WRT 80–307, WRT 80299 dl 2

1874[6]   *Graduel romain...Chant restauré par la Commission de Reims et de Cambrai d'après les anciens manuscrits.* Paris, 1874.
Cited in David Hiley, *Western Plainchant,* 625.

1875[1]   *Graduel romain contenant les Messes du Propre du Temps, y compris celles des féries; les Messes du Propre et du Commun des Saints, les principales Messes Votives, les Messes de supplément, les Matines et les Laudes de Noël et de Paques.* Paris, H. Repos et Cie, Successeurs, 1875.
Paris, Bibl. nat., Mus., 8° E 43
Contains a useful four-page introduction on performance.

1875[2]   *Graduale Romanum : complectens missas et horas omnium dominicarum et festorum duplicium et semiduplicium totius anni....* Parisiis, Jacobum LeCoffre et socios, 1875.
Paris, Bibl. nat., Imp., B–23268

1875[3]   *Organum comitans ad Graduale romanum: quod curavit Sacrorum rituum congregation.* Ratisbon, New York, Pustet, 1875, 1876.
New Orleans (La.), Tulane Univ.; Amsterdam, Openbare Bibliotheek

1876[1]   *Graduale Romanum: juxta Missale et Officia : novissime auctoritate apostolica pro universali Ecclesia approbata. Editio undecima.* Leodii, Spée-Zelis, 1876.
Berkeley (Calif.), Univ. of California

1876[2]   *Graduale Romanum juxta ritum sacrosanctae Romanae ecclesiae. Editio secunda revisa et castigata.* Marianopoli, Joan Lovell.
Toronto, St. Michael's College Library

1876[3]   *Graduale ad normam cantus S. Gregorii, auf Grund der Forschungs-Resultate und unter Beihilfe der Mitglieder des Vereins zur Erforschung alter Choralhandschriften nach den ältesten und zuverlässigen Quellen.* Ed. by M. Hermesdorff, Trier. Leipzig, Wagner, 1876–82.
Mundelein (Ill.), St. Mary at the Lake Seminary; Eichstätt, Katholische Universitätsbibl.; Regensburg, Bischöfliche Zentralbibl.

1877[1]   *Offices de l'église du matin et soir suivant le rit romain: entièrement notés en plain-chant d'après le graduel et l'antiphonaire de la Comission de Reims et de Cambrai. Nouv. éd.* Paris, J. Lecoffre, 1877.
Québec, Univ. de Laval, M2151 L4 1877

1877[2]   *Graduale de tempore et de sanctis juxta ritum sacrosanctae romanae ecclesiae cum cantu Pauli v. pont. max. jussu reformato cui addita sunt officia postea adprobata sub auspiciis sanctissimi domini nostri Pii PP. IX. Curante Sacr. rituum congregatione....Editio secunda augmentata.* Ratisbonae, Neo Eboraci...sumptibus, chartis & & typis Friderici Pustet, 1877.
Cambridge (Mass.), Harvard Divinity School; New York, New York Public Library; Ithaca (N.Y.), Cornell Univ., M2149.R3 1877; Yonkers (N.Y.), St.

Joseph's Seminary; Washington, D.C., Library of Congress; Fort Worth (Tex.), Texas Christian Univ.; Emmitsburg (Md.), Mount St. Mary's College; St. Meinrad (Ind.), St. Meinrad Archabbey and School of Theology; Plymouth (Mich.), Madonna Univ.; Bowling Green (Ohio), Bowling Green State Univ.; Edinburgh, City Library

1877³   *Het Graduale Romanum ten dienste der Katholieke Koorzangers, door L. H. Borking; woordelijk boven den Latijnschen tekst in het Nederlandsch vert.* Leiden, Van Leeuwen, 1877.
Utrecht, Universiteitsbibl., ALV 28–39 [CBDP1 ABTHO]; Nijmegen, Katholieke Universiteit, KDC c 6930; The Hague, Koninklijke Bibl., 537 K 12

1877⁴   *Graduale Romanum… cantu reviso juxta manuscripta.* Parisiis, J. Lecoffre et soc. 1877.
Paris, Bibl. nat., Imp., B–23661

1877⁵   *Supplementum continens Missas proprias trium ordinum S. P. N. in usum Fratrum Minorum Recollectorum Provinciae Sancti Joseph Belgii.* Mechliniae, Dessain, 1877.
Utrecht, Universiteitsbibl., ALV 27–318 dl 2 [CBAB AB], WRT 79–550 dl 2

1877⁶   *Organum comitans ad Graduale romanum: quod curavit Sacrorum rituum congregation,* 2nd ed. [with J. Hanisch]. Ratisbon, Pustet, 1877.
Cited in *New Grove Dictionary of Music and Musicians,* 2nd ed., 10:636.

1878¹   *Graduel romain, contenant les messes de tous les jours de l'année.* … Marseilles, Mingardon, 1878. (See 1872.)
Vatican, Bibl. Apost. Vat., Casimiri V.197 int.1

1878²   *Graduale ad usum sacri ordinis Cartusiensis…, cura et iussu reverendi patris domni Rochi-Mariae correctum et impressum.* Cartusiae sanctae Mariae de Pratis, sumptibus maioris Cartusiae, 1878.
Vatican, Bibl. Apost. Vat., Racc. gen. Liturgia II.49

1878³   *Offices de l'Église du matin et du soir suivant le rit romain entièrement notés en plainchant d'après le graduel et l'antiphonaire de la commission de Reims et de Cambrai. Nouvelle édition.* Paris, imp. Lalure, lib. Lecoffre fils et Cie, 1878.
Paris, Bibl. nat., Imp., B–23761

1878⁴   *Graduel et vespéral romains contenant en entier les messes et les vêpres de tous les jours de l'année… Partie d'hiver.* Rennes, H. Vatar, 1878.
Paris, Bibl. nat., Imp., B–23765

1878⁵   *Graduel romain pour tous les jours de l'année. Nouvelle édition conform à celle in-folio de 1815, augmentée d'un supplément.* Paris, Lyon, Lecoffre fils et Cie, 1878.
Paris, Bibl. nat., Imp., B–23785

1878⁶   *Livre de choeur destiné à rendre facile à tous les fidèles la participation au chant de l'église…* Grenoble, 1878.
Paris, Bibl. nat., Imp., B–23775

1880[1]   *Graduale Romanum quod ad cantum attinet, ad Gregorianam formam redactam....* Parisiis, Poussielgue, 1880.
Paris, Bibl. nat., Imp., B–24106

1880[2]   *Offices de l'Église du matin et du soir suivant le rit romain entièrement notés en plain-chant d'après le graduel et l'antiphonaire de la commission de Reims et de Cambrai. Nouvelle édition.* Paris, V. Lecoffre, 1880.
Paris, Bibl. nat., Imp., B–25028

1881[1]   *Graduale romanum : complectens missas omnium dominicarum et festorum duplicium et semiduplicium totius anni....* Parisiis, Jacobum LeCoffre et socios, 1881.
Paris, Bibl. nat., Imp., B–24197

1881[2]   *Graduale de tempore et de sanctis juxta ritum sacrosanctae Romanae ecclesiae cum cantu Paul V. pont. max. jussu reformato.... Editio stereotypa.* Parisiis, Ratisbonae etc., Pustet, 1881.
Durham (N.C.), Duke Univ.; Provo, Brigham Young Univ., M2148.L4\1881

1882[1]   *Graduale de tempore et de sanctis juxta ritum sacrosanctae Romanae ecclesiae cum cantu Paul V. pont. max. jussu reformato.... Editio stereotypa.* Parisiis, Ratisbonae..., 1882.
Cleveland (Oh.), John Carroll Univ.; Northhampton (Mass.), Smith College; St. Paul (Minn.), Univ. of Saint Thomas; St. Meinrad (Ind.), St. Meinrad Archabbey and School of Theology; Conception [Mo.], Conception Abbey; Philadelphia, Lutheran Theological Seminary; Utrecht, Universiteitsbibl., RIJS 94–243 [CBDP1 ABTHO]

1882[2]   *Epitome ex graduali Romano quod curavit sacrorum rituum congregatio....* Ratisbon, Pustet, 1882.
Baltimore (Md.), St. Mary's Seminary and Univ. Library; Chicago, Univ. of Chicago, Regenstein Library, M2149.H15; St. Louis (Mo.), St. Louis Univ., Pius XII Library; Maynooth, National Univ. of Ireland

1883[1]   *Graduale romanum quod ad cantum attinet, ad Gregorianum formam redactum ex veteribus manuscriptis et duplici notatione donatum notae veteres....* Parisiis, Poussielgues fratres, 1883.
Paris, Bibl.nat., Mus., 8° E 56 (Reprint of 1857 edition; see also, 1902)
London, British Library, D.3395.c.32, is another copy, tentatively ascribed to 1870.

1883[2]   *Liber Gradualis a S. Gregorio Magno olim ordinatus postea summorum pontificum auctoritate recognitus ac plurimus auctus...in usum congregationis Benedictinae Galliarum.* Tournai, Desclée, 1883.
Cambridge (Mass.), Harvard Univ.; Princeton (N.J.), Princeton Univ.; New York, New York Public Library; Berrien Springs (Mich.), Andrews Univ.; St. Meinrad (Ind.), St. Meinrad Archabbey and School of Theology; Paris, Bibl. nat., Imp., B-24481 and Smith Lesouef S–835; Aix-en-Provence, Bibl. Méjanes, P. 187 Pécoul; Vienna, Österreichische Nationalbibl., 395762–B; Nijmegen, Katholieke Universiteit, 470 c 311

1884[1]   *Graduale de tempore et de sanctis juxta ritum sanctae romanae ecclesiae cum cantu Paul V. pont. max. jussu reformato cui addita sunt officia postea adprobata, cura et auctoritate Sacrorum rituum congregationis digestum.* Romae, 1884.
Washington, D.C., Catholic Univ.; Baltimore (Md.), St. Mary's Seminary and Univ. Library; Gainesville (Fla.), Univ. of Florida; Cleveland (Oh.), Case Western Univ.; Detroit, Sacred Heart Major Seminary; Berkeley (Calif.), Graduate Theological Union; Cleveland (Oh.), Athenaeum of Ohio

1884[2]   *Graduel romain, contenant les messes du propre du temps compris celles des féries, les messes du propre et du commun des saints, les principales messes votives, les messes du supplément qui se célèbrent le plus généralment, les matines et les laudes de Noël et de Pâques.* Paris, Société générale de librairie catholique, 1884.
Québec, Univ. de Laval, M2148 L4 1884

1884[3]   *Organum comitans ad graduale romanum...ed. Franz X. Haberl, Ecclesia Catholica, Congregatio Rituum,* 2nd ed., Regensburg, 1884.
Chicago, Chicago Public Library; New Haven (Conn.), Yale Univ., School of Music; Washington, D.C., Catholic Univ.; Bamberg, Universitätsbibl., BS 2030; Regensburg, Universitätsbibl., BS 2030

1886[1]   *Graduale de tempore et de sanctis juxta ritum sanctae romanae ecclesiae cum cantu Paul V. pont. max. jussu reformato....* Rome, Sacrorum Rituum Congregatio, 1886.
St. Meinrad (Ind.), St. Meinrad Archabbey and School of Theology; Eichstätt, Katholische Universitätsbibl., 21.1 ESL III 241; Bamberg, Metropolitankapitel, 0122/Lit. 671

1886[2]   *Epitome ex editione typica Gradualis Romani, quod curavit sacrorum rituum congregatio. Editio stereotypica.* Ratisbonae, Neo Eboraci et Cincinnatii....Typis Friderici Pustet. 1886.
Nijmegen, Katholieke Universiteit, 636 c 127; Passau, Universitäts- und Staatsbibl; Bamberg, Staatsbibliothek, 0122/Lit. 671

1887   *Graduale de tempore et de sanctis juxta ritum sacrosancte Romanae ecclesiae cum cantu Pauli V. pont. max. jussu reformato cui addita sunt officia postea approbata sub auspiciis sanctissimi domini nostri Pii pp. IX curante Sacr. rituum congregatione.* 2nd. ed., aug., Ratisbon, Pustet, 1887
Augsburg, Universitätsbibl., 01/BS 4700 G733(2)

1889[1]   *Graduale de tempore et de sanctis, juxta ritum sanctae romanae ecclesiae cum cantu Pauli V. pont. max. jussu reformato cui addita sunt festa novissima. Editio prima post typicam.* Roma, Cura et auctoritate Sacrorum rituum congregationis, 1889.
Chicago, Newberry Library, VM 2149 G 73 1889; Manchester (N. H.), St. Anselm College; Tübingen, Universitätsbibl., 12 A 12209

1889[2]   *Het Graduale Romanum: ten dienste Katholieke Koorzangers,* 2nd ed. Leiden, Van Leeuwen, 1889.
Antwerp, Staatbibl., H242368

1890[1]   *Graduale romanum, juxta ritum sacrosanctae romanae ecclesiae, cum cantu Pauli V. pont. maximi jussu reformato. Editio quinta.* Mechliniae, Dessain, 1890.
Chicago, Newberry Library, VM 2149 G 73 1890; Utrecht, Universiteitsbibl.

1890[2]   *Graduel dominicain; Graduale iuxta ritum sacri ordinis Praedicatorum.* Tournai, Desclée, Lefevre, 1890.
Lyon, Facultés Catholiques, Bibl. centrale, LFCC 168.A–3, Fonds ancien

1891   *Graduale de tempore et de sanctis juxta ritum sanctae Romanae ecclesiae cum cantu Pauli V. Pont. Max., jussu reformato cui addita sunt festa novissima. Editio prima post typicam.* Rome, Ratisbon, Pustet, 1891.
Washington, D.C., Dominican College; Philadelphia, St. Joseph's Univ.; Eichstätt, Katholische Universitätsbibl., 03/BS 4710 G733.891

1892   *Epitome ex editione typica Gradualis Romani, quod curavit sacrorum rituum congregatio. Editio stereotypica.* Ratisbonae, Neo Eboraci et Cincinnatii.... Typis Friderici Pustet. 1892.
Private collection

1893[1]   *Graduale de tempore et de sanctis iuxta ritum sanctae Romanae Ecclesiae, cum cantu Pauli V. pontificis maximi iussu reformato.* Romae [sumptibus, chartis et typis Friderici Pustet], MDCCCXCIII.
Rochester (N.Y.), Univ. of Rochester, Eastman School of Music; Trent, Bibl. Feininger, FSG 40 (#351); Bamberg, Staatsbibliothek, 19/zqi 03 7069 (93)

1893[2]   *Compendium Gradualis et Missalis romani, concinnatum ex editionibus typicis cura et auctoritate S. Rituum Congregationis publicatis. Ed. 2. stereotypica.* Cincinnati, Pustet, 1893.
New York, Union Theological Seminary; Yonkers (N.Y.), St. Joseph's Seminary; Collegeville (Minn.), St. John's Univ.

1895   *Liber Gradualis juxta antiquorum codicum fidem restitutus. Editio altera.* Solesmes, 1895.
New Haven (Conn.), Yale Univ., School of Music; Pittsburgh, Duquesne Univ.; Washington, D.C., Wesley Theological Seminary; Paris, Bibl.nat., Imp., B–41227

1896   *Graduale de tempore et de sanctis, juxta ritum Sanctae Romanae Ecclesiae, cum cantu, Pauli V.... jussu reformato; cui addita sunt festa novissima. Editio novissima post typicam.* Romae, cura et auctoritate S. Rituum Congregationis, 1896.
New York, Union Theological Seminary, MnCS; Bamberg, Staatsbibliothek, 19/zqi 03 7069

1898   *Enchiridion Gradualis Romani....* Regensburg, New York, Pustet, 1898.
St. Meinrad (Ind.), St. Meinrad Archabbey and School of Theology; Camarillo (Calif.), St. John's Seminary

1902 *Graduale romanum quod ad cantum attinet, ad Gregorianum formam redactum ex veteribus manuscriptis et duplici notatione donatum notae veteres*. . . . Paris, Poussielgue fratres, 1902.
   Paris, Bibl.nat., Mus., 8° E 57 (Reprint of 1857 edition; see also, 1883.)

Graduals of Unknown Date

16— *Graduale Missarum SS. Ordinis Fratrum Minorum*. . . . S.l. s.d., mid-17th cent.
   Copenhagen, Kongelige Bibl.

16— *[Graduale Romanum. . .]*. [Title page lacking.]
   Valognes, Bibl. mun. Julien de Laillier, B 543, Fonds ancien 2

— *Graduel parisien gravé & noté selon le Graduel et le Missel de S. l. m. le cardinal de Noailles*. Paris, s.d.
   Paris, Bibl. nat., Imp., B-4693 (Temporale)

17— *[Cantus Missarum]*. [Title page lacking; the volume is ascribed to the 18th cent.]
   Besançon, Bibl. mun., Arch. P.II.178, Archevêché
   This copy seems to be 6 cm. smaller than the *Cantus missarum* of 1722.

17— *Graduel de Chaalons. . . Propre du temps, Propre des Saints*. Châlons-sur-Marne.
   Besançon, Bibl. mun., Arch. P.II.159 (1, 2) and Arch. P.II.160 (1, 2), Archevêché

[—] *[Graduale ad usum ordinis Sancti Hieronymi.]* S.l., s.d.
   Paris, Bibl. nat., Imp., Velins–806; also R7911 and Microfilm M–10185

[—] *Graduale Romanum*. . . . Dabin Ant.
   Munich, Bayerische Staatsbibl., 4 Mus. pr. 33708

18— *Proprium Sanctorum diocesis Ruthenensis, Cantus vesperarum (et Missarum)* Dijon, Douillier, s.d.
   Paris, Bibl. nat., Imp., B–1012

18— *Graduale Romanum, sive missale romanum ad usum fratrum et sororum Ordinis Discalceatorum Beata Mariae Virginis de Monte Carmelo*. S.l., s.n., s.d. [Barchinonae/ Barduinonae? Ex. Typ. Carmelitarum discalceatorum; thought to be post 1831].
   Madrid, Biblioteca Nacional, 2/13263

1852–70? *Graduale Romanum]*. Dijon. [The title-page and colophon are missing; the basis for the date and place of publication is not stated.]
   Chicago, DePaul Univ.; Dubuque (Iowa), Loras College
   One cannot ascertain whether the two citations are for the same book or for different books. Cf. items listed in accompanying index for possible identifications.

[—] *Graduale Romanum. . . cantu reviso juxta manuscripta vetustissima. (Horae Diurnae)* pp. xxii, 664, 158.
   London, British Library, 3355.aaa.23 (Destroyed in World War II)

INDEX

Cazin: 1852[2]
Chambeau, François: 1782[2], 1789[2], 1821[3]
Chambeau, L.: 1773[2], 1778[3]
Charrier: 1622[1]
Ciera: 1610, 1618[2], 1621, 1629[1], 1643, 1668[1], 1680[1]
Coignard: 1717, 1738[4]
Collignon: 1779[2, 3], 1821[4], 1839
Commission écclesiastique: 1854[3], 1859[4], 1869[1], (see also, 1872[2])
Cornemillot: 1847[8]
Côté, A.: 1854[5]
Courtois, A. P.: 1815[4]
Crajenschot, Theodor: 1751[1, 2], 1755[1], 1763[2], 1770[2], 1770[5], 1781[3], 1788[1, 2]
Cramoisy, Sebastian; Clopeiau, Gabriel and Nicolas: 1662
Dabin: [ ] (following 1902)
Daireaux: 1860[5]
Dalesme, Francis: 1783[1]
Dejussieu, F.: 1844[7]
Delaroche: see Roche
Delarue: 1861[4]
Delorme: 1742[1]
Desbarats, G. & G.: 1864[2]
Desclée: 1883[2], 1890[2]
Desrosiers, P. A.: 1826[5]
Dessain: 1874[5], 1877[5], 1890[1]
Dessain, H.: 1855[1], 1859[1], 1874[2]
Dessaint: 1756[3]
Devillers, L.: 1808[2]
Douillier, J.-M.-Alexandre: 1825[3], 1828[1], 1845[1]
Drimborn, Caspar: 1726
Dubois, A.: 1840[5]
Ederus, Wilhelm: 1630
Eynden, Arnold: 1678
Faulcon, Jean-Felix: 1741[2], 1749[1], 1770[6], 1774[2]
Faulcon & Barbier: 1781[1]
Faure, André: 1747[1], 1753[1], 1789[5]
Faure, André (Vidua): 1753[2]
Faure, Pierre: 1730[1], 1732[2], 1735
Fay, Antoine de: 1753[3]
Fessy, Alexandre Chrales: 1850[2]?
Flandrus, Ioannes: 1597
Fournier, F.: 1777[2]
Galles, Jean-Nicolas: 1766[1], 1773[1]
Gardano, Angelo; 1587, 1591

Garnier, J-B, and Le Prieur, P.-A: 1755[2]
Garon & Lambert: 1860[3]
Gaude (Veuve); 1844[6]
Giraud, (Veuve) & Sons: 1783[5], 1785[1]
Giroud, J. L. A.: 1806[2]
Giunta: 1586[1], 1596, 1606[1], 1611(?), 1618[1], 1626, 1642(?), 1647[1, 2]
Giunta, Bernardo: 1607
Grach, J. B.: 1863[1]
Grande Chartreuse: 1878[2]
Gregoire, Jean: 1674, 1679[1]
Grimblot and Veuve Raybois: 1847[5]
Haener, H.: 1787[1]
Hanicq, P. J.: 1845[3], 1848[1, 2], 1854[2], 1859[2]
Henault, A.: 1822[4]
Henault, Gaspard: 1747[2], 1754[3]
Henault, Jean: 1671[4]
Herissant, Cl. Jean Baptiste: 1732[1], 1749[2]
Herissant, Pierre: 1697[2]
Hubault, Vidua Carolus Caron: 1753[4]
Jacqmain: 1854[1]
Jore: 1727[1]
Journet, Claude: 1738[2]
Kersten, P.: 1843[4], 1851[1], 1865[3]
Kren, Philip: 1696[4]
Küchler, Chr.: 1671[2]
Labau: 1844[4]
La Caille, Jean de: 1650?, 1666, 1668[2]
Lainé: 1869[1]
Lanquement, Nicolas: 1730[7], 1738[3]
Larcher, Nicolas: 1844[8]
La Roche, A. de: 1760[1, 2], 1765[1], 1780[1], 1782[1]
Laurens (Laurent), André: 1718[3], 1724[1]
Laurent, J. & J. F.: 1667
Laurent, Vidua N.: 1616, 1630[2]
Lebaron, C. and Chalopin, P.: 1750[9]
Le Clere, A.: 1869[3]
Le Clere & Soc.: 1857[3], 1858[1, 2, 6], 1860[2]
Lecoffre, Jaques: 1815[2]
Lecoffre, Jacques & Soc.: 1851[2?], 1852[1], 1853[3, 4, 6], 1855[2], 1855?, 1856[1], 1857?,
    1859[3], 1860[1], 1861[1], 1862, 1863[2], 1865[2], 1866, 1869[2], 1872[3], 1874[1], 1875[2],
    1877[1, 4], 1881[1]
Lecoffre fils: 1856[2], 1867[2], 1878[3, 5]
Lecoffre, V.: 1880[2]

Leonardian: 1696[3]
Leeuwen, van: 1877[3], 1889[2]
Le Roux, F. H.: 1868
Le Roux, Louis Francis: 1829, 1844[1], 1855[3]
Le Roy, G.: 1806[1]
Libraires associés: 1826[3], 1846
Libraires associés aux Usages du Diocèse: 1746[1], 1754[2]
Lottin, A. M.: 1770[3], 1782[4]
Lovell, J.: 1864[1], 1865[1], 1867[1], 1876[2]
Mame ainé: 1784, 1827[1]
Mame, Carolus: 1826[9]
Manavit, A. D.: 1835, 1836?, 1852[3], 1854[4]
Mariette: 1750[7]
Masius, Bernardinus (Bunandinus?): 1633[2], 1648
Medicaea: 1614/15
Méquignon-Junior: 1822[1]
Méquignon-Junior & Leroux: 1845[6]
Merson: 1837[3], 1845[4, 5]
Millange, Simon: 1599[1]
Mingardon, J.: 1872[2], 1878[1]
Moerentorf: see Plantin
Mommaert, Joannes: 1623
Moretus: see Plantin
Mosmans: 1873
Neilson, John: 1800[2]
Neilson, W.: 1841
Neilson and Cowan: 1827[2]
Niel, J. J.: 1750[8], 1768[2], 1775[1], 1821[1]
Niel (Vidua): 1756[4]
Nischkowsky: 1870[1]
Nivers, G.-G.: 1687[1], 1687[1, 2, 3, 4], 1696[1, 2]
Nugo, Bonaventura: 1606[2]
Outhenin-Chalandre: 1843[3]
Paravia, J. B.: 1847[1]
Paschal, Louis: 1650?
Pavie, L.: 1817
Pelagaud, J. B.: 1840[4], 1845[2], 1847[3]
Pepie: 1766[2]
Pepie, N.: 1706[2]
Pepie, R. and N.: 1697[3]
Perisse Freres: 1783[4], 1822[1], 1825[2], 1834[1], 1840[2], 1844[2], 1851[3]
Petit, Jean: 1824[1], 1882[4]
Petricovius, see Piotrkowczyk

Peutet-Pommey: 1858[4]
Pezzana, N.: 1690[2], 1703, 1716[1], 1730[2], 1750[1], 1779[1], 1789[3]
Piotrkowczyk, Andreas: 1600[2]
Piotrkowczyk: 1629[2], 1651
Pitrat, Theodore: 1815[1], 1816[1], 1822[2]
Plantin: 1599[2], 1695, 1774[1], 1834[2]
Plomteux, Clement: 1772[1], 1777[1], 1787[2], 1789[1]
Poisson, F. et fils: 1847[6], 1861[4]
Poussielgue Frères: 1857[2], 1880[1], 1883[1], 1902
Pustet, Friedrich: 1865[5], 1871[1], 1872[1], 1875[3], 1877[2, 6], 1881[2], 1882[1, 2], 1886[2],
    1887, 1891, 1892, 1893[1, 2], 1896, 1898
Quentel: 1600[1]
Repos: 1850[1]?, 1851[4], 1859[4], 1875[1]
Rigoine, L.: 1682[2]
Robert, P. G. D.: 1756[2]
la Roche, Aimé de: 1755[3], 1760[1, 2], 1765[1], 1780[1], 1782[1]
Rojat, Abbé: 1858[3]
Rolland. J.-B.: 1871[2]
Sacrorum Rituum Congregatio: 1886[1], 1889
Servant: 1714[2]
Sevestre, Louis: 1673, 1688/89, 1694[1], 1720[5]
Simon: 1734[5]
Societas bibliopolarum: 1670, 1671[1], 1690[3], 1702, 1705, [1739[2]?], 1762[1](?)
Societas Typographicae librorum officii Ecclesiastici: 1608(?), 1640, 1657
Société générale de librairie catholique: 1884[2]
Soffietti, A.: 1826[1]
Soffietti, Ignatio: 1797, 1824[1]
Spee-Zelis: 1857[1], 1863[3], 1876[1]
t'Serstevens, Franciscus: 1771[1]
Stichter, Cornelius (Widow): 1730[3], 1730[6], 1745[1, 2], 1763[1], 1789[4], 1790
Stichter, Johann: 1693, 1694[2]
Sutor, Caspar: 1630[1]
Templeux: 1828[3]
van Tetroode, F. J.: 1780[2], 1781[2], 1791[3], 1792, 1801?, 1808, 1809, 1815[3], 1822[3]
Thibaud-Landriot: 1826[8]
Thibaut-Landriot frères: 1847[7]
Thiboust: 1632
Thomas-Malvin: 1844[5]
Trognes, Joach.: 1609
Valfray, P.: 1669, 1682[1], 1716[3], 1720[4], 1724[3], 1730[4], 1750[6]
Vannier, Veuve: 1826[6, 7], 1827[3]
Varisco, J. and Paganino: 1586[2]
Vatar: 1847[2], 1853[1, 2], 1858[5], 1861[2], 1878[4]

Vedeilhiém, P.: 1774[5]
Verdussen, Hieronymus & Joan. Bapt.: 1674[2]
Verdussen: 1712, 1720[1], 1749[3], 1758
Verdussen, J. P.: 1776[2]
Verhoeven: 1842[1]
Vertua, Joan. Paulo: 1721, 1755[4]
Vigneulle, Claude: 1718[1]
Visscher: 1720[2]
Wade: 1737[?]
Wagner: 1876[3]
Wirth, J. G.: 1855[5]
Zweesardt, A.: 1842[2]
Not known or not given: 1585, 1594, 1605, 1608, 1629[2], 1635, 1644, 1651, 1653[2], 1655[2], 1655, 1668[3], 1669, 1679[2], 1680[2], 1682[3], 1690[4], 1691[1, 2, 3, 4, 5], 1693, 1694[3], 1696[3], 1701[2], 1714[1, 3], 1716[2], 1718[2], 1719?, 1720[4], 1722[2], 1727[2], 1730[5], 1739[1], 1740[1, 2], 1741[1], 1745[3], 1746[2], [1747], 1749[4], 1750[5], 1752[1, 2, 3, 4, 5], 1753[5], 1754[1], 1762[2], 1763[3], 1765[2], 1768[1], 1770[4], 1771[2], 1772[2], 1774[3], 1775[2], 1776[1], 1778[2], 1779[4, 5], 1782[3], 1783[2, 3], 1785[2], 1787[1], 1791[1], 1799, 1800[1], 1804, 1805, 1816[2], 1824[3], 1825[1], 1826[2, 4], 1833[2, 3], 1834[3], 1836[1, 2], 1842[3, 5], 1843[1, 2], 1847[4], 1848[2, 3], 1849, 1853[5], 1857[4], 1861[3], 1863[4], 1869[3], 1870[2], 1874[3, 4], 1874[6], 1877[3], 1878[2, 6], 1884[1, 3], 1886[1], 1889, 1895, 1896

Places of Publication

Agen: 1834[3]
Albertville: 1844[3]
Ambianum: see Amiens
Amiens: 1818[1], 1824[2], 1753[4], 1860[3]
Amsterdam: 1693, 1694[2], 1701[3, 4], 1720[2]?, 1720[3], 1730[3], 1730[6], 1745[1, 2], 1750[3, 4], 1751[1, 2], 1755[1], 1756[1], 1763[1, 2], 1769[2], 1770[1, 2], 1770[5], 1780[2], 1781[2, 3], 1788[1, 2], 1789[4], 1790, 1791[3], 1792, 1801?, 1808, 1809, 1815[3], 1822[3], 1842[2]
Andegavus: see Angers
Angers: 1784, 1817, 1826[9], 1827[1]
Antwerp: 1599[2], 1609, 1620, 1633[3], 1653[2], 1674[2], 1691[2, 3], 1695, 1712, 1720[1], 1749[3], 1758, 1774[1], 1776[2], 1834[2], [—] (following 1902)
Argentorati: see Strasbourg
Auscis (=Auch): 1837[1]
Auselianis: see Orléans
Autun: 1844[7]
Auxerre: 1777[2]
Avignon: 1739[2], 1742[1], 1750[8], 1756[4], 1775[1], 1768[2], 1773[2], 1778[3], 1782[2], 1789[2], 1816[3], 1818[2], 1821[1], 1821[3], 1870[2]
Bayeux: 1861[4]
Beauvais: 1756[3]

Besançon: 1682[2], 1768[1], 1779[4], 1804, 1816[2], 1824[1], 1842[3, 4], 1843[1, 2, 3], 1874[3]
Bourges: 1741[3]
Bordeaux: 1599[1], 1622[1]
Breslau: see Wroclaw
Brussels: 1623, 1771[1]
Caen: 1750[9], 1806[1], 1847[6]
Carcassonne: 1844[4]
Castros: 1756[2]
Châlons-sur-Marne: 1749[4]
Charleville: 1785[2]
Cincinnati: 1893[2]
Clermont-Ferrand: 1742[1], 1744, 1826[8], 1847[7]
Cologne: 1600[1], 1726
Cracow: see Kraków
Coutance: 1860[5]
Digne: 1850[1?], 1851[4], 1854[3], 1859[4], 1869[1]
Dijon: 1753[3], 1825[3], 1828[1], 1845[1], 1849, 1853[5], 1858[4]
Evreux: 1847[8]
Fougères: 1826[6, 7], 1827[3]
Francopoli-Ruthenorum: see Villefranche-le-Rouergue
Ghent: 1854[1]
Grande Chartreuse: 1878[2]
Gratianopoli: see Grenoble
Grenoble: 1730[1], 1732[2], 1735, 1741[1], 1747[1], 1750[5], 1753[1, 2], 1783[5], 1785[1],
    1789[5], 1806[2], 1823, 1840[3], 1878[6]
s'Bosch: 1873
s'Hertogenbosch: 1842[1]
Ingolstadt: 1618[3], 1630[1]
Köln: see Cologne
Kraków: 1600[2], 1629[2], 1651, 1690[4], 1740[1]
Landshut: 1696[4]
Laon: 1774[4], 1815[4]
Leipzig: 1876[3]
Leodii: see Liége
Leyden: 1695[4], 1877[3], 1889[2]
Liége: 1772[1], 1777[1], 1787[2], 1789[1], 1808[2], 1816[4], 1821[2], 1828[2], 1833[1], 1851[1],
    1843[4], 1844[8], 1857[1], 1863[3], 1865[3], 1876[1], 1876[4]
Limoges: 1729[1, 2], 1783[1, 2, 3]
Lisieux: 1752[3, 4], 1753[5]
London: 1737[?], 1847[4]
Louvain: 1633[2], 1648
Lyon: 1606[2], 1669, 1670, 1671[1], 1674[1], 1679[1], 1682[1], 1690[3], 1691[5], 1697[4],
    1701[2], 1702, 1705, 1714[2], 1716[3], 1720[4], 1724[1, 3], 1727[2], 1730[4], 1738[2], 1750[6],

1755[3], 1760[1, 2], 1763[3], 1765[1], 1771[2], 1780[1], 1782[1], 1783[4], 1815[1], 1816[1], 1822[1, 2], 1825[2], 1833[2], 1834[1], 1840[2, 4], 1844[2], 1845[2], 1847[3],1848[3], 1851[3], 1856[2], 1863[4], 1878[5]

Luxemburg: 1865[4]

Madrid: 1595–97

Mainz: 1671[2], 1855[5]

Malines: 1845[3], 1848[1, 2], 1854[2], 1855[1], 1859[1, 2], 1874[2, 5], 1877[5], 1890[1]

Marianopoli: see Montreal

Marseilles: 1872[2], 1878[1]

Meaux: 1840[5]

Mechelen: see Malines

Metz: 1779[2, 3], 1800[1], 1805, 1821[4], 1839

Monasterii (various possible sites): 1852[2]

Montreal: 1864[1], 1865[1], 1867[1], 1876[2]

Moulins (Molinis): 1826[5]

Nancy: 1782[3], 1787[1], 1847[5]

Nantes: 1837[3], 1845[4, 5], 1847[5]

Narbonne: 1778[1]

Nimes: 1833[3], 1844[6]

Orléans (=Auselianis): 1730[7], 1738[3]

Paris: 1608/9, 1632[1], 1635(?), 1640, 1647[3], 1650?, 1655[1], 1657, 1658[1, 2, 3], 1662, 1666, 1668[2, 3], 1671[3, 4], 1673, 1680[2], 1682[3], 1687[1, 2, 3, 4], 1688/89, 1694[1], 1696[1, 2, 3],1697[1, 2, 3], 1706[1, 2], 1714[1], 1717, 1720[5], 1722[2], 1724[2], 1730[4], 1732[1], 1734[1, 2, 3, 5], 1738[1, 4], 1740[2], 1745[3], 1746[1], 1749[2], 1750[7], 1754[2], 1755[2], 1756[3], 1762[1], 1766[2], 1770[3], 1778[2], 1782[4], 1815[2], 1822[1], 1826[3], 1833[2], 1845[6], 1846, 1848[3], 1850[2]?, 1851[2], 1852[1], 1853[3, 4, 6], 1855[2], 1855?, 1856[1, 2], 1857[2, 3, 4], 1857?, 1858[1, 2, 6], 1859[3, 4], 1860[1, 2], 1861[1], 1862, 1863[2, 4], 1865[2], 1866, 1867[2], 1869[1, 2, 3], 1872[3], 1874[1, 4, 6], 1875[1, 2], 1877[1, 4], 1878[3, 5], 1880[1, 2], 1881[1], 1882[1, 2], 1883[1], 1884[2], 1902

Paris, Regensburg: see Regensburg, Paris

Poitiers: 1741[2], 1749[1], 1770[6], 1774[2], 1781[1], 1791[2], 1826[2, 4]

Québec: 1800[2], 1827[2], 1841, 1854[5], 1864[2], 1871[2]

Ratisbona: see Regensburg

Regensburg: 1865[5], 1871[1], 1876[6], 1882[2], 1884[3], 1887

Regensburg, New York: 1875[3], 1877[2], 1898

Regensburg, New York, Cincinnati: 1872[1], 1886[2], 1892

Regensburg, Paris: 1881[2], 1882[2]

Regensburg, Rome: 1891

Rennes: 1847[2], 1853[1, 2], 1858[5], 1861[2], 1878[4]

Rome: 1614/15, 1884[1], 1886[1], 1889[1], 1893[1], 1896

Rome, Regensburg: 1891

Rouen: 1727[1], 1752[2], 1861[3]

Sens: 1746[2], 1844[5]

Solesmes: 1895

Soresina: 1721, 1755[4]

Sorexina: see Soresina

Stena (= Steene): 1828[3]

Strasbourg: 1829, 1844[1], 1855[3], 1868

Tarascon: 1825[1]

Toul: 1622[2], 1627/8, 1633[1], 1656, 1667, 1718[2, 3], 1752[1]

Toulouse: 1747[2], 1752[5], 1754[3], 1770[4], 1775[2], 1776[1], 1779[5], 1822[4], 1835, 1836[1, 2], 1852[3], 1854[4]

Tournai: 1616, 1630[2], 1883[2], 1890[2]

Trier: 1863[1]

Troyes: 1739, 1837[2]

Tullus Leucorus: see Toul

Turin: 1797, 1826[1], 1840[1], 1847[1]

Utrecht: 1632[2], 1678, 1691[1]

Valence: 1858[3]

Venice: 1585, 1586[1, 2], 1587, 1591, 1596, 1605, 1606[1], 1607, 1610, 1611(?), 1618[1, 2], 1621, 1626, 1629[1], 1642?, 1643, 1647[1, 2], 1653, 1655[2], 1668[1], 1680[1], 1690[1, 2], 1701[1], 1703, 1716[1, 2], 1719?, 1722[1, 3], 1725, 1730[2, 8], 1734[4], 1750[1, 2], 1754[1], 1759, 1766[1], 1769[1], 1773[1], 1779[1], 1789[3]

Verdun: 1718[1]

Villefranche-le-Rouergue (Francopoli-Ruthenorum): 1774[5]

Westmalle: 1844[8], 1860[4]

Wratislavia: see Wroclaw

Wroclaw: 1870[1]

Not known or not given: 1594, 1644, 1655[2], 1679[2], 1730[5, 8], [1747], 1762[2], 1765[2], 1772[2], 1774[3], 1791[1], 1799, 1824[3], 1842[3], 1848[2], 1869[3], 1878[2]

THREE

The Third Mass of Christmas

It is appropriate to begin our exploration of the post-Tridentine Mass Proper with a consideration of the chants for the Third Mass of Christmas. This occasion marks one of the most important liturgical moments of the Church Year, and the constituent chants are very well known. It is reasonable to think that they were as well beloved near the turn of the seventeenth century as they are now. By beginning in this fashion we may obtain some measure of the effect of liturgical prominence and familiarity on the nature of melodic preservation.

As is well known, the text of the introit antiphon, *Puer natus,* is taken from the Book of Isaiah, chapter 9, verse 6, although in a form that shows numerous divergences from the version of the Vulgate.[1] The text of the verse is drawn from Psalm 97. To continue with the familiar, the seventh-mode chant exhibits a symmetrically balanced construction. The opening two phrases are clearly rooted on the final, even though the first of these closes on the fifth degree of the mode. This open phrase is followed by a parallel one that is closed. The third phrase moves from the modal final to a contrasting tonal area on *a,* while the fourth phrase ends on a cadence parallel to that of the third. The fifth and final phrase returns to the original modal center. This simple and strong construction encouraged a transmission that is, as far as I know, quite stable. The most interesting of the variants occur in a small group of manuscripts primarily from Chartres.[2] These reinforce the relationship between the first two phrases by allowing the initial phrase to descend to *a* on the second syllable of *natus* thereby extending the parallelism beyond the initial use of the ascending fifth, *g–d'.* The descent to *a* is then carried out systematically later in the chant.

One of the aspects that has already attracted attention with regard to post-Tridentine chant is the heightened emphasis on good prosody, an increased expectation that the strong syllables of the text will be set by a greater number of tones than those that are weak. We will find this to be true in general, but, depending on the source consulted, we will also find a considerable number of exceptions. One of the lesser objectives of this study will be to create a more precise understanding of post-Tridentine practices in this regard. This, however, can be built up only gradually.

The principle of what Willi Apel has called a sustaining accent[3] is followed with reasonable regularity in the normative medieval version of *Puer natus*. Twelve of the seventeen polysyllabic words are set in such fashion that the accented syllable receives a greater number of tones than those that are not accented. There are three instances in which the setting is neutral, although one might argue for an acceptance of one of these—*vocabitur*—into the main group. There are only two instances, *nomen* and *consilii*, that go counter to the general tendency. One may note, however, that some of our earliest sources treat the latter word as having only three syllables. The two last vowels are merged into one in these readings, and this may conceivably have affected the matter of stress. This form of reading is apparently rare in later medieval sources and is seemingly absent among the immediate predecessors of the early "reformed" Graduals. One will note that the strophici characteristic of the early readings of *Puer natus* have already disappeared in the reading of the Liechtenstein Gradual of 1580, and indeed their disappearance goes back considerably further. (See example 1,[4] staff **b**.)

It was possible also for singers to acknowledge the importance of textual shape through the governance of pitch. That is, they could set the stressed syllable by one or more notes that are as high as or higher than the following unstressed syllable. Such shapes would correspond loosely to the principles of the *accentus* that governed the pronunciation of Latin in late antiquity.[5] Given the presence of multiple tones for individual syllables this correspondence can only be loose at best, and the criteria for determining the relative strength of the correspondence may easily vary among different scholars. Those that I propose are modest. I concentrate on the syllable bearing the primary stress and the one immediately following. I consider a parallelism of shape to exist if: (a) the stressed syllable begins at a higher pitch than the following unstressed syllable; or, (b) the stressed syllable contains an upward motion that reaches a level higher than or at least as high as that of the beginning of the unstressed syllable—as in the setting of the first word of *Puer natus est*. I do not insist on broad contrasts in pitch height nor do I downplay the significance of tones that are essentially decorative. In *Puer natus*, we find only one word, *cuius*, in which the unaccented syllable is set by a tone higher than the previous stressed syllable. There are, to be sure, two instances (*super*, *nomen*) that display no variation in height. Nevertheless, we may conclude that on the whole the medieval melody for *Puer natus* displays a very considerable solicitude for the shape of the text.

The earliest known complete "reform" Gradual, which was issued by Angelo Gardano in 1591, presents a reading of *Puer natus* (staff **d**) that is nearly identical with that of the slightly earlier Liechtenstein print of 1580. Indeed, it lacks only two tones in the setting of the word *eius* in the penultimate phrase and a single tone in the setting of the final word, *Angelus*. Variants of such minor scope may easily occur in pre-Tridentine sources.

The version provided by the Giunta Gradual of 1596 (staff **e**) is not much more distant, but the variants do form part of a significant pattern. Late editors of chant were for the most part highly sensitive to textual accents that fell on the antepenultimate syllable. There are multiple examples of this in the text for *Puer natus: filius, imperium, humerum, vocabitur, consilii,* and *Angelus*. One might think that the medieval version, which accords 3, 2, and 1 tones respectively to the syllables of *filius* would have been regarded as satisfactory from the standpoint of prosody. Nevertheless, the contrary is true. While this form of text setting is permitted to stand in the reading of the Gardano Gradual, it is changed not only in the subsequent edition by Giunta, but, except for the Flandrus print of 1597, in all others that participate in reform practices. Even though these utilize, with one exception, the same pitches, there are no fewer than four ways in which these are distributed. In the exceptional instance furnished by the Medicean Gradual (staff **g**), the descent to *a* is delayed so that it takes place on the first syllable of the following word. In all instances of change, the syllable following the stressed antepenultimate is limited to a single tone, a practice that we shall observe time and again. Furthermore, in five of the readings this single tone is further differentiated by using a diamond-shaped form. Often this indication of brevity is present even more consistently. On the other hand, the use of the diamond-shaped form for the final syllable of the following word, *datus*, in the Premonstratensian reading (staff **l**), is unusual, although comparable examples are to be observed within the late Venetian tradition. It seems advisable to interrupt at this point in order to remark that Premonstratensian practice did not remain uniform. The readings of the Verdun Gradual of 1718 are basically identical to those in the 1680 print edited by Nivers, as are those of the edition of 1771. There is, however, a later Gradual of 1787, prepared in Paris for Premonstratensians of Nancy, which contains many neo-Gallican chants. This will be treated in a later chapter. To recapitulate, while reform Graduals may follow medieval practice by retaining basically the same series of pitches, these may be redistributed to suit the changed sensitivity to prosodic values.

In the setting of *cuius imperium*, we may note similar principles at work. In the readings of the Medicean Gradual (staff **g**) and the Belleros imprint of 1620 (staff **i**) the first syllable of *cuius* is accorded an additional tone that reflects its position as an accented syllable. (The latter reading is derived from the Gradual issued four years earlier by Laurent in Tournai.) And one can note the varied ways of setting the accented syllable of the word following, which, while maintaining the same general profile, may have anywhere between three and six tones.

This variability in relative prolixity is even more pronounced when one compares the different treatments of the last word of the segment, *super humerum eius*. The normative medieval version given in the Solesmes editions allots seven tones to the first syllable of this word. These, however, are contained within the interval of a third. Rather than forming a broad gesture, they circle back and forth in a quasi-repetitive fashion. This kind of motion was often viewed with disfavor by seventeenth century-editors of chant. We thus find readings that reduce the number of tones to five, four, and even two. It is worth noting that even though the Giunta edition of 1596 and the one by Ciera in 1610 (staves **e**, **f**) belong to the same Venetian tradition, the two vary notably in their treatment of this word. Similar comments may be made concerning the treatment of the first syllable of the word *eius* that occurs slightly later. Here the Medicean Gradual (staff **g**) reduces what had in previous centuries been a gesture of as many as six tones to a single tone.

Apart from the solicitude for prosody, a trait shared by most post-Tridentine Graduals, the Medicean Gradual presents a notable change in melodic profile. The tonal architecture of the normative medieval version rests on an A–B–A structure, the contrasting element using cadences on *a* for the two interior phrases each ending with the word *eius*. The Medicean editors, Anerio and Soriano, apparently felt that this conjunction threatened the tonal centricity that should reside on *g*. Hence they eliminated the stepwise descent to *a* in the first of these instances and terminated this cadence on *b*, while they raised the level of the second cadence by utilizing repeated *d's*.

The variability to be observed in the setting of the two last words, *consilii Angelus*, demonstrates with considerable clarity the variability of chant practice during the seventeenth and eighteenth centuries. Each of the readings, including the conservative versions of the Benedictines and Carthusians is individual. None is a duplicate of another. Differences in attention to prosodic values are especially apparent with regard to the setting of the concluding word.

Not shown in the example is the reading of the Gradual published by Andreas Petricovius (=Piotrkowczyk) in Kraków, 1600. This is among the more conservative reform Graduals, but it nevertheless is assignable to this group. This is not merely a result of its adherence to the Roman Missal of 1570, but of its attention to the details of prosody. In its reading for *Puer natus*, this new attitude shows clearly in the allocation of tones to six sensitive words: *filius, imperium, eius* (twice), *consilii*, and *Angelus*. In four instances the unaccented penultimates are restricted to a single tone; the remaining instances reduce the number of tones for the unaccented final syllables to two tones.

Viewing the transmission of *Puer natus* as a whole, we observe that when a simple medieval chant displays a strong sense of tonal centricity as well as a respect for prosodic values, the changes that are apt to be wrought during the post-Tridentine period are modest. Striking alterations in melodic profile are rare, although occasional minor changes can be observed. This notwithstanding, minor changes in the allocation of tones to syllables are not only frequent, but vary from source to source. Considerable variety is displayed within a modest framework.

The floridity of the gradual, *Viderunt omnes*, furnishes quite a different set of problems to the chant editors freed of the responsibility for adhering to an established tradition. The text for the chant is taken from Psalm 97. The respond utilizes the latter half of verse 3 together with the first portion of verse 4. The text corresponds to the reading of the Latin Psalter edited by Robert Weber[6] and to Jerome's translation after the Hebrew. The verse utilizes the entirety of verse 2, following the version of the Latin Psalter. The two translations by Jerome differ only in that they employ the word *in* rather than *ante*. My knowledge of the medieval transmission of the melody is limited, but my initial impression is that it was quite stable. I attribute this posited stability to the simplicity and strength of the tonal skeleton.

The melodic profile of the respond builds quickly through the second word. In so doing, it ignores the normal text stress on the second syllable of *Viderunt*, with regard not only to melodic height but also the number of tones per syllable. The remainder of the first broad phrase may be interpreted reasonably in groups of two, one, and two words, each group terminating with the succession $c'-b-c'-a$. The conclusion of the respond may be viewed as two groups of two words each, both groups ending on the final. (See example 2.)

Considered in these terms, we may note the suitability of the melodic and sustaining emphasis on the first syllable of *omnes*, as well as the melodic emphasis on the first syllable of *fines*. But these instances are overshadowed by others that would be viewed with disfavor by those concentrating on prosodic values. These persons would frown on the prominence given to the last syllable of *Viderunt*, and the corresponding weight given to the last syllable of *salutare*, *Dei*, and *nostri*. The tristropha placed on the last syllable of *iubilate*, as well as the weight of the last syllables of both *Deo* and *terra*, would have given equal offense. In arriving at a melodic shape for the respond the medieval singers did not accord a high value to prosody even though careful perusal will disclose that only in the first and last word does the melody fail to reach a peak on the accented syllable at least equal to, if not higher than the following context. And yet one may perhaps see a different set of values for text setting within this more florid framework. The relative numbers of tones accorded to final syllables may have been chosen as a means of setting the various words apart from one another, thus endowing each with a slightly greater sense of unity than might otherwise have prevailed within a melismatic style. Whether this possible view of the medieval aesthetic is valid or not, matters were clearly not viewed in this fashion during the seventeenth and eighteenth centuries.

The discomfort with the medieval conception of the melody for *Viderunt omnes* went far beyond matters of prosody. At least some chant theorists of the seventeenth century—Guillaume Gabriel de Nivers among them—preferred melodies with active profiles. The continued oscillation between a and c' that is so prominent in the first part of the respond—particularly with regard to the setting of *fines terrae*—would have been looked on with distaste by these persons, and their feelings would not have improved greatly even when the modal final, *f*, expanded the tonal skeleton towards the end.

The number of options open to the late editors of *Viderunt omnes* results in a far greater variety in the transmission of this melody than was observed with regard to *Puer natus*. We find again that Andrea Gabrieli and Orazio Vecchi use greater restraint in remodeling *Viderunt* than do their later Italian colleagues. They permitted the setting of the opening word to stand (staff **d**), whereas this segment was revised shortly thereafter. The Giunta print of 1596 (staff **e**), which furnishes the point of departure for the Venetian tradition of the seventeenth and eighteenth centuries, transfers the initial melodic ascent to the accented second syllable, while reducing the number of tones assigned to the final syllable to one. The change wrought by Anerio and Soriano in the Medicean Gradual of 1614 (staff **f**) is more striking because it repeats the initial tone and assigns three tones to the accented syllable. These revisions stand in striking contrast to the normative transalpine editions, whether French, Flemish, or German. Among the northerly sources, only the Küchler and Premonstratensian editions of 1671 and 1680 (staves **l**, **o**) find it advisable to revise the setting of the opening word.

The contrast between southerly and northerly practices is still sharper in the following portions of the melody. The former sources are far more succinct than the latter. When comparing the medieval Gregorian with the Roman and Beneventan repertoires, one finds the southerly melodies to be more florid on the whole than the former. In dealing with later music it is tempting to generalize and to imagine the Italians as the exuberant singers and the northerners as far more reserved. In the music of concern to this study, however, it is the reverse that is true. The Italian editors restrict the floridity of chant to a far greater extent than do their northern counterparts. This is not uniformly obvious at first. Even though the editions of Giunta and Ciera sharply curtail the small melisma on the first syllable of *omnes*, the Medicean edition allows this to stand. However, all agree in curtailing the floridity of the ensuing section, *salutare Dei nostri*. Here we may note the power of the editors to reshape the melodic profile noticeably. We commented earlier on the parallelism of the closes to *terrae*, *salutare*, and *nostri* in the normative medieval version of *Viderunt*. The Medicean version (staff **f**), on the other hand, ends the first of these words on *c'*, rather than descending to *a*, and restricts the following segment to the upper register, ending on *d'*. Similarly, the Medicean reading ends *omnis* on *c'* rather than bringing it down to *g*, as do other versions given in this example except for the earlier Giunta and the later Premonstratensian Graduals. The intermediate tonal goals have been changed considerably.

Viderunt omnes appears no fewer than three times in the Medicean Gradual.[7] It occurs both on the Sunday within the Octave of Christmas (fol. 32v) and on Circumcision (fol. 36v). Each of these later occurrences is written out in full. It noteworthy that the reading for the Sunday within the Octave of Christmas is not a consistent duplicate of the earlier one written for the Third Mass of Christmas. The cadence on *nostri* is sharply altered to d'–c'–b–a–b–c'–a and resembles the cadences of other sources to a greater extent. The final cadence of the respond reads a–f–a–g–f–g–g–f. Changes of this nature cannot be easily ascribed to mistakes. In each of these instances, the version for the Third Mass of Christmas is confirmed by the reading for Circumcision. The final cadence of the verse also submits to change in the Sunday within the Octave of Christmas, reading f–g–a–g–a–g–f. Whereas the reading for Circumcision retains the penultimate neume of the version for Christmas, it too ends g–f rather than with the solitary f. (There are three other changes in the reading for the Sunday within the Octave, but these are quite minor.)

Again, with the exception of the Premonstratensian reading (staff **o**), the northern editions do not find the relative floridity of this gradual to be disturbing. They adhere within reasonable limits to the medieval setting. On the other hand, they do revise the setting of the word, *iubilate*, in order not to contravene prosodic values. Staves **p** and **q**, devoted respectively to Benedictine and Carthusian readings, demonstrate the extent to which some adhered to the earlier traditions for this melody. The Carthusian edition of 1674 is virtually identical to the earlier reading of 1578.

Perhaps the most prominent feature of the verse is the huge melisma (52 tones) on the first syllable of *Dominus*. Within the repertory of Notre Dame polyphony this was to provide the basis for many clausulae. This melisma is greatly reduced in all reform sources, but the manner of reduction varies considerably among the sources. In the Premonstratensian Gradual of 1680 (staff **o**), the flourish is reduced to a mere six notes. The initial descent from d' (essentially an upper neighbor of c') and the repeated hovering in the lower pentachord of the mode is eliminated entirely. Instead we have a turn around the d' that proceeds directly to a peak on the upper octave and a descent from this high point. The gesture is roughly comparable to the end of the medieval melisma. The Cistercian revision published in 1696 (staff **n**) parallels the later portion of this neume but prefaces it with three tones drawn from the opening of the medieval melisma, thus employing a total of seven notes. Despite the somewhat conservative nature of the Flandrus Gradual of 1597 (staff **m**), the sharp curtailment of this melisma to a mere eleven notes, clearly marks this source as a "reform" Gradual. This is confirmed by a variety of small details. In many ways a rather idiosyncratic source, one can only speculate concerning its possible antecedents. The name of the printer, Ioannes Flandrus (=Juan Flamenco), raises suspicions of possible Franco-Flemish influence even though the edition stands clearly apart from the editions of Laurent, Belleros, and Mommaert on the one hand and the edition of Plantin on the other. A native Spanish antecedent cannot be ruled out at this time, but very little is known of late sixteenth-century chant in Spain.

The later transmission of *Viderunt omnes* in Italy warrants a separate example devoted to these sources. (See example 3.) Glancing quickly at the readings for the respond, one can note how consistent the Venetian tradition can be, excepting the Gardano edition. Two notes from the setting of the first syllable of *terra* are generally dropped beginning in 1610, but there is nothing else to detain our attention.

Matters are otherwise with regard to the readings for the verse. The melisma for *Dominus* in the Ciera Gradual of 1610 (staff **f**) is sharply curtailed, but it is likely defective. Like most other readings, it too begins with the same descent from *d'* to *a*. It proceeds with another two tones drawn from the medieval melisma but breaks off abruptly, continuing with a clivis and pes that are only loosely related to the original form. A total of nine tones suffices. A full assessment of the reading is complex. One can readily see that this reading is essentially derived from the earlier reading of the Giunta Gradual of 1596 (staff **e**). The Giunta Gradual, however, descends from the second *d'* to *g* in stepwise fashion, whereas the Ciera reading omits two of the intermediate notes. This seems to be the result of an oversight; the omission does not occur in the Venetian Graduals issued in the surrounding years.

As shown in example 3, the Venetian editors, beginning with the print by Ciera in 1621 (staff **i**) restore the upward motion that had been excised in the Giunta edition of 1606 and its immediate successors. They do not, however, return to the reading of Giunta, 1596, but instead draw on the reading of the Medicean Gradual of 1614 (staff **h**). At this time I am not aware of any seventeenth-century Gradual that takes over in its entirety any chant from this Roman source. There are, however, a limited number of occasions when later Venetian editors create curious hybrid forms, utilizing their own tradition for part of the melody and the Roman reading for the remainder. *Viderunt omnes* furnishes one such example of this practice, and the offertory, *Dextera Domini*, another. It is worthy of note that the later editors do not feel it necessary to follow the Medicean version faithfully. While the Ciera edition of 1621 and the Giunta edition of 1626 parallel the Medicean reading for the setting of *salutare suum*, the later editions by Giunta (1642), Baba, Baglioni, and Pezzana (staves **k–p**) return to the Venetian tradition for this segment. Given this flexibility, the consistency of these later editions is striking.

Among northerly readings those of the Plantin and Angermaier prints of 1599 and 1618 (example 2, staves **j**, **k**) are the most extensive. Not only do they retain the descent, *d'–c'–a* from the opening of the *Dominus* melisma but also the two following four-note neumes. They couple these with eleven tones that represent the main substance of the melisma's end. The varied treatments of this melisma are sufficiently distinctive that one is drawn to explore further. One will then realize that the later of the two prints is simply a derivative of the earlier, not only with regard to this chant, but also all others taken up in this study. One can thus understand the absence from the Angermaier print of the traits of the Germanic chant dialect that are clearly present in the 1671 Küchler Gradual issued in Mainz.

Like the Plantin and Angermaier readings, that presented in example 2 by the Laurent Gradual issued in Tournai in 1616 (staff **h**) also descends to *f* in paralleling the normative medieval version. However, it then leaps up to the fifth of the mode before ascending to the upper octave. Together with the Antwerp Gradual issued by Belleros in 1620 and the Brussels Gradual of 1623 brought out by Joannes Mommartius (Mommaert), these sources constitute a second Flemish tradition that will be continued by later printers. Their readings display occasional variants from one another and do not remain entirely stable. In the present instance, however, their account is consistent. Nevertheless, alterations may be made in the surviving copy of the Belleros Gradual by means of paste-overs; there are none such for *Viderunt*. In the surviving copy of the Mommaert print small passages may be crossed out by hand. The final melismas for both the respond and the verse of *Viderunt* are excised in this fashion. The final syllable of *terra* is reduced to a single tone, *f*, while the final syllable of *suam* is reduced to the neume, *e–f*.

The earliest of the French reform Graduals was issued in Bordeaux by the press of Simon Millange in 1598/99.[8] The title page credits G[uillaume] Bony (more frequently spelled Boni) with the major share of the editorial enterprise. A singer, canon, and *maître de chapelle* for the Cathedral of Toulouse, Boni was a capable composer. In 1565 he took part in a reception for Charles IX and his entourage and attracted the favorable attention of the king. His later *Psalmi Davidici* (1582) was dedicated to King Henri III. Several collections of his music were published in Paris by Le Roy and Ballard.

Within a decade another French reform Gradual was apparently issued in Paris, most likely by the *Societas Typographicae librorum officii Ecclesiastici*. Unfortunately no copy is presently known to survive. Amadée Gastoué mentions such a work, but gives no details.[9] It is unclear whether Gastoué ever had this work in hand or whether he inferred its existence on the basis of a sentence to be found in the preface to one of the later books brought out by the printer Belgrand and his associates in Toul in 1627, 1633, and 1656. The first surviving *Graduale Romanum* from Paris is that issued in 1640 by the *Societas Typographicae librorum officii Ecclesiastici*. This was later to be reissued in 1657. Given the fact that the readings offered by Boni agree basically with those appearing in the 1640 *Graduale,* and also with the intervening books brought out by Belgrand and Laurent, it is quite probable that the 1608/9 Gradual belonged to the same family and that our loss is minimal.

Gastoué was apparently also familiar with a 1622 Gradual brought out by Belgrand in Toul. No copy of this work is traceable either. The readings of the Toul and Paris Graduals were later to appear in other French centers such as Lyon and Grenoble. In the hands of Belgrand and later Parisian editors, the chants submitted to further editorial changes. In dealing with the melisma on *Dominus*, the Bordeaux and Toul readings (staff **g**) descend no further than *a* before rebounding to the fifth of the mode. The ensuing ascent carries only to the seventh degree of the mode. Comparing the northerly readings as a group, one may find small moments in the latter portion of the verse in which the reading in one source may agree with that of another. If one sets aside the derivation of the Angermaier Gradual from the earlier Plantin print, the brief stretches of similarity occurring elsewhere are not lengthy enough to demonstrate a purposive relationship between the remaining pairs.

In the reading given in the Piotrkowczyk Gradual of 1600 (staff **i**), the large melisma on the first syllable of *Dominus* is treated in an individual manner. This is the only source to preserve some of the central portion. In this fashion the reading is also marginally longer than any of its counterparts. The treatment of the final melisma is also individual. The Piotrkowczyk Gradual is the only northern source in which the melody fails to ascend to *b-flat* following the descent from $c'-f$. Only Anerio and Soriano, the editors of the Medicean Gradual (staff **f**) revise the melisma in this manner, but they do it by making a fundamental change in the final cadence.

The *Alleluia Dies sanctificatus* presents still another set of circumstances with regard to its transmission. The source for the text of this chant is yet undetermined, although theories concerning the nature of its origin have been set forth. The chant is quite stable in its medieval transmission, as has been demonstrated both by David Hughes[10] and the present author.[11] Undoubtedly the most striking change that takes place in its late transmission is one that affects the very structure of the work. Every beginning student of chant is informed that the opening *alleluia* is sung first by one or more soloists, who are followed by the choir, taking up the melody from the very beginning and adding the jubilus. The soloist(s) are responsible for the performance of the main body of the verse, while the very end is once again entrusted to the choir. Thereafter the opening *alleluia* and jubilus are sung respectively by the soloist(s) and then the choir. This practice apparently represents not only the normative form of performance in the Middle Ages and Renaissance, but also that during the opening two decades of the seventeenth century.

However, beginning with the Ciera Gradual of 1621, we find that there is no indication of any break between the solo and choral segments of the Alleluia. (See example **4f**, which gives the reading of the Baglioni Gradual of 1690.) Instead, the word *alleluia* is repeated, suggesting that the chorus entered in midstream and not at the beginning. Furthermore, at the end of the verse, we find a highly abbreviated form of the opening *alleluia*, eliminating the need for a full-scale repetition. This changed mode of performance is abandoned in later Venetian Graduals of Baglioni, but it then resumes in the later Graduals brought out by Pezzana in 1730, 1779, and 1789. The setting of the jubilus by the repeated word, *alleluia*, occurs also in the Küchler Gradual of 1671.

The fact that the medieval melody for the *Alleluia Dies sanctificatus* displays a clear sense of tonal focus on the modal final and the pentachord above it—as did the two earlier items of the same Mass Proper—undoubtedly contributed to the relative stability of its later transmission. This generality notwithstanding, one does find various changes that give insight into some of the musical values of the later editors. Anerio and Soriano, for example, were particularly solicitous in their efforts to remain within theoretic descriptions of the mode. While all but one of the other readings consulted begin with the subtonium, the editors of the Medicean Gradual begin on the modal final before descending to the subtonium (staff **g**). The same concern had been demonstrated earlier by Guillaume Boni in the 1598/99 Gradual published in Bordeaux (not illustrated in example 4).

The jubilus for the *Alleluia Dies sanctificatus* is relatively modest in length and the later chant editors preserve its general character reasonably well. There is a tendency to shorten it slightly, but only in the version of the Medicean Gradual, is this markedly noticeable. The final descent from the upper fourth in the reading of the Belleros Gradual from Antwerp (staff **i**) is unusual, but there are medieval precedents for this cadence in sources from northern France. (See, for example, the reading in Cambrai, Bibl. mun., MS 61.)

The individuality of the Medicean reading is more striking in the verse. In conformity with the medieval version of the melody, on the word *sanctificatus* most sources begin an extended, varied recitation on *d,* followed by an ascent to the upper fifth and a compensating descent that reaches a half-cadence on *c.* In the Medicean reading (staff **g**), on the other hand, the varied recitation is soon curtailed by an upward skip to *f,* which serves as an internal breathing point. The revised melody resumes from this tone and continues the ascent to the upper fifth. The complementary descent, however, concludes with a full cadence on the modal final. The phrase beginning with the words *venite gentes* has near its beginning a descent into the plagal range. This is replaced in the Medicean reading by an upward leap from the final to the fifth degree of the mode. With the exception of the Cistercian reading, none of the others find the momentary descent, occupying only a single tone, to be objectionable. The Cistercian solution (staff **m**), which derives from the medieval readings from this Order, is much simpler. The offending tone is simply replaced by the subtonium.

This passage presented still another problem, namely that the opening melisma is on an unaccented syllable. Generally this was found to be quite offensive to the southern editors, but much less so to the northerners. Even so, some of the northern Graduals rework this passage so that the emphasis on the first syllable of *venite* is lessened.

The continuation of the medieval version of the melody terminates a recitation on *f* with a turn that is placed on the last—therefore unaccented—syllable of *adorate*. This is followed to a greater or lesser degree in most post-Tridentine readings. The Medicean editors, on the other hand, transfer the turn to the previous, accented penultimate and add a subsequent descent to the modal final for the last syllable. In the Piotrkowczyk Gradual (staff **k**) the problem is solved by dividing the tones of the turn equally between the last two syllables.

The Medicean Gradual presents a modified shape for the concluding portion of the *Alleluia Dies sanctificatus* (staff **g**). The descent from the upper fifth on the word, *hodie*, is eliminated and we have instead an abrupt downward leap of a fifth to begin the word, *descendit*. Even though the descent to the fourth below the final for the word *venite* had been judged inappropriate, likely because it transcended the boundaries of the first mode, here the opportunity for a bit of text painting was apparently irresistible. The Medicean reading leaps down to this lower fourth for the last syllable of *descendit*, while the most readings are content to remain on the final, in keeping with medieval tradition. The Premonstratensian reading (staff **o**) also indulges in a comparable bit of text painting, although it wends it way downward from *f* rather than *d*. In bringing about these changed profiles, the editors of these two Graduals disrupt the parallelism that exists between the segment beginning *quia hodie* and the opening of the verse both in the medieval version of the melody and in most other seventeenth-century readings. The disregard for the parallelism is further marked by the curtailment of the melisma on *magna* in both sources.

Before going on to consider the offertory *Tui sunt caeli*, I shall interrupt in order to consider the *Alleluia Dies sanctificatus* from a different vantage point. For the sake of simplicity and convenience we have considered the foregoing chants in relative isolation. Yet none of them was actually limited to a single occasion, and none existed totally apart from the repertoire as a whole. Especially the *Alleluia Dies sanctificatus* was part of an extensive nexus of chants. If we are to understand fully the import of the various changes wrought in its transmission after the Council of Trent, we require a much broader context.

We may begin by noting that the Proper chants for the Third Mass of Christmas could serve also for the Sunday within the Octave of Nativity. This is not the situation that obtains in the modern books issued by the monks of Solesmes, but it was one option offered by the Medicean Gradual issued under the direction of Anerio and Soriano. It is not possible to document how widespread a practice this was because many of the printed Graduals of the seventeenth century lack a Mass for this occasion. When we compare the reading for the Alleluia given for the Third Mass of Christmas with that given for the Sunday immediately following, we discover (as observed in connection with *Viderunt omnes*) that the two readings are not identical. There are no fewer than eleven variants of different extent—some of them moderately significant—that distinguish the two versions.

Next we may recall that the *Alleluia Dies sanctificatus* forms part of a very extensive melody type. Even if we restrict ourselves to the period from Christmas to Epiphany, we note that essentially the same melodic materials form the basis for the *Alleluias Video caelos, Hic est discipulus, Inveni David,* and *Vidimus stellam.* If it was found advisable to revise one of these in order better to suit modern tastes, what was the effect on the remaining four?

In accordance with the evidence of several medieval sources, I prefer to regard the normative medieval version of the verse for the *Alleluia Dies sanctificatus* as bipartite, having the form A B A′ C. In the reading of the *Graduale Triplex* the opening syllable is set by a characteristic melisma of eleven tones, subdivisible into groups of 6+5. The latter group and the following group of six recur near the beginning of the second half in association with the second and third syllables of *hodie*, while the opening group is condensed for the setting of the first syllable of this word. The nineteen-note melisma that sets the opening syllable of *nobis* recurs later for the setting of the first syllable of *magna*, while the following punctum is the same for both concluding syllables. The symmetry is easily apparent.

When we examine the normative medieval reading for *Video caelos* reconstructed in Solesmes books, we find that the setting of the opening word is identical with that for *Dies*. The same may be said for the setting of *apertos*, which is equivalent to *nobis*. The first seventeen tones for *stantem* are identical with those for the beginning of *venite* in *Dies sanctificatus*. The fourteen tones for *dextris* are the same as those for *hodie*, and, allowing for the presence of an introductory tone, the setting of *virtutis* corresponds to that of *magna*. The last fifteen tones of the two chants are also identical. Carrying out the same process for the remaining three chants of our group, we obtain very nearly the same results. For example, in *Hic est discipulus*, the setting of the first two words is identical with that of *Dies*, while that for *ille* is identical with that for *nobis*. The setting for *perhibet* corresponds closely with that for *venite*, that for *et scimus* with *quia hodie*, and that for *verum est* with *magna*. These facts and others have been known for decades thanks to the work of Ferretti[12] and Wellesz[13]. Their recall is relevant to our current interests.

It is not possible within the confines of an introductory study to pursue the interrelationships found within all of our sources, and I shall deal only with three of these. In the Medicean Gradual, we find that among the readings of *Video caelos*, *Hic est discipulus*, *Inveni David*, and *Vidimus stellam*, not one preserves the identities or near identities that are present at the comparable moments in their medieval transmission. (See example 5.)

Sometimes the changes are small, at other times they are striking. For example, while the normative medieval version of the *Alleluia Dies sanctificatus* reaches a cadence on *d* for the phrase *quia hodie*, that of the Medicean Gradual cadences on *a*. The corresponding passage of *Video caelos*—associated with the words *a dextris*—begins with an unusual descent from *f* before reaching a cadence on *d*; the other three chants cadence on *f*. *Hic est discipulus* and *Vidimus stellam* begin the comparable passage with an ascent from *d*. *Inveni David*, on the other hand, begins the setting of the word *oleo* on *a*. The reader should consult example 5 to compare the passages that correspond to the sections of the *Alleluia Dies sanctificatus* setting the words, *illuxit nobis*, *venite gentes et adorate Dominum*, and *lux magna* in order to verify how the formulaic materials may change from chant to chant.

In order to demonstrate that this variability is not simply an idiosyncrasy of the Medicean Gradual, I offer an additional two musical examples, the first drawn from the Venetian Gradual issued by Ciera in 1610 (see example 6), the second from a Premonstratensian Gradual edited by Nivers and published in Paris in 1680. (See example 7.) In surveying the former, one will note immediately the inconsistencies involving the opening gesture of the verse. The readings given for the *Alleluias Dies sanctificatus* and *Hic est discipulus* are identical, but their fellows depart from this formula in one way or another. Further exploration shows that this inconsistency is present in various other passages. To the extent that different editors may treat the melismatic portions with a lighter hand, we may find that formulaic nexuses survive to a greater extent. On the whole, the northern editions are more conservative in this respect than the southern ones. Yet even these may be affected, as may be seen in the example devoted to the Premonstratensian readings of 1680. One notes readily that the opening of *Video caelos* omits the opening dip from the final that is characteristic of its counterparts. While *Dies sanctificatus* comes to a cadence on *d* at *nobis*, each of the associated chants cadence on *c*. The decision to indulge in tone-painting at the word, *descendit*, effectively destroys the formulaic nature of the passage in the medieval tradition. Still other examples of inconsistency in the treatment of formulas are easily found.

Although the forms of variability documented in these examples are characteristic of the epoch, they do not constitute a necessary result. We have already pointed out that the gradual for the Third Mass of Christmas is likewise given three times in the Medicean Gradual. As noted previously, the second presentation (for the Sunday within the Octave of Christmas) varies the chant at several points, including three major cadences, but the third (for the Feast of Circumcision) is nearly identical to the first.

The ultimate result of the changes that we have been documenting is a process of individuation. I am convinced that this is a reflection of another kind of change that goes hand in hand. The medieval singer, working within a primarily oral culture, was heavily dependent upon the consistency of formulaic structures in order to retain in his memory the vast amounts of material needed. The singer could, for example, learn thoroughly the *Alleluia Dies sanctificatus*. If he could then retain a sense for the minor adjustments that were occasioned by differences in textual accentuation and length, his knowledge would enable him to sing some thirty or forty additional chants (depending on the nature of the repertoire employed in a specific area) with reasonable security. If, under ordinary circumstances, the singer of the seventeenth century learned the *Alleluia Dies sanctificatus* with equal thoroughness, this knowledge would not necessarily permit him to sing other chants, even if related in general format. Here we have been dealing with inconsistencies in the transmission of similar materials in complete melodies. In the next two chapters, we shall consider comparable inconsistencies on the level of individual phrases. (See especially examples 18–24.) Both forms of evidence lead to the same conclusion. The undermining of the strength and constancy of formulaic structures undoubtedly had as a consequence the change from a primarily oral to a primarily written culture. The singer *had* to read; his memory would no longer suffice for the increased burdens. Certainly the memory remained an important function; but its role was fundamentally diminished. It seems likely that this change eventually influenced a change in the physical dimensions of our sources. Many of the sources from the turn of the seventeenth century are in very large format, suitable for use on a lectern. A century later this format is being abandoned and we have instead small books capable of being held in the hand of the individual singer. We shall mention the change in the balance between memory and reading at later points in this study.

Tui sunt caeli, the offertory for the Third Mass of Christmas, is a fourth-mode chant. The text is taken from Psalm 88, verse 12, and the first part of verse 15. With the exception of the use of *orbem terrarum* rather than *orbem terrae*, the chant text accords with the readings of the Latin Psalter and Jerome's *Hexapla*. Like many other chants of the fourth mode, the melody accords prominence to the *f–d* third at the opening. (See example 8.) This was troubling to several editors at or slightly after the turn of the seventeenth century because of the conflict with their concepts of modality. In the Gradual issued by Joannes Flandrus (= Juan Flamenco) in Madrid, 1595–97 (staff **m**), this problem is solved merely by changing the opening tone to *e*, the modal final. Boni, in his Gradual of 1598/99 (staff **g**), also focuses the opening on *e*. He continues to circle around this tone before ascending to the fifth degree, which is not attained in any other early reading. He then closes with a cadence, *f–e*, on the final syllable of *caeli*. This is a normal close. But only in the Flandrus and Millange prints do we find a tonally closed gesture for the first phrase. Anerio and Soriano, the editors of the Medicean Gradual also open the chant on *e* (staff **f**), the modal final, preceding the initial entry of *f*, in a manner comparable to their treatment of the opening of the *Alleluia Dies sanctificatus*. This accords two tones to the initial syllable, while the normative torculus for the second syllable is reduced to a single tone, thus producing a better accord with normal prosody. The Medicean Gradual, however, closes the first phrase on the third degree of the mode. The elimination of the torculus for the second syllable is found also in Venetian Graduals. Curiously, the modal centricity displayed in Boni's revision is not retained by his successors in Toul and Paris, who revert to a form much closer to the normative medieval version.

We may conveniently return to observe the distinctiveness of the Medicean reading (staff **f**), which will go on to emphasize the importance of the modal final, *e*, and the third above. The first breathing point in the text comes after the third word, *caeli*. In the normative medieval version, the last syllable is set by a clivis and torculus, the latter ending on *e*. This was judged quite acceptable by Gabrieli and Vecchi in their edition brought out by Gardano in 1591 (staff **d**), but unacceptable by later Italian and French editors because of the weight accorded the unaccented final syllable. The Medicean Gradual, however, presents the only reading to recast the setting of the complete word so that it reaches a peak on *a* and then relaxes to *g*. It is also the only reading to begin the next phrase on *e*. The following cadence on the word *terra* demonstrates a bifurcation in the tradition. I have not made an extensive comparison of medieval sources for *Tui sunt caeli*. The normative ending given in the *Graduale Triplex* consists of the single note, *e*. This is the reading adopted by the *Graduale Herbipolense* in 1583. However, a rapid check of readily available facsimiles—Graz, Universitätsbibl., 807, Leipzig, Universitätsbibl., 391, Munich, Universitätsbibl., 2° 56 (Moosburger Gradual), and the *Graduale Pataviense* of 1511[14]—shows that the Germanic preference was for *f*. (The Leipzig reading provides an exception.) In six of our post-Tridentine sources we find the pes, *e–f*. The Medicean Gradual reading is one of a few that uses the single *e*, and it is the only one that begins the following phrase with this tone. This reading also stands alone in using a single *e* both at the conclusion of the sub-phrase, *plenitudinem eius*, and at the final cadence. It is one of two that begins the next sub-phrase on *g*. The Medicean Gradual presents the only reading to end the setting of *justitia* on *g* and *judicium* on *e*. It is singular in ending *preparatio* on *g* and having only a single *e* on the last syllable of text.

One should not, however, overemphasize the individuality of the Medicean reading. The Premonstratensian reading (staff **o**) is also idiosyncratic. Only the readings of the Giunta Gradual of 1596 and the Ciera Gradual of 1610 are nearly identical and even these two display occasional small differences. While the various Graduals compared in this example do show small-scale identities with one or another of their fellows, these are not long enough to be significant in demonstrating lines of influence.

The communion for the Third Mass of Christmas takes for its text the initial seven words of the segment of Psalm 97 that had previously served for the respond of the gradual. The melody is in mode 1 and is tonally stable. While chants for communions tend to be relatively restrained, that for *Viderunt omnes*, is among the more prolix of its kind. No fewer than four syllables—two accented and two unaccented—are set by five or more tones. Thus there are opportunities for abbreviation even in this relatively brief chant. (See example 9.)

Again the reading of the Medicean Gradual (staff **g**) is among the more distinctive. As in the preceding offertory, the first tone of the revised version is given to the modal final, postponing the entrance of *f*, which serves as the initial in both the normative medieval version as well as in the various later readings given with the exception of those issued by Laurent, Belleros, and Mommaert. And the Medicean reading is the only one that consistently assigns but a single tone to the last syllable of each word. The Premonstratensian reading (staff **o**) is likewise among the more original of the re-workings, but is less systematic in its approach to the editorial task. The mildness of the changes wrought in the Gardano edition (staff **d**) by Gabrieli and Vecchi is in keeping with earlier observations, as is the willingness of northern editors to retain much of the earlier medieval fabric. There is a single variant between the Plantin edition of 1599 (staff **j**) and that by Angermaier in 1618. The former has six notes for the second syllable of *terrae*, while the latter omits the third of these (*g*).

Reviewing our initial observations concerning the chants for the Third Mass of Christmas, we find considerable variety to the changes wrought by post-Tridentine editors. When, as in *Puer natus,* the medieval chant is simple, tonally stable, and solicitous of prosodic values, the changes tend to be few and simple. At times these may involve little more than a realignment of tones and syllables in order to effect minor improvements in prosody. Yet, there may also be small changes designed to achieve greater tonal stability. These are especially visible in the readings of the Medicean Gradual, but they are to be found elsewhere as well. Modal propriety, however, is not a constant value. We have observed "violations" of the first mode range for the sake of tone painting in the *Alleluia Dies sanctificatus.* The more ornate the medieval model, the more likely it is to submit to extensive revision. The curtailment of melismas is more drastic among Italian sources and is milder among northerly editions. Particularly among these latter it is possible to find melismas remaining—even if curtailed—on the final syllables of important sections. There are spheres of influence that should be noted. Most striking is the derivation of the Angermaier and Sutor prints from the Plantin model. While we shall find that the last-named influences also the edition of Piotrkowczyk, issued one year later in Kraków, the Polish print retains a much greater degree of editorial freedom. The speed of transmission in this instance is startling. Eventually we shall need to build up a better geographical knowledge concerning the use of important editions in various European locales, such as the presence in Salzburg of liturgical books brought out in Toul and the presence in Vienna of the Medicean Gradual. This, however, is a task that I must leave to later scholars.

FOUR

The First Sunday of Advent

Before considering the transmission of the melodies for the Proper of the First Sunday of Advent, it would be advantageous to treat briefly their texts. The introit, gradual, and offertory for this occasion all draw on the first four verses of Psalm 24. The respective readings of St. Jerome's translations after the Septuagint (the *Hexapla*) and after the Hebrew (*Hebraeos*) are as follows:

Hexapla	*Hebraeos*
1. *Ad te Domine levavi animam meam*	1. *Ad te Domine animam meam levabo*
2. *Deus meus in te confido non erubescam*	2. *Deus meus in te confisus sum ne confundar*
3. *necque inrideant me inimici mei etenim universi qui sustinent te non confundentur*	3. *ne laetentur inimici mei sed et universi qui sperant in te non confundantur*
4. *confundantur omnes: iniqua agentes super vacue vias tuas Domine demonstra mihi et: semitas tuas doce me.*	4. *confundantur qui iniqua gerunt frustra vias tuas Domine ostende mihi semitas tuas doce me.*

The Latin Psalter concords with the Hexapla for the first two verses, but concludes verse 3, *qui expectant Domine non confundentur.* Verse 4 of the Latin Psalter ends, *vias tuas Domine notas fac mihi et emitas tuas edoce me.* (The beginning of this verse differs from the readings of both the *Hexapla* and the *Hebraeos*, but this section is not used as a text for chant.)

The earliest nearly complete textual version of the introit is preserved in the Corbie Gradual, Paris, Bibl. nat., MS lat. 12050, written some time after 850. There it is given as follows:

> *Ad te levavi animam meam Deus meus in te confido non erubescam neque irrideant me*
> *inimici mei etenim universi qui te expectant non confundentur.*
> PSALM: Vias tuas Domine notas fac mihi [. . .].

The still earlier sources of Hesbert's *Antiphonale Missarum Sextuplex* either omit the verse entirely or give only the first two or three words. The Corbie reading is the one employed in the modern editions issued by Solesmes. It is quickly apparent that the chant tradition is closer to the Latin Psalter than to either the *Hexapla* or the *Hebraeos*, but the derivation is not literal. The introit antiphon deletes the word *Domine* from the first verse. The psalm verse of the introit draws on the second half of verse 4. Here the chant text departs twice from the normative version of the Latin Psalter, although the version customarily used for the chant appears in each instance as a variant. The first of these variants involves the words, *demonstra mihi,* given in the Solesmes' reconstructions of the chant. Here the Latin Psalter normally presents *notas fac mihi,* but *demonstra mihi,* is given as a variant reading. A cursory survey indicates that while the musical sources generally employ *demonstra mihi,* the alternative, *notas fac mihi,* does appear, for example, in Benevento, Bibl. capitolare, MS VI.34. Various sources of the St. Gall tradition waver in the psalm verse between Jerome's *doce* and the more prevalent *edoce.* This latter reading is preferred in the Latin Psalter, although the former alternative appears as well.

In contrast to the introit, the offertory retains the word *Domine* as the third word, but it too employs *exspectant* (from the Latin Psalter) rather than *sustinent.* The gradual text begins in the middle of verse 3. We again find *exspectant,* as well as the *notas fac mihi.* Without complete critical editions of these chants we are unable to determine with assurance the extent to which the variants discussed are carried out with consistency in the musical sources of the Middle Ages and Early Renaissance. My own limited knowledge would indicate that changes are rare. This consistency is at least exhibited in various sixteenth-century editions, including the two that will serve as our representative samples. Nevertheless, we shall find that some of these small textual changes still occur among post-Tridentine sources. The *Missale Romanum* of 1570 continues to omit the word *Domine* from the introit antiphon and uses *demonstra mihi* for the psalm verse. On the other hand, this source uses *notas fac mihi* for the corresponding place in the gradual verse. Yet the example of the *Missale* is not followed universally. The offertory text is changed, deleting the customary *Domine,* thus bringing the introit and offertory texts into accord with one another. Again the musical sources do not conform uniformly with this precedent.

The Alleluia verse and the communion draw respectively on verses 8 and 13 of Psalm 84. The former passage reads the same in the Latin Psalter and in both of Jerome's translations as well: *Ostende nobis Domine misericordiam tuam et salutare tuum da nobis.* The chant tradition follows the textual tradition faithfully. With regard to verse 13, there are variants among Jerome's two translations. The version of the *Hexapla* reads, *Dominus dabit benignitatem et terra nostra dabit fructum suum.* This reading is found also in the Latin Psalter and this is the form of text employed in the Mass. The version *iuxta Hebraeos,* on the other hand reads, *Dominus dabit bonum et terra nostra dabit germen suum.*

Armed with the foregoing information, we may now consider the transmission of these chants at the turn of the seventeenth century and beyond. Although the introit, *Ad te levavi,* is not a complex chant, its medieval transmission is not as stable as that for *Puer natus.* There are two families of openings, one that begins on the final and another that begins a fourth below. Each family is further subdivisible, depending on the presence or absence of a descent from the initial tone within the first neume. With one exception, these subdivisions carry through to the seventeenth century and beyond. (See example 10.) The subfamily that descends a fourth from the final within the first neume has not yet been documented. However, both the Gradual issued by Piotrkowczyk in Kraków, 1600 (staff 1), and a distinctive *Graduale Bisuntinum* (=Besançon), edited by Jean Millet in 1682, use this descent at the beginning of the second neume. The former is one of three printed sources of "eastern" provenance to make use of *Hufnagelschrift.* An unusual symbol to be found in this source at the very opening of *Ad te levavi* consists of a pair of diamond-shaped notes at the unison, very closely spaced and connected by a loop with crossed ends at the bottom, loosely comparable in shape either to an inverted gamma or to the Aids ribbon. In the transcriptions this symbol is represented by two closely-spaced note heads bridged by an unbroken slur. All final notes in the Piotrkowczyk print are indicated by the normal diamond shape, followed closely with a heavy descending hook, shaped as a comma.

As a rule of thumb, westerly sources for *Ad te levavi* prefer to begin with the final, while easterly ones tend to begin on the lower fourth. However neither generality holds true uniformly. The opening on *c,* which occurs in the Tournai Gradual issued by the widow of Nicholas Laurent is unusual, but is evidently part of a Netherlandish tradition inasmuch as it appears four years later in the Belleros Gradual (staff i), and also in the slightly later Mommaert Gradual that appeared in Brussels.

The respect for prosodic values is much lower in the normative medieval reading for *Ad te levavi* than was the case for *Puer natus.* There are three instances (*meam, Deus,* and *confundentur*) where there are mismatches between tonic accent and stressed syllable, and another four to six in which the situation is at best neutral. There are six instances in which more tones are accorded to an unstressed syllable than to the one that bears the stress. Late editors will occasionally seek to reform this situation, but their attention to such matters is desultory. The Millange and Toul editions (see staff **g**) stand alone in their revision that allots 4+2 tones to the word *meam* (rather than the former 2+5); the Medicean Gradual (staff **f**) is equally isolated in assigning 1, 1, 5, 1 tones to the word *erubescam,* rather than 2, 4, 3, 1. It is likewise the only source to restrict the final syllable of *neque* to a single tone.

Nevertheless, a number of editors show awareness of prosodic values by assigning a single "semibreve" to unaccented antepenultimate syllables.

On the whole, there are few striking changes in melodic profile that arrest the ear and eye. It is unusual that the Giunta Gradual of 1596 (staff e) closes the penultimate segment (ending with the word *exspectant*) with *c′* rather than *a*, but this is a relatively minor matter. The variability of the tones setting the third syllable of *universi* is also worthy of passing mention. The Solesmes books give the normative medieval reading as *g–b–a–b*. However, the fourteenth-century Premonstratensian Gradual, Vienna, ÖNB 12865, specifies *b-flat* in this region of the chant. The *Graduale Pataviense* of 1511, on the other hand, indicates *b-natural*. The sources comprising our example lean markedly to *b-flat*, but there is no uniformity. Indeed, the *Graduale Herbipolense* (staff c) raises the sensitive pitch to *c′*.

Among the numerous minor variants, perhaps the most significant are those that mark the relative independence of the reading furnished in the Gradual of Cramoisy and Clopeiau (not shown in the example). Instead of following its French predecessors, the latter half of the chant accords quite closely with the readings of the two Netherlandish sources, issued by Laurent and Belleros in 1616 and 1620 respectively. This is another example of hybridization that one may encounter from time to time among seventeenth-century sources. A secure assessment of the extent of this phenomenon must await later studies that may build on this introduction. Worthy of remark is a four-note group setting the last syllable of *levavi*. This is a formulaic group consisting of a leap descending a third, a tonal repetition, and an upward step that is to be met time and again in the Cramoisy and Clopeiau source, one that influences other later French Graduals, including some from the Neo-Gallican orbit.

The gradual, *Universi qui te exspectant*, offers considerably greater insight into the nature of post-Tridentine editorial practices. The chant is classified in mode 1 by virtue of the range of the verse, which extends upward to *e′*. Nevertheless the respond opens with a gesture that descends forcefully into the range of mode 2. (See example 11.) This lack of tonal unity was viewed with disfavor, especially in Italy and a variety of solutions were provided for its avoidance. The descent forms part of a melisma of a dozen tones, and one will note that this melisma is cut in varying extents. The reading of the Medicean Gradual (staff f) provides for five pitches, while that of the Gardano print of 1591 (staff c) for only four, descending to the modal final only on the ensuing syllable. The most laconic versions are those of Giunta and successors, and these too do not descend to the modal final until the following word. In order to emphasize the centrality of the modal final, the opening subtonium is replaced by the final in the Medicean Gradual. This is a characteristic device employed by Anerio and Soriano and we will continue to encounter it on multiple occasions.

The most striking solution to the problem of unified modality is to be found in the Cistercian Gradual (staff m). The Cistercians employ a different opening entirely, one that forms a characteristic first-mode gesture to be found among numerous chants, including the introit, *Rorate caeli*, used also within Advent season. When, however, we proceed one step further, we are brought to the realization that we are not dealing with a post-Tridentine editorial decision but with one that goes back to medieval Cistercian revisions that were completed not later than 1190. This is demonstrated in our example by means of comparison with a late twelfth-century Cistercian Gradual from Morimondo, Paris, Bibl. nat., MS n.a. lat. 1414 (staff **n**). We find that the Cistercian print from Paris, brought out in 1696, does indeed incorporate post-Tridentine revisions. However, the opening one that captures our attention is not among these. We are provided with a vivid warning that our understanding of post-Tridentine practices will necessarily remain incomplete until such time as we have also grappled with the nature of the immediate precedents for these sources. It is necessary for us to acknowledge that at this time we have no broadly based history of Christian liturgical chant, and that it will require a long time, with efforts on the parts of many in order to achieve a basic amelioration of this situation.

Having begun by commenting on sensitivity to modal centricity, expressed in the reworking of the opening of *Universi*, we may transfer our attention to a striking modal problem that occurs at the end of the chant. *Universi* is, as we have already noted, a first-mode gradual. But it is not so treated with absolute uniformity. Example 11 provides one reading from the Giunta Gradual of 1596 (staff **d**) and another from the reading given by Baba in 1653 (staff **e**). (The latter form first occurs in the Ciera Gradual of 1618.) The two versions presented are remarkably close until we get to the final cadence, which is lacking the concluding *d* in the later print, a situation ostensibly comparable to one that will discussed with regard to the offertory, *Ad te Domine*. Surely—one would think—this must be an error. Hardly anything could be clearer! Alas, though this thought is beguiling, it is but a siren's song. Not only is this altered ending duplicated in later editions by Giunta, Ciera, Baba, Baglioni, and Pezzana, but when we reach a Turinese print of 1847 we find that the chant is assigned verbally to mode 3! This is passing strange indeed. Not only does the respond end on *d*, but the verse opens on the same note. And the skeleton tones of *d*, *f*, *a*, and *c'* play an important role in the verse. Moreover, there is very little, if anything, that would encourage one to predict an ending on *e*. Nevertheless, it is this ending that carries through among Venetian Graduals until 1779, and, as mentioned, is later specified in the Turinese print of 1847.

When discussing the text setting for the gradual, *Viderunt omnes*, I suggested that the relative numbers of tones accorded to final syllables may have been viewed as a means of setting the various words apart from one another. In this fashion they might be endowed with a slightly greater sense of unity than might otherwise have prevailed within a melismatic style. This hypothesis seems to fit well with the manner in which text is treated in the present gradual. In the respond, a melisma accompanies the last syllable of *exspectant, confundentur,* and *Domine*. In the verse, the same is true for *Domine, mihi,* as well as the final monosyllable, *me.* Melismas occur also on the accented syllables of *Universi* (respond), *semitas,* and *tuas.* On the whole, the various melismas are viewed with relative equanimity among the French, Netherlandish, and German sources. There are, however, notable exceptions to this rule of thumb. The readings provided in the Graduals from Tournai, Antwerp, and Brussels, issued by Laurent, Belleros (staff **h**), and Mommaert, respectively, agree in eliminating entirely the final melisma for the respond. They provide only one note each for the first two syllables of *Domine,* and a mere three for the last. All reform sources agree in reducing the very extensive melisma on the same word early in the verse. This having been said, with the exception of the Premonstratensian Gradual (staff **o**), the northerly sources are less heavy-handed in their cutting than their Italian counterparts. The same may be said for the treatment of the word, *mihi.* The Italian sources assign between 3–5 tones to this word, whereas the Graduals issued by Plantin and Angermaier (staff **i**) provide twenty-one. Other northern sources employ 10–13 tones, while the Premonstratensian Gradual (staff **o**) is again parsimonious with only eight. It is in the treatment of the melismas of the verse that the Cistercian Gradual of 1696 (staff **m**) diverges from the medieval tradition established by this Order.

Even though the melodic profiles remain reasonably firm among the various readings compared, the truncation of the melismas has marked effect on phrase shapes, particularly among Italian readings. The readings of Gardano, Giunta, and Baba terminate the word *Universi* on *f,* rather than on *d.* The latter two editions together with the Medicean Gradual end *Domine* (the third word of the verse) on *g* and *a,* respectively, rather than on *f.* And the Giunta and Baba editions also end *mihi* on *g* rather than *f.* They also end *tuas* on *e* and *f* rather than on *d.* Despite the overall consistency of profile, the curtailments have a marked effect on tonal organization.

Given our introductory comments regarding the texts for the introit, gradual, and offertory for the First Sunday of Advent, it is of interest to note that the Graduals by Laurent (1616), Belleros (1620), Mommaert (1623), and Angermaier (1618) begin the verse with the words, *Vias tua demonstra mihi.* They thus revert to the translation of Jerome after the Septuagint. (This is equal also to a variant reading of the Latin Psalter.) The use of this text form in the Angermaier Gradual (staff **i**) is surprising inasmuch as its parent source, the Plantin Gradual of 1599 (not given in the example), employs the opposite alternative. Nevertheless, the two musical readings remain extremely close to one another.[1] Since the three syllables of *demonstra* correspond to the three of *notas fac* in the standard Gregorian text, no musical change is required and none is present. The version of the Flandrus Gradual uses the standard Gregorian text, as does the one issued by Küchler. I have previously mentioned the relative distinctiveness of the *Graduale Bisuntinum,* edited by Jean Millet. This individuality is especially apparent in its treatment of *Universi,* not only at the end of the respond, but at many moments throughout the verse.

The observations that may be made regarding the *Alleluia Ostende nobis* fall into the patterns previously described, I shall present the musical account of selected readings with a minimum amount of commentary. (See example 12.) It is appropriate to draw attention to the retention in the Plantin, and Angermaier Graduals (staff **i**) of basically the entire melisma on the first syllable of *tuum*. No other reform sources do likewise, although the version presented by Piotrkowczyk (staff **k**) is fuller than most. Here and elsewhere there are seeming inconsistencies in the use of *b-flat*, and it is not always clear how these may best be resolved. The practice of using an abbreviated return to the opening Alleluia occurs earlier among Venetian sources than was the case with regard to the *Alleluia Dies sanctificatus*. It is present, as one can readily see, in the 1596 edition of Giunta (staff **e**). The texting of the jubilus to be sung by the chorus was described previously in connection with the *Alleluia Dies sanctificatus*.

The offertory, *Ad te Domine*, for the First Sunday in Advent is also among chants of moderately stable transmission. On staff **d** of example 13, I give the reading of the earliest of the so-called "reform" Graduals now documentable, that by Andrea Gabrieli and Orazio Vecchi brought out by Gardano in Venice in 1591. The omission of the word, *Domine* is immediately striking; this, however, is the textual form given in the *Missale Romanum* of 1570. Rather than bringing the text into conformity with the two translations by Jerome, the editorial revision distances itself from these prominent versions of the Psalter. We find instead conformity with the text of the introit. Notable also is the fact that the text does not remain consistent in subsequent publications. This situation is rare, but not unique, and the resultant cautionary flag may be salutary. We have noted word substitution in two readings of the gradual, *Universi*. And the offertory, *Dextera Domine*, inserts an additional phrase, the resultant text form being in closer conformity with the *Hexapla* of St. Jerome. (See the next chapter, example 38.) Glancing at the lower staves of example 13 you will quickly observe the multiplicity of ways in which different editors chose to deal with the melodic problems caused by the omission of the word. The Gardano setting (staff **d**) is quite faithful to the original melodic outline and is only slightly terser, most notably for the second syllable, *te*. The Giunta reading of *Ad te Domine*, (staff **e**) and one by Ciera from 1610 (not shown) are nearly identical. The retention of the word *Domine* is unusual among Graduals that present reformed readings.

The opening of the Medicean reading (staff **g**) is more compact than the other readings offered in this example. In general, however, the Medicean versions are less terse than those in Venetian Graduals. Comparing the latter with the other late readings given in our example shows the relative distinctiveness of this Roman Gradual. See, for example, the opening phrase, the first syllable of *animam* on the second page, the second syllable of *confido* on the third page, and so forth. This is a normal state of affairs and is more strongly marked in other chants. To reiterate, I have yet to observe any print before 1848 that presents readings identical or nearly identical to those of the Medicean Gradual.

We have noted that the Giunta reading of 1596 (staff **e**), which is retained in later editions of 1606 and 1618, is exceptional in its retention of the word, *Domine*. Exceptional too is the retention of two *binariae* for the setting of the unaccented third syllable of *irrideant* (see the fourth page of example 13). In contrast, the accented syllable previous is given but a single tone. These features were looked upon with increasing disfavor, and within three decades they caused a change in the Venetian tradition. If one examines the more modern version of *Ad te Domine*, after the 1629 Ciera Gradual (staff **f**), one will observe a very curious hybrid. The opening is clearly derived from the Medicean reading (staff **g**), while the second phrase, *Deus meus*, follows the earlier Giunta tradition. The setting of the word, *irrideant*, parallels the Medicean reading, while the passage beginning with the word *inimici* again returns to the Giunta tradition. The distribution of the tones setting the final word, *confundentur*, is individual even though the pitch content is standard. This version then becomes standard in the Venetian repertoire, recurring, for example, in Graduals by Giunta, Baba, and Baglioni in 1629, 1653, 1690, and 1725. It continues further with the editions of Pezzana that were published in 1730 and 1779.

The Toul and Parisian tradition for *Ad te Domine* is represented on staff **h**. Later printings by Belgrand were issued in 1633 and 1656. A 1635 print lacking its original title page is clearly part of this tradition, but apparently from a different press. There are further Parisian Graduals, and the tradition was known both in Lyons and Grenoble. The earlier French reading edited by Boni for Simon Millange in Bordeaux, 1598/99 is quite close to that given by Belgrand, with only a six variants of one tone each. On the other hand, the later *Graduale Bisuntinum* of 1682, already singled out as distinctive, departs from the main French tradition by retaining the word *Domine* and its associated melody. Millet, however, redistributes the tones so that the initial six are accorded to the accented opening syllable. The remainder of the first phrase continues to differ strikingly from other French readings. Nevertheless, the later phrases are in reasonably close accord with the main tradition.

Staves **i–k** present two Netherlandish versions published in Antwerp and a German reading issued in 1671 in Mainz. In keeping with the general tendency towards conservatism on the part of eastern sources, the Mainz Gradual retains the word, *Domine*. On the other hand, the much more easterly source from Kraków deletes the word in accordance with the reading of the Roman Missal of 1570. The reading given in the Flandrus Gradual (staff **l**) presents an unusual expansion of the melisma on the accented syllable of *levavi*. Also unexpected is the transposition of the chant to the upper fifth that marks the Premonstratensian reading given by Nivers (staff **o**). Despite the general prevalence of change, not all sources present reform readings. The Carthusian reading (staff **q**) conforms to earlier tradition for this Order, and a Benedictine manuscript version (staff **p**) is also conservative.

Essaying an overview of the late transmission of *Ad te Domine*, we may note that, with the exception of the changes brought about by the omission of the third word of the standard text, there is a fairly close resemblance among the various readings that were sampled. The general outline of the melody remains firm, and the pitch content of the cadence areas is for the most part transmitted faithfully. The Medicean Gradual furnishes a notable exception to this statement. The cadence tones for the phrase endings at *meam, erubescam, mei, exspectant,* are normally *d, f, c, A,* and *d.* The Medicean reading (staff **g**), on the other hand, has a single-minded focus on *d,* with the exception of the penultimate phrase, which terminates on *A.* The final, void square form given for the Giunta reading (staff **e**) represents a tone that is omitted in the source, but one which is supplied in the 1611 reading.

Earlier scholars have remarked on the humanists' demands for good prosody. Within limits, their observations are valid. It would be well, however, not to overemphasize the importance of this element. Flourishes on unaccented syllables continue to occur particularly on final syllables, not only in the conservative Bene-dictine and Carthusian readings, but also—though less frequently—among reform readings. That which stands out is an insistence that following an accented ante-penultimate or earlier syllable, the following syllable should bear but a single tone. More often than not, this tone will be presented as a "semibreve." Examples in *Ad te Domine,* include the treatment of *irrideant* and *etenim.*

The Premonstratensian reading for *Ad te levavi* (staff **o**) is unusual for more than one reason. As indicated previously, it is written a fifth higher than any of its coun-terparts examined here. This places the opening on *e* and the close on *a.* The 1718 edition of this Gradual, issued by Vigneulle in Verdun, is among those that provide modal assignments by means of numbers placed at the close of each chant. (These are not present in the edition of 1680.) It is startling to find that the editor takes the opening of the chant as indicative of mode and thus assigns it to mode 3. Indeed, this assignment is reasonably apt for the opening gesture, but conflicts begin to surface not too long thereafter. Not only is the close clearly in protus, but the placement of the final in the context of the overall range is strong evidence to show that we are dealing with a plagal chant rather than an authentic one. Plagal open-ings on the fourth below the final are quite frequent in Gregorian chant. We have already mentioned this form of opening in conjunction with Germanic sources for the introit of this Mass. *Ecce advenit* furnishes another example, and several more could be adduced were this necessary.

Just as the different reform Graduals vary in their attitudes towards modal centricity, so too do they vary with regard to their attitudes towards floridity and to prosody. It is quickly apparent that editorial pruning is heaviest among the editions of Giunta, Ciera, and their Venetian colleagues. The Medicean Gradual represents a middle stage, whereas Graduals from more northerly areas generally retain more of the medieval flourishes even though these may be redistributed among the sylla-bles. This finding runs directly counter to the popular notion of the exuberant nature of Mediterranean melody and the stolid, simple nature of Germanic singing.

None of the foregoing examples is ideal to demonstrate the ultimate effect of the newer, terser style. As indicated elsewhere, especially with regard to the discussion of *Ex Sion species* in the next chapter, much more is involved than the deletion of a few or even many notes here or there. The building blocks of medieval Gregorian melodies consist of formulas, and these formulas find their most vivid expression in richly neumatic or melismatic passages rather than in syllabic or nearly syllabic passages. And it is these formulas that served as *aide-mémoires* for the largely oral culture in which they arose. By pruning the formulas in many *different* ways, the Baroque chant editors were eliminating an essential support for the singers' memories. As mentioned previously in connection with the discussion of the *Alleluia Dies sanctificatus,* I suggest that we have here a gradual transfer to a culture that was governed more and more by reading. This postulated change went hand in hand with a changed readership. A pious family might not have had a keyboard instrument available and might not have been able to assemble a string quartet for an evening's entertainment, but it was possible to sit around a table and sing Gregorian chant, an occupation that seemed more edifying to many. Whereas most early prints are of large format and are clearly designed for use in the liturgy itself, by the mid-eighteenth century we have the emergence of pocket-sized books that are specifically designed for the musical amateur. A 1756 Gradual by Beekman issued in Amsterdam declares itself to be one such, and its appearance was prompted by the success of an earlier print of 1750. Some of the very small manuscript Graduals of the sixteenth and seventeenth centuries might have been designed for similar purposes.

The transmission of the brief communion, *Dominus dabit benignitatem,* is instructive primarily with regard to details. (See example 14.) In its normative medieval form, as given in the *Graduale Triplex,* the chant is not punctilious with regard to prosody. Of the eight polysyllabic words in the text, three (the first two and the penultimate) have sustaining and tonic emphases on weak final syllables. These mismatches are dealt with in a variety of ways; and no two of the examples illustrated are identical. The Gardano print of 1591 (staff **d**) takes the first two of the three tones for the second syllable in the normative medieval version and sets these to the opening syllable. This leaves a single tone for the second syllable. The small melisma for the final syllable is shortened slightly, but eight tones nevertheless remain. The Giunta print of 1596 (staff **e**), on the other hand, transfers the material for the second syllable in the normative medieval version to the first syllable, and, from the material associated with the final syllable, selects two tones for each of the following two syllables. This solution continues to be employed by its immediate successors. In each instance the first sub-phrase closes on the final rather than on the sub-final, a solution followed by three other prints. Later Venetian Graduals, such as the one issued by Baba in 1653 (staff **f**) and that brought out by Baglioni in 1690, carry the revision further. They group the first five tones together for the initial syllable and apportion the following two among the remaining syllables. An even more extensive revision is undertaken in the version of the Medicean Gradual (staff **g**), which places the opening on the fifth degree rather than on the third.

The entire melodic weight rests on the initial accented syllable, which receives eight tones while each of the two remaining syllables receives only one tone each.

The northern readings to be considered also insist on limiting the second syllable of *Dominus* to a single tone. However, they do not mind closing with a flourish on the unaccented final. This melisma encompasses eight tones in the normative French readings (staff **h**), but eleven in the reading provided by Plantin in 1599 (staff **j**), and a full thirteen in the reading by Laurent, Belleros (staff **i**), and Mommaert, from Tournai, Antwerp, and Brussels, respectively. The Premonstratensian reading (staff **o**) is the most unusual in that it reapportions tones between the last syllable of *Dominus* and the opening syllable of the word following. Thus it ends the first word with a rather brief melisma of five tones, terminating on the third degree of the mode. The remaining tones serve to emphasize the first syllable of *dabit*, continuing the descent down to the sub-final before turning upward. One finds too that by means of minimal changes the Giunta, Medicean, and Millange prints alter the placement of the melodic stress for the word *dabit*.

One might think that there was little in the medieval setting of the word *benignitatem* to have caused offense to the Baroque editors of chant. The accented syllable receives both a tonic and a sustaining accent, and the sub-phrase is modally stable, including the entire modal octave, with suitable use of the final, third, fifth and upper octave. Nevertheless, most of the late readings presented here differ from one another in both subtle and not so subtle ways. The readings of Giunta and his followers (staves **e**, **f**) choose to simplify the passage. The later Venetian readings rise only to the upper fifth, while the earlier ones ascend one tone higher. Furthermore, both traditions are sensitive to the secondary accent that falls on the second syllable. Rather than apportioning one tone to this syllable and two to the unaccented syllable following, they reverse this assignment, allotting two tones to the secondary accent and one to the syllable following. The Piotrkowczyk Gradual of 1600 (staff **m**) and the Premonstratensian Gradual of 1680 (staff **o**) give the greatest emphasis to the secondary text accent by assigning it three tones. The varying number of tones assigned to the final syllable of the word seems to reflect differences that trace back to the late medieval-Renaissance tradition, as shown in the reading of the Liechtenstein print. seems to reflect differences that trace back to the late medieval-Renaissance tradition, as shown in the reading of the Liechtenstein print.

The distribution of melodic material among the Italian readings serves to heighten the importance of the first syllable of *dabit* in the last phrase. And the Venetian prints accord much greater prominence to the opening syllable of the final word than do the others. Despite the fact that the essential melody is seldom much changed, considerable variety is achieved within fairly limited scope.

The treatment of the post-Tridentine transmission of *Dominus dabit benignitatem* has completed our survey of the chants constituting the Mass for the First Sunday of Advent. It may seem abrupt to terminate discussion at this point, but my major conclusions have been stated earlier where they seemed most appropriate. The main purpose of each chapter is to enable the reader to achieve a certain degree of familiarity with the pertinent repertoire. Any worthwhile understanding of and empathy for these chants rests on such familiarity, and this in turn requires coming to terms with the details that have been supplied.

FIVE

The Second Sunday of Advent

The text for the introit antiphon for the Second Sunday of Advent derives in part from the Book of Isaiah, but the derivation is more distant from the version of the Vulgate than is that for the introit for the Third Mass of Christmas. The opening words, *Populous Sion*, are reminiscent of the *Populous enim Sion* that opens verse 19 of chapter 30, but the texts diverge immediately thereafter. The middle portion is more clearly derived from verse 30 of the same Book, *et auditam faciet Dominus gloriam vocis suae*. But again the texts diverge thereafter. The text for the psalm verse, on the other hand, is clearly taken from the first half of the opening verse of Psalm 79 in the version of the Roman Psalter and the *Hexapla*. The textual differences between the Vulgate and the chant text are as follows:

Vulgate	Chant
Populous enim Sion habitabit in Hierusalem plorans nequaquam plorabis miserans . . .	*Populus Sion, ecce Dominus veniet ad salvandas gentes:*
et auditam faciet Dominus gloriam vocis suae et terrorem brachii sui ostendet . . .	*et auditam faciet Dominus gloriam vocis suae, in laetitia cordis vestri.*

A search in a standard Biblical concordance for those portions of the chant text that have no equivalent in the passages quoted from Isaiah proved fruitless. Apparently these additions were created by the early chant editors.

The medieval transmission of *Populous Sion* is diffuse, and this lack of uniformity is germane to our understanding of the readings from the late sixteenth century and thereafter. The notational problems posed by this chant and the various kinds of solutions were outlined in moderate detail elsewhere,[1] and still other multiple readings of the chant were presented earlier by both Delalande[2] and Van der Werf.[3] While the antiphon clearly closes in the tetrardus maneria, it apparently opened in protus. We find that in the initial portion of the melody, some sources use c' for brief recitations and cadence on g, while others use d' as the reciting tone and cadence on a. The first group normally makes frequent use of *b-flat*, so that the ascending tetrachord, g–a–b-*flat*–c' is equivalent to the alternative a–b–c'–d'. As a result, the group reciting on d' has a different tonal focus for each half of the chant, while the group reciting on c' maintains the same tonal focus throughout. The modern reading presented in the Solesmes editions employs a recitation on c', and maintains a uniform tonal reference on g. There is a secondary variant as well. Many sources begin directly on the reciting tone (usually c'), while others (usually reciting on d') begin on the modal final. This latter beginning is apparently attested to by the neumations of our earliest sources, including Chartres, Bibl. mun., 47; Laon, Bibl. mun., 239; and Einsiedeln, Stiftsbibl., MS 121 (together with other sources of the St. Gall orbit). The opening at a higher level appears as early as the eleventh century in the famous bilingual manuscript, Montpellier, Fac. méd., H. 159.

The two primary families of medieval readings continue on into the seventeenth century and beyond. (See example 15.) The Venetian editions, beginning with Gardano (staff **d**) and continuing with Giunta and his successors (staves **e**, **f**), all opt to place the brief recitations on c'. They are joined by the Medicean Gradual of 1614 (staff **g**), the Plantin Gradual of 1599 (staff **j**)—and thus the Angermaier print of 1618—the Flandrus Gradual of 1597 (staff **m**), and the Premonstratensian Gradual of 1680 (staff **o**). Recitations on d', on the other hand, are employed in the normative French tradition begun by Boni in 1599, in the Polish print by Piotrkowczyk in 1600 (staff **l**), in the Netherlandish prints by Laurent, Belleros (staff **i**), and Mommaert, in the edition of Küchler (staff **k**), and in the readings of the Cistercian, Carthusian, and Benedictine Orders (staves **n**, **p**, and **q**, resp.). The normative French readings, together with the Netherlandish group just mentioned, and those from the Cistercian, Carthusian, and Premonstratensian orders begin on the reciting pitch, whereas the remainder approach this pitch by means of a leap from below.

Even if the broad outlines of the melody remain easily recognizable in late sources, one may find significant changes of detail that affect the tonal order of the piece. In the first place, written indications of *b-flat* virtually disappear, although they still occur in the *Graduale Herbipolense* of 1583 (staff **c**). The use of *b-flat* may be obviated by transpositions of a whole tone that maintain the same local succession of intervals, but this is accomplished at the cost of changed relationships to the eventual final. Secondly, the use of a as a tonal reference is sharply restricted. In our main example, it appears as a cadential tone for the word *gentes* only in the readings provided by Küchler (staff **k**), Piotrkowczyk (staff **l**), and the Carthusians (staff **p**). It is to be found also in the *Graduale Bisuntinum*, edited by Millet, who asserts a certain independence from the main French tradition. This is shown in example 16, which compares six French readings, demonstrating the individuality of two of the number and the overall consistency of the tradition, documenting its spread to Lyon and Grenoble.

Despite the lack of truly marked departures from sixteenth-century antecedents, large-scale identities among readings from different traditions are lacking. Many of the small-scale differences revolve about concerns for details of prosody. Only uneven attention is given to prosody in the normative medieval version of *Populous Sion*. On the whole, the melodic shape reflects well the placement of textual accents. Of the sixteen polysyllabic words, twelve find a positive correlation between tonic accent and syllabic stress. Two instances are neutral and two (*gloriam, laetitia*) provide mismatches. The correlation between syllabic stresses and "sustaining" musical accents is less consistent. There are five mismatches and one neutral case.

In one instance the mismatch between the syllable bearing the textual stress and the one bearing the greater number of notes is trifling, and this instance is ignored more often than not. In the normative medieval version, two tones are assigned to the accented syllable of *Sion*, and three are given to the unaccented syllable following. This distinction was an irritant to both Italian and French editors. The two syllables are each given three tones in the reading by Gardano (staff **d**), three and two in the reading by Millange and his successors in Toul (staff **h**) and Paris, four and one in the version proposed by Giunta (staff **e**), and a still more striking five and two in the Medicean Gradual (staff **f**). On the other hand, the medieval reading was perfectly acceptable to Piotrkowczyk (staff **l**), Ciera (staff **f**), Flandrus (staff **m**), Plantin and Angermaier (staff **j**), Belleros (staff **i**), the Cistercians (staff **n**), and the Premonstratensians (staff **o**).

The remaining instances prompting revisions all involve accented antepenultimate syllables: *veniet, Dominus* (two appearances), *gloriam,* and *laetitia.* The normative medieval reading for the first of these words allows four tones for the second syllable. With the exception of the readings provided by Gardano (staff **d**) and Küchler (staff **k**), all other reforming Graduals allow only one tone for this syllable.

The treatment of *Dominus* is more varied. In the second appearance of this word in the normative medieval version and in the versions of Liechtenstein (staff **b**) and the *Graduale Herbipolense* (staff **c**), the three syllables are assigned two, three, and five tones respectively. With the exception of the Küchler Gradual of 1671 (staff **k**), the remaining reforming Graduals agree that the second syllable is to have no more than a single tone. They vary, however, in their choice of this tone. The Gardano, Medicean, Plantin and Angermaier, Piotrkowczyk, and Cistercian Graduals place this tone on *d'*, while the Graduals by Giunta and his successors (staves **e, f**), together with the Belleros (staff **i**) and Premonstratensian Graduals (staff **o**) employ *c'*. The normative French Graduals first edited by Boni employ *a*, although the Rigoine Gradual edited by Millet and the one issued by Cramoisy and Clopeiau use *d'*. These different solutions merely represent alternative choices from the array of tones present in the medieval version; they do not depart fundamentally from the medieval profile. No fewer than six different solutions are found for the final syllable. The Graduals issued by the firm of Plantin (staff **j**), the Cistercians (staff **n**), and the Premonstratensians (staff **o**) reduce the number of tones from five to four by eliminating the first of the tones employed in the medieval version. The Graduals by Gardano (staff **d**) and Belleros (staff **i**), on the other hand, reduce the number of tones to three by eliminating the first two tones of the medieval version. The Medicean version (staff **g**) eliminates the last of these tones and thus terminates the word on *c'*. The version begun by Giunta and continued by later Venetian publishers (staves **e**, **f**), eliminates in addition the antepenultimate tone of the medieval version and thus ends on *d'*. The Boni reading also assigns only a single tone to the final syllable, but this tone is the last tone of the medieval version and of those post-Tridentine readings that employ either four or three tones. The reading of the *Graduale Bisuntinum* again demonstrates its independence from the main tradition. Millet employs the solution adopted by Gardano, Küchler, and Piotrkowczyk, closing with three tones.

The following word, *gloriam*, is also subjected to a variety of treatments. In its normative medieval guise, the three syllables are assigned 3, 5, and 2 tones (the last ending with a liquescent). Again it was deemed essential that the second syllable receive no more than one tone. This was accomplished variously. The Gardano (staff **d**) reading eliminates the tonal repetition on *e'* and joins the four tones following to the three normally associated with the first syllable. This leaves the tone *d'* for the second syllable, and this *d'* is then repeated for the final syllable. The versions of the Graduals issued by the Giunta (staff **e**) and Medicean (staff **g**) presses simply delete the five tones assigned at earlier date to the second syllable and use the single pitches *d'*, *c'* for the last two syllables. The readings of the normative French group (staff **h**) expand the basic medieval profile by beginning with an upper neighbor motion from *c'* and returning before continuing with the ascent to *f'*. The melody then turns downward, has a single *d'* on the sensitive second syllable, and ends with an upward movement equivalent to the medieval liquescent on the final syllable. The Belleros reading (staff **i**) is unusual in it assigns four tones to the final syllable while still retaining the same general profile. These four tones correspond to the last four assigned to the previous syllable in the medieval reading.

The situation is reasonably comparable with regard to the treatment of the word *laetitia*. Again there is a consistent determination that the unaccented antepenultimate is to receive no more than one tone. A variety of means are employed to accomplish this. There is a notable difference between the Italian and northern versions in that the former insist on a single tone for the unaccented final. The northern readings, on the hand, see no drawback to allowing this syllable a full allotment of four tones. The simple lesson to be learned from all of the foregoing detail is that there was considerable independence afforded to chant editors of the very late sixteenth and seventeenth centuries. While we can discern general sets of values, these find numerous individual forms of expression.

The gradual for the Second Sunday of Advent is *Ex Sion species*. The text for the respond is taken from Psalm 49, verse 2 and the first part of verse 3. It corresponds both to one of the variant versions of the Roman Psalter and to Jerome's translation from the Septuagint. The text for the verse is taken from verse 5 of the same psalm. The verb form, *ordinaverunt*, is characteristic of the Roman Psalter; whereas the *Hexapla* uses the form, *ordinant*. The melody, one of a very large group of fifth-mode graduals, seems on cursory examination to have had a fairly stable medieval transmission.

Ex Sion is more prolix than either *Viderunt omnes* or *Universi*, the first two graduals that we have studied to this point. The melody sets no fewer than fourteen syllables with flourishes of between seven and thirty-six tones each. (See example 17.) The two largest are to be found in the verse, where, in the normative medieval version, thirty-six tones are assigned to the accented syllable of *Congregate* and thirty-five are assigned to the final, unaccented syllable of *ordinaverunt*. These, as well as the smaller melismas, presented diverse challenges for the post-Tridentine chant editors.

The study of these readings warns us against the dangers of too rapid conclusions based on small samplings of evidence. And this warning recurs frequently. Depending on what is studied, the Gardano Gradual of 1591 seems to disappear without any progeny. Yet the ending of the Gardano reading (staff **d**) is to be found also in the Toul Graduals issued by Belgrand (staff **g**). The identity is sufficiently distinctive that it causes us to recall the similar identity of the earlier, incomplete close on *eius*, and thus to review the entire melody in these sources. We find to our surprise that, with the exception of the omission of one tone in the verse, the readings are identical.

The readings of the sum total of sources investigated for *Ex Sion* are sufficiently varied that this identity can hardly be ascribed to chance. Apparently the version of the Gardano print was known in France and had won sufficient approval there to be taken over in its entirety. It continues to recur among Parisian Graduals as late as the Christophe Ballard print of 1734. With two minor variants it appears in the Paris, 1668 Gradual by La Caille. Moreover, this reading is to be found in Lyonnaise Graduals of 1690 and 1724, and it is documentable in a Gradual of 1730 from Grenoble. The demonstrable importance of this version notwithstanding, we do find at least one alternative to the Gardano melody in the Parisian Gradual issued by Cramoisy and Clopeiau in 1662 (not given in example 17.). There is a notable difference in the final cadence for the respond. In the Gardano reading, only a single tone is assigned to the last syllable of *veniet*. In contradistinction, the Cramoisy and Clopeiau reading provides for a flourish of eleven tones, comparable to the cadences appearing on staves **k** and **l**. The reading employed in this source is closer to that given in the later Cistercian Gradual of 1696 even though the final cadences vary. (This cadence is more closely akin to the still later Premonstratensian Gradual of 1718 than to any other.) It is difficult—perhaps impossible—to ascertain why only this one chant should have crossed international boundaries and spread in different locales in France. One would suppose that other melodies from the 1591 Gardano print were also known outside of Venice. But, as already mentioned, in the few dozen examples forming the basis for this study no comparable example has surfaced.

In the same vein, one finds that the reading of the Küchler Gradual of 1671 (staff **k**) for *Ex Sion species* is identical in pitch with the reading found in the Flandrus Gradual of 1597 (staff **j**). This information might suggest the conclusion that Juan Flamenco drew on sources from the general Rhine region that were available also to Küchler. Such a conclusion, however, rests on a shaky foundation unless one were to discover other striking resemblances between the two sources.

Before going on to consider further the transmission of *Ex Sion species* in its entirety, I shall take a lengthy excursus to examine the broader contexts relating to several individual readings. The graduals of mode five vary considerably in the density of their formulaic usage. *Ex Sion species* and *Viderunt omnes* are among those that are less dependent than average upon strict formulas. (The same may be said of the first-mode gradual, *Universi*.) Whereas *Ex Sion* contains a number of small melodicles—e.g., c' $c'–a$, c' $c'–a$ or the triadic rise from f to c'—that may be found in other chants of the same genre, only twice do these coalesce into larger formulas. The more interesting of the two occurs on the consecutive melismas setting the word, [*testamentum*] *eius*. In the Solesmes readings this combination occurs identically in the gradual, *Misit Dominus*, for the Second Sunday after Epiphany, in conjunction with the same word [*misericordiae*] *eius*.[4] This and additional comparisons are given in example 18 (see staff **a**). The first portion recurs also in *Ad Dominum* (staff **b**), and in *Respice, Domine* on the words, *labiis* and *judica*, respectively (staves **c**, **d**). In both instances, the continuations vary from each other and from *Ex Sion* and *Misit Dominus*. The use of the first portion of the formula in *Respice, Domine* is of special interest because it recurs almost immediately following its first appearance, this time in the middle of a long melisma on the first syllable of *causam*.

Alerted to the fact that the formula may occur in the middle of a long melisma, we can find still other instances of its presence in *Viderunt omnes* (staff **g**), *Quis sicut* (staff **e**), *Omnes de Saba* (staff **f**), and *Qui operatus* (staff **h**). The second and third of these citations are identical, while the first and fourth are individual in their later portions. (In *Omnes de Saba* the formula enters in the middle of a melisma on the accented fourth syllable of *illuminare*, not shown in the example.) This latter group of four is distinguishable from the first in that it lacks the quilisma in the rise from f to c', as shown in the following example. *Omnes de Saba* is individual in that it has a second statement of the formula that is expanded by a very small interior recitation. Were it not for the insertion of two tonal repetitions, this statement would be identical to that contained in *Viderunt omnes*. We find a verbal link that prompts this memory cue. The text in the Christmas gradual employs the word *Dominus,* while that for the gradual for Epiphany use a different case for the word *Domini.*

The Italian post-Tridentine readings for *Ex Sion* are terser than those from the north. Owing to the very heavy cuts in the melismas, the formulas disappear in both the Venetian and Roman readings, and no new formulas take their place. Consider, for example, the readings of the Gardano Gradual of 1591, shown in example 19. Within the first group of citations given above, hints of the erstwhile medieval formula are observable only in *Ex Sion species* (staff **a**) and in *Ad Dominum* (staff **c**). Even here the allusions are vague. If we did not already know the medieval antecedents, I doubt that we would think of associating these passages with one another. When examining the second group of four graduals we observe a situation that is not too different. The first statement of the formula in *Omnes de Saba* (staff **g**) strongly recalls its medieval antecedent, and this is unusual. However, the near identity with the passage from *Viderunt omnes* has vanished entirely. Gone too is the medieval identity between passages in *Quis sicut* and *Omnes de Saba.* As shown on staff **e**, the former begins on the upper fifth, and has only three tones for the entire final syllable of *Suscitans.* If an analog is to be found in the medieval version, it consists of the sixth to the fourth tones before the melisma's end. In *Qui operatus* (staff **i**), the melisma on the opening syllable of *Dei* corresponds basically to the last portion of the medieval melisma. However, the opening portion, which concerns us most at this point, has been excised.

It is not possible to describe in a few words the formulaic structures of the Giunta Graduals and their successors. The Venetian tradition is a variable one. In the edition of 1596, traces of the original formulas have already disappeared in several instances. (See example 20.) The reading of *Ex Sion* (staff **a**) contains a very brief hint of the medieval formula; depending on the framework of comparison this consists of either two or four notes. There is not much else. There is no comparable segment in *Misit Dominus* (staff **b**); the former identity has vanished entirely. Not shown in the example is the treatment of the melisma on the first syllable of [*sanavit*] *eos* in the respond. In the medieval tradition this syllable is accompanied by a melisma that begins in identical fashion to the one of concern here, becomes looser in resemblance, and, after fifteen tones, becomes unique. In the Giunta reading of 1596 (and also 1606), the former melisma is restricted to two tones, b–c'. In *Ad Dominum* (staff **c**), a few internal tones from the medieval melisma have been transferred back to the previous syllable, and only the last two remain for the opening syllable of *labiis.* The four tones constituting the setting of this word are employed in the 1606 edition of *Quis sicut* for the setting of *Suscitans* (staff **e**), providing a momentary parallel where none had existed before. But the parallel is so brief and its character so loosely defined that it lacks musical force.

The situation is not different in the readings of the Giunta Gradual of 1606, as indicated by the variants given in example 20.[5] If anything, it is exacerbated. As before, the reading of *Ex Sion* contains a very brief hint of the medieval formula, but not much else. There is no comparable segment in *Misit Dominus*. Where the medieval identity had existed, we find an equally terse segment that begins on the fifth degree, leaps up to the seventh, and then turns downward. In *Ad Dominum*, reference to the opening of the medieval formula has been transferred to the previous monosyllable, and the textual counterpart begins with the decoration of the fifth degree. As noted previously, we may see a connection between this segment and comparable passages in *Quis sicut*, and *Respice, Domine* but these bits are so brief and their character so loosely defined that the resemblances could easily pass unnoticed. The same is true of the segment from *Qui operatus* (staff **i**), which is so brief that I have here expanded the preceding context. The first of the passages from *Omnes de Saba* (staff **g**) consists of only three or four notes, quite insufficient to recall the breadth of the medieval formula. And while the second is far more reminiscent of its medieval antecedent, its strength is sapped in the modification given in the issue of 1606. Further revision of *Viderunt omnes* (staff **h**) removes not only the greater part of the medieval formula, but it destroys the near identity that had once prevailed between the relevant segment and its counterpart in *Omnes de Saba*. (The passage is so brief that I am able to give the 1596 reading first, followed by the even terser version of 1606.) We have an extraordinary opportunity to witness the further dissolution of the formulaic nexus within a period of scarcely more than a decade.

These readings continue to recur in the large number of Venetian Graduals issued by the firms of Giunta, Ciera, Baba, Baglioni (Balleoni), and Pezzana through the remainder of the seventeenth and eighteenth centuries, but it is not sufficiently germane to our purpose to trace each of these out in detail.

With the reader's indulgence I intend to continue to pursue our current path with an examination of the readings from the Medicean Gradual. (See example 21.) I am trying to demonstrate that we are dealing with a general practice observed in the revising process and not with a momentary editorial aberration. The excisions to be observed in this source are not as severe as those initiated by the Giunta press, but they are considerable nevertheless. The Medicean Gradual does not duplicate either the opening or succeeding melisma from the medieval version of *Ex Sion*, but does provide a reasonable summary, reorganizing the distribution of tones so that only one is accorded to the final syllable (staff **a**). We have a central tonal axis formed by the third degree, which is used both at the beginning and end. This would have worked equally well for *Misit Dominus*. Instead we find a different passage that circles around the fifth degree and descends to the final (staff **b**). In the corresponding passage in *Ad Dominum* we find hints of the original medieval formula, but in abbreviated form (staff **c**). The broad melisma on the second syllable of *iniquis* is condensed in such fashion that a different overall tonal shape emerges. Neither of the two melismas in *Respice, Domine* (following one another without interruption on staff **d** in example 21) nor the one in *Quis sicut* (staff **e**) survives in anything approaching its original form. On the other hand, we catch glimpses of the medieval antecedents in the two relevant segments from *Omnes de Saba* (staves **f**, **g**). The first of these, however, does not form an identity with what had been a comparable passage from *Quis sicut*. Similarly, the second does not form a near identity with what had been an equivalent passage in *Viderunt omnes* (staff **h**). Lastly, the passage from *Qui operatus* (staff **i**) has been reworked to such an extent that it bears little resemblance either to its fellows or to its medieval antecedent.

When we turn to the reform Graduals issued north of the Alps we find a contrasting situation. The Netherlandish, German, and French editors revised chant, but were less hostile to melismatic flourishes and permitted several to survive only lightly modified. Although the details of construction in the readings of the Gradual issued by the Plantin press in 1599, contrast with those from Italian sources, the general results remain similar. (See example 22.) The version of the compound formula in *Ex Sion* (staff **a**) is similar to that present the medieval tradition. It is unexpected, however, to find that the relationship between text and music has seemingly been altered in such fashion that much less emphasis is accorded to the accented initial syllable and much more is placed on the unaccented final. Furthermore, the conclusion of the second half has an added tone, g, not present in the medieval reading. Matters become still stranger when one examines what had formerly been the identical passage in *Misit Dominus* (staff **b**). Here the initial syllable of *ejus* has been transferred to a much earlier point in the melody. Indeed the transfer is so considerable that in the source the syllable is on the staff previous to the one on which it would be expected. The second syllable occurs only slightly earlier than it had in the normative medieval reading, but this latter placement corresponds to what had been the middle of a "neume" in the Plantin reading of *Ex Sion*. On the other hand, the placement of the comparable melisma in the respond, associated with the first syllable of [*sanavit*] *eos*, remains consistent with medieval practice. It is necessary to consider the disturbing possibility that the syllable underlay in neither *Ex Sion* nor *Misit Dominus* corresponded to the actual performance practice followed by those using this edition. These persons might simply have used their sense of propriety when singing these chants. It is possible to demonstrate that the concern for the "coupures" shaping neumes during the Middle Ages was at a particularly low ebb among printed sources of the seventeenth and eighteenth centuries, that what had once been a single neume could be cut at a line ending, with the remnant spilling over to the next line. But if indeed the modern scholar may not put any trust in the alignment between syllable and tone, we are in a parlous state indeed. The question indeed needs to be raised, but I would be very hesitant at this stage of our knowledge to give free rein to twenty-first-century editorial revisions.

The similarity between the Plantin reading of *Ad Dominum* (staff **c**) and the normative medieval version is immediately apparent, as is that between the first of the two excerpts from *Respice, Domine* (staff **d**) and its medieval counterpart. In the Angermaier reading for the first excerpt from *Respice Domine*—not shown in the example—one finds an unusual upward leap of a fourth—ostensibly augmented—from the second to third tones. Here I strongly suspect the presence of an error despite the fact that one finds a comparable leap in the midst of the melisma on the last syllable of *Suscitans* from *Quis sicut*. (With the exception of these two tones, the Angermaier pitches remain the same as those in the Plantin model.) Apart from the omission of two tones, the opening of the first of the two excerpts from *Omnes de Saba* (staff **g**) is very nearly the same as that from *Respice, Domine*. Furthermore, the relationship between the second of the two excerpts (staff **h**) and its counterpart from *Viderunt omnes* (staff **i**) is stronger than previously seen. Again we find a few tones lacking from the latter chant. In a similar vein, we find a readily discernible relationship between the melisma from *Qui operatus* and the remainder of the family. It would appear that the Plantin Gradual goes to greater lengths than any other edition of its time in preserving the essence of formulaic construction. This notwithstanding, the medieval versions are still stronger in this aspect.

The second of the Netherlandish sources now accessible is the Gradual issued by the widow of Nicholas Laurent in Tournai in 1616. Here we find the original pair of melismas from *Ex Sion* with comparatively minor changes. (See example 23, staff **a**.) The first five tones of the normative medieval reading remain untouched, but the following clivis is eliminated. The rise from the second to the sixth degree remains even though shorn of an interior quilisma and a final liquescent. The second half would be identical were it not for the omission of the sixth tone, a passing note on c'. Nevertheless, the comparable passage in *Misit Dominus* (staff **b**) is no longer identical. The opening melisma has been reduced from nine notes to six, with a resultant modification of the gesture. And, somewhat to one's surprise, two notes have been added to the closing melisma on the unaccented second syllable. The nine notes of the comparable passage in *Ad Dominum* (staff **c**) are identical to those in *Ex Sion* even though the neumation is somewhat different. The first counterpart in *Respice, Domine* is also identical, although the continuation is modified. However, the second counterpart is less easily recognizable. The equivalent passage from *Qui operatus* (staff **j**) is reworked to an even greater extent. On the other hand, the two segments from *Omnes de Saba* (staves **g**, **h**) are again clearly related to their medieval antecedents, the second particularly so. Nevertheless, the near identity that had formerly prevailed in the medieval tradition between this passage and one in *Viderunt omnes* (staff **i**) is curtailed and only the final halves remain the same as each other. The descent from the third to the final that had characterized the melisma on the first syllable of *Dei* in *Qui operatus* (staff **j**) has been excised from the seventeenth-century reading, and only the final portion corresponds closely to its medieval antecedent. Surveying the total, we find that there are significant remnants of formulaic construction, but these are nevertheless lacking the full measure of strength that they had possessed within the medieval tradition.

The last of the "northern" Graduals to be explored is taken from a late representative of the French tradition begun by Millange in Bordeaux and continued in Toul and Paris. (See example 24, taken from a mid-seventeenth-century print from Paris.) The excerpt from *Ex Sion* that has provided the point of departure for this entire section is given in our print (staff **a**) deprived of the first five tones from the medieval reading, an excision characteristic of the French tradition as a whole. The remainder continues in basically the same way as the normative medieval reading. Curiously enough, the reading for *Misit Dominus* (staff **b**) is unaffected by the excision that distinguishes the late version of *Ex Sion* and presents the medieval version in full, adding to it a final repetitive clivis. Examining the remaining excerpts shown in this example we observe a variable response to the medieval formulaic nexus. The segment from *Ad Dominum* (staff **c**) remains quite close to the normative medieval reading, while the continuation of the passage considerably shortens the melisma following and provides a tighter sequential organization. The segment from *Respice, Domine* largely eliminates the opening portion of the formula while providing a simplified account of the remainder (staff **d**). The major cuts for the ensuing section eliminate entirely the second statement of the formula. The first of the two passages from *Omnes de Saba* (staff **f**) presents a simplified, though readily recognizable account of the formula, while the second (staff **g**) is closer still to its medieval antecedent. On the other hand, the reference to the formula in *Viderunt omnes* (staff **h**) is almost entirely eliminated.

Surveying the last group of three examples, we note that in the Plantin readings the formulaic nexus survives in a slightly weakened form. In the other two northern traditions—that of Tournai-Antwerp-Brussels and that of Paris—the nexus, while still identifiable, has suffered noticeable losses. In the three Italian Graduals, only sporadic glimpses of the previous formulaic structures are still present.

The evidence that has been gathered to this point regarding formulaic construction in the post-Tridentine Mass Proper has included two of the genres most heavily affected, the Alleluia and the gradual. When examining the *Alleluia Dies sanctificatus* together with the Advent members of its melodic family, as well as *Ex Sion* species, *Viderunt omnes*, and related fifth-mode graduals, we find a strong reason to conclude that the process of revision proceeded primarily on a chant-by-chant basis, without taking into consideration the repertoire as a whole. There was no strong spur prompting editors to take into account the interrelatedness of the various segments of the repertoire or the underlying function served by formularity in a primarily oral environment. This lack of sensitivity to the medieval gestural vocabulary resulted in a process of individuation and a manifold increase in the demands made on the memory. As indicated previously, I greatly doubt that earlier modes of learning and retention could have survived under the newer conditions, and I have posited that by the turn of the seventeenth century there was a marked shift from performance by memory to performance by reading. A second result of the new editorial procedures was the creation of a new, albeit related, tonal language. Both features merit closer attention.

Having said this much, it is appropriate to shift attention from selected components of *Ex Sion* to consider the transmission of the gradual as a whole, returning to the materials presented in example 17. The respond consists of two broad sections, with the first ending on the word *eius* with an open cadence on the third degree of the mode. The general profile survives moderately well in most sources, although numerous small changes may be observed. These reduce the ambitus from a major seventh to a sixth or a fifth. The "cadence" is not constructed from a familiar formula and several alternatives are to be found. The versions of the Gardano, Medicean, and Millange Graduals (staves **d**, **f**, and **g**) close on *g* rather than on *a*, while those of the Belleros and Premonstratensian Graduals (staves **h**, **n**) approach the cadence from below rather than from the upper fifth. In the readings of the 1596 Giunta Gradual (staff **e**) and its derivative, the 1610 Ciera Gradual, the flourish on the last syllable of *eius*, which in its medieval form had consisted of ten tones, is reduced to a single tone, sharply altering the nature of the cadence. Earlier on there is a similar degree of terseness in these sources in the setting of the word *species*. Whereas the medieval antecedents for this passage had employed a total of eighteen tones for the three syllables (using eight, one, and nine pitches respectively) these sources assign no more than the minimum of three. These are equivalent to the first three pitches of the medieval version. All else has been excised, and this involves the deletion of the ascent from the fifth degree to the seventh, as well as the subsequent descent to the third. This rise is eliminated also in the Premonstratensian reading (staff **n**). The Netherlandish version redistributes the material for the first syllable of *species* so that it covers both the first two syllables as well as the beginning of the third. Again the peak on the upper seventh is avoided.

The second segment of the respond exhibits a similar series of editorial actions. In the normative medieval version, the final syllable of the closing word, *veniet*, is assigned a full ten tones, ending with a familiar cadence on *f*. In the Gardano reading (staff **d**) we find only a single *f*, while the editions of Giunta (staff **e**), Ciera, and the Medicean press (staff **f**) allow a two-note descent from *g–f*. Whereas the Giunta Gradual of 1596 retains the full ascent to the upper seventh that is characteristic of the medieval setting of the opening syllable of *veniet*, this ascent is curtailed at the fifth and reshaped in the Ciera Gradual of 1610. It is again curtailed and further modified in the Baglioni Gradual of 1690 (not shown in example 17).

The major transformations occurring in the verse affect particularly the two huge melismas mentioned much earlier. The thirty-six tones assigned to the accented syllable of *Congregate* are reduced to a mere two in the readings of the early Graduals by Giunta (staff **e**) and Ciera. The reading of the Cistercian Gradual of 1696 (staff **m**) is somewhat more generous, employing six tones, while the Medicean Gradual (staff **f**) provides seven tones and that by Laurent and by Belleros (staff **h**), a total of nine. The reading utilized by Plantin (staff **i**) in 1599, on the other hand, employs twenty-seven tones. Nearly as generous are the readings provided by Flandrus and Küchler (staves **j**, **k**), while that by Piotrkowczyk (staff **l**) is a bit shorter than these. Although three readings terminate the word on *g*, the remainder agree with the medieval precedent and end on *a*.

The melisma on the final syllable of *ordinaverunt* submits to similar changes. The thirty-five tones of the medieval version are reduced to one in readings by Giunta (staff **e**), Ciera (and followers), the Medicean press (staff **f**), and the Premonstratensian reading of 1680 (staff **n**). The readings by Laurent and Belleros (staff **h**) allow four tones, while the Cistercians permit six (staff **m**). The readings by Gardano (staff **d**) and his French followers use five tones. Again the Plantin reading (staff **i**) is the fullest of the reform sources, while those of Flandrus, Küchler, and Piotrkowczyk (staves **j**, **k**, and **l**) occupy an intermediate position. The concluding portion, [*testamentum*] *eius super sacrificia,* is also abbreviated in southerly readings, but the contrast is for the most part less stark. Nevertheless, the reduction to a single tone of the fifteen-note melisma on the final syllable in the readings of Giunta (staff **e**) and Ciera remains striking. And the two notes assigned by the Medicean Gradual are scarcely generous (staff **f**). By contrast, the earlier edition by Gardano (staff **d**) had allowed nine tones for this syllable, while the northern readings permitted a dozen or more.

The Second Sunday for Advent employs as its Alleluia, the *Alleluia Laetatus sum,* a chant with a complex history of transmission during the Middle Ages and Renaissance. From the time of the notationless Senlis, *Antiphonale Missarum* (Paris, Bibl. Ste. Geneviève, MS lat. 111), of the late ninth century, the *Alleluia Laetatus sum* was provided with two verses. The texts of the two were taken from the first two verses of Psalm 121 in the equivalent versions of the Latin Psalter and of Jerome's translation after the Septuagint. From the late Middle Ages on, the use of the second verse, *Stantes erant,* became less and less frequent. Nevertheless, it continues to appear occasionally in sixteenth-century sources, particularly from Germany. It is, however, quite unusual to find the two verses present in the Premonstratensian Graduals of 1680 and 1718. Here, however, we shall consider only the first verse.

It is reasonably certain that the melody to *Laetatus sum* employed a variable second degree during the early decades of its existence. When the second degree was a whole tone removed from the final, the modal character was that of the protus maneria. When, however, it was a half step removed from the final, the modal character was deuterus. This modal ambiguity was exacerbated by the fact that the gestures at the openings of both the Alleluia and the verse are frequent in chants of both maneriae. When diastematic notation came into common use, the solution normally employed was to place the final on *a*. The modal character thus revolved around the local presence or absence of *b-flat*. This solution was especially prevalent in France and only somewhat less so in German lands. However, a number of Italian scribes preferred not to employ the alternative final and they placed the final on *d*. This meant that the passage in the middle of the verse that ended with an unambiguous deuterus cadence had to be written a second higher than was originally intended. The intended final in Aquitanian sources lacking clefs can be determined by the presence (or absence) of this displacement.

We cannot be certain whether the cadences implied by the early adiastematic sources employed the raised or lowered second degree, a matter essential to the modal categorization of the chant. With the advent of diastemy, the cadential structures often underwent change. Thus we have not only cadences on *a*—with or without *b-flat*—and cadences on *d*, but also cadences on *e*. On the whole, cadences on *d* become more prevalent after the fourteenth century. In sixteenth-century Italy, however, it was customary to begin on *d*, but to have the final on *e*, as in the Graduals of 1527, 1546, and 1572 by Giunta and 1525 and 1580 by Liechtenstein. The same is true for the 1524 Turinese print by Dossena and Porro, as well as the 1565 Venetian print by Varisco. On the other hand, there was a tendency for Germanic sources to employ the higher reading with final on *a*. This family of readings is to be found in the Wenssler and Kuchen Gradual (1486?), the Reyser Gradual of 1496, the Pruess Gradual of 1501, the *Graduale Pataviense* of 1511, the Pforzheim Gradual of the same year, and the *Graduale Herbipolense* of 1583. (Various Germanic sources may lack the melody, preferring to employ the *Alleluia Rex noster* instead.) It is necessary to assess post-Tridentine readings in terms of this varied background.

Perhaps the most striking of the post-Tridentine readings for the opening *alleluia* is that of the Medicean Gradual, which goes counter to the normal Italian practice and places the final on *d*. (See example 25, staff **e**.) This source emphasizes the final by curtailing the initial upward rise and returning to *d* as an intermediate final immediately before the choral entry. No other Gradual presently known prior to 1848 takes this route. The beginning of the jubilus picks up with the second ascent to the seventh degree to be found in the normative Solesmes reading and proceeds directly to the cadential neume, deleting the descent to the subfinal and subsequent ascent present in the medieval form of the jubilus. The descent to the subfinal is to be found in both the Liechtenstein Gradual of 1580 (staff **b**) and the Würzburg Gradual of 1583 (staff **a**), even though these two sources close on different finals.

The broad tonal design of the Medicean reading is to be found in readings of the French tradition, appearing initially in the Bordeaux Gradual edited by Guillaume Boni (staff **f**) in 1598/99 and continuing with the Toul prints issued by Belgrand beginning in 1627. It is to be found also in Parisian prints of 1635 and 1640, and it was presumably present in earlier sources from Paris that are not known to have survived. This group of Graduals preserves the first ascent to *c'*, but deletes the second one. The descent to the subtonium is shortened, but there is a brief ascent to *g* prior to a descent to the final, followed by a rebound and a final cadence. The Flandrus Gradual of 1597 (staff **g**) also employs *d* as a final, and it is individual among this group of sources in its fuller treatment of the jubilus.

While the two early Venetian Graduals issued respectively by Gardano and Giunta in 1591 and 1596 (staves **c**, **d**) both begin on *d*, these, like their earlier Italian counterparts, both conclude on *e*. They both shorten the opening *alleluia*, but do so in different fashions. Comparison between these sources and the Medicean and French prints requires that one compensate for the difference in final by an imagined transposition of the cadential area. Although the actual pitches differ between the Giunta and Bordeaux Graduals, the two display similar relationships between these pitches and the respective finals.

The reading of the Plantin Gradual of 1599 (staff **h**), as well as that issued by the same press in 1774 (staff **i**), also belong to the broad family that employ *e* as final. The jubilus is given quite fully in the earlier source, although abbreviated noticeably in the later. In keeping with their general derivation from the Plantin Gradual of 1599, the readings of the Angermaier Gradual of 1618 and the Sutor Gradual of 1630, both published in Ingolstadt, follow the Plantin lead, and thus depart from earlier German tonal practice. The first of the Plantin readings is also noticeably related to that of the Carthusians, who do not avail themselves of the freedoms taken by the reform editors. (Compare the versions given on staves **h** and **k**.) One additional source belonging to the tonal family ending on *e* is that found in the Piotrkowczyk Gradual of 1600 (staff **j**), which presents a quite distinctive account of the jubilus.

Readings that place the final on *a*, once the most numerous of all families of readings for the *Alleluia Laetatus sum*, are to be found among post-Tridentine Graduals, but they are rare. The only "reformed" version is that of the Cistercians, which makes several small excisions from the jubilus. This reading (staff **l**) may be contrasted with the reading of the Benedictine Gradual of 1624 (staff **m**) and its sister MS one year earlier in date, but not given here. These sources resist the reforming tendencies prevalent at the time.

Lastly, we have a few readings that both open and close on *e*. These include the Laurent, Belleros (staff **n**), and Mommaert Graduals of 1616, 1620, and 1623, respectively, together with the Premonstratensian Graduals of 1680 (staff **o**) and 1718. Although these two groups of Graduals share some common traits of tonal structure, they nevertheless belong to different families. Their respective treatments of the *alleluia* section are distinctive, as are their treatments of the verse. Even though they both end on this section on *e*, the Belgian group begins on *d*, while the Premonstratensian group begins on *e*. No other source from the seventeenth or eighteenth centuries is known to begin the verse in this fashion, although there are some comparatively late French sources of the Middle Ages that do so.

The verse is divisible into irregular segments, the first ending with a characteristic protus cadence on *mihi*. Since there are no notably large melismas in this section, the foreshortening among different readings is comparatively minimal. The syllable most often affected is the first syllable of *dicta*, which is abbreviated especially in the readings of Giunta (staff **d**) the Cistercians (staff **l**), the Premonstratensians (staff **o**), and Piotrkowczyk (staff **j**). In the last named, the melodic continuation is unexpectedly employed to extend the following monosyllable, *sunt*, which apparently receives nine tones as opposed to the normal two (or one). The Premonstratensian reading for the initial segment is idiosyncratic in more than one way. First, although the neumation of the first verse differs from that of the Alleluia, the opening eleven tones are identical in pitch. This brings the Premonstratensian version (staff **o**) to a higher peak in pitch than is reached in any other reading. Second, being solicitous of modal unity, the editor, Nivers, replaces the characteristic protus medial cadence on the last syllable of *mihi* by a terse *deuterus* cadence not employed in any other source.

The opposite action is taken by the editor of the Flandrus Gradual (staff **g**) in connection with the cadence on *Domini* at the conclusion of the second segment of the verse. An effusive flourish on the first syllable wends its way downward from the fourth degree to a forceful conclusion on the final. This strengthens the modal unity of the melody as well. It is perhaps ironic that Anerio and Soriano, the editors of the Medicean Gradual (staff **e**), did not take a similar opportunity, even though they are normally the most solicitous of this aspect of chant. They do, however, eliminate the formulaic character of this small segment, thus reducing its overall impact on melodic structure. The Premonstratensian version edited by Nivers (staff **o**) also eliminates the cadential character of this passage. There is a very simple descent from the sixth degree to the fourth, ending with the repeated tone *a*. Like Flandrus, the Belgian editors, including Belleros (staff **n**) employ a protus cadence, even though this is at odds with the overall modality of their readings. The Cistercians, who employ a high final on *a*, could have employed a deuterus cadence by the simple expedient of employing *b-flat*, as in the reading of the *Graduale Herbipolense*. However, no *b-flat* is used either here or at the conclusion to the opening *alleluia* (see staff **l**). Under comparable conditions, the conservative Benedictines obtained their deuterus cadence by notating the relevant segment a second higher, ending on *b* (staff **m**).

The final segment consists of a single word, *ibimus*, with its accented antepenultimate syllable. The normative medieval reading allots two tones to the unaccented middle syllable, and accords the first and last syllables seven and twenty-nine tones respectively. The final twenty of the latter reiterate the close of the jubilus. In typical fashion, the Medicean, French, Belgian, German, and Cistercian readings assign only a single tone to the unaccented penultimate syllable, although the place of that tone in the closing segment varies. On the other hand, the Giunta reading of 1596 (staff **d**) increases the number of tones allotted to this sensitive syllable to six, and this unusual coupling of text and melody recurs in the succeeding edition of 1606 and is found as late as the Ciera Gradual of 1618. However, the Giunta Gradual of 1626 and later Venetian prints, such as the Gradual issued by Baglioni in 1690 alter the text setting so that the middle syllable gets only one tone. The Gardano print of 1591 (staff **c**) employs a modest two tones here. The Plantin Gradual of 1599 (staff **h**) as well as its successors issued by Angermaier and Sutor increase the number of tones assigned to the accented opening syllable to twenty-one, while the Plantin Gradual of 1774 (staff **i**) employs twenty.

More significant is the treatment of the final syllable. Several Graduals close with flourishes ranging from six tones (Gardano, 1591, staff **c**) to nineteen (Flandrus, 1597, staff **g**). On the other hand, the Giunta Gradual of 1596 (staff **d**) and the Premonstratensian Gradual (staff **o**) employ only a single tone, while the Medicean Gradual (staff **e**), together with the 1599 Plantin Gradual and the 1774 Plantin Gradual employ two tones (staves **h**, **i**). In the reading of the Premonstratensian Gradual the setting of the final word occupies a lower than normal register, reaching the final at an unusually early stage, closing with a threefold iteration of that tone. This is a further bit of evidence establishing the idiosyncratic nature of this version of the melody.

With the exception of the Carthusian and Benedictine readings (staves **k**, **m**), post-Tridentine sources bring the chant to a conclusion on the expected final. It is possible that the scribes of the two conservative sources cited expected the singers to complete the verse with the conclusion of the jubilus. This, however, is not a foregone conclusion. In his setting of the *Alleluia Laetatus sum* in the *Choralis Constantinus*, Isaac employs a version of the chant with a foreshortened conclusion and dovetails this ending with the beginning of the second verse in such fashion that it is impossible to insert anything additional. It is significant that Isaac's understanding of the chant is confirmed by various printed sources from the turn of the sixteenth century which end the verse at the same place. In its original form the 1623 reading in the Mommaert Gradual ended, as might be expected, on *e*. However, a later editor has crossed out the last several notes—still easily legible— so that the chant comes to an end with a deuterus cadence on *a!*

In any event, the varied changes taking place in the setting of the last word of the verse exercise a profound effect on the formal structure of the chant. With the possible exception of the Carthusian and Benedictine readings, the symmetry between the end of the jubilus and the end of the verse is destroyed. And in five readings the verse comes to an abrupt halt on the final syllable. Moreover, exceptions to the return of the opening *alleluia* occur with increasing frequency among Venetian sources beginning with the Giunta Gradual of 1596. This return is replaced by a much smaller phrase. Within a quarter century we find the double texting of the word *alleluia* for the opening section, suggesting that the initial choral portion entered in midstream and no longer returned to the beginning.

The last reading to be considered is that of the Küchler Gradual of 1671 (staff **p**). This source does not use the familiar form of the *Alleluia Laetatus sum* in any guise whatsoever. Instead we find a first-mode melody given in such fashion that we are encouraged to think that the chorus entered with the newly-texted jubilus and that the melody ended with a return to the opening *alleluia*, shorn of the jubilus. When summarizing the history of the *Alleluia Laetatus sum* prior to 1600, I noted that its use was not universal. In Germanic lands—and indeed elsewhere in central Europe—the *Alleluia Rex noster* could be employed instead. (Other alternatives could include the *Alleluias Virtutes caeli*, *Deus a Libano veniet*, and *Memento nostri*, but *Rex noster* was apparently more frequent than any of these.) Communities accustomed to *Rex noster* were faced with a dilemma when, in 1570, the *Missale Romanum ex decreto sacrosancti concilii Tridentini restitutuum* was issued in Rome by the firm of Faletto and Varisco. This was to be adopted by all churches throughout Europe. On the one hand it was necessary to accept the new Missal, while on the other a few sought to retain the melody to which they were accustomed. Occasionally the alternative melody was simply adapted to the "new" text, and this is the situation that one finds in the Küchler Gradual. The *Alleluia Rex noster* is a member of the *Alleluia Posuisti* family and employs the melody used as the basis for that family.[6] The melody that is given here is a reworking of the *Alleluia Posuisti* as given in sources such as the Albi Gradual, Paris, Bibl. nat., MS lat. 776,[7] one of the more famous Aquitanian manuscripts. (Curiously, the Küchler reading is more distant from that given in Berlin, Öff. Wiss. Bibl., Q° 664.)

The offertory for the Second Sunday in Advent is *Deus tu convertens*, a moderately lengthy and florid chant in mode 3. I have not explored its transmission among medieval diastematic sources in sufficient depth to offer a meaningful commentary regarding its relative stability. The text is taken from Psalm 84, verses 7–8 in the version of the Latin Psalter. Jerome's *Hexapla* differs only in using *conversus* rather than *convertens*, while his translation after the Hebrew is considerably more distant. *Conversus* occurs as a variant form in the Latin Psalter, which is otherwise identical to the chant text. The concern for prosodic values in the normative medieval version is sporadic at best. Of the thirteen polysyllabic words, only four accord a greater number of tones to the primary accented syllable than to others. A fifth, *salutare*, provides for a succession of 4–1–3–1 tones for the four syllables, and that may also be regarded as acceptable. On the other hand, the extension provided to the middle syllable of *Domine* and to the last syllables of *tua*, *ostende*, and *tuam*, would have been regarded as faulty by musical aestheticians of the late sixteenth and seventeenth centuries.

The text is divisible into four main clauses, each of which is further subdivisible. In the normative medieval reading, these four have cadences respectively on the final, third degree, subfinal, and final. The medial cadence for the third major clause also ends on the final. The reciting tone of mode 3 plays a considerable role in the structure of the melody thanks to its frequent reiterations by *strophici*, and through its appearance as the high point of various local constructions. Apart from the notable reduction in the size of the melisma on *nos*, a superficial glance at the ensemble of readings presented here may indicate little of interest. Nevertheless, there are a number of changes of detail that are of some significance.

The reading of the Medicean Gradual is again distinctive for its emphasis on tonal centricity. (See example 26, staff **f**.) Whereas medieval modal theorists often note that chants may begin on degrees other than the final, the Medicean Gradual views such alternative openings with disfavor. While this trait is not universal, it has been previously observed in the gradual, *Universi*, the *Alleluia Ostende nobis*, the *Alleluia Dies sanctificatus*, and the offertory, *Tui sunt caeli*. It appears in *Deus tu convertens*, and it will appear also in the gradual, *Timebunt gentes*, to be treated in the next chapter. (One should bear in mind that many of the other chants studied to this point open on the final in their normative versions, and the Medicean Gradual is not individual in doing the same.) Except for the Medicean Gradual, all remaining sources listed in our example open with an ascent from the third degree to the dominant, *c'*. The Medicean reading, however, insists on inserting a preliminary tone on the final. Curiously, however, while most sources bring the first main clause to a cadence on the final, the Medicean changes the cadential shape and ends on the third degree. (The Graduals issued by Piotrkowczyk, Küchler, and the Carthusians end here on *f*; staves **l**, **k**, and **p**.) The reverse procedure obtains at the end of the following clause: where the normative versions end on the third degree, there the Medicean closes on the final (staff **f**).

All of the "reform" Graduals exhibit an increased concern for prosodic values, but the Medicean Gradual is the most punctilious of these. It is, however, unusual that the Venetian prints of Giunta, Ciera, and their successors should increase the number of tones assigned to the final syllable of the opening word from one to three. There is a noticeable decline in prolixity for the latter portion of the first main section, especially apparent in the prints by Giunta and Ciera. The solicitude for the brevity of unaccented penultimates (*laetabitur, Domine, misericordiam*) is in keeping with observations made previously.

The text of the communion for the Second Sunday of Advent conflates the opening of the fifth verse of Baruch, chapter 5, with the end of the thirty-sixth verse of chapter 4. In each segment there are changes of word order that depart from the version given in the Vulgate.

Vulgate	Chant text
Exsurge Hierusalem et sta in excelso	*Ierusalem surge, et sta in excelso*
et vide iucunditatem a Deo tibi venientem.	*et vide iucunditatem, quae veniet tibi a*
	Deo tuo.

Inasmuch as the normative medieval version of the melody is not particularly florid, the impetus for change is not as great as in other instances. There are numerous variants among the post-Tridentine readings, but these tend to affect matters of detail. (See example 27.) The most noteworthy departure from the medieval profile occurs in the Premonstratensian reading (staff **n**), which ends the first segment on the fifth degree rather than on the final. The chant is normally classified in mode 2, but the readings of the Giunta and Ciera prints behave as if the editors thought the melody belonged to mode 1; these are the only sources to eliminate the downward descent to A at the end of the word *tibi* (staff **e**).

In this chapter we have touched upon various features of the editorial changes wrought by chant editors of the late sixteenth and seventeenth centuries. We have noted frequently the increased attention paid to modal constructions, affecting especially opening and closing tones of important segments. This feature also drew comment in previous chapters. I have dwelled especially on the dissolution of the formulaic gestures that had provided the medieval repertoire with a tightly-knit melodic vocabulary. Because this constitutes in my opinion such a fundamental alteration of the tonal vocabulary, I have sought to document the change by means of multiple examples. This decision will be carried out further in the next chapter, so that the reader will understand that the documentation that has been furnished here is not limited to an isolated example, but is part of a wide-ranging system.

SIX

The Third Sunday after Epiphany

Among the chants forming the Proper for the Third Sunday after Epiphany, the introit, offertory, and communion have, in their individual ways, unusual histories of transmission. The extra-diatonicism present in the earliest forms of the introit, *Adorate Deum*, posed difficult notational problems for the medieval scribes. The communion, *Mirabantur omnes*, survives with three melodies; the one present in post-Tridentine and modern sources exhibits significant gestural contrasts in our earliest sources. The offertory, *Dextera Domini*, is the most stable of the three among medieval readings, but exhibits an important textual alteration in the post-Tridentine Missal.[1]

Among medieval music theorists, both Goscalcus (= the Berkeley Anonymous) and Anonymous XI indicate that *Adorate Deum* employed the conjuncta on *e'-flat*, and their description of the melody is corroborated by the classification provided by Theinred of Dover. In addition, one finds this *e'-flat* notated in the reading of Toulouse, Bibl. mun., MS 94. In effect, *Adorate Deum* opens in the protus maneria and closes in the tetrardus. This assertion notwithstanding, I have yet to find any tonary, Gradual, or notated Missal that employs a protus classification or psalm tone. Our evidence nevertheless indicates that the second word, *Deum*, originally closed with the gesture, *e'-flat–c'–c'–b-flat*. This did not present a problem to those theorists who were willing to exceed the constraints of the Guidonian gamut or to the very rare scribe who was willing to do likewise. Others had to find alternative forms of notation.[2]

Germanic scribes generally employed the solution entailing the least upset; these persons simply raised the sensitive high tone from *e'-flat* to *f'*. A more complex alternative was to notate the setting of the first five words a second higher than normal, placing the temporary final on *a* rather than on *g*. A much rarer option was to accomplish the same effect by notating the chant a fourth lower than normal, opening on *d* and employing *b-flat*. Still a fourth route was to ignore the need for *e'-flat*, but to specify *b-flat*. Presumably it was left to the stylistic sensitivity of the singers to realize that the succession *e'–c'–c'–b-flat* was inappropriate and to adjust the tone that could not be openly specified. Finally, the scribes could opt to omit both flats; in such cases the conversion to a tetrardus opening was likely to have been fairly rapid. The last solution entailed another problem in its wake. The succeeding segment then had an outline of a diminished fifth. To avoid this lack of euphony, some scribes raised only the second segment of the melody, thereby obtaining a *c'–g'* outline in place of the undesirable *b–f'*.

The text for this chant is drawn from Psalm 97, beginning with the last portion of verse 7 and continuing with the majority of phrase 8. The version employed by the introit differs from that of the Latin Psalter and Jerome's *Hexapla* only in that the second word is *Deum* rather than *eum*. This change does appear as a variant among the readings of the Latin Psalter collated by Robert Weber.

It is instructive to observe several dozens of medieval scribes wrestling with the notation of the opening of *Adorate Deum* and finding their individual solutions. We do not have an equal variety of source material for the post-Tridentine Mass melodies, and the later landscape seems much simpler. Nevertheless, the versions created by chant editors of the sixteenth to eighteenth centuries betray traces of earlier practices. (See example 28.) The most obvious and lengthiest of these is found in the Belgian readings of Laurent (Tournai, 1616) and Belleros (Antwerp, 1620; staff **h**). Although this version allows the opening and closing tones of the double segment ending on the word *eius* to remain on *g*, the interior tones are a second higher than normal. The Carthusian reading (staff **p**), which reflects sixteenth-century roots, avoids the descending tritone between *e'* and *b-flat* by bringing the first segment to a close on *c'* and beginning the second segment (*omnes*) on the same tone. The second segment then appears a second higher than normal. The Premonstratensian reading (staff **m**) also begins the second segment on *c'*, but allows the tones following to remain at normal height.

The close on the word *eius* is treated quite variously in our selected sources. The Liechtenstein Gradual of 1580 (staff **b**) follows the version offered by an earlier print brought out by the same firm in 1525 and ends on *c'*. I have not found a medieval precedent for such a reading. The *Graduale Herbipolense* of 1583 (staff **c**) signs *b-flat* for the entire double segment and closes the second portion with the descent of a minor third from *b-flat* to *g*. The Gardano Gradual of 1591 (staff **d**) avoids flats, but nevertheless manages to end the second portion with the descent of a minor third from *c'* to *a*. The subsequent editions by Giunta (staff **e**) and Ciera sidestep the entire problem neatly by recasting the melodic profile. The initial segment ends with the descent *e'–d'*, thus avoiding the tritone, and the second segment does not ascend as far as f', thus avoiding the outline of a diminished fifth. The two readings are equivalent and both end *eius* on c'. Anerio and Soriano forge still another revision. The opening ascent of the Medicean reading (staff **f**) becomes triadic, and the word *Deum* employs the figure associated with the word *nobis* in *Puer natus*. The second segment (on *omnes*) begins on c', and closes on b, the third degree of the mode. The Plantin Gradual of 1599 (staff **i**) eschews the earlier Germanic practice of employing f' in place of e'/e'-flat, but nevertheless cadences *eius* on a. As is normal, this reading is followed in the German editions of Angermaier and Sutor. The remaining sources cadence on g, which is the most frequent medieval version. I have previously indicated why I believe that the post-Tridentine sources were interpreted through the process of reading, and thus I believe that these contrasting versions were intended to be sung as written.

The various post-Tridentine readings of *Adorate Deum* provide multiple illustrations of the power of late chant editors to reshape melodic gestures. We have already seen examples of this when examining the close on *eius*. The second double segment of the chant consists of the text, *audivit, / et laetata est Sion*. Normally the first half closes on the final by means of a descending flourish of five or six notes on the last syllable of *audivit*. Anerio and Soriano not only consider the flourish to be inappropriate for an unaccented syllable, but they turn the ending upward to finish on the fifth degree (staff **f**). The half immediately following normally closes on the fourth degree, but here Anerio and Soriano bring the melody down from the fifth degree to the final. The effect is to lend a greater weight to this cadence and thereby provide an increased sense of tonal centricity to the series of cadential progressions. The readings of both the Gradual edited by Boni and the one issued by Flandrus bring the segment on *Sion* to a close on b. Just as Anerio and Soriano reject the small flourish at the end of *audivit*, so too do they reject the assigning of four or five tones to the last syllable of *filiae*. They limit this syllable to a single tone, and transfer the ascending gesture that normally occurs here to the beginning of the following word.

In contrast to *Adorate Deum*, the fifth-mode gradual, *Timebunt gentes*, appears to be fairly stable in its transmission. The text for the respond draws on Psalm 101, verse 16, omitting the preliminary *et* of the psalm, while the text for the verse is based on the line immediately following. There are no departures from the reading of the Latin Psalter. One finds, however, two words that distinguish the verse from the translation offered in Jerome's *Hexapla*. Jerome opens with *quoniam* rather than *quia*, and at the end he speaks of *gloria sua* rather than *maiestate sua*.

Unlike the graduals that we have studied previously, *Timebunt gentes* is highly formulaic. The respond is composed of two major subdivisions, the first ending with the word *Domine*. The initial half is subdivisible into two segments, while the second contains three segments of unequal length, the middle one being the shortest of these. The opening subdivision features two formulas, the latter being abbreviated and varied. The flanking segments of the second (beginning *et omnes*) also employ two formulas. The second, associated with the word *tuam*, is quite extensive, but apparently appears elsewhere only in *Vindica Domine*. The verse is composed equally of two major subdivisions, each being further subdivisible into two, each segment employing a formula. These formulas are each associated with a melisma. The respond contains eight flourishes of six tones or more, the longest being the last, on the first syllable of *tuam*. This melisma is thirty tones in length. The verse contains only five melismas, but these are generally longer than their average counterpart in the respond. (For post-Tridentine readings, see example 29.)

The formulaic nexus involving the final cadence to the verse of *Timebunt gentes* encompasses more than two dozen chants and is by far the largest assemblage of its kind. (In addition to the instances listed by Willi Apel under the heading F10,[3] the formula may be found at the close of *Justus non conturbabitur*, no longer retained in modern books.) In its normative medieval form this formula concludes with a segment of twenty-seven notes on the final syllable of text. This segment may vary slightly depending upon whether one is consulting a Western or Eastern source, but seems to remain constant within individual sources. With few exceptions the melisma will be prefaced by one of two introductory segments. In the main, the form of introduction is dependent upon whether the last accented syllable is the penultimate or the antepenultimate. In *Timebunt gentes*, the concluding phrase sets the text, *in maiestate sua*. The last accented syllable is obviously the penultimate. In *Bonum est confidere*, on the other hand, the concluding text consists of the words, *in principibus*, the accent falling on the antepenultimate syllable. Instances of the former sort are much more frequent than the latter. This rule of thumb is not absolute; an exception occurs in *Tollite hostias*, which features a tiny modification in the introductory segment.

As indicated above, the final melisma seems to be fixed in all chants within a given source. Inasmuch, however, as there is a strong tendency for formulaic terminal melismas to be abbreviated in the early sources, our evidence is not as full as one might wish. Because fifth-mode graduals are grouped together in the readings of Montpellier, Fac. Méd, MS H. 159, one can quickly see the extent to which they vary regarding the material they present. In Paris, Bibl. nat., lat. 903, the first two occurrences of the formula—for the graduals *Sederunt* and *Exiit sermo*—are given complete, but the later ones tend to be abbreviated. On the other hand, the Albi Gradual, Paris, Bibl. nat., MS lat. 776, normally gives the melisma in full, as does Verdun, Bibl. mun., 759. Graz, Universitätsbibl., 807 is quite consistent in this respect. If, as in *Timebunt gentes*, there is sufficient text, the introductory portion will recite briefly on *f*, move up to *a*, and thence to *c'* or *d'*. The melisma features a twofold descent from the former tone to the final. Because a detailed examination of all instances of this formula would entail a major detour from our main objectives, I will treat this body of evidence selectively. Representative examples of the readings given in the Solesmes books are presented in the first of a series of examples. (See example 30.)

The coupling of a melisma with a final, unaccented syllable is a frequent phenomenon among melismatic genres of chant and poses immediate problems when one considers the transmission of individual chants in post-Tridentine sources, as given in example 29. With the exception of the Gardano print of 1591 (staff **d**), the Venetian sources accord only two tones to the final syllable. This is accomplished by transferring a greatly modified version of the preceding material to the initial syllable. The Medicean Gradual presents the chant in full twice, the first time with only one tone for the final syllable (staff **f**), the second with two. The Cistercian and Premonstratensian readings (staves **m**, **n**) are equivalent in their last eleven tones and assign a modest melisma of seven tones to the final melisma. According to the notated records, the Benedictines shortened the concluding melisma to some eleven notes (staff **o**). Both manuscripts consulted break off at exactly the same place, ending on the final with an acceptable cadence that may be documented in other chants. Nevertheless, taking into account the nature of the two manuscripts as entities, this writer is inclined to suspect that the singers were expected to complete the singing on the basis of their aural memories. The sources from France, the Low Countries, and Poland all find the principle of a large final melisma to be acceptable, but they modify the melisma variously.

When discussing the gradual, *Ex Sion species,* I focused attention on the tendency—particularly notable among Italian sources—for a formulaic nexus to dissolve and for medieval relationships to disappear or be lessened. In order to provide a counterbalance to this demonstration, I open our present inquiry with an examination of selected appearances of the formula concluding *Timebunt gentes* in the readings of the Laurent Gradual issued in Tournai, 1616. (See example 31.)

Surveying the group of examples as a whole, one finds that despite the occasional presence of a small variant, the nexus itself survives with remarkable constancy. To illustrate the nature of possible variants, I compare the readings for *Timebunt gentes, Sederunt principes, Exiit Sermo, Propitius esto, Protector noster,* and *Christus factus est.* Only few variants are to be observed, and these are mainly located in the flexible initial portion of the formula. Medieval counterparts may be found for each.

Not only does the nexus survive undiminished, it acquires new members. For example, the fifth-mode gradual, *Gloria et honore,* chooses to end with the formula concluding *Timebunt gentes,* abandoning the normative alternative customary among medieval sources. (See example 32, staff **a**.) *Concupivit rex,* normally a first-mode gradual, is provided with an entirely different fifth-mode melody which ends with the formula that we are investigating (staff **b**). In the absence of a critical edition for *Concupivit rex,* one dare not say that this is a *new* melody, only that we have no present knowledge of antecedents. The eighth-mode *Clamaverunt justi* presents a still stranger example (staff **c**). Normally, the conclusion to the verse presents certain gestural affinities with the conclusion to *Timebunt gentes,* but these occur on other pitches. In the reading of the Laurent Gradual, the final word is given as *salvabuntur* rather than *salvabit*, and the pitch framework is momentarily shifted to that of mode 5! Eight tones before the end the modal framework returns to normal and the chant ends with its customary final, *g*. A full-scale investigation of all graduals among post-Tridentine prints might very well unearth further examples. Nevertheless, such an exploration exceeds the bounds of the present study.

Even though, as mentioned, the formulaic nexus remains remarkably constant, the ligating of pitches can vary widely. One encounters this phenomenon time and again with regard to the repertoire as a whole. Apparently notation no longer conveys the nuances of phrasing that were expressed in our earliest sources. The final *figura* for *Timebunt* contains seven tones and this may be considered normative. However, counterparts in other chants may contain anywhere from three to nine tones. Similar contrasts obtain throughout. The grouping of pitches seems to be at the haphazard convenience of the printer. Similarly, there is no consistency in the indication of *b-flat*. This pitch is signed for no fewer than eight chants and I conclude that it was intended, even if not signed, for the entire group.

When examining the same formulaic nexus in the readings of the Gardano Gradual of 1591, several features attract our attention. When discussing the post-Tridentine transmission of the Third Mass of Christmas, we noted that multiple readings survive for *Viderunt omnes* and the *Alleluia Dies Sanctificatus* in the Medicean Gradual of 1614 and that the readings may change from one liturgical occasion to another. This is true for other chants within the same source. The fifth-mode graduals that are of interest to the present inquiry may also occur on more than one liturgical occasion, particularly those that appear both on Lenten weekdays and during the post-Pentecostal season, as well as those that are employed for various Saints, whether within the Proper or Common. In the Laurent Gradual each melody is notated only once; the other appearance(s) are signaled by verbal cues with page references. While the Gardano Gradual uses cues copiously, there are—as noted previously—many occasions when a chant is written out in full more than once. This is true for both *Convertere* and *Protector noster*. As may be seen from example 33, in each instance the formula is modified from the first occurrence to the next. (Compare staves **a**, **b** and **c**, **d**.)

In example 33, I have amplified the citations from *Protector noster* by adjoining relevant excerpts from *Respice Domine* (staff **e**) and *Locus iste* (staff **f**). We note that we have four different musical treatments for an identical pair of words (*servorum tuorum*) serving the same closing function in chants of the same genre and the same mode, all four having their ultimate origin in a single gesture. In this one respect, the medieval originals accord greater attention to word setting than do the post-Tridentine revisions, this despite the fact that the medieval singers were not concerned with the prosodic appropriateness of what Apel has called the sustaining accent. These examples do not, of course, provide an account of the entire chant and thus are not entirely comparable to those drawn from the Third Mass of Christmas. Nevertheless, it is important that we acknowledge the lack of consistency in this important source and that we be attentive to the possibility of similar examples elsewhere.

In the Gardano Gradual of 1591, Andrea Gabrieli, Orazio Vecchi, and Ludovico Balbi did not arrive at a consistent policy concerning melismas appearing on final syllables. In some instances, such as *Sederunt*, *Discerne causam*, *Christus factus*, *Convertere Domine*, *Dominus noster*, *Justorum animae*, and *Suscepimus*, the final syllable is assigned two tones, while in *Locus iste* and in one version of *Protector noster* it receives only one. At other times it may receive between five and twelve tones. The flourishes at the ends of *Convertere* (staff **b**), *Respice Domine* (staff **e**), *Exiit sermo* (staff **h**) and *Propitius esto* (staff **i**) are notable in this regard. Obviously the placement of this sensitive syllable during the course of the melodic line will impact the shape of the terminal formula.

Even greater variety obtains in the readings provided by the Ciera Gradual of 1610. (See example 34.) The versions of *Ecce sacerdos* (staff **b**) and *Protector noster* (staff **c**) remain the most faithful musically to their medieval antecedents. It was a simple matter to shift the placement of the melisma to the final accented syllable while retaining the general shape. On the other hand, the versions of *Omnes de Saba* (staff **d**) and *Justorum animae* (staff **e**) reduce the medieval line to a minimum, leaving little that is recognizable. In between these extremes there is an extraordinary variety of individual realizations, a sampling being given in the example.

The Medicean Gradual provides equal, if not greater, variety in the rendition of the same cadential formula. (See example 35.) The setting of *Justorum animae* (staff **a**), for example, abandons the mode 5 framework for the cadential area and descends into the range for mode 6. The readings for *Qui operatus* (staff **c**) and *Discerne causam* (staff **o**), on the other hand, have the introductory material in an unexpectedly high tessitura, comparable to that for the word *Sion* in *Timebunt gentes*. The Medicean Gradual presents two full readings for our gradual with only very minor variants between the two. In other instances, the final cadence may vary meaningfully between pairs of readings. I present only one of these pairs (drawn from *Protector noster* staves **d**, **e**) in the example.

When we consider the melisma at the close of the respond for *Timebunt gentes*, we are faced with a sharply contrasting situation. The formula in question has been identified in only one other chant, *Vindica Domine*, for the Vigil of the Feast of Sts. Simon and Jude. (The chant may have additional assignments in late sources.) In *Timebunt gentes*, the melisma is associated with the penultimate syllable of text, while the final syllable is set to a single tone. In *Vindica Domine*, the melisma is associated with the final monosyllable. This difference notwithstanding, one finds in the normative medieval version a run of twenty-six tones that are identical in both chants. Inasmuch as only two chants are involved, I present a series of four comparisons in example 36. Among these, the reading of the Laurent Gradual (staves **d1, d2**) best preserves the sense of the medieval original. In each of the chants we find an extensive melisma placed where it had earlier been. The melismas, however, have each been considerably reworked in individual fashions. One can perceive a loose resemblance in the broad profile, but one's attention is considerably distracted by the differences of detail in the way that these profiles are worked out. The Gardano Gradual (staves **a1, a2**) has greatly reduced the size of the melismas. The one for *Timebunt gentes* has surrendered three of its tones to the final syllable. However, in other aspects, one can still see a loose kinship with the terminal melisma for *Vindica Domine*. The changes wrought in the readings of the Ciera Gradual of 1610 (staves **b1, b2**) are still more fundamental. The melisma on the penultimate syllable of *Timebunt* is further reduced while that on the final syllable of *Vindica Domine* has been eliminated to all intents and purposes. The Medicean Gradual employs *Vindica Domine* for a second occasion and writes it out twice in full. None of the three citations (staves **c1, c2,** and **c3**) is identical with another.

If we now turn our attention to the transmission of *Timebunt gentes* itself, rather than on the various ways in which this gradual interacts with others at diverse times and places, our attention is claimed by a variety of details. We note, in example 29, that the respond opens on no fewer than three different pitches. The opening on *c* that appears in the Netherlandish sources (staff **h**), the Küchler Gradual (staff **l**), the Premonstratensian Gradual (staff **n**), and the two Benedictine Graduals (staff **o**) can be documented in several medieval sources of the Germanic orbit. The opening on *d* is perhaps the most common one in the medieval tradition. The Cistercian opening on *f* (staff **m**) is the result of a medieval revision rather than a post-Tridentine one; the same reading is to be found in sources such as Munich, Bayerische Staatsbibl., MS 2541. I judge, however, that the similar opening in the Giunta (staff **e**), Ciera, and Medicean Graduals (staff **f**) is a late revision seeking to strengthen the modal unity of the chant.

In the Venetian Graduals of Gardano, Giunta, and Ciera, the setting of the word *Domine* at the mid-point of the respond is worthy of passing comment. In the normative medieval reading, the gesture constitutes a very frequent fifth-mode cadence. In this form, the middle syllable bears the cadential flourish of six tones despite the fact that it is a weak syllable. Normally this attracts prompt correction on the part of the post-Tridentine editors. In this instance, however, the gesture is permitted to stand unamended in both the 1591 Gradual by Gardano (staff **d**) and the 1596 Gradual by Giunta (staff **e**). When, however, we reach the 1610 Gradual by Ciera (not shown in the example), which is a descendant of the tradition begun by Giunta, we find that the six tones for the middle syllable have been transferred backward to flesh out the initial syllable. A similar treatment is provided in the version of the Medicean Gradual (staff **f**), with only one repeated tone remaining for the weak middle. This is the normative form for most of the later readings of the seventeenth and eighteenth centuries.

The cadence to the respond of *Timebunt gentes* is quite unusual. Within the medieval tradition, it is customary for fifth-mode graduals (and graduals of other modes as well) for both the respond and the verse to end with at least a flourish if not a more extended melisma on the final syllable of text. *Timebunt gentes* stands apart in that it concludes with a single tone on the last syllable of *tuam*.[4] Among the forty-seven medieval graduals in mode 5 examined by Willi Apel in his comparative table of formulaic usage, only *Propter veritatem* and *Fuit homo* do likewise. (*Tribulationes cordis mei* ends the respond with two tones for the final syllable.)

One might be inclined to think that this unusual form of text setting would have met with the approval of all editors of chant of the sixteenth and seventeenth centuries, inasmuch as the single tone for the final unaccented syllable does not attract attention to itself. Nevertheless, the opposite is true. The Liechtenstein Gradual (staff **b**) and the *Graduale Herbipolense* (staff **c**) each assign two notes to the final syllable, and this practice is continued by the Giunta Gradual of 1596 (staff **e**) and the Medicean Gradual of 1614 (staff **f**). The number is increased to three in the 1591 Gardano Gradual (staff **d**), but none of these instances are of major import. Furthermore, as we can see from the first two instances, the use of two tones for the final syllable is evidently a variant from the late Middle Ages or Renaissance. It is, however, surprising to find that the number of tones is increased to six in the 1598/99 edition of Millange, as well as the 1656 edition of Belgrand (staff **g**). Nine tones are assigned to the final syllable by Nivers in his 1680 edition of Premonstratensian chant (staff **n**), a highly unusual step for an editor who proclaims with such ardor the supremacy of the text over the music. Lastly, one finds a total of thirteen tones assigned to the final syllable in the 1600 Kraków edition of Piotrkowczyk (staff **k**). In these instances the emphasis on prosodic values decidedly takes a back seat.

In the Mommaert Gradual of 1623, *Timebunt gentes* underwent a further editorial revision. Major portions of the melismas at or near the close of both the respond and the verse are lightly crossed out. The editorial intent for the second of these is somewhat equivocal. The final syllable of *sua* retains two tones, *c'–a*, seemingly ending on the third of the mode. It is, however, possible that the final note of the chant was appended to these two tones, thus ending the melody on the normal final. The last of the manuscript hatch-marks appears between the two last tones. The melismas on the last syllables of *Dominus*, *Sion*, and *videbitur* are each abbreviated, in extreme instances being reduced to a single tone each.

The normative Alleluia for the Third Sunday after Epiphany is the *Alleluia Dominus regnavit, exultet terra*. This chant occupies this liturgical position among five of the six sources of the *Antiphonale Missarum Sextuplex*, the exception being the Antiphoner of Mont-Blandin, which employs the *Alleluia Beatus vir* instead. Among these six sources, our chant appears occasionally in four other liturgical assignments. Despite its relative fixity of position among medieval sources in general, its position is not fully fixed among post-Tridentine sources. The text, taken from the opening verse of Psalm 96, reflects accurately the versions of both the Latin Psalter and Jerome's *Hexapla*. My slight acquaintance with medieval sources for the melody suggests that it was fairly stable in its transmission.

The reading of the opening *alleluia* presented in the Gardano Gradual of 1591 remains fairly close to its normative medieval antecedents. (See example 37, staff **d**.) In the verse, however, the melismas on the accented syllables of *terra* and *laetentur* are truncated, the latter markedly so. The same is true for the melisma on the final syllable of text. These foreshortenings are, however, of different natures. The first two are traits of new editorial tastes. The last, however, reflects practices of earlier generations. In example 37 (staff **b**) one will note that the final melisma had already been truncated in the reading of the Liechtenstein Gradual of 1580, and this is not a "reform" Gradual. The trait appears at earlier date, as, for example, in the Varisco Gradual of 1565, which presents the identical ending some fifteen years earlier. Indeed, the practice appears at the very opening of the century in the Giunta Gradual edited by Franciscus de Brugis, 1499/1500. Here, however, the abbreviation is far less marked. In the instance of this Alleluia, we seem to be dealing with a specifically Italian practice. Germanic sources, such as the Pruess Gradual issued in Strasbourg in 1501, the Pforzheim Gradual of 1511, and the *Graduale Herbipolense* of 1583, all give the melisma in full. Nevertheless, we are dealing with a variable practice, not limited to this one Alleluia. Occasionally, even Germanic sources may truncate the final melisma of an Alleluia, as in the instance of the *Alleluia Laetatus sum*. Continuing to examine the various post-Tridentine readings of the *Alleluia Dominus regnavit*, we may note that the truncated form of the final melisma in the verse found in the Liechtenstein Gradual of 1580 (staff **b**) recurs in identical form, but with different grouping of tones and different text underlay in the Giunta Gradual of 1596 (staff **e**) as well as the Ciera Gradual of 1610. It is found also in the Medicean Gradual (staff **f**). I judge, however, that the reading of the Carthusian Gradual of 1674 (staff **p**) was meant to be completed in accordance with earlier models. Before leaving this subject, we may pause to remark on the other truncations of melismas mentioned above. These, occurring on the accented syllables of *terra* and *laetentur*, result not from a distaste for poor prosody, but from a more general, though inconsistent disinclination for floridity itself. As we have seen on earlier occasions, the drive for an economical text delivery is strongest in the Venetian editions of Giunta, Ciera, and their successors.

In this chant, as in many others, the Medicean Gradual stands apart from its fellows in its concern for modal centricity. It is a matter of principle for Anerio and Soriano that a chant should open on the final of the mode. If there is more than one clearly definable segment, the same applies to the segments after the first. Thus, in the *Alleluia Dominus regnavit*, the Medicean version (staff **f**) omits the traditional opening tone on the subfinal and begins with the final itself, a pitch that is normally the second of a group of three. The change at the opening of the verse is stronger. Normally this section begins on the fourth degree and continues with a circular motion involving lower and upper neighbors of this tone. The Medicean reading, on the other hand, begins on the final, unlike any other reading, and slightly enlarges the circular motion. A total of six tones are assigned to the opening syllable rather than four. The Medicean revision is unusual in still another regard. The long melisma that had traditionally occurred on the accented syllable of *laetentur* was subdivisible into two, the latter portion opening with an emphasis on *c'* and continuing with an ascent to *e'*. Apart from the reading in the Plantin Gradual of 1599 (staff **i**), its successors issued by Angermaier and Sutor, and the Piotrkowczyk print (staff **k**)—also with ties to the Plantin model—the Medicean Gradual stands out by retaining this portion of the original melody. Whereas the Plantin version continues with an adaptation of the entire second half of the melisma, as does the reading given by Piotrkowczyk, the Medicean Gradual breaks off immediately after the opening and cadences on *c'*. All other sources conclude on the subfinal, *f*.

The offertory for the Third Sunday after Epiphany is *Dextera Domini*. The text for the antiphon is based on lines 16–17 of Psalm 117 as given in the Latin Psalter. In our earliest documents one finds two additional verses that draw respectively on line 5 together with part of 6 and on line 13 together with the last part of 14, again drawing on the Latin Psalter. In the former instance, the chant text adds the word *quia* as a conjunction leading into verse 6. Both of Jerome's translations, the one according to the Hebrew as well as the one from the *Hexapla*, differ from the Latin Psalter in that they provide in verse 16 a threefold reference to the Right Hand of the Lord rather than the twofold reference of the Latin Psalter. This is in keeping with the Hebrew original, which, in modern editions, places the first of the set of three as the last portion of verse 15. None of the sources of the *Antiphonale Missarum Sextuplex* gives evidence of a third statement. None of our early musical sources employs this statement, which is simply a duplicate of the first.

The differences to be observed among post-Tridentine readings for *Dextera Domini* are sufficiently notable that I shall devote three examples to an exploration of this chant, examples 38, 39, and 40. The first will present an overall panorama of selected readings, the second will explore Italian readings in greater number than could be accommodated in the first, and the third will do likewise for the French tradition. I shall begin my discussion with a report on the first of these.

The sixteenth-century basis for *Dextera Domini* is shown in example 38 (staves **a**, **b**). As before, these present readings by Liechtenstein in Venice and a thus far unidentified editor in Würzburg. A Giunta print of comparable date could have been employed with no basic change. Recent Solesmes editions differ from the Liechtenstein reading (staff **a**) mainly in two respects. They are written a fifth higher and they have numerous strophici that are omitted in the reading from 1580. In the early print a quilisma is replaced by a normal note. The Gardano reading of

1591 (staff **c**) begins nearly identically. But the Gardano print now uses as text the threefold statement characteristic of Jerome's *Hexapla*. As indicated earlier, this is not the text form employed in the *Missale Romanum* of 1570. Gabrieli, Vecchi, and Balbi thus have to create a melody for the third statement where none had previously existed. The remainder then presents only minor variants from the earlier melody states. In the Giunta reading (staff **d**) we again find recourse to the threefold statement, set this time to a repeat of the opening phrase. Since there was no earlier precedent for the music for this phrase, editors were free to do as they wished. The necessity for new creation will afford some insights into the relationships between those sources that make use of the revised text. One will note that the threefold statement of *Dextera Domini* is adopted over a broad geographic range, appearing in sources from Italy, France, Spain, Belgium, and Poland. Among the seven sources incorporating new phrases, we find five that are idiosyncratic. A sixth independent reading is provided by the French Gradual issued by Cramoisy and Clopeiau, shown in example 40 (staff **f**). Under these conditions, the very close similarity visible in example 38 between the Graduals by Plantin (1599) and Piotrkowczyk (1600) is unexpected. (See staves **h, j**.) Indeed, the two sources give surprisingly similar accounts of the entire chant. To be sure, variants between the two sources do occur, but these are quite minor. This information is valuable in that it demonstrates a close relationship of the Piotrkowczyk Gradual to the Western chant tradition, even though elsewhere we find clear evidence of the Germanic dialect with regard to minor variants. One may note that, apart from the final cadence area, the relationship between the Plantin and Piotrkowczyk readings for the introit, *Adorate Deum*, is quite close, although not as striking as in *Dextera Domini*. On the other hand, the two readings for the gradual, *Timebunt gentes*, are decidedly more differentiated. With the limited amount of material presently available, it is hazardous to attempt any final pronouncement regarding this subject. Nevertheless, one should make note of the fact that the Plantin and Piotrkowczyk Graduals bear dates only a year apart. Apparently it was possible for knowledge of individual melodies, and perhaps even groups, to travel considerable distances within a short time.

Comparing the readings given in our example 38, one finds that the cadence that precedes the moment of insertion for the new phrase is quite variable. The words *exaltavit me* normally cadence on *c*, as in the readings of Liechtenstein, the *Graduale Herbipolense*, Gardano, Giunta, Millange, Flandrus, Küchler (staves **a, b, c, d, f, g,** and **k,** resp.), as well as the Cistercians, the Benedictines, and the Carthusians (staves **l, n,** and **o,** resp.). However, the Medicean Gradual (staff **e**) ends on *d* in order to strengthen modal centricity, while Plantin and Piotrkowczyk end on *e* (staves **h, j,** resp.), and the Premonstratensian Gradual, edited by Nivers (staff **m**), concludes with an upward gesture to *a*. The same upward gesture is employed in this source for the segment ending on *sed vivam*. For this passage, the Medicean Gradual ends on A an octave lower (staff **e**), while the Giunta Gradual of 1596 descends to *c* (staff **d**). The majority of sources end *vivam* with an ascent from A–c, generally by leap but filled in on one occasion. The first cadence in the Premonstratensian reading (staff **m**) is also idiosyncratic. It closes the word *Domini* on *d*, whereas most sources bring the melody down to G. The Medicean Gradual (staff **e**) and the French Gradual edited by Boni (staff **f**) choose A as an alternative. The combination of these different cadential goals can produce quite varied orientations for the melody, even though most readings are moderately similar in less sensitive areas.

The treatment of words with accented penultimate syllables can also give rise to quite varied distributions of tones. In its medieval form the word *Domini* occurs three times, *dextera* twice, and *moriar* once.

In the normative medieval form provided in the Solesmes books, the first setting of *dextera* has respectively 3, 4, and 8 notes for the three syllables. The second is in better accord with prosodic values, utilizing 2, 2, and 4 notes respectively. In the former instance, the Gardano Gradual of 1591 (staff **c** of example 38) omits the tonal repetitions for the last syllable but still accords the unaccented middle four notes. Tonal repetitions are again ignored in the second instance, with the result that we have 1, 2, and 2 notes assigned to the three syllables. On the first appearance of the word *Domini*, the medieval version allows the greatest expansion for the unaccented second syllable, having a progression of 2, 5, and 2 notes. Gardano's editors are content to leave this unaltered. The second appearance employs a succession of 4, 1, 1 notes for the three syllables. Gardano has at best a marginally acceptable 3, 2, 1 grouping. His is the only one of the reform versions in example 38 with more than one note for the second syllable. The final appearance, as the last word of the text, presents a series of 1, 1, and 9 tones for the three syllables. Not being willing to close with a flourish on the final syllable, Gardano's editors transfer five of the tones backward, assigning them to the unaccented penultimate syllable. This solution is strange but not unique. One finds a similar text underlay in the edition brought out by Flandrus (staff **g**). The editor of this Spanish source also disregards text accent in the setting of the opening, *Dextera Domini*.

The reading of the Medicean Gradual (staff **e**) is again idiosyncratic in several ways. It departs notably from the medieval form of the chant, particularly in the second phrase, which is reshaped considerably. Understandably this source adheres to the text of the *Missale Romanum* of 1570 and thus has only two statements for *Dextera Domini*, rather than the three found in other sources of the seventeenth century.

Dextera Domini is used also for Thursday of Holy Week. Under most circumstances the later use is indicated merely as a cue. In the Medicean Gradual, however, the chant is written out in full. One might expect that the second reading would be either identical to the first or contain a few very minor variants. Instead, we find a major departure in the recasting of one of the later phrases, shown on staff **f** of example 39. (In order to make this passage stand out, I have omitted materials that are identical to the earlier of the two versions.) We have already seen this phenomenon on several previous occasions, and have here a further demonstration of the potential fluidity of chant readings in certain Italian post-Tridentine sources.

In the example 39, one notes that the original readings provided by Giunta and Ciera (staves **c**, **d**) appear in a minimum of five sources from 1596 to 1618. Nevertheless, there is a break in this tradition as early as the Giunta edition of 1626, shown on staff **g**. While the Venetian tradition is not abandoned in its entirety, the reading of *Dextera Domini* in this and later sources is a strange hybrid. The first phrase is clearly derived from the Medicean reading (staff **e**) and from no other. In the 1626 Gradual, the second phrase, *dextera Domini exaltavit me*, continues to draw on the Medicean Gradual. However, the Giunta edition of 1642 reverts to the earlier Venetian tradition and is followed in this regard by the later Venetian Graduals. None of these sources insert the third statement of *dextera Domini*, and in this respect they are again in agreement with the Medicean. The concluding segment, beginning *non moriar*, changes once more. The 1626 Giunta edition (staff **g**) continues to follow the Medicean version, while the later editions again return to Venetian practice. The final word, *Domini*, employs the melodic setting of the Medicean reading either in a literal or a slightly edited version shorn of the first two notes. Beginning with the Giunta print of 1596, no fewer than five sources provide for a final Alleluia that is used when the chant is sung during Paschal time (staves **c**, **d**, **g**, **h**, and **i**). The example is noteworthy for the demonstration of the variability of Venetian practice and the extraordinary discretion open to individual editors. We have previously noted another hybrid reading involving late Venetian sources in the transmission of the gradual, *Viderunt omnes*. As far as one can tell at this moment, these examples are few. Under normal circumstances, the Medicean Gradual, like the 1591 print by Gardano, leaves very little mark on the history of chant outside of Rome between 1615 and 1848, at which time it is rediscovered by northern editors.

In example 40, the normative French tradition for *Dextera Domini* is given on staff **a** after the 1599 version edited by Boni for Simon Millange and issued in Bordeaux. Noting the unusual reading for the cadence on A for the second word, where most other readings conclude on G, one might very well suspect the presence of an error, resulting in the appearance of a five-note segment a second higher than intended. Nevertheless, as shown, the same reading appears in later French Graduals, rendering the postulate of error suspect. Typographical errors do exist, but given the number of instances of willful variation, it is no easy matter for the modern editor to judge their presence. One may remark that both northern editors as well as later Italian editors become very concerned to mark the brevity of syllables that follow stressed antepenultimate syllables by using diamond-shaped "semibreves." The four staves that follow (staves **b–e**) demonstrate the firmness of the central French tradition. The first two of these were issued in Toul, but there are also Parisian Graduals issued prior to 1656 that participate in the central tradition. Of more than passing interest is the 1697 Gradual brought out by Christophe Ballard under the general editorship of Guillaume Gabriel Nivers (staff **e**). The readings of *Dextera Domini* and those others consulted conform closely to the central tradition. Nivers' function was primarily to ensure their accuracy. One will remark that the edition is described as *antiquus Ecclesiae Cantus Gregorianus è puro fonte Romano elicitus*. Yet comparison shows quickly that there is nothing either Roman or even Italian about the chant, and its antiquity is not quite a century old. This tradition continues to find expression in the 1730 Gradual brought out by Pierre Faure in Grenoble (staff **k**), as well as in the 1734 Gradual by Christophe Ballard (not shown), based on the earlier 1697 print.

Readings from staff **f** onward were chosen to demonstrate the number of alternatives to the main French tradition that were present in the seventeenth and eighteenth centuries. The first of these was issued by Cramoisy and Clopeiau in 1662 (staff **f**). This displays a striking degree of individuality, especially in the second and third phrases (the latter devoted to the third statement of *Dextera Domini*). Whereas the Gradual edited by Boni for Millange treats the inserted material as a variation of the initial phrase, the later publication begins at a different height and cadences in an individual manner. The differences between the two editions in the setting of the final word, *Domini*, are of some passing interest. The earlier of the two readings places the entire melodic weight on the initial, stressed syllable. The later one is quite content to retain the character of the medieval readings and to close with a flourish on the unstressed final syllable. One finds, in addition, smaller variants, such as are to be observed at the close of the first word, that are "thumbprints" not only of this Gradual but also of later Neo-Gallican sources.

The readings of the next four sources presented in the third example all return to the textual form of *Dextera Domini* present in the *Missale Romanum* of 1570. The editorial revisions performed by Louis Paschal for the pub-lisher Jean de la Caille (staff **g**) are noteworthy in that they gave rise to a small subfamily, with at least two later members from Lyon, one issued by the *Societas Bibliopolarum* and the other by André Laurens (staves **i**, **j**). This subfamily is nevertheless recognizably French. The variants that distinguish it are of small scope. For example, the final syllable of the opening word receives three tones instead of four; these are equivalent to the first three of the tones in the more widely used tradition. The descent from *d* to *A* on the first syllable of the second word, *Domini*, is accomplished by leap rather than diatonically, but the framing tones remain the same.

The Gradual edited by Jean Millet that was brought out by Rigoine in Besançon in 1682 seems to be quite individual throughout, and this can be seen its reading for *Dextera Domini*. (See staff **h**.) The chant is notated an octave higher than normal. The opening is distinctive, and we have already mentioned the lack of the third statement for the text. Most of the remaining variants, however, are of small scope.

The remaining three readings are each unusual in some fashion. The *Graduale Ecclesiae Rothomagensis*, brought out by Jore in Rouen in 1727, is a Neo-Gallican source. Indeed, it is one of the first (if not the first) printed source of Neo-Gallican Mass Propers to survive. These sources contain varying admixtures of Gregorian and Neo-Gallican chants, the percentages of both varying considerably from one source to another. If we are to understand these sources as entities it will be necessary to investigate their Gregorian contents. We have yet to take the first step in this endeavor, and a representative investigation of this nature lies beyond the bounds of this study.

The *Graduale Ecclesiae Rothomagensis* contains a large percentage of Gregorian chants and is the only Neo-Gallican source available to me to contain *Dextera Domini*. Its reading of this chant (staff 1) is unusual in that it is notated a fifth above the level that is normative for sources of the seventeenth and eighteenth centuries. (There are only two such sources in our sampling.) Apart from this transposition, the *Rothomagensis* reading is very close to that of the unusual *Graduale Bisuntinum*, edited by Jean Millet. The largest variants concern the reduction in the number of tones assigned to the last syllable of *vivam* and the additional tones assigned to the last syllable of *opera*. The relationship thus established with a source from Besançon is unexpected in view of the fact that the contents of the *Graduale Ecclesiae Rothomagensis* as a whole are clearly related to the *Missale Parisiense* of 1685, issued under the authority of Archbishop François de Harlay.

The reading of the *Graduale Sanctae Lugdunensis Ecclesiae*, brought out by Journet in Lyon in 1738 is also drawn from a highly unusual source that will be discussed in some detail in chapter 11. As we shall see, this Gradual contains many features that descend directly from the Early and High Middle Ages. Thus this is one of the very rare late sources to be accepted by the Solesmes monks among those that are mentioned in *Le Graduel romain*, II. Prominent among these elements are a large number of offertory verses. Unfortunately, *Dextera Domini* is one of those offertories that are presented without verses. The reading (staff **m**) stands apart from its fellows in a number of respects. It is presented transposed a fourth higher than normal, with a consequent final on *g* and a consistent use of *b-flat*. I am unable to recall any other instance of a second-mode chant surviving in such a notational form. Transpositions of a fourth do, of course, occur elsewhere, but these few instances seem to involve largely chants of the deuterus maneria, such as the communion, *Beatus servus*, normally notated with a final on *a*. Another unusual feature of the *Lugdunensis* reading is the large number of strophici that are employed. See, for example, the second statement of *Dextera Domini*. These are not singled out by any unusual notational forms but are represented by two or three square neumes that are closely spaced. There are a number of idiosyncratic moments in this reading, but I will comment on only one of these. The reader may note that the setting of the final word, *Domini*, with the flourish on the last syllable, is one of the few among our three examples to correspond identically with the normative medieval version presented in the modern Solesmes books. Among the French sources presented in our third example, there is only one other to do likewise.

The second of the sources to contain a flourish on the last syllable of *Domini* is the *Cantus missarum totius anni*, brought out by the Dominicans in Paris in 1722 (staff **n**). This is the earliest printed Dominican Gradual known to survive. Nevertheless, the existence of a Dominican Antiphonal published in Venice by Ciera in 1643 suggests the likelihood of earlier Graduals that are presently unknown or that have not survived.

That which is known concerning manuscript Graduals for the Dominican order from the thirteenth through the sixteenth centuries indicates a very firm tradition comparable to that of the Cistercians. However, the Dominicans introduce far fewer changes during the period that is of concern to this study than do the Cistercians. On the other hand, they are less conservative than the Carthusians in that they are more responsive to prosodic values than are the Carthusians.

The relationship between text and music for *Dextera Domini* within the medieval tradition opens numerous opportunities for changes in the assignment of tones to syllables. In the medieval Dominican tradition the syllables of the first word are served by 3, 4, and 5 tones, respectively. In the 1722 print, the same tones are regrouped so that 6 are assigned to the opening syllable, 1 to the second, and 5 to the third. The second word is treated likewise; the medieval succession of 2, 4, and 2 syllables is reworked so that we have instead 5, 1, and 2. Even the less disturbing setting of the second appearance of the word, *Domini*, is changed from 4, 2, 1 to the greater contrast of 5, 1, 1. In medieval readings, the word *moriar* receives respectively 1, 3, and 1 tones, while the version of 1722 changes this to 3, 1, 1. Other variants, including the omission of a liquescent are extremely few and minor. The use of a final on *e* is in keeping with the medieval Dominican tradition.

Mirabantur omnes, the communion for the Third Sunday after Epiphany, has an extraordinary history during the Middle Ages and Renaissance. The text for the chant is taken from the Gospel of Luke, chapter 4, verse 22. Together with a simple first-mode melody this chant served at early date as both antiphon and communion.[5] Its use as antiphon was apparently restricted to the area of Benevento, as it is known to survive in only two sources, Benevento, Bibl. capitolare, V.19 and V.21. As communion, it had an international diffusion for a brief period, but was most at home in Germanic lands, where it was retained into the seventeenth century as may be seen in example 41. Nevertheless, the simplicity of the melody was apparently felt to be excessive for a communion, and a replacement melody in the fourth maneria emerged from the time of our earliest notated sources, Chartres, Bibl. mun., 47 and Laon, Bibl. mun., 239. This melody was very loosely defined at the outset, and only gradually coalesced into a form approaching that given in modern chant books.[6] Given the inordinate multiplicity of forms taken by the chant during the Middle Ages, it is very difficult, if not impossible, to trace the antecedents of the much more restricted number of late forms. One can state that in such and such an area of the melody, a particular late version is identical to or is roughly equivalent to a given early version, but one cannot postulate that the editor of the late version knowingly used the specific early version as a model. One cannot peer into the editor's workshop, so to speak, but only take note of his results.

I am not aware of any medieval reading of *Mirabantur omnes* that prefigures with entire accuracy the version presented in the Graduale Triplex, given at the head of the example. At best one can find documentation for individual parts of the chant. For example, the Solesmes readings parallel that of the Albi Gradual, Paris, Bibl. nat., MS lat. 776 for the setting of the first word. If, however, one takes the chant as a whole, then the versions that are closest to the form given in modern books include readings from Paris, Bibl. Arsenal, MS 111; Toulouse, Bibl. mun., MS 94; New York, Morgan Library, MS 795; Turin, Bibl. naz., MS F.III.17; and the lost Beuron Gradual that survives only in the photographic records of Solesmes. This is an unusual grouping of sources; nevertheless, they are each extremely close to the totality of the Solesmes reading. Obviously, the latter is supported by numerous other readings in terms of individual details. The form utilized in the Gardano Gradual of 1591 (example 41, staff **c**) is quite close to the readings of the sources just mentioned, even though the use of *b-flat* at the final cadence may be unexpected to those who have not had the occasion to explore the full range of medieval sources. The slight simplification on the word *de* is without precedent among the Italian sources that I have consulted.

As might be expected, the reading of the Giunta Gradual of 1596 (staff **d**) is the simplest and most laconic among those presented in example 41. It is clearly the product of a thorough-going reworking. The final cadence is especially distinctive. The Medicean reading, on the other hand, has various isolated moments of resemblance to earlier readings. Curiously, it is not close to any of the score of Italian sources that I have consulted. Nevertheless, the opening units loosely resemble the initial gesture of Montpellier, Fac. Méd, H. 159 and Brussels, Bibl. royale, II.3824. The setting of the word *omnes* seems not only to lack earlier precedent, but any late parallel. The versions presented by Boni in the Bordeaux Gradual of 1598/99 (staff **f**) and the La Caille Gradual of 1668 (staff **g**) open in a manner parallel to that of Paris, Bibl. nat. lat. 904, but the resemblance is fleeting and inexact. Somewhat longer are the parallels between the 1662 reading of Cramoisy and Clopeiau and that of Bari, Bibl. capitolare, Santo Nicola, 85. These similarities at least extend through the first half of the chant, but they dissipate in the second half. The relationship between the Piotrkowczyk Gradual (staff **k**) and that issued by the Plantin press one year earlier (staff **j**) is again striking. In the search for antecedents we seem to be chasing phantoms. Having made an effort in good faith, I feel that I can now call a halt to this enterprise. All that can be said is that the variety found among the details of post-Tridentine readings of *Mirabantur omnes* reflects the more considerable variety found in readings prior to 1500.

SEVEN

The Mass for Easter Sunday

Together with the Third Mass of Christmas, the Mass for Easter Sunday marks one of the most important occasions of the liturgical year. The transmission of this Mass Proper subsequent to the closing years of the sixteenth century should be included in our survey if only for this reason and none other.

The text for the introit, *Resurrexi*, is an unusual assemblage of fragments from Psalm 138 (=139) drawn from the Latin Psalter, beginning with the latter portion of verse 18. The readings of the entire verse given in the Latin Psalter (A), Jerome's *Hexapla* (B), and Jerome's translation after the Hebrew (C) differ slightly from one another:.

(A) Dinumerabo eos et super harenam multiplicabuntur *resurrexi et adhuc tecum sum*

(B) Dinumerabo eos et super harenam multiplicabuntur *exsurrexi et adhuc tecum sum*

(C) Dinumerabo eos et harena plures erunt *evigilavi et adhuc sum tecum.*

The frame of reference for verse 18 is seemingly provided by the last word, *rasheihem*,[1] of the preceding line. This has been taken variously to refer either to the leaders of Israel (according to the Targum), or to the thoughts or main ideas of God (following the commentaries of Ibn Ezra [1089–ca.1164] and the Radak [Rabbi David Kimchi, 1160–1235]). Thus one standard translation of the Hebrew runs: "If I could count them [the leaders], they would outnumber grains of sand, I reach the end—but I remain with you." Another reads, "If I would count them [the thoughts of God], they are more in number than the sand; Were I to come to the end of them, I [the Psalmist] would still be with Thee." The Jerusalem Bible (Alexander Jones, general editor; Garden City, 1966), which does not indicate the source of the text being translated, gives, "I could no more count them than I could the sand, and suppose I could, you would still be with me." Another common English source arrives at the following: "If I tried to count them, they would be more numerous than the sand; when I awake, I am still with Thee." The Saint Joseph Daily Missal couples the text, "I arose, and am still with You," with an etching displaying Jesus arisen from the tomb, flanked by a praying angel and Roman soldiers shielding their eyes from the extraordinary light. In any event, the passage has been wrenched from its original significance.

The Hebrew original from which these translations ultimately derive is equivocal in meaning, but the Latin translations are intended to be understood in a fundamentally different manner.

Apart from the interspersed *alleluias,* the remainder of the text for the antiphon is taken from the last portion of verse 5 together with the opening of verse 6. Here the diversity of texts and translations is lessened though not eliminated. Jerome's *Hexapla* concords with the Latin Psalter, and his translation according to the Hebrew is less divergent. Nevertheless, the simple message that seems to be conveyed by the Latin excerpts still conflicts with the broader context furnished by the Hebrew original, which has been understood in different fashions by various early commentators.

Latin Psalter and Jerome's *Hexapla*	*Hebraeos*
tu formasti me et posuisti super me	*. . . formasti me et posuisti super me*
manum tuam	*manum tuam*
mirabilis est scientia tua ex me	*super me est scientia et excelsior est*

The fourth-mode melody to *Resurrexi* is familiar to all who work with chant. Like many other melodies in mode 4, it features prominently an oscillation between the sub-final and the second degree. In this instance, the repeated insistence on the tone *f* entirely overshadows the role of the eventual final. Within the Solesmes reading, only in the setting of the initial *alleluia* does *e* appear in a place of structural prominence and stability. (See example 42, staff **a.**) This somewhat unusual tonal construction is accepted by most post-Tridentine editors with the exception of Anerio and Soriano, who rework the melody considerably for the Medicean Gradual (staff **f.**) In their version the opening oscillates between *e* and the minor third above. The cadence on *e* in conjunction with the word, *alleluia,* is of course retained. The next clause also cadences on *e* on the word *tuam.* Inasmuch as the same cadence had been employed more than a quarter-century earlier in the Liechtenstein edition of 1580 (staff **b**), this is not necessarily a change that should be attributed to the Medicean editors. Nevertheless, the next cadence on the word *alleluia,* cadences on *e* only in the reading of the Medicean Gradual, as do the next two cadences on *tua* and *alleluia.* The relentless determination to rework the melody so as to create a tone center on *e* is unmistakable.

Other readings also demonstrate traits that are characteristic of their individual styles. The readings of the Giunta Gradual of 1596 (staff **d**) and the Ciera Gradual of 1610 (staff **e**) are clearly the tersest of the group. The conservatism of the Benedictine and Carthusian readings (staves **o**, **p**) is demonstrated notably by the retention of the *strophici* which have disappeared elsewhere.

Elsewhere the variants to be observed are chiefly matters of detail. Especially apparent is a much heightened sensitivity to prosodic values. The normative medieval reading reconstructed in the Solesmes editions has at best a desultory attitude towards these. We do, however, encounter an interesting problem at the very beginning. The normal pronunciation of the word *Resurrexi* has the stress falling on the third syllable, with a possible secondary stress on the first. However, the allocation of tones to the respective syllables seems to stress the second and fourth of these. This may easily be attributed to indifference with regard to medieval versions. It is much more difficult to bring such a charge against post-Tridentine readings. Among these, the Giunta Gradual of 1596 (staff **d**) and the Medicean Gradual of 1614 (staff **f**), shift the apportioning of the pitches to syllables. In the first instance, the second syllable receives only one tone, while the accented third receives three. In the latter instance, the first three syllables receive two tones each. Note, however, that the Ciera Gradual of 1610 (staff **e**), which derives essentially from the earlier Giunta model, accords four tones to the second syllable of *Resurrexi*, employing an oscillation between subfinal and second degree reminiscent of the normative medieval version. The reading of the Belgrand Gradual of 1627 (and later Parisian editions, staff **g**) also accords four tones to the second syllable in contrast to the reading of the Boni Gradual of 1598/99 from which it derives. This latter opens with the succession of tones *d, f–d, e–f* assigned to the first three syllables of the opening word. The closely-related Laurent Gradual of 1616 together with the Belleros Gradual of 1620 (staff **h**) assign a total of five tones to the normally weak second syllable. I find it difficult to posit that these various editors all shunned the prosodic values of the pronunciations known to them, and hesitantly suggest that the pronunciation of *Resurrexi* may have fluctuated over time and depending upon area. Certainly the remainder of the introit antiphon gives numerous examples of changes in the number of tones assigned to individual syllables in order to assist a more natural delivery of text.

The gradual for Easter Sunday, *Haec dies*, is a fairly florid chant, as shown in example 43. The respond has seven melismas, including four with more than a dozen tones each, the last (on the final syllable) including no less than thirty-one pitches. The verse likewise has seven melismas, all but the first having a dozen or more pitches, the most extensive being on the first syllable of *quoniam*.

The text for the respond of *Haec dies* is taken from Psalm 117, verse 24, according to the reading of the Latin Psalter. (The two translations by Jerome both employ the verb *est* between the first two words of the chant text; otherwise they are identical.) The text for the verse derives from the first line of the same psalm; here the readings of the Latin Psalter and Jerome's *Hexapla* are identical with the chant text. Jerome's translation after the Hebrew uses *aeternum* rather than *saecula*.

Although a second-mode chant, the *Haec dies* family (and indeed the other members of the so-called *Justus ut palma* family) is notated so that it both begins and ends on *a*. The melody is perhaps the best known example demonstrating the importance and usefulness of alternative notations employed in order to avoid the necessity to notate notes that were not to be found within the Guidonian gamut. In the present case, the melody to the respond begins with a gesture that includes as the third tone a half-step above the final. Were the melody to be notated at the *d* level this would call for an *e-flat*, for which there was no provision within the Guidonian gamut. Shortly thereafter there is a descent to the major third below the final, and this tone recurs several times during the later course of the chant. Were the melody to be notated at the *d* level this would demand a *B-flat*, which again lacks the sanction of the Guidonian gamut. The alternative notation a fifth higher than normal for the mode provides for the half-step above the final and the major third below. I have not seen any medieval or Renaissance source that does not employ this notational solution. Perhaps such a source will eventually be found, but if one does survive, it would be a great rarity. Yet the Flandrus Gradual of 1597 does employ a notation that begins and ends on *d*.[2] (See example 43, staff **h**.) And it does so without any indication of flats. Particularly strange is the cadence at the end of the word *exsultemus*, which is part of a very common formula that employs a downward leap of a perfect fourth, followed by a whole-tone descent. Because of the absence of a symbol for *B-flat*, the notation of the Flandrus Gradual seems to indicate a descent of a perfect fourth followed by a further half-step descent. Surely any competent chant singer of that or any other time would have rejected any such notion and sung the formula as it was originally intended to sound. The same remarks apply to the comparable cadence in the verse at the end of *saeculum*. These remarks point to a major difficulty in constructing a critical edition for purposes of performance. That which is furnished here is simply a diplomatic transcription of the selected sources, keeping editorial intervention at a minimum. I recognize the value and importance of editorial conclusions, but I consider these to be hazardous when made in the absence of a sufficient foundation of data. The little more than a dozen sources employed here for most samplings do not permit the construction of well-informed conclusions regarding either individual sources or melodies, and I hesitate to interject my tentative opinions at this moment. The very rare accidentals that I have added are all based on written indications in the given source that seem to require extensions.

The normative medieval melody is not especially solicitous of prosodic values. Four of six melismas in the respond occur on unaccented final syllables. (A seventh melisma falls on the opening monosyllable.) Three of the seven melismas in the verse do likewise. It may be instructive to look closely at some ways in which the melodic line may be readjusted to the text in order to gain a fit that was deemed acceptable.

Looking at the respond as a whole, the most remarkable variants affect the final cadence, associated with the word *ea*. The final syllable—though unaccented—carries the largest melisma of the chant. In the normative medieval form given in the Solesmes books, the last syllable is associated with a melisma of thirty-one tones. This melisma is retained with only few departures in the readings of the Liechtenstein Gradual of 1580 (staff **b**) and the *Graduale Herbipolense* of 1583 (staff **c**). It is retained also in the reading of the Carthusian Gradual of 1674 (staff **p**), which is not part of the reform tradition. Nevertheless, the melisma is abbreviated more often than not among the reformed Graduals. The Plantin Gradual of 1599 (and its successors brought out by Angermaier and Sutor) stand apart from the rest by presenting a very full account of the melisma (staff **j**). The penultimate segment is excised in the Boni Gradual of 1599 (staff **g**), which otherwise gives a fairly full account. There is still further reduction in the Cistercian and Premonstratensian readings and in the Medicean Gradual, affecting particularly the middle portion. The Gardano Gradual of 1591 does likewise, although this reading retains the ascent to f'. The editor of the Giunta Gradual of 1596, on the other hand, is unwilling to tolerate a large melisma on the unaccented final. In order to avoid this, he introduces a series of changes, each influencing the next as in a group of tumbling dominos. The tones assigned to the accented syllable of *laetemur*, the antepenultimate word, are increased in number. This reduces the number of tones assigned to the final syllable, which is, as always, weak. The two tones given to the final syllable are normally associated with the word that follows. The shift is then passed down the line, with the penultimate word being set by the first two tones normally associated with the initial syllable of the final word. This syllable begins with the third of the normative pitches and carries the melisma itself, truncated somewhat in its initial portion, but preserving the remainder of the main outline. The cadence is reworked in its details, and the concluding syllable enters with the second note from last. This solution is followed in the Ciera Gradual of 1610 and basically carries through the later Venetian sources. By the time that we arrive near midcentury, with the Ciera Gradual of 1642 (not shown), the final melisma, still attached to the accented syllable of *ea*, is shortened further, although only slightly, and the final syllable receives only a single tone.

Others shortenings are more drastic. The Küchler Gradual (staff **l**) assigns only five notes to the final syllable, these being taken from the very beginning of the melisma. The respond thus comes to an end on the third degree of the mode. One might be inclined to think that the singers were expected to make good the remainder on the basis of their memories. However, our evidence casts strong doubt on such a conclusion. The Piotrkowczyk Gradual of 1600 (staff **k**) employs the same ending. Moreover, in this case the last note is followed by the heavy, hook-shaped form that is employed in this source only for the final note of a chant or major section thereof. When we look further, we find that the Benedictine sources of 1623 (staff **o**) and 1624 end on the third degree as well. Their agreement in this matter seems to add further weight to the evidence of the Polish Gradual. Lastly, the Graduals of Laurent (from Tournai), Belleros (from Antwerp, staff **i**), and Mommaert (Brussels), carry out the process of abbreviation to the greatest extent possible. They assign only a single note to the last syllable of *ea* and end on the fourth degree of the mode. As noted in our previous discussion of the *Alleluia Laetatus sum*, evidence pointing to altered endings on degrees other than the final goes back at least as far as the early sixteenth century, both in the chant sources of the period and, convincingly, in the *Choralis Constantinus* of Isaac.[3] Unfortunately, we presently have no information concerning the frequency of the practice or about contemporary views regarding its modal justification. It would behoove us to keep our eyes open for additional examples.

Turning now to some of the details in the construction of the respond for *Haec dies*, we find that in the normative medieval version, the words *quam fecit* are set by a melodic arch that begins on *g* and, following an ascent to *e'*, returns to that tone before concluding with an upward step to *a*. The first syllable of *fecit* is sung to a bistropha on *c'* that marks a midpoint in the ascent that had begun with the previous word. Nine pitches are assigned to the final syllable, beginning with a repeated *c'*. Most, but not all, post-Tridentine editors felt that this relationship between melody and text was overbalanced in terms of the emphasis accorded to the final, unaccented syllable. Gabrieli, Vecchi, and Balbi—the editors of the Gardano Gradual of 1591 (staff **d**)—adjusted the balance by omitting the opening *strophici*, retaining only one *c'*, and dividing the eight pitches that remained equally among the two syllables, repeating the *c'* in the middle of the descent. The unknown editor(s) of the Giunta Gradual of 1596 (staff **e**) chose instead to continue the ascent on the previous *quam* and to begin *fecit* at the high point in the melody. Four tones are assigned to the first syllable of *fecit*, including an interior pair of *c'*s. The concluding syllable is set by the ascent *g–a*. This solution is taken over in the derivative Ciera Gradual of 1610.[4] Anerio and Soriano, the editors of the Medicean Gradual (staff **f**), assign the three note ascent *c'–e'* to the first syllable of *fecit* and leave the remaining four tones to the second. The slight balance in favor of the second syllable was deemed acceptable. This solution was also arrived at in the Belleros Gradual of 1620 (staff **i**).

The French tradition for this passage is variable. Boni, the editor of the Bordeaux Gradual of 1599 (staff **g**), gives a melisma of eight tones on the initial syllable of *fecit*, allowing only a single tone for the final syllable. Later Graduals, however, reverse this revision. The Toul Graduals of 1627 and 1656, as well as the Parisian Gradual of 1657 return to medieval practice, assigning only a single tone to the initial syllable of *fecit* and allowing the final syllable a total of nine. The unknown editor of the French (Parisian?) Gradual of 1635, not shown in the example, follows a middle course. He limited the opening syllable of *fecit* to a single *c'* and assigned an ascent *b–e'*, followed by a return to *c'* to the final syllable. The further descent is simply eliminated. A comparable solution is employed in the Premonstratensian Gradual of 1718 (staff **n**), although this eliminates also the return to *c'*. (This tone serves as the initial pitch for the word following.)

The Plantin Gradual (staff **j**) and its successors adopt an approach comparable to that of Boni, whose Gradual was issued in the same year of 1599. With the exception of the final note, the entire gesture is shifted to the opening syllable of *fecit,* while the second syllable receives the one pitch that had not been previously used. The opposite tack is taken in the Cistercian Gradual of 1696 (staff **m**). Although the editor(s) of this source reworked other areas of this chant, including the conclusion to the respond, they permit the original setting of *quam fecit* to stand, with the exception of the repeated *strophici*. One finds time and again in studying post-Tridentine adaptations that one cannot trace the influence of the medieval precedents if one insists in focusing on the setting of individual syllables isolated from their surrounding contexts. Melodic gestures are frequently transferred from one syllable to another.

Continuing in this vein, we may examine the setting of the word *Dominus*. In the normative medieval version, the opening syllable receives three notes, the second a tristropha, and the third, a melisma of thirteen tones. The Gardano Gradual of 1591 (staff **d**) finds nothing amiss in these general proportions, but substitutes a single tone for the tristropha and reduces the melisma on the final syllable to eight tones. The Giunta Gradual of 1596 (staff **e**), on the other hand, wishes a marked stress on the first syllable. To achieve this it ignores the tristropha for the second syllable and transfers tones from the third syllable to the first, achieving an initial melisma of twelve tones, followed by single tones for each of the second and third syllables. The 1610 Gradual of Ciera may well have intended the same apportionment, but the text underlay is not at all clear. The Medicean Gradual (staff **g**) follows the general plan of the earlier Giunta Gradual, but allows two tones for the final syllable. In his Gradual of 1599, Guillaume Boni finds nothing amiss with a melisma on the final syllable and simply reduces the unaccented syllable to a single tone, which is further defined as weak through the use of a diamond-shaped note. This practice is retained in later French editions. The editors of the Belleros Gradual of 1620 (staff **i**), the Plantin Gradual of 1599 (staff **j**), and the Cistercian Gradual of 1696 (staff **m**) do likewise. The Premonstratensian Gradual (staff **n**) opts for a middle course. The number of tones assigned to the initial syllable is increased to five, and the number of tones for the final syllable is reduced to seven.

The following word, *exultemus,* has melismas on each of the last two syllables among medieval readings, the last encompassing sixteen pitches. In the Gardano edition (staff **d**), this is reduced to five, as in the Premonstratensian Gradual (staff **n**), while in the Giunta edition of 1596, it is reduced to three. In the 1610 edition by Ciera, and in the Medicean Gradual (staff **f**), there are only two pitches assigned to this syllable. In the Italian editions brought out by the Giunta, Ciera, and Medicean presses, the reduction is accomplished in part through the transfer of pitches to the accented syllable, but in the Premonstratensian Gradual, tones that had once been assigned to each of the last syllables are simply excised. On the whole, the Northern presses allow the melismas to remain, albeit with some small reductions.

The various readings for the verse hold few new points for us. The truncation of melismas is already familiar, as is the observation that this truncation is far more extreme in the Giunta edition of 1596 (staff **e**) and those of his successors. All of the early Italian editors go to considerable lengths in order to avoid having a melisma fall on a final syllable. This trait is particularly striking in the setting of the last word, *eius*. In the normative medieval version, the preliminary syllable bears four tones, while the final carries eighteen. The weight is entirely reversed in the Italian readings (staves **d**, **e**, and **f**), which place the final syllable on the final or penultimate tone and use those tones remaining from the original gesture in the service of the first syllable. The northern editors, on the other hand, have no such compunctions; a melisma on the final syllable is perfectly acceptable to them, even though it is often reduced.

Although we have previously examined the ways in which formulaic nexuses are either dissolved or retained, it is instructive to continue this vein with regard to *Haec dies*. I have written earlier of the process of individuation in the editing of post-Tridentine chant. The chants examined, however, have been from diverse parts of the Church Year. It is worth our while to inquire whether chants occurring in close succession are treated in similar manners. We will find that our answers vary according to editor.

As is well known, the respond, *Haec dies*, recurs for each of the five days following Easter Sunday, coupled each time with a different psalm verse. With the exception of the gradual for *Feria III.*, the texts for the verses are all taken from Psalm 117 and proceed in increasing numeric order. The verse, *Dicant nunc qui redempti*, is, however, taken from Psalm 106, verse 2. As a group, the six graduals are well known to share very considerable portions of their melodic substance, especially the opening and closing phrases. The next step is to examine the cadences to this group, enlarging this repertory first with the gradual, *Tollite portas*, and later with this chant and a series of four graduals for the Saturday in the Ember Week in Advent.

The graduals for Easter Week employ two different formulas for the opening phrase of the verse. Those for *Confitemini Domino*, *Dicat nunc*, *Dicant nunc*, and *Lapidem quem reprobaverunt* are closely equivalent. *Dextera Domini* and *Benedictus qui venit* share a different formula which, however, has the same first two tones and the same last two tones as the first. Both groups are included within our next examples. Four of the seven chants excerpted have cadences falling on some form of the word, *Dominus*, surely an incentive to employ similar melodic substance.

When we turn to the readings of the Giunta Gradual of 1596, we find that the initial cadence for [*Confitemini*] *Domino* contains only five tones for the three syllables of the word, as shown in example 44 (staff **a**). Its medieval counterpart, on the other hand, contains twenty-six. The medieval version closes on *d'*, as do all other of the twenty-four mode 2 graduals in the repertoire. The readings of the Giunta print and its successors close, however, on *c'*. A *d'* cadence is achieved in the graduals for each of the next two days, but is approached from opposite directions. There is nothing formulaic here. We ought not be surprised that the cadence to *Dextera Domini* (staff **d**) departs significantly from the previous three; its medieval forbear had employed a different formula. However, as just stated, this formula had terminated on *d'*, while the new cadence ends on *a*. This serves as nothing more than an interior tone in the medieval version, although set apart from that which follows through a change of tessitura. Note, moreover, that although the cadence for *Benedictus qui venit* was identical to that of *Dextera Domini* in medieval sources, it is entirely different in this late reading (staff **f**). In fact, it is drawn from the portion of the medieval phrase that follows the segment ending on *a* that was apparently the model for the cadence given for *Dextera Domini*. Even though *Benedictus qui venit* and *Lapidem quem reprobaverunt* employed different formulas in their medieval states, their profiles are related in their transformed states (staves **f**, **e**). *Tollite portas,* the basis for the last excerpt, serves as gradual for *Feria IV* of the Ember Week of Advent. Its cadence (staff **g**) is equivalent to that of *Dicant nunc*, and is more closely related to that of *Confitemini Domino* than most others from our group. By virtue of their relative extension, the medieval excerpts each have a clear personality even in isolation. The abbreviated equivalents, however, are so terse and bland, that they lack such personality and cannot easily be evaluated apart from their context. They are scarcely memorable.

An examination of the final cadences to a group of eleven mode-2 graduals furnishes us with a somewhat different picture. We are dealing with a cadence that had been universal among all two dozen second-mode graduals. Here we shall examine two sub-groups, the first from Easter Week, and the second from Ember Week of Advent. Our example is of necessity incomplete. On Ember Saturday, *Excita Domine* serves first as the verse for *Domine Deus virtutem*, the second of the graduals for Ember Saturday. The same text serves immediately thereafter as the respond for the third gradual. The persons responsible for the 1596 Gradual apparently became momentarily confused and lost their place. As a result, no verse is given for *Domine Deus*.

Even a brief glance at example 45 quickly shows the formulaic nature of this material in the remaining group of ten. Only the cadence for *Dextera Domini* (staff **d**) stands apart. The reader will recall that the text for this gradual is the same as the one that serves as offertory for the Third Sunday after Epiphany. Not surprisingly, it undergoes the very alterations that were discussed earlier with regard to the offertory. In its normative medieval form, the text for the gradual verse consists of two clauses: *Dextera Domini fecit virtutem*, and *Dextera Domini exaltavit me*. Various post-Tridentine editions restore the original tripartite form of the text, returning to *Dextera Domini fecit virtutem* at the close. This necessitates either the creation of a new musical phrase or a sharply changed adaptation of the older material. In this instance, the phrase that had served for the entirety of the second statement of *Dextera Domini* is transformed and subdivided. The first portion serves for *Dextera Domini*, while the second, which terminates with a standard formulaic cadence on *f*, serves for *exaltavit me*. Each portion is transformed. The remainder, which had served the text *exaltavit me* is transformed more sharply and serves for the "new" third phrase, *Dextera Domini fecit virtutem*. This transformation alters considerably the nature of the final cadence. Taking these exceptional circumstances into account, the remainder of the cadences are reasonably similar. Nevertheless, the strict identities that had marked the medieval versions are no longer present.

Somewhat similar lessons are to be learned when examining the readings of the somewhat earlier Gardano Gradual of 1591. In dealing with the first of the cadences, shown in example 46, the Gardano readings are noticeably more expansive than those furnished by Giunta. Gabrieli, Vecchi, and Balbi do not insist, as do later editors that the syllable following an accented antepenultimate be set by no more than a single tone. In one instance, the middle syllable of *Domini* (from *Tollite portas*, staff **g**), has five tones, in two instances, three tones, and in the remaining instance, two. The cadence for *Confitemini Domino* (staff **a**) stands apart from its fellows in that it is the only one to close on a note other than *d'*. Hints of formularity in a previous life abound, but there are no two cadences that are identical. On the other hand, the cadences for *Dextera Domini* and *Benedictus qui venit* (staves **d**, **f**), which in their normative medieval versions had employed a different formula from the remaining four for Easter week now display various features in common with their fellows. In the Gardano edition, as in the 1596 edition by Giunta, the verse for *Dextera Domini* has a tripartite text. Gabrieli, Vecchi, and Balbi do not, however, foreshadow the editorial decisions made by their successors. Both of the first two statements follow loosely their medieval antecedents, and additional material is furnished for the final statement. While this material is largely new, there is an eight-tone parallelism between the setting of the word *Domini* and the previous setting of the syllables [exal]-*tavit me*.

An examination of the final cadences in the Gardano Gradual for the expanded group of graduals demonstrates even stronger indications of formularity, but here too there is not a single pair of chants that is identical. (See example 47.) The insistence on the brevity of the final syllable that was such a persistent feature of the Giunta readings is not present in this earlier revision. To be sure, there is only one tone for the last syllable of both *Confitemini Domino* (staff **a**), and *Dextera Domini* (staff **d**). And there are three for the final syllable of *Dicat nunc* (staff **b**). But the remaining eight graduals assign between six to fourteen tones for the concluding syllable.

The treatment of the above materials by Anerio and Soriano in the Medicean Gradual departs from earlier editions in several respects. With regard to the initial cadences for the verses of the graduals for Easter Week, shown in example 48, the editors are content to use a single solution to serve for *Confitemini Domino*, *Dicat nunc*, and *Dicant nunc*, together with *Tollite portas* for Ember Week in Advent. And the cadence for *Lapidem reprovaberunt* is closely similar, omitting a tonal repetition because of changed textual structure. The initial cadences for *Dextera Domini* and *Benedictus qui venit*, which had drawn on a different formula in their normative medieval versions, are now brought much closer to the readings of their associated chants. The last ten tones of the cadence for *Dextera Domini* are the same as those for the parallel passage in *Confitemini Domino*. The introductory two tones, however, are suggestive of the gesture that opens the final cadence in each of these chants, and in most of their associated fellows.

In the final cadences we find a strong formulaic consistency, shown in example 49, but not consistent uniformity. Four of these chants, *Confitemini, Dicat nunc, Lapidem quem reprobaverunt,* and *Tollite portas* (staves **a**, **d**, and **f**), use identical terminations, while another three vary from these only in tiny details. The text for the verse, *Dextera Domini* (staff **c**), is bipartite, closing with the words, *exaltavit me*. It is quite startling to find that the original melody for *In sole posuit*—for Ember Saturday in Advent—has been entirely suppressed and a new melody in fifth mode has been inserted in its place. Had the Medicean editors found an unrelieved succession of four second-mode graduals so excessive that they were led to this resort? This, however, is not the only instance in this Gradual of the melody for one chant being replaced by another that is entirely new.

We may briefly contrast the results given for the three Italian Graduals with those to be found in one northern Gradual, using for this purpose the one issued by Millange in 1599 under the editorship of Guillaume Boni. Here the formulaic nexus is retained with reasonable fidelity, although not on all occasions. The initial cadences for the verses of the graduals for Easter Week (example 50) are in fair accord with the medieval tradition. *Dextera Domini*(staff **d**) and *Benedictus qui venit* (staff **f**) agree with one another, while contrasting with their counter-parts from other days of Easter Week. This is as it had been formerly. *Confitemini Domini* (staff **a**) and *Dicant nunc* (staff **c**) are quite similar, although not identical. However, *Dicat nunc* (staff **b**), the intervening gradual, is considerably less close, although resembling *Lapidem quem reprobaverunt* (staff **e**) in many respects. *Tollite portas* (staff **g**), from Advent, sharply curtails the melisma on the final syllable and breaks with the medieval tradition in this respect.

With regard to the nexus of final cadences (example 51), we find that with the exception of one variant in *Dextera Domini* (staff **d**), the remaining melismas for the graduals for Easter Week correspond to one another, as do those for *Tollite portas* and *A summo caelo* (staves **g**, **h**). However, the concluding melisma of *In sole posuit* (staff **i**) is somewhat curtailed, while those for *Domine Deus* and *Excita Domine* (staves **j**, **k**) are shortened more drastically, each in an individual way. Reviewing the entire complex of material surveyed, we find that the response to the retention of formulaic materials among chants in close calendaric proximity is variable. At times the formulaic character may be disregarded, as in the Giunta editions. More frequently, the formulaic character is retained, but not in as strict a manner as is observed among medieval sources, and with individual idiosyncratic examples. It is somewhat surprising to find that on occasional instances, a medieval formulaic nexus may acquire new members that previously had been somewhat independent.

The Alleluia for Easter Sunday is the well-known *Alleluia Pascha nostrum,* which had two verses from a very early date. The text for the first is drawn from 1

Corinthians, chapter 5, verse 7, while that for the second is drawn from the verse following. To be sure, the second verse vanished from most sources long before the Council of Trent. It is surprising to find, however, that it is still present both in conservative Germanic sources of the seventeenth century and in a Premonstratensian Gradual of 1718 (staff **m** of example 52).

The post-Tridentine transmission of this chant presents a number of familiar features that have been dealt with on several prior occasions, and we shall eventually touch upon these. I prefer, however, to begin by reflecting on two highly unusual readings, the first from the Medicean Gradual, and the second from the group of three Graduals from the region of present-day Belgium. These pose questions regarding modality and regarding the nature of relative pitch in interpreting the notation of adjacent musical sections.

Whereas all sources except for the four mentioned above begin the verse on *c'*, the fourth degree of the mode, the three sources from Tournai, Antwerp, and Brussels begin startlingly on *b-flat*. (See staff **g** of example 52 for the first of these.) This is not a mistake because the aberrant opening continues through the setting of the words, *Pascha nostrum,* remaining a second lower than normal. A total of nineteen tones is involved. Upon reaching the word, *immolatus,* the normal notational level resumes and continues for the remainder of the piece.

If this unusual passage had appeared in a medieval source prior to the fourteenth century, one might suspect that the chant contained a combination of tones involving pitches other than those notatable within the Guidonian gamut. Under unusual circumstances, when a chant requires a combination of tones not notatable within the confines of the Guidonian gamut (even allowing for alternative notation a fifth or fourth higher than normal), scribes would be forced either to distort the recalcitrant gesture or to employ a sectional transposition, either a second, fourth, or fifth higher or lower. Thus we find instances in which the respond and verse of a given gradual may lie a fourth or fifth apart, the notation seeming to prescribe a large leap between the two even if this was not to be realized in performance. A trope may be notated at one level and the chant with which it is to be associated at another. Again the visual appearance belies the intended result.

Such an explanation will not, however, account for the present anomaly. The use of a notation a second lower than expected would make notatable a passage that at normal height used *f-sharp.* In transposition this tone would then become *e*. Yet no *e* occurs within this stretch of nineteen tones. The proffered explanation is without foundation. If we are dealing here with an intervallic relationship between the final of the Alleluia and the opening tone of the verse that does not represent the intended sonic reality, then this extraordinary occurrence is without a sustainable justification. It is my opinion that the opening of the verse was intended to be sung as written. Although this example is understandably rare, it is not unique. Whereas the average post-Tridentine source begins *Anima nostra*, the gradual for Holy Innocents, on *c'*, a fifth higher than originally intended, the same three sources begin on *b-flat*. This is noteworthy in that during the Middle Ages the chant was intended to open on the final. Whether there are still additional comparable examples can only be determined by a thorough study of the Graduals in their entirety.

The melody given for the *Alleluia Pascha nostrum* in the Medicean Gradual (staff **p**) would indicate strongly that by the early seventeenth century, relative pitch relationships were regarded as fixed, and the dissembling conventions that permitted partial transpositions were seldom used. In order to understand the Medicean reading by Anerio and Soriano it is necessary to remember that following the singing of *Victimae paschali laudes*, there was a return—written out in the print—to the opening *alleluia* and the jubilus. Anerio and Soriano could thus conceptualize the whole as one large structure. Under these circumstances, there was a conflict between the mode-7 character of the Alleluia and the mode-1 character of the sequence. Given the drive of these composers for modal unity and centricity, one of the two elements had to be eliminated. It is startling to find that at this time the melodic tradition for the sequence had greater attraction than that for the Alleluia. The melody for the *Alleluia Pascha nostrum* is eliminated except for certain loose references and is replaced by a new melody in mode 1. From the standpoint of historical precedence, the tail was permitted to wag the dog! It seems clear that here the notation was to be taken at face value, and it governed the performance. As for the liberty taken in supplanting the original melody for *Pascha nostrum*, the reader will recall the prior mention of a similar liberty taken with regard to the gradual, *In sole posuit*, for the Ember Week of Advent.

The same problem in modality was posed to the other reforming editors of the *Alleluia Pascha nostrum*, though these took far less drastic solutions. These editors were apparently willing to begin *Victimae Paschali* a fourth below the final of the preceding Alleluia. They were not, however, willing to leap back up a fourth for the repetition normally expected of the Alleluia form. The solution was simple: remain at the level employed by the sequence. This could be accomplished in various ways. The editor of the Plantin Gradual (staff **h**) duplicated the gesture of the solo portion of the initial Alleluia a fifth lower. The new melody thus began on *c'*, which now served as the subfinal in its new function. Having paid homage to the original chant, a new ending was crafted that brought this small section to an end on the desired final, *d*. The new ending has loose affinities with the jubilus, but one would not wish to draw too close comparisons between the two. This solution is adopted within the year following by Piotrkowczyk in his Gradual issued in Kraków (staff **j**). Apart from Angermaier and Sutor, no other editors employ the Plantin solution, and its appearance in the Kraków is thus a strong indication of the Plantin influence in still another quarter of Europe. With this evidence in hand one can compare other readings contained in the two Graduals and note how frequently the readings in both are similar. Piotrkowczyk, however, exercises a greater degree of independence in the governance of details than do the two German publishers.

In Küchler's Gradual of 1671 (staff **k**), we find a phrase for the repeat of the Alleluia that loosely resembles the opening of the first Alleluia, albeit in a much reduced form. The remaining solutions have no such resemblance and are all still terser. The most laconic is that appearing in the Laurent Gradual from Tournai (staff **g**), together with its successors from Antwerp and Brussels. These sources employ only a single tone for each of the four syllables of the Alleluia. The Boni Gradual from Bordeaux (staff **f**) is one step more expansive and employs a total of five tones. This is the pattern followed by Nivers in the Premonstratensian Gradual of 1680 (staff **m**). Gardano in Venice is more generous, allotting a total of nine tones for the four syllables (staff **d**). The Gradual issued by Giunta in 1596 allots respectively 4, 1, 1, and 1 tones for the second Alleluia (staff **e**) In the version brought out by the same firm in 1642, the proportion is changed, bringing greater emphasis to the second syllable; the proportion is 2, 3, 1, and 1 (staff **f**). The Cistercians did not employ either *Victimae paschali* or any other sequence for Easter Sunday, and thus had no problem in modality. The Flandrus Gradual brought out in Madrid stands apart from the remainder. It does employ *Victimae paschali laudes*, but it returns to the opening *alleluia* following the sequence without a modification to avoid the modal problem.

Returning now to a consideration of the new melody provided in the Medicean Gradual (staff **p**), we observe that it opens on the final and concludes the solo portion on the fifth of the mode, as does the medieval melody. Nevertheless, the details of the ascent differ from those in the traditional melody. Each of the following three neumes returns to the modal final, and there is a twofold return to the modal final in the medieval melody as well. Nevertheless, the medieval chant is much more expansive and repetitive than the one from the seventeenth century. The final ten tones of the Medicean version do parallel the comparable ten tones of the medieval version, allowing for difference of mode and small detail. Whereas the medieval version begins the verse on the fourth degree of the mode and oscillates repeatedly between the fifth and sixth degrees, the Medicean melody begins on the final and climbs directly to a turn around the fifth degree. The medieval melody features a major melisma on the accented syllable of *immolatus*, a segment well-known as a source of numerous discant clausulae in the Parisian polyphonic repertory of the late twelfth and thirteenth centuries. This melisma rises from the fifth degree to the upper ninth, circulates between these two tones, and then circuitously wends it way downward eventually to reach the final. The motion in the Medicean melody is quite different. Encompassing only nine tones for the full word, it plunges down from the seventh degree, touches upon the final and rebounds to the fourth. The setting of the word *Christus* also differs in overall profile from its more florid counterpart in the medieval melody. Punctilious respect is accorded throughout to word accent in the text.

A similar concern for prosodic values is exhibited in the reworking of the normative medieval chant in the 1596 edition of Giunta (staff **e**) and its successors. The only polysyllabic word in the text to be accorded more than one tone for the final syllable is *Christus*, whose final syllable has two notes. In contrast, the Venetian edition by Gabrieli, Vecchi, and Balbi (staff **d**), issued only five years previously, has small flourishes on the final syllables of *nostrum*, *immolatus*, and *Christus*. The parallelism between the end of the Alleluia and the end of its verse disappears in this reworking and in many other of the post-Tridentine sources. Likewise, the northern sources are not hesitant to retain flourishes on final syllables, even though these may be somewhat curtailed. Quite striking is the major expansion of the first syllable of the verse in the reading given by the Flandrus Gradual (staff **i**). This creates a loose parallelism with the opening of the Alleluia itself, a feature not found in any of the other sources that I have consulted. The recasting also contributes to a heightened sense of modal centricity.

The text for the offertory for Easter Sunday is taken from Psalm 75, the last portion of verse 9 and the opening of verse 10, in a variant version of the Latin Psalter. The two translations of Jerome are further removed. The variant reading of the Latin Psalter is given as (A), that of the *Hexapla* as (B), while that after the Hebrew is represented in (C):

> (A) terra tremuit et quievit / dum [resurgeret] in judicio Deus
>
> (B) terra timuit et quievit / cum exsurgeret in judicium Deus
>
> (C) terra timens tacebit / cum surrexerit ad judicandum Deus

(The preferred form of the Latin Psalter also uses the verb form *exsurgeret*.)

The familiar fourth-mode melody presents many traits similar to those of the introit, *Resurrexi*. The structural skeleton rests to a considerable extent on a *d–f–a–c′* chain of thirds. The opening gesture, setting the words, *Terra tremuit*, relies on the lower three tones of this chain, while the following gesture expands to include all four. The setting for *dum resurgeret* also uses the full complement, and like the first, closes on *a*. The fourth gesture likewise extends over the full chain, and concludes on *d*, in a manner similar to the second phrase. It is only at the end of the setting of the final word, *alleluia*, that we find a strong, familiar, deuterus maneria cadence. All of the post-Tridentine editors with the exception of Anerio and Soriano accept this tonal structure without question. (See example 53.) But the tension between the *e* final and the consistent chain of thirds founded on *d* is beyond the realm of the acceptable for these two musicians. In reworking the introit *Resurrexi*, the two editors changed a number of sensitive pitches, particularly at the very opening in order to create a reasonable focus on *e*. In this offertory, however, such a procedure would encounter too many tonal contradictions. Thus the Medicean editors take the opposite route and simply alter the final cadence so that one comes to a logical conclusion on *d*. The reader will remember that the later Venetian editors of the gradual, *Universi*, excised the final tone of that chant, thus ending on *e* rather than *d*. It was necessary to comment on the strangeness of this ending because there was little in the previous melodic fabric to establish the tonal suitability of the *e* ending. Here, however, the ending on *d* falls in readily with the earlier melodic ductus. No wrench is felt, despite the distortion of the original model.

The normative medieval melody for *Terra et tremuit* is little concerned with the niceties of prosodic stress. Of the seven polysyllabic words (including the final *alleluia*), only one, *Deus*, accords a greater number of tones to the stressed syllable than to any other. Each of the first two syllables of *tremuit* is accorded three tones. There is, to be sure, a lengthening of the accented syllable of *iudicio*, but it is the final syllable of that word that bears the greatest tonal weight. In the setting of the final word, *alleluia*, it is the first and especially the second of the syllables that carry the greatest weight, and not the accented third. This situation is largely reversed in the Italian and French Graduals, and at least ameliorated in the other "reform" editions. Using bold face to indicate the number of tones for the accented syllables, the apportioning of tones in the Gardano edition (staff **c**) may be indicated as **4**–1, **3**–3–1, 1–**5**–2, 1–3–2–**4**, 2–3–**1**–1, **7**–1, and 2–5–**4**–4. The Giunta Gradual of 1596 (staff **d**) employs the successions: **3**–1, **3**–1–1, 2–**4**–1, 2–2–**1**–1, 2–2–**1**–1, **6**–1, 2–6–**3**–2. The reading of the Pezzana Gradual of 1779 (staff **e**) demonstrates a consistency of tradition that extends for nearly two centuries. The Medicean Gradual exhibits the successions: **4**–2, **4**–1–2, 1–**7**–1, 1–3–**1**–1, 2–3–**1**–5, **5**–1, 2–6–**10**–1. The Gradual edited by Boni and associates runs as follows: **3**–4, **6**–1–1, **3**–10–1, 2–3–**1**–5, 1–3–**1**–5, 1–3–**1**–5, **7**–1, 8–13–**3**–2. The brevity of the penultimates in *resurgeret* and *iudicio* is emphasized through the use of "semibreves." Nevertheless, Boni does not have the aversion to small flourishes on the final syllables that generally characterizes the work of his Italian predecessors. The Praemonstratensian Gradual of 1718 (staff **n**) also follows the general tendency, with successions: **3**–2, **3**–1–2, 1–**4**–1, 2–3–**1**–1, 1–1–**1**–5 (the unaccented penultimate note is indicated by a semibreve), **6**–1, 4–8–**3**–2. Among this group, only the Medicean Gradual accords a sustaining accent to the penultimate syllable of *alleluia*, suggesting that there may have been an alternative pronunciation with the accent falling on the second syllable. In all of these reshufflings of the allocations of tones per syllable, the general melodic profile persists. To be sure, different portions of the profile drop out by virtue of the greater brevity of the late reworkings, but the tonal goals tend to remain reasonably consistent. An exception to this rule of thumb is found in the reading of the Premonstratensian Gradual (staff **n**), which omits the rise that marks the final syllable of *resurgeret*. This, however, is transferred to the following monosyllable, *in*.

The communion for Easter Sunday utilizes the text previously employed for the two verses of the Alleluia that precedes it. Although, as noted earlier, the second of these dropped out for the most part long before the seventeenth century, I mentioned its surprising survival into the eighteenth century in the Premonstratensian Gradual, first issued in 1680 and then re-issued in 1718. As mentioned earlier, the text derives from 1 Corinthians, verses 7 and 8.

The sixth-mode melody clearly revolves around the final with frequent closes on that tone at syntactical significant points, such as the ends of *Christus*, *alleluia*, *itaque*, *sinceritatis*, and *veritatis*. We find once more that little heed has been paid to the stressed syllables, as each of the first four polysyllabic words ends with a small flourish on the final syllable. With the exception of the Gardano edition, the melisma on the middle syllable of *itaque* was regarded as particularly egregious by the Italian and French editors. Thus, while the general melodic profile remains reasonably constant in the various editions consulted, there is considerable variety in apportioning the tones to the individual syllables and also in determining which tones are to be retained, and which may be cut. (See example 54.)

Consider, for example, the setting of the word, *immolatus*. The normative medieval version assigns, 2–1–2–7 tones respectively to the four syllables, ending on *g*. The Gardano print of 1591 (staff **d**) employs 1–1–3–4 tones, lessening the contrast between the accented penultimate and the unaccented final, which here falls on *f*. The Giunta edition of 1596 (staff **e**) has a stronger revision, with 1–1–4–1 tones, respectively, while the Medicean Gradual (staff **f**), employs 1–1–5–2. The Gradual edited by Boni for Millange (staff **g**) is fuller, using 1–1–9–1 tones, emphasizing the brevity of the antepenultimate by means of a semibreve. The later print issued by Cramoisy and Clopeiau (staff **h**) employs 1–2–5–1 tones. The Netherlandish and derivative German versions are both concerned with the brevity of the antepenultimate syllable, indicated by the use of a semibreve, but neither is offended by the length of the final syllable. They exhibit the successions 1–1–4–7 and 1–1–2–7, respectively (staves **i**, **j**). The Premonstratensian editor, Nivers, on the other hand, was much concerned with the brevity of the final syllable, not only employing the succession 1–1–3–1, but employing a semibreve at the very end (staff **n**). This is not normal practice, but the Nivers uses semibreves in other unusual placements at various times. The Cistercian Gradual (staff **m**) presents the succession 2–1–2–5. We find no complete agreement between any pair of editions.

Comparison between the Pezzana Gradual of 1779 (not shown in example 54) and the Giunta Gradual issued nearly 180 years earlier demonstrates how faithful the Venetian tradition could remain when exactness was deemed appropriate. I have chosen to omit the reading given in the Piotrkowczyk Gradual of 1600, having established earlier in this chapter its close relationship to the Plantin Gradual of 1599. In the present instance the Polish reading diverges from its antecedent in only two quite minor variants.

EIGHT

A Selected Miscellany

The five Mass Propers examined in the previous chapters did not include any representative from Lent. Nor was there any taken from the Sanctorale. The two lacunae thus formed are of serious scope, and the purpose of this chapter is to provide a partial remedy. Rather than select a Mass from Lent and another from the Sanctorale, I propose to study a group of selected chants, not limiting myself to representatives from the aforementioned two groups. In this fashion, I intend to take into account genres of chant that have not thus far been considered, to examine some chants that had notably unstable musical transmissions during the Middle Ages, to consider a chant that underwent a significant textual change and, finally, to consider three chants from the Sanctorale. In order to address these diverse needs, it is necessary to relinquish the thread of liturgical unity that provided a connective element in previous discussions. The chants to be examined are as follows: (1) the second-mode tracts, *Domine audivi* and *Qui habitat*; (2) the antiphon, *Immutemur habitu in cinere*; (3) the communions, *Qui biberit* and *Oportet te*; (4) the introit, *Deus in adjutorium*; (5) the offertory, *Jubilate Deo universa terra*; and 6) the gradual, *Suscepimus Deus*, the tract, *Nunc dimittis*, and the communion, *Responsum accepit Simeon*, the latter three having been taken from the Mass for the Purification of the Blessed Virgin Mary.

We have not thus far had occasion to examine any tract. As all informed readers know, these are elaborate and heavily formulaic melodies, which come down to us in only two modes, mode 8 and mode 2. Although the former group is the more numerous, I shall discuss two examples from the latter group in order to take advantage of prior experience with these chants. When dealing with chants for the Sanc-torale, I shall take up a tract that is in mode 8.

Our first example, *Domine audivi auditum tuum*, is—according to hypotheses set forth in earlier work of mine[1]—one of the three earliest second-mode tracts. *De necessitatibus* and *Domine exaudi orationem meam* are the other members of this group; all three were distinguished in our earliest sources by rubrics identifying them either as responsories (or gradual responsories). I have concluded that *De necessitatibus*, the most idiosyncratic of the entire group, was the earliest of the three, the formal traits that were to characterize the later members of the family not yet having been fixed.

The five verses of *Domine audivi* draw their text from the Book of Habakkuk (Abacuc), chapter 3, verses 2–3, subdivided and with significant departures from the texts commonly known in Latin, Hebrew, and English. The latter present a sufficient number of problems in interpretation that their meanings are not always immediately clear. Obviously there are different philosophies of translation, and renderings into vernaculars are dependent upon the translator's objectives. Below, I compare the chant text with an English translation to be found in two Daily Missals (English-1), with a common English translation from the original Hebrew (English-2), with a critical reading of the Latin Vulgate, and with an additional two English renditions based on various sources.[2] Unfortunately, the books of the *Vetus Latina* that have been available to me do not include the Book of Habakkuk. Should such a version be extant, it might be germane to present considerations. It is worth noting that only Chapters 1 and 2 survive in the Dead Sea Scrolls, but not Chapter 3, which is generally thought to be an independent addition. Before beginning we may remark that Teman, mentioned in verse 4 of the tract, is thought to be northwest of Edom, and hence God was envisaged as proceeding from the south to the north. This is captured in the Vulgate, *ab austro*, but is reversed in the chant text, *"a Libano."* (Reference to Lebanon had occurred in verse 17 of the preceding chapter.) The word *Selah* is found primarily here and in the Psalms, and it has been suggested that it was originally some form of musical direction. (The word occurs also in various prayers appearing in modern *Siddurim* [Hebrew prayer books].)

> Chant: *Domine, audivi auditum tuum, et timui*
> English-1: O Lord, I have heard Your hearing and was afraid:
> English-2: O Lord, I have heard the report of Thee, and am afraid;
> Vulgate: *Domine, audivi auditionem tuam et timui*
> English-3: O Lord, I have heard the report of thee, and thy work, O Lord, do I fear
> English-4: Yahweh, I have heard of your renown, your work, Yahweh, inspires me with dread
> English-5: O LORD. I have heard thy speech and was afraid

> Chant: *consideravi opera tua et expavi.*
> English-1: I have considered Your works and trembled.

Chant: *In medio duorum animalium innotesceris: dum appropinquaverunt anni,*
                cognosceris:
English-1:   In the midst of two animals You shall be made known: when the
                years shall draw near, You shall be known:
English-2:   O Lord, revive Thy work in the midst of the years, in the midst of
                the years make it known;
Vulgate: *Domine opus tuum in medio annorum vivifica illud in medio annorum*
                notum facies
English-3:   In the midst of the years renew it; in the midst of the years make it
                known;
English-4:   Repeat it in our own time, reveal it in our time.
English-5:   O LORD, revive thy works in the midst of years, in the midst of
                years make known.

Chant: *dum advenerit tempus, ostenderis.*
English-1:   when the time shall come, You shall be manifested.

Chant: *In eo, dum conturbata fuerit anima mea: in ira, misericordiae memor*
                eris.
English-1:   When my soul shall be in trouble, You will remember mercy, even in
                Your wrath.
English-2:   In wrath remember compassion.
Vulgate: *cum iratus fueris misericordiae recordaberis*
English-3:   in wrath, remember mercy.
English-4:   For all your wrath, remember to be merciful.
English-5:   in wrath remember mercy.

Chant: *Deus a Libano veniet, et Sanctus de monte umbroso et condenso.*
English-1:   God will come from Lebanon, and the Holy One from the shady
                and thickly covered mountain.
English-2:   God cometh from Teman, And the Holy One from mount Paran.
                Selah
Vulgate::   *Deus ab austro veniet et Sanctus de monte Pharan Semper*
English-3:   God came from Teman and the Holy One from Mount Paran.
English-4:   Eloah is coming from Teman, and the Holy One from Mount Paran.
English-5:   God came from Teman, and the Holy On[e] from mount Paran.
                Selah

Chant: *Operuit caelos majestas ejus: et laudis ejus plena est terra.*
English-1:   His majesty covered the heavens: and the earth is full of His praise.
English-2:   His glory covereth the heavens, And the earth is full of His praise.
Vulgate: *operuit caelos gloria eius et laudis eius plena est terra.*
English-3:   His glory covered the heavens, and the earth was full of his praise.
                Selah.
English-4:   His majesty veils the heavens, the earth is filled with his glory.
English-5:   His glory covered the heavens and the earth was full of his praise

The chant text not only enlarges on both the Hebrew original and the Latin
Vulgate, but it distorts the sense as well. The most serious instance involves verse
2, in which the critical word in Hebrew is chaiyehu (spelled: cheyt, yod, yod, heh,
vav [bear in mind that vowels are not ordinarily indicated in Hebrew]). We may

perhaps understand how the chant text came to be if we subdivide this word into its component parts. The first two letters form the word chai, for "life," as in the toast, *"L'chaim"* (To life). This noun is converted into a verb, "to give (restore) life" or renew, by means of the next two letters. The Amidah, a central prayer in Jewish liturgy, refers to God as "One who restores life (mechayei) to the dead." The suffix "hu" normally indicates the third person singular. Nevertheless, there are times when normal grammatical rules distinguishing plural from singular are ignored. "Elohim" is the best known of these words. The form itself is a plural and reference may be intended to (other) gods, but in Scripture, the word most often refers to the One God, and in this context it is consistently accompanied by a verb in the singular. In the present instance we have another word of ambiguous number, and medieval Jewish commentators do not agree whether the reference is singular (him) or plural (them).

If we alter the spelling of the critical word, dropping the final letter, eliminating one of the *yods* as superfluous, and misreading the penultimate *heh*, we come up with "chayot," meaning creatures, beings, or animals. "Chayot hakodesh," is a reference to the holy beings in service of God, while "chayot hasadeh" are beasts of the field, or, in the chant text, animals. To make the transformation complete, one need merely misinterpret the unspecified vowels of the text. In place of "shanim" (years), we come up with "shnaim" (two), and we have the text of the chant. (This interpretation was kindly suggested to me by Professor Tikva Frymer-Kensky and Rabbi Allan Kensky.) According to the *Jerusalem Bible* (p. 1517), this mistranslation appeared earlier in the Septuagint, apparently the source for the chant text. Within the Hebrew tradition, these words could conceivably bring to mind the Covenant Between the Parts that was sealed between God and Abraham, but this is highly tenuous. The fit is very poor. However, within a Christological framework, the mangled sentence apparently gave rise to the image of two animals standing near the crib at Bethlehem.

There is a further problem in verse 4 of the tract. Teman is thought to be northwest of Edom, and hence God was envisaged as proceeding from the south to the north. This is captured in the Vulgate, *ab austro*, but it is reversed in the chant text, "a Libano." (Reference to Lebanon had occurred in verse 17 of the preceding chapter.) The word Selah is found primarily here and in the Psalms, and it has been suggested that it was originally some form of musical direction. (The word occurs also in various prayers appearing in modern Siddurim [Hebrew prayer books].)

The text itself has much of the character of a psalm, and in Scripture it has a superscription comparable to that of a psalm: "A prayer of Habakkuk the prophet. Upon Shigionoth." Psalm 7 begins with a similar heading, "Shiggaion of David," and the two terms are thought to refer to the impassioned style of a dithyrambic poem and melody.

The process of chant reform gave rise to many and varied effects with regard to *Domine audivi*. On the largest scale, one may be taken aback to find that in the reading given by Cramoisy and Clopeiau in 1662 the last verse is lacking! Suspicion of an oversight may spring readily to mind. One can, after all, find an oversight of such nature elsewhere when dealing with the graduals for the Ember Week of Advent as presented in the Giunta edition of 1596. Yet the problem does not have such a simple solution. When we consult the Flandrus Gradual of 1597, we find that this source lacks the last two verses. And the reading of *Eripe me*, which follows on Good Friday, gives only the first three verses. Curiously enough, text is supplied for four more verses without space for music, but verses 8–11 are lacking entirely. Furthermore, the reading of *Qui habitat*, which we shall consider next, consists of only the first three verses. Still more surprising is the treatment of these and other second-mode tracts in the 1840 Gradual published by Canfari in Turin. In this print *Domine audivi* consists of only the first two verses, *Qui habitat* of verses 1–4, and *Deus, Deus meus* of verses 1–7. *Eripe me*, another of the longest tracts, presents only verses 1–6, while *Domine non secundum*, a much briefer chant, presents only the first two verses. Evidently we are dealing with a broader issue.

This problem is not restricted to sources that are associated with chant reform. When one consults the readings of the *Graduale Herbipolense*, published in 1583, one finds that the tracts *Domine audivi* and *Eripe me* are given complete. However, the tract, *Qui habitat*, for the First Sunday of Lent, gives the first two verses and then jumps to the last two, subdividing the final verse and treating *Longitudine dierum* as a separate verse. Following this chant is an annotation, "Non plus cantatur in choro Herbipolensi." The reading for *Deus, Deus meus*, the tract for Palm Sunday also gives the first two verses, followed by the last two, *Annuntiabitur Domino*, and *Populo qui nascetur*. There is no annotation here. The very same readings appeared nearly a century earlier in another Würzburg Gradual brought out by Georg Reyser in 1496.

Knowledge of the practice of excising verses may, on occasion, give rise to difficulties in the interpretation of a specific reading. Here, I have consistently employed readings from Würzburg, Universitätsbibl., MS ch. 283 in order to demonstrate the nature of conservative German Benedictine practice of the early seventeenth century. In this source, we reach the very end of verse 8, *Quoniam Angelis suis*, at the bottom of fol. 72r. When we turn the leaf, we do not find the next verse, *In manibus portabunt te*, but instead verse 13, *Eripiam eum*, the final verse. Is this unexpected juxtaposition the product of error or of a deliberate editorial policy? A companion source, compiled for the same monastery within a year or so, presents *Qui habitat* complete, suggesting that error is a more likely explanation.[3] Where possible, I shall amplify example 55 with material drawn from the more complete source. Nevertheless, given the conditions that we have been describing, we cannot be certain that error is involved. Without a greater knowledge of chant practice in the fifteenth through sixteenth centuries we do not know how often the longer tracts may have been abbreviated. This is a striking reminder of the dangers posed by our lack of a comprehensive history of chant.

The next smaller structural level concerns the tonal arrangement of the individual verse. Although the most frequent structure for verses of second-mode tracts consists of a series of four phrases ending on the tones, *d*, *c*, *f*, and *d*, the verses of

Domine audivi have longer than average texts and hence a greater number of subdivisions each. Nevertheless, the overall progressions correspond reasonably well to the norm.

Examination of the readings assembled in example 55 demonstrates rapidly that the characteristic melismas of this chant are cut most heavily in the three Italian sources issued by the Gardano (1591), Giunta (1596), and Medicean (1614/15) presses (staves **c**, **d**, and **e**). Indeed, the cuts in the Giunta reading are so severe that on only four occasions among the five verses do we find more than three tones assigned to a single syllable.[4] The most effusive has a mere six. This is a style that could easily be associated with a communion or antiphon were it not for the length of the text. By contrast, the initial melisma of verse 1 in the restored Solesmes reading has twenty tones, while its counterpart in verse 2 has twenty-five. The cuts in the Giunta edition, and those of the Gardano and Medicean readings, strike at the heart of the formulaic structures characteristic of the medieval version, basically destroying these. It is not surprising therefore, to find that the tonal progressions mentioned in the previous paragraph are subjected to a variety of modifications.

The first of the problems to face us concerns the very opening of the Gardano reading (line **c** of example 55), which lies a third higher than one might expect, beginning on *f* and descending to *c*. One's first reaction is to declare this a simple clef-reading error and to provide an editorial correction that would have the chant open on *d* and progress to *A*. This is very possibly the correct solution and would undoubtedly be readily adopted if one were dealing with a medieval source. Such editorial correction would have the advantage of corresponding loosely to the reading in the Medicean Gradual. When, however, one is dealing with a source in which the editors have been given a free hand to change according to their will, matters are considerably less certain. One may well be suspicious of a supposed clef-reading error when dealing with the very opening of a chant and the reading does make quite acceptable musical sense as it stands. The editorial decision is far chancier under these conditions.

The truncation or virtual abolition of melismas creates other difficulties. It is the melisma on the last syllable of *Domine* that basically constitutes the opening phrase of the medieval melody and the phrase is defined largely, if not entirely on the basis of an easily recognizable formula. One is much more reluctant to think of a group of 4–6 tones apportioned among three syllables as a phrase. Thus the subdivision of any of the Italian readings into phrases must be considered anew. In dealing with the medieval melody the first phrase sets the word, *Domine*, and cadences on *d*. The second and third phrases terminate on the final syllable of *tuum* and *timui*, respectively, employing standard medial formulas that cadence on *c*. The second half of the opening verse is devoted to the setting of the word, *consideravi*, and concludes with a cadence on *f*, employing one of two familiar formulas for this purpose. It is perhaps best to view the setting of *opera tua* as a separate phrase even though it does not employ a standard formula; this segment too reaches a cadence on *c*. The final phrase sets the text, *et expavi*, ending with a standard formula leading to *d*.

Since it can be difficult to compare the early and late versions of *Domine audivi* in terms of phrases, I will treat the final notes of phrases in the normative medieval version as "markers" and seek their late equivalents in comparable places in the revised melodies. Depending upon whether we regard the version in the Gardano print as erroneous or not, the first marker is either A or c, in either event a mismatch for its medieval counterpart. Both the Medicean reading (staff e) and that of the Premonstratensian version (staff n) place their first marker on A, again a mismatch. The Giunta edition of 1596 (staff d) has the first marker on d as in the medieval version, but reaches this marker in a far different manner.

The reading for the second marker, which falls at the end of the word *tuum*, again displays alternatives among the Italian versions. Whereas we normally find here a medial formula cadencing on c, the Gardano print (staff c) gives d at this point, while the Medicean Gradual (staff e) carries up to g. The third marker, which occurs at the end of the word *timui*, is replicated more consistently in the late readings. However, the Premonstratensian version (staff n) concludes this segment on d, rather than the customary c, and employs d also at the fourth marker (at *consideravi*), which normally cadences on f. The Giunta Gradual of 1596 (staff d) reaches c at three successive markers for *timui*, *consideravi*, and *tua*.

In the medieval readings of second-mode tracts one normally finds *consideravi* associated with either of two cadences concluding on f. The most common consists of a simple turn around this note, while the less frequent one leads up to a *b-flat* before descending. In tracts belonging to later chronological layers the formula displaying the upward extension is generally to be found in the last verse of the chant. *Domine audivi*, however, is unusual in this regard and employs this formula early on in the chant. In contrast to other northern readings, the French versions of Millange (staff f) and Cramoisy and Clopeiau (staff g) substitute the common formula for the less frequent one at this point. Briefly stated, the late revisers of chant were not consistently concerned with maintaining the most significant reference points in the melody, or at least they did not view these as crucial to the melodic shape. The openings of subsections also submit to change. The Premonstratensian version of *Domine audivi* (staff n) begins *consideravi* on a low A, rather than the customary c, and thus achieves a longer upward sweep that carries beyond this word.

The lessons to be learned from an examination of the later verses of *Domine audivi* are similar to those commented upon with regard to the first. In order to demonstrate this point I shall treat the second verse in similar detail, but mention only the most prominent aspects of the three last verses. There are seven "markers" for the second verse, *In medio duorum animalium;* these occur at the ends of the words, *medio, animalium, innotesceris, anni, cognosceris, tempus,* and *ostenderis.* Only the last of these remains fixed throughout all of the sources studied. One exception may be found for the second marker, which normally falls on d. The 1591 Gardano edition (staff c) reaches f at this point. The fourth of the markers, on *anni*, normally concludes on d, but the Medicean Gradual of 1614 (staff e) rises to g. Similarly, the penultimate marker, on *tempus*, which normally falls on *f*, terminates on *g* in the Gardano reading (staff **c**). The antepenultimate marker, at the end of *cognosceris*, falls on *d* in the Premonstratensian reading (staff **n**) rather than on the customary *c*. The initial marker, normally *d*, is *f* in both the readings of the Giunta Gradual of 1596 (staff **d**) and the Premonstratensian Gradual of 1680 (staff **n**). The third marker, which closes *innotesceris*, is the least stable of the group. Normally this falls at the end of a medial formula leading to *c*, this occurs on *d* in the French editions of Millange (staff **f**) as well as Cramoisy and Clopeiau (staff **g**), and also in the Netherlandish edition of Laurent (1616, staff **i**). Much more unusual, the Giunta Gradual (staff **d**) ends this segment of the melody on *g*.

The least stable of the markers for the later verses are the opening segment of verse 4, *Deus a Libano*, and the second segment of verse 5, *Operuit de caelos*. In the normative medieval version, the opening marker of verse 4 falls on *d*. In both of the French sources employed here (staves **f**, **g**), it falls out on *f*, whereas in the 1596 Giunta Gradual (staff **d**) and in the 1680 Premonstratensian Gradual (staff **n**), this marker occurs on *g*. The version of the 1591 Gardano Gradual (staff **c**) is most unusual in that the marker is found on *e*. (A marker on *e* occurs in the Premonstratensian reading—staff **n**—of verse 3 at the end of *fuerit*.) In verse 5, the second marker, found at the end of *caelos*, is customarily associated with a medial cadence on *c*. However, the Laurent, Premonstratensian, and Cistercian Graduals (staves **i**, **n**, and **m**) all reach *d* at this point in the melody, while the 1596 Giunta Gradual (staff **d**) ascends to *f*.

The destruction or weakening of the formulaic cadences in *Domine audivi* affects not only the tonal direction of the individual verses, but also the formal relationships of the chant as a whole. Formulas are important elements that contribute to the unity of tracts by virtue of their multiple appearances in different verses. Thus their destruction, weakening, or substitution has a fundamental effect on overall unity.

One of the lesser instances of this effect involves a small formula leading to a cadence on *d* that appears in verses 2 and 3. The earlier of the two instances is associated with the setting of the word *animalium*, while the later is associated with the words *conturbatur fuerit*. In the normative medieval version represented by the Solesmes readings the two passages are not identical.[5] The first consists of twenty tones, while the second has only seventeen, the pitches 14, 15, and 19 are lacking. These differences notwithstanding, the recurrence still carries force.

When one examines the selected post-Tridentine readings, the situation is different. Neither the 1591 Gardano Gradual (staff **c**) nor the 1614 Medicean Gradual (staff **e**) exhibits this near identity. In the earlier of these two editions, the passage from verse 2 ends on *f*, while that from verse 3 ends on *d*; in the later print, the situation is reversed. In both cases the lengthy near-identity is lacking. The same is true of the reading presented in the 1680 Premonstratensian Gradual edited by Guillaume-Gabriel Nivers (staff **n**). The relevant segment of verse 2 occupies a low tessitura and ends on *d*. Its counterpart in verse 3, on the other hand, reaches a peak a third higher, and closes on *e*. Again the element of unification is absent.

The two passages in question both close on *d* in the 1596 reading by Giunta (staff **d**), but only the last two notes in each are identical, and this is entirely insufficient to establish a large formal resemblance. In Boni's revision of 1598/99 (staff **f**), one catches vague glimpses of a broader resemblance, and there is a broader parallelism of tonal profile, but the distribution of the melody among the respective syllables is such that there is no extended stretch of identity. The reworking accomplished in the Cramoisy and Clopeiau Gradual of 1662 (staff **g**) is such that moments of near identity appear. These occur near the openings of the two passages, but are lacking at the cadential points. Their unifying force is thus undermined. There is somewhat greater resemblance between the two passages in the Plantin Gradual of 1599 (staff **h**), but this consists of a few fleeting moments. Only in the Graduals of the Cistercians (1696), Flandrus (1597), Küchler (1671), and Laurent (1616)—staves **m**, **l**, and **k**, resp.—is the relationship between the two passages fairly extensive. Even in these sources, our attention may be distracted from the similar melodic profiles owing to the different ways in which the various pitches may be distributed among the relevant syllables. The unifying force still fails to achieve the levels to be observed in the medieval versions.

An examination of other passages will corroborate the same simple observation. In the normative medieval version, verses 3–5 of *Domine audivi* each end with a melisma of twenty-one tones that coincides with the final syllable of the respective verses. (The identity between the conclusions of verses 3 and 5 is more than fifty percent longer, but the segment that is common to all three is sufficient for our needs.) Helmut Hucke[6] has pointed out that this formal feature is characteristic of responsorial structures, and this fact lends significance to the early rubrics that designate *Domine audivi* as either a gradual or gradual responsory. Given the prominent placement of the melisma, it exercises an important function in shaping the tonal profile of the work and in accounting for a sense of unity. The melisma begins with a lower neighbor motion from the final to the sub-final and continues with an ascent to the fifth degree, followed by a relaxation, and concludes with a second ascent to the fifth degree, followed by a descent to the final, a rebound to the second degree, and a return to the final.

The treatment of this passage varies considerably among the readings of post-Tridentine Graduals. In verses 3 and 4, the final syllable is frequently set by no more than one to four tones. This syllable may, however, be treated more generously in the final verse. Nevertheless, in order to get a sufficient idea of the various cadences, it is necessary to expand our frame of reference in order to include the last two syllables, rather than focus exclusively on the last one. As might be expected from the observations made in all of the previous chapters, the Italian Graduals are cut the most heavily. Neither the Gardano, Giunta, nor Medicean versions (staves **c**, **d**, and **e**) features a rise from the final to the fifth degree. In verse 3, we find in both the

Gardano and Medicean readings a descent from the fourth to the final that takes place over the last two syllables. The Giunta reading (staff **d**) takes its point of departure from the subfinal, but it reaches only the third degree. The last four tones of all three passages are the tones that end the normative medieval reading, i.e., *d–e*, *e–d*, the last two of these being assigned to the final syllable. In the Giunta and Medicean readings of verse 4 (staves **d**, **e**), these four tones are constitute the entire ending for the last two syllables. The Gardano reading (staff **c**) is slightly more expansive, employing a turn around the final for the penultimate syllable and limiting the final syllable to a single tone on the final. The concluding verse is less restricted. The Gardano and Medicean readings (staves **c**, **e**) rise from the third degree to the fifth before descending to the final, turning, and then reiterating the final one last time. There is an affinity between the endings to the last three verses, but this is limited to four tones, ascending from the final to the upper neighbor, followed by a tonal repetition and return. This is not even one fifth of the expanse of the normative medieval melisma, and these four tones cannot achieve the architectural significance and the importance as a unifying factor present in the earlier melody.

Roughly similar comments may be made regarding the readings of the Laurent and Cistercian Graduals for verses 3 and 4 (staves **i**, **m**) even though these are less succinct than the readings of their southern counterparts. In the final verse, however, each of these Graduals presents a reading that follows the general profile of the medieval melisma, without, however, employing a twofold ascent to the fifth degree. And both editions permit the abbreviated melisma to fall entirely on the last syllable. The Laurent Gradual (staff **i**) employs thirteen tones, while the Cistercian (staff **m**) uses fifteen. A comparable situation exists also in the Premonstratensian Gradual edited by Nivers (staff **n**), which employs twelve notes for the melisma.

The remaining editions are each more expansive. The Mainz Gradual issued by Küchler (staff **k**) manages to follow the concluding profiles for the last three verses, although grouping the relevant tones in rather idiosyncratic manners. In all three verses, the passage begins in mid-stream during the setting of the penultimate syllable, and in all three, the final syllable is accorded only two tones. The Gradual edited by Boni (staff **f**) accords five and two tones respectively to the last two syllables of verse 3; it begins with a descent from the fourth degree. However, this Gradual presents a reasonably full account of the final melisma of verse 4, although assigning all but the last two tones to the penultimate syllable. It follows the same profile while adding three supplementary tones to the final verse, and here the editor follows medieval practice in assigning the entire melisma to the final syllable.

The Plantin Gradual (staff **h**) is the most unusual of the selected group.[7] It presents the profile of the full melisma, with two ascents to the fifth degree, in all three verses, and verses 3 and 4 are identical. Verse 5 lacks only two tones from its predecessors, and all three verses place the melisma on the final syllable in keeping with the medieval tradition. Here the melisma retains nearly its full force in providing a sense of unity to the work. Whereas in other, briefer chants, we have clear evidence of the interrelatedness of the Piotrkowczyk Gradual and its Belgian predecessor, the treatment of *Domine audivi* in the Polish source (staff **j**) shows the extent to which it could maintain a degree of independence. Although the readings continue to belong essentially to the Plantin family, the final melismas of the last three verses are much curtailed.

Considering the work as a whole, including all of the readings provided here, we find numerous other, less striking variants to be observed. Much more could be said regarding various details of the editorial revisions, but I have preferred to expend my efforts in dealing with those larger aspects that I have deemed most important.

The tract, *Qui habitat in adjutorio Altissimi*, for the First Sunday of Lent, presents a comparable series of problems. A significant difference lies in the fact that, with thirteen verses, this chant is more than two-and-a-half times the length of *Domine audivi*. Having laid out a ground plan for the previous example, I feel that brevity is necessary here. The text of *Qui habitat* is taken from Psalm 90, verses 1–7 and 11–16. In both the Roman Psalter and the *Hexapla, Eripiam eum*, the opening of the last verse of the chant is given as the last portion of verse 15. (There is a textual variant at this point in Jerome's translation from the Hebrew.) Verse 16 begins rather with the words, *Longitudine dierum*, and this fact helps explain why some chant sources treat this as a separate verse, as has been noted previously in the discussion of the abbreviated forms of this chant. Nevertheless, the tonal ordering of the chant demonstrates clearly that the singers responsible for the formation of the Gregorian tradition were of the opinion that verse 16 was to begin with *eripiam*. Were one to accept the division given in the textual sources, then verse 15 would come to an end with a medial cadence on *c*, rather than a final formula on *d*.

With very minor exceptions the chant text follows the Roman Psalter; it is also close to the reading of Jerome's *Hexapla*, although here the small variants are somewhat more numerous. One of the small distinguishing variants occurs near the beginning of verse 2. The Roman Psalter reads, *Susceptor meus es*, while the two translations by Jerome provide the additional word, *tu*. This is the form adopted in the Roman Missal of 1570, and it is not surprising to find that this word is supplied in the Graduals issued by Gardano, Giunta, and the Medicean Press (staves **c**, **d**, and **e**). It is not, however, to be found among the northern sources. (See example 56.)

In the normative medieval version of *Qui habitat*, we find a total of sixty phrases distributed over the thirteen verses. In barely over half of these instances there is a mismatch between the respective "markers" in one or another of the post-Tridentine sources. The Graduals by Giunta, the Medicean Press, and the Nivers edition of the Premonstratensian Gradual (staves **d**, **e**, and **n**) are the sources most affected, but mismatches are to be found in the Millange Gradual (staff **f**), as well as in those issued by Küchler, Cramoisy and Clopeiau, and the Cistercians (staves **k**, **g**, and **m**). The greatest contrast is perhaps to be found in the setting of the last verse. Here the entire chant reaches a climax in pitch on the second syllable of the word *illi*, relaxing thereafter to a cadence on *f*. Not only does the Giunta reading (staff **d**) end on *d*, but the entire upward thrust is lacking. The opening markers are particularly vulnerable to change, especially when two formulas ending on *d* follow one another.

Even when the marker may remain constant, one may find notable changes in the associated melodic shape. In the normative medieval version, verses 5 and 7 feature a descent to A as part of the final phrase. This descent is lacking variously in the versions of Giunta, the Medicean Press, and Nivers (staves **d**, **e**, and **n**). On the other hand, the penultimate marker in verse 10 is associated with a cadence on *d*; here, the Medicean and Nivers versions (staves **e**, **n**) descend to A. In other instances when the "marker" remains constant, one may find that it is reached by means of a contrasting phrase. In verse 10, the word *ambulabis* ends with an unusual medial formula. The cadence on *c* is retained in the Cramoisy and Clopeiau reading (staff **g**), but it is associated with a different phrase.

Instances such as the one just described lead one to realize that the unification provided by the same or similar phrases in the normative medieval version of *Qui habitat* are often lacking in specific post-Tridentine reworkings. I will confine myself to one example and leave it to the individual reader to pursue others to the extent to which these are of interest. In the normative medieval reading, the third phrase of verse 4, ending with the word *ejus*, begins in the manner of the most frequent formula cadencing on *f*. When, however, we reach this tone, the melody continues downward and concludes on *c*. The same phrase, with the same unusual ending appears also in verse 9, in conjunction with the word *lapidem*. It is not at all surprising that the post-Tridentine editors chose to rework this phrase in a variety of ways. The sum total of all of the changes, including the sharp curtailment of many melismas, produces a more diffuse melody than that of the medieval predecessor.

Another genre not considered previously is that of the antiphon, whether associated with use in procession preceding Mass or having some other function. The example that we shall consider here is *Immutemur habitu in cinere*, which forms part of the ceremony blessing and distributing the ashes that marks the beginning of Lent.[8] The chant has a tortuous history of transmission caused by the fact that it had two variable degrees. It employed not only a major and a minor third above the final, but also a major and minor sixth. Thus there were no means by which it could be notated accurately within the Guidonian gamut. We learn of the unusual construction of the chant through the writings of Theinred of Dover, Anonymous XI, and Szalkai.[9] Their information is confirmed by the presence of an extremely rare *e-flat* in the fragmentary Gradual, Arras, Bibl. mun., MS 437.

In addition, the difficulties experienced by the medieval scribes become vividly apparent when we compare their various efforts to notate the chant.[10] There were some who notated the chant with a final on *d*, in agreement with its classification as a protus chant. This permitted a variable sixth degree, but not a variable third degree. Others notated the chant with a final on *g*. This permitted a variable third degree, but sacrificed the variability of the sixth degree. Still other scribes split the chant in two. By notating the opening centered on *g* and the second, larger portion centered around *d*, it was possible to have available both a variable third degree for the opening and a variable sixth degree for the second portion. This, however, was achieved by means of a disjunction between the two parts that began as an artificial sort of notational code and eventually became a sounding reality. Although the chant appears in four of the earliest six sources for the texts of the chants of the Mass Proper, the chant is not employed in all medieval Graduals. Nor is it ubiquitous among post-Tridentine sources; it is lacking in the Gradual issued by Cramoisy and Clopeiau as well as in the Carthusian Gradual preserved in the Feininger library in Trent, and perhaps in other sources that I have not checked.

The two late sixteenth-century sources that are included in example 57 for the sake of comparison exemplify the two main branches of medieval readings. The Liechtenstein Gradual presents a reading in which the opening and closing tones are a fourth apart, whereas the *Graduale Herbipolense* presents a reading that corresponds more closely to the original conception of the piece, opening and closing on the same tone. Five of the six post-Tridentine sources that open on *g* close on *d*. The sole exception is the Premonstratensian Gradual edited by Guillaume Gabriel Nivers in 1680 (staff l). This source retains the original form of the melody in which the opening and closing tones are the same. Three readings open a fourth lower on *d*. Two of these are from the eastern chant region, namely the Polish reading furnished by Piotrkowczyk (staff j) and the one from Mainz published by Küchler (staff k). The third reading is that given by Joannes Flandrus and published in Madrid (staff i). The link thus established may lend support to a theory that this "John from Flanders" was using source materials from his native region—at least for this chant—and not drawing on a tradition in his adopted country. While the support should be noted, one would require considerably more evidence before reaching any firm conclusion.

The remaining three sources are individual. The Medicean Gradual (staff f) insists, as is its custom, on a modally unified melody and achieves this by moving the opening down a fourth by eliminating the opening two tones and redistributing the remainder slightly. This informs us further about the tastes of Anerio and Soriano, the editors, but says little about the sources familiar to them. The entire reading of *Immutemur* is highly idiosyncratic in this source. The opening, inclusive of the setting of *jejunemus*, is clearly related to other readings, even if not identical. The remainder, however, becomes increasingly individual, with only occasional resemblances to the mainstream. The Cistercian reading (staff n), mentioned previously, achieves modal unity in a different fashion, drawing on the medieval Cistercian tradition, which employs a standard first-mode formula for the opening. The last of the individualistic readings included in our example is that furnished by Jean Millet, the editor of the *Graduale Bisuntinum* published by Rigoine in 1682 (staff m).

Millet begins *Immutemur* on *d'*, an octave higher than the remaining *d* readings. This unusual choice permits him to end the melody on *a*, contrary to the practice of the other readings that open on *d*. The reading of the late *Graduale Lugdunensis* of 1738 (staff **o**) will be taken up when that source is discussed in chapter 11.

The crucial moment in the construction of the melody for *Immutemur* occurs at the end of the word *cilicio*, which concludes the opening clause. At this point an upward leap followed to the beginning of the word, *jejunemus*, a leap that is indicated in some early adiastematic sources by the presence of the Romanian letter, *l*, as in Einsiedeln, Benedikterkloster, MS 121. In later sources this leap is customarily that of a fifth, but the interval is variable. In the revised version we tend to find a more restrained movement of an upward second, but a unison or even a downward second are likewise possible.

Not only are the overall tonal outlines variable in both the medieval and post-Tridentine versions of *Immutemur*, but the smaller details are as well. Among the readings chosen for presentation, I have included one from the Baglioni Gradual of 1690 (staff **e**). Previous experience with late Venetian prints has indicated that these tend to adhere fairly closely to the readings of the early Giunta prints of 1596 and 1606, although we have earlier observed notable exceptions to this rule of thumb. In the present instance, the general resemblance between the Venetian readings of 1596 and 1690 is apparent enough. However, the changes of detail do affect our perception of the tonal organization of the chant. In the Giunta print (staff **d**), the setting of the word *cinere* concludes on *d*, as is the general practice. (The alternative, A, reflects a simple transposition of the whole.) The Baglioni reading, on the other hand, continues downward to *c*. This is followed by two consecutive leaps, *g–c'*, which combine to provide a momentary tonal focus on *c* that is lacking in other readings. And this feeling of a changed tonal orientation is enhanced when the succeeding word, *cilicio*, concludes on *a* in the Baglioni reading, as opposed to *g* that is customary elsewhere. The close of the opening syllable of *Dominum* in the Baglioni reading features a descent to *f* followed by an upward leap to *b-flat*. This results in a descending half-step cadence on the final two syllables. This form of cadence is specified by signed flats in the readings of Gardano, Plantin, and Rigoine (staves **c**, **h**, and **m**), but is contradicted in the Premonstratensian Gradual of 1680 (staff **l**), which closes *e'–d'*. Other sources employ a falling minor third, while still others do not specify the presence or absence of *b-flat*. Were we considering the Giunta reading devoid of the context provided by contemporaneous or later sources, we would have little specific reason to supply editorial flats at this juncture. The variability that we have noted makes such editorial decisions fraught with risk. Yet such decisions play a vital role in forming our impressions of the sound of *Immutemur*.

Another detail worthy of comment concerns the setting of the word, *jejunemus*. The reform editors' concern for prosodic values has been noted time and again by scholars dealing with this repertoire. To judge accurately the extent of this concern, one would need to have a comprehensive account of word accent in the practice of the late sixteenth and early seventeenth centuries. In the present instance, it would appear that this practice was not entirely consistent. In the readings of the Liechtenstein Gradual of 1580, the *Graduale Herbipolense* of 1583, the Gardano Gradual of 1591 (staves **a, b**, and **c**), the Plantin Gradual of 1599 (staff **h**), the Piotrkowczyk Gradual of 1600 (staff **j**), and the Cistercian Gradual of 1696 (staff **n**), the third syllable of *jejunemus* is treated as short, and is restricted to a single tone. However, in the remaining eight readings provided in example 57, this syllable is treated as long, and is accorded between two and seven tones. (A long syllable may have as few as two tones if surrounding syllables have only one.)

The communion, *Qui biberit*, is the next example in our order of discussion. It has been chosen by virtue of a complex history of melodic transmission that also includes textual variability. Employed for the Friday following the Third Sunday of Lent, *Qui biberit* is one of four Lenten communions with texts drawn from the Gospels that were set with multiple melodies during the Middle Ages. I propose to study the post-Tridentine transmission of both this chant and *Oportet te*—another of the group—in order to learn whether the post-Tridentine editors sought to conform to a single melodic version for these gospel communions or whether they were content to remain with multiplicity.

The text for *Qui biberit* is a conflation of verses 13–14 of chapter 4 from the Gospel according to John. In the Vulgate, the passage reads as follows: *qui autem biberit quam ego dabo ei non sitiet in aeternum / sed aqua quam dabo ei fiet in eo fons aquae salientis in vitam aeternam.*

Among the sources of the *Antiphonale Missarum Sextuplex*, the chant is lacking from the Monza Cantatorium; it is given only as a cue in the source from Senlis (Paris, Bibl. Ste.-Geneviève, 111), and as a somewhat longer fragment in Mont-Blandin (Brussels, Bibl. royale, lat. 10127–10144). However, the three remaining sources—Rheinau (Zurich, Stadtsbibl., Rh. 30), Compiègne (Paris, Bibl. nat., lat. 17436), and Corbie (Paris, Bibl. nat., 12050)—all agree on the text: *Qui biberit aquam quam ego do, dicit Dominus Samaritanae, fiet in eo fons aquae salientis in vitam aeternam.* (The spellings are modernized and punctuation added in accordance with recent practice.) Despite this agreement—and the incomplete corroboration of Mont-Blandin—the textual practice of the Middle Ages was variable. The word *Samaritanae* is omitted early on in sources such as Darmstadt, Hessische Landes- und Hochschulbibl., 1946, and St. Omer, Bibl. mun., 252, as well as in some later manuscripts that follow in this tradition. And instead of the words, *ego do,* one may find variously *ego dabo, ego dabo ei,* and *ego dabo vobis.* The *Missale Romanum* of 1570, regarded as the *Editio Princeps,* reads, *Qui biberit aquam quam ego dabo, dicit Dominus ei, fiet in eo fons aquæ salientis in vitam æternam.* The *Graduale Auscitanum,* printed by Garnier and Le Prieur (Paris, 1755), is a Neo-Gallican source, which however contains numerous chants from the Gregorian tradition. This work presents still another text for *Qui biberit,* which reads: *Qui biberit ex aqua quam ego dabo ei, non sitiet in aeternum: sed aqua quam ego dabo ei, fiet in eo fons aquae salientis in vitam aeter-nam.* The accompanying melody clearly has Gregorian roots, but it is highly distinctive nonetheless.

It has been claimed that six melodies survive in connection with *Qui biberit,* but this statement awaits confirmation from further studies yet to be published.[11] The actual number will ultimately depend upon the number of sources consulted and upon decisions regarding the respective roles of sameness and difference that would determine the classification of any given reading. Suffice it to say that one can find sources that end respectively on *c, d, e, f,* and *g.* And different readings may open on *d, e, f, b, c',* and *d'.* The use of any given opening tone is not necessarily a guarantee of the final that will eventually follow.

Casting only a cursory glance at the post-Tridentine readings given in example 58, one can quickly note openings on *e, f, a, c', d',* and *e',* while there are endings on *d, e, g,* and *a.* The variety here is almost as great as that among medieval sources. The prolixity of the medieval sources is often greater than that of the post-Tridentine prints. Nevertheless, the readings in the Graduals brought out by Millange (=Boni), Plantin, Rigoine (=Millet), and the Cistercians (staves **f, h, m,** and **n**) are fairly florid.

A comparison between medieval and post-Tridentine sources is, sad to say, potentially misleading. We have many hundreds of the former, the majority of these created independently of copying. Moreover, these sources come from many different locales. The number of independent post-Tridentine sources is unlikely to be more than a few score, and these come from a more restricted number of places.

If we survey the sources present in our sample, we find that only the *Graduale Herbipolense* of 1583 (staff **b**), the Benedictine manuscript of 1624 (staff **o**, also of Germanic origin), and the Carthusian Gradual of 1674 or 1679 (staff **p**) retain the text present in both our earliest sources and in the *Missale Romanum* of 1570. These conservative readings constitute three of the four sources that end with a final on *g.* The Küchler Gradual of 1671 (staff **j**) uses the same final even though this reading uses the alternative text form, *ego dabo ei.*[12] Together, these four sources place pitches 2–4 on *d', c',* and *b.* (With the exception of the Carthusian Gradual, which opens on *c',* this group begins on *d'.*) Disregarding for the moment variants brought about through the difference in text, the remaining variants are all minor in nature. We are dealing basically with four versions of a single melody.

Like the reading in the Küchler Gradual, that in the Gradual issued by Laurent in 1616 (staff **g**) uses the alternative text form, *ego dabo ei.* The latter reading, however, begins a second higher, and it concludes a second higher, with a cadence on *a.* The details of the Laurent reading are confirmed in the Graduals issued both by Belleros in Antwerp (1620), and by Mommaert in Brussels (1623), so that it is highly unlikely that we are dealing with a series of mistakes. The comparison between the Netherlandish and German readings takes on greater interest when we find that there are interior moments when the two are at the same pitch level. Furthermore, the reading furnished by the Laurent Gradual for the words, *ei, dicit Dominus*, uses a series of pitches that closely parallels the *Herbipolense* and other conservative readings for the text, *Dominus Samaritanae*, despite the contrast in texts.

The reading furnished for *Qui biberit* in the Flandrus Gradual of 1597 (staff **k**) is unusual. More than half of the sources given in example 58 end on *e*, and most of these begin on the same tone, with the progression, *e, g, f, e*. (The Boni reading—staff **f**—decorates the *g*, by providing the equivalent of a torculus.) The Flandrus reading, on the other hand begins essentially a tone lower. It also ends a tone lower, with a cadence on *d*. Furthermore, the phrase, *quam ego dabo ei*, begins with a descent of a fourth, whereas most readings based on *e*, begin with an ascent. This descent is, however, to be found in variant forms among the four readings that begin on a higher level. A tangled series of variable relationships among the different readings lie before us, and it will be extremely difficult—if not impossible—to trace each of these back to earlier antecedents. Distinguishing between differences that are the result of the fractured early traditions and those that are the products of recent editorial emendations will be for the most part speculative. The reading given in the Premonstratensian Gradual edited by Nivers (staff **l**) is one of the more distinctive ones of the group, even though one may remark that it basically begins and ends a fourth lower than the Benedictine and Carthusian group that opens on *d'* and closes on *g*. Nevertheless, interior points demonstrate a fair amount of independence, and the texts do not match throughout. I have access to reproductions of only half of the Premonstratensian sources listed in *Le Graduel romain, II: Les Sources*. It is noteworthy that all four of the manuscripts for this order preserving *Qui biberit* belong to the textual tradition that uses the text, *ego do dicit Dominus Samaritanae*. The diastematic source, Vienna, Österreichische Nationalbibl., Pal. 12865 begins on *e'* and ends on *a'*, while Paris, Bibl. nat., lat. 833 begins on *a* and ends on *d*. The latter source, however, was not originally intended for Premonstratensian usage. The print of 1680 corresponds in its overall outlines to the French source, but not in its details. Furthermore, in keeping with the reading of the *Missale Romanum* of 1570, it employs a different textual tradition, employing *ego dabo ei, dicit Dominus*.

Although the broad tonal outlines of the melody presented by Jean Millet in the *Graduale Bisuntinum* of 1682 (staff **m**) agree with others that begin and end on *e*, several details are idiosyncratic. The flourish on the opening syllable of *biberit* is more extensive than in any other reading, and the descent on the final syllable of *aquam* goes counter to the ascent that is present in most other sources. It is the only source to assign more than one note to the opening syllable of *dicit*, employing four tones at this juncture. In other respects, however, it loosely parallels the version in the Cistercian Gradual.

The communion, *Oportet te*, for the Saturday following the Second Sunday of Lent, employs a text taken from the Gospel according to Luke, 15:32. The opening words have been modified slightly by those responsible for the earliest tradition for the chant. However, apart from the omission of the word *hic*, the main body is faith-ful to the Scriptural passage. According to present information, there are no fewer than ten melodies for this text to be found among various medieval sources.[13] Again this claim awaits corroboration or modification from studies that are yet to appear. Again the number will depend upon the breadth of the sources consulted and the definition of sameness and difference.

The medieval readings of *Oportet te* display considerable modal variety, although less than that encountered in *Qui biberit*. The sources that I have consulted open on *f, g, a,* and *c′*. Finals may be found on *d, e, g, and c′*. (The last-named of these finals occurs in Montpellier, Fac. méd., MS H. 159, where the chant is classified as *tritus*.) All of the post-Tridentine sources consulted open on *g*, and most close on that tone. However, alternative endings may be found on *d* and *e*.

Despite this relative agreement, the chants contain considerable elements of diversity, as shown in example 59. The four sources that present the simplest, most conservative readings for *Qui biberit* behave in a like manner with regard to *Oportet te*. These include the *Graduale Herbipolense* (staff **b**), the Küchler Gradual of 1671 (staff **j**), the Benedictine manuscript of 1624 (staff **o**), and the Carthusian Gradual of 1679 (staff **p**). Only seldom do these sources employ more than a single tone per syllable, and never more than two. As one might reasonably expect, three of the four sources are from the Germanic orbit, and the melody is to be found in more than a half-dozen medieval Germanic sources. (It is found also in an equal number of sources from Italy and France.)

The Premonstratensian reading edited by Nivers (staff **l**) follows the phrase shapes employed by first-named Graduals, but it is slightly less austere. The first portion of *Oportet te* in the reading of the Laurent Gradual (staff **g**) is also fairly laconic, whereas the closing portion is noticeably more florid. This reading is distinctive in the comparatively low tessitura adopted for *quia frater tuus*, which may be viewed as a foreshadowing of the unusual ending on *d*. Such an ending is to be found in medieval manuscripts now housed in St. Petersburg and Vercelli, but these contrast strongly with the Laurent reading for the major part of the melody. Near the opposite side of the spectrum, the reading in the Flandrus Gradual of 1597 (staff **k**) is among the most florid. In its broad tonal plan, it resembles the readings of vari-ous Aquitanian manuscripts—including Madrid, Real Academia de la Historia, 18—in that it opens on *g* and closes on *e*. However, the Flandrus reading lacks the numerous interior closes on *g* that are to be found in the Aquitanian sources at the ends of the words, *gaudere, fuerat,* and *perierat*. One could perhaps point to the downward leap of a fourth that immediately precedes the first of these words, and posit that this is the result of a clef-reading error, which is remedied at the begin-ning of the next phrase, *quia frater*. Nevertheless, this leap is signaled by means of a custos at the end of the first staff and is clearly confirmed by the subsequent nota-tion. An attempt to create reconciliation by means of such a hypothesis is thus forced and weak. By ending *gaudere* on *e* and by closing *fuerat* and *perierat* on *b*, the Flandrus editor prepares the singers and listeners for the final cadence on *e*.

Six post-Tridentine sources—including Liechtenstein, 1580; Gardano, 1591; Giunta, 1596; Medicean, 1614; Millange, 1599; and Plantin, 1599 (staves **a**, **c**, **d**, **e**, **f**, and **h**, resp.)—share the same or nearly the same opening. However, the Medicean Gradual (staff **e**) soon distinguishes itself from the other sources displaying this beginning. There is an individualistic rise on the word *gaudere*, and an equally individualistic descent on the words, *mortuus fuerat*. Keeping in mind other instances of tone painting to be found in this source (as in the descent on the word *descendit* in the *Alleluia Dies sanctificatus*), I am inclined to view these idiosyncrasies as further examples of the same mind set.

Not all of the medieval Graduals and notated Missals contain the liturgy for the week-days of Lent, and in other instances the relevant folios may be lost. I have had occasion to review readings for *Oportet te* in nearly fifty notated sources, both adiastematic and diastematic. Among these, only one, Paris, Bibl. nat., lat. 10503, furnishes a close parallel to the reading of the Liechtenstein Gradual of 1580 (staff **a**). Through this striking relationship one can gain a better appreciation of the transformations that have been wrought in the four later sources (staves **c**, **d**, **h**, and **i**) that belong to the same family. According to information furnished by the Solesmes monks in *Le Graduel Romain, II: Les Sources* (p. 103), lat. 10503 is a Franciscan manuscript of the second half of the thirteenth century, originally intended for use in the Holy Land. I should report at the same time that Vercelli, Bibl. capitolare, 162 belongs to the same overall family, although apparently written a fourth lower and with many significant variants. It is to be hoped that a more intensive study of melodies with diffuse histories of transmission may yet yield more information concerning the immediate and more distant forebears of other post-Tridentine readings.

In the previous discussion of the communion, *Qui biberit*, we had occasion to note the similarities between the reading provided by Millet and that offered by the Cistercians. The same similarities are to be observed for the greater part of *Oportet te*. However, in this chant Millet departs markedly from the Cistercian tradition for the setting of the last three words, and parallels instead the readings of Boni, Plantin, and Piotrkowczyk (staves **f**, **h**, and **i**), although with a changed distribution of tones for the word, *inventus*. Having commented on the independence of the Piotrkowczyk readings for our two selected tracts, we may pause to note its close relationship here to the Plantin Gradual issued a year earlier.

The last of our Lenten examples is taken from the introit, *Deus in adjutorium*, which serves both the Thursday (*Feria V.*) following the Second Sunday of Lent and the Twelfth Sunday after Pentecost (example 60). The text is taken from Psalm 69, verses 2–3 in the version of the Roman Psalter. It reads there, *Domine Deus in adjutorium meum intende Domine ad adiuvandum me festina / confundantur et revereantur inimici mei qui quaerunt animam meam*. Allowing for the omission of the initial word, this is the version that appears in the sources from Rheinau, Compiègne, and Corbie in the *Antiphonale Missarum Sextuplex*. (The remaining sources either omit the chant or give an incomplete text.) This version of the text differs from Jerome's

Hexapla in that Jerome omits both the initial word, and the words *inimici mei*. The *Missale Romanum* of 1570, on the other hand, not only includes the latter two words but prefaces them with the word, *omnes*.

This chant is among the *cantus nothi* cited by Regino of Prüm, chants that begin in one mode and end in another. This lack of modal unity posed problems to both singers and theorists during the Middle Ages. As a result we have two contrasting families of readings for the antiphon and no fewer than seven different ways of coupling these readings with the psalm tone that follows. In my previous treatment of this chant,[14] I provided an account of one medieval reading for each of the seven families and cited transcriptions of an additional dozen readings in two other locations.

In brief, it was possible for the chant to begin on *c'* and to close on *g*, followed by an eighth-mode psalm tone founded on the opening pitch. For reasons enumerated previously,[15] this is undoubtedly the form that was known to Regino. More frequently, antiphon readings having the tonal shape just described are followed by seventh-mode psalmody based on the final. Exceptionally, the antiphon may open and close on *c'* followed by seventh-mode psalmody based on that tone. Alternatively, this shape may be followed by a mode 8 psalm tone, again based on *c'*. In other instances the antiphon may open and close on *g*, followed by either seventh- or eighth-mode psalmody based on that tone. Finally, one finds a strange pair of readings in Paris, Bibl. nat., MS lat. 13254, that open on *d'*, close on *a*, and are provided with a seventh-mode psalm tone based on *g*.

This bewildering variety of alternatives is much reduced among post-Tridentine sources, but remnants of it remain nonetheless. Of the sixteen sources surveyed in example 60, five begin at the upper level on *c'* or—as in the case of the Gradual edited by Millet (staff **n**) and the Carthusian Gradual (staff **p**)—on *d'*. The main nucleus of this conservative group consists of the *Graduale Herbipolense* (staff **b**), the Laurent Gradual (staff **i**), and the Benedictine manuscript (staff **o**). All four sources end on *g*. The last three all take the surprising step of providing an eighth mode psalm tone based on *c'*. This agrees perfectly with Regino's advice to the effect that the mode of an introit is to be sought at its beginning, but it blithely disregards modal theory from the time of Guido onward. The Gradual edited by Millet and published by Rigoine (staff **n**), together with the Carthusian Gradual (staff **p**), employ a seventh mode psalm tone based on *g*. The remaining eleven sources all begin and end on *g*, and provide seventh-mode psalmody based on that tone. The Cistercian Gradual of 1696, not given in the example, begins on *a* in a fashion comparable to that of Carthusian practice.

A far less divisive issue concerns the minor addition in the *Missale Romanum* of 1570 of a single word, *omnes*. It is ironic that this added word does not appear in the Medicean Gradual itself. It is, however, found as early as the Liechtenstein Gradual of 1580, and recurs in the French and Belgian Graduals included in the sampling and in the 1597 Gradual by Flandrus. In contrast to the major changes brought about by the addition of a text phrase for certain readings of *Dextera Domini*, discussed above, this small addition is hardly noticeable in its overall effect. While there is no lack of small-scale variants, none seem sufficiently important to be singled out of comment.

We move outside the period of Lent for the next chant to be discussed in this chapter, the offertory, *Jubilate Deo universa terra*, employed for the Second Sunday after Epiphany. This chant has been chosen because it undergoes a striking textual change. *Jubilate Deo universa terra* has a text pieced together from Psalm 65, verses 1, 2, and 16. Among our earliest textual sources for this chant, the Compiègne and Corbie Graduals feature a repetition of the opening verse that is not part of the Latin Psalter or either of Jerome's two translations. The Mont-Blandin and Senlis give only incipits for the antiphon, while the repetition is absent from Rheinau. The sources for the chant text all employ the word *universi*, rather than the customary *omnis*. (The Compiègne and Mont Blandin Graduals also give texts for two verses, drawn respectively from lines 13–15 of Psalm 65, divided in an unusual manner.) The textual repeat, a well-known feature of a small group of offertories, including *Jubilate Deo omnis terra*, employed for the previous Sunday within the Octave of Epiphany. In both instances the repeat is set to a different melody with a huge melisma on the third syllable. The repetitions are dropped from the *Missale Romanum* of 1570.[16] Among post-Tridentine Graduals the textual repetition is normally lacking.

It is noteworthy to find that the Liechtenstein print of 1580, given on staff **a** of example 61, returns to the Scriptural form of the text. One may reasonably posit the influence of the Roman Missal issued a decade earlier. Indeed, it is to be noted that the first word of the introit for the Feast of St. Stephen, *Etenim sederunt*, is lacking in both the Roman Missal of 1570 and the Liechtenstein print. The pitches associated with this word are retained, resulting in a small melisma on the first syllable of *sederunt*, where none had existed previously. I have not had the occasion to study the 1580 Gradual as a whole from this standpoint and cannot report on the consistency of this policy. In terms of editorial decisions concerning the melodies, the print does not normally exhibit other reform characteristics. We may recall, moreover, that the extraneous repetition present in the normative chant form for *Jubilate Deo universa terra* was excised during the Middle Ages by both the Cistercian and Dominican Orders. Nevertheless, the Liechtenstein reading is unrelated to either of form of revision. Three years later, the Würzburg Gradual still retains the medieval structure and basic melody, as shown on staff **b**.

In a normative medieval reading, the first phrase begins with a typical first-mode gesture, rising from the sub-final to the fifth degree, which is decorated by an upper neighbor, and then by an upper third. The phrase eventually cadences on the fifth degree. The repeated text begins on this degree and proceeds to a melisma spanning a twelfth. As one proceeds further, one finds a second, much more modest, melisma on the accented syllable of *terra*, leading shortly thereafter to a formulaic conclusion on the third degree. The reforming editors each had to decide what was to be retained from the setting of the first statement and how this was to be joined to that which followed. Most opted to revise the opening phrase of the music, and ignore the second phrase entirely; the descent of a third from the closing *a* to the *f* that opens the third phrase of the normative medieval was simple and could be negotiated without strain. This solution, however, was not followed universally. The Liechtenstein print of 1580 (staff **a**) chooses instead to follow the opening phrase for the first three words, and proceeds with the melody accompanying the fourth word of the textual repeat. The Cistercian print that appeared in 1696 (staff **m**) works similarly but with different details. There the editor seized on the fact that the setting of the final word (*terra*) begins in the same fashion in both textual statements, and proceeds at this point to the second of the statements, while greatly curtailing the small melisma mentioned above. The editions of Giunta (staff **d**) and his followers do likewise, while curtailing the setting of *terra* to a mere two notes for each of the syllables The conservative editors of the Benedictine and Carthusian sources employed here (staves **o**, **p**) had no problems; they simply retained the textual repetition to which they were accustomed.

The most unusual of the readings for the opening of *Jubilate Deo* is that cited by Guillaume Gabriel Nivers in his *Dissertation sur le Chant Gregorien*, published in 1683. The first five tones are those given in staff **m**, from a German Benedictine manuscript. To these are adjoined a version of the melisma associated with the repeated text phrase. This melisma is not associated with the opening phrase of *Jubilate Deo* among any of several dozen sources consulted. To add to this mystery, Nivers presents the first six tones of our chant in a seventeenth-century version, 'corrected after the Roman.' These, however, do not correspond to the Medicean reading, but rather to northern incipits. Unless, by some remote chance, there was another modernized Roman version of *Jubilate*, it would appear that "romain" did not have the same meaning for Nivers as it does for us. In all probability, 'the Roman' refers to the text form of the Roman Missal.

There are, of course, many differences between the several reform versions that are unrelated to the excision of the textual repetition. Particularly the Italian readings are terser than others. Although early reform Graduals began to institute changes in the relationship between music and text, favoring prosodic values, these changes are carried out more systematically in the version of the Medicean Gradual (staff **e**). See, for example, the setting of the word *Deo*, or the phrase, *psalmum dicite nomini eius*. While the opening of the chant was an instantly recognizable first-mode formula, not even this was sufficient for Anerio and Soriano; they felt that an initial emphasis on the final had to be stronger and thus reversed the position of the first two tones. However, in the setting of the words, *nomini eius*, the Medicean reading departs from all others in opting for a lower tessitura, with a cadence on *e* rather than the customary one on *a*. In the setting of the word *Dominus*, this version departs from most others in terminating on *f*, rather than the normative *d* final.

Thus the concern for the strength of the modal final is uneven. Other sources may also reshape individual segments. The Giunta Gradual of 1596 (staff **d**) ends the words *narrabo vobis omnes* on g, d, and e, respectively, whereas these words normally terminate on c', g, and g. Comparable instances are also to be found later in the antiphon.

In contradistinction to the variability of the Venetian tradition, the French tradition remained reasonably firm, with only occasional minor variants. As noted in earlier chapters, this originated in a Bordeaux print by Millange in 1599, edited by Guillaume Boni, and is then found in a print from Toul edited in 1627 by Belgrand. This was reissued in 1633 and again in 1656. Other printers join in at early date; we find an edition by an unknown publisher in 1635, and two others issued by the *Societatis Typographicae Librorum Officii Ecclesiastici* in 1640 and 1657. Robert Ballard published a Gradual in 1655. The tradition continues late in the century in a print of 1697 by Christophe Ballard and thereafter in another that was issued in 1734 by the same firm.

The readings of the *Graduale Romanum* issued by Cramoisy and Clopeiau in 1662 (staff **g**) demonstrate that the primary Parisian tradition did not hold universal sway in that city. While the reading of *Jubilate Deo* is clearly related to the form established earlier by Boni and Belgrand, the departures are evident. It was apparently founded on a different editorial enterprise. Another Gradual that also stands somewhat apart from the mainstream Parisian tradition was first issued by la Caille in 1666. Still a third distinctive reading is provided by Millet for the print issued by Rigoine in 1682.

The choice of chants has thus far been governed in part by a desire to have available as many readings of different origins as possible for each chant to be discussed. For this reason, I have focused on chants from the older portions of the Temporale, these being more stable in assignment than their counterparts for the Sanctorale. I do not, however, wish to ignore entirely the latter segment of the liturgy. Hence, I have selected for discussion three chants from the Mass for the Purification of the Blessed Virgin Mary, celebrated on February 2. The Mass itself is one of five Marian Feasts documented in the sources of the *Antiphonale Missarum Sextuplex*.

In these early textual sources for the Mass Proper, 2 February is given different assignments. The Monza Cantatorium simply presents the rubric, *In Sancti Simeonis*. The Rheinau Gradual, on the other hand, reads *IIII Nonas Februarias Purificatio Sancta Maria*. The Compiègne Gradual, provides fuller information, *IIII. Nonas Februarias Purificatio Sanctae Marie Collecta ad Sanctum Adrianum*. The opposite counterpart is to be found in the Mont-Blandin Gradual, *IIII Nonas Februarias Natale Sancti Simeonis Collecta ad Sanctum Adrianum Statio ad Sanctam Mariam in Purificatione*. The Corbie Gradual is similar, though lacking the specification, *in Purificatione*. Finally, the Senlis Gradual combines both elements in its rubric, *IIII Nonas Februarias Purificatio Sanctae Dei Genetricis Maria et natale Symeonis. Collecta ad Sanctum Adrianum. Statio ad Sanctam Mariam.*

Despite this relative diversity in rubrication, the Mass Propers that follow remain relatively constant, though not entirely so. Taking into consideration the fact that the Monza source provides information concerning only the soloistic gradual and Alleluia, all five remaining sources give as the introit, *Suscepimus Deus*. All six sources employ the same text for the gradual, adding *Sicut audivimus* as the verse. Five of the six sources employ the *Alleluia Adorabo ad templum*, while the Monza Cantatorium stands apart by providing a cue for the *Alleluia Adducentur*. Only the Rheinau Gradual takes into consideration the possibility that the Feast might occur following Septuagesima Sunday, and provides a cue for the tract, *Jubilate Domino*. This chant is employed for Quinquagesima Sunday both among the sources of the *Antiphonale Missarum Sextuplex* as well as among modern books. The offertory, *Diffusa est gratia*, is given by four of the five Graduals. The Rheinau Gradual furnishes the sole exception, employing *Tollite portas*, from the Mass for the Vigil of Christmas. All sources cite *Responsum accepit Simeon* as the communion for this day.

This relative consistency was not destined to remain unbroken over the centuries following. While the introit, gradual, and communion were not—in my experience—replaced by substitutes, alternatives were employed for the Alleluia, tract, and offertory. The last-named was the most stable of this group, but even here one may find at least two alternatives, including *Offerentur regi* and *Dextera Domini* as replacements. There are at least four Alleluias, the *Alleluia Senex puerum* being probably the most frequent of these, the *Alleluia Post partum* being another. And at least four different tracts may be found for this Feast. The one employed in modern books, and the one best represented in sources of the Renaissance and Baroque is *Nunc dimittis*. However, one finds also *Diffusa est gratia*, *Audi filia*, and *Gaude Maria* as alternatives. (This is why the reader will not find entries in example 63 for either the Carthusian or Benedictine sources that are customarily cited for other chants.) We may note as an aside that in dealing with the Mass for the Purification of the Virgin, both the introit and the offertory are frequently given as cues.

The text for the respond of *Suscepimus Deus*, a fifth-mode gradual, is derived from Psalm 47, verse 10 and the major portion of verse 11. The gradual verse takes its text from verse 9 of the same psalm. The version of the first of these passages reads as follows in the Roman Psalter: *Suscepimus Deus misericordiam tuam in medio templi tui / secundum nomen tuum Deus ita et laus tua in fines terrae....* In St. Jerome's translation after the Septuagint, the word *sic* substitutes for the word *ita*. In his translation after the Hebrew, the same variant appears, together with two others. The first word is now given as *aestimavimus*, and the antepenultimate and penultimate words are replaced by *usque ad extremum*. Among the sources of the *Antiphonale Missarum Sextuplex*, only the readings of Compiègne and Corbie are complete and these follow the reading of the Roman Psalter. If we take a momentary detour and examine the preceding introit, we find that this chant uses the entire text of verse 11, finishing *justitia plena est dextera tua*. Again the chant follows the Roman Psalter. The introit uses *Magnus Dominus* as the psalm verse in all five sources for the Sextuplex. Compiègne and Senlis both give cues for a versus ad repetendum, *Sicut audivimus*. This is the text that serves the verse of the gradual.

In the Roman Psalter, verse 9 of Psalm 47 reads: *sicut audivimus ita et vidimus in civitate Domini virtutum in civitate Dei nostri Deus fundavit eam in aeternum*. In Jerome's *Hexapla*, the words *ita et* are replaced by the word *sic*, while in the version after the Hebrew *ita* is retained and *et* is dropped. However, the last portion in this translation reads, *Dei exercituum in civitate Dei nostri Deus fundavit eam usque in aeternum*. The chant text, as given in Compiègne and Corbie abbreviates somewhat and gives: *Sicut audivimus ita et vidimus in civitate Dei nostri*. The Rheinau Gradual, on the other hand, ends with the words, *civitatem Domini virtutum*.

If now we jump ahead chronologically and look at the texts provided in modern books, we find both small and significant changes. In the *Graduale Triplex*, we note an intermediate version of the respond, which substitutes the word *Domine* for the word *Deus*. The Solesmes editors document this in the readings of St. Gall, Stiftsbibl., MS 359 and Laon, Bibl. mun., MS 239. The variant is further confirmed in the later readings of Montpellier, Fac. méd., MS H. 159; Benevento, Bibl. capitolare, MS VI.34; and Verdun, Bibl. mun., MS 759, among others. The melody accompanying this small snippet consists of a cadential formula common to several maneriae, with a flourish of six tones assigned to the unaccented penultimate. This will obviously be of concern to editors around the turn of the seventeenth century and later. On the other hand, the reading of Chartres, Bibl. mun., MS 47 and Rome, Bibl. Angelica, MS 123 hold to the reading of the Roman Psalter, shared by the two translations of St. Jerome. This version is to be found in various diastematic manuscripts, including Paris, Bibl. nat., MS lat. 903 and Graz, Universitätsbibl., MS 807, and the Cistercian family of sources, among others. In these versions the cadential flourish falls on the accented syllable of *Deus*.

A more substantial variant concerns the end of the verse, *in civitate Dei nostri, in monte sancto eius*. Clearly, the last four words are nowhere to be found among the early Latin translations of Psalm 47. These words seem to have a familiar ring, but an electronic concordance for the Vulgate indicates that they are to be found as a group only in Psalm 97, in the middle of verse nine. In the *Graduale Triplex* this variant is brought to the reader's notice by means of a large bracket that encompasses the words, *Dei nostri, in monte*. No adiastematic reading is provided for this portion of text, and a handwritten insertion shows that in the version adhering to the Latin Psalter, the words *dei nostri* are placed under the tones setting *sancto eius* in modern sources. This version is supported by the readings of St. Gall, 359 and Laon, 239, neither of which gives the closing melisma complete. (These sources are corroborated by numerous others.)

When we consult the readings assembled for example 62, we find that the great majority of the readings for the respond are in accordance with the textual practice of the sources constituting the *Antiphonale Missarum Sextuplex*. Only four employ the word *Domine* at the first of the two junctures just discussed. These include the *Graduale Herbipolense* (staff **c**), the Piotrkowczyk Gradual of 1600 (staff **m**), and the arch-conservative Benedictine and Carthusian Graduals (staves **o**, **p**). Both the *Herbipolense* and Piotrkowczyk Graduals are Eastern, and the Benedictine Gradual was likely created for an Eastern house, even though not employing the characteristics of the Eastern dialect that one would ordinarily expect.

The four extra words of text that are to be found in modern readings of the verse occur in all but three instances. Again the *Graduale Herbipolense* (staff **b**) and the Benedictine Gradual (staff **o**) are among the exceptions, preferring the early medieval version. Here these two are joined by the Küchler Gradual of 1671 (staff **k**). Two of the three are thus Eastern. Although a preliminary search did not turn up an early medieval representative of the fuller reading, apparently this reading had become well established by the Renaissance and was a major factor in determining the later history of the chant.

There is a third instance of textual variability, albeit one limited to the three sources of the Netherlandish family. Examining the verse in the reading of the Laurent Gradual (staff **i**), one will note that immediately after the melisma on the last syllable of *audivimus*, the word *ita* has been omitted. The same omission occurs seven years later in the Brussels Gradual of Mommaert. While it is possible that this reading may have originated as an oversight, it appears then to have become deliberate.

Apart from these instances of textual—and hence musical—variability, a survey of the late readings for *Suscepimus Deus* serves largely to confirm earlier findings. In the respond, the "sustaining accent" for each of the last two words, *fines terrae*, falls on the final, weak syllable of the word. Less striking mismatches are associated with the words *medio*—the middle syllable receives the greatest number of notes—and *nomen*. In the verse, as just mentioned, we find a major melisma on the last syllable of *audivimus*. There is a smaller one on the last syllable of *ita*, again on the last syllable of *vidimus*, and, as noted previously, another large melisma on the last syllable of *nostri* (=*eius*). All of these instances invite alterations, although the treatment of *nomen*, which originally accorded one tone to the initial syllable and two to the final, is more often than not left untouched.

In providing an overview of the resultant emendations, one will again note that the Italian sources of Giunta and followers, together with the Medicean Gradual of Anerio and Soriano are much more stringent in their concerns for prosody than are others. Despite the airs flaunted on the title pages of the Gardano Gradual and the one by Millange, these editors are less consistent in their adherence to prosodic propriety. The northern editors pay only token respect to these principles. Indeed, they may even go counter to these principles on occasion. In the normative medieval version of *Suscepimus Deus*, the second word awards five tones to each of the two syllables. In later readings the first group of five is often reduced to four (or less). See, for example, the versions of Gardano (staff **d**), Plantin and Angermaier (staves **h**, **j**), Piotrkowczyk (staff **m**) and Laurent (staff **i**). But it is quite unexpected to find that in the readings of Plantin, Angermaier and Piotrkowczyk, the tones allotted to the final syllable are *increased* to seven. By way of contrast, the reading in the Medicean Gradual (staff **f**) provides eight tones to the initial syllable, leaving only a single tone for the last.

The most unusual and fascinating reading for *Suscepimus Deus* is that adopted by the Cistercians. The reader will recall that in the Cistercian version of the gradual, *Universi*, the normative opening gesture, which descends into the lower region of mode 2, was replaced by an entirely different gesture characteristic of mode 1. Furthermore, this replacement was found to be attributable to the medieval revision of Cistercian chant and not to any seventeenth-century editor. Even though the medieval version of *Suscepimus* shares its opening gesture with *Propitius esto*, also a fifth-mode gradual, and is reasonably similar to *In Deo speravit*, the three chants open on *d*, a third below the final and come to an initial caesura on the same tone. One can easily understand why certain medieval musicians considered this gesture to be more characteristic of modes, 1, 6, and 8, rather than of mode 5.[17] Hence the medieval Cistercian chant editors found the opening of *Suscepimus* to be disturbing and revised it. In the readings of manuscripts such as Munich, Bayerische Staatsbibl., clm 2542, the chant opens on the final, *f*, and ascends through a triad to the fifth degree of the mode, which is embellished by an upper neighbor. The portion setting the words, *Deus, misericordiamn tuam*, is essentially transposed up a fifth, and the normal height is reached only with the passage beginning *in medio templi tui*. With some modifications, this is the approach taken by the post-Tridentine Cistercian reading of 1696. Yet the late reading is not a slavish copy of an earlier original. Having been sensitized to the textual modifications affecting *Suscepimus*, it is illuminating to note that the medieval Cistercian version uses the word *Domine* at the critical juncture of the respond, while the post-Tridentine version employs *Deus*. In the medieval reading of the verse, we find the ending, *in civitate Dei nostri*, while the post-Tridentine print employs the expanded version, *in civitate Dei nostri, in monte sancto ejus*. Beyond these changes, one finds various melismas trimmed and shifts in the numbers of tones accorded to the unaccented syllables.

I have indicated previously that several different tracts are assigned to the Feast of the Purification of the Blessed Virgin Mary. The one in most widespread usage is *Nunc dimittis*, whose text is taken from the Luke, 2, verses 29–32. Neither this chant nor any of the alternatives are to be found among the repertory contained in the *Antiphonale Missarum Sextuplex*, nor is the chant to be found among our earliest musical sources, such as Chartres, Bibl. mun., 47; St. Gall, Stiftsbibl., MS 359; Laon, Bibl. mun., MS 239; or Einsiedeln, Benedikterkloster, MS 121. At present we know of two melodies for the *Nunc dimittis* text. The one in modern usage is preserved in the St. Yrieix Gradual (Paris, Bibl. nat., 903); Rome, Bibl. Angelica, 123; Montpellier, Fac. méd., H. 159; and in a Sarum Gradual (Oxford, Bodleian Library, Rawl. lit. d.3). It is probable that the same melody is found also in London,

British Library, Harley 4951; Madrid, Real Academia, MS 18; Paris, Bibl. nat., lat. 904; Rome, Bibl. Vallicelliana, C52; Modena, Bibl. capitolare, O.I.13; Bologna, Bibl. univ., 2551; and Milan, Bibl. Ambr., S 74sup.; among others. In short, it appears in selected sources from northern and southern France, Italy, and Great Britain, but not consistently in any of these regions. The second melody is documented in Benevento, Bibl. capitolare, VI.34 and is likely the one appearing in two other sources from the same library, the manuscripts V.19 and VI.35, as well in Beneventan sources in the Vatican library, lat. 6082, and Ottoboni, lat. 576. Strangely enough, the melody for the second verse of this chant is basically similar to the reading for the alternative melody, allowing for the fact that the Beneventan chant recites on *b* while the international reading recites on *c'*. I have not had occasion to note the presence of either melody in any Germanic source, but only five dozen manuscripts were included in the source survey.

The other three tracts known to have served for the Mass for the Purification include *Audi filia*, *Diffusa est gratia*, and *Gaude Maria*. All three are second-mode chants. *Audi filia* is found in St. Gall, Stiftsbibl., MSS 359 and 339, as well as in Einsiedeln, Benedikterkloster, MS 121. It appears in numerous other Germanic sources, both adiastematic and diastematic (e.g., Graz, Universitätsbibl., MS 807), but it seems not to have been known west of the Vosges or south of the valleys of northern Italy. *Diffusa est gratia* appears in the prefatory section to Laon, Bibl. mun., 239, Mont Renaud, in a number of Aquitanian sources, including Paris, Bibl. nat., MS 903, and in several manuscripts from central and northern Italy, France (e.g., Brussels, Bibl. royale, MS II.3823), and England. I am not aware of its presence in any Germanic source. *Gaude Maria*, apparently the latest of the three, occurs in sources from northern France and Germany, the earliest likely being Cambrai, Bibl. mun., MS 60. (It occurs also in Verdun, Bibl. mun., MS 759.)

Turning now to the late sources that constitute the focus for this study, we find that *Nunc dimittis* is present consistently among the various Italian sources consulted from 1580 (Liechtenstein Gradual) to 1779 (Pezzana Gradual). Indeed, the reading of the Pezzana Gradual of 1779 presents only four variants of one note, and one of two, from the reading of the Giunta Gradual of 1596. The predominance of this chant in Italy is easily understood since *Nunc dimittis* is the chant that is given in the *Missale Romanum* of 1570.

Nunc dimittis is generally present among French sources, beginning with the Gradual edited by Boni for Millange in 1598/99. It occurs in the subsequent publications of Belgrand in Toul beginning in 1627, as well as in later Parisian publications and in prints from both Lyon (1690, 1724) and Grenoble (1730). In the Low Countries, *Nunc dimittis* is the tract of choice for both the Plantin Gradual brought out by Moretus in 1599 and the contrasting tradition begun by Laurent in Tournai in 1616. As we have noted on numerous previous occasions, the influence of the Plantin Gradual was felt in Kraków in the edition of Piotrkowczyk in 1600 and in Ingolstadt in the editions of Angermaier and Sutor (1618, 1630, resp.). Closer to home, the Plantin Gradual served as a model for B. Masius beginning in 1633 in nearby Leuven. It influenced Dutch publications as early as the Utrecht Gradual of Arnold van Eyndam in 1691 and as late as the Amsterdam Gradual of F. van Tetroode in 1780. In all probability its influence was felt well beyond. No post-Tridentine source draws on the Beneventan melody.

Nunc dimittis was not a universal choice in northern countries. In France, the Gradual brought out by Cramoisy and Clopeiau in Paris, 1662, uses instead the tract, *Gaude Maria*, as does the Dominican Gradual of 1722. The Carthusians (1679) and Premonstratensians (1680) choose instead *Diffusa est gratia*, while the Benedictine manuscript source of 1623 employs *Audi filia*. The sources given in example 63 are thus fewer in number and variety than is normally the case.

In the Küchler Gradual of 1671, *Nunc dimittis* is unexpectedly provided with a second-mode melody (staff **n**). This idiosyncratic pairing is capable of a simple explanation once we recall that in this source the *Alleluia Laetatus sum* is provided with a melody other than the customary one. In dealing with *Laetatus sum* I suggested that the diocese of Mainz had previously been accustomed to using the *Alleluia Rex noster* for the Second Sunday of Advent. While the editor of the Gradual was willing to accept the assignment of the text of the *Alleluia Laetatus sum*, he (or she) was not willing to give up the melody that had traditionally been used in this locale. I suggest that the use of a second-mode melody for *Nunc dimittis* is a further instance of the same phenomenon. Given the geographic locale of Mainz, I am inclined to suspect that the chant that had previously been used for the Feast of the Purification had been *Audi filia* and that it was this melody that was transformed for use in the changed liturgy. *Diffusa est gratia* is an alternative possibility, but this tract has eight verses while *Nunc dimittis* has only four, and *Diffusa est gratia* is associated primarily with Aquitanian sources, occurring only rarely among the Germanic manuscripts. There is no echo of the highly idiosyncratic opening of *Gaude Maria* in the Küchler version of *Nunc dimittis*.

The use of a second-mode melody for *Nunc dimittis* is not an entirely happy fit. To be sure, one can easily recognize some of the standard formulas of the second-mode tract, including several characteristic phrase beginnings and endings. Nevertheless, the four verses of *Audi filia* are built on a four-phrase ground plan, generally with endings on *d, c, f,* and *d*. (The same is true of *Gaude Maria* and *Diffusa est gratia*.) Willi Apel[18] and others have shown that the normative ground plan for *Nunc dimittis* is founded on verses of two main phrases, with the last verse having three main phrases and a smaller one. Inasmuch as the texts for the four verses are all comparatively brief, it is difficult to fit into the restricted space the entire complement of phrases for a second-mode tract.

A survey of the available reworkings of the normative melody for *Nunc dimittis* serves to recall to the reader points raised in earlier discussions. The most striking change is the fundamental change of style that occurs in the Giunta Gradual of 1596 (staff **d**) and its many later successors through the Pezzana Gradual of 1779.

While the medieval tracts are florid, melismatic chants, it is not until the antepenultimate syllable of the final verse that the Giunta rendition assigns as many as five tones to a syllable. At the end of verse 3 we find two groups of two tones each set to the first syllable of *populorum*, even though it is the third syllable that receives the primary stress. Normally each syllable carries either one or two tones, although occasionally three. The reader will recall that a similar observation was made earlier in this chapter when examining the second-mode tract, *Domine audivi*. On the opposite side of the ledger, those sources that previously furnished the most conservative, and thus the fullest renditions of the individual chants, namely the Carthusian and Benedictine sources, do not include *Nunc dimittis* but present alternative tracts instead.

We have noted on previous occasions the tendency of some post-Tridentine editors, especially Anerio and Soriano, who were responsible for the preparation of the Medicean Gradual, to introduce changes that would strengthen a sense of modal centricity. *Nunc dimittis* offers comparatively little incentive for such forms of tinkering. To be sure, the Medicean Gradual (staff **e**) has the opening phrase of the third verse develop downward from the final to the fourth below rather than upward to the fourth (and fifth) above with a return to the final. But this change does not actually strengthen the sense of the eighth mode. However, the unusual opening of the reading of the 1690 Gradual from Lyon (staff **g**) was apparently designed to achieve such a goal. Rather than beginning with an upward motion from the fourth below the final to the final itself, the Lyon editor begins the melody on the final before leaping down to the fourth below. Although there are other distinctive moments in this reading, the edition as a whole follows the main features of the French tradition that had been begun approximately ninety years earlier. I have included the reading of *Nunc dimittis* appearing in the Solesmes *Graduale Sacrosanctae Romanae Ecclesiae* of 1943 partly out of a sense of contrariness. As shown in staff **a**, the second verse ends with a cadence on the sub-final. This accords with the reading of Montpellier, Fac. méd., MS H. 159, noted for its bilingual notation in adiastematic neumes and alphabet letters. However, a cursory survey of other important manuscripts available in facsimile would indicate that a greater number of sources prefer an alternative cadential gesture ending on the final. In this instance, the contrast between the Solesmes reading and those of post-Tridentine sources is not attributable to changes initiated in these late sources. We are not in a position to assert that this striking variant is the only one of major import to affect the transmission of this chant. Thus the lack of a uniform consensus among medieval readings for *Nunc dimittis* proves troublesome when seeking to evaluate the readings of our various late sources. One could devote an entire volume to the construction of a critical edition for this chant.

As can reasonably be expected, a major number of revisions among post-Tridentine sources reflect a desire for increased attention to prosodic values. Nevertheless, as we have noted on previous occasions, this attention is only occasionally systematic and consistent. In the version presented by the Solesmes editors, only one tone is assigned to the accented middle syllable of *dimittis,* whereas the following unaccented syllable is accompanied by a melisma of seventeen tones. The general proportion is accepted with minimal change not only in the Liechtenstein Gradual of 1580 (staff **b**), but also in the Gardano Gradual of 1591 (staff **c**). The melisma is also retained in large part by in the 1597 Gradual issued by Flandrus, where it is divided among two staves. In the copy in the Lilly Library of the University of Indiana, a late hand has inserted two rough ovoids marking the excision of the last ten tones of the melisma, and this hand has entered the last letter of the word at the point immediately prior to the first of these. The area concerned is marked on staff l by a pair of horizontal brackets. In general this source is much less sensitive to prosodic concerns than its counterparts.

On the other hand, the editions of Giunta (staff **d**) and followers, assign a total of three notes to *dimittis.* The Medicean Gradual (staff **e**) is slightly more prolix, employing one tone each for the initial and final syllables and three for the accented penultimate. Sources belonging to the French tradition solve the problem in prosody by transfer rather than by excision. The offending melisma is divided unevenly into two, with the lion's share going to the accented middle syllable, leaving a residue of two notes for the unaccented final. The same is true for the Cistercians. However, the Netherlandish editors for Plantin and Laurent and those influenced by their early prints are perfectly willing to let matters basically stand, with the melisma being assigned entirely to the final syllable and trimmed to only a slight degree. Küchler's editor had the problem of adjusting a pre-existent text to a gestural form for which it had not originally been intended. Even so, the normal practice for second-mode tracts is to associate a melisma with the syllable *following* the first major accent. This is disregarded in the 1671 print and the first melisma is placed on the accented syllable of *dimittis.* Slightly later in the first verse we find a smaller problem with the setting of the word, *Domine.* In the medieval form given in staff **a**, the weak second syllable is assigned five tones, whereas the initial, accent-bearing syllable receives only one. The editions of Liechtenstein (staff **b**), Gardano (staff **c**), and Flandrus (staff l) reduce this disparity, without, however, eliminating it. All remaining examples restrict the middle syllable to a single tone.

The second verse, *Quia videret,* provides an object lesson in problems that may arise when dealing with an unstable transmission. We shall concern ourselves with the setting of the last two words of the verse, *salutare tuum.* Even though, as noted previously, the Solesmes reading of this verse can be traced back to that appearing in Montpellier, Fac. méd., MS H. 159, a source of high value, this reading is of little service to us inasmuch as it appears to be atypical. While keeping this state of affairs in mind, we may briefly note that the last word concludes with a melisma on the final (and therefore unaccented) syllable of *tuum.* The reading provided in the divergent Benevento, Bibl. capitolare, VI.34 also ends with a melisma on this syllable. The same is true for the version of Oxford, Bodleian Lib., Rawl., lit. d.3. But the reading provided in Paris, Bib. nat. lat. 903 is different, the final syllable is delayed so that it coincides with the fourth tone from last. (Other sources still remain to be explored.)

Surveying the readings of the Liechtenstein and Gardano Graduals (staves **b**, **c**), we may judge that medieval Italian sources were likely closer to the reading of Rawl. lit. d.3 than they were to the reading of lat. 903. They each conclude with a flourish of nine tones on the final syllable, outweighing the four or five tones assigned to the initial syllable. The Plantin Gradual (staff **h**), together with the derivative readings of Piotrkowczyk and Angermaier (staves **j**, **k**) assign seven tones to the final syllable, while the Laurent Gradual (staff **i**) employs only one less. I would judge that the northern antecedents for these sources had featured a slightly longer melisma which was trimmed somewhat. The versions of Giunta (staff **d**) and successors and the Medicean Gradual (staff **e**) employ respectively one and two tones for the final syllable. The French versions (staves **f**, **g**) assign three and four tones to the syllable. The Flandrus reading (staff **l**) for this verse presents a melisma containing nineteen tones for the accented syllable, with four for the final syllable. Again, the copy in the Lilly Library marks the last fourteen of the melisma for excision together with the four that follow and transfers the final syllable so that it coincides with the fourth of the tones remaining. As before, the excision is marked by a horizontal bracket in example 63.

The penultimate word of the second verse features a totally unexpected alteration wrought by Anerio and Soriano, the editors of the Medicean Gradual. The accent for *salutare* obviously falls on the third of its four syllables. According to the sketchy information we possess concerning medieval readings for *Nunc dimittis*, the setting of this word in medieval sources might be described as neutral with regard to prosody. The accented syllable may have as few as two tones (or even one), but no syllable carries more than three. Whereas the Medicean readings are normally quite solicitous of prosodic values here we find that the editors have expanded the setting of the final (unaccented) syllable to a flourish of eight tones. This goes directly counter to the principles normally governing this edition.

The last two verses of *Nunc dimittis* contain few passages that arouse comment. In the reading of Montpellier, Fac. méd., MS H. 159, reflected in the Solesmes books, the final word of verse 3, *populorum*, is provided with an excellent prosodic fit. One tone is assigned to each of the first two syllables, while the accented syllable following is provided with a lengthy melisma. The final syllable receives four tones.[19] This form of text setting is continued in the Liechtenstein and Gardano Graduals (staves **b**, **c**) and in the Plantin and Laurent Graduals (staves **h**, **i**), together with the derivative publications of Piotrkowczyk and Angermaier (staves **j**, **k**). The French, on the other hand, assign five tones to the initial syllable, only four to the one bearing the primary accent, and eight or nine to the unaccented final (staves **f**, **g**). The Cistercians arrive at a similar reading (staff **m**), although providing only three tones to the initial syllable. The Flandrus print (staff **l**) belongs to the same family, and is indeed the earliest of the group.

The Solesmes reading of verse 4 does not derive entirely from that presented in Montpellier, Fac. méd., H. 159, although the beginnings are in accord. At any rate, our various sources do not agree in their identification of the syllable bearing the primary accent in the word, *revelationem*. In principle, this should fall on the penultimate syllable. This is reflected in the reading of Paris, Bibl. nat., lat. 903. However, the readings of Montpellier, Fac. méd., H. 159 and Oxford, Bodleian Lib., Rawl., lit. d.3 accord a greater number of tones to the third syllable, which in principle bears only a secondary accent. Among our late sources, this policy is followed notably in the reading of the Medicean Gradual (staff e), although I would not wish to postulate a direct link between any of these three sources. The version of the Flandrus Gradual (staff l) is idiosyncratic in that it is the only source to place a flourish on the weak fourth syllable.

The final word of *Nunc dimittis* poses a similar problem but of different origin. The word *Israel* is one of a very few Hebrew words taken over into the Latin liturgy. (*Adonai*—the Lord—is another.) A conflict arises in pronunciation inasmuch as Latin practice treats the final syllable as weak, whereas the Hebrew practice is opposite. There are numerous exceptions to the general rule, but in Hebrew the final syllable is more often strong than not. Neither the Giunta nor Medicean editors (staves d, e) are able to accept the concept of a strong final syllable and therefore place the melodic weight on the first syllable. The Medicean reading is especially unusual in that the word previous is *tuae*. Alone among all post-Tridentine editors, Anerio and Soriano expand the number of tones setting the final syllable of this word so that it receives six tones to the five accorded to the accented initial. The version of the Flandrus Gradual (staff l) is unusually close to that presented in the Solesmes books, and indeed expands somewhat the closing melisma.

The communion for the Feast of the Purification is *Responsum accepit Simeon*. With minor changes the text is taken from Luke, 2, verse 26. The Vulgate reads *et responsum acceperat ab Spiritu Sancto non visurum se mortem nisi prius videret Christum Domini*. The eighth-mode melody provided for the chant text is relatively simple, but even so, it provides impetus for changes wrought by later editors.

The most extensive of these appear in the Medicean Gradual edited by Anerio and Soriano. (See example 64, staff f.) The normative medieval melody presented in the *Graduale Triplex* does have various breathing points in accordance with the subdivision of the text. Nevertheless, these do not combine to furnish a cohesive account of an eighth-mode structure. Following a beginning on the lower fourth of the mode, there are breathing points on *d* (the end of *Simeon*), on *f* (the end of *Sancto*), and *b* (the end of *mortem*), none of these taking the form of a standard cadence. In their reworking, Anerio and Soriano have the melody proceed from *d* through *g* (on *accepit*) and up to *c'* for the first breathing point. The second breathing point falls on *g* and is reached through a recognizable cadential gesture. The third breathing point is on *c'*, and the melody then turns downward with an emphasis on *g* before a final rise to *c'* and a fall to the final. Reminders of the medieval original occur only occasionally.

The Medicean reading is exceptional also in the degree of attention paid to prosodic values. It is the only version to accord five tones to the accented syllable of *Responsum;* other readings use either one, two, or three tones. The word *accepit* receives respectively one, two, and one tones for the three syllables. Other sources may accord three tones for the final syllable, while the Plantin and Piotrkowczyk Graduals (staves **i**, **k**) employ four at this juncture. Alone of all the Graduals, the Medicean print provides five tones for the initial syllable of *Simeon,* and one each for the two later syllables. Most of the other post-Tridentine Graduals have the greatest melodic extension on the final syllable, as in normative medieval practice. The setting of the word *Spiritu* breaks from the principle of assigning a greater number of tones to the accented syllable inasmuch as it provides two tones for the final syllable. But the following word, *Sancto,* again emphasizes prosody emphatically by assigning six tones to the initial syllable. Other sources employ only one or two at this juncture. Only twice in the last half of the melody do we find disparities of similar order. The Medicean Gradual provides only one tone for the last syllable of *mortem,* whereas most other sources provide six, five, or four. Finally, Anerio and Soriano assign six tones to the middle syllable of *videret,* with one tone for each of the flanking syllables. The medieval tradition has emphasized the final syllable of this word by providing it with four tones, using only one tone for each of the two previous syllables. This tradition is preserved in nine of the post-1580 sources provided in the example. In general it was frequent for medieval practice to assign more tones to the weak middle syllable of *Domini* (and other cases of the same word) and fewer to the flanking ones, and we find a further instance of this practice at the conclusion of *Responsum accepit Simeon.* As might be expected, the Medicean Gradual—and indeed the majority of the post-Tridentine sources—"rectifies" this situation. Nevertheless, the medieval tradition persists among the conservative sources of the period. In the exemplar of the Flandrus Gradual preserved in the Lilly Library of the University of Indiana, one finds three notes that have been added by a later hand. These are enclosed in parentheses in example 64.

Having completed our examination of the chants mentioned at the outset of this chapter, we have now reached the end of the first—indeed the major—portion of this book. It seems appropriate at this point to step back and review what has been learned.

The latter part of the sixteenth century was witness to a major break in the ongoing transmission of medieval chant. Although not universal, this break was widespread and affected mainstream chant practice for more than three centuries. There were, to be sure, earlier hints that foreshadowed this deep disruption. By the very late fifteenth and sixteenth centuries, one finds some of the longer tracts curtailed in some sources, and the final melismas of Alleluias may be cut. But the first document marking the imminent broader changes that were to take place is a letter of 25 Oct. 1577 from Pope Gregory XIII to Palestrina and Zoilo requesting that these highly respected musicians revise current liturgical books in order to rid them of abuses that had supposedly crept in over the ages. Although this commission was considered carefully, in the end it was not honored. In the aftermath, however, the Pope's desires were to be fulfilled by others.

Because censorship in Venice was less stringent than in other Italian centers, this city became a major publishing center during the sixteenth century, arguably the most important in Europe. A greater number of Graduals were published there than in any other European center, issued by firms such as Giunta, Liechtenstein, Varisco and others. In 1587, the firm of Angelo Gardano brought out a revised Gradual and Antiphonal of some thirty folios, edited by Ludovico Balbi and presenting selected Feasts celebrated by the Franciscan order. This was followed four years later by a complete Gradual under the editorship of Andrea Gabrieli, Orazio Vecchi, and Ludovico Balbi, the earliest of the reform Graduals now known. The readings were generally more succinct than those representative of the medieval tradition, and the prosody was improved, but at the same time, these readings tended to be clearly related to the earlier Venetian readings for the same chants.

The developing movement for chant revision did not emanate from one authoritative edition or one powerful center. Within five years the firm of Giunta brought out a new edition embodying far more drastic revisions. This 1596 Gradual went on to provide the standard for nearly two centuries, not only for editions issued by the firm of Giunta, but for most later Venetian publishers such as Ciera, Baba, Baglioni, and Pezzana. Even though most Venetian publishers clearly adhered to a single tradition, this tradition was not immutable. Significant changes may occasionally be documented for readings of problematic chants.

Contemporary with the Giunta print, a certain Joannes Flandrus (= Juan Flamenco) brought out a four-volume Gradual in Madrid, 1595–97, that differs fundamentally from both Venetian readings. We can only speculate concerning the source(s) from which this print was derived. By 1599, two additional sources appear, one from the press of Millange in Bordeaux, the other from the Plantin press in Antwerp, then under the direction of Johannes Moretus (Moerentorf), each distinct from the other and from each of the sources noted previously. The lack of a centrally imposed "official" version is unmistakable. While there are certain goals that are held more or less in common, each editor or group of editors has comparative freedom to do as wished. Not even the texts of the 1570 *Missale Romanum* published by the Medicean Press held universal sway.

Unlike the firm of Giunta, the firm of Plantin did not follow up its first Gradual with other editions brought out within a short space of time. However, the Plantin Gradual seems to have had excellent distribution among northern countries. Its readings are picked up not only by later Netherlandish publishers, beginning in Leuven with Graduals of B. Masius, and continuing with later publishers in Antwerp itself, but spreading elsewhere as well. The first of the derivative publications is that of Piotrkowczyk, issued in Kraków one year later. This print demonstrates the extraordinary rapidity of diffusion of influence that could occur during this period. At the same time it also documents the retention of the right to further emendations on the part of the Polish publisher. By 1618 the Plantin readings have spread to Ingolstadt, then an important center in Bavaria. The Bavarian University was founded there in 1472 and moved to Landshut and then Munich in the nineteenth century. The edition issued by Elizabeth Angermaier was basically duplicated by Caspar Sutor in 1630. Neither exhibits the freedoms utilized by Piotrkowczyk. Thus, the necessity of tracing out lines of influence in the transmission of the post-Tridentine chant repertoire is evident.

Given the prominence of the Medicean Gradual edited by Anerio and Soriano in early studies of post-Tridentine chant, it is somewhat surprising to find that it exercises comparatively little influence on the later development of the repertoire. In later Venetian sources we find interesting examples of hybrid chants that combine passages from the Medicean Gradual with others representative of the Venetian tradition, but we seem not to find chants that follow Medicean practice consistently, nor do we find entire books that take over the editorial contributions of Anerio and Soriano. A year following the publication of the second volume of the Medicean Gradual, the widow of Nicholas Laurent brought out a Gradual that features a second Netherlandish revision of chant. This is taken up in short order by the Belleros brothers in Antwerp and by Mommaert in Brussels. These three publications of 1616, 1620, and 1623, seem to bring the first wave of chant revisions to a momentary halt.

Nevertheless, the movement itself continues at later date. We have Cistercian Graduals from 1668 and 1696 that revise medieval Cistercian practices and are to be understood in light of the latter. I am inclined to suspect that the revisions of 1668 had still earlier roots, but this hypothesis does not presently have documentary support. The Premonstratensians also issue a revised Gradual in 1680 under the editorship of Guillaume Gabriel Nivers. Medieval Premonstratensian sources do not seem to exhibit idiosyncratic features comparable to those of the Cistercians, and the revised Gradual apparently emerges out of the variegated practice known during the seventeenth century. During the interim between the issuance of the Cistercian and Premonstratensian publications, Christian Küchler issued in 1671 a reformed Gradual in Mainz. The dearth of complementary material from Germanic regions is startling, even taking into consideration the swift growth of Protestantism in the region and the consequent religious conflicts.

As noted previously, the desire for chant revision in order to meet humanistic values with regard to prosody was not universal. It was notably absent from the chant sources of various religious orders, including especially the Carthusians, but also the Benedictines. We shall see in chapter 11 that the Dominican tradition remains relatively conservative, even though submitting to change. In the same chapter we shall encounter also a Lyonnaise print of 1738 that is extraordinarily archaic in its account of chant, transmitting practices that are rarely found after the twelfth century. We have to ponder whether there were not other sources that did likewise, but it seems improbable that we shall ever arrive at a definitive answer to this question. At the very end of this study we shall mention a manuscript source that enlarges the panorama that has been presented to this point. We cannot now tell how many other manuscripts may exist that do likewise. We do not even have a firm basis for speculation. This notwithstanding, that which is known to remain offers a picture of a rich variety of chant practices varying according to locale and religious order. Our main lessons concern a certain independence of action partially balanced by spheres of influence.

The musical consequences of the liberty to revise medieval chant in accordance with one's individual tastes were far reaching. These may be subsumed under two main headings and a subsidiary one: (1) a desire for greater succinctness; (2) a desire for improved prosody; and (3) a willingness to recast the shapes of individual phrases. Editors were seldom scrupulous in the uniform application of any of these principles. As a rule of thumb, the larger a flourish or melisma in a medieval chant, the more likely it was to be reduced or even eliminated. Italian editors, whether Venetian or Roman, were much more concerned with brevity than their northern counterparts. French, Netherlandish, and German editors were willing to allow moderately significant chunks of melismas to remain intact. There seems to have been no governing principle or principles that determined which areas were to be cut and which areas were to remain, or how the remnants were to be pieced together. These decisions seem to have been made on a case by case basis. While derivations from specific points in the medieval originals are frequently clear, this is not always the case.

This variability of practice holds true also for decisions regarding what was deemed acceptable in terms of prosody. These decisions interacted with those concerned with greater brevity. In principle the primary accented syllables (and also the secondary accents) were to receive more notes than those that were unaccented. But this principle was not followed with equal consistency. It was at its most consistent when dealing with words having accents falling on the antepenultimate syllable. Under these circumstances the syllable following was not to receive more than one tone, and this note was normally written as a semibreve, indicating a time value only half that of normal. In general, the unaccented last syllables received the least consistent attention to their weakness in terms of grammar. This is especially true of final syllables of words that end major sections or entire chants. Among most northern sources, syllables ending sections or chants could retain a reasonably significant flourish. The Premonstratensian Gradual edited by Nivers constitutes an exception to this general rule. Indeed Nivers occasionally emphasizes the brevity of a final syllable during the course of a phrase by setting it with a single tone shaped as a semibreve. On a few occasions, different treatments of specific words by various editors seems to suggest that these persons were not in agreement regarding the accentuation of the word in question.

Adjustments to the prosodic fit between text and music were made in a variety of ways. The tones assigned to unaccented syllables could simply be decreased in number. Or these tones could be transferred from the unaccented syllable to a nearby accented syllable. In the latter instance, the setting of more than one word could be altered through the reassignments of portions of the melodic line.

Changes in phrase shape were of various kinds. Most frequently the editors were concerned to have the melodies adhere to theoretical constructs governing the eight Church modes. This set of values is most apparent in the Medicean Gradual edited by Anerio and Soriano, but we have seen examples in other sources as well. In the Medicean Gradual a major effort is made to ensure that each chant opens on the final of the mode. Furthermore, it was thought desirous that some interior cadences should also end on this tone. Still other interior cadences could be adjusted in order to present a more cohesive account of the mode. We have seen too that, in the Medicean Gradual, the traditional melody for the *Alleluia Pascha nostrum* was abandoned in favor of a new one that was cast in the mode of *Victimae paschali laudes*, the sequence that follows. Chants in mode 4 seem to be affected in greater proportion than those in other modes. Generally various d's and f's in crucial points in the melody are replaced by e's and g's. However, the reverse may also be found: the d's and f's may be taken as the primary modal indicators and the ending may be altered so that the conclusion is on d. Lastly, we may note that a few changes in phrase shape seem to be occasioned by a desire for text painting. The numerous possible combinations of these three forms of freedom resulted in a highly variegated landscape of chant practice.

NINE

Guillaume Gabriel Nivers and *Plainchant musical*

The most distinctive of the numerous branches of chant practiced in France during the seventeenth century is that which was brought into being through the work of Guillaume Gabriel Nivers, and generally referred to under the rubric, *plainchant musical*. I use this term with a sense of unease, however. It has broad application with regard to melodies for the Mass Ordinary, with those by Henry Du Mont being among the best known. Within the realm of the Mass Proper, we apparently have almost nothing except for the publications by Nivers. There are some precedents to be found in François Bourgoing's *Brevis psalmodiae ratio* (Paris, 1634), but there is no complete Gradual among those noted in the checklist given in the second chapter of this study that is representative of *plainchant musical* beyond those of Nivers. These are *sui generis*.

Guillaume Gabriel Nivers (ca. 1632–1714), now best known as an organist and composer of organ music, was active in the editing and composition of chant for a major portion of his life, beginning as early as 1658. In that year three related Graduals of his, intended respectively for the use of French nuns of the Franciscan, Augustinian, and Benedictine orders, were issued by Robert Ballard in Paris. A series of Graduals either by Nivers or associated with him continued to appear in 1671, 1680, 1687, 1696, 1697, and 1706. There is even a posthumous publication that was issued in 1734. In addition to these editions, he brought out a comparable series of Antiphonals, as well as more specialized publications: Processionals, Passions, Lamentations, etc. These publications are surveyed from many points of view in an excellent dissertation by Cécile Davy-Rigaux,[1] who does much to illuminate the place of Nivers in his time. Nivers' role in these publications varied considerably. Davy-Rigaux seems to have had access to all of the editions brought out by Nivers and also to some earlier Graduals that I have not been able to consult. On the other hand, it would seem that the early French Graduals that have furnished the basis for my work were not available to her. Our aims differ, and, given the differences in the sources consulted, it is not surprising that our findings should vary on some points. Resolution of these differences will require further research. Obviously, Davy-Rigaux is able to address the subject in much greater depth than can be attempted here.

In the Graduals for the nuns of the Franciscan, Benedictine, and Augustinian orders, Nivers acted essentially as a composer. His association with the 1697 *Graduale Romanum* issued by Christophe Ballard requires clarification. Nivers' name does not appear anywhere on the title page, but rather in the two final paragraphs of the prefatory matter. In the first of these, the *Approbatio,* the work is credited to the "opera et studio Guillelmi Gabrielis Nivers" In the second he signs himself as censor. Here he states that he has gone over this Parisian Gradual in its entirety with greatest care. These passages provide reasonable justification for regarding Nivers as "editor." However, such action entails a price. The readings that I have examined in this Gradual derive directly from the tradition of the earlier Toul prints of Belgrand, the print of unknown origin of 1635, as well as those of the Parisian *Societas Typographicae librorum officii Ecclesiastici* of 1640 and 1657. This does not mean that they are without any variants or that all variants are minor. We shall find an example to the contrary when we explore the readings of the gradual, *Anima nostra,* in the following chapter dealing with Neo-Gallican chant. However, differences with the readings found in the earlier prints mentioned seem normally to be inconsequential. The melodies do not represent Nivers' philosophy of chant as set forth in his *Dissertation sur le chant grégorien,* published in 1683. His principal function here was to oversee the accuracy and acceptability of the edition in the light of mainstream French practice of his day. Likely he contributed small changes at various points, but his input seems to have been minor. His function was not equivalent to that of A. Gabrieli, Vecchi, and Balbi in the Gardano print of 1591, nor of Guillaume Boni in the Millange print of 1599, nor yet of Anerio and Soriano in the Medicean Gradual of 1614–15. Nor did he function in the manner of the unknown editors of the Giunta Gradual of 1596, the Flandrus Gradual of 1595/97, the Plantin Gradual of 1599, and the Laurent Gradual of 1616. All of these persons were responsible for major recastings of the Gregorian melodies. Should we wish to describe Nivers as the "editor" of the 1697 Ballard Gradual, we must keep clearly in mind that we would then be using this word in two quite separate senses, and it becomes necessary to distinguish between these. In light of this view, I shall not deal here with the 1697 publication. Nor shall I mention here his connection with the reform Gradual of 1680 intended for the Premonstratensian order. The chants contained here and in subsequent derivative publications have already been examined during the course of the preceding chapters. In this publication Nivers may very well have been responsible for the shape of the melodies as they are presented.

The Graduals destined for use by the nuns of the Augustinian, Benedictine, and Franciscan orders are of distinctive character. While adhering to the Roman liturgy of the time, they generally replace or fundamentally rework the traditional melodies. Some of this has already been demonstrated both by Davy-Rigaux and also by Richard Sherr,[2] who offered two useful examples. I shall attempt to supplement these two works by offering complementary material.

The chants in these Graduals have austere, declamatory melodies. Except for the jubilus of the Alleluia, they rarely exceed three tones to a syllable, and the more normal upper limit is only two. Yet, if taken literally, the preceding statement is misleading. One finds sprinkled throughout signs indicating the presence of ornaments. Some of the melodies are modal—in the Gregorian sense—but others seem to hover in a no-man's land, being neither fully modal nor tonal. Nivers was unquestionably a highly learned man, and—as demonstrated in his *Dissertation sur le chant grégorien*—far more aware of the historical panorama of Gregorian chant than his average contemporary. The prefatory matter to the 1697 Ballard Gradual contains a small section entitled *Observationes* that succinctly outlines the structural underpinnings of the various modes. Nivers may well have been responsible for this section. In his various Graduals for the Augustinian, Benedictine, and Franciscan nuns, he shows an awareness of the modes, if only through the use of standard recitation formulas for the psalm tones. This notwithstanding, his modal practices are quite unusual. For one thing, his pitch vocabulary exceeds that of Gregorian chant, employing not only *f-sharp*, but *c-sharp* and *g-sharp* as well. These are generally employed as half-step decorations, and a few result in unexpected outlines such as diminished fourths that are foreign to the Gregorian language. Although he retains the Gregorian texts, very frequently the modality of his melodies differs from that of the Gregorian repertoire.

I propose here to examine Nivers' melodies for two Masses taken up in earlier chapters, beginning with the Mass for Easter Sunday, transcribed in example 65. As all familiar with chant are aware, the Gregorian introit, *Resurrexi*, is in mode 4 and, like many others in this mode, it gives a prominent place to the *d–f* third. Nivers, however, provides the text with a melody in mode 2 that begins a fourth below the final and ascends through the subtonium to the final and the minor third above, a gesture that is familiar from the Gregorian repertoire. After having subsided to the final at the close of the intonation, the choral portion begins with a rise to the fourth degree, a fall to the subtonium, and a full turn around the final that includes the subsemitonium, *c-sharp*. The following section begins on the final and circulates between the lower fourth and the second degree. We then begin again on the final and ascend to the fifth above before gradually descending to the subtonium; there is an ascent to the upper fourth and a last descent to the final, which again features a subsemitonium, and the outline of a diminished fourth between *f-* and *c-sharp*. We have here a piece with a sharply focused tonality—using this term in a broad sense—and a consistent sense of melodic movement. There is only one point when the same pitch is presented three times in succession, and the same pitch is not used for successive cadences. (Nivers criticizes the occurrence of both practices in Gregorian chant.)

The Gregorian melody for the gradual, *Haec dies*, is a member of the well-known *Justus ut palma* family belonging to mode 2. Nivers fashions in its place a new melody in mode 5. This begins on the final and leaps up immediately to the fifth degree; there is then an upper neighbor motion and a return to the fifth. It is surely obvious that the leap of a fifth constitutes a fairly common opening in Gregorian chant. Nevertheless, the leap is customarily associated with the pitches *d* and *g*. Very rarely does one find it beginning with the pitch *f*, as in the hymns, *Exsultet jam angelica* and *Katherinae solemnia sancta*. The Bryden and Hughes, *Index of Gregorian Chant*, does not cite a single appearance in conjunction with a mode-5 chant of the Mass Proper. Although the interval is not jarring, it is out of place if considered in terms of a Gregorian context. The verse, *Confitemini Domino*, begins on the fifth degree and leaps up to the upper octave. Again the interval and the opening shape are well designed and mellifluous, but both belong to a tonal realm that is apart from the Gregorian tradition. This is new and different, and I do not wish to suggest anything further, because an aesthetic judgment needs to take other criteria into consideration. Nevertheless, the readings that we have considered heretofore, and most that we shall consider in the next chapter, all have reference to a common melodic language which is manipulated in various manners. It is clear that here we are dealing with a new melodic vocabulary.

It is common knowledge that the respond, *Haec dies*, is reused for each of the five graduals in Easter Week; these repetitions are indicated in medieval sources by means of cues. The verses of these graduals are also closely linked by means of common melodic formulas. Nivers loosely continues this practice with reference to his new melody. The responds are signaled by cues. The melody for the verse for Easter Monday, *Dicat nunc Israel*, remains quite close to that for *Confitemini Domino*, apart from a few incidental adjustments necessitated for the different text structures. The melody for *Dicant nunc qui redempti*—for Easter Tuesday—opens with the same initial figure. Whereas *Confitemini Domino* delays the upward leap to the octave above the final for a very brief recitation on *c'*, *Dicant nunc* opens with the upward fourth, descends promptly, and then recites on *d'* for four pitches. The remainder of the verse is largely fresh in profile, although the closing phrase loosely resembles the closing phrase for *Confitemini*. The procedure is different again for *Dextera Domini*, the gradual verse for Easter Wednesday. This chant retains the opening phrase of *Confitemini Domino* (minus the opening repeated tones), and omits the material for *quoniam bonus*, hastening on to that for *quoniam in seculum*, which is modified slightly to accommodate the text structure. A new close follows for the second text clause, and Nivers allows himself to paint the text, *exaltavi*, by means of an upward leap of a fifth, *g–d'*, that then descends diatonically to the final. *Lapidem quem reprobaverunt*, for Easter Thursday, has still another text structure and hence different melodic treatment. It too, opens with the same upward leap of a fourth, followed by an ensuing descent, which this time proceeds directly downward to the opening tone. The second segment, *quem reprobaverunt*, is loosely comparable to the second segment of *Dextera Domini*, but the following material is individual. Among the entire group of *Haec dies* graduals for Easter Week, only *Benedictus qui venit* fails to employ the common opening gesture. It is related to others of the family in that it too opens on the upper fifth and ascends to the upper octave; the ascent, however, is accomplished in an individual manner, and the continuation is also distinctive. However, the closing segments, *Deus Dominus, et illuxit nobis*, are loosely comparable to the close of *Lapidem quem reprobaverunt*, setting the text, *et est mirabilis in oculis nostris*.

Comments similar to those made concerning the Easter gradual are applicable also to the melody that Nivers furnishes for the *Alleluia Pascha nostrum*. This, too, is a melody in mode 5. (The Gregorian model is a well-known chant in mode 7.) The verse, like that for *Haec dies*, begins on the upper fifth and leaps to the upper octave. This is a more florid melody than most, with two syllables being accorded five tones each, and one having four. It is worth remarking that the opening of the verse uses the music previously provided for the solo portion of the opening *alleluia*, creating a formal structure not present in the original. This melody, like that of *Haec dies* is well crafted and entirely diatonic.

The treatment of the ensuing sequence, *Victimae Paschali laudes*, is astonishing in more than one respect. Nivers builds consistently on the well-known Gregorian model, though he adjusts this in various ways. The chant is traditionally classified in mode 1 even though it twice uses the fourth below the final. Most surprising are the modifications of the melody brought about by the use of *f-sharp, c-sharp,* and *g-sharp*, as well as *b-flat*. The familiar chant opens with a lower neighbor motion that descends from the final to the subtonium and returns. Nivers, however, enjoys half-step motion, so he raises the *c* to *c-sharp*. To be sure, composers had been using leading-tone cadences in polyphony for more than two centuries without feeling that they were destroying a sense of modality. However, previous use of accidentals in chant, treated by late-medieval and Renaissance theorists under the heading of *conjunctae*, was not of this nature. We can hardly treat the second note of the melody as cadential, and the outline of a diminished fifth that is created between the *c-sharp* and the ensuing peak on *g* is mildly disturbing.

In both halves of the second versicle we have further instances of the same practice. Here we find a lower neighbor motion that departs from *a* and returns. Following either one or two tonal repetitions, the melody then proceeds to the half step above, as part of a balancing upper neighbor motion. The resulting chromatic sequence of two successive half steps is totally foreign to chant and a sense of chant modality. The older principles of melody leading have ceded place to a newer sense apparently seeking a heightened emotional effect. In the relevant portion of example 65 (given in section **d**), Nivers' melody is contrasted with the version of *Victimae paschali* that appeared two years earlier in Toul in the Gradual issued by Belgrand (1656). The same reading is to be found also in the 1657 Gradual issued by the *Societas Typographicae Librorum Officii Ecclesiastici*. One is tempted to think of the first four segments of the Nivers' version in terms of D-minor. However, such a framework does not fit the fourth segment comfortably. In the setting of *Sepulchrum Christi viventis*, the appearance of *f-sharp* preceding *g* is disturbing to the overall progression. This had originally been conceived within the framework of a first-species pentachord on *d*, and the *f-sharp* is jarring within such a context. It leads one to focus on small details rather than on a larger progression. Similar uses of accidentals continue throughout, as demonstrated in the example.

Despite these features, one suspects that Nivers was thinking in terms of a new form of modality. In the medieval form of the chant, the sections beginning *Dic nobis Maria* and *Angelicos testes* begin on the fourth below the final. This tradition continues through the Graduals of Belgrand and those of the *Societas Typographicae Librorum Officii Ecclesiastici*. Even in the Medicean Gradual, which in other ways is extremely solicitous of modal unity, these phrases stand unaltered. (The Cistercian Gradual of 1696, which shares similar concerns, does not contain any sequences.) Nevertheless, I suspect that it is significant to find that Nivers alters this well-established practice by twice replacing the lower fourth with a beginning on the final. The only reason that I can suggest for this action is that of a desire for modal unity. This desire, however, operates only with regard to range, and not with regard to the vocabulary of available pitches.

The second unusual aspect of Nivers' reading concerns its rhythmic shape. The use of more than one time value is by no means an innovation on the part of Nivers. In France, we find the usage already in the 1599 Gradual edited by Boni which forms the point of departure for the ensuing editions by Belgrand. Still earlier examples from the sixteenth century are to be found. Nivers is, however, distinctive in the frequency with which he makes use of rhythmic contrasts. The 1656 Gradual of Belgrand, given in example 65**d** for purposes of comparison, uses three different rhythmic values, whereas Nivers uses only two. But Nivers changes values much more often than does his earlier counterpart. In his *Dissertation sur le chant gregorien*, he insists steadfastly that the chant melodies have been created for the sake of the texts rather than the texts being created for the sake of the melodies. His scansion of the *Victimae paschali* text is far more nuanced than other rhythmical versions. Inasmuch as this text is not metrical, various phrases may have asymmetrical constructions, and the element of asymmetry is increased when syllables having two tones follow an initial "semibreve" with a "breve." Repeated melodic clauses appear with changed rhythms in both of the Graduals given in example 65**d**.[3]

The offertory, the familiar *Terra tremuit*, opens with the same torculus as does its Gregorian counterpart. But the ensuing melodic profile is much changed. Although the medieval melody emphasizes the *d–f–a–c'* chain of thirds until the very end, it concludes on *e*. While not descending below *c*, and ascending only to *c'*, the melody is classed in mode 4. Nivers, on the other hand, ends the first subphrase (*Terra tremuit*) on *e*. Subsequent segments end respectively on *d*, *a*, *g*, *c*, and the finish is on *d*. With *c-sharp* used twice in this rather brief melody, the result is very akin in feeling to D-minor.

The communion, *Pascha nostrum*, is in mode 6, as is its medieval counterpart. Little of the main substance is equivalent. In Nivers' chant, the segment *immolatus est Christus* descends to a cadence on *d*, preceded by the semitone below. The medieval counterpart ends with the porrectus *f–d–f*. The ensuing segment in Nivers' melody attains the fifth degree before descending, while its medieval counterpart does not rise above the third. The penultimate *alleluia* in the chant created by Nivers proceeds from *d* to *c*; in its counterpart we find a more ornamental rise from *d* to *a*. Given the general solicitude for prosody that is displayed in both the writings and editions of Nivers, we may spare a few moments for a quizzical look at the treatment of the word *alleluia*, which appears once following the end of the opening text phrase and in threefold succession at the end of the chant. In the first appearance the second syllable is set by a single "semibreve," as is normative practice. The same mark of brevity appears in connection with the second of the three closing iterations of the word. The first of these, however, lacks any indication of brevity, using a normal square form, while the last increases the length of the syllable by employing two tones having normal shapes. This is hardly a model of consistency. Among the six items for the Proper, only the sequence—not part of the mandatory Proper—has any relationship to medieval chant other than a very brief opening figure. In four of the remaining five items, only one is in the same mode as its medieval counterpart.

The second Mass that I propose to survey is that for the Second Sunday of Advent. The melodies created by Nivers are given in example 66. In its medieval transmission, the introit, *Populus Sion*, is a seventh-mode chant that survives with a variety of openings.[4] Nivers' melody—also in mode 7—leaps upward from the final to the fifth and completes a turn around this tone. On the surface this seems quite reminiscent of one or another of the Gregorian openings. Yet French practice, from the time of the Boni Gradual of 1599 onward, omits the opening leap and begins directly on *d'*. Still, some sense of relationship persists, although a rather loose one. This, however, dissipates from *veniet ad salvandas gentes* onward, at which point the profile of Nivers' melody becomes quite independent. A vague affinity with earlier practice seems to return for the final phrase, but this may appear questionable to others.

The Gregorian melody for the gradual, *Ex Sion species,* is in mode 5, and Nivers replaces this with a melody in mode 2. Nivers uses the subsemitonium, *c-sharp*, three times as part of a lower neighbor cadence, and once en route from the final to the fourth below. He also uses *f-sharp* as a decoration to *g*, even though it is approached by a stepwise descent from a previous *b-flat*. The sensation produced is akin to that of a harmonized melody segment in G-minor.

The medieval transmission of the *Alleluia Laetatus sum* is unstable—it appears with finals on both *e* and *d*. The Solesmes restorations give preference to the latter, in keeping with later French practice that extends into the eighteenth century and beyond. Nivers' melody is also in mode 1. The setting of the opening *alleluia* contains reminiscences of the medieval melody in terms of its outline, although the laconic form of text setting eliminates the possibility of a close match of details. The jubilus contains a mere nine tones, barely a third of its medieval equivalents. The opening and closing tones of the phrase, *Laetatus sum in his*, correspond to their medieval counterparts, but the details of the melodic profile differ. The verse ends succinctly on the fifth degree, with no remnant of the melisma that contributes to the rounded form of the medieval melody. One should note, however, that this curtailed ending is to be found in numerous sources of the Renaissance. It is fairly common for Nivers to end a verse on a tone other than the final, relying on the return to the opening section to reestablish the needed sense of full closure. When one compares the first three sections of the Mass Proper to each other, one finds that the introit is very nearly as long as the gradual, and is as long, if not slightly longer, than the Alleluia, even taking the repeat into account. The former sense of relative balance between movements and the sense of stylistic differentiation that had prevailed during the Middle Ages is absent. Again, this observation should be taken as a neutral description and not an aesthetic evaluation, as a broader account needs be furnished for that purpose. The traditional balances and differentiation are not indispensable to good melodies in pious religious service.

In Nivers' Gradual, the offertory, *Deus tu convertens*, is a first-mode chant that opens as does the preceding Alleluia. The Gregorian melody, on the other hand, is in mode 3. Not only is it much more florid, but the profile is quite different. Whereas the medieval chant continues to recite on *c′* for *vivificabis nos*, Nivers returns to a varied melody that begins and ends with the final. The communion, *Jerusalem surge*, is set by a mode-2 melody within the Gregorian tradition. Nivers, on the other hand creates a new melody in mode 5. Both the older and newer melodies ascend on the segments *Jerusalem surge* and *et sta in excelso*, but they do so in different ways. Nivers contrives a nearly uninterrupted ascent to the upper octave, which is reached on the first syllable of *excelso*. He seems to be indulging intentionally in text painting.

The selection of the Masses for Easter Sunday and the Second Sunday of Advent has emphasized the individuality of Nivers' contributions as composer and the distinctiveness of his style. While the descriptions given seem to be reasonably representative of the Gradual as a whole, it might be appropriate to comment on other aspects that have received less coverage. The Mass for the Fourth Sunday of Advent employs *Rorate caeli desuper* as introit. The normative medieval melody opens with a familiar mode-1 formula that includes an upward leap from the final to the fifth. This is an opening that Nivers enjoys. Not only does he use it here, but also, as pointed out by Richard Sherr, for the introit, *Gaudeamus omnes in Domino*, for the Feast of the Assumption.[5] The Gregorian version of *Gaudeamus omnes* uses the same formula. A third instance of this formula is to be found also in Nivers' melody for *Dominus dixit ad me*, for Midnight Mass on Christmas. In its Gregorian form, this melody has quite another opening. Returning to a consideration of *Rorate caeli*, one may note that the initial resemblance is short-lived, Nivers' melody returns to the final, whereas the Gregorian melody cadences on the upper seventh. This fact notwithstanding, one continues to find other resemblances to the Gregorian melody in the segments that follow, even though these are brief and are interrupted. Whether these similarities are entirely coincidental or not, is perhaps arguable. I suspect that the answer will depend upon whether one is deliberately looking for them, as I was, or whether one desires stricter standards of similarity. I am inclined here to think that here the Gregorian melody has at least exerted subliminal influence on Nivers' thinking.

In dealing with the introit for the Third Mass of Christmas, Nivers retains the well-known opening leap from *g-d'*. However, he descends promptly to the final, as he did in *Rorate caeli*. He avoids the parallelism between the two opening elements that is present in the Gregorian melody, beginning *et filius datus est* directly on the upper fourth. Nevertheless, he retains the upper neighbor motion present in the Gregorian version, together with the diatonic descent to *a*. Whereas he replaced the initial Gregorian cadence on *d'* with one on the final, he does the opposite in the second segment, employing a cadence on the upper fifth, rather than one on the final. Still, the opening of the segment on *cujus imperium* employs the same general profile as does the Gregorian melody. Again, more independent material follows.

We have had occasion to observe small elements of formulaic structure in Nivers' work. The gradual for the Fourth Sunday of Advent is *Prope est Dominus*. Within the Gregorian tradition, this is a fifth-mode gradual, as is *Ex Sion species*, for the Second Sunday, a chant mentioned above. Nivers, on the other hand, furnishes a first-mode melody for *Ex Sion species*, and does the same for *Prope est Dominus*. The openings of both the respond and verse are remarkably similar for the two chants. (We may note that in *Prope Dominus*, the respond ends on the fifth degree; the verse is required in order to bring a sense of completion.) The *Alleluia Veni Domine*, also for the Fourth Sunday of Advent is a mode-3 chant within the Gregorian tradition. Although it is a member of the family containing the *Alleluias Paratum cor meum* and *Adducentur*, and not at all closely related to the *Alleluia Laetatus sum*, for the Second Sunday of Advent, there are certain elements of similarity relating the opening sections, depending upon the melodic version consulted. Here I am referring to those readings that open on *e*. In Nivers' Gradual the respective Alleluias and the openings of the verses have much in common.

It is my hope that the chants selected for discussion are reasonably representative of the whole, and that I have been able to offer the reader a serviceable introduction to a repertoire that has not been fully explored even now.

TEN

Neo-Gallican Chant

The realm of the Neo-Gallican liturgy, including both texts and their associated music, is so little known that the appellation itself may arouse varied expectations on the parts of different readers. The purpose of this chapter is to forge a basis for a common understanding. We are concerned here with a liturgy that was designed for use in nationalistic French churches that sought to maintain a degree of independence from Roman practice. The movement flourished from the late seventeenth to the middle of the nineteenth century. We are thus dealing with prayers, readings, chants, and all other aspects that make up a liturgy. These each require individual consideration, and the results need then to be coordinated. The full task would require a large volume of its own and cannot be undertaken here.

We may appropriately begin by defining what constitutes a Neo-Gallican source and what constitutes a Neo-Gallican chant. The former term is applicable to any source that includes non-Roman elements of French origin in one degree or another. These need not pertain to music, and they do not involve the entire content. A Neo-Gallican chant is one that differs from its authorized Roman counterpart in any of three ways: (1) in terms of both text and melody; (2) in terms of a new melody set to a familiar text; or (3) in terms of a familiar melody set to a text not authorized by Roman practice for the particular assignment. Chants of these kinds never constitute the totality of a chant book and, as we shall see, they often vary considerably from source to source. Here, I shall deal with both traditional melodies and newly created ones, but the emphasis will be on the former. It is prudent to begin by considering briefly the non-musical contents of Neo-Gallican sources inasmuch as these provided the point of departure for the movement, together with its justification.

The preface to François de Harlay's Missal of 1685 informs us that the French had their own tradition of readings for the Epistle and Gospel on Wednesdays and Fridays that differed from that of Rome.[1] Understandably, these do not appear in the post-Tridentine *Missale Romanum* of 1570. However, two years prior to the issuance of the *Missale Romanum*, Pope Pius V had issued a bull, *Quod a nobis* (9 July 1568), that permitted churches having liturgical uses of more than two centuries standing to retain their individual traditions. This provided whatever sanction might have been needed for the continued retention of the earlier French readings. Over the course of time, the French seized on this opening as an opportunity not only to retain their accustomed readings—disregarding those provided by the Roman standard—but also to replace various chants for the Mass Proper with others for which there was no prior authority. It is this latter process that for the moment floats in a chronological haze.

Missals obviously provide our main sources for the prayers, readings, and texts for the chants of the Mass. Gaston Fontaine has furnished a very helpful account of French diocesan Missals of the seventeenth through the nineteenth centuries, providing also information regarding libraries in which these sources are to be found, as well as relevant bibliography.[2] His article represents a diligent and honorable work. Nevertheless, the development of Internet resources over the past two decades makes it now possible to go beyond what the author accomplished, both in terms of sources and library holdings. It would be highly useful were some scholar in liturgical history to embark on a revised bibliography. Fontaine gives as his fourth item an edition of 1696 of a *Missale Aurelianense* issued under the authority of Pierre du Cambout de Coislin. There appears, however, to be a prior edition of this Missal issued in 1673 (Paris, Bibl. nat., Imp., B–201) under the authority of the same cleric.[3] Should this identification be correct, this book would be entitled to pride of place. (A third *Missale Aurelianense* appeared in 1732.) The *Missale Parisiense* issued in 1685 under the authority of François de Harlay de Champvallon (more precisely, 13 November 1684) is considerably better known. Nevertheless, we cannot ascertain accurately its impact on this movement until we have inventories of the relevant sources, ordered according to the respective liturgical categories. Such a tool appears to be far off in the future.

A minimum of eighteen diocesan Missals appear through the year 1738. These come from such diverse places as Vienne, Paris (3), Besançon, Orléans (3), Meaux, Sens, Angers (2), Nevers, Rouen, Cluny, Troyes, Lyon, and Auxerre. In brief, we seem to be dealing with a diffuse phenomenon rather than one radiating out from a single powerful center. The year 1738 marks the appearance of a watershed publication, the *Missale Parisiense* issued under the authority of Archbishop Charles-Gaspard-Guillaume de Vintimille du Luc.[4] According to the best of present knowledge, this volume exerted substantial influence on later Neo-Gallican practice for more than a century.

The classification of the two earliest editions of the *Missale Aurelianense* may pose problems. I have had the opportunity to review the chant texts contained in the 1673 edition from the First Sunday of Advent through Easter and can report that all of these follow standard Roman practice. I did not feel that I could afford the expenditure of time for a full-scale exploration of the readings, although the prefatory matter does encourage one to think that these contain new materials. Father Fontaine does not provide specific information concerning the contents of the 1696 edition and this source has not been available to me. Whether or not either or both of these editions belongs to the Neo-Gallican orbit will eventually be determined by a detailed examination of the readings chosen for Mass.

The *Missale Aurelianense* of 1673 was followed by a *Missale Viennense* of ca. 1680 (cited by Dom Guéranger, but not known to survive), and the *Missale Parisiense* of 1685. We, thus, have available information of French provenance concerning texts for the Mass Proper at the end of the third quarter of the seventeenth century, as well confirmed evidence of Neo-Gallican texts not later than 1685.

Our earliest evidence for the melodies themselves is of somewhat later date in a pair of manuscripts preserved in the Bibliothèque nationale de France under the siglum, fr. 14097/98. The opening leaf of the first volume bears the inscription, "Livre d'Eglise a L'Usage de Paris, Contenant Les Vespres Des festes et Dimanches, A Commencer Le Premier Dimanche de L'Avent jusqu'au Mardi d'apres Pasques."[5] (It is entitled *Antiphonaire de Paris* in the published catalogue.) In point of fact, the contents of the source are much more varied than is indicated in the title. Not only are there chants for Offices other than Vespers, including invitatories and responsories for Matins, but also occasional chants for the Mass. Indeed, one finds the entire Midnight Mass for Christmas, as well as three items for Easter Mass. Those texts for the Office that I have had occasion to check have coincided uniformly with those found in "Roman" sources. It would take much more work to ascertain the status of the melodies, but I suspect that most of these will also have origins in the Roman liturgy. On the other hand, the Midnight Mass for Christmas corresponds entirely with the Mass formulary for that occasion that is found in François de Harlay's *Missale Parisiense* of 1685. Both the *Alleluia Cui Deus dixit aliquando*, and the communion, *Natus est vobis hodie Salvator*, are Neo-Gallican chants. (The introit, gradual, and offertory, on the other hand, offer revised versions of standard melodies.) On page 164 of the source we find a tantalizing reference to a Mass book, presumably one that would have contained other Neo-Gallican chants,[6] but it is not known whether such a book has survived or where it might be located.

The earliest Neo-Gallican printed Gradual that I have been able to consult is the *Graduale Ecclesiae Rothomagensis* of 1727.[7] The next is the *Graduale insignis Ecclesie Nivernensis*, issued in Orléans in 1730, under the authority of Bishop Carol Fontaine des Montées, not quite sixty years after the appearance of the first Orléannais Missal.[8] (The chants in the sources of 1727 and 1730 seldom correspond with one another.)

The first Neo-Gallican printed Graduals from Paris that are now known were published in 1738, the year that marked the appearance of the Missal brought out under the sponsorship of Archbishop Charles Vintimille du Luc. One of these was issued by the little-known printer, Coignard, whose only other musical publication for the Mass appeared in 1717. The surviving portion of the 1738 book, the *pars hiemalis*, is entitled, *Graduale Parisiense, illustrissimi et reverendissimi in Christo Patris D.D. Caroli-Gaspar-Guillelmi de Ventimille, ex Comitibus Massiliae Du Luc, Parisiensis Archiepiscopi, Ducis sancti Clodoaldi, Paris Franciae....* Unfortunately, the known copy is too fragile to be photographed, and I have not had access to it. The other of the two volumes survives in a copy lacking a title page; this I shall dub *Antiphonaire-Graduel de Paris* in consideration of the fact that the rubrics are in French. We learn the date and publisher, J. C. Ballard, from the Explicit. The first segment of this volume is devoted to chants for the Office, although most responsories are lacking. The second segment of the Ballard imprint is given a separate pagination and is devoted to the Mass Proper. The various Masses are generally prefaced by an antiphon for Terce and are followed by an antiphon for Sext. The book proves to be of fundamental importance.

The difficulties that we face in trying to ascertain the origins of the Neo-Gallican musical traditions become quite apparent when we compare the contents of the two Parisian Missals and seven Graduals of 1727, 1730, 1738, 1738, 1741, and 1756, issued respectively in Rouen, Orléans, Paris (2), Auxerre (though printed in Orléans), Bourges, and Beauvais. Leafing through the early pages of the Temporale of the *Missale Parisiense* of 1685, one notes only a single instance among the first five Masses given where a chant text appears to differ from Roman practice. This is the offertory for the First Sunday of Advent. The text given begins *Dirige me in veritate tua*. The same text appears in the *Missale Parisiense* of 1738. In point of fact, *Dirige me* is not new. Rather it is the first verse of the customary offertory, *Ad te Domine levavi*. Music to this text is to be found in the Rouennaise Gradual of 1727 and in two Graduals brought out in 1738. In the *Graduale Lugdunensis*, the text is accompanied by the traditional Gregorian melody, whereas in the Ballard *Antiphonaire-Graduel* of the same date, it appears in conjunction with a new melody.

Continuing with the 1685 *Missale Parisiense*, non-Gregorian texts appear with greater frequency beginning with the Saturday of Ember Week in Advent. There we find that two of the four graduals have texts that were previously unknown, *Salutare tuum expectabo* and *Orietur in diebus ejus*. From this point on, non-standard texts appear with greater frequency. As a rule of thumb—not without exceptions—the higher the rank of the feast, the fewer the number of new texts. The three Masses for Christmas Day have a total of three new texts—leaving aside the sequence *Laetabundus*. By way of contrast the three Masses for St. Stephen, St. John Evangelist, and St. Thomas have a total of twelve new texts. Subsequent Masses for Saints' days are more susceptible of being reworked than those of the Sundays of the Church Year, and such major feasts as Circumcision and Epiphany.

In constructing a summary of the initial portion of the Harlay *Missale* it is neces-sary to set aside the Mass for the Five Sacred Wounds of Christ, occurring in this source on the first Friday in Lent. We do not presently have any known Gregorian counterpart.[9] Some 160 chants for the Mass remain for the portion including the First Sunday of Lent. Of these, forty-seven (just under thirty percent) have Neo-Gallican texts. In evaluating this Missal, one receives the impression that we are witnessing rather tentative beginnings of a development that will attain full growth only in the second quarter of the eighteenth century.

Furthermore, we find, instances in which we cannot be certain of the correct text of a given item. The communion given for the Mass at Dawn has the text *Exulta Sion* [sic]. The normative Roman text is of course *Exulta filia Sion*, but the remain-der is the same in both versions. Are we dealing with a printer's oversight, or is the missing word indicative of a changed melody? Similarly, the *Missale Parisiense* gives *Video caelos apertos* as the communion for the Feast of St. Stephen. The text follows normative Roman usage until we reach the end, at which point we find the last four words lacking.

The changed text in the Harley Missal for *Video caelos apertos* is confirmed by the *Graduale Rothomagensis*, but the omitted word for *Exulta [filia] Sion* is present. The Rouennaise source also points out some likely errors in the Parisian Missal. The latter gives for the Feast of St. John, Apostle and Evangelist, an *Alleluia Scimus quoniam Filius Dei venit*, and an offertory, *Hic est discipulus ille*. Apparently the two chants are out of order. The Rouen Gradual gives the *Alleluia Hic est discipulus* (a member of the *Dies sanctificatus* family), and the offertory, *Scimus quoniam Filius Dei venit*. Only close examination will reveal how many other traps for the unwary may lie in this and other publications.

When we compare the eight sources mentioned a few paragraphs earlier, we note a very considerable amount of independence among them. Under these conditions, the extraordinarily close relationship between the Harlay Missal and the 1727 Gradual from Rouen stands out sharply. While the two are by no means identical in content, they retain most of the same chants from the Gregorian repertoire, and they share many highly distinctive Neo-Gallican items that are apparently rare or non-existent elsewhere.

The Missal issued a half-century later in Paris under the directive of Charles Vintimille du Luc presents a much-changed account of the chants to be used for Mass. Only occasionally do the two Missals agree on texts, even though they both come from the same city. Much of the musical content of the Harlay Missal can be reconstructed mainly from the *Graduale Rothomagensis* of 1727 with occasional melodies in Paris, Bibl. nat., MSS lat. 14097/98. We are fortunate in possessing musical counterparts for the 1738 Missal in the *Antiphonaire-Graduel* of Ballard, but the two sources are unfortunately not identical with regard to the sung texts. The Ballard print lacks the Masses for Ember Days that are present in the Missal. It lacks also Masses for the weekdays following Ash Wednesday. This means that the Proper items for the Five Sacred Wounds of Christ remain tantalizing mysteries, with surviving texts but no melodies. I have not had the opportunity to compare the Gradual and the Missal in their entireties, but I can report that their musical contents are otherwise identical through Quadragesima Sunday. It is premature to comment on the origins of the materials common to the two sources.

In contrast to the Missal of 1685, issued under the direction of François de Harlay, the 1738 Missal consists primarily of Neo-Gallican texts. Among the 171 Proper chants employed through the First Sunday of Lent, no fewer than 140 are non-Roman, barely under eighty-two percent. (The reader will recall that the percentage for the 1685 Missal was less than thirty percent.) The figures cited need to be used with caution inasmuch as they deal with both text and melody. I have classified a chant as Neo-Gallican if it has either a Neo-Gallican text or a Neo-Gallican melody. The communion for the Second Sunday of Advent is the familiar *Jerusalem, surge et sta in excelso*. The Gregorian melody is in mode 2, but the one given in the *Antiphonaire-Graduel de Paris* is in mode 5. The offertory for the First Sunday of Advent has a text equivalent to the first verse of its counterpart in the Gregorian repertoire, but its melody is different. How does one classify the gradual for the Midnight Mass of Christmas? Its respond is based on both the text and melody of *Tecum principium*, a familiar second-mode gradual. However, its verse has a new text whose melody is only roughly comparable at beginning and end to the Gregorian melody. How does one treat instances in which the entire text is new, but the melody contains echoes of a Gregorian counterpart? In short, when this repertory is studied more intensively in the future, the numbers given above may change in small part. My sense of the matter is that they will not be modified to a meaningful extent. The two-volume MS 14097/98 antedates the 1738 Missal by nearly forty years, and raises unsettling questions concerning the *modus operandi* employed by the clerics entrusted with the preparation of the latter.

The foregoing comparisons are, unfortunately, insufficient to give the reader a sense of the variety possible within liturgical books existing within the Neo-Gallican orbit. Since so little is known about this subject, I shall at least furnish some information concerning the contents of five Graduals. The *Graduale Nivernensis* of 1730 gives for the First Sunday of Advent, the offertory, *Tollite hostias et adorate Dominum*, rather than *Dirige me in veritate*, mentioned previously. In this Gradual, the initial group of five Masses contains no fewer than sixteen chants of Neo-Gallican origin. As mentioned previously, the Harlay Missal of 1685 contains only one. In the *Graduale Nivernensis*, not a single chant in the initial group of five Masses recurs in the same liturgical function in the Ballard print issued eight years later. Indeed, in the portion leading up to and including the First Sunday of Lent, there are only thirty-seven texts that serve the same liturgical functions in the two Graduals. Five of these occur in connection with the Mass for Ash Wednesday and four for Quadragesima Sunday. More instances occur in connection with introits than in any other genre of the Mass Proper; graduals stand in second rank in this respect.

We shall observe that identity of text does not necessarily go hand in hand with identity of melody.

Nicolas Lanquement, the Orléannais publisher of the *Graduale Nivernensis*, brought out eight years later a *Graduale Autissiodorense* (=Auxerre). This contains a much higher percentage of Neo-Gallican chants. Among the 140 chants of the Proper from Advent through Quadragesima, only five have Gregorian antecedents. Three of these are the introits, *Sederunt principes*, *Ex ore infantium*, and *Dominus dixit ad me*. The last of these has been transferred from the Midnight Mass for Christmas and serves instead for the Vigil for Epiphany. The remaining two of the group of five are the tracts, *Ad te levavi oculos* and *Qui habitat*. In the period that extends to Easter Sunday there are eight further Gregorian tracts that are presented in modernized form, as well as the offertory, *Perfice Domine*, which is transferred from Sexagesima Sunday to the Third Sunday of Quadragesima. The Neo-Gallican chants in this publication have no commonalities with those of the earlier publications previously discussed.

In 1741 a *Graduale Bituricense* (=Bourges) was brought out by the widow of J. Boyer and by J. B. Cristo. This presents a repertory that is almost entirely different from those of the three Graduals discussed previously. Among the first 175 chants for the Mass Proper—putting aside a few Sequences and the *Benedictus es*—a group that goes through the First Sunday of Lent, only three have readily demonstrable Gregorian origins. These are the introit, *Ex ore infantium*, for the Holy Innocents, and the tracts, *Domine non secundum* and *Qui habitat in adjutorio altissimi*, for Ash Wednesday and the First Sunday of Lent, respectively.[10] Two other chants may possibly be added to this total. To be sure, casual perusal of later pages shows a few more chants that have Gregorian antecedents, but the number is small. The independence of the *Graduale Bituricense* from the *Antiphonaire-Graduel de Paris* is equally striking. Only a small handful of chants have the same texts and melodies, and serve the same liturgical functions in the two sources. These include the introit, *Deus, docuisti me*, for St. John the Apostle, the introit, *Ex ore infantium*, for Holy Innocents, and the communion, *Ecce Agnus Dei*, for the Octave of Epiphany, together with the two tracts cited above, *Domine non secundum* and *Qui habitat*. The concentration of new chants seems to reach a peak with the Graduals from Auxerre and Bourges.

The *Graduale Bellovacense* of 1756, brought out in Paris and Beauvais by the Fratres Dessaint, is less individualistic than the *Graduale Bituricense*. In the portion that carries through the First Sunday of Lent, there are some fifteen chants that have Gregorian antecedents, five times the number found in the *Bituricense*. Moreover, there are no fewer than thirty-eight chants that are traceable in the *Antiphonaire-Graduel de Paris*. Many of these are clustered in individual Masses. The Mass for Ash Wednesday is the most striking of these, in that the content of the *Graduale Bellovacense* is in complete agreement with that of its Parisian predecessor. The Second Sunday after Epiphany and Quinquagesima Sunday each share three chants with the Ballard print. Granted that the sum total is no more than one quarter of the total content, nevertheless it is sufficient to demonstrate a decided influence of the earlier print on the later. The independence of the *Graduale Bellovacense* is not to be doubted, but the editor was clearly knowledgeable of the Parisian repertoire and did not hesitate to draw upon it for his own purposes.

Quite opposite to the determined independence of the *Graduale Autissiodorense* and the *Graduale Bituricense* is the *Graduel de Lyon,* published in 1780 by Aimé de la Roche. The preponderant majority of the contents for the pre-Lenten period of the Church Year is drawn directly from the Missal of 1738 authorized by Charles Vintimille du Luc and the Gradual of the same year brought out by Ballard.

I have not had occasion to search for Neo-Gallican Antiphonaries, and I have not had access to the *Antiphonarium* of 1681. The article by Monique Brulin, "L'an-tiphonier de Paris en 1681," provides a series of very brief excerpts. The segments from the responsory, *Jerusalem surge,* the antiphon, *O Radix Jesse,* and the hymns, *Regum progenies* and *Terra tremuit,* all use standard Gregorian texts set with reformed versions of Gregorian melodies.[11] I judge therefore that this print also belongs to the "Gregorian" tradition. There are subsequent French Antiphonaries issued in 1722, 1723, and 1724, brought out respectively in Lyon, Paris, and Grenoble by the firms of B. Martin, J.C. Ballard, and P. Faure. These specify in their title pages that they are each following the Roman Breviary. While bearing in mind the two-volume manuscript Antiphonal described earlier, the earliest Neo-Gallican publications known to me are a pair of multi-volume Antiphonaries issued in 1736/37 that were issued by the *Bibliopolae Usuum Parisiensum (Libraires associés pour les usages du Diocèse),* one with Latin rubrics, the other with French. Both acknowledge that they are based on the Breviary of Charles Vintimille du Luc.[12] Ballard's publication of 1738 follows soon thereafter and remains one of the earliest Parisian Neo-Galli-can publications to give the melodies for the chants.

In dealing with our earliest medieval sources, scholars are generally willing to grant that those responsible for our first surviving textual manuscripts for the Mass likely knew the melodies in forms close to those in which they appeared approxi-mately a century later, when our first major surviving musical sources came into being. This assumption is based in part on the highly conservative nature of the manuscripts containing the melodies. Moreover, the suggestiveness of identities of text is reinforced by important information regarding identical modal classifica-tions. It is unfortunate that a parallel assumption is dangerous when dealing with the materials that are of present concern. In the seventeenth and eighteenth centuries, conservation was of very minor concern. We may think instead of free-dom as the rallying cry of the day. Furthermore, we shall later observe once more that two settings of the same Neo-Gallican text appearing within eight years of one another have very different melodies. (In this instance, both the text and the two melodies appear to be new.) We do not yet know how many of these cases exist,[13] but we ought not ignore these cautionary flags.

Although we have sufficient reason to be cautious with regard to the dating of the melodies for the Mass Proper, it would appear that activity in the creation of new hymns (appearing in the first section of the 1738 Ballard print) was considerably earlier. Eighty-five of these are attributable to Jean-Baptiste de Santeuil, who died in 1697. Indeed, P. Clairé's *Hymni ecclesiastici novo cultu adornati*, published in 1676, is one of the earliest specialized Neo-Gallican books.[14] In this sphere it seems likely that text and melody were transmitted hand-in-hand.

Pulling together these various threads, we may observe that we cannot treat the Neo-Gallican liturgy as if it had sprung full-grown from the forehead of Zeus. We have dates for the publication of texts, and a *terminus ante quem* for the creation of some hymns. We have quite different dates for the earliest recorded appearances of the chant melodies for the Mass Proper. At the present moment we are best off in treating the various segments separately and in seeking to establish the relationships between different segments as our studies mature. This point becomes even more important when we investigate the melodies and their texts, for we find that the repertoires of the *Graduale Nivernensis*, the *Antiphonaire-Graduel de Paris*, the *Graduale Autissiodorense* and the *Graduale Bituricense* are quite distinctive. Furthermore, even though the repertoire of the second of these volumes exercises influence over the succeeding decades into the nineteenth century, the use of alternative chants remains substantial. As I have already noted, even when the texts remain the same, the melodies do not necessarily do so. It is prudent therefore to think of a family of repertoires rather than one monolith.

Turning now to textual matters, we may note that the little that is known concerning Neo-Gallican chant texts emphasizes the abandonment of non-Scriptural texts and a focus on texts of Scriptural derivation. This is correct as far as it goes. But unless the reader has further information at his or her disposal, he or she may well imagine a rather literal derivation from Scripture. This is seldom the case. In the *Graduale Nivernensis*, the Alleluia for Christmas Vigil (*Confidenter state*) and the offertory for the same Mass (*Lauda et laetare*) have texts corresponding closely to the Vulgate.[15] But instances such as these are in the minority. More often, the texts are edited, and sometimes heavily so. Words may be inserted or omitted, similar words may be substituted, and segments from comparatively separate locations may be brought together. Similar statements may of course be made concerning some Gregorian texts.

The search engines available on the Web for the Vulgate are a great boon to scholars seeking to identify textual sources,[16] but even so the process can on occasion be lengthy. Eighteenth-century spelling practices are not necessarily identical with those followed now, and numerous alternative searches may be needed in order to pierce the veil erected by the editing processes. When texts are drawn from the Book of Psalms, difficulties may arise because of the existence of multiple Psalters. The one drawn on for the chant may not be the one employed by the search engine.[17] (An edition of the *Vetus Latina* by Pierre Sabatier [1682–1742], the *Biblia*

Sacrorum Latinae Versiones Antiquae, was published one year after his death; it is difficult to determine how much of this pioneering work had circulated at earlier date.)

To give one instance of editorial practice, consider the text for the offertory for the First Sunday of Advent in the *Graduale Nivernensis.* It reads as follows (I employ the spellings of the sources, which are not consistent with one another):

> *Tollite hostias, et adorate Dominum in atrio sancto ejus: commoveatur a facie ejus universa terra; et enim judicabit populos in aequitate.*

Most of this is derived from 1 Chronicles, verses 29–30. The equivalent in the Vulgate[18] reads:

> *... levate sacrificium et venite in conspectu eius et adorate Dominum in decore sancto [30] commoveatur a facie illius omnis terra ipse enim fundavit orbem immobilem.*

Levate sacrificium has been replaced by an equivalent, *Tollite hostias;* the next five words have been deleted; *decore sancto* has become *atrio sancto;* the word *ejus* is added; *universa* is substituted for *omnis;* *ejus* replaces *illius;* and the remainder is ignored. Nevertheless, the last two words of the passage in the Vulgate triggered the editor's memory of Psalm 95, verse 10, which reads, *adpendit orbem immobilem iudicabit populus in aequitate.* Without using the words in common, he attached the last portion of the psalm verse as a close.

Working with the texts for chants from Advent through Epiphany, I have been able to identify the great majority of texts employed in both the *Graduale Nivernensis* and the *Graduale Parisiense,* but there have been a few that have eluded my best efforts. Some of this number give the impression of being of Scriptural origin, but we cannot yet confirm that all texts are based on Scripture. As an aside, we may note that most texts for the Gregorian Mass Proper are of Scriptural origin, so that it is difficult to differentiate between Gregorian and Neo-Gallican chant simply by determining which texts are based on Scripture.

Surveying the chant texts in the *Graduale Nivernensis,* and limiting ourselves to the section up to Epiphany, we find that the editors have consulted a very wide variety of sources. The Book of Psalms continues to be by far the most important; in part this is owing to the presence of a number of chants retained from the Gregorian repertoire. From the Pentateuch, we have texts derived from Genesis, Exodus, and Deuteronomy. There is also one chant text taken from Joshua and two from 2 Samuel. First Chronicles furnishes two texts and 2 Chronicles an additional one. As might perhaps be expected, the Book of Isaiah is drawn upon more frequently than any other with the exception of the Book of Psalms. Other prophets include Jeremiah, Zechariah, Zephaniah, Habbakuk, and Baruch. Perhaps unexpected are passages taken from Job, Lamentations, and Wisdom. Christian Scripture yields texts from Matthew, Luke, and John. There are, furthermore, excerpts from 1 Timothy, 1 John, Titus, Hebrews (no fewer than six), 1 Thessalonians, Galatians, Colossians, Ephesians, Romans, and Revelation (three instances). In all, passages are drawn from no fewer than thirty books of Scripture.

The extent of the Parisian repertoire is only slightly less rich, drawing on some twenty-seven books. Books not previously drawn upon include Amos, Haggai, Micah, Hosea, Joel, Mark, Philippians, and Acts, while excerpts from Genesis, Exodus, 2 Samuel, 2 Chronicles, Zephaniah, Wisdom, 1 Timothy, Titus, 1 Thessalonians, and Romans are absent. In both instances, the richness of the Scriptural repertoire is amply evident, and the sum total for the various derivations would likely be higher for each if the entire liturgical year was included.

Both the *Graduale Nivernensis* and other Neo-Gallican books contain an admixture of revised Gregorian chants and new substitutions. The *Graduale Nivernensis*, for example, opens with the customary introit for the First Sunday of Advent. As we have remarked in the chapter dealing with this liturgical occasion, the normative medieval text for the introit omits the third word, *Domine*. Not only is this editorial decision retained in the *Missale Romanum* of 1570, but also in each of the post-Tridentine sources selected in our transcriptions. We begin to get a tiny inkling of changes that we shall find in the *Graduale Nivernensis* when we find that the Neo-Gallican editors have restored this word as part of the chant text, and have modified slightly the opening of the melody in order to suit. The remainder of the reading, however, is quite similar to the readings of earlier French Graduals, from 1599 on. Among the more noticeable of the few variants is the reallocation of tones for the word *erubescam* in order to emphasize prosodic values.

The fact that we are not dealing here with a revised source of Gregorian chant is brought home forcefully at the bottom of the opening page of music (p. 3), when we find that the gradual is not the familiar *Universi qui te expectant*, but *Dulcis et rectus Dominus*,[19] whose respond is drawn from Psalm 28, verses 8 and 9. The familiar gradual has not been excised, however, but rather reassigned. It occurs later in conjunction with the Mass for the Third Sunday of Advent, which in the Gregorian tradition employs *Qui sedes, Domine* in this function. Except for incidental changes at interim cadences for the words, *Universi* and *tuas*, and a small excision of three tones in the setting of the word *fac*, the *Graduale Nivernensis* reading of *Universi* is in basic accord with the French tradition. Even the changed cadences follow patterns characteristic of the Parisian Gradual issued in 1662 by Cramoisy and Clopeiau.

Not only does one find changes of liturgical assignment in the *Graduale Nivernensis*—*Dominus dabit benignitatem* is given for the Second Sunday of Advent rather than the first—but also changes in function. *Dominus dabit* now serving as communion for the Second Sunday rather than *Jerusalem, surge*, we find that a variant of *Jerusalem surge* has replaced *Deus tu convertens* as the offertory for this occasion. Changes can occur also within the context of an individual chant. The use of Gregorian materials for an antiphon or respond does not guarantee that the psalm or the verse that follows will also draw on equivalent materials. The introit antiphon for the Midnight Mass for Christmas is the familiar *Dominus dixit ad me*. The psalm verse that follows in the *Graduale Nivernensis*, however, is *Servite Domino in timore*—drawn from Psalm 2, verse 11—rather than *Quare fremuerunt gentes*. The gradual that follows has the traditional respond, *Tecum principium*. But the verse is *Dabo tibi gentes hereditatem tuam*, rather than *Dixit Dominus Domino meo*. The melody for the former text is in the same mode as that of the latter, and there are other points of resemblance, including recitations on *d'*, but the differences between the Neo-Gallican and Gregorian melodies far outweigh their similarities. (I remind readers that we are proceeding segmentally and are only dealing with the *Graduale Nivernensis* for the present moment.) The presence of a text used in Gregorian chant is not a guarantee that the music will be used. *Dicite pusillanimes* functions as a communion text for the Third Sunday of Advent in the Gregorian repertoire. In the *Graduale Nivernensis* it serves—with small changes—as the gradual respond for the Sunday previous. The Gregorian melody, which is in mode 7, is not at all related to the Neo-Gallican melody, which is in mode 5. (We shall later note that this melody is based on that for the Gregorian, *Ex Sion species*.)

It is possible for the Neo-Gallican editor(s) to draw on the same Scriptural passage for more than one function. I mentioned at the beginning of the previous paragraph the displacement of *Jerusalem surge*. When we reach the Mass for Vigil of Epiphany in the *Graduale Nivernensis*, we find that the same textual source has been drawn upon for the introit, *Exsurge Jerusalem*. This time a different selection of phrases to supplement Baruch 5, verse 5 is employed, but the basic derivation is the same.

Having provided the reader with a partial overview of the contents of the *Graduale Nivernensis*, I shall now embark on an excursus in order to examine the first three chants for the Third Mass of Christmas. My purpose is simple: I wish to demonstrate the complexities of the webs that may arise when one seeks to view a Neo-Gallican chant not as an isolated entity, but in a broader historical context. Unfortunately the complexity of the materials does not lend itself to a light prose style. Moreover, the reader should keep in mind that I have not had access to the full range of Neo-Gallican sources; the full picture may perhaps prove to be even more convoluted than what is outlined here.

In the *Graduale Nivernensis*, the introit, *Puer natus est nobis*, is one of a total of twenty-five chants during the period from the First Sunday of Advent to the First Sunday after Epiphany with Gregorian antecedents in both text and music. (The total number for the period in question is more than a hundred.) As shown in example 67, the version presented is extremely close, although not entirely identical, to that edited by Boni in 1599. The second syllable of *Puer* employs a cadential form that did not come into being before the mid-seventeenth century. There is a minor redistribution of tones for the second appearance of the word *nobis*. And a passing tone is inserted in conjunction with the first syllable of *humerum*. That is all.

One is not surprised to find the presence of this introit for the Third Mass of Christmas. Yet we find that by 1738, the date marking the issuance of the *Antiphonaire-Graduel de Paris* by Jean-Christophe Ballard, this well-known chant has been replaced by *Parvulus natus est nobis*, whose incipit corresponds more closely to the Vulgate text for Isaiah 9, verse 6 than does the Gregorian. In the Parisian

Gradual the traditional melody has been replaced by a new one (staff **c**), this time in mode 1. The two melodies are distantly related through the use of the familiar leaps of a fifth that are associated with the openings of the first two phrases, at *Parvulus* and *et Filius*, respectively; furthermore, there is a parallel in a later cadence at *nomen eius*. As far as my limited consultation of sources indicates, *Puer natus* is not employed again as an introit among subsequent Neo-Gallican sources. The first-mode setting of *Parvulus natus est nobis*, while not universal, is more frequent. This notwithstanding, certain editors felt a sufficient affection for the well-known melody of *Puer natus* that they sought to adapt it to the extent possible to the changed text. At least three different solutions were found, in the *Graduale Bellovacense* of 1756, the *Graduale Auscitanum* of 1755, and in the *Graduale Praemonstratense* of 1787. (See staves **d**, **e**, and **f** of example 67.) The resemblance to the traditional melody continues uninterrupted for a greater distance in the two earlier of these three sources. However, in the *Graduale Bellovacense*, *Parvulus natus est* has traded place with *Dominus dixit ad me* and is assigned to the Midnight Mass. In the *Graduale Bituricense* of 1741, on the other hand, the text of *Dominus dixit ad me* (normally for Midnight Mass) replaces that of *Puer natus* for the Third Mass (staff **h**). It does not, however, bring with it the accustomed melody but uses instead a revision of the melody for *Puer natus*. In the *Graduale Autissiodorense* of 1738 a further reworking of the melody is presented in conjunction with the text, *Tecum principium* (staff **j**). If we enlarge further the scope of our survey, we may come on the introit, *Ecce Dominus ascendet*, to be found on the Sunday between Circumcision and Epiphany in the *Graduale Bellovacense* of 1756 (staff **i**). The text is new, but not the melody. We have an unexpected contrafact of *Puer natus*, adjusted to the idiosyncrasies of the new text structure. Lastly, we find the text and melody of *Parvulus natus* serving as a gradual respond in the Poitiers Gradual of 1774 (staff **g**).

We may now move on to consider the ensuing gradual for the Third Mass of Christmas. In the *Graduale Nivernensis* we find the familiar *Viderunt omnes* whose text is drawn from Psalm 97, the second half of verse 3 and verse 4 for the respond, as well as verse 2 for the verse. The wording corresponds to that of the Roman Psalter. The melody given in the *Graduale Nivernensis* corresponds quite closely with the version provided by Boni more than a century earlier, although with the more modern cadence for the opening word and the deletion of the last four tones from the concluding flourish on *omnis*. The *Graduale Nivernensis* is not the earliest Neo-Gallican Gradual to contain *Viderunt omnes*. It appears three years earlier in the *Graduale Rothomagensis* of 1727. Furthermore, the chant is to be found also in the *Graduel de Lyon noté*, published in 1780 by Aimé de la Roche, in the *Graduale Lemovicense* (Limoges) of 1783, and in a still later Lyonnaise Gradual published in 1822 by Pitrat. There is a still further use of the melody in the *Graduale Autissiodorense* of 1738, where it appears in conjunction with the Mass for Epiphany. The customary text for the respond has been replaced here by a new text, *Mysterium Christi*. The verse, on the other hand, retains the traditional text, *Notum fecit Dominus*.

The readings cited above are compared with one another in example 68. One will note promptly that the number of tones assigned to the final syllable of the opening word have been increased to either four or five. Furthermore, these tones represent a cadence for the soloists, utilizing an adaptation of the cadential formulas employed in the Cramoisy and Clopeiau Gradual of 1662. Neither the Boni Gradual of 1599 nor the Belgrand Gradual of 1627 provide any clear indication of the end of the solo portion of the respond, which in the Solesmes editions comes with the close of the second word. This is its position in the 1738 *Autissiodorense* setting of *Mysterium Christi* (staff **f**) and is signaled by the same cadential formula. It is of mild interest to note the use of the word *termini* (rather than *fines*) in the Lyon readings of 1780 and 1822. This word appears in Jerome's *Hexapla*, whereas the normative *fines* is taken from his translation according to the Hebrew. *Termini* is employed in a related Neo-Gallican chant that I shall discuss shortly, but I have not had occasion to note this substitution in any other reading of *Viderunt omnes* that has come my way.

The readings of the *Rothomagensis* and the *Lemovicensis* Graduals (staves **b** and **d**) for the opening portion of the respond are very closely related, as are those of the two Lyonnaise sources (staves **c** and **e**). But we find numerous indications of independent editorial activity beginning with the setting of the word *jubilate*. Despite their early date, neither the *Graduale Nivernensis* nor the *Graduale Rothomagensis* serves as a model for the later Neo-Gallican sources. These are each independent in individual ways. The individuality of the *Graduel de Lyon* of 1780 is particularly striking.

The relationship between *Mysterium Christi* and *Viderunt omnes* is obvious from the outset and would be so even if the verses of the two chants were not the same in text. But the necessity of expanding a melody intended for a text of twenty-seven syllables into one capable of adapting to a text of sixty syllables necessitates a certain degree of freedom in the middle section. Even so, one can recognize the adaptation of the melody for *salutare Dei nostri*, to the new text, *non est agnitum, nunc revelatum*. Smaller related chunks appear elsewhere. The form of the final cadence, setting the word *Jesu*, offers a minor mystery. The reader will recognize promptly the repeated triadic ascent from the final to the fifth degree that begins the setting of the last syllable. It is familiar from the normative medieval version as presented in the Solesmes books, as well as in the Liechtenstein and Würzburg Graduals of the early 1580s. Yet this twofold ascent is not present in any early Neo-Gallican source. Nor is it to be found in the readings of the early French reform Graduals by Boni and Belgrand or in their later successors. It is lacking also from the quasi-independent readings of the Gradual issued by Cramoisy and Clopeiau, as well as the *Graduale Bisuntinum* edited by Millet. It is present in the Graduals for the Carthusian order, as well as in a conservative German Benedictine Gradual and in the Plantin Gradual, together with others that derive from it. It turns up much later in the Neo-Gallican Gradual of 1780 from Lyon (staff **c**) even though it had been absent from an earlier reform print of 1690 from that city. I am inclined to suspect Carthusian influence for reasons of geographical proximity, but I cannot help but wonder whether the twofold triadic ascent is not the result of influence from some hitherto undocumented local practice.

Within eight years of the issue of the *Graduale Nivernensis* (eleven years after the appearance of the *Graduale Rothomagensis*), we find a different gradual for the Third Mass of Christmas in the *Antiphonaire-Graduel de Paris* of 1738. This chant incorporates the text of *Viderunt omnes*, but begins with the first half of verse 3 of Psalm 97. The opening words, *Recordatus est misericordiae suae*, conform to the text of Jerome's *Hexapla*, in contrast to *Memor fuit misericordiae*, the version of the Roman Psalter. However, the reading given in the Roman Psalter is used for both the remainder of the new part as well as the continuation. We find in this source a basically new melody in mode 7. The latter half, containing the *viderunt* text, opens with a reminiscence of the mode 7 psalm tone, and a relationship to the earlier chant remains quite tenuous until the end. When, however, we come to the setting of the final word, we find a conclusion that makes clear reference to the Gregorian *Viderunt*, albeit a second higher than normal. The upper neighbor motion and return, followed by the triadic ascent from the final to the fifth degree are clear markers.

This version of *Recordatus* continues in use well into the nineteenth century. There are late appearances in Parisian Graduals of 1754 and 1846. Elsewhere it is to be found in a Gradual of 1779 from Metz. I have not had access to later sources from this city rich in chant history, but we may reasonably suspect the presence of *Recordatus* in at least some of these. The chant is also to be found in a Gradual of 1827 from Angers. Knowledge of this chant is useful to us in three ways. First, it helps to demonstrate the influence of chants based on the 1738 Missal of Charles Vintimille du Luc and the contemporaneous 1738 *Antiphonaire-Graduel* issued by Ballard. Second, in contrast to the freedom of transmission observed in the previous example, there is only a single variant to be observed in the transmission of this version of *Recordatus*. The fifth tone for the setting of the first syllable of *terrae*, placed in parentheses in example 69, is lacking in the 1738 reading. All else remains constant for more than a century.

Lastly, we find no fewer than three alternative melodies for the *Recordatus* text. The first to be discussed appears in the *Graduale Auscitanum* (=Auch) of 1755. Recognizing the textual relationship with the Gregorian *Viderunt*, the editor of the *Auscitanum* provides a melody that is in mode 5. When we reach the portion of the text that is equivalent to its Gregorian predecessor, we find another version of the Gregorian melody, as shown in example 69 (staff **b**). The verse as well is clearly modeled after the Gregorian prototype, albeit with changes comparable to those wrought by other seventeenth- and eighteenth-century chant editors.

The second of these melodies occurs in the *Graduale Bellovacense* (=Beauvais) of 1756, where it is employed for the *Dominica in Octavam Nativitatis Domini*. This chant too is in mode 5. Here, however, the text of the respond concludes with the word *Israel*, the last word previous to the concluding half, *viderunt omnes*. The second half—beginning with *Viderunt*—is instead reserved for the verse, which goes on to include the following segment of Psalm 97, *cantate et exultate et psallite*. This verse is the third of three sources to follow Jerome's *Hexapla* in the use of the word *termini* (rather than *fines*). One notes immediately in example 69 (staff **c**) that in the *Bellovacense*, the *Recordatus* text is accommodated to an edited version of the Gregorian *Viderunt omnes*. Having used this melody for the respond, the editor is faced with the quandary of what to do for the verse, for whose text the melody was originally intended. Undaunted, the editor employs tiny bits of the Gregorian melody, pieced together with newly contrived materials. Thus, for example, the verse opens with a triadic ascent from the final to the fifth degree, but it turns downward immediately, only to repeat the ascent in a different neumation.

In point of fact, the reduced portion of the *Recordatus* text, ending immediately prior to the word *viderunt* had been used some fifteen years earlier in the *Graduale Bituricense* of 1741. Here it appears in conjunction with the Midnight Mass for Christmas. We find associated with this text (staff **d**) a quite different melody, in mode 2, with a final based on *a*. The verse is based on a non-psalmic, Christological text, *Ubi venit plenitudo temporis, misit Deus Filium suum, factum ex muliere*. One can catch occasional faint echoes of the melody for *Haec dies*, both at the outset and at the setting of *[veritatis] suae*. However, these are sufficiently vague that they may well be the result of coincidence. If not, we have an entirely new line of inquiry to pursue, something I shall leave for a colleague.

Our third example from the *Graduale Nivernensis*, concerns the *Alleluia Dies sanctificatus*. The reading presented here is quite close to that of the earliest of the revised French post-Tridentine Graduals. This is not always the case. Even though we are not dealing with strict identity, the number of variants that separate the two readings is small. The most extensive occurs at the words, *hodie descendit*. Even this is not disturbing. Among the well known aspects of the *Alleluia Dies sanctificatus* within the Gregorian repertoire is its close relationship with many other chants that are members of the same melody family. This is particularly evident during the week that follows Christmas. In the *Graduale Nivernensis*, we find the *Alleluia Protexit me Dominus* given for the feast of St. Stephen, the *Alleluia Ad praeceptum Domini*, for St. John Evangelist, and the *Alleluia Populus, quem non cognovi*, for Epiphany. All three are obviously Neo-Gallican texts; but their melodies are all crafted on the Neo-Gallican version of the *Alleluia Dies sanctificatus*. (See example 70.)

When we survey the Alleluias from Christmas to Epiphany in the *Graduale Ecclesiae Rothomagensis* of 1727, we find the *Alleluia Dies sanctificatus* absent. In its place there is instead an *Alleluia Verbum caro factum est*. This new text is, however, set to the *Dies sanctificatus* melody. In the *Antiphonaire-Graduel de Paris* of 1738, however, we find the new text set instead to a fifth-mode melody, which then becomes normative among later sources for the Third Mass. In the 1738 Parisian Gradual we find for the Feast of St. Stephen on the following day, the *Allelluia Video caelos*, another member of the *Alleluia Dies sanctificatus* family within the medieval tradition. This is clearly based on late Gregorian antecedents. For 27 December, the Feast of St. John Evangelist, we find another Neo-Gallican chant, the *Alleluia Nos vidimus et testificamur*. The melody to this new text is nonetheless based on the *Dies sanctificatus* melody family. Within the medieval tradition, the Alleluia for Epiphany is *Vidimus stellam*, still another member of the same melody family. In the 1738 Paris Gradual, this gives way to the *Alleluia Confiteantur tibi*. Unlike its counterpart in the *Graduale Nivernensis*, this chant has a new first-mode melody. This is vaguely similar to the medieval *Alleluia Qui timent Dominum*, but the relationship dissipates in the latter part of the verse.[20] We are again enmeshed in a complex web. When the *Alleluia Confiteantur tibi* appears in the *Graduale Bellovacense* of 1754, it is accompanied by a melody from the *Dies sanctificatus* family. The *Graduale Autissiodorense* of 1738 makes only one contribution to this family. For the Third Mass of Christmas, it chooses as text, *Sic Deus dilexit mundum, ut Filium suum unigenitum daret*; this is set to the melody of the *Alleluia Dies sanctificatus*, whose text it replaces. The Beauvais Gradual mentioned just previously has another Alleluia text that is set to the same melody family, namely the *Alleluia Qui diligit* (for St. John Evangelist). The *Alleluia Notum fecit Dominus* (for the Sunday within Christmas Week) presents a special case. The latter text appears within the Gregorian tradition as the second verse in two settings of the *Alleluia Cantate Domino*.[21] The first of these survives only in four Aquitanian sources, but the second, listed as No. 121 in the *Thematische Katalog* by Karlheinz Schlager, is of quite broad distribution.[22] The *Graduale Bellovacense* uses for this text the introductory Alleluia melody characteristic of the *Dies sanctificatus* text. This is coupled with a new second-mode melody that, while containing some brief, vague reminiscences of the *Dies santificatus* tune, is essentially new. One of the major tasks that will face future investigations of the Neo-Gallican repertoire is the identification of contrafacta and the separation of these from new compositions. In many instances the contrafacta are based on well-known melodies and their identification is simple. I dare not suggest that this is true in all instances.

We have now reached the outer bounds of this excursus and may begin to return. En route, I present in table 1 the assignments for Christmas from four Neo-Gallican Graduals that I have mentioned to this point. The table is only a small sampling, taking in as much as can fit within a page, but it should serve to make graphic the diversity that I have tried to describe for the Neo-Gallican repertoire. We find that individual chants may appear in a pair of sources in seemingly unpredictable fashion, but in no instance do we find consistency in the content of three sources, let alone four. Even if we were to expand this table through the inclusion of the *Graduale Rothomagensis* of 1727 and the *Graduale Bituricense* of 1741, two more of our earliest sources, the picture would remain essentially similar. For the Midnight Mass, the *Graduale Rothomagensis* presents *Dominus dixit ad me*. This conservative choice is repeated in the *Graduale Nivernensis* and *Graduale Parisiensis*. The gradual, *Tecum principium*, retains the medieval verse, *Dixit Dominus Domino meo*, in

Table 1. The Contentes of Four Neo-Gallican Prints for the Three Masses of Christmas

	Nivernensis	Parisiensis	Bellovacense	Autissiodorense
Midnight Mass				
Introit	Dominus dixit ad me	Dominus dixit ad me	Parvulus natus est	Misericordia et veritas
Gradual	Tecum principium / Dabo tibi gentes	Tecum principium / Cui Deus dixit	Cum medium / Ubi venit	Parvulus natus est / Misit Deus Filium
Alleluia	Minuisti eum	Christus, cum in forma	Verbum caro	Gloria in altissimis
Offertory	Laetentur caeli	Tollite hostias	Christus ingrediens	Christus ingrediens
Communion	Ecce Deus noster	Domine, ego credidi	Laetare et exulta	Laetare et exultare
Mass at Dawn				
Introit	Populus qui ambulabat	Populus qui ambulabat	Benedictus qui venit	O Domine, salvum me
Gradual	Benedictus qui venit / A Domino factum	Benedictus qui venit / Deus meus es tu	Populus qui habitabat / Tenebrae transierunt	Populus qui ambulabat / Vita manifestata
Alleluia	Vocabitur nomen eius	Laudate caeli	Visitavit nos Oriens	Manifeste magnum est
Offertory	Christus ingrediens	Transeamus usque	Laudate caeli	Laudate coeli
Communion	Deus meus es tu	Invenerunt Infantem	Vidimus et testificatur	Vidimus et testificamur
Mass of the Day				
Introit	Puer natus est	Parvulus natus est	Dominus dixit ad me	Tecum principium
Gradual	Viderunt omnes / Notum fecit Dominus	Recordatus est / Notum fecit	Tecum principium / Cui Deus	Scimus quoniam Filius / Hic est Deus
Alleluia	Dies sanctificatus	Verbum caro factum	Hic est verus Deus	Sic Deus dilexit
Prose		Votis Pater annuit	Votis Pater annuit	
Offertory	Confitebor tibi	Hostias et oblationes	Ecce Deus noster	Lauda filia Sion
Communion	Dominus Deus tuus	In hoc apparuit	Cantate Domino	Verbum caro factum

contradistinction to the two different substitutions in the first two Graduals in our table. The *Alleluia Dominus dixit ad me* does not correspond to any of the four given in the table, and the communion, *Natus est vobis*, is equally idiosyncratic. The offertory, however, is equivalent to that given in the *Graduale Nivernensis*. In the *Graduale Bituricense*, only the offertory, *Christus ingrediens*, has a counterpart among the sources being considered.

For the Mass at Dawn, the conservative *Graduale Rothomagensis* retains all five of the medieval chants. Of these five, only the gradual is retained in the *Graduale Nivernensis*. The *Parisiensis* retains the respond but not the verse. There are no counterparts in any of the remaining sources. The *Graduale Bituricense* is not quite as independent. The introit and Alleluia recur in the *Graduale Bellovacense*, and the gradual in the *Graduale Autissiodorense*, although with a different verse. The offertory and communion are idiosyncratic.

The number of concordances expands somewhat for the Third Mass. In the *Graduale Rothomagensis*, the introit, *Puer natus*, is presented in a form quite similar to that in the *Graduale Nivernensis*. The same is true for the gradual, *Viderunt omnes*. The *Alleluia Verbum caro factum est* is based on the *Dies sanctificatus* melody, as we have already seen and does not use the Neo-Gallican melody that became customary only eleven years later. The offertory is the one known in the Middle Ages, and it is not used elsewhere in our sample. The communion is an idiosyncratic Neo-Gallican contribution. All of the chants in the *Graduale Bituricense* are without known counterparts.

When beginning to discuss the subject of Neo-Gallican chant, I pointed out that we cannot treat the surviving melodies as if they formed one monolithic tradition. I also pointed out that we are apparently faced by a very troubling gap between the earliest dates for the textual traditions, including the readings and prayers, and those for the melodies of the Mass Proper. We may make a preliminary attempt to sort out those dates that we do possess.

The checklist of printed Graduals in chapter 2 cites some fifty-two sources that are either known to belong to the Neo-Gallican tradition or whose titles lead one to suppose that they do.[23] I have had access to only fifteen of these, and cannot claim to have studied any one in its entirety. I have, however, had access to eight of the earliest ones. As indicated previously, the first verified Neo-Gallican printed Gradual dates from 1727. The latest is a *Graduel de Paris*, published in 1846. Careful scrutiny of the list raises a few questions. We have a *Nouveau Graduel à l'usage du diocèse d'Angers* (1827) as well as an *Editio Nova Graduale Erecense* (1837), but in neither case are we able to trace a previous edition. This notwithstanding, my sense of the matter is that the list is at least eighty percent complete. I may well be wrong, but I doubt that we are missing more than six to ten items.

If we divide the time span into quarter centuries, allowing a few years at either end, we come up with the following summary. From 1725–50, we have twelve potential Graduals; from 1751–75, there are eight; from 1776–1800, there are nine;

from 1801–25, there are six; and from 1826–50, there are no fewer than seventeen. The numbers for each of these periods do not vary greatly until we reach the last, which is much greater than any of the preceding. Even if we allow for the loss of material, activity seems to be markedly greater from 1826–50 than at any other period, and then there is an abrupt end after 1846.

As we begin to explore these sources we find that several are not fully sufficient to the liturgical needs of the day; they lack materials for Masses that one would imagine were celebrated. The *Graduale Nivernensis*, for example, has Masses for the three Ember Days in Advent, but these are lacking from the *Parisiense*. Yet texts for these Masses are given in the *Missale Parisiense* issued in 1738 under the direction of Charles Vintimille du Luc. On the other hand, the *Graduale Nivernensis* does not provide a Mass for the Sunday within the Octave of Epiphany, while the *Parisiense* does. What was done on days such as these? We are not dealing here with Masses for local saints, but with the regular succession of Masses for Sundays; nor are the Ember Days to be skipped over lightly.

If one compares the contents of the *Graduale Nivernensis* with those of the *Parisiense*, one is struck by the fact that among the materials given for the four Sundays of Advent, only the introit antiphon for the First Sunday, remains constant, and this is borrowed from the Gregorian repertoire. Among the materials given for the four Masses for Christmas (including the Vigil for 24 December), the introit for the Mass at Dawn and the introit antiphon for Midnight Mass remain constant. So too do the gradual responds for the first three: the Vigil, Midnight Mass, and the Mass at Dawn. The verses in all instances are new. This is not a stable repertoire that we are describing. Of the ninety-five chants from the First Sunday of Advent through the Third Sunday after Epiphany, eleven texts remain constant from the earlier print to the later, and an additional seven carry over in their antiphons or responds. This is not a large harvest. Among the prevailing currents of change, the Mass for Holy Innocents stands out. The first four of the five items of the Proper relate to one another, and three of these are drawn from the Gregorian repertoire. A panoramic view of the repertoire becomes even more diffuse when one factors in the *Graduale Ecclesiae Rothomagensis* of 1727.

In contrast to the situation just outlined, we find that the Neo-Gallican tradition in Paris remains fairly constant. The contents of the Parisian Graduals of 1738, 1754, and 1846 remain stable. But even here one finds problems that call for attention. The Gradual of 1846 is extraordinarily rich in sequences, whereas fewer of these chants are to be found in its predecessors. Other late sources seem to form a middle ground. Among the four Masses for the Sundays of Advent, the Lyon Gradual of 1822 departs from Parisian practice in only two instances. But among the following four Masses for Christmas, we find no fewer than seven instances of independence.

The fluidity of the Neo-Gallican repertoire that is exhibited in the earliest sources continues, albeit to a much more limited extent in later Graduals issued into the nineteenth century. This seems to suggest that this body of music was still in process of formation in the second quarter of the eighteenth century. And this hypothesis is supported by the variable practice we have documented with regard to the text and music for *Viderunt omnes,* as well as the treatment of the various members of the *Alleluia Dies sanctificatus* family It may be of note that the *Graduale Rothomagensis* and *Graduale Nivernensis* draw more directly and more often on the Gregorian repertoire than their successors. While earlier melodies may have been created in the last quarter of the seventeenth century, it is difficult at present to imagine these as definitive promulgations.

We have already considered the use of a handful of Gregorian melodies among Neo-Gallican sources. It would, however, be useful to take up a few additional examples before turning to a sampling of a few non-Gregorian melodies. In order to maintain some focus, I shall discuss three chants from the Mass for the Holy Inno-cents, namely the introit, gradual, and Alleluia. The introit, *Ex ore infantium,* is a brief and simple chant in mode 2. It unfolds within the range of a sixth, from the subfinal to the fifth degree. Only at the penultimate syllable does the normative medieval version have more than four tones per syllable. Under these conditions, the chant editors from the turn of the seventeenth century and later had little impulse to use a heavy hand. To be sure, the flourish of ten notes on the penulti-mate syllable is trimmed to seven, and the pair of notes on the penultimate, unac-cented syllable of *lactentium* is reduced from two to one. A more striking change arises out of the fact that the word *Deus,* which normally occurs as the third word in the text, is here placed sixth; nevertheless the tones associated with this word are retained, albeit in a new context. With these two exceptions, the reading in the *Graduale Nivernensis* accords closely with that furnished more than a century previ-ous in the edition of Boni, 1599.

The gradual that follows, *Anima nostra,* presents a different set of circumstances. We have here a fifth mode chant that is fairly closely related to seven others of its class. The verse, *Laqueus contritus est,* is very clearly in the authentic form of the mode, reaching e' at numerous points and attaining the octave once. In its medieval form, the solo portion of the respond opened with a recitation on the final and then descended to the lower fourth. (See example 71, staff **a**.) In the eyes of many musi-cians of the sixteenth and seventeenth centuries this was a distasteful violation of modal unity. The problem was a frequent one since the descent is part of a formula that recurs in another eight graduals of the fifth mode, and in part in a ninth.

Conformance to theoretical strictures concerning modality was also important to the Cistercians in their medieval reform of chant. Their solution was to begin on the final, but to employ a triadic ascent as the first neume, thus permitting a trans-fer of the recitation to the fifth degree and a descent from that point. A simpler solution was employed among Italian Graduals at the turn of the sixteenth century, beginning with the Giunta and Emmerich Gradual edited by Franciscus de Brugis in 1499/1500. One simply began directly on the fifth degree of the mode. This solution was used in later Graduals such as the one brought out by Porrus in Turin in 1524, and the one published by Varisco in Venice in 1565. The same practice may be observed in Italian Graduals of the turn of the seventeenth century, including the Gardano Gradual of 1591, the Giunta Gradual of 1596 and the Medicean Gradual of 1614 (example 71, staves **b**, **c**, and **d**). It is this practice that is employed by Boni in the Gradual issued by Millange in 1599 (staff **h**), and it continues in use in most of the later French Graduals issued during the seventeenth century. (The one exception known to me occurs in the Gradual edited by Millet and published by Rigoine in 1682; see example 72, staff **e**.) The descent brought the termination of the solo portion down to the second degree above the final. Instead of a subsequent upward leap of a fourth to the tone beginning the choral portion, there was a simple descent of a whole step to the note following. This melodic form occurs also in the Plantin Gradual of 1599 and in its descendants (staff **e**). A striking variant solution is to be found in the second Belgian tradition which begins with the 1616 Gradual of Laurent. Here the recitation is moved instead to *b-flat*, an action that would hardly have occurred to any medieval scribe. The solo portion thus ends on the final, lending an additional element of tonal unity to the chant, and picks up on the same tone at the choral entry. Among other atypical post-Tridentine reform readings given in example 71 are those by Flandrus in 1597, Piotrkowczyk in 1600, and Küchler in 1671 (staves **g. i**, and **j**). Like the version by Millet, these recite on the final and move downward. In the first of these, the closing melisma is reworked and extends down only to the third below the final rather than the fourth.

Even though we find relative consensus in the way most reform Graduals approach the treatment of the opening of *Anima nostra*, there is no systematic approach among post-Tridentine Graduals to the modal problem posed by this melody. I have already remarked on the fact that the sensitive melisma constitutes a formula within the Gregorian repertoire. It is to be found in the gradual, *Prope est Dominus*, with the verse, *Laudem Domini*, that serves for the Fourth Sunday of Advent. When we trace out the ways in which this chant is treated among post-Tridentine sources, we find that these agree on beginning with the final. The French sources from the time of the Boni Gradual (1599) on, all open on *f*, and progress downward to *c*. It may be significant that these sources do not specify in their layout the presumed juncture between the solo and choral portions of the respond; we can only speculate concerning this aspect of performance practice. The Italian sources—Gardano, Giunta et al., and Medici—likewise begin on the final; these too make no distinction between the presumed solo and choral portions. And although these sources do descend below the final, they dispense with the thorny melisma and do not descend to the lower fourth.

Turning to the situation among Neo-Gallican sources, when we examine the reading of *Prope est* in the *Graduale Nivernensis*, we find that here too the chant opens on *f*. The same is true elsewhere in the same source. Here the *Graduale Nivernensis* terminates the solo portion very early on. The choral conclusion begins with the third word, *Dominus*, and the melisma appears at this point, as it does in the normative Gregorian version. We encounter another comparable chant in the Mass for *Feria IV.* in the Ember Week for Advent. There the gradual is *Respexit Dominus in orationem humilium,* with the verse, *Respexit humilitatem ancillae suae.* Neither text is to be found among those listed in the Bryden and Hughes, *Index of Gregorian Chant;*[24] the chant is undoubtedly of Neo-Gallican origin. Yet the melody opens as does *Anima nostra;* here, too, it is permitted to recite on the final. The end of the solo portion comes very early on, and the melismatic descent to the lower fourth occurs at the close of *Dominus,* the first word sung by the chorus. Even though the melisma is not identical to either its medieval predecessor nor to any of the post-Tridentine forms, it remains clearly recognizable. On *Feria VI.* of Ember Week in Advent, we find another Neo-Gallican gradual, *Quis dabit ex Sion,* with the verse, *Dominus judex noster.* This too is a fifth-mode gradual that presents the same problem in modality. Again the end of the solo portion comes very early on, and the characteristic melismatic descent to the lower fourth is postponed to the fourth word of the choral portion. Although the melisma is now distributed among three syllables, it retains the melodic form that it assumed in *Respexit Dominus.* Tongue in cheek, we may note that the post-Tridentine sources are consistently inconsistent in dealing with the modal problems presented by *Anima nostra* and related chants. This accords with much earlier observations concerning the varied treatments accorded other melodic formulae, particularly among melismatic passages.

The relative floridity of the normative medieval version of *Anima nostra* gave rise circa 1590–1627 to other revisions of the chant. Within the French tradition, exemplified by the Boni Gradual of 1599, the changes wrought to the respond, though numerous, are chiefly minor. The most significant of these concerns the reworking of the first neume of the final melisma. (See example 72.) The verse, however, does not escape so easily. The thirty-seven note melisma associated with the final syllable of *Laqueus* is trimmed to a mere twelve tones. Again one is dealing with a formula that would have been well known to medieval musicians inasmuch as it appears in no fewer than eight chants. The three smaller melismas that appear thereafter are also trimmed, but much more lightly. The word *Domini* comes to an end on *b* rather than *c',* and the conclusion of the terminal cadence is reworked so that it descends in stepwise fashion.

Examining the various French readings of *Anima nostra* given in example 72, one can see that the influence of the Boni Gradual of 1599 remains remarkably strong through the 1657 edition of the *Societas Typographicae* (staff **b**). Significant variants are relatively infrequent. The specification of *b-flat* in some later editions where the sign is absent from the 1599 print is welcome. The version of the Gradual issued by Cramoisy and Clopeiau in 1662 (staff **c**) is much more individual. Although the opening remains stable, the melisma that closes the solo portion is sharply revised and features a cadence that is frequently to be found in the Neo-Gallican repertoire. The version of the Ballard print of 1697 (staff **d**) abbreviates the melisma that is of concern to us. When we come to the reading in the *Graduale Nivernensis* (staff **f**), we find that this matches the 1697 version at the outset, but it couples this beginning with the cadence that had appeared in the 1662 print. We find the same cadence in the 1738 reading, but here it appears at the conclusion of the first word rather than the second. Indeed, the double bar immediately following in the print indicates that the solo portion of the respond has now been limited to only the first word. All six Neo-Gallican readings given in our example recite on the final. Ranging over a century, these remain reasonably consistent with one another despite varying in the length of the solo portion. Two readings restrict the solo portion to the first word, while the two others include the first two words.

In the choral portion of the respond, we again find the reading given by Cramoisy and Clopeiau (staff **c**) to be individual. In seeking to establish the best prosodic fit for the setting of the word *laqueo* the editor limits the final syllable to a single tone; he thus shifts the descent, $d'-c'-a$, to the opening of the following word. There is a further shift, and the descent to the final is postponed until the third syllable, while the subsequent triadic ascent is eliminated. Instead we find a new shape given to the melody for the accented syllable of *venantium*, one that accords this syllable a greater number of tones. This solution is taken over in the 1697 Ballard print as well as in the *Graduale Nivernensis* of 1730. The *Graduel de Paris* (staff **h**) opts for a compromise solution, following a course comparable to that of Cramoisy and Clopeiau at the outset, but then retaining the descent to the final and the ensuing triadic ascent.

The version of the concluding melisma in the Cramoisy and Clopeiau print (staff **c**) is idiosyncratic; it is the only source among those given to eliminate the final ascent to the seventh degree that appears both in the Boni Gradual of 1599 and in the normative medieval version of the melody. The Ballard Gradual of 1697 as well as five of the six Neo-Gallican Graduals in the example each retains this feature. The *Graduel de Paris* (staff **h**) is surprisingly close to Boni's version of this passage, although by no means identical to it. Variants among the different readings are to be found for the verse of *Anima nostra*. These, however, are fewer and are of lesser consequence. We may note that the reading of the *Graduale Rothomagensis* (staff **g**) trims certain melismas mildly, but the remaining variants do not warrant remark.

The Alleluia for the Feast of the Holy Innocents is *Laudate pueri Dominum*. The medieval melody, in mode 4, is comparatively restrained and formally balanced, with the jubilus returning at the close of the verse. Like many other chants of the same mode, it opens on the subfinal and skips to the second degree before ascending higher. The jubilus twice features a descending leap of a fifth from $a-d$, and tones of the $d-f-a-c'$ series of thirds are moderately prominent at various points of the structure. The final is not entirely without weight in the melodic construction. In addition to its role in the two major sectional cadences, it appears as the cadential goal of interior cadences for each of the two appearances of the word, *laudate*.

The revisions undertaken by Boni for the 1599 Gradual issued by Millange do much to strengthen the role of the final in the melodic construction and to reduce the importance of the chain of thirds on d. These result in sharp changes of profile, particularly in the jubilus. The downward leaps of a fifth disappear, together with the subsequent ascents to *a*. The jubilus begins on *a*, as does its medieval predecessor, but proceeds to an upper neighbor (probably *b-flat*), before descending to *g* and skipping to *e*. There is a parallel profile beginning on *g* and descending from *a* to the final, before a last rebound and return to the final.

In the verse, the Boni revision parallels its medieval predecessor at the beginning, but it simplifies the setting of the unaccented penultimate of *pueri* so that it receives only a single tone having the shape of a semibreve. The setting of *Dominus* is revised so that the emphasis is on the first syllable, the second syllable being accorded a single semibreve, and the final descending to *e*. The setting of the second appearance of the word *laudate* opens in a manner that parallels the opening of the Alleluia, and this segment also closes on *e*. The same is true for the segment on the word *nomen*, which shifts the entire melodic weight onto the opening syllable instead of distributing it equally. As we approach the end of the melody, we realize that the tones beginning just before the choral close in the medieval version are closer to the shape of the revised opening than is the counterpart at the medieval beginning. This shape appears also in conjunction with the second *laudate*, and, in modified form in the setting of the final word. As the reader will have already surmised, the final melisma of the medieval melody is cut and the two downward leaps of a fifth are eliminated. The relationship between the medieval version and its later successor nevertheless remains readily evident despite the numerous changes in detail.

Prior to the advent of the Neo-Gallican sources for the Mass Proper, one finds little variation in the transmission of the *Alleluia Laudate pueri*. In the 1627 Gradual issued by Belgrand, the opening *Alleluia* is identical to the reading provided by Boni. The verse is also identical in the two readings until we reach the setting of the final word, which contains a tonal repetition in the later print. That is all. A comparison with the 1697 Gradual issued by Ballard yields similar results. In the opening Alleluia the later print omits a single repeated tone. In the verse, there is an omission of a repeated tone for *Laudate*, and the suppression of the descent to the final at the close of the word *Dominus*. Moreover, the initial tone of the final word is discarded. Four tones present in the 1599 version are absent in the reading of a century later.

As shown in example 73, the version present in the *Graduale Nivernensis* also stays quite close to its seventeenth-century heritage. The cadence preceding the jubilus adopts a form seen in *Anima nostra* that follows the policy of the Cramoisy and Clopeiau Gradual of 1662. In keeping with the 1697 reading, the jubilus eliminates a tonal repetition that had been present in the Boni reading, but nothing else is changed. Similarly, another tonal repetition is discarded for the setting of the opening *Laudate*. And, like the version of 1697, the descent of a second at the close of the word *Dominus* is omitted. The cadence characteristic of the readings in the Cramoisy and Clopeiau Gradual appears at the close of the word, *nomen*. The setting of the final word parallels exactly the form of the 1697 reading, i.e., it omits the initial note. Evidently the editor of the *Graduale Nivernensis* was thoroughly familiar with French seventeenth-century practice and remained very close to earlier models. The assignment of an Alleluia for the Feast of the Holy Innocents is quite variable. Nevertheless, the text is set in the *Antiphonaire-Graduel de Paris* issued in 1738 and in a number of later sources that are dependent on it. Although the melody given here is very likely derived from earlier French readings for the *Alleluia Laudate,* the contrast is remarkably strong. The 1738 print and its Parisian successors write out the opening Alleluia twice, drawing attention to the minor differences between the solo and choral statements. This repeat could not be shown in the example owing to a lack of space, and the omission is indicated by a pair of brackets. In the choral statement, the second neume lacks the opening tone, and the final neume lacks the two repeated f's. Both readings are in mode 4. Both open the verse on *a,* a tone that is repeated immediately. From this point forward, however, the two Neo-Gallican versions diverge considerably. This is especially apparent in the setting of the word *pueri* and the text that follows. Nevertheless, the stretches in which the relationship becomes tenuous are limited, and points of resemblance occur periodically. All in all, the comparison demonstrates forcefully the degree of independence that could occur in the transmission of a single framework.

Thus far we have compared the *Graduale Nivernensis* readings of the introits, graduals, and Alleluias for the Third Mass of Christmas and for the Mass for the Holy Innocents with earlier counterparts for the French tradition of reformed chant. For the most part the readings in the Neo-Gallican source were found to be reasonably close to those of their predecessors. This closeness is not, however, without exceptions, as we have observed in dealing with *Anima nostra.* I propose to conclude this section with a discussion of the fifth-mode offertory, *Reges Tharsis,* first because offertories drawing on Gregorian melodies seem to be infrequent in Neo-Gallican sources, and second, because it affords an opportunity to examine the treatment of a single chant in a sizeable number of sources.

Example 74 permits the comparison of several readings for both the standard "reform" practice in France, and their counterparts in Neo-Gallican sources. The offertory for Epiphany, *Reges Tharsis,* is not to be found universally among Neo-Gallican sources; it is lacking, for example, from sources coming from Auxerre, Bourges, and Poitiers. Nevertheless, it does occur in the majority of sources that I have been able to examine, and I have given accounts of ten of these in the example.

Within the reform tradition, the variants encountered in *Reges Tharsis* are somewhat fewer and less consequential than those found in *Anima nostra.* The version presented by Cramoisy and Clopeiau (staff **c**) again stands apart from its fellows. The cadential neume for *Reges* departs from previous practice, and the flourish on the last syllable of *insulae* is shortened to two tones. On the other hand, the flourish on the initial (accented) syllable of *offerent* is enlarged. The setting of the word

Saba is considerably changed, and it is unusual to find the tones allotted to the first syllable reduced to one, while those for the final syllable are increased. The reading in the Ballard print of 1697 (staff **d**) is again quite close to those of its predecessors, especially taking into consideration the minor variants that appear beginning with the edition by Belgrand in 1627.

The earliest of the readings from Neo-Gallican sources available to me is that of the *Graduale Ecclesiae Rothomagensis*, issued in 1727 (staff **e**). This is an unusual version of the melody. Though beginning in standard fashion, with a descent from the fifth degree to the third, followed by an immediate return to the opening tone, it becomes idiosyncratic not long thereafter. The reading follows the general melodic plan of the traditional melody, but varies the details at numerous junctures. This version of the chant seems to disappear immediately thereafter, but it resurfaces unexpectedly in 1783 in the *Graduale Lemovicense*, issued by Francis Dalesme (staff **k**). This is not an idle happenstance. Apart from minor typographical details the two versions are identical.[25]

The next version in chronological order is provided by the *Graduale Nivernensis* of 1730 (staff **f**). This follows the French tradition fairly faithfully, allowing for the changed cadence on the last syllable of *Tharsis*. Here the shape given in the Gradual by Cramoisy and Clopeiau is given preference.

This closeness is not, however, characteristic of the Parisian Gradual published eight years later (staff **g**). A variety of variants occur in the first large phrase despite a general adherence to the general profile. Nevertheless, more substantial changes appear in the phrase following, beginning with the words *reges Arabum*. The descent to the final at the end of the word *Saba* that occurs in previous French readings is here curtailed, and an ascent to the upper octave ensues, reaching a melodic peak well in advance of that attained in the other readings given in the example. It is not until we reach the area of the final cadence that we again find a correspondence in shapes between the *Graduale Parisiense*, its predecessor—the *Graduale Nivernensis*—and the remaining body of French reform sources.

One of a few sensitive points in the chant occurs at the end of the word *insulae*. In the reform tradition, the last syllable is set by five tones. This number is reduced to two in the Paris 1738 reading. This reduction is then followed by several later sources, including those from Beauvais, Metz, Lyon, and Angers. These appear essentially to be copies of the Ballard print, and are one of the telling indices of the influence of the Vintimille du Luc *Missale Parisiense*, together with the *Antiphonaire-Graduel de Paris* published in the same year.

I believe that the selection of comparisons given up to this point show characteristics that are reasonably representative of the full repertoire, but verification of this needs to be sought through later studies. In the *Graduale Nivernensis*, the Neo-Gallican versions of chants having Gregorian antecedents in text and music show, by and large, close correspondence to earlier French reform readings. This is not to deny the existence of various exceptions. The *Graduale Parisiense*, on the other hand, seems to take greater liberties with the traditional melodies. Although our comparisons took their points of departure from a limited number of texts and melodies, our discussion ranged more widely, taking into consideration related uses of the same musical materials in conjunction with Neo-Gallican texts. This is an area that is worthy of considerably more study, and here, I have been able to offer only a sampling of the kinds of results we may obtain.

As the reader will recall, within the Gregorian tradition, the Mass Proper for the Second Sunday of Advent includes the introit, *Populus Sion*, the gradual, *Ex Sion species*, the *Alleluia Laetatus sum*, the offertory, *Deus tu convertens*, and the communion, *Jerusalem surge, et sta in excelso*. In the *Graduale Nivernensis*, one finds for this date, *Populus Sion, Dicite pusillanimis, Alleluia Deus manifeste, Jerusalem, surge, et circumspice*, and *Dominus dabit benignitatem*. The normative medieval version of the introit begins on the final and leaps upward, attaining the fourth, the fifth, and then the sixth, but there are various alternatives to this reading. The one chosen by the Boni Gradual of 1599 begins directly on the fifth. The *Graduale Nivernensis*, on the other hand, begins with an upward leap from the final to the fifth and it continues with the cadence form found in the Cramoisy and Clopeiau Gradual of 1662. Otherwise it remains quite close to the French reform tradition.

The gradual respond presented by the *Graduale Nivernensis* has the text, *Dicite pusillanimis: Confortamini et nolite timere*. (Here I am using the capitalization and punctuation of the source.) This is familiar to us as the text of the communion for the Third Sunday of Advent, albeit with minor changes in the latter half. When we study the melody associated with this re-edited text, we perceive that we are dealing primarily with a revised version of the traditional melody for *Ex Sion species*. To be sure, the incipit is distinctive and again uses the Cramoisy and Clopeiau cadence for the end of the first word, which marks the close of the solo section. But, beginning with the accented syllable of *pusillanimis*, we find a series of twenty-two tones that, apart from one tonal repetition, are identical with their counterparts in the Boni reading of *Ex Sion*. After omitting a pair of tones marking the cadence in the Boni Gradual, the *Graduale Nivernensis* continues to parallel the reading of the Boni Gradual quite closely, allowing for an occasional exception here or there. The gradual verse in the *Graduale Nivernensis* is *Tunc aperientur oculi cœcorum*. Its melody begins idiosyncratically with a recitation on the final, *f*. But after the introductory section we again find a close correspondence with the reformed melody to the Gregorian verse, *Congregate ille*. (This situation is by no means as apparent should one try to use the Solesmes readings as a basis of comparison, but such comparison is inappropriate inasmuch as no one active in chant in the 1720s and 1730s would have had any foreknowledge of the Solesmes restorations.)

A comparable relationship exists with regard to the *Alleluia Laetatus sum* and its Neo-Gallican counterpart, the *Alleluia Deus manifeste*. The editor of the latter was not willing to forego his assumed right to tinker with the melodic details prescribed by his immediate predecessors, but his indebtedness to the reform Gregorian tradition is quite clear nevertheless. The Neo-Gallican editor did, nevertheless, have to account for differences in the structures of the two texts. The result is that one finds a reasonably close correspondence between the opening halves of the two verses, whereas the latter halves are reasonably distinctive.

The offertory for the Second Sunday of Advent has, as indicated previously, a text comparable to that used by the communion for the same day in Gregorian practice. There are notable variants in the middle section, which reads *circumspice ad orientem*, rather than *et sta in excelso*. These changes notwithstanding, it proved possible to retain the Gregorian melody in a form reasonably close to that of the Boni Gradual. The communion in the *Graduale Nivernensis* is simply borrowed from that for the previous Sunday in the Gregorian tradition.

On other occasions, the relationship between a Neo-Gallican chant and a Gregorian counterpart may be more nebulous. In the *Graduale Nivernensis*, the gradual for *Feria VI.* in the Ember Week of Advent has for the text of the respond, *Quis dabit ex Sion salutare Israel*, while the text for the verse is *Dominus judex noster, Dominus legifer noster*. In the Gregorian repertoire, the former appears as the text for a communion used on *Feria II.* following the Third Sunday of Lent, while the latter appears in modern books as an antiphon for the Feast of our Lord, Christ the King— a Feast instituted in 1925.[26] Minus the first three words, the remainder of the text serves as an antiphon for *Feria V.* in the third week of Advent, and this is to be found in numerous medieval sources. In the Gregorian tradition one finds the gradual, *Ostende nobis Domine*, with the verse, *Benedixisti Domine*. When one compares this latter one with its Neo-Gallican counterpart, one finds a series of short-term relationships that flicker in and out.

These are sufficiently numerous that it is reasonable to think of the Neo-Gallican editor having *Ostende nobis* in mind while working on his melody, and yet not wishing to make his borrowing overly obvious. It is not possible at the present time to judge how many instances similar to this are lurking in the repertoire as a whole, but it is likely that perceptive study will yield further examples in the future.

In addition to instances of loose borrowing, the melodic vocabulary of the *Graduale Nivernensis* includes many brief melodic snatches—particularly at the openings of chants—that draw on Gregorian formulas, although again in their reform guise. I feel, however, that the mention of their presence is sufficient for the moment and do not propose to go into a detailed examination of individual examples.

The task of selecting for discussion a few examples of Neo-Gallican chant that do not appear to have recognizable Gregorian antecedents may be loosely comparable to playing a game such as pin-the-tail-on-the-donkey or blind man's buff. The likelihood of finding something worthy of attention seems largely a matter of chance. Nevertheless, we need to begin somewhere.

We have previously considered the introit, gradual, and Alleluia from the Mass for the Holy Innocents; these all have links to the Gregorian tradition. I should like now to focus on the offertory for this occasion, *Sicut in millibus*. According to a marginal note provided in the *Missale Parisiense* of 1738, the text was taken from the Book of Daniel, chapter 3. However, I have not been able to locate the relevant citation either through a perusal of the chapter or by means of the Internet search engine available to me.

In the *Graduale Nivernensis* of 1730, the text is set by a simple melody in mode 7, as shown in example 75 (staff **a**). Prior to the final cadence there are only three syllables that are set by as many as four tones; the norm per syllable is one or two. The melody begins on the fifth degree and the first two phrases circulate from the third and sixth degrees of the mode. Only when we reach the cadence for the third phrase do we encounter the final for the first time. Thereafter the melody leaps up a fourth to return to the initial tessitura, reaching an interim breathing point on the third degree, and closing with a very common Gregorian cadence, 1–2–3–2–1–2, 2, 2–1. With a single exception, meticulous attention is paid to prosodic principles, and the one exception is not jarring.

The same text recurs eight years later in the *Antiphonaire-Graduel de Paris* (staff **b**), and it continues to recur in later Parisian publications. In the 1738 Gradual we find an entirely new melody, this time in mode 1. This melody is considerably more florid, with no fewer than eleven syllables being set by between four and thirteen tones. The melody opens on the final, and separates the solo intonation from the choral continuation by means of the familiar cadential figure that had been instituted in the Cramoisy and Clopeiau Gradual of 1662. The melody circulates initially between the sub-final and the fifth degree, but then ascends to the seventh degree by means of two successive skips of a third. This represents the melodic peak, but the chant continues to move in reasonably active fashion between the sub-final and the sixth degree for the remainder of its course. Although this melody recurs verbatim (allowing for different note-groupings, which were a matter of indifference to printers and singers alike) in several later Graduals, it is not entirely fixed. When we consult the reading of the *Graduale Bellovacense* of 1756 (staff **c**) we find that the segment setting the text *agnorum pinguium* has been altered considerably. Instead of a triadic ascent that carries us up to the seventh degree, as mentioned previously, we have a diatonic ascent that reaches only the fifth degree, and the subsequent descent takes us down to the region of the final and subfinal rather than cadencing on the fifth degree. Having exerted a bit of independence, the later editor relents and provides for the remainder a version that is similar to the Parisian reading of 1738, although with numerous small variants.

While we can discern a mainstream to the transmission of the 1738 melody, its acceptance in whole or in part was not mandatory. The same text occurs in the Premonstratensian Gradual published by Haener in 1787. Here we find a melody in mode 6 (staff **d**) that is quite unlike both of its predecessors. It is more active than the melody given in the *Graduale Nivernensis*, but it is somewhat less active than that presented by the *Antiphonaire-Graduel de Paris*. It begins on the final and leaps down immediately to the lower fifth degree, then circulating between this tone and the fourth degree above, cadencing on the lower fifth at the end of the word *nostrum*. The melody resumes its earlier upward trajectory, reaching a peak on the sixth degree of the mode, and subsiding gradually as it reaches its end.

Still a fourth melody is associated with *Sicut millibus* in the Neo-Gallican tradition. The text, which is altered and expanded at the end, is employed as the offertory for the Second Sunday after Epiphany in the *Graduale Autissiodorense* of 1738 (staff e). The chant is considerably more florid than those considered earlier and is in mode 4. We thus have four basically different melodies for the text, set in four different modes. We can thus appreciate why the presence of a given text in the Harlay Missal of 1685 or some other Missal of early date does not inform us reliably of the nature of the melody that accompanied it.

To continue with our examination of the chants for the Feast of the Holy Innocents, we may turn our attention to the communion. In the *Graduale Nivernensis*, we find the text, *Hi sunt qui cum mulieribus*. We are accustomed nowadays to think of offertories as relatively florid, extended chants and of communions as briefer, simpler chants. In the *Graduale Nivernensis*, however, this communion is almost twice as long as the offertory that precedes it. The melody is in mode 2 and opens on the fourth below the final, skipping upward a third, and then arriving at the final. This is a standard Gregorian opening for second-mode chants, as, for example, in the introits, *Salve sancta parens* and *Veni, et ostende*, but I am not aware of any larger scale borrowing in the communion. The melody begins with a brief intonation for soloist(s), and the main section is subdivided into unequal halves. The point of division is indicated both by a double bar and by a star. This suggests that the performance may have been apportioned between two halves of the choir. This layout is customary for the communions in this source.

The communion found for this Feast in the *Antiphonaire-Graduel de Paris* is *Agnus, qui in medio throni est*. The melody is in mode 3, and opens with the succession *g–a–c′*. Again this is a frequent Gregorian opening, but one that is characteristic of mode 4 (particularly among antiphons) rather than mode 3. Large-scale borrowing seems to be absent. The subdivision of the main body of this chant into two sections is not present. The melody reaches the final only near its midpoint, and does not cadence on the final before the close. Among later Graduals this chant becomes normative for this occasion. Nevertheless, it is not universal.

The communion for the Holy Innocents in the *Graduale Autissiodorense* is *Prædestinavit nos Deus*, with a text somewhat longer than average. In this source the text is set by a protus melody that circulates mainly between the subfinal and the fifth degree. However, late in its unfolding it rises twice to the seventh degree, and for this reason is perhaps best classified as mode 1, despite its generally low tessitura. The opening solo intonation, setting the first three words, dips down to the subfinal and rises to the fourth degree, eventually coming to a cadence on the subfinal. The gesture is one familiar in a number of Gregorian chants, but this brief similarity seems not to be part of a longer reference to a specific medieval melody. The melody then develops the space around the fifth degree before descending again to the subfinal. The next upward exploration carries up to the seventh degree on two occasions. However, the melodic energy subsides in advance of the close, descending again to the subfinal before rising to the third degree and descending stepwise from that point.

We find the text of *Præedestinavit nos Deus* again in the *Graduale Praemonstratense* of 1787. Here it is set by a mode 7 melody that opens on the final and continues on the second syllable with the familiar upward leap of a fifth. This gesture recurs near the halfway point of the structure, endowing the chant with a small element of formal unity, but the creator does not build on this feature. Again large-scale borrowing seems to be absent.

Before closing, I propose to discuss briefly the chants for the Mass for the Second Sunday of Advent that are given in the *Graduale Autissiodorense*, published by Nicholas Lanquement in 1738. (See example 76.) The introit for the day is *Laetentur coeli, et exsultet terra*, which is set by a melody in mode 7. The text is an edited version of Psalm 71, verses 3–4. The opening closely parallels that of *Viri Galilei*, although with a changed cadence that adopts the form characteristic of the Cramoisy and Clopeiau Gradual. Inasmuch as this gesture runs roughly parallel to the opening of the seventh-mode introit tone, one finds large numbers of chants that open in comparable fashion: introits, Alleluia verses, communions, antiphons, invitatories, responsories, and even hymns. The tonal plan of *Laetentur* is reminiscent in various ways of *Puer natus* in that we have an opening portion concluding on the fifth degree, followed by a second small phrase that concludes on the final (following a descending skip of a fourth). The third phrase opens and closes on *a*, and the tonal shape leading to this cadence is not dissimilar to that for the comparable phrase in *Puer natus*. However, the third phrase in *Puer* is more closely paralleled in *Laetentur* by the segment setting the words *quoniam venit*. In short, the introit seems to fit comfortably within a vocabulary cultivated in medieval chant.

The same is not equally true for the gradual, which sets the text, *Attendite ad me, populae meus*, with the verse, *Ecce venio cito*. The respond opens with the first five of the eighteen words of Isaiah 51, verse 4, and continues with the first four of the twenty words of verse 5. The first five words of verse six then follow, together with two other snippets drawn from later sections of this lengthy verse. The verse, on the other hand, is based on 1 Chronicles, verses 31 and 33. The melody opens on the fourth degree of mode 3, leaps gently to the sixth degree, and returns to the opening via an intermediate tone on the third degree; it cadences on the sixth degree, again using the form that was popularized in the Cramoisy and Clopeiau Gradual. There is little that is strongly reminiscent of any Gregorian formula here. Indeed, given the general distaste for lengthy melismata during this general period, there is little to bring to mind the salient characteristics of Gregorian graduals. With the exception of the closing melisma that extends to fifteen tones, other syllables rarely are set by more than six to nine. The group of Gregorian graduals in mode 3 is a small one, with only a dozen members present in modern books. None of these either open or close in a manner that corresponds closely to *Attendite ad me*. The Neo-Gallican melody develops within a range from the subfinal to the octave above, and is fairly active within these bounds. It utilizes the two highest degrees to a considerable extent, but does not have the lengthy *strophici* on *c'* that are to be found in Gregorian graduals. While there is an important cadence on *e* associated with the final syllable of the word *vestros*, the basic skeleton rests on the fourths, *d–g–c'*. The verse opens with a diatonic ascent from *g–c'* and, with occasional exceptions develops within this space. The concluding cadence on the fifth degree of the mode might be unexpected by some, but this is moderately characteristic of the repertoire as a whole; tonal closure is brought by the return to the opening respond. This return is accomplished quite smoothly by a simple descent of a whole step. A double bar is provided in the print to mark the point of separation between the solo introduction and the choral continuation, but no such device is employed at the end of the verse. Inasmuch as a double bar marks the choral close to the verse of the following Alleluia, it would appear that the verse of the gradual was entrusted entirely to soloists. Even though I have not been able to discern any notable large-scale resemblances to Gregorian chants, the small gestural content of *Attendite ad me* fits reasonably smoothly with its earlier antecedents.

The Alleluia for the Second Sunday of Advent is unusual in that it employs two verses. During the period from the opening of Advent through the Sixth Sunday after Epiphany, there is no other comparable chant in this print that has a second verse. The texts are taken verbatim from Psalm 71 according to the version of Jerome's *Hexapla*. The opening verse, *Suscipiant montes*, presents verse 3 in its entirety, while the second of the pair does likewise for verse 4. The melodies are again instantly recognizable renditions of well-known Gregorian gestures. The opening of the Alleluia descends stepwise from the mode 1 final, skips up to the third degree, and then snakes upward to the fifth. This opening is characteristic of numerous Gregorian antiphons in mode 1,[27] while the end of the jubilus is loosely comparable to similar segments of the *Alleluia Dies sanctificatus*. The opening of the first verse is also a common formula, comparable to the opening of the *Alleluia Timebunt gentes* and its verse, and also to the verse of the *Alleluia Laetatus sum*. The last thirteen tones of both the first and second verse are equivalent to the last thirteen tones of the jubilus, a unifying device that is quite common among Gregorian Alleluias. The second verse, *Judicabit pauperes*, opens with a "thumbprint" formula providing instant modal identification for mode 1 chants in the Gregorian repertoire. Beginning on the subfinal, it proceeds to the final and then leaps up a fifth, circulating around that degree. Various forms of this opening are quite common and it is to be found also in a group of Alleluia verses that one suspects are modern Solesmes compositions.[28]

If one were to disregard liturgical function and placement, one might conceive of the Mass Proper for a particular occasion as constituting one large artistic unit possessing certain inherent balances. One might perceive an arch shape, proceeding from a modest beginning and progressing to a still more modest ending. The middle portions would carry the greatest artistic weight in terms of expansiveness. The avoidance of major melismata both in the general reform practice and in the Neo-Gallican sources in particular, results in quite a different set of balances between the various movements. These become dependent not so much on style, but on the mere length of the texts to be set, and these lengths may vary unpredictably. In the present instance, the Alleluia with the verse, *Suscipiant montes*, is only barely longer than the initial introit, and is dwarfed by the preceding gradual, *Attendite ad me*. Even without its verse, *Ecce venio cito*, the gradual respond is approximately twice as long as the succeeding movement, and is nearly as long as the Alleluia with both of its verses. The offertory that follows, *Adonaï Domine*, is fully as large as the Alleluia with its two verses.

Adonaï Domine, the offertory for the Second Sunday of Advent, is a third-mode chant. Its text is based on the Book of Judith, Chapter 16, verses 17–19, but is heavily edited.[29] Some of its musical characteristics are similar to those of the gradual for the same day. The final plays a relatively small role in the melodic construction. Not one of the interior cadences ends on *e*, and none of the major phrases begins on this tone. At best *e* serves to begin a few subphrases. The melody does not depend upon repetition of gestures or common goals for cadences in determining its shape and unity. The opening, which ascends diatonically from the third degree to the sixth, only to fall back to the third degree and curl upward one step, is found frequently enough among Gregorian melodies, but it is not distinctive and does not appear elsewhere within a mode 3 context. The chant is moderately florid, with a melisma of eighteen tones on the antepenultimate syllable, and a handful of briefer flourishes of eight to eleven tones.

The communion for this Sunday, *Ego pascam oves meas*, creates a text that brings together passages from Ezekiel, chapter 34, verses 15 and 22. The melody in mode 5 is a simple one that begins on the fifth of the mode and occupies the octave range above the final. The melody does not seem to have a strong personality and there is little to note that stands out as being especially characteristic of either a Gregorian or Neo-Gallican ductus. It is pleasant but not memorable.

One cannot, within the framework of a study of this nature, account for the totality of chants for the Neo-Gallican Mass Proper. I hope, however, to have provided a representative panorama of this repertoire that has previously been lacking. Since it was necessary to interrupt the discussion by pursuing numerous tangents, a brief closing summary may be in order. Our information concerning the texts for this branch of chant comes to us from sources possibly as early as 1673, and clearly documentable from 1685. The first musical sources now known containing chants for the Mass date from no earlier than 1698. The prints circa 1727–54 disclose a repertory in a state of flux, lacking fixity in both choice of text and accompanying melody. Under these conditions it is hazardous to project the existence of the known melodies back to a period some fifty years earlier than their first appearance. That which survives is likely to be mainly the product of work in chant carried out in the second quarter of the eighteenth century. While this family of chant seeks independence from the Roman liturgy, the early sources each demonstrate an awareness of the reform tradition of chant as practiced in France during the seventeenth century. A small, variable percentage of chants can be related to Gregorian antecedents in both text and music. Furthermore, new texts may be set by melodies rooted in the French reform tradition. An instinctive awareness of medieval principles governing melodic creation-such as formulaic interrelationships and melody families-often makes it presence felt on both large and small scale. From the musical standpoint there is much that is conservative, even though we are dealing with the retention of melodic practices of the seventeenth century and not those of the Middle Ages. If this chant is viewed in its own right and not simply in comparison with the creations of the more distant past, it will—I believe—be found worthy of more attention than it has received.

ELEVEN

A Retrospective Glance and the Eighteenth Century

The transcriptions that have accompanied chapters 3–8 have emphasized largely the readings of Graduals brought out between 1591 and 1680 and more especially between 1591 and 1630. The more limited period was crucial to the formation of the post-Tridentine Mass Proper. This focus notwithstanding, I have commented from time to time on certain later readings that have reworked traditions begun early in the seventeenth century, if not from before the turn of that century. Before moving on to a consideration of chant history in the eighteenth and—in the next chapter—in the nineteenth centuries, I wish to reflect on what has been accomplished to this point and to provide information on materials not previously discussed.

The reader has been offered an opportunity to peruse a sizable number of chants from various sources printed in Italy, France, the Low Countries, Germany, Poland, and Spain. Given the seeming fixity of music inscribed on the printed page, an incautious person might easily think that the transcriptions represent music that was equally fixed for a number of generations. Such a conclusion, however, is not warranted.

The transcriptions record more transient phenomena, and we receive various reminders of this fact. First, we observe that the best represented traditions do not remain constant over any broad period of time. When the firm of Giunta brought out the Graduals of 1606 and 1611, these did not retain the readings of the 1596 print unchanged. The alterations are rarely substantial, and they are not omnipresent. Having once submitted to major change before the turn of the seventeenth century, the idiom can revert to the conservatism of earlier days. The Giunta style remains clearly identifiable. Nevertheless, change does occur, both in terms of small details, and in terms of entire phrases, as we have seen in our discussions dealing with late hybrids that contained mixtures of the Medicean and Giuntan traditions. The unknown persons responsible for overseeing the Italian Graduals of the late seventeenth and eighteenth centuries, retained prerogatives for change even though they exercised these only intermittently.

The situation in France is roughly comparable. The Gradual edited by Boni for Simon Millange in 1598/99 set a precedent for a general French style of chant. We no longer know the whereabouts of the first successors to this pioneering publication—a Parisian Gradual of circa 1608 and a Toul Gradual of 1622 known to Amadée Gastoué—but the Toul Gradual of 1627 issued by Belgrand clearly follows in the footsteps of its earlier predecessor. Its readings are clearly molded by Boni's work, but they do not adhere to it literally. The changes are generally of modest nature, but they should not be attributed to "mistakes" made by the publishers. The tradition that we are discussing carries on into the late seventeenth century and beyond. At the same time, the publishing scene in France was apparently more diverse than in Italy. While some of the later seventeenth-century publications of Belgrand and Laurent, the *Societas Typographicae librorum officii Ecclesiastici,* and Christophe Ballard continue to follow in the paths laid out at earlier date, there were others that exhibited greater independence. The Gradual issued in 1662 based on the Missal of Archbishop Jean François Paul de Gondy is notable in this respect. Its indebtedness to the past is clear, but so too was the will of the unknown editor to depart from this tradition on a moderately frequent basis. Similar comments apply to the distinctive Gradual edited by Jean Millet and published by Rigoine in Besançon in 1682. Because only the *Pars aestiva* is known to survive from the Gradual issued in 1688/89 by the two L. Sevestres, my work with this publication has been limited. I have had extremely little access to the various publications edited by Louis Paschal and issued by Jean de la Caille, and the 1655 Gradual issued in Paris by Robert Ballard was not available to me. Exploration of these Graduals may well yield further insights.

In Italy, the publication scene was dominated by Venetian firms throughout the seventeenth and eighteenth centuries, apart from the solitary Medicean Gradual, issued in Rome, 1614/15. Only in 1797 does the first post-Tridentine Gradual from Turin appear,[1] and at that time the Venetian publishers had just ceased their activity in the field of chant. In France, on the other hand, a print from Lyon was issued in 1606 and—after a considerable hiatus—Graduals were issued on a moderately frequent basis beginning in 1669. No fewer than nineteen appear by the end of the eighteenth century. (Some of these belong to the Neo-Gallican orbit.) I have been able to examine somewhat superficially two that follow the Roman liturgy, and preliminary results would indicate that these follow normative Parisian practice rather closely. Ten Graduals are issued in Grenoble between the years 1730–89, chiefly by various generations of the firm of Faure. Again, the two that I have been able to see correspond closely to the readings of Paris. I nevertheless suspect that neither the publications from Lyon nor those from Grenoble are mere mechanical duplications of earlier editions. Far fewer Graduals appear in various other French cities.

Our evidence concerning flexibility in chant practice in the Lowlands comes in different forms. The earliest of the Graduals issued from the area of present-day Belgium is that brought out by the firm of Plantin in 1599. After this, the firm lapses into inactivity in this area of publication until it belatedly produces a second Gradual in 1774[2] and a third in 1834. During the interim, other firms enter the scene for brief moments. In 1616 the firm headed by the widow of Nicolas Laurent brings out a Gradual in Tournai. This is followed by another issued by two members of the Belleros family in Antwerp in 1620, and a third published by Jan Mommaert in Brussels in 1623. The sole copy of the Belleros Gradual that is known to survive is of considerable interest because of the many paste-overs that dot its pages. Some later user was not entirely satisfied with what he found in the edition, and changed it to his taste. The Mommaert Gradual does not employ this practice, but we find various instances scattered throughout where a later user has opted for a terser style of melody and has therefore crossed out brief portions of the offending melismas. In these two instances we have clear evidence that users of printed Graduals did not feel bound by the printed page, but insisted on small editorial prerogatives. I suspect that other choir directors may well have acted in similar fashion even though they did not record their changes on our surviving documents. I may mention here that the manuscript Gradual now at the Biblioteka Jagiellonska ascribed to 1600 (olim Berlin, Staatsbibl., 40103) began life as a conservative Gradual much in the fashion of the two Benedictine Graduals in Würzburg. At some later date, however, the manuscript was revised and the lengthier melismas were truncated. A sign was placed at the point where the cut was to begin and the same sign was placed where the cut ended. Some measure of variability continues to exist into the early twentieth century. There is a copy of the *Liber Gradualis juxta antiquorum Codicum* of 1895, formerly owned by Joseph J. Pierron of Milwaukee, but now in the library of Duquesne University. The former owner has apparently neatly crossed out the final syllable of the third word of the offertory, *Deus tu convertens*, and replaced it neatly with the syllable "sus," thus reverting to an alternative form known previously. In placing our sources in context, we need to allow for processes of change in their later use.

However frustrating our early adiastematic sources may appear to us, they do have the virtue of providing us with precious hints concerning details of phrasing in performance. This information continues to be furnished by later diastematic neumes. When printed chant sources first began to appear, a certain amount of this information survived. These remnants became fewer and fewer as the vocabulary of notational signs decreased. In many publications of the seventeenth and eighteenth centuries, there are basically only one or two signs present, the omnipresent square (breve) and the diamond (semibreve). Except for the separation points between syllables, the square forms tend to be crowded together as closely as possible so that the maximum number may be fit onto a line. If there are many notes to one syllable, there may be no interruption between them. Obviously, when the printer comes to the end of a line there is a division in the printed music, but this visual division does not function to illuminate the musical phrasing. Indeed, there are numerous instances where the seeming "division" is entirely inappropriate, subdividing what had in earlier times been a single neume. I cannot help but think that this lack of sensitivity to the nuances of phrasing was both a mirror to a less nuanced form of musical phrasing as well as an encouragement to more mechanical, less sensitive phrasing. Indeed some writers—e.g., Nivers—inform us of a performance style that depended on equal time-values. In his *Dissertation sur le chant grégorien*, Nivers campaigns against such a style.

In his *Directorium chori* of 1582, Guidetti advocates a much more flexible style of performance, distinguishing between no fewer than four different rhythmic values. The mode of notation that he advocates and the resultant mode of performance is not, however, documented in the printed Italian Graduals that follow. I do not believe, however, that their silence necessarily testifies to a lack of willingness on the part of chant singers to follow his rhythmic style in performance. But this style would likely have been dependent upon the oral instruction that would have been provided by the choirmaster.

This chapter has begun with a caution not to transform the seeming fixity of musical notation into an equivalent fixity in performance. It is proper that we continue with another caution: we need be careful not to confuse the place of publication for any given print with the broader area in which the print was known, either directly or by means of influence on a later publication. It is reasonable enough to describe the chant style of a particular edition as a style from Venice, Rome, Bordeaux, Toul, or Antwerp, etc. But we should keep in mind that the knowledge and influence of this edition likely radiated well beyond the confines of the city of origin, and that, on the other hand, the city of origin may well have known more than one version of chant. Aspects of this topic have been touched upon tangentially on multiple occasions in previous chapters, but it seems appropriate to devote at least some brief space to focus directly on the problem. I suggest that one long-term future goal of chant scholarship would be to create a sense of the geography of chant performance traditions to whatever extent may be possible. This will not be an easy task.

I doubt strongly that we would think of the early sixteenth-century publications of Petrucci, for example, as being directed exclusively to a Venetian audience, nor would we think of the products of other major printers and publishers of the sixteenth century as being equally restricted to the various locales in which their products were issued. There is no reason that I know of why we should posit artificial restrictions on the purchasers of chant editions. Indeed, we do have evidence that demonstrates the contrary. We have been informed that the Cathedral of St. Stephen in Vienna had purchased a copy of one of the late Graduals by the Venetian printer, Baglioni. The Cathedral of St. Peter in Salzburg owned multiple copies of both a Gradual and an Antiphonal issued by Belgrand in Toul. There are occasional records of comparable northern purchases of the Medicean Gradual issued in Rome. Indeed, we have drawn attention to occasional hybrid Venetian readings that make use of the Medicean model. In the discussion of the various readings of the gradual, *Ex Sion species*, I had occasion to draw attention to the very close resemblance between the Gardano reading of this melody and the somewhat later reading in the French Gradual edited by Guillaume Boni. I am skeptical that this relationship is coincidental and am inclined to posit some form of relationship between the two editions. It remains, however, to find out whether there is any additional evidence that would corroborate such a relationship.

In 1766 the firm of Johannis-Nic. Galles brings out in Venice a print entitled *Epitome Gradualis Romani, seu Cantus missarum dominicalium et festivarum totius anni*. On the title page we read the description, "*cantui Romano simillima*." The print was successful enough that three editions appeared within seven years. My curiosity was piqued by the description, and I was able to put my mind to rest thanks to the kindness of a librarian who was willing to provide me with a handful of reproductions. As one might perhaps infer from the name of the publisher, the Gradual simply gives readings that accord with the main French tradition! The descriptive phrase, *cantui Romano simillima*, refers not to the music, but to the text. I suspect that Galles is distinguishing his publication from the contemporary Neo-Gallican publications that had become frequent in France by the 1760s, though it is hard to say why this should have been thought advantageous in a print issued in Venice. The only thought that occurs is that Galles wanted his book to be saleable not only in Italy but in France as well.

We shall eventually have to ponder more closely the readings of the three Polish Graduals issued by the firm of Piotrkowczyk in Kraków from 1600 to 1651. Preliminary findings suggest that these are not purely local products issued in isolation from the chant practice of Western Europe, but that they reveal the varied influence of different Western traditions. All of these matters belong to the realm of a geographical history of chant, but they are not matters that can be addressed fully in the context of this book. It is necessary to draw a line here and to proceed with a discussion of two eighteenth-century prints that afford unusual opportunities to broaden our knowledge of chant during the interim period, 1590–1890.

The *Graduale Sanctae Lugdunensis Ecclesiae* published in 1738 provides an extraordinary contrast to its many counterparts from circa 1690–1790, both visually and in terms of its contents and readings. Although its ultimate importance resides in the latter elements, we will do ourselves a disservice if we skip over the first. I shall devote a very lengthy excursus to this print because I believe that it poses unusual and meaningful challenges to our thinking regarding the history of chant.

This Gradual is presently known to survive in three locations: the Bibliothèque Ste.-Geneviève in Paris, the Abbey of Solesmes, and the Bibliothèque municipale of Lyon. The copy preserved in the Bibliothèque Ste.-Geneviève contains no introductory matter, no *Approbation, Imprimatur,* or *Privilège,* no identification of the editor(s) responsible for the print, no mention of its intended audience. Directly following the title page we find the *Asperges me* and then the Mass for the First Sunday of Advent. The first impression one receives in perusing its opening pages is that of marked elegance. This is not a frequent characteristic of liturgical prints of this era. The *Graduale Romanum* published in Lyon by André Laurens in 1724 (*sic*) is more representative.[3] This book is printed by single impression, with small type segments that combine bits of a four-line staff and an individual square- or diamond-shaped note. These are generally crammed together as tightly as possible, and the breaks between type elements give the work a coarse appearance. If no major rubrics are required to mark the liturgical occasion, one will find fifteen staves crowded onto a single page. It is a strictly utilitarian work, with little regard for the reader's ease or pleasure of use. The same description holds true for the earlier *Graduale Romanum* issued by the Societas Bibliopolarum of Lyon in 1690. And the *Epitome Gradualis Romani* issued in Grenoble by Pierre Faure in 1735 is no more handsome. The books issued by Christophe Ballard and J. C. Ballard in 1734 and 1738 are not as parsimonious in their use of space, but neither are they exemplars of the printer's art at its best. They are workaday books.

By contrast, the *Graduale Lugdunensis* is extraordinarily generous in its use of space. A maximum of seven staves are placed on pages that are somewhat over sixteen inches high.[4] The work has been printed by double impression, with the staves in red and the neumes in black. This makes for an infinitely more attractive page. Still more important, there is ample space given to the individual neumes, and long melismas are clearly subdivided into their component parts rather than being presented as undigested lumps. Visually speaking, the music has room to breathe. Even more significant, we are given a Gregorian notation comparable to that which one might find in a careful French manuscript of the late thirteenth century. Not all printed sources circa 1600–1750 are poverty-stricken in the breadth of their notational apparatus. Among northern sources, the *Graduale Romanum integrum* and the *Graduale Romanum de Tempore et Sanctis,* published in 1599 respectively by Millange in Bordeaux and the firm of Plantin in Antwerp employ a fairly broad notational apparatus, as do a number of Venetian prints by Giunta and his competitors.

Nevertheless, the notational apparatus of the *Graduale Lugdunensis* is broader still. For the First Sunday of Advent, the opening neume of the introit, *Ad te levavi,* is a *cephalicus,* while on the following page we find two further instances of this neume and two examples of an *epiphonus.* This remark about liquescents might seem quite trivial until one tries to recall earlier instances of these neumes in the history of chant prints over the previous two hundred years. I have not made a search of every source available to me on microfilm, nor have I seen all sources from this period. Nevertheless, I cannot recall any other examples from the period 1475–1850. Another unusual feature is the frequent presence of *strophici*, both bistrophae and tristrophae. For the most part, these have largely disappeared by the turn of the seventeenth century, with the exception of prints for the Carthusian order. There are no fewer than seven instances of these in the opening introit. None are to be found in the post-1590 sources selected for the examples accompanying chapter 4 except for the conservative Benedictine and Carthusian sources, and most are lacking from the first of these. The most prominent symbol lacking from the 1738 *Graduale* is the quilisma. But if the model employed by our source was in square chant notation, this lack is not surprising.

Unless we are able to identify a possible model for liquescents during the 150–200 years preceding the Lyonnaise source, we must ask not only from whence the printer derived his awareness of such symbols, but also the significance that such symbols would have had for users that had possibly not seen them theretofore. To be sure, there were musical antiquarians of the general period who were greatly interested in old sources of Gregorian chant. Guillaume-Gabriel Nivers springs instantly to mind as one of these, and there were several others as well. Nevertheless, these men distinguished sharply between their interests in the old forms of chant and the requirements of then contemporary performance. Nivers would have recoiled in horror at the thought of reviving twelfth- and thirteenth-century readings for purposes of Parisian services of the late seventeenth century. This is amply clear from his criticisms of medieval chant in his *Dissertation sur le chant grégorien* of 1683.

The hints that we are dealing with a notational vocabulary descended from the Middle Ages are reinforced when we begin to consider the readings themselves. Even a superficial comparison of the gradual, *Universi qui te expectant*, shows that we are not dealing with any counterpart to the reform readings that were prevalent from 1590 onward. We are given instead a reading comparable to those from early diastematic manuscript sources.

The ensuing Alleluia furnishes us with a minor surprise. In place of the normal *Alleluia Ostende nobis* we are given the *Alleluia Excita Domine potentiam tuam*, which is generally associated with the Third Sunday of Advent. The two chants have simply traded places in the *Graduale Lugdunensis*. A similar change of place affects the fourth of the graduals for the Saturday in the Ember Week of Advent. Here the standard chant, *Excita Domine*, is replaced by *Ostende nobis Domine*, which is repeated from the Friday immediately preceding. Indeed, for the pre-Lenten period, one finds some twenty-nine chants that appear in other than their customary liturgical assignments. (Fifteen of these fall on the Fourth, Fifth, and Sixth Sundays after Epiphany.)

In the previous chapter I mentioned that in the *Graduale Lugdunensis* the offertory for the First Sunday of Advent is *Dirige me in veritate tua* rather than the expected *Ad te Domine levavi anima meam*. As noted then, *Dirige me* is customarily the first verse of *Ad te Domine*. When we page through this source we find no fewer than fifty-five offertories that either have verses or, exceptionally, that consist of an offertory verse. Normally these verses are serving their customary liturgical function, but at least one exception may be found. For Trinity Sunday, the offertory verse *In multitudine virtutis* is coupled with the antiphon, *Jubilate Deo omnis terra*, rather than with the normative *Benedicite gentes Dominum*. These verses are only rarely to be found after 1400, and the number appearing here is truly extraordinary.

The most unusual of the Masses to be found in the *Graduale Lugdunensis* are those for Easter and Pentecost. As expected, *Resurrexi et adhuc tecum sum* serves as the introit antiphon for Easter Sunday. And, as expected, the psalm verse is the traditional *Domine probasti me*. An abbreviated Gloria Patri follows. But this is not all. We have a second psalm verse (rubricated *Superps.*), *Intellexisti*, that is also given in full. Shades of the old *Versus ad repetendum!* When we consult Hesbert's edition of the *Antiphonale Missarum Sextuplex* we find that the word *Intellexisti* is given as a cue in the manuscripts from Compiègne (Paris, Bibl. nat., MS 17436) and Senlis (Paris, Bibl. Ste.-Geneviève, MS 111), but not elsewhere. There is then a gap in time. Our earliest adiastematic sources rarely provide any record of *Intellexisti*. It is lacking from Laon, Bibl. mun., 239; Chartres, Bibl. mun., 47 (destroyed); Angers, Bibl. mun., 91; St. Omer, Bibl. mun., 252; and St. Gall, Stiftsbibl., 339. However, the verse is present in Einsiedeln, Benedikterkloster, 121 and it later surfaces in two of our famous Aquitanian sources. It is present as a two-word cue in the Albi Gradual, Paris, Bibl. nat., MS 776, f. 71v and is given complete in London, Brit. Lib., Harley 4951, f. 215, both sources of the eleventh century. The verse is absent from both Paris, Bibl. nat., MS 780 and 903,[5] which employ only a single verse. Paris, Bibl. nat., 1132 still retains a second verse for *Resurrexi*, but it uses *Haec dies* rather than *Intellexisti*. I have not felt it incumbent to make a thorough search for other appearances, but the verse seldom appears after the eleventh century. And yet, as we shall see, knowledge of this second verse did remain alive in Lyon perhaps as late as the early sixteenth century and was later drawn upon for our mid-eighteenth century source.

The gradual for Easter Sunday presented in the *Graduale Lugdunensis* is of course the traditional *Haec dies*, with the verse, *Confitemini Domino quoniam bonus*. There is no surprise here. Nevertheless, when we come to look closely at the reading itself, we shall note a very small detail that bears on the nature of the source employed by the eighteenth-century editor(s). This we shall discuss at a later point. The Alleluia is, as one would expect, the customary *Alleluia Pascha nostrum*. Again we are taken back in time inasmuch as the Alleluia is given with two verses, the second being *Epulemur in azymis*. This verse was quite well known during the Middle Ages, but it had disappeared from average practice many centuries before 1738.

If the foregoing two items have been conventional, the succeeding one is not. The prosa given for Easter is neither *Victimae paschali laudes* nor *Fulgens praeclara*. We find instead *Immolatur Pascha novum*. This is the first item in a tiny Prosarium/Sequentiarum that occurs at the back of this volume with a fresh numeration. Calvin Bower was kind enough to inform me that this prose is not to be found in *Analecta Hymnica* (or in any medieval source that he has explored), but is listed in the *Repertorium hymnologicum* by Ulysse Chevalier (item 8465). The source cited for this text is a *Missale Sanctae Lugdunensis Ecclesiae*, published in Lyon in 1737 by the same Claude Journet who has provided us with our Gradual. The one surviving copy that is known is preserved in the Bibliothèque municipale of Lyon. *Immolatur* appears in a later source from this city, namely the Neo-Gallican *Graduel de Lyon* published in 1780. A second prosa from the small group of seven preserved in our source is also traceable to the Journet Missal. Thus our Gradual contains not only many items rescued from a nearly vanished medieval heritage, but also a few of the most up-to-date creations of its day.

The offertory for Easter Sunday is of course *Terra tremuit*. The *Graduale Lugdunensis* presents this chant complete with its three verses: *Notus in Judaea*, *Et factus est*, and *Ibi confregit cornu*, each of these concluding with the refrain, *alleluia*. Normative Aquitanian sources—indeed normative sources in general—open with a torculus, *d–f–e*. Our print, on the other hand, follows the opening *d* with a bistropha on *f*.

Before one reaches the communion, the *Graduale Lugdunensis* presents an *Antiphona ad Eucharistiam*. This function is often found among Aquitanian sources, but Paris, Bibl. nat., MSS lat. 776, 780, 903, and 1132, together with London, Brit. Lib., MS Harley 4951, all use the antiphon, *Venite populi*, for this purpose. The *Graduale Lugdunensis*, on the other hand, employs *Gustate et videte*. This chant is not to be found in the earlier Lyonnaise Graduals of 1690 and 1724, but the text appears in the Neo-Gallican *Graduel de Lyon* of 1780. Here, however, it is accompanied by a melody in mode 6, whereas in the *Graduale Lugdunensis* the melody is in mode 1. I have not located this antiphon in a medieval source, but the chant may perhaps be medieval nevertheless.[6]

While the communion antiphon, *Pascha nostrum*, is of course familiar to nearly all, it is presented here with the psalm verse, *Expurgate vetus fermentum*. Following the verse, one is directed to return to the latter half of the antiphon, beginning with the word *Itaque*. The Gloria Patri then follows, given in abbreviation, and the final return begins with the first word of the triple *alleluia* that closes the antiphon. Among our main Aquitanian sources, the psalm verse is already missing from Paris, Bibl. nat., MS lat. 1132. The manuscripts 776 and 903 both use *Haec dies* as a psalm verse, and the repetition structure in 776 is quite different. The first return is to the beginning of the communion antiphon, while the second is to the *Itaque*. Manuscript 780, on the other hand, uses *Expurgate*, as does Harley 4951. Neither source is explicit with regard to the repetition structure. Regardless of possible doubts concerning its reliability, the *Graduale Lugdunensis* presents us with information about early chant practice not otherwise available.

The Mass of the Day for Pentecost has a structure comparable to that of Easter Sunday. The introit, *Spiritus Domini*, is given with two psalm verses, *Exurgat Deus* being the first, and *Confirma hoc* the second. These two verses appear in Paris, Bibl. nat., 776, 780, and 1132, together with London, British Library, Harley 4951. The St.

Yrieix Gradual, Paris, Bibl. nat. 903, on the other hand, uses only the second of these. Following the second of two Alleluias, the *Graduale Lugdunensis* presents another unusual prosa, *Quis auditur tantus fragor*, known at present through the 1737 Lyonnaise Missal mentioned previously. Again we are dealing with a contemporary product.

The offertory, *Confirma hoc*, is presented together with three verses, and the *Antiphona ad Eucharistiam* is the same *Gustate et videte*, given here only by cue. Again the communion is presented with a verse. Such a verse is frequent among Aquitanian sources, although it is not present in Paris 1132. All of the remaining sources that have been cited above agree on using the verse, *Et apparuerunt illis*, as the verse for this occasion. The *Graduale Lugdunensis*, on the other hand, uses the verse, *Terra mota est, etenim coeli distillaverunt*. A total of five Masses in this print couple a verse with the communion. The remaining three include *Feria II*. of Easter Week, *Dominica in albis*, and Ascension. Even though this is not a large harvest we are prompted once more to inquire from whence this knowledge comes.

It is possible to take preliminary steps to respond to this question even though many of these will of necessity be speculative. Since our Gradual originated in Lyon, it is not surprising that much of our information concerning the communion verses and the *versus ad repetendum* for the introit should come from southern French sources. Furthermore it is possible to substantiate a southern French connection in other ways. As is well known, the gradual, *Haec dies*, contains many melismas. The one concluding the word *exultemus* is given in modern editions with an ending, $c'-g-g-f$. I have no reason to think that this is not the normative form. However, the Aquitanian equivalent is $b\text{-}flat\text{-}g\text{-}g\text{-}f$, and it is this form that is given in the *Graduale Lugdunensis*. The ending is a common formula. It is to be found, for example, in the gradual, *Universi qui te expectant*, as the conclusion to the melisma on the last syllable of *Domine*, and in the offertory, *Deus tu convertens*, on the last syllable of *tua*. On both occasions the *Graduale Lugdunensis* presents the southern French form of the formula. This form is best known from Aquitanian readings, but, as we shall see, it is found elsewhere in the general region. This mode of inquiry may be expanded, and I am confident that similar results will be obtained.

In Volumes II and IV of *Le Graduel romain*, the editors place our Gradual as one of a small group of three coming from Lyon. The other two are the manuscripts Vatican, Barberini 559 and Lyon, Bibl. mun., 513. The former is a notated Missal probably compiled between 1173 and 1223, employing an adiastematic notation in franco-lyonnaise neumes. The latter is a Gradual in square notation, unfortunately incomplete at the beginning and end. The *Graduel romain*, II, adopts a cautious stance and places Lyon 513 after 1312 on the basis of the appearance of the Feast of Corpus Christi in the hand of the main scribe. The inside cover of the manuscript, however, contains a handwritten annotation by Abbé R[obert] Amiet, dated 30 April 1969, that boldly attributes the source to the early sixteenth century.[7] The note states that the list of Alleluias following Pentecost is identical to that given in the *Missale Lugdunense* of 1487. (The *Graduel romain* had earlier indicated such a relationship regarding both graduals and Alleluias, but it did not specify any one source as the basis for comparison.)

A preliminary glance at the two manuscript Graduals cited above quickly confirms their close relationship to the eighteenth-century print, while demonstrating at the same time that neither could have been a direct progenitor. Barberini 559 gives the introit, *Resurrexi*, with both the customary psalm verse, *Domine probasti me*, and a second verse, *Intellexisti*. It presents two verses for the *Alleluia Pascha nostrum*. The manuscript has an *Antiphona ad Eucharistiam*, but this is *Venite populi* rather than *Gustate et videte*. It also presents the communion, *Pascha nostrum*, with the psalm verse, *Expurgate*. For Pentecost, the introit, *Spiritus Domini*, is provided with two psalm verses, *Exurgat Deus* and *Confirma hoc*. The singer is provided a choice among three Alleluias, including *Emitte spiritum tuum*, *Spiritus Domini replevit*, and *Veni Sancte Spiritus*. The *Graduale Lugdunensis* does not employ either of the latter two but has instead an *Alleluia Spiritus Domini, spiritus sapientiae*. This verse is not to be found among the early sources indexed in Karlheinz Schlager's *Thematischer Kataloge*. Barberini 559 does not present a verse for the communion, *Factus est repente*.

The later Lyon, Bibl. mun., MS 513 also has ties to the *Graduale Lugdunensis*. It does not provide a *versus ad repetendum* for *Resurrexi*. It does give two verses for the *Alleluia Pascha nostrum*. And, like Barberini 559 and other sources, it uses the antiphon, *Venite populi*, prior to the communion. *Expurgate* is employed as a verse to the communion, *Pascha nostrum*. The relationship between Lyon 513 and its counterparts is less close for Pentecost. It does not provide either a *versus ad repetendum* for the introit, or a verse for the communion, *Factus est repente*. However, the source does contain a verse for the communions, *Surrexit Dominus* (music lacking) and *Mitte manum tuam*, but not for *Psallite Domino*. The reading for the close of the melisma on *exultemus* for *Haec dies* is the same as that in the *Graduale Lugdunensis*. The loss of the opening folios prevents us from knowing whether the formula was treated in the same fashion in *Universi qui te expectans* and *Deus tu convertens*.

The reshuffling of liturgical assignments that is found in the *Graduale Lugdunensis* does not apparently find a precedent in either Barberini 559 or Lyon 513, or, for that matter, among any of our Aquitanian sources. Nevertheless, even a cursory perusal will uncover additional evidence of some form of relationship between Lyon 513 and the printed Gradual of 1738. At the same time, this evidence will be found to be conflicting. Our editor(s) evidently drew on multiple traditions; the source—and likely its immediate model—is contaminated. Various forms of evidence attract our attention, from rather small variants to major ones.

Beginning at the lower level, we may consider the transmission of second-mode tracts, a subject that has been of concern to me in previous years. With the exception of a few late members of this genre, the remainder of the family open with a gesture that proceeds from the final to the lower fifth degree via a *pes subipunctis* with the content, *c–d–c–A*. In my limited experience, this neume is fixed and without variants in any of the major sources that I consulted at an earlier time. In such well-known chants as *Qui habitat; De necessitatibus; Deus, Deus meus; Domine exaudi*; and *Domine audivi* this statement holds true for the *Graduale Lugdunensis*. However, for *Eripe me*, which appears immediately following *Domine audivi* on Good Friday, the descent to A is entirely diatonic. It is found thus in Lyon 513 as well. It may be that with more diligent exploration of the sources for this chant we shall find other sources with this variant, but it is my impression that these will be few in number. Also on a level of small detail, we may consider the opening of *Deus, Deus meus*. Immediately subsequent to the descent to A, it is normative practice for the melody to ascend to *c*, continuing *c–d–c, d–e–d*, and so forth. However, the Lyon Gradual of 1738 instead descends to G before leaping up to *d* and continuing *c, d–e–d*. Lyon 513 is similar, though not identical. It continues *A–d–c, d–e–d*. It is my impression that this variant, though infrequent, may appear more often than the one discussed previously. Examples 16 and 40 from previous chapters present readings for the introit, *Populus Sion*, and the offertory, *Dextera Domini*, taken from the *Graduale Lugdunensis*.

The antiphon, *Immutemur habitu in cinere*, for Ash Wednesday, presents us with a curious textual variant at its opening. In the version of 1738, it reads *Immutemus habitum*, and it is this reading that is to be found in Lyon 513. Nevertheless, more is at issue with regard to the readings for this chant, discussed previously in chapter 8. Example 57 was introduced at that point, giving selected readings from sources published between 1580 and 1738. The *Graduale Lugdunensis* was the last of these. As indicated in the prior discussion, the melody presented grave problems to medieval scribes because it had both a variable third degree and a variable sixth degree. As a result, these scribes have left us with readings beginning and ending on *g*, readings beginning and ending on *d*, and readings beginning on *g* and ending on *d*. Still other solutions were possible, as we shall see immediately.

The version of *Immutemur* presented in the *Graduale Lugdunensis* and Lyon, Bibl. mun., MS 513 opens on *g* and closes on *a*. Among approximately fifty readings that I have consulted,[8] this form of reading is to be found in Arras, Bibl. mun., 437; Provins, Bibl. mun., 12; Troyes, Bibl. mun., 1947; and Monza, Bibl. capitolare, K 11. It is lacking from Germanic and insular sources, and, strikingly, from the Aquitanian sources examined by me.[9] It seems likely that this sampling is large enough to prove representative. Should that prove true, the version that is of interest to us occurs in barely over ten percent of the surviving sources, and it is best represented in northern French sources.

The antiphon, *Collegerunt pontifices*, for the procession for Palm Sunday, is another chant that exists in several different notational families. Like *Immutemur*, the use of *Collegerunt* is not mandatory, even though it is typical.[10] The normative readings begin and close on *d*.[11] There are, however, others that begin on *g*, *a*, and even on *middle c'* and *d'*.[12] And, in an exceptional instance, there is a reading that presents the verse on a level higher than that of the opening antiphon, despite the fact that the two parts share material in common. The theorist, John (pseudo-Cotton), was sufficiently convinced that the chant was to begin on *d* that he framed his brief discussion of the opening gesture in these terms. In decrying the practice of singers who would open with the downward leap of a fifth (rather than a fourth), he points out that such an opening would result immediately thereafter in the use of F, a tone not sanctioned within the Guidonian gamut, and therefore automatically incorrect. But John's objection does not hold water if one begins on any of the four higher alternatives.

Collegerunt pontifices furnishes an extraordinarily useful example for our purposes inasmuch as it displays an unstable transmission on several different levels. The differences affect not only the general pitch height, which does not remain constant among all readings, but the gestural content, and the details of gestures that are basically similar. In this confusing welter, it is striking to see how close the readings of Lyon 513 and the 1738 print are to one another. The variants are few and entirely inconsequential. In the antiphon itself, the majority concern the presence or absence of liquescents. None affect more than a single tone. Although the two readings begin on the *g* level, they transfer to the level a second above by the end of the fifth word. Other readings may also vary in relative height, as noted previously, but I have yet to observe any other reading that presents this particular shift.

There is, to be sure, other evidence of the close relationship between these two sources. This would include the relatively restricted use of the tract, *Domine non secundum*, which is to be found with great frequency during Lent in most medieval sources. It is time, however, to consider opposing evidence, which distinguishes with equal clarity the two Lyonnaise sources. The *Graduale Lugdunensis* has a number of unusual chants, especially among the Alleluias. By the time that we reach the Second Sunday of Advent, we note the use of an *Alleluia Levate et capita vestra*, which takes the place of the normative *Alleluia Laetatus sum*. If we have no more than modest knowledge, this may not appear surprising unless we look more closely. The text appears not long thereafter in a Neo-Gallican Gradual, and several Neo-Gallican Graduals begin the text at a slightly earlier point, *Respicite et levate capita vestra*. But when we examine the melody, we find that it is medieval and not Neo-Gallican. Furthermore, the medieval melody is extremely rare. According to the catalogue of Karlheinz Schlager, it survives in the adiastematic Rome, Bibl. Angelica, MS 123 (from the region of Bologna) and in the diastematic Rome, Bibl. Vallicelliana, C. 52 (from central Italy).[13] Professor Schlager was kind enough to inform me that he has not found this melody in any of the later sources that he has consulted. And yet, it pops up unexpectedly in 1738! At this point we may wish to recall that the Lyonnaise version of *Immutemur* corresponds in its tonal outline with the reading of Monza, Bibl. capitolare, K 11. Only a much more systematic search will reveal other possible Italian connections for our late print.

There is more to the web of evidence that we have touched upon. The *Alleluia Laetatus sum* has not disappeared. It is given instead as the Alleluia for the Twelfth

Sunday after Pentecost. This is true also for Lyon, Bibl. mun., MS 513—although with a marked difference. This Alleluia is also an unstable chant, surviving in a number of variant versions. That given in the *Graduale Lugdunensis* is surprising in that it not only ends the opening Alleluia and the verse on *e*, but begins on that tone as well.

Among some five dozen diastematic French sources listed in *Le Graduel romain, II*, that I have been able to examine, only Orléans, Bibl. mun., MS 121 begins the *Alleluia Laetatus sum* on *e*. Some three other French sources (Paris, Bibl. nat., MS lat. 17312 and Arsenal, MS 111, together with Toulouse, Bibl. mun., MS 94) begin on *d*, but terminate on *e*. Among much later sources, not listed in this bibliography, Paris, Bibl. Ste.-Geneviève, MSS 2668 and 2669 also begin and end the Alleluia portion on *e*; these sources, however, unify the melody tonally, by beginning the verse on *e*, which is decidedly unusual. The *Graduale Lugdunensis*, on the other hand, begins the verse on the much more frequent *d*. Except for Brussels, Bibl. royale, MS II.3823, which is of Cluniac origin, none of the more than a dozen sources employing Aquitanian notation that were studied share the tonal features of our Lyonnaise Gradual, nor do any of the several dozen Graduals that I have examined from Italy, Germany, and Britain. While not unique, the reading presented to us by the 1738 Gradual is quite rare.

I have reserved mention of the situation in Lyon 513 for last because it is frustrating. The *Alleluia Laetatus sum* appears there in connection with the Twelfth Sunday after Pentecost, but it does so only in the form of a verbal cue, referring the user to the beginning of the manuscript. As I mentioned early on, the opening folios are, however, missing. We are left to guess what this reading might have been like. It seems clear, however, that this manuscript did not present the *Alleluia Levate et capita vestra* for the Second Sunday of Advent, and this is one of several points of fundamental disagreement between the two Lyonnaise sources.

Other points concern broad levels of content. The 1738 Gradual contains some Feasts not present in Lyon 513; these are presumably reasonably contemporaneous with the publication itself. It also presents individual masses for Feasts that are not normally assigned such. For example, the Fourth, Fifth, and Sixth Sundays after Epiphany are each accorded a Proper Mass. The first of these gives as introit, *Exsultate Deo adjutori*, which in modern books appears in conjunction with the Mass of *Feria IV., Quatuor Temporum Septembris*. The gradual is *Esto mihi in Deum protectorum*, which in modern books is assigned to the Eighth Sunday after Pentecost. The offertory is *Laudate nomen Domini*, which is the first verse of *Jubilate Deo omnis terra*. In normative practice this functions as part of the Mass for the Sunday within the Octave of Epiphany. The communion carries the text *Quam magna multitudo dulcedinis tuae*. The associated melody is not, however, the one given in modern books; nor is it the same as any of the other chants utilizing the same incipit that are given in the Bryden and Hughes, *Index of Gregorian Chant*. The Alleluia has the verse, *Notum fecit Dominus salutare suum*. When we seek to place this within context, we find that this is the second verse of the *Alleluia Cantate Dominum* (Schlager, *Katalog*, Nr. 121). This chant is part of a three-member family, the other members being *Exivi a patre* and *Qui timent dominum*. The family has reasonably broad distribution throughout France, Italy, and Germany, and is to be found in one insular source, Oxford, Bodleian Library, MS 775. While the *Alleluia Cantate Domino* has early roots, as demonstrated by its presence in Chartres, Bibl. mun., 47, the *Alleluia Qui timent dominum* is by far the better represented of the two in the sources. Nevertheless, the *Alleluia Cantate Domino* is to be found in a good half-dozen of the most important Aquitanian sources and in the Benevento, Bibl. capitolare, MS VI.40 as well. Insofar as the present study is concerned, it is quite striking to find that the second verse has been preserved in the *Graduale Lugdunensis*, while the first has disappeared. This goes counter to all of the tendencies observed until now with regard to Alleluias with multiple verses. The version of the St. Yrieix Gradual (Paris, Bibl. nat., MS 903) has been presented by Karlheinz Schlager in his *Alleluia-Melodien I (bis 1100)*, while Benevento VI.40 is available in a handsome color facsimile edition.[14] The reading of the *Graduale Lugdunensis* contrasts strongly with both of these sources in terms of the neumation. This notwithstanding, the melodic gestures remain reasonably constant.

I have taken this topic as far as I dare go within the present context. It should be obvious that I have merely begun to outline approaches that can help us place the Lyon print of 1738 within context. It may be that even when we have exerted ourselves to the fullest, we shall not have attained a secure account of the roots of this important source.

In what way or ways does knowledge of the *Graduale Lugdunensis* affect our perception of chant history? The sources for chant are so multitudinous that we cannot possibly assimilate each one in all its details. The best that we can hope for is to grasp the essentials of the main trends. It is, however, necessary to realize that when we treat the main stream we are not encompassing the totality; unexplored subsidiary waters might help us to realize a far richer heritage than we would otherwise envisage. It is of course out of the question to think of Lyon as subsidiary. To the contrary, it has been one of the major primatial Sees of France. It contributed significantly to the tradition of reform chant in France as well as to the Neo-Gallican movement. But in addition to these contributions, it managed also to preserve to an astonishing degree reminders of early medieval traditions that had seemingly disappeared from view practically everywhere else. This allows a ray of hope that we may perhaps find in the future one or two additional late sources that do likewise. Even should this not materialize—and I do not wish to ignore how fragile this ray of hope may be—we are still left with a much richer vision of the field of chant history than we would otherwise have.

Other forms of conservatism may be found among eighteenth-century prints. It has been long known that the liturgical and musical practices of the Dominican Order were firmly fixed during the Middle Ages. From relatively early date new sources were created through accurate copying of existing exemplars, thus extending medieval practices into the Renaissance. It is startling to find that there are no printed Dominican Graduals among the seventeenth-century sources located to this point. Apparently the earliest post-Tridentine source for the Mass according to the Dominican order is that provided by a *Cantus Missarum Totius Anni ad usum Sacri Ordinis FF. Praedicatorum*, published in 1722 by the Parisian Chapter of the Order situated in the Rue St. Jacques. As we shall see, this source demonstrates a limited influence of contemporary ideas concerning prosodic values in chant, but an influence that is contained within very narrow bounds. A very superficial survey of the contents shows that the editors did not follow the *Missale Romanum* of 1570 in all respects. The fact that the 1722 print eliminates the textual repetitions found in the offertories, *Jubilate Deo omnis terra* and *Jubilate Deo universa terra*, common to most medieval sources, but lacking in post-Tridentine prints is of no help here. These repetitions had not formed part of the Dominican tradition from the outset. However, it does appear significant that the print retains the first word of the introit, *Etenim sederunt*, which is excised from the *Missale Romanum* of 1570 and from most of the later Graduals, even when these are not part of the oncoming wave of reform. It may be that there was a supply of late Renaissance Graduals for the Dominican Order that was sufficient for the needs of the order for yet an extended period of time. Nevertheless, we would need much more evidence before reaching any safe conclusion on this matter.

As is well known, the Dominican Order took shape under the guidance of St. Dominic at two General Chapters, which met at Bologna in 1220 and 1221. Its musico-liturgical practices were fixed not long thereafter, and it was general practice for a manuscript to be created by the process of copying from an accredited exemplar. In this respect, a consistency similar to that of the Cistercians was reached and maintained through several centuries. In order to place the readings of the 1722 print in context, we shall compare these with a medieval exemplar together with the Gradual published in Ghent in 1854—the next known Dominican source—and the modern Dominican Gradual, published in Rome in 1950. From the various medieval Dominican sources available to me, I have opted to use the Steinhardt Gradual, preserved at the University of Kansas Library in Lawrence.

For purposes of this comparison we shall explore the chants for the Second Sunday of Advent.[15] The medieval Dominican version of the introit, *Populus Sion*, belongs to the family that recites on d' and that begins on the reciting tone, without any preliminary upward leap. When we compare the reading of 1722 (see example 77) with that given in the medieval source, we find that the successions of pitches are virtually the same. There are a few differences but these are trifling. In the setting of the fourth word, *Dominus*, one finds in the eighteenth-century reading the second tone is written as c' rather than b. There is no liquescent for the first syllable of either *salvandas* or *cordis*. (In this regard one may recall the previous remarks concerning the absence of liquescents as a general feature of seventeenth-

and eighteenth-century sources, with the exception of the *Graduale Lugdunensis* published in 1738.) But there is nothing more substantial. We do, however, find notable changes in the ways in which the various tones are assigned to respective syllables. The medieval reading assigns two tones to the first syllable of *veniet* and four to the second. We are once again dealing with an accented antepenultimate. The revised version understandably assigns five tones to the first syllable and only one to the second. The same problem occurs thrice in succession with the text segment *faciet Dominus gloriam*. On each occasion the multiple tones occurring in conjunction with the unaccented penultimate are shifted in their assignment so that only one remains with this unaccented syllable and the rest are chanted together with the accented antepenultimate. These changes leave no doubt that we are dealing with a product of the reform movement in chant. This notwithstanding, the assignment of five tones to the last syllable of *laetitia* is accepted without compunction.

The lessons to be learned from a study of the gradual, *Ex Sion species*, are comparable. With only occasional exceptions, the successions of pitches remain reasonably consistent. (See example 78.) In the respond, the pitch successions are identical, even though their neumation will vary. The medieval version of this chant assigns only a single tone to the unaccented penultimate syllable of the word *veniet* and there is no need for any change. The situation regarding the verse is comparable. Not a single tone is cut from the major melisma on the third syllable of *Congregate*. On the initial syllable of *eius*, one finds a torculus in the medieval source, but only a pes in the 1722 version. Since the latter form recurs both in the 1854 reading and in the modern reading from 1950, I am inclined to suspect that the torculus in the Steinhardt Gradual represents a minor variant in that source. When, however, we come to the melisma on the final syllable of *ordinaverunt*, we find that the 1722 reading lacks a group of nine tones present in its medieval counterpart. Curiously, we find that the 1950 reading lacks two of these nine tones. I would judge that this passage was not frozen in its medieval transmission and can only wonder whether an intensive search through multiple medieval manuscripts might not reveal a small area of flexibility here. It remains possible that we are dealing with a small excision in the 1722 print, but this is miniscule in terms of the major cuts that we have observed in other sources and in other chants. One may observe in passing that the 1722 print is much more generous than the medieval source in the indication of the use of *b-flat*, and that its readings are confirmed by our two late sources on multiple occasions.

The Dominican version of the *Alleluia Laetatus sum* draws special comment with regard to its treatment of modality. The reader may recall that this chant posed problems to medieval scribes in general. When dealing previously with the Mass for the Second Sunday of Advent, I pointed out that the *Alleluia Laetatus sum* apparently had at its origin a variable second degree. This could be accommodated if the chant were written with a final on *a*, and this is by far the most frequent medieval solution. It was not, however, a universal solution and there were scribes who preferred to place the final on *d* or on *e*. When dealing with the first of these two solutions, it was generally necessary to notate the passage closing the word *Domini* a second higher than normal in order to preserve the deuterus character of the cadence. The Dominicans, however, took a different tack. They permitted this passage to close on *d*, thereby producing a protus cadence and providing the chant with a modal unity that was previously lacking. (See example 79.) This version carries over to the prints from 1722, 1854, and 1950. The 1722 print emphasizes the nature of the protus melody by utilizing *b-flat* at the beginning of each staff. We find again that the liquescent present on the very first syllable is lacking in this print, although present in both the medieval model as well as in the most recent print. The 1854 *Cantus Missarum* from Ghent also lacks the requisite symbol, but compensates by indicating the liquescence through the use of a diamond-shaped note form adjoined to the first main note. Apart from this one difference the opening segment of this chant remains the same in all versions examined.

A comparable lack of a liquescent occurs in the verse in conjunction with the word *in*. When we reach the penultimate word, *Domini*, we find that the 1722 print has taken note of the accented antepenultimate, allowing only one tone to the syllable following and leaving two for the final syllable. A similar reduction occurs in the word following, *ibimus*. The final cadence is also worthy of comment. In its earliest form the verse concluded with a passage identical to the one that closed the jubilus of the Alleluia. By the turn of the sixteenth century this melisma seems to have been excised more and more often, with the result that the verse could apparently conclude on the fifth degree of the mode, without any reference to the tone progression that had originally followed. The Dominicans, on the other hand chose to produce a modally unified melody without resorting to the early parallel form. They brought the melody to a prompter, more economical close with an independent first-mode cadence.

The treatment of the offertory, *Deus tu convertens*, in the 1722 print remains consistent with everything that we have observed to this point. (See example 80.) The assignment of four tones to the third syllable of *laetabitur* is again regarded as unacceptable, following, as it does, an accented antepenultimate. These notes are therefore shifted back so that they are associated with the accented syllable, while the third syllable is restricted to a single note. The same process is repeated in connection with the setting of the words, *Domine* and *misericordiam*. The pitch successions remain constant. The fact that there is no tinkering with melismatic lengths in these last two chants lends support to the conclusion that the minor instance observed in the verse of *Ex Sion species* is not the result of a changed editorial policy.

The examination of the communion, *Ierusalem surge*, does not contribute anything basically new to our discussion. Again we find that the 1722 lacks equivalents for the medieval liquescents. Differences in pitch successions are tiny. (See example 81.) Again scrupulous attention is paid to limiting the tones following an accented antepenultimate. It is fascinating, I think, to find that all of the small changes that we have discussed are dismissed in the following Dominican print of 1854. Without fanfare the Dominicans returned to their medieval readings. It was a return, however, that affected only this order and not the Church as a universal institution. It was to remain for the Benedictines to affect this latter change during the decades that followed.

It may seem surprising, if not premature, to close this chapter at this point, after having focused on two atypical prints. However, the reader will recall that we have already considered numerous other eighteenth-century prints in previous chapters. We have taken note of the 1725 and 1730 editions of Baglioni, the 1779 and 1789 editions of Pezzana, the 1734 edition of Ballard, and numerous eighteenth-century editions associated with Neo-Gallican chant. We have dealt with the introduction of the French tradition into the Venetian orbit through the editions of Johannis-Nic. Galles beginning in 1776. This is as much as I can hope to achieve within an introductory work of the present nature.

TWELVE

The Nineteenth Century: The Road Back

How does one determine the validity of a chant reading? This question is seldom asked openly even though it requires answers by virtue of the choices that must be made by those responsible for our sources (including those of the present day) and for the performances based thereon. The answers have varied considerably over time. During the ninth to eleventh centuries, the imprimatur took the form of the legend of St. Gregory receiving the chant through divine inspiration. The reading presented in the source was—if only by silent implication—supposedly that handed down by the revered Pope. No higher form of validation could exist. From the eleventh century through the fifteenth, it was often necessary for chant to submit also to the dictates of chant theory, thus acquiring sanction from a second authority. If a given chant did not conform to these dictates it might well be judged corrupt and be submitted to editorial revision in order to remove the assumed corruption(s). During the sixteenth through the eighteenth centuries, the chant reading was required to follow a different law, that of contemporary taste, which emphasized prosodic values at the expense of musical ones. (There were various sixteenth-century precedents for the major overhauls that were undertaken at the turn of the seventeenth.) By the mid-nineteenth century, standards were again in process of change. Chant practice was to be justified by its relative antiquity, by its historical pedigree.

This last kind of validation could take different forms. In 1845, the firm of P. J. Hanicq published an *Ordinarium Missae e Graduali Romano*, **announ**cing its pedigree in the title, *typis Plantinianis anno 1599, edito, depromptum*. Three years later, the same firm issued a Gradual that was based on the readings of the Medicean Gradual issued in 1614/15.[1] This book was brought out under the authority of Cardinal Engelbert Sterckx, who, in a prefatory open letter, named Edmund Duval, F. de Voght, and C. Bogaerts as the editors responsible.[2] Its validation depended on the authority of Pope Pius V, the acceptance of the legend of Palestrina's involvement with the revisions, and a respect for the editors, Anerio and Soriano, who were well-known composers in their day. This Gradual was later taken over by Hanicq's successor, H. Dessain, in 1855 and appeared in later editions until at least 1890. According to the best of our present knowledge, the 1848 edition was the first to submit to an overall influence by the Medicean Gradual. A much wider acceptance of the Roman readings was brought about by their adoption in 1871 by the press of Friedrich Pustet under the editorship of Franz Xaver Haberl. This was singled out by Pope Pius IX as the only version to be recognized officially by the Vatican, a fact proudly announced in the lengthy title: *Graduale de tempore et de sanctis juxta ritum sacrosancte Romanae ecclesiae cum cantu Pauli V. pont. max. jussu reformato cui addita sunt officia postea approbata sub auspiciis sanctissimi domini nostri Pii pp. IX curante Sacr. rituum congregatione. Cum privilegio.* Later editions continued to appear into the early twentieth century, well past the first editions brought out by the Solesmes monks.

    In the instances just cited, age had only a relative meaning, stretching back little more than two centuries. Moreover, there were concurrently many sources that were perfectly content to go on employing readings that had essentially arisen around the turn of the seventeenth century and which still continued to be in use. An effort to return to medieval readings was first mounted by a Commission ordered by the Archbishops of Reims and Cambrai, which resulted in the publication of a *Graduale Romanum . . . Cantu reviso juxta manuscripta vetustissima,* issued in Paris, 1851, by the firm of J. Lecoffre et Socios. Even though later reissues of this Gradual were frequent, the restored versions were not regarded with universal approval and the subject was to be debated passionately for decades to come.

    Appeals to standards of taste continued to be made for some time after the general interest in historical validation had come into play. And it is likely that in France Neo-Gallican chant continued to be performed a decade or more after the appearance of the last-known Neo-Gallican Gradual in 1846. At the end of the last chapter we remarked that in 1854 the Dominican Order went back quietly to the medieval tradition that had characterized the chants of that order. We shall not deal with this process as part of the present exposition for two reasons. First, as mentioned then, the process affected only the Dominican Order and did not impinge on the Catholic Church as a whole. Second, the Dominican tradition was essentially a late medieval tradition. The efforts led by the Benedictines of Solesmes, on the other hand, were aimed at the restoration of the earliest accessible chant tradition for the use of the Church as a whole. When dealing with the changing scene that eventually witnessed the restorations accomplished by the Solesmes monks who produced the editions that scholars and performers of chant use most often, it would be well to keep in mind that we are dealing not only with music, but also with details of text, and even notation. All three elements play a role.

Notation can perhaps be dealt with swiftly, and the matter then set aside. Publishers of the early nineteenth century quite naturally began with the fonts that had been employed by their predecessors. These consisted primarily of square shapes for the individual notes that were crowded together to form the equivalent of ligatures. Stems, generally facing downward, could be added. These might indicate a longer than normal value, but often had no clearly ascertainable musical purpose apart from serving a connective function when a leap occurred within a group of notes. In addition, diamond-shaped forms were employed to specify shorter than normal values. This small assortment of shapes continued to be employed as the basis of notation even when the editors sought to return to the musical readings of the Middle Ages, as in the various Graduals issued by Lecoffre. A historical curiosity, *la méthode arithmographe de plainchant*, arose momentarily in an edition prepared by J. E. Miquel jeune, in a Gradual brought out by J. M. Blanc in Albertville in 1844. In this system the various tones were represented not by notes on a staff, but by numbers, based on a solmization system with a "fixed do" (1=c, 2=d. etc.). This system allowed for two octaves, these being separated by a horizontal line drawn across the page, and this range could be extended on the lower end. The tones of the lower octave were indicated by numbers placed below the line, while those for the upper octave were placed above. (When a tone lower than *c* was required, this was indicated by writing the requisite number on a lower than normal level and placing a small dash above it.) The sequence, *g–a–c′*, *c′*, for example, was represented by the numbers 5–6–1, 1, the first two being placed below the line, the last two on top. Above the numbers the editor might place (or withhold) either of two symbols borrowed from metrical scansion, a small dash to indicate relative length, and an upward-facing curved arc to indicate relative brevity. This system was apparently received with little enthusiasm. Although it is apparently to be found in some hymnals, the system has no known successors among Graduals. The standard notational forms were used in new constellations in the Lecoffre Gradual. The diamond shape, for example, could be used where one would find a liquescent or quilisma in a medieval source.

The two editions edited by Michael Hermesdorff, brought out respectively in 1863 and then (in fascicles) from 1876–82, employ a variety of shapes having different rhythmic significance. Their meanings are set forth in a valuable preface that informs us also about Hermesdorff's editorial principles and the nature of sources consulted for the edition. A square with a tail is equated with the longa, the square without tail is a brevis, the diamond shape is a semibrevis, and the small diamond indicates a portamento. (A maxima may be used on rare occasions. corresponding to a *pressus major* in the sources.) In the examples to be given here, the long is indicated by a void rectangle, the breve by the normal oval shape, the semibreve by a diamond, and the portamento by a void diamond. In his second Gradual, Hermes-dorff added elegantly drawn German neumes above the respective tones of the melody, without employing these to designate pitch. It is during the period encom-passed by this latter Gradual that the activities at Solesmes reached an initial peak and it was through the efforts of the Solesmes monks that the square chant nota-tion currently employed came into being.

It is not possible to deal fully with changes in chant texts within a study such as this. We can do no more than take sample instances into consideration. The reader will remember that we have mentioned these previously on an occasional basis. Recall, for example, mention of the omission of the word *Domine*, as the third word in the offertory for the First Sunday of Advent, or the omission of the second state-ment of the phrase, *Dextera Domini fecit virtutem*, from the offertory for the Third Sunday after Epiphany. Or the repetition or lack thereof of the opening phrase of the offertory, *Jubilate Deo universa terra*, for the Second Sunday of Epiphany. Nor are such changes limited to offertories. The first word of the introit, *Etenim sederunt principes*, for the Feast for St. Stephen, is customarily omitted in sources of the seventeenth and eighteenth centuries. Still other examples will undoubtedly be found when scholars begin to investigate more thoroughly the sources of this interim period. For the moment, when dealing with the variegated panorama of chant during the nineteenth century, we can do no more than comment on a hand-ful of individual examples. My initial impression, offered only hesitantly, is that the sources of the latter half of the nineteenth century are more reluctant to restore text that had been cut by previous generations than they are to restore the truncated melismas. (Available Missals seem to have had considerable effect on textual details.) They may even retain the earlier redistribution of tones among syllables. In an unusual instance, the editor of the *Graduale Romanum* issued by Spée-Zelis in 1876 sought to have his cake and eat it at the same time. When dealing with the offertory, *Dextera Domini*, the third text phrase, previously omitted, is now restored. It is, however, placed in parentheses, and the reader is informed that the parenthet-ical material may be omitted. On the other hand, no such restoration is attempted for *Jubilate Deo universa terra*, where the medieval text repetition remains excised. (This lack of consistency is striking in that these two examples occur on successive Sundays.) Changes in text obviously have an effect on melodic shapes. However, the total number of examples that can be addressed within the course of this chap-ter is very limited, and I cannot devote much attention to the topic of text within the present framework.

Seeking to hold within manageable limits the number of examples to be exam-ined, I propose to focus on the Mass for the Second Sunday of Advent, emphasiz-ing the introit, gradual, and Alleluia, while giving only cursory treatment to the offertory and communion. The first source to be discussed for the introit, *Populus Sion*, is a Turinese Gradual published by Canfari in 1840 (see staff **a** of example 82). The publication of Venetian Graduals ceased after the issuance of the 1789 imprint by N. Pezzana, and there is no present knowledge of any activity during the nineteenth century. The resultant void was filled for a time by the publication of four Graduals in Turin, brought out in the years 1797, 1826, 1840, and 1847. After this, we meet with no further Italian publications until we reach the *Graduale de Tempore et de Sanctis . . . cum cantu Paul V. pont, max.*, published in Rome in 1884. With the exception of two neumes setting the first and last syllables of the word, *Dominus*, the reading presented by the Canfari Gradual is identical with that in the Baglioni Gradual of 1690. Indeed, the Canfari reading is only very slightly more distant from that present in the Giunta Gradual of 1596.

Staff **b** gives the reading of the previously-mentioned Gradual edited by Miquel jeune for the firm of J. M. Blanc in Albertville in 1844. I chose to investigate this source because I wished to ascertain whether its unusual numerical notation was matched by an equally idiosyncratic musical reading. This proves not to be the case. The handful of readings examined here derive on the whole from the main French tradition, and can be traced back, for example, to the Ballard Gradual of 1734 and its earlier antecedents. The adherence to tradition can be determined by comparison with other nineteenth-century editions. What sets the present reading apart from the others is its choice of opening pitch. Rather than beginning on the final and then leaping upward, this version begins directly on the fifth. This gesture adheres more faithfully to the French tradition of the seventeenth and eighteenth centuries than those alternative nineteenth-century readings that begin on the final.

As noted above, the first major attempt to return to the medieval tradition began as the result of a Commission brought into being by the Archbishops of Reims and Cambrai. It is desirable to allow these scholar-clerics and their deputies to speak directly to us, employing for this purpose passages taken from the Introduction to the edition brought out by J. Lecoffre and Associates in 1851 and 1852.

> Wishing to provide a suitable edition of Choirbooks for their Dioceses, and not being able to accept any of those in current use because of the numerous variants that are to be found among them, the grave alterations Gregorian chant has undergone in them, and the textual inexactitudes that one encounters even in the most recent and most respected of them, these two prelates, following the counsel of the sovereign Pontiff, established in 1849 a commission charged with the preparation of a new edition of the Gradual and Antiphonal, more accurate and, as much as possible, in conformity with bygone ages. . . .
>
> Ecclesiastical chant being essentially a traditional genre, in order to reestablish it in its original purity it is necessary to return to its source, that is the Antiphonal of Saint Gregory. However, the manuscripts generally thought to be the oldest are notated in neumes, which have not yet been translatable to date, and which very probably are untranslatable. It is thus necessary to have recourse to later manuscripts, whether notated in letters, in dots, or in forms analogous to ours.
>
> The editors have taken as their point of departure the celebrated Montpellier manuscript, a complete repertoire of all the genres (*types*) and formulas of Gregorian chant. As is well known, this manuscript indicates chant by means of a double notation: the first in neumes, the second in letters, which are a translation of the neumes. They have compared it with other manuscripts in the public libraries of Paris, Cambrai, Reims, etc. . . ., and, in the last instance, with several manuscripts in Swiss monasteries. They

have also consulted early printed editions, particularly the choirbooks of Chartreux, where Gregorian chant has been preserved with greater fidelity than elsewhere.

A long and minute examination has led them to the happy certainty that apart from certain trifling differences, all these manuscripts resemble one another. This unanimity manifestly attests to an identical origin; and to what origin can they be ascribed other than the Antiphonal of St. Gregory?

It is this chant that the editors have reproduced, almost always with scrupulous exactitude. Nevertheless, as we are not dealing with an archeological work, but with a practical book capable of adoption for use in churches and to be performed by the congregation, they have felt it necessary to permit themselves slight modifications in certain cases, these being, properly speaking, no more than a simple typographical arrangement. Here is the reason for this. Gregorian melodies are generally rich and flowing, especially in the graduals, tracts, and Alleluias. It was to be feared that if one were to reproduce these melodies in their entire lengths many persons would find— undoubtedly wrongfully—their length to be excessive. On the other hand, to abbreviate and thus mutilate them would be to lose them; it would be to fall back into the errors of the past, to act as vandals in arbitrary fashion, and thus place still another obstacle to the restoration of ecclesiastical chant. The editors have avoided these twin perils. The length of the melismas (*neumes*) being due, most frequently, to the repetition of certain subphrases, or complete phrases of chant, they have on occasion suppressed these repetitions, generally indicating them by the notation r*, which will permit one to perform them in their entire length should one so wish.

This was indeed a worthy enterprise. Greater detail concerning its management was apparently provided in a separate *Mémoire,* reported to be in press at the time of publication of the Gradual. Unfortunately, I have had not had access to this document. Nevertheless, several points in the abbreviated description of aims and methods may attract our attention. Perhaps first is the awareness of the various parties of differences between the chant readings that were then available. These we can confirm. Next is the observation that the readings adopted by the Carthusians were more faithful to the medieval tradition than others of late origin. This too can be verified. (It is necessary to recall, however, that the Dominican Gradual of 1854 had not yet been issued.) We are informed about the primary source used as the basis for the edition, Montpellier, Fac. méd., MS H. 159, and this is still regarded as a source of high value. The lack of information concerning the complementary sources is a potential irritant, or it may be dismissed with an indulgent smile. The sources available in the municipal libraries of Reims and Cambrai are easily identifiable and not impossibly numerous. We are on much shakier ground should we attempt to speculate on those sources in the Bibliothèque nationale de France that may have been consulted. The hint that the congregation was to participate in the singing of Mass is deserving of attention. The notion may appear quite startling to some who have had in their hands the very large Graduals that were published near the turn of the seventeenth century. We shall find that the unnamed author of this introduction has not been entirely forthcoming about the editorial processes employed, but this will emerge gradually in the course of the discussion below. Suffice it to say for the moment that the struggle between conflicting forces of taste and those of history is not entirely resolved in this edition.

When one compares the reading of *Populus Sion* found in the Lecoffre Gradual of 1852 (staff **c**) with that given in the Montpellier manuscript, one will observe that the opening segments of the two are identical. However, when we come to the setting of the word *veniet*, the medieval source assigns respectively 2, 4, and 1 tones to the three syllables, the largest number falling on the unaccented penultimate. This continues to be anathema to post-Tridentine taste. As a result, the tones are regrouped in the Lecoffre Gradual, so that the first five are assigned to the accented syllable, and one each is left for the remaining two. Thereafter the identity resumes until we reach the word, *Dominus*, again involving an unaccented penultimate. In the manuscript reading the three syllables receive 2, 3, and 5 tones respectively; the nineteenth-century version provides 5, 1, and 4 tones for the three syllables. The word immediately following is *gloriam*. The unaccented penultimate here receives no fewer than six tones in the medieval reading. Again these are reduced to a single tone in the Lecoffre version, but in this instance the initial tones assigned to the first syllable are reworked slightly. In the setting of *laetitia* the medieval version happens to follow the form of prosody that was to be advocated systematically at later date and thus no change was necessitated.

If, on the other hand we compare the reading of the LeCoffre Gradual with other French readings of the nineteenth-century, whether before or afterward, we immediately notice fundamental differences. The most basic of these concerns the identity of the recitation pitch, *c′* in Lecoffre and *d′* in most other French sources. This difference will by extension control the pitch height of the surrounding tones. There are numerous other variants between the various sources that affect chiefly matters of detail. Viewed as an ensemble, these clearly establish the independence and value of the Lecoffre edition. It is not at all surprising that Katherine Bergeron should report that prior to the creation of their own edition of the Gradual the Solesmes monks sang from the Lecoffre Gradual.[3]

The next two sources represented in our example are drawn respectively from a Gradual printed in Évreux in 1858, and another, better known, that was issued in 1869. The latter (staff **e**) presents the fruits of a Commission authorized by Marie-Julien Meirieu, Bishop of Digne, and apparently first brought out in 1848. The 1869 volume issued by Lainé is marked as the fifth printing, but no records of the four earlier ones have surfaced as of yet. The firm of Mingardon in Marseilles also produced Graduals incorporating the results of the Digne Commission, the earliest surviving of these having been published in 1872. Together, these readings reflect the conservative aspect of French practice in the mid-nineteenth century. The philosophy underlying this approach is set out firmly in the Preface to the Lainé Gradual.

> The programme of the Ecclesiastical Commission of Digne deals with the traditional chant of the Roman liturgy in France. This encompasses an entire doctrine, and the warm feelings that are associated with it do not in any way permit its abandonment.
>
> Moreover, of what use is a reversal of opinion in a matter that all of the recent polemics have elucidated with such an uproar? Is it not uncontestable that a return to

the earliest chant, attributed to St. Gregory faces serious and perhaps insurmountable difficulties? Cannot it be said, without wounding anyone, that even if the efforts of the scholars who concern themselves with musical archeology are praiseworthy, one need not think that these result in clear advantages for contemporary practice? Experience itself has demonstrated that the prolixity of the earlier chant, called Gregorian, is sometimes insufferable, even with the rhythmic expedients that have been put into use in these last years. That which one must, above all, seek in this chant is not so much the number of notes that make it up but the secret of bringing these alive. Well, this secret, whatever one says about it, has been lost forever. Some obscure expressions, some vague or undecipherable notational signs, different or contradictory practices, rules that are sometimes arbitrary and sometimes manifestly in poor taste—this is what one finds in the old liturgical chant manuscripts that have come down to us. As long as a musical theory held sway in the Middle Ages, it made the laws, and the oral teachings of the chant masters transmitted the small details; but at each transformation of the art, that which was relatively new constantly caused one to forget that which was relatively old.

It will always be thus. To transport backward the musical liturgy eleven or twelve centuries is to create a veritable anachronism; it is to wish that the music be as immutable as the dogma, which it is not. Undoubtedly there are some eternal principles in art, but one should not confuse the fundamental with the accessory, nor the general character with the details of embellishment, which have varied in their essence from century to century.

The foundation and general character of plainchant is the tonality, it is the melodic dignity, it is an austere and calm rhythm; and these three traits exist in the Roman chant that the episcopate of France had caused to be edited following the Council of Trent for use in contemporary times. It is to the propagation of this chant that we have dedicated ourselves. We believe firmly that if a liturgical chant is to reign in France, it is this one, because, placed above all personal vanity, it represents the religious art in its definitive form and is sufficiently rooted in the memory of the faithful to bring about, without shock, the unity that is so desirable in the musical liturgy.

The manuscript discoveries of the decade preceding the Commission are dismissed firmly as archeological curiosities, incapable of sustaining life, and indeed unsuited to the needs and tastes of the then contemporary society. Obviously, this point of view did not prevail, but it is useful to have it clearly and fervently stated if we are to understand the variegated panorama presented in this century. It may elicit a smile on the part of some to note the very unobtrusive dismissal of the Gregorian legend of the Divine Creation of chant. Even if one were to project backward twelve centuries from 1860 (the upper limit envisaged by the writer of the Preface), one would reach only 660, fully a half-century after the pontificate of Gregory I, and the minimal projection of eleven centuries would take one back to 760, the approximate date presently assigned for the Frankish adoption of Roman chant. A more direct statement would have stirred up an additional hornet's nest, and the topic was contentious enough that there was no desire to do that. Nevertheless, the implicit effect of the dating of "Gregorian" chant is sufficient to undercut the argument that the early chant should be retained because of its holy status. In a very restricted sense the editors of this Gradual are also claiming a historical validation for their work, but it is a validation that takes us back no further than 1598/99.

When one turns to the readings given for *Populus Sion,* we find that, with a single exception, these are identical with the version presented in the Boni Gradual of 1598/99 and transmitted thereafter through the main body of sources from Toul and Paris. The single exception involves the opening pitch, which is given here as the final. This variant was mentioned previously in the discussion of the version edited by Miquel.

The reading presented on staff **f** is that given in a *Graduale Romanum: quod ad cantum attinet ad gregorianam formam reductum ex veteribus mss. undique donatum,* edited by Louis Lambillotte (1796–1855) and published posthumously in Paris in 1857. The editor is well known to scholars by virtue of his pseudo-facsimile edition of St. Gall, Stiftsbibl., MS 359, a source then thought to be the Antiphoner of St. Gregory sent in the care of Romanus.[4] The technology required for photographic facsimiles not having been available prior to 1870, Lambillotte's pseudo-facsimile had to be produced by hand. He was able to find a copyist whose eye and hand he trusted, a M. Naef, and confided the enormously time-consuming labor of copying the manuscript by hand, seeking to reproduce faithfully every detail. This copy was then traced with an oily ink that could be transferred onto a stone, thus providing the inverted image to be used in lithography. This complex and costly process was thus open to error at multiple stages. It is not surprising that when Dom Joseph Pothier first had the opportunity to compare the pseudo-facsimile with the original, he noted several dozens of errors. It was only in 1907, when the Benedictine monks had the opportunity to study the copy made by Naef, that they found his "original" to have been far more accurate than the printed edition. The basic point of this historiographical information is to establish Lambillotte's credentials as a scholar familiar with medieval sources. It remains to be learned the use to which he put this knowledge.

Even a cursory inspection of Lambillotte's *Graduale Romanum* shows it to be an idiosyncratic work. Though titled as a Gradual, modern scholars would be more likely to call it a notated Missal inasmuch as it furnishes the prayers and readings required for each Mass. In addition, it contains also the Offices for a few Feasts of the highest importance. Given the fact that the work was published posthumously, it is difficult to know how much of the opening matter represents the thinking of the original editor and how much is attributable to the person(s) responsible for overseeing the completion of the work. There is an extensive preface that bears the name of J. Dufour, but we are not told the extent of this man's association with Lambillotte, or whether Lambillotte might have been responsible for part or all of what is set forth in the preface.

The copyright notice states that "All reproduction, even partial, whether in square notation or in modern notation of the GREGORIAN CHANT restored by the R. P. Lambillotte, is entirely forbidden." The key word for us is of course "restored," and this takes us back to the claims of "restoration" made at the turn of the seventeenth century. As we shall see, what Lambillotte has accomplished is not a restoration, but a complete revision, not only of medieval chant, but of French chant practice of the previous two and a half centuries. The preface mentions specifically consultation of Paris, Bibl. nat., MS lat. 1134 (from St. Martial of Limoges) and is critical of some of the melodic features to be observed on fol. 7. It then cites an extensive passage from the opening of the verse to *Misit Dominus*, the gradual for the Second Sunday after Epiphany, both according to Carthusian reading(s) and according to Montpellier, Fac. méd., MS H. 159. This sets up a distinction between antiquarianism—a seeking of knowledge about things in the past—and the practicalities of chant performance in the mid-nineteenth century. If one were to judge from this one example, the two realms were apparently to be kept separate. The version of *Misit Dominus* given in the main body of the Gradual has little to do with any medieval version known to me; and it does not correspond either to any chant reading known to me originating in the period 1590–1855. Further study suggests, however, that knowledge of source readings does impinge on Lambillotte's editorial decisions, but this knowledge is not permitted to be a controlling factor.

The reading given by Lambillotte for *Populus Sion* is not fully equivalent at the beginning to any of the French versions given in staves **b–e**. It is closer to the reading offered by Lecoffre than to any other, but it opens with a leap from the final, whereas the Lecoffre reading opens on the fourth degree, the reciting tone. There are further variants in the settings of the first syllables of *Dominus* and *veniet,* and other small variants sprinkled throughout. The opening gesture parallels the one employed in the Medicean Gradual that forms the basis for the editions by Dessain and Pustet, but significant variants occur in the passages that follow. The opening is found also in the editions of Baglioni and in the later print by Canfari that reflects the Venetian tradition. Again the material that follows displays numerous variants. The two editions by Michael Hermesdorff, issued later, also recite on c' but again the reading by Lambillotte varies from these for the setting of the word *veniet* and elsewhere.

The next two staves (**g** and **h**) of our example present the readings of the Dessain Gradual of 1859 and the Pustet Epitome of 1892. These, to be sure, are not the first of their kind, as has been made clear previously. However, to the best of present knowledge, they are accurate reflections of their immediate predecessors. Comparison with the readings of the Medicean Gradual of 1614/15 shows that the two families of nineteenth-century Graduals provide a faithful rendition of the earlier source. While they seem not to be entirely without occasional fault, their accuracy is high. One may, however, note that versions of Hanicq (=Dessain) and Pustet are not consistent with one another in terms of neumation. This was apparently regarded as incidental.

Next in order I present two readings from Graduals brought out in Liége (staves **i, j**), the first issued in 1821 by the firm of C. Bourguignon, the second issued in 1876 by the firm of Spée-Zelis. The latter is the eleventh of its kind; earlier ones survive from 1857 and 1863. Though the two are separated by more than a half-century, comparison shows them to be virtually identical. When we seek to place these readings in historical context, we find that they are direct descendents of the second branch of the Belgian chant tradition, that represented by the Laurent Gradual of 1616, the Belleros Gradual of 1620, and the Mommaert Gradual of 1623.

It is more difficult to assess the readings presented in the Graduals edited by Michael Hermesdorff. The editions seek to represent the best of the medieval tradition that was known in Trier and that is preserved in sources available in the libraries of that city. David Hiley has already demonstrated the presence of significant differences between the versions of the opening of the gradual, *Exsurge, Domine, non praevaleat* in the two editions.[5] They represent different stages in the process of recovering a preferred medieval state.

The title page of the *Graduale ad normam cantus S. Gregorii* of 1876 informs us that Hermesdorff was the President of the *Verein zur Erforschung alter Choral-Handschriften* [Society for Research into Old Chant Manuscripts], that he was the Cathedral organist and Music Director, and that he taught chant both at the Cathedral Music School and the Seminary for Priests; furthermore he was President of the Caecilian Society for the Diocese of Trier. The edition is proclaimed to be founded on the researches conducted on the oldest and most trustworthy sources. We are not yet at the point where the editor feels it obligatory to give citations for his main sources. Hermesdorff thus refers to only some of the earliest adiastematic manuscripts from St. Gall (not otherwise identified), and two others that were to be found in the Cathedral and Town Libraries of Trier. Neither of the latter has been available to me. While it is notable that the editor was solicitous of the neumations to be found in our precious adiastematic sources, my main concern has been for the way in which he and his colleagues went about determining pitches for the various chants.

The range of subjectivity that has reigned among different views of chant history is astonishing. In the late seventeenth century, a chant scholar such as Guillaume Gabriel Nivers, could examine a sizable number of primary sources—identities unspecified—and summarize his findings in terms of heterogeneity, a total lack of agreement between readings, and thus a scene of massive corruption. These conclusions were then used to support a call for the editorial "correction" of chant in order to bring it into agreement with the principles of science and taste. Two centuries later, Hermesdorff and his colleagues could also examine a large number of chant sources—identities largely unspecified—of the "9th, 10th, 11th, and 12th-14th centuries" and find them to be in essential agreement in their readings. This agreement, it is claimed, extends to the numbers of tones contained in the individual melodies, the subdivision of the melodies and the assignment of tones to the various syllables, and to the layout of the melody, that is, the rise and fall of the tones in the individual phrases. We may perhaps concede to Nivers that if one consults a sufficient number of readings for an individual chant, one will find few that are identical throughout all sources. Nevertheless, it is likely that scholars working in the twenty-first century will find Nivers' claims to be gross exaggerations; he is seeing and describing that which he wishes to see. In their initial statement, the descriptions of Hermesdorff are also too broad and over generalized, but they are far closer to the mark. And Hermesdorff does modify somewhat his initial remarks. He does acknowledge the difference between what are commonly known as "Eastern" and "Western" chant dialects, citing two brief excerpts that are cobbled together. The first is taken from the opening of the introit, *Statuit ei,* with its initial upward leap of a fifth, followed variously by either a minor third or a minor second. The second I have not been able to identify inasmuch as it comes from the interior of a (protus?) chant and only a single syllable, "e-" is given. At issue is a neighbor motion, again contrasting the minor third with a second. In his view, variants such as these do not disturb the essential unanimity between readings, and I think that most would agree with this point of view. Except for a group of quite unusual, unstable chants, the majority of the Gregorian repertoire can be viewed quite reasonably in terms of Hermesdorff's descriptions.

One cannot hope to uncover Hermesdorff's working procedures by means of a cursory study except through an extraordinary stroke of good fortune, and this has not been vouchsafed to me. However, it is possible to offer a preliminary evaluation of his work even on the basis of limited comparisons. A casual perusal of his two Graduals is sufficient to indicate that the editor is according preference to the "Eastern" or "Germanic" dialect of chant. Instances spring to light on many pages. For purposes of comparison I have thus focused on those sources from this region that have appeared in facsimile edition. These include the St. Thomas Gradual from Leipzig; Graz, Universitätsbibl., MS 807, and Munich, Universitätsbibl., MS 2° 56. To this group I have added a source preserved in Trier itself, Bistumsarchiv, MS 404, a notated Missal from the latter half of the thirteenth century, and Wolfenbüttel, Herzog August Bibl., MS Helmstedt 40, a thirteenth-century Gradual.

If we compare the various manuscript readings of *Populus Sion* with one another, we find that they do not all belong to the same family. Trier 404, Graz 807, Leipzig 391, and Wolfenbüttel 40 all belong to the group of sources that recite initially on c'. Munich 2°56 (the Moosburger Gradual), on the other hand, employs a recitation on d'. While not identical, the remaining four sources are in basic agreement with one another, and the versions presented by Hermesdorff agree quite closely with these, though not identical to any one.

The small differences are, however, of some importance. I have elsewhere suggested that in its earliest form, *Populus Sion* began in the protus maneria and ended in the tetrardus.[6] In the family of readings that recites on c', the presence of protus gestures is signaled by the frequent use of *b-flat* until the first major subdivision at the word *gentes.* The family of readings that recites on d' accomplishes much the same goal by employing *a* (rather than *g*) as a temporary tonal reference. The four sources that I collated for comparison with the readings given by Hermesdorff are unanimous in their use of *b-flat.* Even though this accidental appears only once in the Leipzig Gradual, the expectation that it was to hold good for the first two phrases is made clear by the use of a natural that appears in the third phrase in conjunction with the word, *auditam;* this accidental is employed also in the Graz and Wolfenbüttel readings, again emphasizing the importance of *b-flat* in the previous section. The two versions presented by Hermesdorff, on the other hand, are serenely in tetrardus throughout (staves **k**, **l**). Without critical editions and without access to the Trier sources cited in Hermesdorff's preface, we have no means of determining the basis for his decision to avoid the normative *b-flats*. The version that he presents is quite singable and possibly accords with late medieval practice.

The second kind of individuality to be found in Hermesdorff's readings concerns the nature of upper neighbor cadences. For the close at the word *gentes*, Hermesdorff employs the progression, *g–a–g*, while the manuscript sources that I consulted agree on *b-flat* as the middle tone. On the other hand, most sources give the progression *d'–f'–d'* for the setting of the first syllable of *suae*, while the Trier Missal gives *e'* as the middle tone. There are occasional other instances of variants between the reading given by Hermesdorff and those of our test sample. For example, the print is the only one to offer two tones for the first syllable of *veniet*. Note, however, that Hermesdorff allows four tones to be assigned to the second, unaccented syllable, in contradistinction to the practice of his earlier predecessors. As far as one can judge from this limited comparison, he does not seem to have a preexistent agenda. The sources that he has used are apparently speaking for themselves.

The lowest staff of example 82 furnishes one of the early restorations under Solesmes editorship. I have unfortunately had only very brief access to the 1883 printing of the *Liber Gradualis S. Gregorio Magno*, printed in Tournai by the firm of Desclée, which I saw for only a few minutes at the Vienna, Nationalbibliothek. For present purposes I am using instead the subsequent edition, the *Liber Gradualis juxta antiquorum codicum fidem restitutus*, published in Solesmes in 1895. The reading for *Populus Sion* found in this edition is identical with that given in later sources issued by the Solesmes monks, including the valuable *Graduale Triplex*. It is worth noting that the Solesmes reading is also very close to that present in the later of the two Hermesdorff editions.

The gradual for the Second Sunday of Advent, *Ex Sion species* (with the verse, *Congregate illi*), presents a contrasting set of conditions for nineteenth-century chant editors. This notwithstanding, the comments made with regard to the historical antecedents for the selected readings of *Populus Sion* largely hold true for *Ex Sion species* as well. (See example 83.)

The reading given in the Canfari Gradual of 1840 (staff **a**) is again quite close to those given by its Venetian predecessors of the sixteenth and seventeenth centuries. The use of an upward third in place of a downward one for the second syllable of the respond catches one's attention, as does the use of a lower neighbor motion in place of an upper neighbor motion for the second syllable of *decoris*. But neither these nor the few other variants are truly consequential. Again we are reminded how much terser are the Venetian readings than those from France. This was obvious when we first compared the early readings for the Mass for the Second Sunday of Advent, but it may bear repeating once more.

The three readings representing the conservative French practice of the nineteenth century are again quite similar indeed (staves **b**, **d**, and **e**). Only in the setting of the word, *manifeste,* in the respond does one find again marked variants between them. Again, the readings are quite close to those of the Boni Gradual of 1598/99 and its successors of 1627, 1633, 1656, etc.

We find more to occupy our attention when we consider the reading of *Ex Sion* representing the fruits of the Reims-Cambrai Commission and published by the firm of Lecoffre (staff **c**). Here the editors had to deal with a considerable number of melismas of varying sizes. As one would expect from the information provided by the introduction to the volume, comparison with the reading of the Montpellier manuscript provides excellent insights into their procedures. The solo portion of the respond is identical in the two sources, as is the opening of the choral continuation. But matters are otherwise when we reach the final syllable of *species.* In the manuscript version, we find a small melisma that begins with a *podatus,* implying an upward movement in which the two tones are closely linked. In the printed reading, on the other hand, the first of these two tones is set apart from the remainder by a thick partial bar-line. A hasty glance at the page creates the false impression that the last syllable is served by a single tone. The melisma itself begins with the second tone, which is grouped together with the four-note descending neume that follows in the manuscript. Following a momentary turn, the line descends to *a* and then repeats the last two tones of the descent, a repetition that is absent from the Montpellier source. It is here that the vagueness of the description of sources consulted becomes an irritant; the possibilities of models are too numerous to encourage one to track down whether another early manuscript version has momentarily been used as a basis. (The two tones are absent from the reading of the *Graduale Triplex.*) The question is vexing because the same figure recurs as part of the small melisma appearing in conjunction with the last syllable of *Deus.* Here the Montpellier manuscript remains consistent, while the Lecoffre Gradual changes to accord with it. There are a few other instances of departures from the manuscript reading, but these seem to this writer to be inconsequential. They are worthy of mention only to document the fact that the editors of the printed Gradual have not surrendered their privileges to make changes in accordance with their discretion.

Comparable lessons are to be derived from a study of the verse, *Congregate illi.* The accented third syllable of the opening words receives a large melisma of thirty-six tones in the version given by the *Graduale Triplex.* This is presented nearly intact in the Lecoffre Gradual. Twice we find that a bistropha in the Montpellier reading is reduced to a single tone in the printed Gradual. And at the beginning of the fourth staff of Montpellier one finds a series of five *strophici* in the neumatic notation that are represented in the alphabetic notation by a single letter followed by a series of dots. These *strophici* are absent from the Lecoffre reading and also from the reading of the *Graduale Triplex.*

Allowing for the elimination of the tonal repetitions present in a tristropha, the next segment of the Montpellier reading is presented accurately in the Lecoffre Gradual up to the point where one reaches another large melisma on the last syllable of *ordinaverunt*. This begins with a varied repetition of the initial segment—such as mentioned in the introduction—and this repetition is indicated only by means of the symbol r*, placed both at the beginning and end of the segment. We find shortly thereafter that a segment that reads a–b, c'–d'–c' in Montpellier is revised to read c'–b, c'–d'–a in the printed Gradual. It is instructive to find that it is the latter reading that has been adopted in the *Graduale Triplex*. As far as one can tell, the Lecoffre editors have emended the Montpellier reading through consultation of one of the manuscripts that they studied "in the public libraries of Paris, Cambrai, Reims, etc."; we seem to be dealing with a conflation. This suspicion is strengthened when we note the omission of the flat given in Montpellier for the ascent associated with the first syllable of the final word. In the reading given in the *Graduale Triplex* one does not find any flat, but the oblique form of i is quite clear in the manuscript itself. Again we find both at the close of the verse and elsewhere, various occasions when the neumation of the Montpellier manuscript is blatantly disregarded in the print. This notwithstanding, we can still appreciate the thoughtful scholarship that has gone into the edition.

There is little to detain us with regard to the readings given in the editions of Hanicq, Dessain, and Pustet (staves **g, h**). As noted previously, these are based on the readings provided in the Medicean Gradual of 1614/15. The Gradual issued in Liége by the firm of C. Bourguignon in 1821 (staff **i**) is on the whole related to the earlier Graduals of Laurent, Belleros, and Mommaert, but it does display elements of individuality. Similarly, comparison shows that the reading presented in the Spée-Zelis Gradual of 1876 (staff **j**) displays remarkably few variants from those presented in the Graduals of Laurent, Belleros, and Mommaert over a century and a half earlier. The only one of consequence concerns the allotment of tones to the third word of the respond. In the seventeenth-century Graduals two notes are assigned to the first syllable of *species*, one to the second, and seven to the final syllable. In the Gradual by Spée-Zelis, on the other hand, six tones are given to the first syllable, a repeated c' to the middle syllable, and four tones are allotted to the last syllable. One may reasonably suspect that this change occurred not in this printing, which is identified as the eleventh of its kind, but at an earlier stage of transmission.

I propose to continue the examination of the two Graduals brought out by Michael Hermesdorff and his associates in order to improve our understanding of his editorial practices, using for this purpose the same group of five sources that were employed in connection with the examination of *Populus Sion*. Even within this limited number of sources one does find numerous variants. But there is none that disturbs any fundamental property of the melody. Many of the variants concern small details of performance, e.g., whether a tone is to be performed in normal fashion or as a quilisma. Others contrast *strophici* with standard neumes using the same pitches. The *strophici* occur on c' and there are instances where b may be used instead of one of the c's. (The most prominent example occurs at the beginning of the verse in the reading of Munich, Universitätsbibl. 2°56.) But despite the proliferation of the variants, especially in neumations, I am unable to point to any one that effects a basic change. In this respect, the reading of Graz, Universitätsbibl. 807 is somewhat more individual than those of the remaining sources, as is that of Munich 2°56.

The readings provided by Hermesdorff (staves **k, l**) are not identical to any of those in our small test group. However, the reader deserves a caution in this matter. In the later of his two Graduals, Hermesdorff provides a double notation. The primary one consists of squares and diamonds placed on a four-line staff headed by a C-clef. The secondary one consists of neumes that have elements of heightening, but not in consistent fashion. The two notations are not always in full agreement with one another. For example, the neume for the final syllable of *decoris* clearly shows a quilisma, but Hermesdorff does not have the type font that will allow him to show this in staff notation. (He does, however, devote considerable space in the preface to a discussion of the way in which the quilisma is to be performed.) Similarly, some readers might prefer another equivalence for the opening of the melisma on the third syllable of *Congregate*, rather than the translation given in the edition. Again one is dealing with the limitations of a type font. Surveying the total, it is possible to declare that the reading provided by Hermesdorff is at least in close agreement with those of the various sources in our sample.

A second major melisma in the verse of *Ex Sion* occurs on the final syllable of *ordinaverunt*. Among medieval readings the first segment is repeated immediately. This repetition is present in the second of the two versions published by Hermesdorff, but is lacking from the first. Apart from this discrepancy, the two readings are fairly close to one another in major respects. The later will occasionally present *strophici* on *c'* that are indicated by single tones in the earlier edition, and it may break a downward diatonic movement by a brief upper neighbor motion that is lacking in the earlier reading. But these are matters of detail. The general closeness notwithstanding, the two readings differ frequently with regard to the interpretation of rhythm.

Although the 1821 readings of Bourguignon (staff **i**) and the 1876 readings of Spée-Zelis (staff **j**) are generally remarkably close to one another, they differ in their treatment of the melisma just mentioned. The former gives a fuller reading for the passage than does the latter, and the two differ in the way in which text is adjusted to the music. These differences notwithstanding, they remain within the same general family as in *Populus Sion*.

The reading for *Ex Sion* given in the Solesmes *Liber Gradualis* of 1895 (staff **m**) is, as one might expect, quite close to that given in more modern editions brought out by the Benedictines. Here, however, one finds a handful of variants. One may note that the quilismas on *b* that are to be found on the accented syllables of *species* and *eius* (the second of the occurrences in the verse) in the later editions are lacking in the 1895 print. Their place is taken by ordinary neumes on *c'*. One might be tempted to think that the requisite symbol was lacking before the turn of the twentieth century, but this is not the case. The 1895 print gives this neume form for the final syllable of *decoris*, and had given it for the preceding introit on the first syllable of *Dominus*.

Of somewhat greater interest is the presence in the verse of liquescents on the first syllable of *sanctos* and the third syllable of *testamentum*. A glance at the *Graduale Triplex* (or the relevant facsimile editions) indicates that these neumes are indeed present in the readings of both Laon, Bibl. mun. 239 and Chartres Bibl. mun. 47. (They are also given in Einsiedeln, Benedikterkloster, 121 and St. Gall, Stiftsbibl., 339.) This notwithstanding, the later Solesmes editions omit the two liquescents. Preference is presumably being given to other, later sources.

The Alleluia for the Second Sunday of Advent, *Laetatus sum*, is an unusual chant in several respects. As noted in chapter 5, medieval scribes had difficulties in conveying the modality of the chant and used several different pitch levels. Even when the general level remained the same, the finals might vary. Furthermore, when the final was placed on *d*, sources were likely to use partial transposition for one phrase. It is also necessary to reckon with the fact that this chant had two verses at its origin, and the second survived into the period that is of concern to this study.

The reading given for the *Alleluia Laetatus sum* provided by the Canfari Gradual (see example 84. staff **a**) is virtually identical with that in the Pezzana Gradual of 1779, allowing for the fact that the page of the exemplar available to me for the Pezzana edition was not aligned with sufficient care. This reading is quite similar to the one presented in the Baglioni print of 1690, although variants are to be found. Indeed, despite the presence of variants, the verse displays a strong family resemblance to that present in the Giunta Gradual of 1596. The opening Alleluia, however, is significantly changed. This notwithstanding, I find impressive the relative fixity of the chant over a period of a century and a half.

The reading presented in the Lecoffre Gradual (staff **c**) is worthy of closer consideration. The main source for the editors, Montpellier, Fac. méd., MS H. 159, classifies the chant among those of the deuterus maneria. The final is placed on *a*, and *b-flat* is signaled frequently by the use of the italic form of *i*. This is especially important at the cadence to the Alleluia itself. The flat is indicated also at the end of the verse, but the closing melisma, which duplicates the jubilus, is slightly truncated. The use of *a* as final is necessitated by the fact that the second degree of the chant is variable. In the Alleluia itself, and in the latter portion of the verse, the melody employs a half step above the final; hence the assignment to the deuterus maneria. In the opening portion of the verse, however, the melody employs a whole tone above the final. This variability is indicated by the change between *b-flat* and *b-natural*. Although the character of the melody is clearly indicated in the Montpellier manuscript, its nature was altered during the course of its later transmission. By the late Middle Ages the French especially preferred to notate the chant with a final on *d*, transforming it into a first-mode melody. This late tradition apparently exercised a considerable hold on the editors of the Lecoffre Gradual. While present-ing the melody on the *a* level in accordance with the reading of the Montpellier manuscript (and other early sources), *b-flat* is nevertheless avoided. Indeed, the chant is prefaced by the notation, M[ode] IX ([=]1). Apart from this fundamental alteration of modality, the pitch names otherwise remain faithful to the Montpel-lier source throughout the opening Alleluia. The reading presented for the verse is largely faithful to the source—again apart from the avoidance of *b-flat* in the latter portion. There are, however, exceptions to the general rule. Montpellier presents the upward liquescent for the word *sunt* at the same height as the *pes* for the close of the preceding word, *dicta*. The more frequent reading has the liquescent a tone lower, and this is the reading presented both in the Lecoffre Gradual and in the *Graduale Triplex*. The Reims-Cambrai reading reverses the direction of the liques-cent for the word *in*. A much graver departure involves the treatment of the passage setting the word *Domini*. In the Montpellier reading and in other early sources, this passage leads to a *deuterus* cadence on *a*. Not wishing, however, to use the *b-flat* specified in the source, the editors basically transpose the passage up a second so that it ends *c'*–*b-natural*. In a strange, almost prescient way, the reading accords with that of the current *Graduale Triplex* and the 1974 *Graduale Romanum*. The normal height resumes thereafter. The *strophici* indicated in the neumatic notation provided by Montpellier for the opening of *ibimus* are disregarded as they were in a parallel instance noted previously with regard to *Ex Sion*. Obviously, the conclusion to the final melisma is supplied by the editors. The reading provided is conflated from multiple sources, but the conflation may be deemed a reasonable one. The interest in the historical practices of the Middle Ages is restrained, and the editors had no wish to give the second verse that is presented in the manuscript.

The first of the versions edited by Hermesdorff in 1863 (staff **k**) employs a final on *d*. Strikingly, the 1876 version edited by this scholar (staff **l**) is notated so that the final falls on *a*. As in the Lecoffre reading, *b-flat* is avoided, and Hermesdorff classifies the melody in Mode 1. Here, however, we can find some justification for this action. While *b-flats* appear in the five medieval Germanic sources that we have been using as a basis for comparison, they are indicated only inconsistently. Furthermore, with the exception of Munich 2°56, the other sources provide a cadence to the Alleluia that descends a minor third from *c*, as does Hermesdorff. For the most part the general outlines of the chant remain constant in the medieval sources despite the presence of a fair number of variants in matters of detail. The most significant departure occurs in the reading of Graz 807, which presents a sizable segment near the opening of the verse a second lower than normal, rising from *b-flat* to *d'* (rather than from *c'* to *e'*), and then recites on *d'*. After conclud-ing the brief recitation, the reading returns to the normal level. Even though the 1876 reading provided by Hermesdorff is not in complete agreement with any one of our five sources, apart from the consistent omission of *b-flat*, each of its details finds confirmation in one source or another, and usually in multiple sources. As before, the two readings differ in their interpretations of rhythmic detail.

Of considerably greater importance is the fundamental difference in the endings to the verse. The 1863 version brings this section to an abrupt end with the first tone of the final syllable of *ibimus*. This corresponds to practices that may be observed in readings of the late fifteenth and sixteenth centuries. The 1876 edition, on the other hand, presents a very full melisma on this sensitive syllable. This is the equivalent of much earlier medieval readings that conclude the verse with a melisma parallel to that of the jubilus.

The readings in the Bourguignon Gradual of 1821 (staff **i**) and the Spée-Zelis Gradual of 1876 (staff **j**) are idiosyncratic. They both begin and end on *e*, emphatically establishing the deuterus nature of the mode. As mentioned previously, such form of modal construction is seldom to be found among the sources studied here. (The Premonstratensian readings of the seventeenth and early eighteenth century are similar, but only partially so.) Nevertheless, these late readings are nearly identical to those of the second family of Belgian Graduals, differing only in the addition of two tones near the end of the jubilus. The protus element in the verse is handled by opening this section on *d* and by continuing a fifth rather than a fourth lower than the versions with final on *a*. There is an important adjustment to the cadence on *Domini*. The melisma that concludes the verse is truncated and reworked.

There are, to be sure, a few medieval sources, such as Orléans, Bibl. mun., MS 121; Brussels, Bibl. royale, MS II.3823; Paris, Bibl. St.-Geneviève, MSS 2668 and 2669, that begin the Alleluia on *e* and conclude the jubilus on the same tone. These, however, are rare and relatively late. Furthermore, the correspondences in the two Parisian sources are only partial, inasmuch as they begin the verse on *e*, and thus have no need for the ongoing partial transposition.

The Solesmes Gradual of 1895 presents a reading (staff **m**) that is basically identical with that of more recent editions. One finds occasional instances in which the grouping of tones into neumes varies slightly from one reading to another, but nothing more substantial. The reading is based on a *d* final and thus corresponds basically to normative French readings of the High and Late Middle Ages. It is not, however, in accordance with earlier French readings, which give decided preference to finals on *a*.

As shown in examples 85 and 86, the readings for the offertory, *Deus tu convertens*, and the communion, *Ierusalem surge*, reveal practices that are basically in keeping with those outlined in the discussion of the three chants preceding in the Mass for the Second Sunday of Advent. For example, the reading of the Canfari Gradual of 1847 (staff **a**) is quite close to that for the Baglioni Gradual of 1690, but it is more distant from that of the Giunta Gradual of 1596. The reading of the Blanc Gradual of 1844 (staff **b**) is similar to that of the Boni Gradual of 1598/99, but with several variants nevertheless. Lacking much that is both noteworthy and new, I shall try to be brief.

Because the editors of the Lecoffre Gradual (staff **c**) were the first to seek to recapture the medieval heritage of chant, and because we can identify their primary source, it seems worthwhile to learn a bit more about their editorial techniques. The melody for *Deus tu convertens* is marked by the use of numerous *strophici*, especially near the beginning. (See the setting of *convertens vivificabis*.) While generally adhering to the lines of the Montpellier melody, the Lecoffre edition suppresses these tonal repetitions and uses instead only a single tone each. If our samplings from this source are representative, we may conclude that the description of the editorial practices afforded in the introduction to the edition is not sufficiently accurate for our purposes. The Montpellier manuscript does indeed furnish a point of departure for the editors; they do indeed seek to come closer to medieval practice than do their contemporaries, but they continue nevertheless to claim their prerogatives as editors in determining the final shapes of the chants.

The earlier of the two editions by Hermesdorff (staff **k**) basically follows a route parallel to that taken in the Lecoffre Gradual. The *strophici* are eliminated and single tones are used in their place. (For that matter, the *strophici* are lacking in most other readings presented in the example; these, however, make no pretense of following medieval practice.) The *strophici* are, however, to be found in the Hermesdorff edition begun in 1876 (staff **l**). They are to be found also in the Solesmes Gradual of 1895 (staff **m**). These two late nineteenth-century prints contain readings that are relatively close to one another without, however, being identical. We may single out a few of the variants for discussion. The first of these involves the second syllable of *convertens*. In the edition by Hermesdorff, this is set by the tones $c'–c'–a$. The 1895 Solesmes edition, on the other hand, has $c'–c'–c'$. This comparison is worthy of remark inasmuch as the *Graduale Triplex*, which shows Solesmes practice as of 1979, gives $c'–c'–(a)$, the last being a liquescent. Yet the accompanying neumations for Laon, Bibl. mun. 239 and Einsiedeln, Benedikterkloster, 121 give no indication of this liquescent. The modern diastematic version is based on readings in other sources. In a somewhat comparable way, the Hermesdorff edition gives $c'–g$, $a–c,'$ $c'–a$ for the beginning of the setting of the opening syllable of the first occurrence of the word *nobis*. Again the Solesmes edition of 1895 omits the descent from c' to a. Neither of the two adiastematic sources reported on in the *Graduale Triplex* gives evidence for such a descent. Furthermore, both Solesmes editions begin on b rather than on c. This appears to be a contrast between the French and Germanic dialects of chant. In setting the first two syllables of the word *misericordiam*, Hermesdorff employs single tones on the pitch f. In both of the Solesmes editions we find a repeated podatus, $e–f$. The neumes of Einsiedeln, Benedikterkloster, 121 support the former interpretation, while those in Laon Bibl. mun. 239 support the latter.

In the modern notation of the Solesmes editions, we find eight instances of a torculus, although we must hasten to add that in several of these instances the equivalents in the early adiastematic manuscripts give these as parts of larger compound neumes. Thus the use of the term, torculus, to describe these varied appearances is simply a concession to convenience rather than a fully accurate descriptor. The reason why it is convenient to treat these gestures as a group is that in fully half of the instances, the pitch constellations vary from the 1895 Gradual to the 1979 *Graduale Triplex*. In short, the process of change that we have charted over the course of three centuries does not come to an abrupt halt when we reach the publication of the 1883 *Liber Gradualis S. Gregorio Magno*, issued by the monks of the great Benedictine Abbey. Change continues, although at a much reduced pace as the Solesmes editors continue to refine their procedures and criteria. On occasion these changes may be on a relatively large scale. The *Liber Gradualis* of 1895 still lacks the repeats for the opening text phrase of the offertory, *Jubilate Deo omnis terra*, for the Sunday within the Octave of Epiphany. The same is true for the opening text phrase for *Jubilate Deo universa terra*, for the Second Sunday after Epiphany. The restoration of these repeats had to await the issuance in Rome of the *Editio Vaticana* in 1908.

It would indeed be pleasant were it possible to report that with the *Editio Vaticana* all the problems in the editing of chant had reached definitive solutions and that unanimity reigned supreme throughout the Church of Rome. Such a state would be possible only in the realm of the fairy tale. The historian must unfortunately wrestle with a much more complex and confusing state.

EPILOGUE

Having bombarded the reader with an unending succession of minutiae throughout the book, I should like to close in a somewhat lighter vein, with an autobiographical anecdote. It was possible for my wife and I to preface our attendance at the 2002 Leuven Congress of the International Musicological Congress, with a few free days spent visiting some family members and paying very brief visits to cities that we had known in previous decades. One of our day trips took us to the city of Antwerp, where I was able to spend a few hours at the library of the Plantin Museum. Another took us to Ghent and to the Cathedral of St. Bavo. There I was delighted to see a few volumes from a five-volume set of huge chant books for use in the choir of that Cathedral. The volume displayed on the lectern bore a title page reading, *Graduale Romanum ad usum exemptae Ecclesiae Cathedralis S. Bavonis, pars Lateris dextri*, dated 7. April 1659. The calligraphy of this and other volumes that I saw was done with such exquisite care that I thought at first that I was dealing with a print. Not so, I was informed. These are manuscripts. I had not budgeted much time for studying the source, and there were limits beyond which I could not impose on the kind courtesy of the conservator. Nevertheless, we were permitted to take two pictures from an opening that contained parts of the Masses for the First and Second Sundays of Advent. My remarks are made possible by these photographs, which were successful beyond our expectations.

It was immediately obvious that these volumes were devoted not to late copies of some medieval source, but rather to some contemporary form of post-Tridentine practice. Jumping the gun, my first assumption was that I was seeing antiquarian items that had been out of use for perhaps a century. Fortunately, I did not voice this hypothesis inasmuch as I was soon astonished to be informed that the books had been in regular use at the Cathedral until 1960, when they were made obsolete by the rulings of the Second Vatican Council requiring Mass to be said in the vernacular. Was this situation replicated elsewhere in Europe? We can only wonder.

Inasmuch as I have carefully documented the existence in our printed survivals of two Belgian chant traditions, the reader may wish to know which of these the Ghent manuscript follows. It accords with neither. The evidence is quite unequivocal in this regard. If we return to a consideration of the *Alleluia Laetatus sum*, we will recall that in the Plantin reading of 1599, the Alleluia opens on *d*, contains a very full jubilus that corresponds reasonably well to the medieval form, and closes on *e*. The Belleros Gradual of 1620 (and its siblings of 1616 and 1623), both opens and closes on *e*. Again the jubilus is relatively full. In the Ghent Gradual, on the other hand, the Alleluia both opens and closes on *d*, but the jubilus has been drastically shortened, consisting of no more than five notes. The treatment of the *Alleluia Ostende nobis* for the previous Sunday is parallel. The jubilus is again restricted to five tones. The Plantin Gradual, on the other hand, uses fifteen tones for the jubilus, while the Belleros Gradual employs sixteen. In the verse for the *Alleluia Laetatus sum* the Plantin Gradual utilizes ten tones for the setting of the opening word, *Laetatus*, before leaping upward and continuing in a basically upward direction, though with small decorative neighbor motions. The Ghent source proceeds in a uniformly upward direction. Indeed, the terseness of the Ghent verse is remarkable. There is only one syllable that is set by more than two notes, and that is the first syllable of the final word, *ibimus*. Both Belgian sources that we have discussed previously are infinitely richer. Both end on *e*, while the Ghent source ends on *d*. Even though the tonal structure of the three readings for the *Alleluia Ostende nobis* remains constant, the stylistic difference between the relatively full versions found in the early prints and the markedly laconic version in the Ghent manuscript is striking.

A study of the introit, *Populus Sion*, reveals similar disparities among the three readings that we are considering. Here we can say that the tonal structure of the Ghent manuscript is akin to that of the Plantin Gradual, while it contrasts with that of the Belleros Gradual. But again there are major contrasts in relative prolixity. To cite merely one example among many, the Plantin and Belleros Graduals each employ four tones for the setting of the first syllable of *ecce* (the third word of the text). The Ghent Gradual employs only one. Another instance: the Plantin and Belleros Graduals use respectively four and five notes for the first syllable of *veniet*. The Ghent Gradual finds that one will suffice. Similar comments may be made for the offertory for the First Sunday of Advent, *Ad te levavi*. Here too the Ghent Gradual stands apart from the others by virtue of its terseness.

Given the severity of the melodies in the Ghent Gradual, perhaps they derive from some Italian tradition? One may observe a certain similarity between the openings of the *Alleluia Ostende nobis* in the Giunta Gradual of 1596 and the Ghent Gradual of 1659. But this similarity dissipates by the time that we reach the jubilus, which is markedly briefer in the Ghent reading than in the one from Venice. The verses do not encourage us to think that the later was derived from the earlier. The Gardano and Giunta Graduals begin the *Alleluia Laetatus sum* on *d*, but they both end the jubilus on *e*; furthermore, they both end the verse on *e*. They thus employ tonal structures that differ from that present in the Ghent Gradual. Comparison with the Medicean Gradual is equally fruitless. And the Ghent Gradual is terser than the Italian Graduals in its readings of *Populus Sion*. The readings for both the *Alleluia Ostende nobis* and the offertory, *Ad te levavi*, also contrast with those of Italian sources, although to a slightly lesser extent. In the latter chant, the Ghent source omits the word *Domine*, which is present in the Giunta edition, but is lacking from the editions by Gardano, the Medicean Press, and Ciera (1629), but it is present in medieval sources and in the Giunta Gradual of 1596. Although I am obviously working with only a very slim corpus of evidence, it is the contrast in the treatment of text that leads me to posit that the differences that we have been documenting are typical of the Ghent source as a whole.

This evidence returns us in aria da capo fashion to cautions stated in the introduction. I pointed out at that juncture that the study being presented does not represent the totality of what needs to be accomplished to gain a balanced perspective on the post-Tridentine Mass Proper. The reader was forewarned that, among other matters, it would remain to explore the manuscript evidence for the period. In serendipitous fashion, one of the very few manuscript sources that I have had the opportunity to consult turns out to contain a highly distinctive repertoire whose existence could not have been predicted from the evidence of the printed sources.

It is my belief that this book represents a significant advance in knowledge over that which was heretofore available to the scholarly community. There is much more that remains to be done before we can claim to have achieved a balanced view of the post-Tridentine Mass Proper. All worthwhile contributions to this endeavor are to be welcomed.

Notes

Notes for Chapter 1

1. A questionable seventh, the 1594 print cited in the Checklist, was reported missing as of January 2001.

2. Translation after Oliver Strunk, *Source Readings in Music History* (New York, 1950), 358. The original text was published in Raphael Molitor, *Die nach-Tridentinische Choral-Reform zu Rom* (Leipzig, 1901–2), I, 297–98.

3. *Graduale Romanum Integrum, Complectens cantum Gregorianum officii totius anni, tam de Tempore, quam de Sanctis, A nonnullis viris piis Musicæ peritissimis, præcipueque a D. G. Bony Cantore & Canonico Ecclesiae Metropolitanæ Tolosatum Musico celeberrimo ad vetustissimorum exemplarium fidem accurate emendatum, ac pristino nitori restitutum, correctis ubique pravis accentibus.*

4. "...*et a multis erroribus temporis lapsis. Magno studio ac labore multorum Eccellentissimorum Musicorum emendatum.*"

5. See, for example, George Huppert, *The Idea of Perfect History* (Urbana, [1970]), and *The Style of Paris* (Bloomington [Ind.], ca. 1999).

6. See especially Katherine Bergeron, *Decadent Enchantments: The Revival of Gregorian Chant at Solesmes* (Berkeley, Calif., 1998), together with the earlier works on the Solesmes restoration cited there.

7. See Raphael Molitor, *Die nach-Tridentinische Choral-Reform zu Rom*, 2 vols. (Leipzig, 1901–2).

8. A still earlier reform publication under the general editorship of Ludovico Balbi was issued in Venice by Angelo Gardano in 1587, but this includes only a few Masses for Franciscan feasts. We do not yet have specific information concerning what is apparently a similar print issued two years earlier. A brief account of the

1591 print is given by Annarita Indino in "Il Graduale stampato da Angelo Gardano (1591)," in *Il Canto piano nell'era della stampa*, edited by Giulio Cattin, Danilo Curti, and Marco Gozzi (Trent, 1999); a fuller account is available in the same author's doctoral dissertation mentioned above.

9. For available information see the Internet data base, RELICS (REnaissance Liturgical Imprints Census) housed at the University of Michigan under the direction of Professors David Crawford and James Borders.

10. See RELICS.

11. Facsimile edition available in *Missale Romanum, Editio Princeps (1570)*, edited by Manlio Sodi and Achille Maria Triacca in *Monumenta Liturgica Concilii Tridentini*, 2 (Città del Vaticano, 1998).

12. See, for example, David G. Hughes, "Evidence for the Traditional View of the Transmission of Gregorian Chant," *Journal of the American Musicological Society*, 40 (1987), 377–404.

13. For the last-named category, see my essay, "An Unknown Late Medieval Chant Fragment," *Cantus Planus: Papers Read at the 9th Meeting, Esztergom & Visegrád, 1998* (Budapest, 2001), 173–88. For the two preceding categories, see my, *Aspects of Orality and Formularity in Gregorian Chant* (Evanston, 1998), chs. 5 and 6.

14. I have not had access to the 1668 edition but have used one from 1696.

15. Bénédicte Mariolle provides a detailed list of the contents of eighty-three treatises in her "Bibliographie des ouvrages théoriques traitant du plain-chant (1582–1789)," *Plain-chant et liturgie en France au XVIIIe siècle*, ed. by Jean Duron (Paris, 1997), 285–356. A much briefer, though still useful listing of plainchant treatises of the seventeenth and eighteenth centuries is given by Bennett Zon in *The English Plainchant Revival* (Oxford, 1999), 28–29 and 32–33.

Notes for Chapter 2

1. *Le fonti liturgiche a stampa della Biblioteca musicale L. Feininger* (Provincia Autonoma di Trento–Servizio beni librari e archivistici, 1994), 2 vols.

2. *Niels Jesperssøns Graduale*, edited by Erik Abrahamsen (Copenhagen, 1935). I thank Professor Christian Troelsgard for having made me aware of this publication.

3. *The English Plainchant Revival* (Oxford, 1999), 50ff.

Notes for Chapter 3

1. In the *Biblia Sacra iuxta vulgatam versionem* (2nd ed., ed. R. Weber, [Württembergische Bibelanstalt Stuttgart, 1975], II: 1105) the text reads, *Parvulus enim natus est nobis filius datus est nobis et factus est principatus super umerum eius et vocabitur nomen eius Admirabilis consiliarius Deus fortis Pater futuri saeculi Princeps pacis.* This form of the text will later be drawn upon in various printed Graduals for the Neo-Gallican rite.

2. These include Provins, Bibl. mun., 12; Chartres, Bibl. mun., 520 (destroyed, but available in facsimile edition); Paris, Bibl. nat., lat. 17310; and Paris, Bibl. nat., lat. 9437 (from Foicy in the diocese of Troyes) .

3. Willi Apel, *Gregorian Chant* (Bloomington, Ind., 1958), 279ff.

4. In extended discussions of a single chant, I shall normally provide only one reference to the relevant musical example in the accompanying volume.

5. Christopher Page, *Latin Poetry and Conductus Rhythm in Medieval France*, Royal Musical Association Monographs, 8 (London, 1997), 50–52. Apel, *Gregorian Chant*, 289ff.

6. *Le psautier romain et les autres anciens psautiers latins*, Collectanea Biblica Latina, 10 (Vatican, 1953), 239f.

7. There are other instances of this nature in this Roman Gradual, but I have not had the occasion to examine each of these. Moreover, Annarita Indino lists a considerable number of both double and triple presentations of the same melody in "Il graduale stampato da Angelo Gardano," (Indino, Annarita. "Il Graduale stampato da Angelo Gardano [1591]," *Il Canto piano nell'era della Stampa*, Atti del Convegno internazionale di studi sul canto liturgico nei secoli XV–XVIII, ed. Guilio Cattin, Danilo Curti, and Marco Gozzi [Trent, 1999], 209f), while providing two highly useful musical examples demonstrating the degree of musical freedom that could obtain in revising the same melody. The same phenomenon is also observable among medieval sources. (Cf. my "Communication," *Journal of the American Musicological Society*, 53 [2000], 674.) Thus it is not attributable to a striking change in editorial policies taking place post-1565. I doubt, moreover, whether we shall be able to discover a single covering law that will explain all instances.

8. The title page gives the date 1599, while the explicit states more precisely the Nones of October, 1598.

9. Amadée Gastoué, *Le Graduel et l'antiphonaire romains* (Lyon, 1913), 186.

10. David Hughes, "The alleluias Dies sanctificatus and Vidimus stellam as examples of late chant transmission," *Plainsong and medieval music*, 7 (1998), 101–28.

11. Theodore Karp, *Aspects of Orality and Formularity in Gregorian Chant* (Evanston, 1998), 135–80.

12. Dom Paolo Ferretti, *Esthétique Grégorienne*, trans. by Dom A. Agaësse (Solesmes, 1938), 107.

13. Egon Wellesz, *Eastern Elements in Western Chant*, Monumenta Musicae Byzantinae: Subsidia, 2 (Oxford, 1947), 38–39.

14. See, respectively, *Paléographie Musicale: Les principaux manuscrits de chant grégorien, ambrosien, mozarabe, Gallican*, I, 19: *Le Manuscrit 807, Universitätsbibliothek Graz (XIIe siècle)*, (Bern, 1974); *Das Graduale der St. Thomaskirche zu Leipzig (XIV. Jahrhundert)*, ed. by Peter Wagner, (1930, 1932; repr., Hildesheim, 1967); *Moosburger Graduale, München, Universitätsbibliothek, 2° Cod. ms. 156*, ed. by David Hiley (Tutzing, 1996); *Graduale Pataviense (Wien, 1511)*, ed. Christian Väterlein, (Kassel. 1982).

Notes for Chapter 4

1. A striking exception to this generalization occurs at the opening of the verse, where the Angermaier Gradual begins on *e*, rather on the customary *d*. I suspect this unusual opening to be the result of an error.

Notes for Chapter 5

1. See my *Aspects of Orality and Formularity in Gregorian Chant* (Evanston, 1998), esp. 200–204, including example 66).

2. Dominique Delalande, *Le Graduel des Prêcheurs* (Paris, 1949), 198–207 and Tableau xxvii.

3. Hendrik van der Werf, *The Emergence of Gregorian Chant*, I:2 (Rochester, 1983), 81–84.

4. In using the Solesmes readings for this example, I recall to the reader the remarks made in the course of the introduction concerning both the limitations and the usefulness of modern editorial conflations. The reader will have observed in the meantime that when information has been available to me concerning the unstable transmission of certain chants, this information has been placed at the reader's disposal.

5. The absence of a variant on any given staff indicates that the 1606 reading is the same as that in 1596.

6. Karlheinz Schlager, *Thematischer Katalog der ältesten Alleluia-Melodien aus Handschriften des 10. 11. Jahrhunderts*, (Munich, 1965), 54, 90–91.

7. Karlheinz Schlager, *Alleluia-Melodien I bis 1100*, (Kassel, 1968), 390–91.

Notes for Chapter 6

1. The change is not yet to be found in the *Missale Romanum ex Decreto Sacrosancti Concilii Tridentini restitutum* (Romae, Apud Heredes Bartholomei Faletti, Joannem Variscum, et Socios, 1570), p. 52 (= p. 108 of the facsimile edition).

2. See the discussion of this chant in my *Aspects of Orality and Formularity in Gregorian Chant* (Evanston, 1998), 204–9, including example 68.

3. Willi Apel, *Gregorian Chant* (Bloomington, Ind., 1958), 346–49.

4. Because this situation is unusual I took the precaution of checking the passage against the readings of Paris, Bibl. nat., lat. 903; Benevento, Bibl. capitolare, VI.34; Graz, Universitätsbibl., 807; Verdun, Bibl. mun., 759; and London, British Library, Add. 12194. The Solesmes text underlay is confirmed by all.

5. James McKinnon, "The Eighth-Century Frankish-Roman Communion Cycle," *Journal of the American Musicological Society* 45 (1992), 179–227.

6. See my "*Mirabantur omnes*: a Case Study for Critical Editions," *CANTUS PLANUS, Papers read at the 6th Meeting, Eger, Hungary, 1993* (Budapest, 1995), II, 493–516; and my *Aspects of Orality and Formularity in Gregorian Chant* (Evanston, 1998), 13–15, including example 1.

Notes for Chapter 7

1. The root of the word is *rosh*, meaning head, as in *Rosh Hashanah*—the "head" of the Year, thus New Year—or *rosh yeshiva*—the head of a religious school. The case is the genitive plural.

2. One may note that the reading for *Tollite portas* in the Giunta Gradual of 1596, another of the family of second-mode graduals, is seemingly notated with the final on *d*. Each of the five staves containing the chant has an f-clef clearly marked at the

beginning. Stranger still, an *e-flat* is plainly marked at the beginning of the word, *vestras* (corresponding to the *b-flat* for the previous syllable in the normative medieval version). The subsequent descent to B produces the extraordinary outline of a diminished fourth. The following Giunta edition of 1606 shows, however, that this reading is erroneous; there the f-clefs have been replaced by the proper clefs on *c'*.

3. See my "Some Chant Models for Isaac's Choralis Constantinus," *CANTUS PLANUS: Papers Read at the 7th Meeting, Sopron, Hungary, 1995* (Budapest, 1997), 337–41.

4. The notation of the 1596 Giunta Gradual is quite crowded and the intended alignment of syllable and tone is subject to question. The 1610 Ciera Gradual, on the other hand, uses more space and the alignment is clear.

Notes for Chapter 8

1. Theodore Karp, *Aspects of Orality and Formularity in Gregorian Chant* (Evanston, 1998), 103–8.

2. The sources used are: [English-1a]: *Saint Joseph Daily Missal*, ed. by Hugo H. Hoever (Catholic Book Publishing Co., New York, 1957), 318–19; [English-1b] *Saint Andrew Daily Missal*, ed. by Dom Gaspar Lefebvre (Liturgical Apostolate, Bruges, 1952), 482; [English-2]: *The Twelve Prophets* (Soncino Books of the Bible), ed. A. Cohen; translation after an earlier version issued by Jewish Publication Society of America (London, Soncino Press, 1970), 224r; [Vulgate]: *Biblia Sacra iuxta Vulgatam versionem*, ed. Robert Weber, 2nd. ed. (Stuttgart, Württembergische Bibelanstalt, 1975), II, 1410; [English-3]: *The Holy Bible, Revised Standard Version* (New York, Thomas Nelson & Sons, 1952), 977; [English-4]: *The Jerusalem Bible* (Garden City, Doubleday & Co., 1966), 1517. [English-5]: The Holy Bible, 1611 Edition, King James Version (Nashville, Thomas Nelson, 1993); orthography modernized.

3. Unfortunately, many stretches of the intervening verses are unreadable on microfilm owing to the fact that material from the recto side is clearly visible and conflicts with the material on the verso (and vice-versa). I have not had the opportunity to work on site with the manuscript.

4. A still simpler reading is to be found in a *Processionarium monasticum* of 1727 for which Raphael Molitor published a facsimile page. Cf. *Reform-Choral: historisch-kritische Studie* (Freiburg in Breisgau, 1901), 64. Unfortunately the author provides no further information regarding his source, and I have not been able to locate a copy.

5. The Solesmes readings are in keeping with those of the Montpellier, Fac. méd., MS H 159 and with Graz, Universitätsbibl., 807, to cite only one manuscript from the Western dialect and one from the Eastern that are readily available to all through volumes 8 and 19 of *Paléographie Musicale*. As is normal in the Eastern chant dialect, the last two tones in the Graz manuscript read *f–d* rather than *e–d*. The same lesson is duplicated in numerous other sources.

6. Helmut Hucke, "Tractusstudien," *Festschrift Bruno Stäblein*, ed. by Martin Ruhnke (Kassel, 1967), 116–20.

7. This remark pertains also to the derivative Graduals issued by Angermaier and Sutor.

8. The origin of the text is as yet unknown. *Iuxta vestibulum*, the antiphon that follows immediately, is drawn from the Book of Joel, chapter 2, verse 17, and the editors of the *Graduale sacrosanctae Romanae Ecclesiae* of 1974 and the *Graduale Triplex* of 1979, find in *Immutemur* reminiscences of the same Book, four verses earlier; there are, however, no identities of wording. This attribution to Joel, 2 is found at early date in the *Missale Romanum* of 1570 and, somewhat later, in the Plantin Gradual of 1599.

9. See further, my *Aspects of Orality*, 209.

10. See *ibid.*, example 69, 208–11. Eight of the twelve readings presented there open on *g*, but close variously on *g*, *a*, and *d*. Three begin on *d*, a fourth lower, all of these ending on the same tone. Lastly, there is a Cistercian reading that replaces the normative opening with a different one, as had been done with regard to the gradual, *Universi qui te expectant*.

11. I have provided an account of seven medieval readings for *Qui biberit* in my, *Aspects of Orality*, example 199, 414–17. Another reading, from an unspecified source, is given in the *Graduale Sacrosanctae Romanae Ecclesiae* (Solesmes, 1974), 99. It is doubtful that readings of the sixteenth and later centuries have been taken into account when estimating the number of surviving melodies for this and similar chants.

12. It is strange to find that the *Graduale Auscitanum*, mentioned above, does not follow French precedents, but instead places the final on *g* in accordance with three Germanic sources (plus one from the Carthusian order), and occupies the same tessitura as well. The opening gesture is clearly recognizable, but subsequent portions are individual; the ending in particular is idiosyncratic. The *Graduale Rothomagensis* of 1727, also a Neo-Gallican source, provides a reading of *Qui biberit* that draws much more clearly on French medieval chant practice.

13. I have provided an account of eight medieval readings for *Oportet te* (including one from the Old Roman repertory) in my, *Aspects of Orality*, example 198, 410–13. The *Graduale Auscitanum*, mentioned previously in connection with its reading of *Qui biberit*, provides a Neo-Gallican substitute for *Oportet te*.

14. Ibid., 240–45.

15. Ibid., 240–41.

16. See the facsimile edition, *Missale Romanum: Editio Princeps (1570)*, ed. Manlio Sodi and Achille Maria Triacca, Monumenta Liturgica Concilii Tridentini, 2 (Vatican, 1998), 50, segment 424.

17. Readers consulting vol. 2 of the Bryden and Hughes, *An Index of Gregorian Chant* (Cambridge [Mass.], 1969) will note that several of the entries for fifth-mode graduals sharing the same opening gesture likely refer to modern graduals, inasmuch as they are not to be found in any of the facsimile editions of medieval manuscripts included in this fine database. Although *Domine Dominus* opens in a manner somewhat similar to *Suscepimus*, the former opens on the final and comes to its first caesura on the same tone.

18. Willi Apel, *Gregorian Chant* (Bloomington, Ind., 1958), 319.

19. The reading of Paris, Bibl. nat., lat. 903 is basically similar with regard to text underlay, although with melodic variants.

Notes for Chapter 9

1. Cécile Davy-Rigaux, "L'oeuvre de plain-chant de G. G. Nivers" (Ph.D. diss., Université de Tours, 1999).

2. "Guillaume-Gabriel Nivers and his Editions (and Recompositions) of Chant "pour les Dames religieuses," *Plain-chant et liturgie en France au XVIIIe siècle*, ed. Jean Duron (Paris, 1997), 237–45.

3. A more broadly based comparison of four readings for the first two phrases of the sequence, *Veni Sancte Spiritus* is offered by Patricia M. Ranum in her article, "'Le Chant doit perfectionner la prononciation, & no pas la corrompre.' L'accentuation du chant grégorien d'après les traités de Dom Jacques Le Clerc et dans le chant de Guillaume-Gabriel Nivers," *Plain-chant et liturgie en France au XVIIe siècle*, ed. Jean Duron (Versailles, 1997), 79.

4. Karp, *Aspects of Orality* example 66 (p. 203) presents transcriptions of the opening of *Populus Sion* according to eight medieval sources.

5. Richard Sherr, "Guillaume-Gabriel Nivers and his Editions (and Recompositions) of Chant *"pour les Dames religieuses"*," *Plain-chant et liturgie en France au XVIIIe siècle*, ed. Jean Duron (Paris, 1997), 241.

Notes for Chapter 10

1. *Missale Parisiense illustrissimi et reverendissimi in Christo Patris D.D. Francisci de Harlay, Dei et Sanctae sedis Apostolicae gratia Parisiensis Archiepiscopi Ducis ac Paris Franciae Autoritate...editum.* (Lutetiae Parisiorum, apud Sebastianum Mabre-Cramoisy..., 1685), 101.

2. Gaston Fontaine, "Présentation des Missels diocésains français du 17e au 19e siècle," *La Maison-Dieu*, 141 (1980), 97–166. The bibliography does not deal with French Missals that follow Roman practice.

3. *Missale Aurelianense, Illustrissimi ac Reverend. in Christo Patris et Domini D., Petri du Cambout de Coislin, Episcopi Aurelianensis, ...authoritate editum* (Aureliae, Claudii et Jacobi Borde..., 1673).

4. Facsimile ed.: *Missale Parisiense anno 1738 publici iuris factum*, ed. Cuthbert Johnson and Anthony Ward, Ephemerides liturgicae: Instrumenta liturgica quarreriensia, Supp. 1 (Rome, 1993).

5. I owe my acquaintance with this source to the kindness of Dr. Robert Gallagher, who found a reference to it in the preface to a volume of organ works by Louis Marchand edited by Jean Bonfils.

6. The passage reads, *Comme dans le livre des Messe. Le Graduel Haec dies, les Versets, & les Alleluia qui sedisent a Vespres ces trois jours sont differens en chant de ceux qui sont marqué a chaque jour. J' ay cru les devoir ajouter icy pour que le chantre se puissent conformer au choeur en l'un des deux chants.*

7. It is possible that the *Graduale Meldense* of 1714 is Neo-Gallican, but I have not been able to gain access to this source.

8. It has been alleged that a Gradual of 1689, issued in Paris under the authority of Archbishop de Harlay, is a Neo-Gallican source. This, however, is incorrect. To be sure, the Paschal Alleluia cycle does not correspond to the cycle of Alleluias to

be found in modern Solesmes books. But the variability of the Alleluia cycles following Easter is well known from the Middle Ages on. A better index of the nature of this source is to be found in an investigation of the introits, offertories, and communions. As of now, we know only the *Pars aestiva* of what had once been a two-volume work. If we investigate the three genres of chant just named from *Dominica in Albis* up to Trinity Sunday, we find few instances in which the chants given in the 1689 Gradual differ from those given in modern books. Every introit is the one familiar to us. The communions, *Spiritus ubi vult* and *Non vos relinquam*, have traded places, as have the offertory, *Portas caeli*, and the communion, *Spiritus qui a Patre*. I would attribute the last-named exchange to a printer's error. Otherwise, there is only one communion, *Talem habemus* that would be unfamiliar to most singers of chant, and two offertories. The melodic readings are not related to the conservative versions of the Carthusians, but they accord quite well with the main branch of "reformed" French readings of the period. The *Graduale Bisuntinum* of 1682, ed.Jean Millet, is, as documented previously, a Roman book.

9. *The Oxford Dictionary of the Christian Church*, 2nd ed., ed. F. L. Cross and F. A. Livingstone (London, 1974), 1500f., does not indicate when this Feast was first observed, although presumably after the fifteenth century. It does, however, state that the Feast "is still observed in some places on the fourth Friday of Lent." The Feast is still indicated for the first Friday in Lent in the *Missale Parisiense* of 1738, together with the same Mass Proper. Unfortunately, the *Graduale Rothomagensis* of 1727, which unquestionably derives from the Harley Missal, does not include this feast.

10. The text of the seldom-found *Alleluia Levate capite vestra* is employed in the *Graduale Bituricense*, but the accompanying melody is new.

11. Monique Brulin, "L'antiphonier de Paris en 1681," *Plain-chant et liturgie en France au XVIIe siècle*, ed. Jean Duron (Versailles, 1997), 117 and 119.

12. For further information, see Marco Gozzi, *Le fonti liturgiche a stampa della Biblioteca musicale L. Feininger* (Trento, 1994), I, 250–52, with reproduction of one opening from No. 32 (=FSA 41–43). (These volumes were reprinted elsewhere, including a Dijon publication issued by Douillier in 1827.)

13. Multiple examples of this phenomenon will be discussed as this investigation unfolds, but these by no means constitute the sum total.

14. Cf. Bennett Zon, *The English Plainchant Revival* (Oxford, 1999), 25.

15. The former is taken from 2 Chronicles, 20:17 and the latter from Zecharia, 2:10.

16. Both the 1685 and the 1738 Missals from Paris indicate the sources of their texts in the margins, but the information will not suffice for all of the melodies given in the Graduals.

17. For example, when dealing with the gradual verse, *Vox Domini in virtute*, used for the Octave of Epiphany, the versions according to the Septuagint and the Hebrew differ sufficiently that it is not readily apparent that the text is drawn from Psalm 28.

18. I am employing the *Biblia Sacra iuxta Vulgatam versionem*, ed. Robert Weber, 2nd ed., (Stuttgart, 1975).

19. This is not the same text that serves in modern books for the Feast of the Sacred Heart of Jesus, instituted in 1765.

20. Cf. *The Liber Usualis with Introduction and Rubrics in English*, No. 801 (Tournai, 1934, and various later dates), 1072, or *Graduale Sacrosanctae Romanae Ecclesiae*, No. 696 (Tournai, 1943 and later dates), 385.

21. See Karl-Heinz Schlager, *Thematischer Katalog der ältesten Alleluia-Melodien aus Handschriften des 10. und 11. Jahrhunderts* (Munich, 1965), 123f., Nos 120 and 121.

22. Of course the best-known use of this text is as the verse for the Gregorian gradual, *Viderunt omnes*, whose Neo-Gallican transformation occurs immediately preceding in the Beauvais source.

23. Cf. 1727[1], 1730[7], 1738[1, 3, 4], 1740[2], 1741[3], 1742, 1744, 1745, 1746[1–2], 1753[4], 1754[2], 1755, 1756[3], 1768, 1774[2, 4, 5], 1775, 1778[4], 1779[2, 3], 1780[1], 1785[2], 1787[1], 1804, 1805, 1816[2], 1822[2], 1824, 1825[2], 1826[3–6, 8], 1827[1], 1833[3], 1835, 1836[1,2], 1837[1, 2], 1839, 1843[1, 2], 1844[4], 1845[2, 4], and 1846.

24. John Bryden and David Hughes, *An Index of Gregorian Chant* (Cambridge, Mass., 1969), cf. I, 365.

25. We have previously noted a close relationship between the two sources in the settings of *Viderunt omnes*.

26. *The Oxford Dictionary of the Christian Church*, 2nd ed., ed. F. L. Cross and E. A. Livingstone (London, 1974), 278. The Bryden and Hughes, *Index of Gregorian Chant*, does not provide a source citation for any of the items of this modern Mass; it is highly unlikely that they were drawn from medieval models. Furthermore, the antiphon is not to be found in any of the sources presently catalogued in *Cantus*.

27. See Bryden and Hughes, *Index of Gregorian Chant*, II, 85.

28. Ibid., 249. Bryden and Hughes do not cite any late medieval source for these melodies, and they do not appear in Karlheinz Schlager's *Thematischer Katalog der ältesten Alleluia-Melodien*.

29. I thank my friend and colleague, Professor Calvin Bower, for this identification.

Notes for Chapter 11

1. There were, of course, four Turinese Graduals issued during the early sixteenth century, from 1512–24.

2. During the interim the firm of Plantin did issue pamphlet-sized prints of the *Proprium Missae*, devoted to local practices. These were deemed to be too limited to merit a place in our checklist.

3. A facsimile page from this Gradual has been published in the highly useful catalogue by Marco Gozzi, *Le fonti liturgiche a stampa della Biblioteca musicale L. Feininger* (Trent, 1994), I, 463. This work is an indispensable resource for those wishing to inform themselves of the appearance of printed liturgical sources from ca. 1500–1890. Facsimiles of a pair of successive pages were published at earlier date in *Paléographie Musicale: Les principaux manuscrits de chant grégorien, ambrosien, mozarabe, Gallican, Le Répons-graduel Justus ut palma. deuxième partie*, 3 (Solesmes, 1892; repr. Bern, 1974), pl. 211.

4. By contrast, the *Graduale sacrosanctae Romanae Ecclesiae* of 1943, fits as many as nine staves on pages that are 8 1/8 inches high.

5. The source is conveniently available in facsimile in *Paléographie Musicale: Les principaux manuscrits de chant grégorien, ambrosien, mozarabe, Gallican, Le Codex 903*

de la Bibliothèque Nationale de Paris (XIe siècle): *Graduel de Saint-Yrieix*, 13 (Solesmes, 1925; repr. Bern, 1971).

6. As a precaution, I checked for this chant in the CANTUS database, but, as expected, found nothing.

7. Amiet is the respected author of well over a dozen books on liturgical subjects, several being devoted to Lyon and Aosta. Among these are an *Inventaire général des livres liturgiques du Diocèse de Lyon* (Paris, 1979), and *Les manuscrits liturgiques du Diocèse de Lyon: description et analyse* (Paris, 1998).

8. The reader should keep in mind that the use of this antiphon was not mandatory and that there are several sources in which it is lacking.

9. To be sure, one cannot be certain of the pitch names that might have been in the minds of scribes who were writing without the use of clefs. Nevertheless, the family of readings that we are discussing is characterized by a final that is notated a second higher than the opening pitch. This I have not found among the Aquitanian sources consulted.

10. In the table given by Terence Bailey, *The Processions of Sarum and the Western Church* (Toronto, 1971), 167, *Collegerunt* appears in fourteen of the earliest sixteen sources cited.

11. *Collegerunt* is discussed in my, "The Cataloging of Chant Manuscripts as an Aid to Critical Editions and Chant History," in *Foundations in Music Bibliography*, ed. Richard D. Green (New York, 1993), 241–69. (It appeared simultaneously in *Music Reference Services Quarterly*, 2 (1993), 241–69.) A selection of sixteen readings is given in example 3, pp. 251–64.

12. The last of these is to be found in Oxford, Bodleian Library, MS lat. liturg. b. 5; the facsimile edition of this source had not been available to me at the time that I wrote my article.

13. Karlheinz Schlager, *Thematischer Katalog der ältesten Alleluia-Melodien aus Handschriften des 10. 11. Jahrhunderts* (Munich, 1965), 216.

14. *Benevento, Biblioteca Capitolare 40, Graduale*, Codices Gregoriano, ed. by Nino Albarosa and Alberto Turco (Padua, 1991).

15. The 1722 Dominican reading of the offertory, *Dextera Domini*, is given as staff **n** of example 40 (ch. 6).

Notes for Chapter 12

1. The prefatory matter (p. 9) mentions also consultation of the Plantin Gradual of 1599 with regard to chants of the Mass Ordinary.

2. The more substantial preface was written by Father de Voght; this mentions Duval, but not Bogaerts.

3. Katherine Bergeron, *Decadent Enchantments: The Revival of Gregorian Chant at Solesmes* (Berkeley, Calif., 1998), 39.

4. The information given in this paragraph has largely been derived from Bergeron's book, 72–75.

5. David Hiley, *Western Plainchant* (Oxford: Oxford University Press, 1993), 625.

6. Theodore Karp, *Aspects of Orality and Formularity in Gregorian Chant* (Evanston, 1998), 200–204.

Selected Bibliography

Abrahamsen, Erik, ed. *Niels Jesperssøns Graduale* (Copenhagen, 1935).

Apel, Willi. *Gregorian Chant* (Bloomington, Ind., 1958).

Bailey, Terence. *The Processions of Sarum and the Western Church* (Toronto, 1971).

Benevento, *Biblioteca Capitolare 40, Graduale* (Codices Gregoriani, ed. by Nino Albarosa and Alberto Turco; Padua, 1991).

Bergeron, Katherine. *Decadent Enchantments: The Revival of Gregorian Chant at Solesmes* (Berkeley, Calif., 1998).

Biblia Sacra iuxta Vulgatam versionem, ed. Robert Weber, 2nd ed., 2 vols. (Stuttgart, Württembergische Bibelanstalt, 1975).

Brulin, Monique. "L'antiphonier de Paris en 1681," *Plain-chant et liturgie en France au XVIIIe siècle*, ed. by Jean Duron (Paris, 1997), 109–23.

Bryden, John and David Hughes. *An Index of Gregorian Chant*, 2 vols. (Cambridge [Mass.], 1969.

Il. cod. Paris Bibliothèque Nationale de France lat. 776: sec. 11: graduale de Gaillac (*Codices gregoriani*), ed. by Nino Albarosa, Heinrich Rumphorst, Alberto Turco (Padua, 2001).

Cohen, A., ed. *The Psalms: Hebrew Text & English Translation, with an Introduction and Commentary* (Soncino Books of the Bible; London, 1945).

Davy-Rigaux, Cécile. *L'oeuvre de plain-chant de G. G. Nivers* (doctoral dissertation, Université de Tours, 1999).

Delalande, Dominique. *Le Graduel des Prêcheurs: Recherches sur les sources et la valeur de son texte* (Bibliothèque d'histoire Dominicaine, 2; Paris, 1949).

Fellerer, Karl G., ed. *Geschichte der katholischen Kirchenmusik*, 2 vols. (Kassel, 1976)

Ferretti, Dom Paolo. *Esthétique Grégorienne*, (transl. by Dom A. Agaësse, Solesmes, 1938).

Fontaine, Gaston. "Présentation des Missels diocésains français du 17e au 19e siècle," *La Maison-Dieu*, 141 (1980), 97–166.

Gastoué, Amédée. *Le Graduel et l'antiphonaire romains* (Lyon, 1913).

Goovaerts, Alphonse. *Histoire et bibliographie de la typographie musicale dans les anciens Pays Bas* (Antwerp, 1880).

Gozzi, Marco. *Le fonti liturgiche a stampa della Biblioteca musicale L. Feininger*, 2 vols. (Trent, 1994).

Graduale Pataviense (Wien, 1511), ed. by Christian Väterlein (*Das Erbe deutscher Musik*, 87; Kassel. 1982).

Graduale Sacrosanctae Romanae Ecclesiae de Tempore et de Sanctis (Rome, 1908).

Graduale Sacrosanctae Romanae Ecclesiae, No. 696 (Tournai, 1943).

Graduale de Sanctis iuxta ritum Sacrosanctæ Romanæ Ecclesiæ: Editio Princeps (1614-1615), ed. by Giacomo Baroffio and Eun Ju Kim (*Monumenta Studia Instrumenta Liturgica*: 11; Vatican City, 2001).

Graduale de Tempore iuxta ritum Sacrosanctæ Romanæ Ecclesiæ: Editio Princeps (1614), ed. by Giacomo Baroffio and Manlio Sodi (*Monumenta Studia Instrumenta Liturgica*: 10; Vatican City, 2001).

Graduale Sarisburiense: A Reproduction in Facsimile of a Manuscript of the Thirteenth Century, with a Dissertation and Historical Index Illustrating its Development from the Gregorian Antiphonale Missarum, ed. by Walter Howard Frere (London, 1894).

Graduale Triplex (Solesmes, 1979).

Le Graduel romain, édition critique par les moines de Solesmes; II: *Les Sources* (Solesmes, 1957); IV: *Le Texte neumatique*, i: *Le Groupement des manuscrits* (Solesmes, 1960); ii: *Les Relations généalogiques* (Solesmes, 1962).

Hesbert, Dom René. *Antiphonale Missarum Sextuplex* (Rome, 1935).

Hiley, David. *Western Plainchant* (Oxford, 1993).

The Holy Bible, Revised Standard Version, (New York, 1952).

Hucke, Helmut. "Tractusstudien," *Festschrift Bruno Stäblein* , ed. by Martin Ruhnke (Kassel, 1967), 116–20.

Hughes, David. "The alleluias Dies sanctificatus and Vidimus stellam as examples of late chant transmission, " *Plainsong and medieval music*, 7 (1998), 101–28.

Huppert, George. *The Idea of Perfect History* (Urbana, [1970]).

———. *The Style of Paris* (Bloomington, Ind., ca. 1999).

Indino, Annarita. "Il Graduale stampato da Angelo Gardano (1591)," *Il Canto piano nell'era della Stampa (Atti del Convegno internazionale di studi sul canto liturgico nei secoli XV-XVIII)*, ed. by Guilio Cattin, Danilo Curti, and Marco Gozzi (Trent, 1999), 207–22.

The Jerusalem Bible (Garden City, 1966).

Karp, Theodore. *Aspects of Orality and Formularity in Gregorian Chant* (Evanston, 1998), 135–80.

———. "The Cataloging of Chant Manuscripts as an Aid to Critical Editions and Chant History," *Foundations in Music Bibliography*, ed. by Richard D. Green (New York, 1993), 241–69. (Also in *Music Reference Services Quarterly*, 2 (1993), 241–69.)

———."Communication," *Journal of the American Musicological Society*, 53 (2000), 671–75.

———. "*Mirabantur Omnes*: A Case Study for Critical Editions," *CANTUS PLANUS: Papers Read at the 6th Meeting, Eger, Hungary, 1993* (Budapest, 1995).

———. "On the transmission of some mass chants, c. 1575–1775, " *Il Canto piano nell'era della Stampa (Atti del Convegno internazionale di studi sul canto liturgico nei secoli XV-XVIII)*, ed. by Guilio Cattin, Danilo Curti, and Marco Gozzi (Trent, 1999), 81–98.

———. "Some Chant Models for Isaac's Choralis Constantinus," *CANTUS PLANUS: Papers Read at the 7th Meeting, Sopron, Hungary, 1995* (Budapest, 1997), 337–341.

Liber Gradualis juxta antiquorum codicum fidem restitutus, editio altera (Solesmes, 1895).

Maciejewski, Tadeusz, and Tadeusz Chrzanowski, eds. *Gradual Karmelitanski z 1644 roku Stanisawa ze Stolca* (Warsaw, 1976).

Mariolle. Bénédicte. "Bibliographie des ouvrages théoriques traitant du plain-chant (1582-1789)." *Plain-chant et liturgie en France au XVIIIe siècle*, ed. by Jean Duron (Paris, 1997), 285–356.

McKinnon, James. "The Eighth-Century Frankish-Roman Communion Cycle," *Journal of the American Musicological Society* 45 (1992), 179–227.

Missale Aurelianense, Illustrissimi ac Reverend. in Christo Patris et Domini D., Petri du Cambout de Coislin, Episcopi Aurelianensis, . . . authoritate editum. Aureliae, Claudii et Jacobi Borde..., 1673.

Missale Carnotense (Chartres Codex 520), ed. by David Hiley, *Monumenta Monodica Medii Aevi*, IV (Kassel, 1992).

Missale Parisiense anno 1738 publici iuris factum (Ephemerides liturgicae: Instrumenta liturgica quarreriensia, Supp. 1), ed. by Cuthbert Johnson and Anthony Ward (Rome, 1993).

Missale Parisiense illustrissimi et reverendissimi in Christo Patris D.D. Francisci de Harlay, Dei et Sanctae sedis Apostolicae gratia Parisiensis Archiepiscopi Ducis ac Paris Franciae Autoritate... editum. Lutetiae Parisiorum, apud Sebastianum Mabre-Cramoisy..., 1685.

Missale Romanum: Editio Princeps (1570), ed. by Manlio Sodi and Achille Maria Triacca (*Monumenta Liturgica Concilii Tridentini*, 2; Vatican City, 1998).

Molitor, Raphael. *Die nach-Tridentinische Choral-Reform zu Rom*, 2 vols. (Leipzig, 1901).

———. *Reform-Choral: historisch-kritische Studie* (Freiburg in Breisgau, 1901).

Moosburger Graduale: München Universitätsbibliothek, 2° Cod. ms. 156 (*Veröffentlichungen der Gesellschaft für Bayerische Musikgeschichte*), Facsimile ed. by David Hiley (Tutzing, 1996).

Oxford, Bodleian Library MS. Lat. liturg. b. 5, ed. by David Hiley (*Publications of Mediaeval Musical Manuscripts*, 20; Ottawa, 1995).

The Oxford Dictionary of the Christian Church, 2nd edition, ed. by F. L. Cross and F. A. Livingstone (London, 1974).

Page, Christopher. *Latin Poetry and Conductus Rhythm in Medieval France* (Royal Musical Association Monographs 8: London, 1997).

Paléographie Musicale: Les principaux manuscrits de chant grégorien, ambrosien, mozarabe, gallican (Solesmes, 1889–1958, Bern, 1968– ; repr. Bern, 1971–). First series:

I. *Le Codex 339 de la Bibiothèque de Saint-Gall (Xe siècle): Antiphonale Missarum Sancti Gregorii* (Solesmes, 1889; repr. Bern, 1974).

III. *Le Répons-Graduel Justus ut palma: Deuxième partie* (Solesmes, 1892; repr. Bern, 1974).

IV. *Le Codex 121 de la Bibliothèque d'Einsiedeln (Xe-XIe siècle): Antiphonale Missarum Sancti Gregorii* (Solesmes, 1894; repr. Bern, 1974)

VIII. *Antiphonarium tonale missarum, XIe siècle: Codex H. 159 de la Bibliothèque de l'École de Médecine de Montpellier. Phototypies.* (Solesmes, 1901–5; repr. Bern, 1972.)

X. *Antiphonarium missarum Sancti Gregorii, IXe-Xe siécle: Codex 239 de la Bibliothèque de Laon.* (Solesmes, 1909; repr. Bern, 1971).

XI. *Antiphonarium missarum Sancti Gregorii, Xe siécle: Codex 47 de la Bibliothèque de Chartres.* (Solesmes, 1912; repr. Bern, 1972).

XIII. *Le Codex 903 de la Bibliothèque Nationale de Paris (XIe siècle): Graduel de Saint-Yrieix.* (Solesmes, 1925; repr. Bern, 1971).

XV. *Le Codex VI.34 de la Bibliothèque Capitulaire de Bénévent (XIe–XIIe siècle): Graduel de Bénévent avec prosaire et tropaire.* (Solesmes, 1937; repr. Bern, 1971).

XVIII. *Le Codex 123 de la Bibliothèque Angelica de Rome (XIe siècle)* (Bern, 1969).

XIX. *Le Manuscrit 807, Universitätsbibliothek Graz (XIIe siècle)* (Bern, 1974).

Second Series

II. *Cantatorium, IXe siècle: No 359 de la Bibliothèque de Saint-Gall*. (Solesmes, 1924; Bern, 1968).

Ranum, Patricia M. " 'Le Chant doit perfectionner la prononciation, & non pas la corrompre.' L'accentuation du chant grégorien d'après les traités de Dom Jacques Le Clerc et dans le chant de Guillaume-Gabriel Nivers." *Plain-chant et liturgie en France au XVIIIe siècle*, ed. by Jean Duron (Paris, 1997), 59–83.

Saint Andrew Daily Missal, ed. by Dom Gaspar Lefebvre (Bruges, 1952).

St. Joseph Daily Missal, ed. by Hugo H. Hoever (New York, 1957).

Schlager, Karlheinz. *Thematischer Katalog der ältesten Alleluia-Melodien aus Handschriften des 10. 11. Jahrhunderts* (*Erlanger Arbeiten zur Musikwissenschaft*, 2; Munich, 1965).

———. *Alleluia-Melodien I bis 1100* (*Monumenta Monodica Medii Aevi*, VII; Kassel, 1968).

Sherr, Richard. "Guillaume-Gabriel Nivers and his Editions (and Recompositions) of Chant *"pour les Dames religieuses"*," *Plain-chant et liturgie en France au XVIIIe siècle*, ed. by Jean Duron (Paris, 1997), 237–45.

Strunk, Oliver. *Source Readings in Music History* (New York, 1950).

The Twelve Prophets, ed. A. Cohen (Soncino Books of the Bible; London, 1970).

Verdun, Bibliothèque Municipale 759: Missale (*Codices gregoriani*, ed. by Nino Albarosa and Alberto Turco; Padua, 1994).

Wagner, Peter. *Das Graduale der St. Thomaskirche zu Leipzig* (*XIV. Jahrhundert*), *Publikationen älterer Musik*, V, VII (1930, 1932; repr., Hildesheim, 1967).

van der Werf, Hendrik. *The Emergence of Gregorian Chant*, 2 vols. (Rochester, 1983).

Weber, Robert, ed. *Biblia Sacra iuxta vulgatem versionem*, 2nd ed., 2 vols. (Württembergische Bibelanstalt; Stuttgart, 1975).

———, ed. *Le Psautier romain et les autres anciens psautiers latins* (*Collectanea Biblica Latina*, 10; Vatican City, 1953).

Wellesz, Egon. *Eastern Elements in Western Chant* (*Monumenta Musicae Byzantinae: Subsidia*, 2; Oxford, 1947).

Zon, Bennett. *The English Plainchant Revival* (Oxford, 1999).

Index

Chants

MS Sources